The History of the Christian Missions

Vol. 1

SALZWASSER
VERLAG

William Brown

The History of the Christian Missions

Vol. 1

Reprint of the original, first published in 1864.

1st Edition 2022 | ISBN: 978-3-75259-144-6

Verlag (Publisher): Salzwasser Verlag GmbH, Zeilweg 44, 60439 Frankfurt, Deutschland
Vertretungsberechtigt (Authorized to represent): E. Roepke, Zeilweg 44, 60439 Frankfurt, Deutschland
Druck (Print): Books on Demand GmbH, In de Tarpen 42, 22848 Norderstedt, Deutschland

THE HISTORY

OF

CHRISTIAN MISSIONS.

THE HISTORY

OF THE

CHRISTIAN MISSIONS

OF THE

SIXTEENTH, SEVENTEENTH, EIGHTEENTH, AND NINETEENTH CENTURIES,

CONTAINING

ACCOUNTS OF THE PROPAGATION OF CHRISTIANITY BY THE VARIOUS MISSIONARY SOCIETIES OF ENGLAND, IRELAND, SCOTLAND, AND AMERICA; ALSO THOSE OF AN EARLY DATE BY THE SWISS, SWEDES, DUTCH, DANES MORAVIANS, ETC., ETC., AND OF THEIR VICISSITUDES AND SUCCESSES IN THE EAST AND WEST INDIES, NORTH AND SOUTH AMERICA, SOUTH AND WEST AFRICA, THE INDIAN ARCHIPELAGO, CHINA, TARTARY, PERSIA, CEYLON, TURKEY, GREECE, EGYPT, ABYSSINIA, RUSSIA, LAPLAND, GREENLAND, AUSTRALIA, NEW ZEALAND, SOUTH SEA ISLANDS, AND MANY OTHER PORTIONS OF THE GLOBE.

TO WHICH IS ADDED,

A LIST OF THE TRANSLATIONS OF THE HOLY SCRIPTURES INTO THE LANGUAGES OF HEATHEN AND MOHAMMEDAN NATIONS.

BY THE

REVEREND WILLIAM BROWN, M.D.

SECRETARY OF THE SCOTTISH MISSIONARY SOCIETY.

THIRD EDITION,

Greatly Enlarged and Improved.

WITH CONTINUATION BROUGHT DOWN TO THE LATEST PERIOD.

IN THREE VOLUMES.

VOL. I.

LONDON

1864.

PREFACE.

The propagation of Christianity in the world is the most important subject which can engage the attention of a historian. The rise, the progress, and the downfal of empires; the discovery of unknown countries; the lives of philosophers, of senators, of princes; the improvements of the arts and sciences, may furnish useful and interesting materials for history; but nothing is so momentous as the diffusion of the gospel in the world, which at once brings "glory to God in the highest, peace on earth, and good will toward man." The transcendent importance of this subject is stamped by no less than Divine authority. In the New Testament, we have only two branches of history; the Gospels, containing the life of our Lord and Saviour Jesus Christ, and the Acts of the Apostles, exhibiting a view of the propagation of Christianity in the world.

During the interval which has elapsed between the publication of the last and the present edition of this work, the Author has spared no pains in improving it. The preparation of the present edition has been the labour of many years, and he trusts it will be found vastly improved as compared with the preceding editions. The history of the previously existing missions, is not only brought down to the latest period, but accounts are now given of numerous missions which had formerly no existence, or which had been only lately begun. Among these are some of the most interesting and important missions now in the world. Though much of the old materials of part of the work remain, yet the alterations and additions are so many and so great, that the present edition is, to a large extent, a new work. With respect to alterations, it may be proper to state, that though in some instances they refer to very material points, he has made them without calling the attention of the reader to them, not because he was ashamed to confess former errors, which no man ought to be ashamed to do; but simply for the sake of brevity, being anxious not to lengthen out the work by any unnecessary statements or discussions, and also not to interrupt the course of the narrative.

Missionary Societies, and especially individual missionaries, will, perhaps, be disappointed on finding in the following work so general and brief an account of their labours. Many circumstances which, in the minds of those more immediately concerned, excited the deepest interest, they will here find passed in silence; even the names of many useful missionaries they will seek in vain in the following work. Sensible as the Author is of its imperfections, he is apprehensive that some, in consequence of this, may deem it much more imperfect than it really is. He believes, indeed, he has more frequently erred in being too minute than too general.

There are so many things common to all missions, that in a History of the Propagation of Christianity, it is necessary to omit innumerable circumstances, which it would be natural to introduce in the life of the individual missionaries, the narrative of a single mission, or even the account of a particular Society. In a general History of Missions, it must be the object of the writer to avoid as much as possible circumstances which are common to all, and to seize on those which are, in some degree, characteristic of each.

As there are many things common to missions in general, there are also some which are common to missions in the same country; and hence when considerable details have been entered into in regard to the earlier missions established in a country, for example, as to the Danish and the Baptist missions in India, the London Society's mission in China, the Church Society's mission in New Zealand, it is often unnecessary to go into much detail in regard to other missions subsequently established in the same country. To do so would only be to repeat over and over again the same or similar facts. To avoid such repetitions is one of the special difficulties which attends the writing of a general history of missions, and notwithstanding all the care which the historian may employ, he will often find it impossible to avoid it altogether.

It has not been for the sake of ease to himself that the Author has given so general and so brief an account of many missions. The truth is, it would have been incomparably more easy for him to have given a detailed and minute history of the various missions which have been established throughout the world, than the account which he has given of them. It would have been far more easy for him to have written the History of Missions in three volumes folio than in three volumes octavo. As some evidence that it was not with a view to his own ease that he has given so brief a notice of many missions, he may mention that he has expunged or generalized, in the present edition, the accounts which he had given in the former editions of a number of missions, particularly in South Africa and in the East and West Indies; and he has also left out a number of missions which have since been established, of which he had, with considerable labour to himself, drawn up an account. Of many of the missions, however, which are merely enumerated, or perhaps even not named at all, general accounts will be found in the Concluding Chapter, particularly of those in India, China, and South Africa.

In preparing the following work, there is nothing in regard to which the author has been so anxious as TRUTH. His object has been to present to his readers a correct and faithful picture of missions. He has not concealed their faults and imperfections; he has been as ready to state unfavourable as favourable circumstances, to mark failure as to note success. He will probably, however, be censured by some for having brought out so broadly, and in so much detail, the errors and defects of particular missions; but he may be allowed to say, that in giving such statements he has not been actuated by a love of detraction, nor yet by any sectarian spirit. Many of the statements now referred to, though painful, are highly instructive, and he trusts they will be useful in checking similar evils in time to come. He is convinced that the friends of missions often draw much too glowing pictures of their triumphant progress, of their past success, and of their future prospects, and that by this means they produce fallacious impressions on the public mind, and excite hopes which can terminate only in disappointment. The Author is sensible that by such a system important purposes are served, but he is no less convinced, that by an impartial statement of facts, inexpressibly greater advantages would ultimately be gained. The common observation that honesty is the best policy, is applicable to truth in general. It may be attended with temporary inconveniences, but on the whole, the advantages will far more than counterbalance the disadvantages. Missionary Societies might by such a system be rendered less popular, but they would probably be more useful. Fewer individuals might offer themselves as missionaries, but those who came forward would, it is likely, be more select. Less money might be raised, but less also would be spent by the employment of unsuitable agents. Besides, were more correct pictures drawn of the nature of the missionary work; were its difficulties and discouragements, its trials and disappointments, its imperfections and its failures, faithfully portrayed, we trust, that the spirit of prayer would be awakened among Christians in another manner than it is at present, in behalf of missionaries,—that men may be raised up, endowed with all those gifts and graces which so great an undertaking requires,—that they may be preserved from falling in the hour of temptation and trial,—that they may not only preach the gospel with their tongues, but in their daily conduct exhibit a living picture of Christian principle and Christian practice,—that they may be zealous, and active, and faithful in their work,—and that they may behold the fruit of their labours, in the conversion of multitudes to the Saviour. Christians in general, know but little of the difficulties, the trials, and the temptations to which missionaries are exposed; and hence, it cannot be expected that they should bear them in any suitable manner on their hearts before God in prayer. There is in fact an unhallowed confidence in that magnificent apparatus of means, which is at present in operation, as if it *must* produce a mighty change in the state of the world; a confidence which, there is reason to fear, may prove an occasion of the influences of the Holy Spirit being withheld from our exertions, until we are humbled to the dust before God, and brought to renounce every thing like self-sufficiency and self-dependence, and to trust with simplicity of heart to the divine blessing, as that without which all human endeavours will be utterly fruitless.

If it were necessary to state any thing further in vindication of the course which the Author has pursued, he would appeal to the example of the sacred historians. They tell the simple truth; they give us an unvarnished story; they write without exaggeration and without concealment. If one of the disciples of Christ betrays him into the hands of his enemies, they tell it. If another denies him, and that with imprecations and oaths, they tell it. If the rest forsake him and flee for their safety, they tell it. If even men of the highest rank in the church, as Paul and Barnabas, quarrel with one another, the fact is related with all the simplicity of truth, "The contention was so sharp between them, that they departed asunder one from the other." If Peter is chargeable with bigotry, and pusillanimity, and dissimulation, another apostle candidly tells us that he "withstood him to the face, because he was to be blamed." From these simple statements of truth, the sacred writers apprehended no injury to the great cause in which they were engaged, the propagation of Christianity in the world; and the result has shewn the wisdom of the principles on which they acted, for the honesty of their representations has not only furnished most instructive lessons to the Church in all ages, but forms an irrefragable proof of the truth of the Gospel history itself.

Though the Church of Rome carried on missions on an extensive scale during the period to which the following work relates, it was no part of the Author's design to give any account of them. The history of them would not be without interest nor without instruction; yet it is well that the fact should be known, that there would often be no possibility of distinguishing between truth and falsehood in the narrations of the missionaries. This is a heavy charge, and ought not to be made except on adequate grounds. It is, however, not only alleged by Protestant writers, but is supported by Catholic authorities of so high an order, that even members of the Church of Rome can scarcely question the fact. "It seems," says M. Cerri, Secretary to the Congregation *de Propaganda Fide*, in a Report which he gave of the state of the Roman Catholic Religion throughout the world to Pope Innocent XI. in the latter part of the seventeenth century, "It seems to be the *constant* opinion of ALL the members of the Congregation, that *little credit* is to be given to the *Relations*, *Letters*, and *Solicitations* that come from the missionaries. Hence it is, that the *usual* answer of the Congregation consists *only* in *asking further information*, which *often proves of no use*. For besides the time lost in expecting a reply from the missionaries, they frequently send back the same informations without giving a new light into the matter. I add, that the *Nuncios* and *other persons* receiving those informations from the parties concerned, are *not able to give a better account of things* than what the Congregation had before. These inconveniences have often moved that Society to send Visitors into the missions, who being *disinterested* and *impartial* men, have given a *true* relation of the state of those missions, by which means several disorders have been effectually removed. Give me leave, Most Holy Father, to represent to your Holiness, that this remedy *is now more necessary than ever* in *many Provinces and Kingdoms*, as I have intimated in several parts of this Discourse."—*Account of the State of the Roman Catholic Religion throughout the World, written for the use of Pope Innocent XI., by Monsignor Cerri, Secretary of the Congregation de Propaganda Fide*, London, 1715, p. 182.

DUDDINGSTON, *April* 20. 1854.

CONTENTS OF VOLUME I.

CHAPTER I.

PROPAGATION OF CHRISTIANITY BY THE SWISS.

CHAPTER II.

PROPAGATION OF CHRISTIANITY BY THE SWEDES.

CHAPTER III.

PROPAGATION OF CHRISTIANITY BY THE DUTCH.

CHAPTER IV.

PROPAGATION OF CHRISTIANITY BY THE ANGLO-AMERICANS.

CHAPTER V.

PROPAGATION OF CHRISTIANITY BY THE DANES.

CHAPTER VI.

CHAPTER VII.

HISTORY OF MISSIONS.

CHAPTER I.

PROPAGATION OF CHRISTIANITY BY THE SWISS.

BRAZIL.

At the Reformation, the light of the Gospel burst forth on the nations of Europe, like the sun in the morning, after a long and darksome night. By degrees, it spread from country to country, and dispelled the shades of ignorance and error, in which they had been enveloped for a series of ages. Fired with a sacred zeal for the cause of religion, the Reformers followed Superstition to her most secret haunts, brought her forth to the view of the world, and exposed her in all her native deformity. In the prosecution of this object, they were appalled, neither by difficulties nor dangers: they triumphed while stretched on the rack; they sung in the midst of the fire. By the vigorous efforts which they made, the authority of the Pope was shaken to its centre; his throne was seen to totter; and ever since that period, his influence has been diminished, even in those countries which continued to acknowledge his spiritual sway.

Engaged in propagating the light of the Gospel through the benighted kingdoms of Christendom, the Reformers could scarcely be expected to direct their attention to the Heathen world. But notwithstanding the magnitude of their other exertions, this object was not entirely overlooked by them.

In September 1556, Philip Corguilleray, Peter Richer, William Chartier, Peter Bourdon, Matthew Verneuil, John du Bordel, Andrew de la Fond, Nicholas Denis, John Gardien, Martin

David, Nicolas Raviquet, James Rousseau, Nicolas Carmieau, and John de Lery, took their departure from Geneva with the view of proceeding to Brazil on the coast of South America. A colony had been sent to that country the preceding year, by Henry the Second, King of France, under the command of Nicolas Durand de Villegagnon, a man of distinguished talents and high in the French naval service. The Admiral de Coligni had promoted this measure with all his influence at Court, in the hope of providing in a distant country an asylum for his Protestant brethren, who were at that time persecuted and proscribed in their native land. Villegagnon himself had embraced the Reformed religion, and was eager to co-operate with the Admiral in accomplishing so desirable an object. On his arrival at the Rio de Janeiro, he wrote to Coligni, requesting further re-enforcements, particularly some good divines from Geneva, to plant the Christian faith in the New World. He addressed a letter to the same effect to Calvin, the Genevan reformer; and in consequence of the prospects he held forth, the individuals now mentioned resolved to proceed to America, in the hope of establishing the doctrines of the Reformation on that extensive Continent, and of introducing them among the Natives. On their way through France, they were joined by a considerable number of other persons, who, in consequence of the influence of Coligni, and the uneasy situation of the Protestants in that country, resolved to accompany them, and establish themselves in the new colony. The whole company embarked from Harfleur in three ships, furnished by the crown; and on arriving at the Rio de Janeiro, they were received by Villegagnon with the greatest demonstrations of joy. Scarcely, however, had they landed, when they began to experience the difficulties and hardships which commonly attend a new settlement, in a distant and uncultivated country. Before they had recovered from the fatigues of their voyage, they had to engage in severe manual labour, in order to complete the fort which the first settlers had begun; and they had, at the same time, to live on the hardest fare, their only food consisting of a little meal, which they had either to eat dry, or to boil in dirty water.[1]

[1] Histoire Generale des Voyages, tom. xiv. p. 185; Thuani Historia, tom. i. p. 500; Southey's History of Brasil, vol. i. p. 270, 275.

During their residence in Brazil, the Geneva divines appear to have had some intercourse with the Natives; but as they were ignorant of their language, their means of communication with them were very imperfect. They endeavoured, however, to convey to them some ideas concerning the principles of Natural and Revealed religion; but though the savages expressed great astonishment at what they heard, it does not appear that any of them manifested the slightest disposition to embrace the Christian faith. Some of them, indeed, promised to become worshippers of the true God; but there is no reason to suppose that their understandings were enlightened, or their hearts impressed by the Gospel.[1]

In the mean while, Villegagnon, won over, it is supposed, by the Cardinal of Lorraine, began to express doubts concerning some articles of the Reformed Church, particularly with respect to the nature of the Sacraments, and the manner of their administration. From the protector he became the persecutor of the Protestants; they were obliged to hold their assemblies for divine worship without him, and even, like their brethren in France, to celebrate the Lord's Supper during the night. Incensed at these proceedings, he declared he would not suffer a Protestant within the fort; and he accordingly obliged them to leave that very place, which they had assisted in building for their mutual security, and to retire to the open country. But as others of the people, provoked by his tyranny, deserted to them, he resolved, from dread of further revolt, to hasten their departure out of the country. With this view he gave permission to the captain of a vessel, which was lying in the river, to carry them back to France; but with a baseness seldom paralleled, he delivered to the master a small coffer, containing, among other articles, a formal process against them, with orders to the first judges in France to whom it should be presented, to seize them as heretics, and commit them to the flames.[2]

In January 1558, they embarked from Brazil, after a residence in that country of only about ten months; but scarcely had they sailed, when they began to experience fresh disasters. After being tossed about for seven days, the vessel was dis-

[1] Lerii Historia Navigationis in Brasiliam, p. 221, 230.

[2] Thuani Historia, tom. i. p. 501; Histoire Generale des Voyages, tom. xiv. p. 192, 196.

covered to have sprung a leak, and appeared to be sinking so rapidly, that there seemed nothing before them but a watery grave. Happily the sailors succeeded for the present in stopping the principal leaks; but the carpenter stated, she was so old, and worm-eaten, that she was quite unfit for so long a voyage. The master, however, afraid that, should he again land, he might be abandoned by his crew, declared his resolution to prosecute the voyage; but offered to grant a boat to any who might wish to return to America, from which they were as yet only nine or ten leagues distant. It was at the same time stated, that as the voyage was likely to prove much longer than ordinary, there were not provisions on board for the whole of the passengers and crew. On learning these circumstances, several of them, among whom were Peter Bourdon, John du Bordel, Matthew Verneuil, and Andrew de la Fond, returned to Brazil; but after escaping the dangers of shipwreck, the first three were, by the orders of Villegagnon, thrown into the sea and drowned.

In the mean while, the vessel proceeded on her voyage to France; but for weeks together she was driven about by incessant storms, and she was at the same time so leaky, that had she not been cleared of water a hundred times a day, she must inevitably have been swallowed up by the waves. Night and day the crew were employed at the pump; yet with all their exertions, they scarcely saved her from sinking. One day as the carpenter was mending a place which needed repair, a plank suddenly gave way; the sea in a moment gushed into the ship with the impetuosity of a torrent; the sailors rushed upon deck exclaiming in terrible consternation, "We are lost! we are lost!" Meanwhile the carpenter, who maintained more presence of mind, thrust his coat into the hole, and treading on it with all his might, resisted the force of the torrent; then crying to the sailors as loud as he was able, to bring him other articles, he succeeded in stemming the water, until he prepared a board to fill up the gap. On another occasion, some powder which was drying took fire; the flame ran from one end of the ship to the other, and communicated to the sails and the cordage. Four men were burnt, one of whom died a few days after. Had the ship taken fire, the whole of the passengers and crew must either have been burnt alive, or drowned in the midst of the ocean.

Meanwhile the apprehensions of famine, which had been entertained soon after their embarkation, began to be realized. Even at an early period of the voyage, it was agreed that part of the monkeys and parrots which they carried home with them as curiosities should be killed and eaten, in order to spare their provisions. Worms and excrements of rats were at length found in greater abundance in the storeroom, than particles of food ; yet they collected the sweepings together, and made them into a kind of pottage, which, though black and bitter as soot, they were glad to use. Such as possessed bucklers of the skin of the Tapiroussou, an animal peculiar to South America, cut them to pieces and devoured them. Others ate the coverings of their trunks, the leather of their shoes, and even the horn of the ship lanterns. They hunted the very rats and mice, which, as they had now nothing to eat, ran up and down the vessel in great numbers dying of hunger, and being so enfeebled, became an easy prey to their pursuers. Such was the value set on these repulsive animals, that a single rat sold for three and four crowns. Could the famished crew have obtained grass or hay, Lery supposes, they would have eaten them, like the brute creation. Nothing now remained to them except Brazil wood, which is represented as the driest of all woods. They were, however, so pressed with hunger, that to satisfy the cravings of nature, they endeavoured to gnaw it with their teeth. One day Philip Corguilleray, on putting a piece of it in his mouth, said to Lery with a sigh: "Alas! my friend, I have 4000 livres due me in France; yet I would gladly give a discharge for the whole, for a glass of wine and a pennyworth of bread." Peter Richer, one of the ministers, lay extended in his little cabin, so deprived of strength, that he was scarcely able to raise his head in prayer to God, though while thus prostrate, he was almost constantly engaged in that sacred exercise.

Meanwhile five or six of the crew died of absolute starvation, and from the disposition of the survivors, as well as the necessity of their circumstances, it seems truly wonderful that they did not devour the bodies of their unfortunate companions. They had now, as often happens in cases of famine, acquired such a degree of ferocity, and such an irritability of temper, that they could scarcely speak to each other but in passion, and without a particular cast of the eye, as if they were ready to devour one another.

After a voyage of near five months, they at length discovered the coast of Bretagne; but as they had already been often deceived by the pilot, they scarcely believed the person who first announced the joyful tidings. Nothing could be more seasonable than this discovery, for the master of the vessel declared, that had they remained another day in the same wretched condition, he had resolved to kill one of the ship's company, not by lot, as has sometimes been done by persons in similar circumstances, but by stealth, in order to provide food for himself and his fellow-sufferers. Having steered for the shore, they landed at Blavet near Henbonne, where the relation of their sufferings, excited, as might be expected, the tender sympathy of the inhabitants. They were warned not to indulge freely in food at first; but to repair by degrees their wasted strength. This salutary caution many of the sailors neglected; but they paid dearly for their folly, for of twenty who arrived in port, more than one half died in a short time. Others were affected with various complaints, as swellings over the whole body, weakness of stomach, diarrhœa, partial deafness, and blindness; but by the use of suitable remedies, they gradually recovered. As to the process against the Geneva divines, it so happened that the judges to whom it was delivered were not unfavourable to the Protestants, and, instead of executing the treacherous designs of Villegagnon, they treated with kindness the unfortunate victims of his malignity.[1]

Such was the termination of the first attempt of the Protestants to plant the Christian faith in the New World. The primary design of the undertaking appears, indeed, to have been the securing an asylum to the Reformed from persecution in Europe: the conversion of the natives was only a secondary object. The colony itself was of short duration. The Portuguese who had previously settled in Brazil, and who at first, had allowed the French to remain unmolested, soon afterwards attacked them, and expelled them from the country.[2]

[1] Lerii Historia, p. 267, 275; Histoire Generale des Voyages, tom. xiv. p. 196; Laval's History of the Reformation in France, vol. i. p. 106.

[2] Southey's History, vol. i. p. 278.

CHAPTER II.

PROPAGATION OF CHRISTIANITY BY THE SWEDES.

LAPLAND.

In the year 1559, Gustavus Vasa, King of Sweden, sent a missionary of the name of Michael into Lapland, with the view of extending Christianity in that country; for though it had been introduced some ages before the Reformation, yet most of the inhabitants were still sunk in the depths of Pagan ignorance and superstition. That prince, therefore, issued a royal mandate, ordaining them to assemble at a certain period of the winter, in order to pay their annual tribute, and to receive instruction in the principles of religion. His successors on the throne of Sweden followed his example in promoting Christianity in Lapland; and about the beginning of the seventeenth century, they were at the expense of erecting churches in different parts of the country, for the accommodation of the inhabitants. Hitherto, however, the labours of the missionaries had been of little use, as they preached in the Swedish language, which the people in general did not understand; while the Lapland youth, who were sent to the University of Upsal, died, either in Sweden, or soon after their return to their own country; and thus the hopes which were formed of them proved abortive. Gustavus Adolphus, therefore, who ascended the throne in 1611, began to establish schools in the country itself; and in order to encourage the people to send their children to them, he allotted a certain sum of money for the maintenance of the scholars, as well as for the support of the teachers. Besides establishing schools for the education of the young, he ordered some useful books to be translated from the Swedish into the Lapponese language; and these were afterwards followed by others of still greater importance. In 1648, a Manual was printed at Stockholm, containing the Psalms of David, the Proverbs of Solomon, the book of Ecclesiasticus, Luther's Catechism, Sacred Hymns, and the Lessons from the Gospels and Epistles, with the History of Christ's Passion, and of the Destruction of Jerusalem, the Ritual, and various forms of prayer, translated into the Lapponese language by John Tornæus, minister of Torna. In 1669, Olaus Stephen Graan, a native minister of Lapland, published a work under a similar title, containing the Lessons from the Gospels and Epistles, the Collects, the Ritual, the History of Christ's Passion, and some prayers. It differs from the other chiefly in this, that the language is nearer the dialect of the Lapmark of Uma and Pitha.[1]

In the eighteenth century, some new measures were adopted for the spread of Christianity in Lapland. In 1738, the Swedish diet resolved, that the whole Bible should be translated into the Lapponese language; that a contribution should be made throughout the kingdom, for the support of the missionaries and the schools; and that the superintendence of the work should be committed to a College, consisting of some of the principal dignitaries in the kingdom. To this object the inhabitants of Sweden contributed so liberally, that, in a short time, no less a sum was raised than 300,000 rixdollars. In 1755, the New Testament was published in the Lapponese language: part of the impression was sold, and part given away, to encourage the people to diligence in reading.[2]

The inhabitants of Swedish Lapland, when young, are in general, it is said, taught to read; but afterwards, for want of books, they often forget what little learning they acquired in early life. In order, therefore, to supply the want of the Holy Scriptures in that country, the British and Foreign Bible Society, published, in 1811, a large edition of the New Testament in the Lapponese language, consisting of five thousand copies. One half of the impression was immediately sent to the different ports in the vicinity of Swedish Lapland, from whence, by the special orders of Government, copies were for-

[1] Scheffer's History of Lapland, 1704, p. 60, 63, 65, 67, 72; Fabricii Lux Salutaris toti orbi exoriens, p. 598.

[2] Bock Missions Geschicht, p. 267; Miss. Mag. vol. xiv. p. 377.

warded, free of expense, by inland carriers, and distributed in fair proportions among the various parishes of that extensive country.[1]

But though it is now near three centuries since the Swedes began to extend the gospel in Lapland, it has hitherto made little progress. The inhabitants, it is true, are professed Christians; but their Christianity is merely nominal, and among some of them the form of it may be sought in vain. Traces of their having offered sacrifices to the gods of their fathers are occasionally discovered among them. Few of them reside in the neighbourhood of the churches; and, indeed, they seldom attend them, unless on the solemn festivals, or at a fair, when they have the sacraments administered to them. To ensure their attendance, they are subjected to a heavy fine and a severe penance, if they neglect the appointed festivals. The clergy, such as they are, go little among them, except during their short summers: they are careful, however, to attend the winter markets to receive their pay, and to sell them spirituous liquors, of which the Laplanders are immoderately fond, and of which, it is said, they can drink an enormous quantity without being intoxicated.[2]

[1] Miss. Mag. vol. xiv. p. 377; Report of the British and Foreign Bible Society, 1812, p. 2. Appendix, p. 43, 88.

[2] Miss. Mag. vol. xiv. p. 419; Periodical Accounts relative to the Missions of the United Brethren, vol. ii. p. 203; Scheffer's History, p. 83; Linnæus' Tour in Lapland, vol. i. p. 114, 158.

CHAPTER III.

PROPAGATION OF CHRISTIANITY BY THE DUTCH.[1]

SECT. I.—CEYLON.

In the beginning of the seventeenth century, the inhabitants of the United Provinces, after having thrown off the yoke of Spain, carried their victorious arms into the East, and wrested from the crown of Portugal some of her most valuable possessions in that quarter of the world. Among these were the maritime parts of the Island of Ceylon. In 1636, the King of Kandy sent a letter to the Dutch Governor of Palliacatta, on the coast of Coromandel, in which, after recounting the violent and dishonourable acts of the Portuguese, he invited the Dutch to enter into an alliance with him for the purpose of expelling them from off the Island.[2] In carrying out this design, however, the Dutch were guilty of an act of perfidy, not less flagrant than any which had been committed by the Portuguese. In open violation of the express terms of their engagement, they retained possession of their conquests, and precipitated a fresh war with their ally, who had called them to his assistance. They established themselves at Galle, Colombo, and Jaffna, and having driven the Portuguese from all their fortresses, they laid claim, by right of conquest, to the whole of their possessions on the coast;[3] but the interior of the island still remained subject to the King of Kandy.

[1] It is not unworthy of mention, that, so early as 1612, a Missionary Seminary was formed at Leyden, for the purpose of preparing missionaries for the East and the West. It was projected by Antonius Walæus, Professor of Divinity at Leyden, who was also the first Principal of the Institution.—*Grant's Bampton Lectures*, 1843, p. 389.

[2] Baldæus' Description of the Coasts of Malabar, Coromandel, and Ceylon, *in* Churchhill's Collection of Voyages, vol. iii. p. 703.

[3] Tennent's Christianity in Ceylon, p. 39.

The population of Ceylon consisted chiefly of two distinct classes. The northern part of the island was occupied by the same race as inhabited the opposite coast of India: they were of the Hindu faith, and spoke the Tamil language. The southern parts of the island were inhabited by a people called Cingalese: they professed the Budhist faith, and their language, like themselves, was named Cingalese. In all accounts of efforts for the propagation of Christianity in Ceylon, it is of importance to bear in mind this distinction in the character, religion, and language of its inhabitants.

As the Portuguese, while the country was in their possession, had sought to bring over the natives to the Church of Rome, so the Dutch now attempted to convert them to the Protestant faith, and they early established the Reformed Church of Holland as the religion of the country. In October 1642, the first Dutch minister, Antony Hornhonius arrived in Ceylon, and in the course of a few years, he was followed by others, who were employed by the Government in establishing and organizing schools and churches on the island. In the northern part of the island, they took possession of the Roman Catholic Churches, some of which were noble and spacious stone buildings; and great numbers of the people were brought over to the profession of the Protestant faith. But while the Dutch endeavoured to bring the natives to the profession of Christianity, the qualifications they required in the catechumens were so very slender, that most of them, it is probable, were little superior, either in knowledge or practice, to the Romish converts in heathen countries. Nothing more was required of them, than that they should be able to repeat the Lord's Prayer, the Ten Commandments, a Morning and Evening Prayer, and a Grace before and after meat. When the ministers, in the course of their visitations, were certified by the schoolmasters that the poor people had committed these things to memory, they proceeded to baptize them without further ceremony!

Among the Budhist population in the southern parts of the island, the Dutch did not find the same readiness to come over to the Protestant faith, as among the Hindus in the north. With the view of overcoming their objections, a Proclamation was issued, ordaining that no native should be raised to the rank of a Modeliar, or admitted to any employment under Government, or even be permitted to farm land, unless he joined the Reformed Church, and subscribed the Helvetic Confession of Faith. This absurd and impolitic order, so well calculated to make the people hypocrites not Christians, was attended with the desired success. Many of the chiefs, who had been baptized by the Portuguese, came forward and abjured the errors of the Romish Church. The landowners, and those who aspired to be petty headmen and police vidahus in the villages, were equally ready to qualify themselves for enjoying these civil advantages.[1]

The Dutch ministers laboured under great disabilities in communicating instruction to the natives. With a few exceptions, they never acquired a knowledge of the Tamil or the Cingalese languages, and consequently were very imperfectly qualified for instructing the people; while the smallness of their number, combined with the extent of their districts and the variety of their duties, devolved upon them an amount of work which it was scarcely possible for them to overtake.[2]

The education of the Natives was an object to which the Dutch directed considerable attention. The country having been divided into parishes, their plan was to establish a school in each parish, and in some there were two or more, according to the extent of the population. The education given in the village schools was but limited, seldom amounting to more than reading and writing. It was also gratuitous; but the attendance of the scholars was compulsory, and was enforced by fines. In the southern parts of the island, and especially at Matura, which has always been a stronghold of Budhism, the opposition of the people was manifested more openly and strongly than in most other places; and the evil was aggravated by an edict of the Dutch, prohibiting the marriage of the professors of Christianity with the worshippers of Budhu. Where religious prejudices did not interfere, the natives, in general, shewed a desire to have their sons educated; but it required many years to

[1] Tennent's Christianity in Ceylon, p. 43, 45; Cordiner's Description of Ceylon, vol. i. p. 155; Conferences of the Danish Missionaries, p. 347; Mather's History of New England, book iii. p. 195.

[2] Hough's History of Christianity in India, vol. iii. p. 75, 80, 103.

Valentyn gives a Catalogue of 97 ministers, between the years 1642 and 1725, but he states that of all these, only eight acquired the native languages, four the Tamil, and four the Cingalese.—*Hough's History of Christianity in India*, vol. iii. p. 103.

overcome the aversion even of the nominal Christians to the education of their daughters, and especially to their being taught to write. According to some accounts, the education of the females was entirely neglected. It was deemed enough for them if they were able to repeat certain Prayers, and to explain the Catechism and Creed before they were allowed to be married.[1]

Besides these Common Schools, the Dutch established two Seminaries of a higher order, one at Jaffna, the other at Colombo, for the education of Native youths of promising talents in the Dutch language, in order that, by obtaining through it more extensive knowledge, they might be better qualified to labour as schoolmasters, catechists, and preachers among their countrymen. Some were even sent to Europe, where they re-

[1] Hough's Hist. vol. iii. p. 75; Tennent, p. 43, 46, 69.

Baldæus, who was a number of years one of the Ministers in this Island soon after it fell into the hands of the Dutch, informs us, in his "Description of the Coasts of Malabar, Coromandel, and Ceylon," a work published at Amsterdam in 1672, that in the province of Jaffnapatam, there were thirty-four Native churches, besides those of the Dutch and the Portuguese. Of most of these, he has given an Engraving in that splendid work; and as they served alternately, as a place of worship on the Sabbath, and a school-house during the week, he has given us the following statement of the number of the hearers and scholars who attended them :—

Churches.	Hearers.	Scholars.	Churches.	Hearers.	Scholars.
Telipole	2000	1000	Warranni	2500	800
Mallagam	600	200	Tenmarache . . .	1150	650
Maylette	1550	750	Catavelli	1100	600
Achiavelli	800	450	Ureputti	850	690
Oudewil	950	600	Paretiture . . .	3000	1000
Batecotte	2000	850	Pælepolay . . .	600	300
Paneterpou . . .	1250	600	Mogomale . . .	500	450
Changane	...	700	Tambamme . . .	900	500
Manipay	750	560	Mulipatto . . .	350	215
Vanarpone . . .	550	200	Alleputti, Welane, Ourature . . .	2600	800
Nalour	...	590			
Sundecouli . . .	400	450			
Copay, Pontour . . .	...	800	Caradwa	1050	490
			Pongardwa . . .	800	200
Navacouli . . .	750	400	Analativa . . .	...	...
Chavagatzery . .	2500	1000	Nainatwa . . .	300	70
Cathay	1150	550	Nindundiva . . .	...	...

This Table we have drawn up from Baldæus; and where he has stated different numbers, we have taken the medium between them. These churches, or at least most of them, were originally built by the Portuguese: some of them were noble buildings. To most of them was attached a house for the minister, with, in some cases, a garden. There were at that time only two or three Ministers for all these churches: so that they were obliged to travel from place to place, and to preach three sermons every Sabbath, and once on a week day, besides constantly visiting the congregations in the country. Most of the Churches being by this means without a Minister on the Sabbath, the ceived a more complete education, and returned to the island ordained to the ministry.

The Dutch Government, and also the Ministers and the Consistories, appear to have been at all times ready to exercise coercion in matters of religion. Severe measures were adopted, from the very first, against the Roman Catholic priests: the object appears to have been nothing less than the extinction of the Romish religion in the island. Measures of a similar kind were resorted to for the suppression of Budhism. In compliance with the wishes of the Consistory, the Government issued an edict, imposing penalties on devil-dances and other heathenish ceremonies. When the King of Kandy, in 1688, sought permission to erect a temple to Budhu in the Dutch territories, his request was refused. The proscription both of Popery and of Budhism having attracted the attention of the Clergy in Holland, the Classis of Amsterdam, in 1700, addressed a remonstrance to the Consistory of Colombo, in which they reminded them that such measures were not of Christ, nor calculated to advance his kingdom; that compulsion can never produce conviction, nor penalties induce belief; and that those who are constrained by such means to call themselves Christians, were still in heart the enemies of Christ. Measures of coercion, however, still continued to be employed. The schools having been found in a very defective state, the parents were made responsible for the better attendance of their children, on pain of being heavily fined, employed as convicts in the public service, or even cast into prison. The local authorities were also directed to keep the Jogees, Brahmans, and other pilgrims, as much as possible, from going at the annual festivals to Ramnadkovil, and other places of resort out of the island; because the example of these

Schoolmaster, to supply this want, used to read a Sermon to the people in their own language, for which purpose a certain number of Discourses was allotted to each of the Churches. With regard to the schools, Baldæus informs us, that, in 1663, there were in the province of Jaffnapatam alone, 15,012 children who attended them, exclusive of those in Manaar and the country of the Wanier, where, in 1665, there were 1315. At the time of his departure from the Island, the children in the Schools had increased to 18,000.—*Baldæus' Description of the Coasts of Malabar, Coromandel, and Ceylon*, in *Churchhill's Collection of Voyages*, vol. iii. p. 713, 719. The gross number of scholars in the Cingalese districts, varied from 30,000 to 40,000, and at the close of the Dutch Government in Ceylon, the number of children in all parts of the Island, was little short of 85,000.—*Tennent*, p. 48.

[1] Hough's Hist. vol. iii. p. 96, 99.

pilgrimages was found to have an injurious influence on the minds of the Christians, and were also the occasion of considerable sums of money being carried out of the Dutch territories. A Proclamation was even issued, declaring a Christian convicted of participating in any of the ceremonies of heathenism, liable to be publicly whipped, and imprisoned in irons for the space of a year.[1]

In 1722, the number of Native Christians connected with the Dutch Church in Ceylon was as follows:—

Tamil Christians in Jaffna, . .	189,388
Christians in other places, . .	179,845
Christians in the Galle District, .	55,159
	424,392

Besides these numbers, there were 2799 young men, and 1493 young women, candidates for baptism.[2] After the accounts, however, which we have already given, no one will be surprised to find that the generality of these professed adherents of the Reformed Church, were Christians only in name.

In 1730, the Consistory of Galle took occasion to place on record their views of the character and condition of the Cingalese Converts to the Reformed Church. The Native chiefs, who had assumed the name of Christians in compliance with the wishes of the Government, they state, were still incorrigible Budhists, and, in their pride of Caste, they required separate churches to be erected specially for themselves, to which even their own wives were not to be admissible. The Christians generally adhered secretly to idolatry, notwithstanding their profession of Christianity. Every action of their lives was regulated by the precepts and practice of Budhism. "When a child is born they still consult the astrologer; when it is sick, they hang charms around its neck. Even after baptism, they discontinue the use of its Christian name; and a heathen name is, according to the usual custom, given to it on the first occasion of its eating rice. They will undertake no work, without ascertaining a lucky day for commencing it; and when sick or

[1] Tennent, p. 39, 50, 54; Hough's Hist. vol. iii. p. 91, 95, 99.

[2] Valentyn Keurlyke Veschryving van Choromandel, Pegu, Arrakan, &c., C. 17, in Hough's Hist. vol. iii. p. 100.

in adversity, they send for the devil-dancer in preference to their minister. When they marry, it must be in a propitious hour; and when they die, their graves are decorated with the leaves of the tree sacred to Budhu, and cocoa-nuts and rice are piled around as food for the departed. They make offerings to the idols at Kattragam; they bestow gifts on the mendicant servants of the temple; and, in short, the highest benediction they can pronounce on their friends is, May you become a Budhist."[1]

If any further proof were necessary of the low state of Religion among the Dutch Converts in Ceylon, we might state the small number of them who were communicants. In 1760, of 182,226 Natives who were enrolled as Christians at Jaffna, only 64 were members of the Church; of 9820 at Manaar, there were only 5; and at Galle and Matura not more than 36.[2] We do not consider great numbers of communicants as any sign of the spiritual prosperity of a Church; but certainly such small numbers do shew that religion is at a low ebb.

With a view to the instruction of the Natives, the Dutch published a considerable part of the Holy Scriptures in the Tamil language, which is spoken in the north of Ceylon; and also in the Cingalese, which is the common language of the island. In 1743, the New Testament in Tamil was printed at Colombo, under the auspices of the Dutch governor. Previous to this, the Four Gospels were translated into Cingalese; and in 1783, the whole of the New Testament, with the books of Genesis, Exodus, and part of Leviticus, was published in that language at Colombo. These, with a version of the Psalms of David, are the whole of the sacred writings which the Dutch printed in Cingalese; but there was a version of a number of other books of the Old Testament left in manuscript by one of their ministers. The New Testament in Portuguese by John Ferreira d'Almeida, a Romish priest who joined the Dutch Church in Ceylon, was also printed; and he likewise prepared a version of the greater part of the Old Testament in the same language.[3]

[1] Tennent, p. 56. [2] Tennent, p. 65.

[3] Le Long Bibliotheca Sacra, Edit. Maschii, tom. i. part ii. p. 201; tom. ii. part ii. p. 210. Rep. Bib. Soc. 1810, App. p. 86. Ibid. 1813, App. p. 18. Niecampii Historia Missionis Evangelicæ in India Orientali; Hough's Hist. vol. iii. p. 76.

In 1795, the Dutch possessions in the island of Ceylon surrendered to the arms of the British; and for a considerable time, the religious instruction of the natives occupied no part of the attention of their new masters. The European ministers became prisoners of war; the native catechists and schoolmasters no longer received their salaries; the duties of public worship, and the education of the young, were either feebly discharged, or entirely neglected; thousands of the natives, who had once called themselves Christians, relapsed into heathenism; and the prohibition of the Dutch against erecting any new Pagan temples being no longer in force, the number of them was, in a short time, greatly augmented.[1]

After some time, however, the schools were re-established at the expense of Government; the Dutch ministers resumed the charge of their congregations; several new preachers were educated in the island; and others still better qualified were brought over from the coast of Coromandel. There was also a very flourishing academy at Colombo, consisting of three different classes of young men, Cingalese, Tamil, and European. They were all taught the English, as well as the native languages. The Cingalese scholars were the sons of the Modeliars, and of the people of the first rank in the island, and made respectable progress in learning.[2]

In baptizing the Natives, the old system of the Dutch was still pursued; or perhaps it was even still further corrupted. The Government native preachers, called Preponents, sometimes baptized two or three hundred infants and elder children at a time, while making the circuit of their districts, and took any one whom they might happen to find as sponsors. Persons passing along the road, and never seen before by the parties bringing the children, were often called on to be godfathers and godmothers; persons as ignorant of Christianity, as if there were no such religion in the world, and who perhaps had never been baptized themselves; though almost all the Budhist priests in the maritime provinces, were persons who had been baptized in their infancy.[3]

[1] Cordiner's Description, vol. i. p. 159.—Proceedings of the Church Missionary Society, vol. i. p. 231. Rep. Bib. Soc. 1815, App. p. 24.

[2] Cordiner's Description, vol. i. p. 165.—Proceed. Ch. Miss. Soc. vol. iii. p. 415.

[3] Selkirk's Recollections of Ceylon, p. 515.

In 1812, a Bible Society was instituted at Colombo, under the patronage of Sir Robert Brownrigg, the Governor, and other distinguished persons, with a particular view to the supply of the natives with the Holy Scriptures. Of such an Institution, the need was most urgent. There were scarcely, it was supposed, twenty copies of the New Testament on the whole Island. To supply this want, a new edition of the Cingalese New Testament was printed, for the use of the Native Christians; but as the translation was deemed very incorrect, a new version both of the Old and the New Testament was executed. If, however, the old translation was often so low as to disgust Cingalese of moderate literary attainments, the new version was so high as not to be intelligible by ordinary readers. In a second edition, however, it was revised, and the language was brought nearer to that in ordinary use.[1]

With regard to idolatry, the British Government pursued an opposite course to that of the Dutch. The Dutch sought to suppress it; the British, at first, tolerated, and after some years, countenanced and supported it. In the maritime parts of the island, which were originally possessed by the British, there was little or no encouragement given to idolatry by the Government; but, in 1815, when the kingdom of Kandy was subjected to the Crown of England, the following article was introduced into the Treaty with the Kandian chiefs: "The religion of Budhu, professed by the chiefs and inhabitants of these provinces, is declared inviolable; and its rites, ministers, and places of worship, are to be maintained and protected." In compliance with this Treaty, the British Government appointed the principal Budhist priests in the interior provinces, and the lay chiefs of the principal Dewalas or demon temples, granted monthly allowances for the support of Budhist priests, and was also at some expense for various festivals, both Budhist and Hindu. The Maligawa or great temple at Kandy, was guarded by soldiers in the British service; and the Delada or Tooth of Budhu, with all its rich appendages, was in the keeping of the Government agent, and could not be exhibited without his permission. Though nothing more than a piece of discoloured ivory, slightly curved, nearly two inches long, and one inch in diameter at its

[1] Rep. Bib. Soc. 1813, App. p. 59, 61. Ibid, 1824, p. 54. Ibid, 1831, p. 55.

base, it is worshipped by the Budhists with the most intense devotion, and is considered by them as the palladium of their country. In 1828, during the government of Sir Edward Barnes, this precious relic was publicly exhibited by order of Government, and vast crowds of devoted worshippers collected from all parts of the Island to witness the sight. It had not been exhibited for fifty years before. In 1843, it was again publicly exhibited by the authority and under the auspices of the Government, on occasion of the presentation of offerings by a number of Siamese priests, who had come to the island on a kind of pilgrimage, as a deputation from the King of Siam.[1]

[1] Selkirk's Recollections, p. 100, 102, 532; Quarterly Review, vol. lxxxviii. p. 100; (Wesleyan) Missionary Notices, 1844, p. 418; (Baptist) Missionary Herald, 1846, p. 293; Ibid. 1849, p. 170.

Of this precious relic, the Rev. Mr Selkirk gives the following account in his Journal:—"Oct. 19, 1838. The third Adigar, the highest native at present in the Kandian country, and the lay head of Maligawa, called to pay me a visit a few days ago. I then said that I should like to see the Maligawa, and went for this purpose, this evening, at the time he was making his offerings. On my arrival about seven o'clock, I was led up stairs, and the Adigar, by special favour, admitted me into the very *penetralia*, where the *Ran Karanduwa*, or golden case is, in which is contained the precious relic of Budhu. This relic is enclosed in the seventh of a set of Karanduwas, which are put one into another. It is only taken out on great occasions. The small Dagoba in which the six Karanduwas are enclosed, is about a yard and a half high, and, as nearly as I can guess, about a yard and a half round the case. There is a beautiful bird made of precious stones, set in gold, hanging over it; and the front of the Dagoba is covered with gold and precious stones. I was told it was worth two or three lacs of rupees, (£20,000 or £30,000). The *Asana*, or table for offerings, on which it is placed, is covered with plates of gold and edged with silver, beautifully cut and worked. Near the Asana, in front, are the altars on which are presented the offerings of flowers that are made, morning and evening, by the Adigar. When I went in, there was a large table before the altar, which was covered with a white cloth, and on which were placed by the Adigar and the servants of the temple, about fifty small silver cups, each having a spoon in it, and containing honey or lime juice, or other small things as offerings. After remaining here for some time, these were removed, and the contents became the portion of the priests, and would be used by them when they ate their rice and curry. They thus 'eat things offered to idols.' A small silver salver was then placed on the table, with all the little implements made use of, by persons accustomed to eat betel. These were all of gold. The plates on which flowers were brought by the Adigar's attendants, were of gold. The large massy doors, which opened into the splendid *Adytum*, were gilt with gold. The door frames were inlaid with ivory, beautifully carved. In short, every thing is of the greatest richness and splendour, and is well calculated to impose upon the senses of the worshippers.

"After leaving this place, I went to another temple, still within the precincts of the Maligawa, where is an image of Budhu in a sitting posture, about four feet high, covered with gold, and a great number of other images of Budhu, some an entire precious stone, others of gold or silver. On one of those made of silver, is the following Cingalese inscription, which I copied while the image was before me: 'Awayana

The connection of the Government in Ceylon with the religion of the Kandians, having been brought under the consideration of the Government in England, it resolved that this connection should entirely cease; that full protection should be afforded to them in the exercise of their religion; but that they should be left to manage their own religious matters; that every facility should be afforded to them for this purpose; and that they should retain the whole of their property, and enjoy every other immunity which previously belonged to them. But this was a scheme which the Kandian chiefs and priests were not disposed to agree to voluntarily, nor indeed on any terms that could be proposed or suggested to them. As they knew it could not be carried into effect without a breach of the treaty made with them, they were exceedingly difficult to deal with, probably believing that if they were firm in starting objections to every plan that was proposed to them, the convention would not be broken at all. There were, however, positive instructions from Earl Grey, the Colonial Secretary, that the connection of the Government with the idolatry of Ceylon should terminate forthwith, whatever might be the cost to England. The dissolution was accordingly announced, to the great annoyance of both the Kandian chiefs and the priests. The Delada was placed under their own custody, and thus matters remained until there happened to be an insurrection in the country, when it was unhappily resumed, not, however, as a trophy of war,

desayehi Rakkaduwe maha Dagoba Wihara Sthanayen gat me Pilima wahanse Barnes Kumarikawa wisin Dalada Mandiriyata pradanayakale warusha ek dahas ata siya wisi hatediya, *i. e.*, 'This image of Budhu, taken from the Great Dagoba and Wihara at Rakkaduwa, in the country of Ava, was presented to the Dalada Mandiriya (temple) in the year 1827, by Miss (the princess) Barnes.' Miss Barnes was the daughter of Sir Edward Barnes, who held the Government of Ceylon from 1823 or 1824 to 1831. The priests shewed me two other images made of silver, presented to the Temple by the Maha Modeliar, the highest Native in the maritime provinces, and a *Christian.* In this place were also several images of gold, some in splendid cases, with small glass doors.

"The number of priests attached to this temple is forty. There are also twenty persons in daily attendance to collect flowers, &c., for offerings, and who wait upon the Adigar when he goes morning and evening. On festival occasions, there are 150 or 200 priests in attendance. The chief revenues of this temple arise from lands left by various Cingalese kings. The twenty persons just mentioned are changed every month, so that in the year there are nearly 250 persons engaged in the performance of the services of this one temple, in addition to the priests."—*Selkirk's Recollections of Ceylon*, p. 529.

but for its safe keeping. Thus the question was thrown back again.[1] Sir G. W. Anderson, the Governor, afterwards resumed the practice of appointing the priests; an oppressive system of service on the Temple estates was thereby once more introduced, and the temples themselves were adorned by forced labour.[2]

With respect to the number of Christians in Ceylon, it is not easy to form any opinion, the accounts are so very contradictory. In 1801, the native Protestant Christians on the island, according to the general returns in the Ecclesiastical department, amounted to upwards of 342,000.[3] In 1811, the Protestant Christians were estimated at about 250,000, and the Roman Catholics at 85,000; in this instance, the computation of the Protestants was founded on the returns from the schoolmasters of the several districts. In 1813, according to similar returns, the native Protestants amounted only to about 146,000, and the Roman Catholics to 37,469, exclusive of children under seven years of age. What is still more singular, the Christian inhabitants of Jaffnapatam had fallen below 5000, though not more than twelve years before, there were said to be in that district 138,896 Protestants, 9632 Catholics, and only 11,362 Pagans;[4] and about twenty years before that, the Christian inhabitants of this province were still more numerous, amounting to no fewer than 186,877, besides 5201 heathen slaves under instruction.[5] This great diminution in the number of professed Christians in Ceylon, we apprehend, is to be attributed partly to numbers of them having relapsed into paganism; but chiefly to the circumstance, that vast multitudes of them differ so little from the heathen, that in one enumeration, the same persons may have been reckoned Christians, who in another, were

[1] Lord Torrington, who was then Governor, expressed the following opinion on the subject in one of his despatches to the Home Government:—"In itself the Budhist religion is a mild and harmless one, and had as *few objectionable points* as any heathen doctrine. *Unless we interfere with it, it will be destroyed* before another and a purer one is built upon its place; and I am sure, I need not point out to your Lordship, the danger and misery that must overtake a country *divested of any spiritual control.*"—*(Bapt.) Miss. Her.* 1852, p. 54. Budhism, of which all this is spoken, let it be remembered, is a system of Atheism.

[2] Calcutta Review, vol. xii. p. 200. (Bapt.) Miss. Her., 1852, d. 19.

[3] Cordiner's Description, vol. i. p. 193.

[4] Rep. Bib. Soc. 1815, App. p. 24.—Christian Observer, vol. i. p. 329.

[5] Neure Geschichte der Evangelischen Missions-Anstalten in Ostindien, tom. iii. p. 144.

accounted Pagans. The fact is, that a large proportion of those who are called Protestant Christians, are in reality heathens; for though they may have been baptized in their infancy, they are entirely ignorant of the principles of the Gospel, and are worshippers of the idol Budhu.[1] Not a few avow themselves both Christians and Budhists, and are willing to be sworn as either in a court of justice.[2]

Though the Dutch ministers, who remained in Ceylon after it was taken by the British, have all either died or left the island, yet a number of missionaries, of various denominations, have settled upon it, so that the natives are no longer so destitute of Christian instruction as they were some years ago. To some of them grants were made by Government of the ancient churches; but many of these are now in a state of dilapidation and decay. In the province of Jaffnapatam may be seen, here and there, the mouldering remains of a forsaken church or house, inaccessible from the surrounding jungle, and now the undisturbed habitation of wild beasts and noxious reptiles. There appears, in general, only a ruinous pillar, or a desolate wall, over which grows spontaneously the aged ivy, as if to bespeak the compassionate inquiries of the Christian traveller; while to heighten the melancholy of the scene, hosts of images, mosques, and pagodas, rear their heads, the monuments of the ignorance, superstition, and idolatry of the wretched natives.[3]

SECT. II.—JAVA.

In 1619, the Dutch established themselves on the Island of Java, and they soon afterwards founded the city of Batavia, the capital of their possessions in the Eastern Archipelago. One of the first objects to which their attention was directed, was the religious instruction of the inhabitants. In obedience to the Governor's orders, the ministers took immediate steps for the introduction among them of the Doctrines of the Dutch

[1] Transactions of the Missionary Society, vol. ii. p. 265.
[2] Proceed. Ch. Miss. Soc. vol. iii. p. 414.
[3] Missionary Register, vol. vi. p. 4.—Report of Methodist Missions, 1817, p. 9.

Reformed Church. The Island was divided into districts, and in each district, a church was erected and a school established. After some time, the most promising Converts were employed as catechists; and a selection was made of the scholars to take charge of the schools, though it does not appear that they had all embraced Christianity. These teachers were distributed over the districts, and Dutch ministers were appointed to superintend the whole.[1]

In 1721, the number of Christians on this island was stated to be upwards of 100,000; in Batavia, there were two churches, in which public worship was performed in the Dutch language; two in which the Portuguese was employed; and one or two in which the Malay was used.[2] The number of ministers at Batavia, when the list was full, amounted to twelve; but, some years ago at least, they were men nowise distinguished either by their learning or their piety.[3]

In propagating Christianity in Java and the neighbouring countries, there is nothing for which the Dutch were more distinguished than by their efforts to furnish the natives with the Holy Scriptures. Not many years after the commencement of their labours on this island, the Gospels and other parts of the Sacred writings were published in the Malay language, which is spoken not only in Malacca, but through all the adjacent islands. In 1668, the New Testament was printed in that language at Amsterdam, at the expense of the East India Company; and, in 1733, a translation of the whole Bible was published in that city, in Roman characters. This version was afterwards printed in 1758, at Batavia, in five volumes, in the Arabic alphabet, with the addition of the letters peculiar to the Malay, under the direction of the Governor-general of the Dutch possessions in the East.[4] Besides the Malay translations, the Dutch printed editions of the Sacred writings in the Portuguese language, a corrupt dialect of which is spoken by many of the inhabitants of Java, and of the neighbouring islands, in

[1] La Croze Histoire du Christianisme des Indes, p. 521, 522. Hough's Hist. vol. iii. p. 54.

[2] Millar's History, vol. ii.; Fabricii Lux Salutaris, p. 594.

[3] Stavorinus' Voyages to the East Indies, vol. i. p. 305, 306.

[4] Le Long Biblioth. Sacra, Ed. Maschii, tom. i. part ii. p. 193; Asiatic Researches, vol. x. p. 183.

consequence of their having once been subject to the Crown of Portugal.[1]

In June 1814, a Bible Society was instituted at Batavia, with a view to the circulation of the Holy Scriptures throughout Eastern Asia, and particularly among the native Christians of this island. Large editions of the Old and New Testament, in the Malay language and the Arabic character, were printed. But as this version was in the high Malay, which is spoken in the interior of the island, and is not understood in Batavia, the Java Bible Society procured also a translation of the New Testament into the low Malay, the dialect that is used in that city, and in the neighbouring country. Two translations of the New Testament were also made into the Javanese language, and a small volume of Extracts from the Old Testament.[2]

In 1816, the Island of Java, which had been taken by the British a few years before, was restored to the Dutch, and though they had in former times promoted measures for Christianizing the Natives, yet of late years their policy has been to discountenance efforts for that end; and the regular clergy were unwilling to do any thing without the sanction of the authorities.[3]

In 1834, the Rev. Mr Wentink was stationed by the Government at Depok, near Batavia, as minister of two small native congregations at that place and Togoe; but there was no other minister known to be employed by it among the native population. Imperfectly instructed as the Javanese converts originally were, and neglected as they have long been, it is not surprising that they should be found unworthy even of the Christian name.[4] Their moral character is awfully depraved; they indulge in the grossest vices, and possess as little of Christianity as their Heathen and Mahommedan neighbours.[5]

[1] Propagation of the Gospel in the East, part ii. p. 15; Fabricii Lux Salutaris, p. 591; Niecampii Hist. p. 275.

[2] Rep. Bib. Soc. 1815, App. p. 116; Ibid. 1816, App. p. 27; Ibid. 1818, p. 26, App. p. 22, 236; Ibid. 1832, p. 42; Ibid. 1842, App. p. 90; Ibid. 1849, p. 47, 51, 59.

[3] Calcutta Christian Observer, 1839, p. 435; Missionary Register, 1835, p. 146, 147.

[4] Netherland's Missionary Society, 1841; Ms. penes me, p. 26.

[5] Baptist Periodical Accounts, vol. vi. p. 239.

SECT. III.—FORMOSA.

IN 1626, George Candidius was appointed minister to a settlement which the Dutch had lately formed on Formosa, where they had taken possession of a harbour on the south side of the island, and for the purpose of protecting it, they built a fort which they called Fort Zealand. It is stated that he took great pains to introduce Christianity among the inhabitants, and that he was successful in bringing a considerable number of them to embrace it.[1]

In 1631, Mr Robert Junius[2] was sent by the Senate of the United Provinces to Formosa, with the view of carrying on the same good work. He endeavoured for about two years to instruct the natives through the medium of the Dutch language; but as they were in general ignorant of it, he at length acquired the Formosan language, which enabled him to convey his instructions with better effect. Many of them, particularly in the northern parts of the island, acquired, it is said, a considerable knowledge of the principles of Christianity; and were led to profess themselves Christians. Mr Junius baptized no fewer than 5900 adults, besides numbers of children. He also instituted schools, in which, in the course of a few years, about six hundred of the natives learned to read; and besides a few Dutchmen, whom he had employed as teachers, there were about fifty of the converts, whom he trained to the same office. He collected the principal heads of religion, wrote some prayers, and translated several Psalms into the Formosan language. It was chiefly in the northern parts of the island that he carried on these operations; but he also planted churches in twenty-

[1] Chinese Repository, Canton, 1834, vol. ii. p. 410; vol. vi. p. 587.

[2] Robert Junius is said to have been of a Scotch family which had settled in Holland, whose name was Young. In the Cottonian MSS. in the British Museum, there is a draft of a Letter from James I. King of England, to the Emperor of Abyssinia, one great object of which was to recommend to that prince a certain Robert Junius, probably the individual who afterwards went to Formosa. After making requests in reference to trade, his Majesty particularly desires that he may be allowed to examine the great library "on the mountain Amhara," and to make a Catalogue of the Books, especially of the early Fathers of the Church.—*Edinburgh Review*, vol. lxvi. p. 331.

three towns in the south. After labouring about twelve years on this island, he returned to Holland; but the work was carried on by other ministers from that country or from Batavia.[1] The Gospels of Matthew and John, translated into the Formosan language, by David Gravius, and also a Catechism, were printed at Amsterdam;[2] but it is probable these works never reached Formosa, or at least were never of much use to the inhabitants, as about the period of their completion, the Dutch were expelled from the island, under circumstances of peculiar barbarity.

In May 1661, Koxinga, a noted Chinese pirate, appeared off Formosa with a force of 20,000 men, and after a severe engagement with the Dutch, effected a landing on the island. In a short time the fort of Province was compelled to surrender to him; but the Dutch in the fort of Zealand, resolved to defend themselves to the last extremity. Koxinga now laid siege to that place; but as he was unsuccessful in all his attacks, he turned it into a close blockade. In the meanwhile, he laid waste the open country, took the Dutch inhabitants prisoners, and treated them in the most barbarous manner. Anxious to bring the war to a close, he sent Mr Hambrocock, one of the ministers, whom he had taken captive, to the governor of the fort, to persuade him to surrender, promising to allow the garrison to depart with the whole of their property; and threatening, in case of a refusal, to revenge himself upon the prisoners. With these instructions, Mr Hambrocock, repaired to the fort, leaving his wife and children behind him as hostages; but though he knew that, if the negotiation failed, he had nothing to expect but death, he was so far from persuading the garrison to surrender, that he encouraged them to make a brave defence, assuring them that the tyrant had already lost many of his best soldiers; that he began to be weary of the siege, and was afraid lest they should obtain succours from Batavia. After hearing his statements, the Council of war left it to his own choice, either to remain in the fort, or to return to the camp of the enemy. Some entreated him to stay; but with singular magnanimity, he turned a deaf ear to all their solicitations. Two

[1] The Conversion of 5900 East Indians in the Isle of Formosa, London, 1650, p. 3, 12.
[2] Fabricii Lux Salutaris, p. 595.

of his daughters who were in the fort, hung about his neck, overwhelmed with grief, and bathed in tears, at seeing him ready to commit himself into the hands of a merciless tyrant, to whose fury he was likely to fall a sacrifice. He represented to them, that as he had left his wife and two other children as hostages in the camp of Koxinga, nothing but immediate death would await them, if he did not return. He, therefore, tore himself from their arms, and left the fort, exhorting the garrison to make a resolute defence, and expressing his hope, that he might be useful to his unfortunate fellow prisoners.

On his arrival in the camp, Mr Hambrocock informed Koxinga, that the besieged would not treat with him, unless the possession of the fort was secured to them, and that, rather than surrender, they would defend it to the last extremity. As some of the Formosans had killed several of his followers, the tyrant, under the pretext that they had been incited to insurrection by the prisoners, ordered all the men among the Dutch, to the number of five hundred, to be massacred. Among the slain, were Mr Hambrocock, two other ministers, and a number of schoolmasters, all of whom were beheaded. Many, even of the women and children, were put to death; others were reserved for the use of the principal officers, or sold to the common soldiers.

In the mean while, the fort of Zealand made a resolute resistance; but it was at length forced to surrender to the enemy, after sustaining a siege of nine months, during which upwards of sixteen hundred persons perished by famine, by disease, or by the sword. Agreeably to the terms of capitulation, the besieged returned to Batavia, where the governor, and the members of the Council, notwithstanding the brave defence they had made, and the aggravated sufferings they had endured, were thrown into prison, and their property was confiscated. The Governor was even condemned to perpetual imprisonment in the Isle of Ey; but through the intercession of the Prince of Orange, he was at length set at liberty.[1] The grandson of the Pirate who expelled the Dutch from the Island of Formosa, was afterwards obliged to surrender it to the Emperor of China;

[1] Nieuhoff's Voyages *in* Churchhill's Collection, vol. ii. p. 160.

and as it has ever since remained in his possession, it is probable no traces of Christianity are now to be found among the inhabitants.[1]

SECT. IV.—AMBOYNA.

In 1647, the Dutch, who had obtained possession of Amboyna some years before, began to introduce Christianity into this island.[2] The inhabitants, both Heathen and Mahommedans, submitted to baptism in great numbers. In 1686, one of the ministers in the capital town, had, it is said, no fewer than 30,000 of the natives under his pastoral care, who had been converted by him to the Christian faith.[3] Few Romish missionaries could boast of a more splendid triumph!

The Government of Amboyna included several Islands, almost all of them within sight of each other. The number of churches on these islands, according to Captain Hamilton, was no fewer than fifty; and the inhabitants shewed a great readiness to embrace Christianity, especially after some of the Native youths, who were sent to Holland for their education, returned ordained to the ministry, and instructed them in the principles of religion. Such of the inhabitants as professed themselves Christians, lived in distinct villages; and in each of these there was a church, where they assembled for Divine worship. They were obliged to attend the church and the catechetical exercises, otherwise their absence was reported to the person in authority, a practice which is continued to the present day.[4]

In 1775, when Stavorinus was at Amboyna, public worship in the Malay church, was confined to the reading of a sermon in that language by one of the visitors of the sick, as the minister did not understand it, and had little inclination to learn it. It had lately been ascertained by a church visitation, that the number of Christians in a part of the places under this Govern-

[1] Modern Universal History, vol. viii. p. 507.

[2] Nieuhoff's Voyages in Churchhill's Collection, vol. ii. p. 156.

[3] Millar's History, vol. ii. p. 475.

[4] Hamilton's New Account of the East Indies, vol. ii. p. 142; Bapt. Period. Accounts, vol. v. p. 493, 616.

ment, amounted to 21,124; but of these only 843 were members of the church. Indeed, the superstitious respect which they paid to the ministers, together with a few external forms of religion, were the chief circumstances which distinguished them from the rest of their countrymen. Few of them had a tolerable knowledge of the doctrines of Christianity, or even of the ordinary duties of morality. Unchastity was universal among the women as well as the men; theft was extremely common, and was generally managed with great dexterity; and, like all the Malay tribes, they were distinguished by a peculiar malignity of character. The superstitions of Heathenism, appeared still to maintain their original sway over their benighted minds. When they sailed past a certain hill on the coast of Ceram, they used to propitiate the Evil Spirit, who, they believed, had his dwelling in that quarter, by setting afloat a few flowers, and a small piece of money in cocoa-nut shells; and if it was the evening, they also put oil into them with little wicks, and set them to burn on the water. After presenting this offering to the Demon of the hill, they proceeded on their voyage, satisfied that he would do no harm to them or their vessels.[1]

Besides the converts in the islands already mentioned, the Dutch made a multitude of others in Sumatra,[2] Timor, Celebes, Banda, Ternate, and the neighbouring Molucca Islands;[3] but they were left for many years in a great measure destitute of the means of religious instruction. Churches were still standing on some of these islands; but they were without ministers. The schoolmasters were not paid their salaries, and hence many of them neglected their schools, and turned their attention to husbandry. Copies of the Scriptures were so extremely scarce, that some even of the schoolmasters possessed only a few leaves

[1] Stavorinus' Voyages, vol. ii. p. 365, 388.

[2] In 1718, Jacob Vischer, a Dutch minister at Batavia, wrote that, in the island of Sumatra, and at the Castle of Badan, he was employed to administer the Sacraments; and that many came to be baptized, presenting, at the same time, offerings of great value unto the Lord; that they received the Lord's Supper only once in two years, and that he was very acceptable to them; that he ordained elders and deacons, provided golden cups for administering the communion, and obtained teachers from the neighbouring islands to instruct the young; that ships full of heathens came there to be baptized, who willingly embraced the Christian religion, bringing gifts in gold and precious stones, which, on their knees, they offered to the ministers of the gospel.—*Bib. Hist. Phil. Theol. Classis Tertiæ*, p. 917, *et seq.* in *Hough's Hist.* vol. iii. p. 60.

[3] Fabr. Lux Salut. p. 594; Niecampii Hist. p. 275; Paget's Christianographie, p. 275.

of the Bible, though it was part of their duty to read it to the people. In some of the villages, which were left without schoolmasters, it is said the best educated boys used to read a portion of the sacred volume in the church every Sabbath.[1]

Within the last thirty years, however, the Dutch have renewed their efforts for bringing over the natives of Amboyna, and of the neighbouring islands, to the profession of Christianity; and if the numbers baptized by them were to be held as a criterion of their success, it might be admitted they had been eminently successful; but there is reason to believe that most of the converts were Christians only in name, and were little improved by the change in their character or conduct. It is to be feared, indeed, that the practice of the Dutch in baptizing the natives without any proper instruction, and without any evidence of piety, has inflicted a deep and lasting wound on the cause of Christianity in the East India Islands, which there is no likelihood will soon be remedied, thus presenting to Missionaries a solemn warning of the evil and danger of not exercising due discrimination in the admission of heathens into the Church of Christ.

Before closing our account of the efforts of the Dutch for the propagation of Christianity in the East, it is proper to state, that their labours extended also to the Continent of India. In 1630, we are told, they had a congregation of Native Christians at Pulicat, twenty-five miles north of Madras.[2] In 1660, Philip Baldæus proceeded from Ceylon to Negapatnam on the coast of Coromandel, with the view of introducing the Reformed religion; and while there he preached both in Dutch and Portuguese. One of his successors, Nathaniel de Pape, made considerable progress in the Portuguese and Tamil languages, and by the encouragement, and under the protection of Cornelius Speelman, the Governor, spread a knowledge of the gospel in the neighbouring villages.[3] Thus the Dutch had the honour of being the first Protestants who made any efforts for the evangelization of India.

[1] Evangelical Magazine, vol. xxii. p. 296; Miss. Trans. vol. v. p. 280, 283, 285.
[2] Methodist Magazine, 1832, p. 340.
[3] Baldæus *in* Churchhill, vol. iii. p. 587.

CHAPTER IV.

PROPAGATION OF CHRISTIANITY BY THE ANGLO-AMERICANS.

SECT. I.—MASSACHUSSETS COLONY.

After the House of Stuart ascended the Throne of England, the tyranny of the government, both in Church and State, was so intolerable, that numbers of the people left their native land, and sought an asylum in the Wilds of America, in the hope of enjoying that liberty of conscience among savages, which was denied them by their own countrymen. Having left their friends and their country, chiefly for the sake of religion, they could not behold with indifference, the Indians living without God, without Christ, and without hope in the world.

Considerable interest in their conversion was also felt by many in England. Among others, Dr Lake, the Bishop of Bath and Wells, had the object so much at heart, as to declare that nothing but his old age hindered him from going to America and devoting himself to the work. Even the Government professed to be zealous for the conversion of the Indians. James I., in a proclamation which he issued in 1622, declared that the special motive which led him to encourage the plantations in the New world, was his zeal for the extension of the gospel; and his son, Charles I., in the Charter which he granted to the Colony of Massachussets in 1628, gave directions that the people from England "may be so religiously, peaceably, and civilly governed, as their good life and orderly conversation may win and incite the Natives of the country to the knowledge and obedience of the only true God and Saviour of mankind and the Christian faith, which in our Royal intention, and the Adventurers' free profession, is the principal end of the Plantation." It is also not unworthy of mention, that the device on the seal of the Massachussets Colony, was an Indian with a label at his mouth, containing the words "Come over and help us."

For some years, however, the difficulties attending a new settlement in a wild uncultivated region, the quarrels in which the settlers were unfortunately involved with the Indians, the disputes that arose among themselves, and various other circumstances, prevented them from making those early exertions for evangelizing the natives, which the nature and importance of the object demanded. A few of the savages, indeed, in different parts of the country, were instructed in the principles of our holy religion; but there were no systematic efforts made to convert them to the Christian faith. In 1646, the General Court of Massachussets passed the first act encouraging the Propagation of the Gospel among the Indians, and recommended to the Elders of the Churches to consider the means by which this might best be effected.[1]

In October 1646, Mr John Eliot, minister of Roxbury, in the neighbourhood of Boston, who by assiduous study had acquired some knowledge of the Indian language, proceeded, with two or three of his friends, to visit some Indians, at a place about four or five miles from his own house, to whom he had previously given notice of his design to come and instruct them in the Christian faith. As they approached the place they were met by a Chief named Waban, and others of the Indians, and were conducted by them to a large wigwam, where a great number of their countrymen were assembled, to hear the new doctrine which the English were to teach them. After a short prayer, Mr Eliot delivered a discourse to them in the Indian language, which lasted upwards of an hour, and comprehended many of the most important articles of Natural and Revealed religion. He spoke to them of the Creation of the world, and the Fall of man; of the greatness of God, the maker of all things; of the Ten commandments, and the Threatenings denounced against the transgressors of them; of the Character and Office of Jesus

[1] Winslow's Glorious Progress of the Gospel amongst the Indians in New England. London, 1649, p. 1; Collection of the Massachussets' Historical Society, 1st Series, vol. vii. p. 223, 2d Series, vol. vi. p. 650; Francis' Life of John Eliot *in* Spark's Library of American Biography, vol. v. p. 36; Hazard's Historical Collections of State Papers, &c. as Materials for a History of the United States, vol. i. p. 252; Hutchinson's History of the Colony of Massachussets Bay, vol. i. p. 151.

Christ; of the last Judgment, the Joys of heaven, and the torments of hell. Having finished his discourse, he desired them, as was afterwards his ordinary practice, to ask him any questions they might think necessary with regard to the sermon. To the inquiries which some of them proposed, he then endeavoured to give as plain and simple answers as possible; and, after a conference of about three hours, he and his friends returned home highly delighted with their visit. Mr Eliot afterwards repeated his visits to the Indians, and on these occasions, they not only listened to him with great attention, but some of them appeared deeply affected with what they heard.[1]

Encouraged by these auspicious circumstsnces, the General Court of Massachussets, on the application of Mr Eliot, gave the Indians in that neighbourhood some land on which to build a town, where they might live together, enjoy the privilege of religious instruction, and cultivate the arts of civilized life. Having now the prospect of settling in one place, a number of them met together to form some laws for the government of their little community, and agreed on the following regulations, some of which are singular enough:

1st, If any man be idle a week, or at most a fortnight, he shall pay a fine of five shillings.

2dly, If any unmarried man lie with an unmarried woman, he shall pay twenty shillings.

3dly, If any man beat his wife, he shall be carried to the place of justice with his hands tied behind his back, and severely punished.

4thly, Every young man who is not a servant, and is unmarried, shall be obliged to build a wigwam, and to plant some ground for himself, and not shift up and down in other houses.

5thly, If any woman shall not have her hair tied up, but shall allow it to hang loose, or to be cut as men's hair, she shall pay five shillings.

6thly, If any woman go with her breasts uncovered, she shall be fined in two shillings and sixpence.

7thly, If any man wear long hair, he shall pay five shillings.

[1] Day-breaking of the Gospel in New England, London 1647, p. 1, 7, 18. Gookin's Historical Collections of the Indians in New England *in* Collections of the Massachussets Historical Society, vol. i. p. 168.

Lastly, Whoever shall kill their lice between their teeth, shall be fined in five shillings.[1]

Though to us some of these fines may seem inconsiderable, yet to the Indians they must have appeared very heavy, considering their general poverty, and the value of money at that period. Some of the regulations, indeed, are frivolous enough, and certainly had better have been omitted; but let it be remembered, every age has its follies.

The seat of the town, which they called Noonatomen, or *Rejoicing*, being marked out, Mr Eliot advised them to surround it with ditches and a stone wall, promising to furnish them with spades, shovels, mattocks, and iron crows, for this purpose; and he likewise gave money to such as wrought hardest. The wigwams which they erected, were in a considerably improved style; they were built not with mats, as formerly, but with the bark of trees, and were divided into several apartments. The women also began to learn to spin, to make various little articles, and to carry the natural productions of the country to market for sale. In spring they sold cranberries, strawberries, and fish; in summer, whortleberries and grapes; in autumn, venison; in winter, brooms, staves, baskets, and turkeys. Besides, several wrought with the English in haytime and harvest; but it was observed, they were not so industrious, nor yet so capable of hard labour, as those who had been accustomed to it from early life. It is worthy of remark, that Mr Eliot, while he laboured for the conversion of the Indians, was fully sensible of the importance of, at the same time, civilizing them. "I feel it absolutely necessary," he says, "to carry on civility with religion."[2]

Influenced by the example of their countrymen, the Indians in the neighbourhood of Concord expressed a similar desire of uniting together, in a regular society, of receiving the Christian faith, and of learning the arts of civilized life. With this view they requested Mr Eliot to come and preach the Gospel to them; and they begged the Government to grant them a piece of land, on which they might build themselves a town, in the neighbour-

[1] Day-breaking of the Gospel, p. 22.

[2] Shepard's Clear Sunshine of the Gospel breaking forth upon the Indians in New England, London 1648, p. 28, 32.

hood of the White people. Several of their Sachems and other principal men met at Concord, and agreed on the following regulations for their government in civil and religious matters:

1st, That no powawing or conjuring should be allowed among them, under a penalty of twenty shillings for each offence.

2dly, That whoever should be drunk, should pay a fine of twenty shillings.

3dly, That whoever should be convicted of stealing, should restore fourfold.

4thly, That whoever should profane the Sabbath, should be fined in twenty shillings.

5thly, That whoever should commit fornication, should pay twenty shillings if a man, and ten shillings if a woman.

6thly, That wilful murder, adultery, and lying with a beast, should be punished with death.

7thly, That no person should beat his wife, under a penalty of twenty shillings.

8thly, That they would lay aside their old ceremonies of howling, greasing their bodies, adorning their hair, and follow the customs of the English.

Lastly, They agreed to pray in their wigwams, and to say grace before and after meat.[1]

Among the evils prohibited by these laws, it will be remarked, was the vice of drunkenness. The North American Indians, previous to their intercourse with the English and other Europeans, had nothing among them of the nature of intoxicating drinks; but these, which have long been proving their bane and ruin in all parts of the country, were, even thus early, found to be a hinderance to the success of the gospel among them. In Massachussets, indeed, the sale of spirituous liquors to the Indians was prohibited, or at least restricted, by the Government, under the penalty of heavy fines; yet, says Gookin, "Some-ill disposed people, for filthy lucre's sake, do sell unto them secretly, though the Indians will rarely discover these evil merchants; they do rather suffer whipping or fine than tell;" and Mr Eliot says, "These scandalous evils greatly blemish and intercept their entertainment of the Gospel, through

[1] Shepard's Clear Sunshine of the Gospel, p. 2.

the policy of Satan, who counter-worketh Christ that way, with not a little uncomfortable success."[1]

Though Mr Eliot still retained the pastoral charge of the church at Roxbury, he usually went once a fortnight on a Missionary excursion, travelling through the different parts of Massachussets, and of the neighbouring country, as far as Cape Cod, and preaching the gospel of the kingdom to as many of the Indians as would hear him. Many were the hardships and dangers which he encountered in the prosecution of his Evangelical labours. In a letter to Mr Winslow, he says, "I have not been dry, night nor day, from the third day of the week to the sixth, but have travelled from place to place in that condition ; and at night I pull off my boots, wring my stockings, and on with them again, and so continue. The rivers also were raised so as that we were wet in riding through them. But God steps in and helps me. I have considered the exhortation of Paul to his son Timothy, *Endure hardness as a good soldier of Jesus Christ*, with many other such like meditations." When travelling through the Wilderness, without a friend or companion, he was sometimes treated very harshly by the Indians, and, in some instances, they even threatened his life. Both the Sachems and the Powaws were greatly opposed to the gospel ; the chiefs were jealous of their authority, the priests of their gain. Sometimes the Sachems thrust him out from among them, saying, It was impertinent in him to trouble himself with them or their religion, and that should he return again, it would be at his peril. To such threatenings he used only to reply, That he was engaged in the service of the Great God, and therefore he did not fear them, nor all the Sachems in the country, but was resolved to go on with his work, and bade them touch him if they dared. To manifest their malignity, as far as possible, they banished from their society such of the people as were called Praying Indians ; and in some instances, it is said, they even put them to death. Nothing, indeed, but the dread of the English prevented them from murdering the whole of the converts ; a circumstance which induced some to conceal

[1] Gookin *in* Mass. Hist. Coll. vol. i. p. 151 ; Francis' Life of Eliot *in* Sparks' Lib. Amer. Biog. vol. v. p. 351.

their sentiments, and others to fly to the colonists for protection.[1]

While Mr Eliot, in the course of his labours among the Indians, had to encounter so many hardships and dangers, he sought to win the confidence and affections of the savages, by manifold acts of kindness. There is something very simple, yet very pleasing, in the account which he gives of his way of treating them: "The work of converting the Indians," says he, "is difficult not only in respect of the language, but also on account of their poverty and barbarous course of life: there is not so much as meat, or drink, or lodging, for them that go to preach among them; but we must carry all things with us, and somewhat to give unto them. I never go unto them empty, but carry somewhat to distribute among them; and when they come to my house, I am not willing they should go away without some refreshment. Neither do I take any gratuity from them unrewarded; and indeed they do account, that they have nothing worth the giving unto me: only once, when I was up in the country, a poor creature came to me, as I was about to take horse, and shaking me by the hand, with the other thrust something into my hand. I looked what it was, and found it to be a pennyworth of wampum,[2] upon a straw's end. I seeing so much hearty affection in so small a thing, kindly accepted it, only inviting him to my house, that I might shew my love to him."[3]

It is delightful to observe the spirit of humility in which Mr Eliot carried on his labours. Mr Winslow having given him the appellation of *Indian Evangelist*, he declared it to be a "redundancy," and protested against its use with the greatest earnest-

[1] Whitfield's Light appearing more and more towards the Perfect Day, London 1651, p. 21, 37. Neal's History of New England, vol. i. p. 249.

[2] A wampum is a small cylinder, about one-third of an inch long, with a hole drilled through the middle of it, and is made of the shell of some sea fish, polished very smooth. A number of these strung together on threads, is called a belt of wampum. Some of them are black, others white; but the former are reckoned most valuable. They were the only Money used by the Indians before the country was visited by Europeans; they were also used as ornaments about their necks, wrists, and other parts of their bodies; they are uniformly employed in all their treaties as a confirmation of them, and are the only records kept by the savages. Without a belt of wampum, a message or an agreement would be reckoned null and void.—*Hopkin's Memoirs relating to the Housatunnuk Indians*, p. 4.

[3] Winslow's Progress of the Gospel, p. 10.

ness. "I do beseech you," he writes, "to suppress all such things if ever you should have occasion of doing the like. Let us speak and do and carry all things with all humility. It is the Lord who hath done what is done; and it is becoming of Jesus Christ to lift up Christ and ourselves to lie low."[1] Well were it for the cause of Christian missions, if they were generally carried on in this spirit of humility and self-emptiness. Few things are more closely connected with their success: "God resisteth the proud, but giveth grace unto the humble."

In 1651, a considerable number of the Indians, who had embraced the Gospel, united together in building a town, which they called Natick, on the banks of Charles' river, about eighteen miles from Boston. This village consisted of three long streets, with a piece of ground for each family. A few of the houses were built in the English style, but most of them were after the Indian fashion; for, as the former were neither so cheap nor so warm as their wigwams, they generally preferred their own mode of building. There was, however, one large house in the English style; the lower room was a great hall, which served for a place of worship on the Sabbath, and a school-house during the week; the upper room was a kind of wardrobe, in which the Indians deposited their skins and other articles of value, and in one of the corners there was an apartment for Mr Eliot, with a bed for his use. Besides this building, there was a large fort of a circular form, palisadoed with trees; and a small bridge over the river, the foundation of which was secured with stones.[2]

In 1660, the Converted Indians were formed into a Christian church, and had the Lord's Supper administered to them. The Churches of New England, were at that period extremely strict in the admission of persons to church fellowship, and required of them decided evidence of personal religion; but in the case of the Indians, they rather increased than abated their usual strictness. After Mr Eliot had himself heard several of them make confession of their sins, and give an account of their knowledge of the principles of religion, and of their Christian

[1] Whitfield's Light appearing, p. 18.

[2] Strength out of Weakness, London 1652, p. 17. Gookin in Mass. Hist. Coll. vol. i. p. 180.

experience, the ministers of the neighbouring churches assembled by his desire, on a day appointed for the purpose, when several of the converts made similar declarations before them. With these the hearers were not only highly pleased, but much affected. Mr Eliot afterwards published their Confessions, in order to obtain the sentiments of the good people in England and America with respect to them. After a considerable time had elapsed, the ministers of the neighbouring churches held another assembly, for the purpose of examining the Indians; and on this occasion, the converts gave most satisfactory answers to the questions which were proposed to them. Having passed through this severe ordeal, several of them were at length baptized and admitted to the Lord's Supper; but as so much strictness was exercised in receiving them, the number was never very great. About ten years after their little church was incorporated, it consisted of only between forty and fifty members.[1]

Soon after the formation of the church at Natick, Mr Eliot had the pleasure of completing a work on which his heart had long been set, and which was intimately connected with the success of his labours, the translation of the Holy Scriptures into the Indian language. In 1661, the New Testament was printed at Cambridge in New England; and two years after, it was followed by the Old Testament. This was the first Bible ever printed in America. Besides the Old and New Testament, he translated into the Indian language various other useful works, as Primers, Catechisms, Baxter's Call to the Unconverted, the Practice of Piety, Shepard's Sincere Convert, and Shepard's Sound Believer. He also published a Grammar of the Indian language; and at the close of it wrote these memorable words, "Prayers and pains, through faith in Christ Jesus, will do any thing."[2]

Besides instituting schools, where many of the Indians learned to read and write, Mr Eliot and the other gentlemen who had

[1] Tears of Repentance, London 1653, p. 1. Eliot's Further Manifestation of the Progress of the Gospel amongst the Indians, London 1655, p. 3, 20. Mather's History of New England, book iii. p. 197. Hutchinson's Hist. of Massachussets Bay, vol. i. p. 167.

[2] Mather, book iii. p. 197; Holmes' American Annals, vol. i. p. 318, 327. Works of the Hon. Mr Boyle, vol. i. p. ccxii.

the superintendence of the mission, were at much expense in educating some of them for the work of the ministry, with the view of employing them as preachers among their own countrymen. This plan, though highly laudable, was not so successful as might have been expected. Several of the youth died, after being some years at their education; others relinquished their studies when they were nearly ready for the college; some, however, persevered, acquired considerable knowledge of the Latin and Greek languages, and were qualified for being employed as schoolmasters and teachers among their own countrymen. At Cambridge in New England, a building was erected at an expense of between three and four hundred pounds, under the name of the Indian College. It was large enough to accommodate about twenty persons with convenient lodgings; but for some years, at least, it was occupied chiefly by English students, on account of the death and failure of the Indian youths.[1]

In 1674, the number of towns, within the jurisdiction of Massachussets colony, inhabited by Praying Indians, had increased to no fewer than fourteen, to all of which Mr Eliot appears, in a greater or less degree, to have extended his labours. Of these, seven were of considerable standing; the other seven had begun to listen to the Gospel only within the last three years. Many of the Congregations in these places had pastors, elders, and deacons of their own nation, settled among them. It is necessary, however, to remark, that under the appellation of *Praying Indians* were included all who merely submitted to be catechised, attended public worship, read the scriptures, and prayed in their families morning and evening, even though they were not admitted either to Baptism or the Lord's Supper. Estimating each family in these towns to consist on an average of five persons, the whole number of individuals enjoying the means of Christian instruction was supposed to amount to about eleven hundred; but among them there were as yet only two churches.[2]

In 1675, Philip, one of the principal chiefs of the Indians,

[1] Gookin *in* Mass. Hist. Coll. vol. i. p. 172, 175, 176, 217.

[2] Gookin *in* Mass. Hist. Coll. vol. i. p. 182, 189, 195. Eliot's Brief Narrative of the Progress of the Gospel among the Indians in the year 1670, London 1671, p. 6.

commenced war upon the English, and being joined by the Natives in various places, he was at first generally successful in his attacks, and spread terror and dismay throughout the whole country. Many were killed on both sides: the Indians in some instances exercised great cruelties on the White people; they laid waste their plantations, and burnt their houses to the ground. Though the great body of the Praying Indians remained true to the English interest, and on many occasions rendered good and faithful service during the war, yet there were some who went over to Philip. Many of the English who had long indulged in unfriendly feelings toward the Indians, not excepting the Praying Indians, now became much exasperated against the latter, and treated them in many cases with great inhumanity, in some instances even putting them to death. After a severe struggle of about a twelvemonth, the war was brought to an end by the death of Philip, who was killed by one of the Indians in the interest of the English. This war was a heavy blow to the cause of the gospel. Many of the towns of Praying Indians were broken up, and a feeling of discouragement weakened those that remained. Mr Eliot was called to lament the total defection of some whose professions had previously cheered his heart, to observe that the love of others had waxed cold, and to mourn over the premature death of others who had promised to be useful in advancing the cause of Christ among their own people. It does not appear, indeed, that they ever entirely recovered the blow. In 1684, their stated places of worship in Massachussets were reduced to four; but occasional meetings were held in other places, when numbers of them came together to fish, hunt, or gather chestnuts.[1]

Notwithstanding these discouraging circumstances, Mr Eliot persevered in his labours among the Indians as long as his health and strength would permit; but being, at length, worn out with the infirmities of age, he was scarcely able to visit them oftener than once in two months, instead of every fortnight, as had been his ordinary practice. Even at Roxbury he was no longer able to perform the duties of the pastoral office to his

[1] Mather's History of the War with the Indians, London 1676, p. 2, 20, 26, 29, 46. Wilson's Life of John Eliot, p. 193. Francis' Life of Eliot *in* Spark's Lib. Amer. Biog. vol. v. p. 274, 277, 282, 286. Boyle's Works, vol. i. p. ccxii.

own satisfaction; and, therefore, he very disinterestedly urged his people to call another minister, as he could not die with comfort till he saw a good successor settled among them. "'Tis possible," he said, "you may think the burden of maintaining two ministers too heavy for you; but I deliver you from that fear. I do here give back my salary to the Lord Jesus Christ; and now, Brethren, you may fix it on any man whom God shall make pastor for you." His church, much to their honour, assured him, that they would consider his very presence among them worth a salary, when he should no longer be able to do any further service among them. Having obtained an excellent young man, Mr Nathaniel Walter, for his colleague, Mr Eliot cherished him with all the care and affection of a father toward a child. For a year or two before his death, he could hardly be persuaded to undertake any public service in the congregation, humbly pleading, that it would be wrong to the souls of the people for him to do any thing among them, when they were otherwise so much better supplied. One day, (Dr Mather thinks it was the last time he ever preached,) after a very distinct and useful Exposition of the eighty-third Psalm, he concluded with an apology to his hearers, begging them, "to pardon the poorness, and meanness, and brokenness of his meditations; but," added he, with great humility, "my dear brother, here, will by and by mend all."[1]

Being, at length, attacked with some degree of fever, he rapidly sunk under it, combined as it was with the infirmities of old age. During his illness, when speaking about the evangelizing of the Indians, he said, "There is a dark cloud upon the work of the gospel among them. The Lord revive and prosper that work, and grant that it may live when I am dead. It is a work I have been doing much and long about. But what was the word I spoke last? I recall that word, *My doings.* Alas! they have been poor, and small, and lean doings; and I will be the man who will throw the first stone at them all." One of the last expressions which were heard to fall from his lips were these emphatic words: "Welcome joy." He at length expired, 20th May 1690, in the eighty-sixth year of his age, and has

[1] Mather, book iii. p. 180, 194, 206.

since been known by the honourable, yet well earned title of THE APOSTLE OF THE INDIANS.[1]

Previous to the death of Mr Eliot, the church at Natick had a Indian minister, named Daniel Takawompbait, settled among them; but it appears to have been in a languishing state.[2] In 1698, there were at that place about a hundred and eighty persons, a number greater than what they were estimated to be upwards of twenty years before; but the church was reduced to ten members, namely, seven men and three women.[3]

In 1721, Mr Oliver Peabody was settled as Missionary at Natick. There was then no church at that place, nor even a single individual among the Indians, who was known to have been baptized. The church formed by Mr Eliot was now totally extinct. Besides labouring to Christianize the Indians, Mr Peabody endeavoured to promote civilization among them. He was anxious to induce them to abandon their barbarous modes of life, and he happily lived to see numbers of them, possessed of comfortable houses, cultivated fields, and flourishing orchards. Many of them were much impressed with divine things, and a number of them, it was hoped, became partakers of divine grace. During the thirty years that Mr Peabody laboured among them, about one hundred and ninety of the Indians were baptized; but of these, only thirty-five were admitted to full communion with the church.[4]

In 1763, according to a census then taken, there were in Natick only thirty-seven Indians; but in this return, it is pro-

[1] Mather, book iii. p. 173, 194, 207.

Mr Eliot had several sons, and it was his earnest wish that they might all be employed in his favourite work of evangelizing the Indians. His eldest son was not only the pastor of an English church, at a place now called Newtown, but, for several years, he regularly preached to the Indians once a fortnight at Pakemitt, and sometimes at Natick, and other places. He was highly esteemed by the most judicious of the Christian Indians, but died in early life, twenty years before his venerable father. Indeed, most of Mr Eliot's children left the world before him; but not until they had given satisfactory evidence of their conversion to Christ. Hence, when some person asked him, how he could bear the death of such excellent children, the good old man replied, "My desire was that they should have served God on earth; but if he choose rather that they shall serve him in heaven, I have nothing to object against it: His will be done."—*Gookin* in *Mass. Coll.* vol. i. p. 171. *Mather*, book iii. p. 174.

[2] Mather, book iii. p. 194; book vi. p. 61.

[3] Holmes' American Annals, vol. ii. p.37.

[4] Panoplist, vol. iv. (*N. S.*) p. 50, 53.

bable, the wandering Indians were not included. Indeed, they so frequently change their place of abode, and are so intermarried with Blacks and Whites, that it is next to impossible to ascertain the precise number who may still remain. In 1797, it was supposed that there were about twenty of the Natick Indians who were of pure blood, and either resided in that town, or belonged to it. Few of them, however, attended public worship ; none of them were remarkable for piety ; and, indeed, only two or three of them were members of a Christian church. There were none among them who retained the knowledge of their original language, so as to be able to speak it, though one old woman said she could understand it when spoken by others. We notice these circumstances, minute as they are, because it is interesting to know the history and the ultimate fate of the Indian flock of the excellent John Eliot Since that time, the Natick Indians may be said to have entirely disappeared. In 1836, one miserable hut or wigwam, inhabited by three or four persons of mixed Indian and Negro blood, was the only remnant of a settlement which its venerable founder probably hoped would prove a lasting source of Christian and social blessings to the Aboriginal inhabitants of the country, and even this one hut, it is likely, may now be sought in vain.

Besides the Indians at Natick, there were, in 1764, eight or ten families at a place called Grafton ; and in 1792, there were still about thirty persons who retained a part of their lands, and received an annual quitrent from the White inhabitants. These, with a few other Indians at Stoughton, it was believed, were all the remains of the once numerous and powerful tribes which inhabited the colony of Massachussets ;[1] and it is not improbable that the whole are now extinct.[2]

[1] Mass. Hist. Coll. vol. i. p. 195, vol. v. p. 43 ; Francis' Life of Eliot *in* Spark's Lib. Amer. Biog. vol. v. 297.

[2] Before leaving this part of our history, we cannot help noticing a curious specimen given by Dr Mather, of the method of instruction employed by the Roman Catholics in converting the Indians of America. It was extracted by him from the Manuscript of a Jesuit missionary, containing a Catechism relative to the principles in which they were to be instructed, and Cases of conscience with regard to their conduct in life. From the Chapters concerning Heaven and Hell, we shall select a few particulars :—

Q. How is the Soil made in Heaven ?

A. It is a very fair soil. They want neither for meat nor clothes ; we have only to wish and we have them.

SECT. II.—MARTHA'S VINEYARD.

In 1642, Mr Thomas Mayhew senior, who had obtained a grant of Martha's Vineyard, Nantuket, and Elizabeth Isles, placed his son, a young man of considerable learning and piety, with a few other English people, in Martha's Vineyard. Being invited by his fellow-settlers to become their pastor, young Mr Mayhew was not satisfied that his labours should be confined to so small a handful of his countrymen, but acquired the Indian language with the view of Christianizing the natives,

Q. Are they employed in Heaven?

A. No. They do nothing. The fields yield corn, beans, pumpkins, and the like, without any tillage.

Q. What sort of trees are there?

A. Always green, full and flourishing.

Q. Have they in Heaven the same sun, the same wind, the same thunder that we have here?

A. No. The sun ever shines; it is always fair weather.

Q. But how are their fruits?

A. In this respect they excel ours, that they are never wasted. You have no sooner plucked one, but you see another hanging in its room.

In this manner the Catechism goes on with regard to Heaven. Concerning Hell there are, among others, the following questions:

Q. What sort of a Soil is Hell?

A. A very wretched soil; it is a fiery pit in the centre of the earth.

Q. Have they any light in Hell?

A. No. It is always dark: there is always *smoke* there: their eyes are always in pain with it; they can see nothing but devils.

Q. What shaped things are the devils?

A. Very ill shaped things; they go about with vizards on, and terrify men.

Q. What do they eat in hell?

A. They are always hungry; and the damned feed upon hot ashes and serpents.

Q. What water have they to drink?

A. Horrid water. Nothing but melted lead.

Q. Do they not die in hell?

A. No. They eat one another every day; but God immediately restores and renews those that were eaten, as a cropt plant in a little time shoots out again.—*Mather*, book iii. p. 203.

Such is a specimen of this singular work. Had not Dr Mather assured us, that a copy of it in the Iroquois language, with a translation annexed to it, had fallen into his own hands, we could scarcely have believed, that even Jesuit missionaries would have had recourse to such artifices for alluring the Indians to the profession of the Romish faith.

who were numerous on this and the neighbouring islands. He began by endeavouring to win their affections by kind and gentle usage; and, in a short time, he had the pleasure of witnessing the good effects of this plan on one of the Indians, named Hiacoomes. This young man having come one day to the plantation of the White people, Mr Mayhew invited him to his house, entertained him in a very friendly manner, and conversed with him concerning the excellence of the Christian religion, as compared with the Indian mode of worship. Hiacoomes was much impressed by this conversation; in a short time he renounced the religion of his country, and made frequent visits to Mr Mayhew with the view of obtaining further instruction in the principles of the gospel.[1]

The revolt of Hiacoomes from the religion of his fathers, alarmed the whole island. All his countrymen were roused with indignation against him; they loaded him with insults and reproaches, with hatred and contempt. By degrees, however, they cooled in their resentment; and, at length, their indignation was changed into reverence, their hatred into respect. Hiacoomes and his family happening to escape a particular disorder which spread over the whole island, his countryman began to conceive a more favourable opinion both of him and of the Christian religion; and after holding a consultation together, the inhabitants of a neighbouring town sent a messenger to him, desiring him to hasten to them, and tell them of the God whom the English worshipped. On his arrival, he found the chief and a great number of the people assembled together, and when he stated to them some of the leading principles of Christianity, they listened with great attention; and appeared in some degree convinced of their sinfulness.[2]

In 1646, soon after this event, the chief sent for Mr Mayhew, and requested him to establish a meeting among them, and to make known the word of God to them in their own language. "Thou shalt be to us," said he, "as one that stands by a run-

[1] Whitfield's Light appearing towards the Perfect Day, p. 3; Neal's Hist. New England, vol. i. p. 262; Mayhew's Indian Converts, p. 280.

[2] Whitfield's Light appearing towards the Perfect Day, p. 6; Neal's Hist. New England, vol. i. p. 263; Mayhew's Ind. Con. p. 282.

ning stream, filling many vessels; even so shalt thou fill us with everlasting knowledge." These proceedings were not, indeed, equally agreeable to all the Indians. Numbers, on the contrary, opposed them with the utmost bitterness and zeal. They mocked and derided such as attended the meetings, and blasphemed the God whom they worshipped. The chief who had invited Mr Mayhew, was in a particular manner the object of their indignation and rage. An attempt was even made against his life, on account of the attachment he shewed to the new religion; but this, instead of frightening him from his purpose, only strengthened his resolution, and increased his zeal.

In 1649, at a meeting of the Indians, both of such as opposed and of such as favoured Christianity, the authority of the powaws was publicly debated, many asserting their power to hurt and kill their enemies, and alleging numerous stories of this kind, which they said were plainly undeniable. Some of them stood up and asked, "Who does not fear the powaws?" To this, others answered, "There is no man who does not fear them." The eyes of the whole assembly were now turned to Hiacoomes. He therefore rose from his seat, and boldly said, "Though the powaws may hurt such as fear them, yet he trusted in the Great God of heaven and earth, and therefore all the powaws in the world could do him no harm: he feared them not." The whole assembly were astonished at this bold declaration, and expected some terrible judgment to overtake him immediately; but finding that he remained unhurt, they began to change their views, and to esteem him happy in being delivered from the power of their priests, of whom they all stood in such awe. Several even declared they now believed in the same God, and would fear the powaws no more. Being desired to tell them what the Great God would have them to do, and what were the things that offended him, Hiacoomes began to represent to them a number of the sins of which they were guilty: and, at the close of the meeting, no fewer than twenty-two of the Indians resolved to renounce the religion of their fathers, and to embrace that of the White people. Enraged at these proceedings, the powaws threatened to kill the praying Indians; but Hiacoomes and his friends challenged them to do their worst, telling them they would abide their power in the face of the whole island.[1]

Encouraged by these auspicious circumstances, Mr Mayhew now pursued his labours with more zeal and energy than ever. He spared not himself, neither by day nor night, travelling among the Indians in different parts of the island, lodging in their smoky wigwams, and partaking of their homely fare. He possessed singular sweetness and affability of manners, by which he wonderfully gained their affections. Besides catechising their children, he preached to them every fortnight; and after sermon, he usually spent more time than in the discourse itself, reasoning with them in a plain familiar manner, answering their questions, removing their doubts, silencing their cavils, and resolving cases of conscience put to him. Every Saturday morning, he also conferred privately with Hiacoomes, who preached to his countrymen on the Sabbath, directed him in the choice of his subject, and furnished him with materials for illustrating it.[2]

About 1650, a circumstance occurred which amazed the whole island, and wonderfully promoted the progress of Christianity among the Indians. This was the conversion of two of the powaws. These poor creatures, who had been the slaves of Satan from their infancy, now professed themselves the servants of God, revealed the mysteries of their diabolical art, and expressed the utmost abhorrence of their past conduct. It rejoiced the Christian Indians to behold the powaws beginning to turn to the Redeemer, and it no less confounded their Heathen countrymen. Many of them, and even the powaws themselves, it is said, began to acknowledge, that since the gospel was preached among them, they had been singularly foiled in their conjurations; and instead of curing, had often killed their patients.[3]

In 1657, Mr Mayhew undertook a voyage to England, with the view of giving a more particular account of the state of the Indians than it was possible to do by letters, in the hope of

[1] Whitfield's Light appearing towards the Perfect Day, p. 9; Neal's Hist. New Eng. vol. i. p. 264; Mayhew's Ind. Con. p. 282, 284.

[2] Neal's Hist. New Eng. vol. i. p. 266; Mayhew's Ind. Con. p. 285.

[3] Strength out of Weakness, p. 23; Mayhew's Letter *in* Tears of Repentance; Mayhew's Ind. Con. p. 287.

thereby promoting the cause of religion among them. But, alas! how mysterious are the ways of Providence! Neither the ship nor any of the passengers were ever heard of more. It was, therefore, concluded that she had foundered at sea, and that all on board had perished. Thus came to a premature and melancholy end, Mr Thomas Mayhew, a man so justly and so affectionately beloved by the Christian Indians, that for many years after his death, they seldom named him without shedding tears.[1]

The Indians of Martha's Vineyard were not, however, left to wander as sheep without a shepherd. His venerable father, Thomas Mayhew, Esq., the patentee of this and the neighbouring islands, though he had hitherto taken no active part in evangelizing the Indians, had yet felt a deep concern for their welfare, and had, in various ways, promoted their interest. After the gospel had made some progress in the island, he persuaded the chiefs to admit into the council some of the most judicious of the Christian Indians; and in cases of more than ordinary difficulty, to introduce trial by jury. By means of his exertions, a regular civil government was established among them; and records were kept of the proceedings of their courts by some of themselves, who had learned to write. But as he now saw no probability of their obtaining a regular minister, he was induced, by zeal for the glory of God and the salvation of souls, to undertake the oversight, not only of their temporal, but of their spiritual concerns. Though about seventy years of age, he began with unwearied diligence to perfect himself in their language, of which he had already some knowledge; and though a governor, he was not ashamed to become a preacher among them, sometimes travelling on foot near twenty miles through the woods to visit them. The Indians were so pleased and edified with his ministrations, that, a few years afterwards, they requested him to accept of the pastoral office among them; but, apprehending this would not correspond so well with the chief place which he held in the civil government, where they also greatly needed his assistance, he advised them to choose such of the Indian preachers as he thought most judicious, and promised to be most useful among them. Agreeably to his ad-

[1] Mayhew's Ind. Con. p. 291.

vice, they made choice of Hiacoomes and John Tackanash, who accordingly were both ordained to the work of the ministry among them, while old Mr Mayhew continued to labour as an evangelist, both in Martha's Vineyard, and in the neighbouring islands.[1]

In 1674, the whole number of native families on Martha's Vineyard was about three hundred, of whom more than three-fourths were Praying Indians. Among these, there were fifty in full communion, whose exemplary life bore favourable testimony to the inward work of grace in their hearts. It may also be proper to add, that there were ten Indian preachers, seven jurisdictions, and six meetings, every Lord's day.[2]

At Nantuket, an island about twenty miles distant, which was often visited by Mr Mayhew, there was also a church of Christian Indians. The whole number of families in that quarter, at the period now mentioned, was also estimated at about three hundred. Among these there were about thirty individuals in full communion, forty children who had been baptized, and about three hundred persons, including both old and young, who prayed to God and observed the Sabbath. They had meetings in three different places, and four Indian teachers among them.[3]

In 1680, the venerable Mr Mayhew died, in the ninety-third year of his age, to the great grief of the inhabitants of the island. Previous to his death, however, one of his grandchildren, Mr John Mayhew, was settled as the pastor of the English families, and the Indians would not be satisfied until he became a preacher to them likewise, even though his grandfather still laboured with great acceptance among them. After the death of that good man, as he had now both the Indians and the English under his pastoral care, it became necessary for him to redouble his diligence and zeal, especially as some erroneous opinions threatened to spread in the island. His course on earth, however, was short. During his last sickness, he expressed a wish that, "if it were the will of God, he might live a little longer, and do some more service for Christ in the world." Such, however, was not the

[1] Mather, book vi. p. 57: Mayhew's Ind. Con. p. 298.
[2] Gookin *in* Mass. Hist. Coll. vol. i. p. 205; Mather, book iii. p. 200.
[3] Gookin *in* Mass. Hist. Coll. vol. i. p. 206, 207.

appointment of Heaven. After a few months' illness, he died, in the thirty-seventh year of his age, and the sixteenth of his ministry.[1]

In March 1694, Mr Experience Mayhew, his eldest son, succeeded him as a missionary among the Indians. They were now greatly diminished in number on Martha's Vineyard, as well as in all the English settlements; yet, such was the progress of the gospel among them, that, a few years afterwards, out of a hundred and eighty families who still lived on that island, there were only two individuals who continued heathens. As Mr E. Mayhew was considered one of the greatest masters of the Indian language that had appeared in New England, having been familiar with it from his infancy, he was employed to make a new version of the book of Psalms, and of the Gospel of John. Besides this, he published a small volume, entitled *Indian Converts*, in which he gives a particular account of a considerable number of the Natives who had embraced the gospel, and appeared to adorn their Christian profession. It is written with great candour, and evidently with a strict regard to truth; and though the examples of piety which it records are not so distinguished for holiness, nor so free from imperfections as might be wished, yet, on the whole, it may be considered as affording pleasing evidence of the power of the gospel, in changing the hearts of savages, and conforming them to the divine image.[2]

In November 1758, Mr E. Mayhew died of apoplexy, after labouring among the Indians for the long period of nearly sixty-five years. He was succeeded by his son, Mr Zechariah Mayhew, who continued to labour among them until near his death, which took place March 6. 1806, in the eighty-ninth year of his age. With him terminated the missionary career of the Mayhew family, which had been distinguished for five successive generations, during upwards of a century and a half, by their labours for the conversion of the heathen, an honour which, perhaps, no other family has enjoyed since the first promulgation of Christianity.[3]

To this account of the Mayhew family, it may not be uninterest-

[1] Mayhew's Ind. Con. p. 302. [2] Ibid. p. 306; Millar's History, vol. ii. p. 461.
[3] Biblical Magazine, vol. ii. p. 365; Mass. Hist. Coll. (*2d Series*) vol. iii. p. 69.

ing to add what little information we possess respecting the Indians under their care. In 1720, there were on Martha's Vineyard six small towns, containing a hundred and fifty-five families, and about eight hundred souls. In each of these villages there was an Indian preacher. There was also a small meeting on Winthrop's Island; another, composed of twelve or fourteen families, on Tucker's Island and Nashaun, which lie adjacent to each other; and a third, consisting of a few Baptists, at Gayhead.[1]

About the middle of the eighteenth century, there were still five small congregations on Martha's Vineyard; but in 1800 they were reduced to three, two of which had countrymen of their own as pastors over them. The whole number of persons in full communion with these different churches was about forty. Most, if not all, of the Indians on the island were professed Christians, but many of them appeared to have nothing more than a form of godliness; yet still there were a few who, it was hoped, were no strangers to vital piety.[2]

With regard to the Indians on the Island of Nantuket, the accounts are still less favourable. Soon after the settlement of the English among them, they greatly decreased in number, and now the whole race is nearly extinct. In 1694, the adult persons on that island were reduced to about five hundred. Even then not a single powaw was to be found among them; but there was a great decay of vital religion. Many of the most pious Indians had died; and such as remained regarded more the form than the power of godliness. Numbers of them were sadly addicted to the use of spirituous liquors. Some, however, appeared of a serious character; and they had still five assemblies and three churches among them, two of them Congregational and one Baptist.[3]

In 1763, there were still three hundred and fifty-eight Indians on the Island of Nantuket; but a fever, which attacked them about that period, committed such terrible ravages among them, that, in the course of a few months, no less than two hundred and twenty-two of them died. In 1807, there were only two Indian men and six Indian women left on the island.[4]

[1] Mass. Hist. Coll. vol. i. [2] Bib. Mag. vol. ii. p. 366; Miss. Mag. vol. vi. p. 384.
[3] Mather, book vi. p. 56.
[4] Mass. Hist. Coll. vol. i. p. 207, vol. iv. p. 66, vol. iii. (*2d Series*) p. 36.

In 1831, Mr F. Baylies was labouring as teacher and missionary to the several Indian tribes on Martha's Vineyard, the Island of Nantuket, and at Narragansett in Rhode Island. The Indians on Martha's Vineyard were estimated at 340, and at Narragansett at 420.

SECT. III.—NEW PLYMOUTH COLONY.

ANIMATED by the example and exhortations of Mr Eliot, some ministers and others in the colony of New Plymouth, engaged in the same noble undertaking, the christianizing of the Indians. Among these was Mr Richard Bourne, a man of some property, in the vicinity of Sandwich. Having, with great industry, acquired a knowledge of the Indian language, he began to preach the gospel to some of the savages in his own neighbourhood; and, meeting with considerable encouragement and success among them, he extended his labours to those in other quarters, and succeeded in bringing numbers of them to the profession of the Christian faith.[2]

Sensible, however, of the importance of the Indians possessing some territory of their own on which they might fix their residence, in order both to the evangelizing and civilization of them, Mr Bourne, about the year 1660, procured for them a grant of land at Mashpee, a place about fifty miles from Boston; and, not content with the Indian deeds according to the forms usual at that period, his son afterwards obtained a ratification of them by the Court of Plymouth, and an entailment of the property to the Indians and their children for ever; so that no part of it could be sold to any White person without the consent of all the Indians, not even by an act of the General Court itself. Never, perhaps, was a place better chosen for an Indian town. It was situated on the Sound, in sight of Martha's Vineyard, and not only lay contiguous to the sea, but was watered by three rivers and three lakes, in the centre of the territory. In the bays were abundance of fish of every description; in the

[1] (American) Missionary Herald, vol. xv. p. 292, vol. xxi. p. 87, vol. xxix. p. 69.

[2] Mass. Hist. Coll. vol. iii. p. 189; Gookin in Mass. Hist. Coll. vol. i. p. 196.

rivers were trout, herring, &c.; in the woods were plenty of game; and adjacent to the rivers and lakes, were otters, minks, and other amphibious animals, the furs of which furnished the Indians with a valuable article of commerce.[1]

In 1666, Mr Eliot, accompanied by the governor and several other magistrates and ministers, and a great multitude of people, held a meeting at Mashpee, when a considerable number of the Indians made a public profession of their faith in Christ, and their obedience to him, with such understanding and seriousness, as proved highly gratifying to the pious auditory. Yet such was the strictness of the good people in this affair, that they would not countenance the admission of them into Christian fellowship, until their confessions were written and circulated among all the churches in the colony, and had obtained their approbation. As these, however, were highly approved of, the Indians were afterwards formed into a church, and Mr Bourne was ordained as their pastor.[2]

The Indians among whom Mr Bourne laboured, appear to have been scattered through a number of towns and villages. In 1674, they amounted to about five hundred, who lived in upwards of twenty different places. Of these, ninety were baptized, and twenty-seven were in full communion; no fewer than one hundred and forty-two were able to read Indian, seventy-two had learned to write, and nine could read English. Besides these, there were upwards of a hundred children, who had lately begun to read and write, but were not included in this enumeration. Some of these Indians, by their general conduct, afforded pleasing evidence of a work of grace in their hearts; but many of them, on the other hand, were very loose in their behaviour, and occasioned their best friends much sorrow.[3]

During the eighteenth century, the inhabitants of Mashpee continued to enjoy, in a greater or less degree, the means of religious instruction. They are still called Indians; but very few of the pure race are now left: there are Indians, Negroes, Mulattoes, and Germans. In 1808, the Indians, Negroes, and Mulattoes amounted to 357. Notwithstanding the care which

[1] Mass. Hist. Coll. vol. iii. p. 189, 190.

[2] Mather, book iii. p. 199; Mass. Hist. Coll. vol. i. p. 198, vol. iii. p. 190; Eliot's Narrative of the Progress of the Gospel, p. 3.

[3] Gookin in Mass. Hist. Coll. vol. i. p. 196; Mass. Hist. Coll. vol. iii. p. 191.

was originally taken to secure to the Indians their lands in perpetuity, part of them have been alienated to the White people. Neither the lands nor the persons of the Indians in Mashpee, Martha's Vineyard, or in any part of Massachussets, are taxed, nor are they required to perform services to the Government in any way. They are not, however, a free people. The Government views them as children who are incapable of taking care of themselves: they are placed under guardians and overseers, who will not permit them to do many things which they wish, and who in particular will not allow them to sell their lands to any one. Religion was at a low ebb among them. In the seventeenth century, the converts were called Praying Indians; but this is a name which could not now be applied to the inhabitants of Mashpee, for family prayer was almost, if not altogether, unknown among them. Very few of the children were baptized, and there were among them not more than ten or twelve communicants. Even the state of morals among them was low. Though there were some who were industrious, yet, in general, they were not distinguished for their industry: they were at the same time very improvident, and many of them were addicted to drinking. If they were left to themselves (and the remark may be extended to the Indians of Martha's Vineyard), they would soon divest themselves of their land and spend the capital. The women were more temperate than the men; but not a few of the young women, the married as well as the unmarried, were unchaste. Some of the women led a vagabond life in the country, where they at last found Negro husbands, whom they brought home to enjoy all the privileges and immunities of Mashpee. Considering how generally the Indians in other parts of the country have melted away before the White people, it may appear surprising that Mashpee should keep up its numbers; but this admits of an easy explanation. In consequence of its enjoying many peculiar privileges and immunities, in particular that those who dwell there are sure of a living by their labour, if they are willing to work, and from the charity of their guardians if they are not, it has, during a great number of years, been an asylum for lazy Indians from all parts of the country.[1] This, too,

[1] Mass. Hist. Coll. (*2d Series*) vol. iii. p. 4, 8.

will help to explain the low state of religion and morals among the inhabitants.

Besides the missionary efforts of which we have given an account, there were various other attempts made in the course of the seventeenth century to christianize the Indians in different parts of New Plymouth Colony. In this important work, several of the ministers honourably distinguished themselves by their activity and zeal, as Mr John Cotton of Plymouth, Mr Samuel Treat of Eastham, Mr William Leverich of Sandwich, and Mr Thomas Tupper, and some of them beheld their labours crowned with considerable success. In 1685, the number of Praying Indians in this colony amounted to no fewer than 1439, exclusive of children under twelve years of age, who were supposed to be more than three times that number. Since that period, however, the Indians have greatly diminished in number; and, except at Mashpee, there is at present no native church in the whole district.[1]

In Connecticut several ministers, as Mr Abraham Pierson and Mr James Fitch, were likewise employed in evangelizing the Indians; but their labours were attended with little success. Though some individuals embraced the gospel, yet no church of Indians was collected in that colony. Some efforts were also made in Rhode Island, Long Island, New York, and even in Virginia; but, so far as we know, with no particular success.[2]

[1] Mather, book iii. p. 200, book vi. p. 50, 60; Strength out of Weakness, p. 2; Millar's History, vol. ii.; Hutchinson's History, vol. i. p. 349; Mass. Hist. Coll. vol. i. p. 201.

[2] Trumbull's History of Connecticut, vol. i. p. 494; Tracy's History of the American Board for Foreign Missions, p. 8; Wilson's Life of John Eliot, p. 172, 233, 239, 280, 294, 297.

In 1649, an Ordinance was passed by the English Parliament for the erection of a *Corporation for the Propagation of the Gospel in New England*, and a collection was appointed to be made for it throughout England and Wales. The ministers were required to read the Ordinance from their pulpits, and to exhort the people to contribute liberally in aid of it. The Universities of OXFORD and CAMBRIDGE also addressed letters to the ministers, calling upon them to stir up their congregations to the good work. But notwithstanding the weight of these high authorities, the collection proceeded heavily and slowly. In fact, it met with warm opposition. The whole plan of converting the Indians was alleged by many to be merely a scheme to raise money by an appeal to the piety of the nation. So discouraging was the prospect of contributions from the people, that an effort was made to raise something from the ARMY. After all, however, a very considerable sum was collected: and lands were purchased with the money to the value of between five and six hundred pounds a year. On the restoration of Charles II. the Corporation being considered dead in law, Colonel Bed-

SECT. IV.—NEW STOCKBRIDGE.

In October 1734, Mr John Sergeant proceeded among the Indians, on the river Housatunnuk, in the province of Massachussets, who had lately agreed to receive a minister among them, to instruct them in the principles of religion. Previous to this, the zeal of Mr Sergeant for the conversion of the heathen was not unknown, as he had freely declared in conversa-

ingfield, a Roman Catholic, who had sold to it an estate of £322 *per annum*, basely repossessed himself of it, and refused, at the same time, to repay the money which he had received for it. In 1661, however, the Corporation was revived by a new Charter from His Majesty, the estate which Bedingfield had so unjustly seized was restored to it, and the Hon. Mr Boyle, a man distinguished at once as a philosopher and a Christian, was chosen Governor, an office which he held for about thirty years. (*Hazard's Hist. Coll.* vol. ii. p. 147, 175, 311.—*Gookin* in *Mass. Hist. Coll.* vol. i. p. 211.—*Francis' Life of Eliot* in *Spark's Lib. Amer. Biog.* vol. v.—*Boyle's Works*, vol. i. p. 68, 151.) It was this Society which supported the various missionary undertakings in New England during the seventeenth century; and as an illustration of the nature and extent of its operations, as well as a specimen of the expense attending exertions of this kind at that period, we shall here subjoin a copy of the Accompt sent by the Commissioners of the United Colonies to the Corporation in London, of the Expenditure for the year 1661:

"September 12: 1661

To John Latimore a messenger sent from Newhauen to Boston to cary letters to bee sent to the Corporation the ship being Reddy to sett sayle	2 10 00
To six coates given to the Pequott Indians for theire encurragement .	3 02 06
To mistris Bland of the vinyards for her paines and care amongst the Indians there and for Physicke and Surgery not brought to account last year	05 00 00
To mr. Mayhew that hee distributed to well deserueing Indians . .	02 10 00
To sundry Disbursments upon the account of printing as appears by account now sent	196 19 01
To seuerall bookes deliuered to the Indian Scollers and Mathew Mayhew as by accounts appeers	08 17 11
To the Gouernor of Newhauen in lue of fiue pounds alowed him in our last yeares account to distribute amongst well deserueing Indians which was sent to him from Boston by Joseph Alsop whoe was cast away att Sea	05 00 00
To Mr. James of Easthampton for his paines in Instructing the Indians att Long Iland and fitting himselfe for that worke the last yeare ending September (60) but not brought to account till now . .	10 00 00
To Mr. Peirson for extreordinary paines attending publicke meetings of the Indians in the bay, &c. which was not brought to account; which was allowed him the last yeare	10 00 00
To him for his Sallery this yeare ending September 1661 . .	30 00 00
To Mr. John Elliot senr. for his Sallery now due	50 00 00
To Job his interpreter and 4 scoolmasters viz. Robert sometims a scool-	

tion, he would rather be employed as a missionary among the Indians, than settle in any English congregation; and long before he had any prospect of being engaged in that capacity, it had been a petition in his daily prayers, that God would send him to these unenlightened Pagans, and render him instrumental in turning them from the error of their ways to the wisdom of the just. He had already finished his course of

master att Cambridge, John Magus, Ponanpam and vpacowillin ten pounds a peece	40 00 00
To Mr. John Elliot Junr. for his Sallery for the yeare past ending September 61	25 00 00
To Mr. Joseph Elliot for the like	10 00 00
To Mr. Thomas Mayhew of the vinyards for his sallery	30 00 00
More for his extreordinary paines charge and trouble for the time past amongst the Indians there	10 00 00
To 8 Indian Scoolmasters and Teachers of the Indians there viz: To Sakomas Memeekeen Takanah Kisquich Samuell Manaso James and Annawanitt	30 00 00
To wheele Cards and Cotten woole to Imploy the Indian weemen att the vinyards to bee kept as a comon Stocke for them	10 00 00
To mistris Mayhew the Relicte of Mr. Thomas Mayhew for her Incurragement and support	10 00 00
To Fesenden of Cambridge for the Diett of Mathew Mayhew	08 00 00
To Peter Folger a Teacher att the vinyard	20 00 00
To mistris Bland for her paines care and Physicke for the Indians att the Vinyard for this yeare and to satisfy her for what was short of her expectation and expence the last yeare	05 00 00
To mr. Danforth of Cambridge for the Diett and Clothing of 4 Indian Scollars for one yeare ending att October next att 15lb. a pece	60 00 00
To the clothing of Mathew Mayhew for the yeare past	05 00 00
To woode to the Scoole	00 18 00
To clothing an Indian att his first coming	1 00 00
To mr. Corlett for teaching 4 Indians and Mathew Mayhew	12 00 00
To mr. Weld of Rocksbury for the Diett Clothing and Teaching of 2 Indians Boyes one year ending the 10th December next	30 00 00
To mr. Bourne of Sandwich for his constant Teaching and Instructing the Indians in those parts	25 00 00
To mr. Willam Tompson for teaching the Indians there	20 00 00
To major Atherton for keeping courts amongst the Indians and instructing them	15 00 00
To the Gouernors of Plymouth Connecticott and Newhauen to distribute amongst well deserueing Indians 5lb a peece	15 00 00
To Thomas Staunton for his sons maintenance according to former agreement	25 00 00
The totall is	733 08 01

It is proper, however, to add, that besides the monies remitted from England for the propagation of Christianity among the Indians, considerable sums were raised in the Colonies for promoting this important object.—*Hazard's Hist. Coll.* vol. ii. p. 442, 459, 495, 508.—*Mass. Hist. Coll.* vol. i. p. 213.

study at Yale College, and was now employed as a tutor in that seminary; but no sooner was he invited to go as a Missionary among the Housatunnuk Indians, than he consented to the proposal, cheerfully exchanging the pleasures of a College life, which to him was no small sacrifice, for a residence among savages. "I should be ashamed," said he, "to call myself a *Christian*, or even a *Man*, and yet refuse to do what lay in my power to cultivate humanity among a people naturally ingenious enough, but who, for want of instruction, live so much below the dignity of human nature, and to promote the salvation of souls perishing in the dark, when yet the light of life is so near them."[1]

Scarcely, however, had Mr Sergeant entered on his labours among the Indians, when the Dutch traders in the neighbourhood endeavoured to frustrate his exertions, and to ruin his character by the basest and most artful insinuations. As they derived great profits from selling the Indians rum, and by striking bargains with them when they were in a state of intoxication, they were justly apprehensive that, should Christianity prevail among them, they would be able to make gain of them no longer. They, therefore, told them, that the religion which Mr Sergeant taught them was not a good religion; that the friendship he professed for them was merely pretended; and that his design was to make slaves of them and their children. By these and similar insinuations, they so prejudiced the minds of the Indians, that many of them were greatly incensed against him. By his friendly behaviour and prudent representations, he succeeded, however, in allaying their resentment, conciliating their affections, and regaining their confidence.[2]

But it was not long before there arose a new source of uneasiness. Among the Indians, it is customary not to conclude any affair of importance, without consulting the several branches of the nation; but as the Indians of Housatunnuk had accepted of a missionary without the consent of their brethren, they were now apprehensive lest their conduct should be condemned at the general meeting of the tribe, which was soon to take

[1] Hopkin's Memoirs relating to the Housatunnuk Indians, and to the ministry of the Rev. John Sergeant, 1753, p. 2, 5, 8, 149.

[2] Hopkin's Memoirs, p. 15.

place, especially as it was reported that the Indians of Hudson's River were highly incensed against them on this account; and that there was even a design on foot to poison their two principal men. Happily, however, when the assembly met, they were so far from condemning the measure, that they expressed themselves thankful on account of it, and even gave some ground to hope that the whole nation would submit to religious instruction.

This meeting, however, was concluded with a frolic and a drinking match, agreeably to the custom of the Indians. Their dancing, on these occasions, is not only a laborious, but a dangerous exercise; and it is a striking proof of the power of habit over the human frame, that it is not more frequently followed by fatal consequences. They dance round a large fire till they are nearly ready to faint, and are completely drenched with sweat. They then run out of the house, strip themselves naked, expose their warm bodies to the cold air; or, if there be snow on the ground, roll themselves in it, till they are perfectly cooled. They then return to the dance; and when they are again hot and tired, cool themselves in a similar manner. This operation they repeat, probably, four or five times in the course of the night, concluding the whole with excessive drinking; and when they are drunk, they often fall asleep in the open air, perhaps buried in snow.

Soon after this meeting, several of the Indians were taken ill, and two of them died suddenly of a violent fever. Easy as it was to account for their death from natural causes, especially as, at the time of their dance, the weather was extremely cold, and there was a deep snow on the ground, the savages were persuaded it was the effect of poison, and resolved to apply to the invisible powers for the discovery of the murderers. Mr Sergeant was then absent; but Mr Woodbridge, his assistant in the Indian school, having heard of their design, rode to the place of their meeting. On his arrival, he found upwards of forty of the Indians assembled in the wigwam of one of the chiefs. The house was swept clean, large fires were kindled, and they were sitting round them from one end of the hut to the other; only in one quarter, a space of about five or six feet, was left for the powaws or conjurers. Each of the Indians had two sticks, about a foot and a half long, one of them split at the end, which he held under his legs. When Mr Woodbridge arrived, they were all prepared for the exercise; but had not as yet begun it. He asked them, whether they would allow him to be present at the ceremony; but before they returned him an answer, the oldest priest lifted up his eyes to heaven, and spoke with great earnestness, after which they told him he might remain. They then began to sing and rap with their sticks; and in the mean while, the eldest powaw was sitting, and talking, and acting a different part from all the rest. This lasted about an hour. The priest then rose from his seat, threw off all his clothes, except a flap about his middle, and in this naked state passed from one end of the hut to the other, with his eyes closed, to appearance in exquisite agony, and employing the most frightful and distorted gestures it is almost possible to imagine. This continued about another hour. The first powaw being exhausted, at length retired; a second then rose and acted the same part; afterwards a third, and finally a fourth. In this manner they spent the whole night, except a few short intervals, during which they either smoked a pipe, or they all rose up in a body and danced. They did not appear, however, to gain their object; and on Mr Woodbridge representing to them the folly and criminality of such a mode of worship, they promised never again to have recourse to it, and some of them even seemed extremely sorry for the step they had taken.[1]

In the course of a short time, Mr Sergeant's hearers greatly increased in number; many of them appeared to be seriously impressed with religion; and within a few months, he baptized upwards of fifty of them, among whom were the two principal men with their wives and children. Most of them appeared anxious to obtain religious instruction; a remarkable reformation of manners ensued among them; and vice, especially drunkenness, the sin to which, of all others, they were most addicted, seemed for the present nearly banished from among them. They themselves were surprised at the change; and expressed the difference between their former and their present

[1] Hopkin's Memoirs, p. 21.

state, by the terms infancy and manhood, dreaming and waking, darkness and light, and other similar metaphors.[1]

Even at an early period of his labours, Mr Sergeant had perceived, that the plan he was at first obliged to adopt of preaching to the Indians through the medium of an interpreter, would answer his purpose very imperfectly, being not only a slow, but a very uncertain method of communicating instruction. He was himself unable to judge of the accuracy of what was delivered to them; and he had even reason to fear, that the truths which he sought to teach them were conveyed to their minds in a very inadequate manner; for the best interpreter he could then find, possessed but an imperfect knowledge of the principles of religion, as well as of the English terms by which they were expressed. Influenced by these considerations, he had early engaged in the study of the Indian language, and prosecuted it with the utmost assiduity. It was extremely difficult to learn, being entirely different from every other language with which he was acquainted. After about three years' study, however, he attained so much knowledge of it, as to be able to pray with his people in their own tongue, and even to preach in it with some little assistance from his interpreter. He at length became so great a master of it, that the Indians used to say: "Our minister speaks our language better than we do ourselves."[2]

With the help of his interpreter, Mr Sergeant translated some prayers into the Indian language for the use of his people, and Dr Watts' First Catechism for the instruction of the children. Besides these small pieces, he afterwards translated a great part of the Bible into their language; namely, such portions of the Old Testament as appeared most useful and necessary, as the history of the creation, of the fall of man, of the call of Abraham, of the conduct of Providence to the patriarchs and the children of Israel, the prophecies concerning the coming of Christ; and the whole of the New Testament, unless we are to except the book of Revelation, which we are uncertain whether he ever finished.[3]

Pleasing as were Mr Sergeant's prospects in the early period

[1] Hopkin's Memoirs, p. 10, 28, 34, 42, 54.
[2] Ibid. p. 59, 154.
[3] Ibid. p. 59, 156.

of his labours, he afterwards met with no small trials from the Indians, as well as from other quarters. The Dutch traders in the neighbourhood, though they had failed in fomenting the jealousy of the savages, never relaxed in their endeavours to corrupt them with rum; and though the Indians passed strong resolutions against drinking, and even kept them for a considerable time, yet some of them relapsed into that and other vices, even after they appeared to be completely weaned from them. One of the chiefs, who had been peculiarly zealous against drunkenness, and seemed firmly established in the ways of godliness, conducted himself for a year or two in a very disorderly manner, was frequently intoxicated, and in other respects extremely troublesome. Afterwards, indeed, he was reclaimed from his apostasy, acknowledged his guilt, was restored to the communion of the church, and walked like a Christian till the day of his death. These painful occurrences were a source of much distress to Mr Sergeant. Nothing, he said, affected him with such pungent grief, his own sins excepted, as the disorderly and wicked conduct of his poor people. Many were the days he spent on this account in fasting and prayer; many the tears he shed; sleep departed from his eyes, and he forgot to eat his bread.[1]

But while Mr Sergeant's expectations were often miserably blasted with regard to the elder Indians, he still cherished the hope of better success among the children. The Rev. Mr Hollis, a Baptist minister near London, having generously offered to be at the expense of educating and supporting twelve Indian boys, he had accepted the proposal with joy, and was now anxious to extend the plan, by establishing a charity school for a still greater number of youth, in which they should be taught not only to read and write, but also the more common arts of life. Experience had convinced him, that the opinions and habits of the Indians were a powerful hinderance to the progress of Christianity, as well as of civilization among them. Extensive success could scarcely be expected, among a people who thought it a disgrace to follow any employment except hunting or war, while the men, at other times, indulged in absolute indolence and inactivity, and the women were obliged to perform all the

[1] Hopkin's Memoirs, p. 159.

manual labour, as gathering wood, planting, hoeing, &c., yet never learned the common arts of housewifery. Mr Sergeant's plan, therefore, was to take their children when young, to train them from their early years to habits of industry, and to instruct both sexes in such employments as were suitable to the station they ought to occupy in society. By this means he hoped they would not only be enabled to provide more comfortably for themselves and their families, but would be preserved from the numerous and powerful temptations to which they were exposed by their present mode of living. He was apprehensive, indeed, that the prejudices of the Indians would prove a strong, if not even an insuperable obstacle, in the way of the execution of his plan; but their aversion to it by degrees unexpectedly vanished.[1]

In 1743, Mr Sergeant circulated a more particular account of his plans, which display very enlarged and comprehensive views. He proposed to procure about two hundred acres of land in that quarter of the country; to erect upon it a building large enough to contain a number of young persons, not under ten, nor above twenty years of age; to place these youth under the care of two masters, one to take the oversight of them in their hours of labour, the other in their hours of study; and to have the day divided in such a manner between these employments, as to render the one a recreation from the other, that so as little time as possible might be lost in idleness. In the school, he proposed that they should not only all be taught to read and write, and such other branches of learning as were useful in common life; but that some, at least, should be prepared to receive an academical education, with the view of being at length employed in spreading the gospel among the more distant tribes. He also proposed, that the produce of their labour should be appropriated to their maintenance and to the general purposes of the Institution; that, with the view of lessening the expense, all kinds of provisions should be raised, and a stock of cattle, sheep, hogs, and other animals, kept on the farm; and that, if they could be afforded, premiums should occasionally be distributed among the youth, as a reward and as an incitement to industry. If this plan succeeded, he pro-

[1] Hopkin's Memoirs, p. 55, 63, 83, 95.

posed to extend the establishment so as to take in girls as well as boys; for he was fully sensible of the vast importance of the female sex in society, of the power they possess over the men, and of the influence they have in forming the character of their children. He therefore designed that they should receive an education suited to their situation and circumstances, that they should be placed under the care of a skilful matron, who should instruct them in housewifery, and that they should be employed in manufacturing the wool, flax, milk, and other articles raised on the farm. By cultivating both the sexes, he thought they would have a natural and reciprocal influence in further improving each other. In this manner, he hoped that, after some time, they would, in a great measure, support the Institution by their own labour, that they would be formed to habits of industry from their early years, acquire the English language, learn our manners, and when arrived at a suitable age, be able to manage farms of their own.[1]

Such is a sketch of Mr Sergeant's plan for the conversion and civilization of the Indians. With the view of carrying it into execution, a subscription was begun in England, and met with considerable encouragement from the friends of religion, and even from some members of the Royal family;[2] but the whole sum raised was by no means adequate to carry Mr Sergeant's plan into execution, even on the smallest scale. Thus were his fond hopes again threatened with disappointment.[3]

Mr Hollis, however, with singular generosity, requested Mr Sergeant to take other twelve boys from nine to twelve years of age, and engaged to be at the whole expense of their education and support. But war having soon after broken out with France, and Stockbridge, as the Indian settlement was now called, being

[1] Hopkin's Memoirs, p. 97, 139, 141.

[2] The Prince of Wales was applied to through the medium of the Rev. Dr Ayscough, Clerk of the Closet, and First Chaplain to his Royal Highness. When that gentleman was informed that Mr Sergeant was not a minister of the Church of England, but a Dissenter, he replied, "What though he be a Dissenter? He is a good man; that is every thing. It is time such distinctions were laid aside, and the partition wall thrown down, that so Christians may love one another. For his part, he loved all good men alike, whether they were Churchmen or Dissenters." Dr Ayscough, accordingly, continued to the last a distinguished friend of Mr Sergeant, and of the School among the Indians.—*Hopkin's Mem.* p. 119, 122, 140, 146.

[3] Hopkin's Memoirs, p. 113, 117, 122.

much exposed to the depredations of the enemy, it was deemed expedient to defer the execution of this proposal till the return of peace. In consequence, however, of the remonstrances of Mr Hollis,[1] Mr Sergeant, notwithstanding the war with France, prepared to carry into execution, on a small scale, the plan which for some years had lain so near his heart. With this view he obtained from the Indians at Stockbridge about two hundred acres, as a situation for the building, and as a plantation to be cultivated by the children. Here he erected a house, containing a number of apartments adapted to the purpose for which it was designed, and removed to it some Indian boys, whom, on account of the war, he had previously committed to the care of a person in Connecticut. But while he was pleasing himself with the hope of beholding the consummation of his favourite plan, the establishment of an Indian Charity School, a period was unexpectedly put to his valuable life.[2]

In July 1749, this excellent man died after an illness of about four weeks, in the thirty-ninth year of his age, and the fifteenth of his labours as a missionary among the Indians. His success among them, though not equal to his desires, was not inconsiderable. When he first visited them, their whole number, including old and young, was under fifty; they lived in miserable huts, were scattered over the country, and often moving from place to place, and were all sunk in the depths of heathen ignorance and barbarity. When he died, they amounted to two hundred and eighteen, were collected together into a town, and,

[1] On being informed of these circumstances, Mr Hollis wrote Dr Coleman of Boston, insisting that his proposal should be carried into effect without further delay. "If my money," says he, "lie unemployed till the conclusion of the war, it may be a long time indeed. Do you see the least prospect in the world of it? Would you not wish to behold the Redeemer's work carried on while you live? I am not willing to have my money of £350 your currency, lying useless till the war is ended." In a subsequent letter, he says, "I request that the £300 of my money in your hands may be employed in the education of twelve new boys, of heathen parents, with all convenient speed. Yea, I absolutely insist upon it, and promise hereby to make a remittance for further charge of education and maintenance, my estate being very much increased of late, as I have had a great deal left me by a relation deceased. As to the war with France, let not that hinder it. I request it may be done speedily, if there are Indian parents willing to have their children educated."—*Hopkin's Mem.* p. 131. Such was the zeal of Mr Hollis in this good work. How few are so anxious to have their money expended in promoting the glory of Christ, and the salvation of souls!

[2] Hopkin's Mem. p. 114, 131, 133, 143.

instead of bark wigwams, possessed twenty houses built in the English style. In the course of his labours, he baptized one hundred and eighty-two of the Indians; of whom, a hundred and twenty-nine were still alive, and resided at Stockbridge; and forty-two were communicants. At a small distance from the town there were also twelve or thirteen English families, who were encouraged to settle there, with the view of promoting, by their example, the arts of industry among the Indians.[1]

In June 1751, the Rev. Jonathan Edwards, of Northampton, removed to Stockbridge, having been appointed to succeed Mr Sergeant at that place. Though a man of distinguished talents and piety, his connection with the church, of which he was pastor in the former town, had some time before been dissolved, on the ground of a difference of sentiment between him and them, concerning the qualifications necessary to the admission of persons to communion with the church, which, along with some other circumstances, had, for several years past, excited violent opposition to him on the part of many of the people.

When Mr Edwards entered on his labours at Stockbridge, there appeared a fair prospect of usefulness at that place. In consequence of an invitation which had been sent to the Mohawk Indians, then residing about forty miles west of Albany, to bring their children to be educated at the Charity School, a number of them had lately come thither with their children; and the Provincial Legislature, on learning this fact, made provision for the maintenance and support of the children. Besides the Mohawks, a number of the Oneida Indians from Onohquaga, near the head of the Susquehanna river, came and settled at Stockbridge. There appeared, in fact, at this time, a fair prospect of a large and flourishing colony of the Iroquois, or Six Nations, being established at this place, drawn thither for the education of their children, of which they appeared very desirous.[2] But their hopes were entirely blasted through a train of circumstances of a very harassing and extraordinary nature.

One of the most wealthy of the English settlers appears to have removed to Stockbridge, with the view of still further improving his circumstances by forming a large trading establish-

[1] Hopkin's Memoirs, p. 143, 147.

[2] Edwards' Works, London 1839, vol. 1. p. clvi, clxxvii.

ment in the neighbourhood of the Indian settlement. In consequence of his wealth and locality, affairs of some moment relating to the Indians at that place were, on various occasions, entrusted to his management; but, while he amassed considerable wealth, he acted in a manner so injurious to their interests, that he entirely lost their confidence, and also alienated so completely the English inhabitants, that every family in the place, his own excepted, was opposed to him.

Immediately after his settlement at Stockbridge, Mr Edwards, in consequence of the misunderstandings and jealousies which subsisted between some of the principal inhabitants of the town, and of the confusion in which the Indian affairs were involved, was led to recommend the appointment of two or more Trustees, "men perfectly impartial, and no way interested in, or related to, the contending parties," to superintend the affairs of the place. The necessity of some such measure to the welfare of the Mission, and of the Indian schools, soon became apparent. In consequence of the growing importance of the Indian Establishment at Stockbridge, the funds appropriated to it were greatly augmented, and were likely to be still further enlarged. By the increased numbers of the Housatunnuk Indians, and the accession of the Mohawks, it had become the principal mission of the Corporation for the Propagation of the Gospel in New England, and appeared destined to receive the chief portion of its revenues. Mr Hollis had increased his annual grant to £160 sterling for the support of thirty-six boys in the school; another gentleman, Mr Paine, was proposing to support a female boarding-school; the Legislature of the Province had just voted £500 currency for the school-house, and would probably assist in supporting the schoolmistress; adequate support was now given to the teacher of the Housatunnuk school; an annual stipend was given to the Housatunnuk Indians, to be expended at Stockbridge for their benefit; a similar stipend was to be paid for the Mohawks, if they removed in considerable numbers to that place; a school to be supported by the colony for the education of their children was not only pledged but actually begun; and hopes were entertained that the yearly stipend of £500 sterling, granted by the King of England to the Mohawks, might be expended under the direction of an agent residing at Stockbridge, and not, as before, at Albany. It required no great discernment to foresee, that the prospect of engrossing the agency through which such large sums would pass, and of converting this into a source of private emolument, might excite the cupidity of individuals, and lead them to adopt every means in their power for securing so great an advantage to themselves. Accordingly, the person already referred to, whose influence in the town had long been nearly extinct, was, through the recommendation given of him by his nephew, while in London, to the Corporation for the Propagation of the Gospel in New England, appointed one of the Board of Commissioners of that Society; the nephew himself was another of the same Board; one of his family was, through the same recommendation, appointed teacher of the female school, provided the Commissioners at Boston approved of the nomination; one of the Trustees of the Indian establishment was about to connect himself with the family; and if the nomination was confirmed, it was his intention to remove to Stockbridge, in order to take the superintendence of Indian affairs, which, in the absence of his colleagues, would be nearly sole and exclusive. Such were the prospects, at this time, of these individuals engrossing the direction and the profits of the whole establishment, that they threw off their wonted caution, and did not conceal their purpose of removing every obstacle in the way of the fulfilment of their designs.

Mr Edwards knew that the influence of these individuals was most formidable, two of them being now members of the Board of Commissioners, on which, as Indian missionary, he was dependent; one of them being one of the Trustees for the Indians at Stockbridge; one of them being personally acquainted with the Directors in London; and two of them having considerable influence with the Provincial Government. Yet he saw just as clearly, that if they succeeded in their designs, the funds appropriated to the improvement of the Indians would be perverted to the purpose of their personal aggrandisement. The Indians too had, as already mentioned, the strongest prejudices against the head of that family, in consequence of his having often molested them in regard to their lands and other matters, and, as they thought, treated them very unjustly. These prejudices were extended to the family, and that to such a degree, that though an offer was made to feed and clothe such of their children as should be sent to the school, which was attempted to be established, only four could be procured, and even their parents complained loudly of the manner in which they were treated. The monies contributed by Mr Hollis were shamefully misapplied. He had made large remittances, but to no good purpose, and he was kept in entire ignorance of the actual state of things at Stockbridge. Capt. Kellogg, an illiterate man, originally a farmer and afterwards a soldier, about sixty years of age, very lame, and wholly unaccustomed to teaching, and utterly unqualified for it, who had previously been engaged temporarily in instructing the Indian children, was employed as teacher. He had received the money, and boarded and professed to instruct the children; but he had never established a regular school, and had never kept any proper accounts of his expenditure. He taught the boys only occasionally and incidentally, employing them chiefly in cultivating his own land. The Mohawk Indians were so dissatisfied with the neglect of their children, that the whole scheme was in danger of miscarrying; but having been assured that a regular school would be established speedily, and a competent teacher procured, they were again conciliated. Mr Gideon Hawley, a young man of liberal education, and of great prudence, firmness, and integrity, having accordingly been appointed teacher, they, after his arrival, took away their children from Kellogg; but the captain wishing to have some pretext for still drawing the money of Mr Hollis, and not being able to procure any of the Indian boys to form a school, went regularly into Mr Hawley's school, and proceeded to treat the children as if they were under his care, alleging that he was the superintendent of the school. No one had been louder in speaking of his unfitness and uselessness as a teacher, and in declaring that it was high time he should be removed, than the resident Trustee; but he now suddenly changed his tactics, and declared he must be retained. In like manner, though he had for many years professed the highest respect for Mr Edwards, yet now his whole conduct in reference to him was suddenly altered, and he took part in all measures of opposition to him.

Singular management was also employed as to Mr Hawley. Before his coming, dark representations were carried to him of the state of things at Stockbridge, in order to discourage him from accepting the appointment of teacher; and after he came thither, it was openly given out that he would soon be removed. The resident Trustee warned him not to depend on Mr Edwards, and challenged to himself the whole authority of directing the schools and the affairs of the Indians.

Still more strange were the arrangements as to the school for girls. When the Corporation in London recommended the teacher proposed to them, they could not be aware that her nearest kinsmen were to be the committee to examine her accounts. But the state of matters grew to be still more preposterous. She being the schoolmistress, her nearest relatives were to be her council, and her husband the only auditor of her accounts, and also the person who was to make a report to the Legislature.

During the spring of 1752, the state of affairs at Stockbridge, instead of improving, grew worse. The interference of Captain Kellogg with Mr Hawley's school produced so much confusion, that one-half of the Mohawks left Stockbridge in utter disgust with him and his friends, fully resolved never to return. A few days after their departure, an intimate friend of Kellogg and his associates, when visiting the school, struck a child of the chief Sachem of the Oneidas on the head with his cane, without any cause or provocation. This roused the general indignation of the remaining Iroquois, and all of them appeared resolved to pack up their effects immediately and be gone. At length the aggressor, in order to pacify them, was persuaded to pay them a sum of money. But the resident Trustee was so angry at what had been done in reference to this matter, that he came to the school and proceeded to abuse Mr Hawley before the whole of the children, in a very violent manner, telling him he was a man of no judgment and of no prudence, and that he was unfit for his office; and continued his attack for three hours together. As he was very loud in his abuse, the Iroquois heard him, and came to the spot expressing their fears for the personal safety of Mr Hawley, to whom they had become very much attached; and apprehending that, in consequence of this attack, he might be led to leave Stockbridge, they declared in a body, that if he went away, they would go also. By these occurrences, the Indians were as completely alienated from the resident Trustee, as they had previously been from his new friends.

In consequence of these measures, and of a settled determination on the part of the resident Trustee to take, in the absence of his colleagues, the whole management of Indian affairs on himself, they also were disgusted. One of them relinquished all connection with the concern, and gave up visiting Stockbridge altogether. The other openly announced his utter discouragement in regard to the establishment, and declared that he would do his utmost to induce the Government to withdraw its patronage from it. This led to an attempt to procure the dismission of the latter, and the appointment of a connection of the resident Trustee, which, however, proved unsuccessful. At the same time, it was announced that Mr Edwards himself would be removed from the mission. The firm and undeviating course pursued by him with regard to the Indian schools and the general concerns of the mission, had convinced the resident Trustee and his friends that they had nothing to expect from him, but that, on the contrary, he would be in the way of the accomplishment of their designs. With the view, therefore, of effecting his removal from Stockbridge, that person repaired to Boston and endeavoured in conversation, not only with the Commissioners, but with some of the principal men in the Government, to produce on their minds very unfavourable impressions concerning him, particularly that he was a man of an unyielding temper, and unwilling to be reconciled to those from whom he had differed, and that in consequence of this he was likely to ruin the Indian mission. But happily the attempt utterly failed. Mr Edwards' character was too well established to be undermined by such insidious measures.[1]

Of the selfishness and unblushing impudence with which the resident Trustee carried on his designs, we have the following striking illustration in a letter from Mr Edwards ; they are in fact so gross, that had not the statement rested on the authority of a man who was so careful in forming his opinions, and so strict in his regard to truth, we would scarcely have ventured to quote it. " The resident Trustee," he writes, " has plainly discovered many designs tending to bring money into his own pocket,

[1] Edwards' Works, London 1839, vol. i. p. clxx, clxxvii, clxxxiii.

namely, a design of taking care of Mr Hollis's boys himself; a design of being steward of both boarding-schools" (*i. e.* the one for boys the other for girls), "by which he will have the opportunity of supplying the Indians out of his own shop, and of getting his pay from the British funds; a design of introducing his son as the master of the boarding-school, under the idea of a present supply, another person not appearing; and an expectation of diverting the King's bounty of £500 sterling to the Six Nations from New York. The former schoolmaster has given hints of an agreement between himself and him to resign the care of Mr Hollis's scholars to him when things are ripe for it; he providing for their maintenance and taking care of their instruction by his son. Besides these things, his wife is to be mistress of the female school; and two of their sons to be maintained and educated at the public expense, and two of their girls, in like manner, to be maintained in the female school; and one of his family to be his wife's usher; and his servants to be paid for, under the character of servants employed in the affairs of the female school; and the house for the boarding-school set on his wife's land; and then the farm to be bought by the country for the school, with the advantage of selling it at a high rate; and yet the family in a great measure to be maintained on the produce of it; besides the advantage of carrying on a trade, both with the Stockbridge Indians and the Mohawks. A man had need to have a great stock of assuredness, to urge a public affair under so manifold temptations of private interest."[1]

Of the boldness, if not the wisdom, with which the original head of the party could act, we have scarcely a less striking illustration in the following singular fact. Differences had long subsisted between him and Mr Woodbridge, the teacher of the Housatunnuk school, and perhaps no one circumstance had been more mortifying to him, or had a more direct tendency to defeat all his schemes, than the fact that the White inhabitants of the town (his own immediate family connections excepted), as well as the Indians of both nations, were to a man opposed to himself and friendly to Mr Woodbridge. This discouraged every attempt to carry through his plans at the public meetings of the

[1] Edwards' Works, vol. i. p. clxxxvi, clxxxviii.

town. For the purpose, therefore, of meeting this difficulty, and with a special view to the removal of Mr Edwards from Stockbridge, he made the extraordinary attempt to change the English inhabitants of the town, by suddenly and unexpectedly buying out the old inhabitants. "To this end," writes Mr Edwards, "he rose very early one morning, and went out before day and called some of them out of their beds, offering to buy their farms. In this manner he went from one to another, until he had been to almost all the inhabitants of the town that forenoon, offering them very high prices and cash in hand, vehemently pressing that the bargain should be immediately closed and the writings drawn, and the affair completed without delay, urging it most pressingly on each one. One of the inhabitants completed the affair with him. Some others came to a verbal agreement on conditions. But notwithstanding the great and extraordinary vigour with which this matter was carried on, the design was discovered before it could be completed, and so was disappointed, and then his friends, and himself too, were glad to ascribe his conduct to distraction." [1]

The chagrin and mortification, and entire loss of influence and respect, consequent upon the complete discomfiture of this shameless attempt to drive Mr Edwards away from Stockbridge, had, in connection with the infirmities of age, such an effect upon the individual referred to, that he was induced soon after to part with his property in the town and remove to a distance. His children, however, though somewhat disheartened by the defeat of the scheme, and though they perceived that if help came to them, it must be from some other quarter than Stockbridge, appear to have resolved that they would not lose all their labour, nor give up all their hopes without a vigorous struggle. The Commissioners at Boston of the Corporation in England, were now to a man firmly opposed to them; but their kinsman, who was a member of the Society in London, was well acquainted with its Board of Directors, and had written to them in behalf of his cousin. He had also applied to Mr Hollis to secure to her husband the management of his benefactions. The latter gentleman also, and the brother of the former, had considerable influence at Boston, and this influence

[1] Edwards' Works, vol. i. p. cxc.

they had exerted for a considerable period to procure the removal of Mr Edwards from Stockbridge. At the opening of the General Court in the autumn, all the influence and all the efforts of the family and of its friends had been brought to bear on this one point, and representations most unfavourable to his character and qualifications were made to many of the principal men of the Province. The annual report of the resident Trustee was also drawn up with a direct and immediate reference to this object, and was read to the Legislature when Mr Edwards knew nothing of its contents, and, being at the distance of 150 miles, had no opportunity of answering it. Mr Woodbridge, however, was on the spot, as were also the Commissioners of the Corporation, and they made such counteracting statements as were required by the circumstances. Mr Woodbridge was likewise now informed, that the author of the report had solicited Sir William Pepperell, the Governor of the Province, to write to England, and to use his influence with the Corporation in London, that Mr Edwards might be removed from the office of missionary, and that Sir William had engaged to do it.[1]

[1] Mr Edwards, on learning this fact, addressed a letter to Sir W. Pepperell in his own vindication, in which, after referring to the great disadvantage under which he lay, in attempting to defend himself at such a distance, and when he did not so much as know what had been said to his prejudice, he states among other things the following :—That since the revival of religion in 1734, the family with which the writer of the report was now connected had discovered an unceasing hostility towards himself and his family, notwithstanding the best endeavours he could use to remove it ; that they deeply engaged themselves in the controversy at Northampton on the side of his opponents, upholding, directing, and animating them in all their measures ; that two of them especially had been the confidential advisers of the opposition, in procuring his dismission ; that when his removal to Stockbridge was proposed, the whole family there and elsewhere opposed it with great vehemence, though when they saw an entire union and general engagedness in all the rest of the inhabitants, both English and Indians, for his settlement there, and that, when there was no hope of preventing it, they appeared as though their minds were changed ; that the author of the report, during the whole controversy at Northampton, in direct opposition to the family with which he was now connected, had remained his zealous friend and advocate ; that he warmly advocated his removal to Stockbridge, and expressed a strong desire of living under his ministry ; that this confidential friendship lasted until his connection with that family, and then was suddenly changed, first into secret, and afterwards into open opposition ; that he had personally blamed him for preaching to the Mohawks, as intermeddling with what was none of his business, although Mr Edwards produced the note of the Commissioners expressly desiring him to preach to them, until a distinct missionary was appointed over them ; that the reason openly assigned for the very great resentment of the author of the Report, and that of his friends, against Mr Edwards, was his having opposed the appointment of the wife of that gentleman as teacher of the

But notwithstanding these and other efforts to ruin Mr Edwards, his character for integrity was too well established to be shaken by unsubstantiated statements and covert attacks, and the replies which were made to the charges brought against him completely unmasked their falsehood. The attack made thus directly upon him, and indirectly on all his associates in the mission (for had they suceeeded in removing him, it was expected the removal of the others would be easily effected), not only failed of its design, but, by leading to a manifestation of the mercenary scheme of their opponents, for diverting to the purpose of private emolument the charities of the Province and of benevolent individuals, recoiled with increased violence on its unprincipled authors.[1]

The Mohawks, however, who had manifested much patience under the disappointments and vexations to which they had

female school, although he neither said nor did any thing respecting it, until his opinion was expressly desired in writing by the Commissioners, and then, that he opposed it on the ground that it was impossible for an individual who had the care of two numerous families of children, to instruct and govern the children of an Indian school; and that, as to his qualifications for the office of a missionary, his *communicative* faculty, &c., which were now denied, he could only appeal to those who had the best opportunity of judging from their own experience, particularly to every man, woman, and child in Stockbridge, that had any understanding, both English and Indian, except the families of the opponent of Mr Woodbridge, and of the author of the report. Mr Edwards then added, "Now, sir, I humbly request that if you had resolved on endeavouring to have me removed from my present employment here, you would once more take the matter into your impartial consideration. The ruin of my usefulness, and the ruin of my family, which has suffered greatly in years past, for righteousness' sake, are not indeed things of equal consideration with the public good. Yet certainly I should first have an equal, impartial, and candid hearing, before I am *executed* for the public good. I must leave the matter, dear sir, to your justice and Christian prudence; committing the affair to Him who knows all the injuries I have suffered, and how wrongfully I now suffer, and who is the Great Protector of the innocent and oppressed, beseeching him to guide you in your determination, and mercifully to order the end."—*Edwards' Works*, vol. i. p. cxcvi.

[1] Edwards Works, vol. i. p. cxcvi. cciv.

We have entered into these details regarding this unhappy contest, partly on account of their extraordinary nature, and partly as forming an interesting and instructive chapter in the life of one of the greatest and best men who have appeared in the Church of Christ. It is one of the mysteries of Divine Providence that such a man as Jonathan Edwards, whose talents and piety so admirably fitted him for usefulness, and whose heart was so much set on being useful, should have for so many years been harassed, first at Northampton, and afterwards at Stockbridge, with incessant opposition and contention, instead of being allowed to pursue his labours in peace and quietness. Yet how frequently have been severely tried the greatest and the best men in every age. "Even so, Father, for so it seemed good in thy sight."

been subjected, were at last wearied out, and the greater part of them gave up their lands and settlements at Stockbridge, and returned to their own country, never having been able to obtain a redress of their grievances. Thus were blasted, through the selfish and unprincipled conduct of these individuals, the fair prospects which appeared, two or three years before, of establishing a large and flourishing colony of the Iroquois Indians, and of extending among them the blessings of education, for which they then manifested a great desire.[1]

In 1754, the war, which then raged between France and England, proved very disastrous to the British Colonies, and Stockbridge, in common with the other frontier settlements of New England, was subjected to unceasing anxiety and alarm, being constantly exposed to an attack from the Indians in the interest of France. Several of the inhabitants of Stockbridge were killed by these marauders; it was judged necessary to garrison the town, and every family had quartered upon it a part of the soldiers required for its defence. The Indians, in consequence of various occurrences, had their minds greatly alienated from the English; and there was an apprehension, that should the Iroquois, or Six Nations, go over to the French, the Stockbridge and other Indian tribes in North America would follow their example. This, in fact, seemed to be the most critical period of the British dominion in North America, since the first settlement of the colonies.[2]

In January 1758, Mr Edwards removed from Stockbridge to Princetown, to undertake the Presidency of New Jersey College. His success at Stockbridge, especially among the Indians, was not great. Few of them appear to have been brought under the power of religion through his labours among them. Nor is this wonderful. During nearly the whole period of his ministry among them, the Indians were placed in circumstances very unfriendly to their moral and religious improvement. Yet when the proposal was first made to him to become the head of a college, he was struck with the greatest astonishment and concern, for though he was a man of distinguished talents and learning, he was no less remarkable for his modesty and humility. He considered himself as so unqualified for this important

[1] Edwards' Works, vol. i. p. cxcix, cci, cciv. [2] Ibid. vol. i. p. ccvi, ccvii, ccviii.

station, that he wondered how gentlemen of so much judgment, and so well acquainted with him, as some of the trustees were, should have thought of him for a moment. He did not, however, positively reject the invitation, but agreed to take the advice of some of his friends in the ministry on the subject. By his desire, a number of them met at Stockbridge, and after hearing his representation of the matter, and the objections of his people to his removal, they determined that it was his duty to accept of the presidency of the college. When they made known this opinion to him, Mr Edwards was uncommonly moved, and burst into tears, a thing very unusual with him in the presence of others. He soon after said to them, it was matter of wonder to him, how they could so easily get over the objections he had made against his removal to be the head of a college; but as he thought it was incumbent on him to be directed by their advice, he should now endeavour cheerfully to undertake the office, believing that he was in the path of his duty.[1] Scarcely, however, had he arrived at Princetown, when it was thought necessary to inoculate him with the small-pox, as he had never had that disease, and it was then prevailing in the town. He had it in a favourable form, and was even considered as out of all danger; but the secondary fever was accompanied by alarming symptoms, and put a period to his invaluable life, about two months after his removal from Stockbridge.[2]

In June 1759, the Rev. Stephen West was ordained pastor of the church at Stockbridge; and like his predecessor, he had under his care not only the Indians, but the English inhabitants of the settlement. He preached to the Indians through an interpreter, but as the animosities which had so long threatened the ruin of the mission, still subsisted and clouded his prospects of usefulness, and as the number of the English rapidly increased, by the coming of families from different parts of the country, and became able to support a minister for themselves, he, in 1775, gave up the Indians to the care of Mr John

[1] It is a fine though a quaint observation of a Scotch preacher, "It's a braw thing for a man's face to shine, and him no to ken it." Of this Jonathan Edwards was a noble example.

[2] Edwards' Life and Character, prefixed to Eighteen Sermons, p. 88, 93; Miller's Life of Jonathan Edwards in Spark's Library of American Biography, vol. viii. p. 140.

Sergeant, the son of the original founder of the mission, who possessed the rare qualification of understanding their language, while he himself continued the minister of the White people until his death.[1]

During the war of Independence which now commenced, the Indians suffered materially, both in their temporal and spiritual interests, by serving a few campaigns in the army of the United States. A large proportion of their most promising young men were killed in battle, while the others were confirmed in their habits of idleness and intemperance.

In 1785, the Indians removed from Stockbridge to the country of the Oneidas, in the western part of the State of New York, they having there granted them lands on which to settle. Here they built a town, which was called New Stockbridge. By their removal to this part of the country, they were materially benefited in a temporal point of view. They possessed more territory than before, having a tract of land six miles square; they were, for some time, less exposed to temptations, in consequence of their greater distance from the White people; they made a division of their lands, so that each held his property as his own individual right; and they became more industrious sober, and comfortable.[2]

During the last thirty years, the Stockbridge Indians have been in a very unsettled state. In consequence of the White people settling around them, they found themselves obliged to remove from New Stockbridge: successive parties accordingly left that place, and proceeded to the westward. The great body settled near Green-bay, on the western shore of Lake Michigan; but within a few years, they were once more overtaken by the tide of American emigration, and found themselves obliged to retire before it. By a new arrangement with the United States Government, they now removed to a part of the country on the east of Lake Winnebago.[3]

[1] Spirit of the Pilgrims, vol. iii. p. 382.

[2] Mass. Hist. Coll. vol. i. p. 195; vol. iv. p. 55; vol. v. p. 26; vol. vi. p. 69.—Fraser's Sermon before the Society in Scotland for Propagating Christian Knowledge, App. p. 46.

[3] Maclagan's Sermon before Society in Scotland for Propagating Christian Knowledge, 1831, p. 65; Report American Board for Foreign Missions, 1833, p. 120, 122. Ibid. 1836, p. 104.

In 1844, the number of Indians residing at Lake Winnebago did not much exceed 200. Death, and emigration to other parts of the country, had for some years past been diminishing their numbers. They might be called an industrious community, and their moral and social condition was much improved. Nearly all of them enjoyed the necessaries, and most of them the comforts of life. Though some of the characteristics of the Indian were found still to cleave to them, yet they may be regarded as substantially a transformed people. There have, however, for many years been much dissension and party strife among them, arising chiefly out of questions connected with their repeated removals and other political matters, a state of things which proved very injurious to their peace, good order, and social and religious improvement.[1]

SECT. V.—NEW JERSEY.

We now come to the history of a mission which exhibited a singular display of the power of divine grace among the Indians; and which has justly commanded the admiration of the Christian world, on account of the faith and patience, the zeal, the self-denial, the elevated piety displayed in the conduct of it, as well as by the remarkable success with which it was attended.

In April 1743, Mr David Brainerd entered on his labours as a Missionary among the Indians, under the patronage of the Society in Scotland for propagating Christian Knowledge, at a place called Kanaumeek, about twenty miles from Albany, in the province of New York. The situation was extremely lonely: it was in the midst of a wilderness, surrounded by woods and mountains, about twenty miles from the nearest English inhabitant. Here he lodged with a poor family who had lately come from the Highlands of Scotland, sleeping on a bundle of straw, and living on the coarsest fare; while almost the only language

[1] (American) Missionary Herald, vol. xxx. p. 416; Rep. Board For. Miss. 1831, p. 9; Ibid. 1839, p. 151; Ibid. 1840, p. 184; Ibid. 1844, p. 224; Ibid. 1847, p. 197; Ibid. 1848, p. 271.

he heard was Gaelic or Indian, neither of which he understood. As he was naturally of a melancholy temper, the dreariness of the country, the solitariness of the place, and the uncomfortableness of his circumstances, contributed not a little to cherish that unhappy state of mind. After he had been about three months in this quarter, he drew the following gloomy picture of his views and feelings: "My soul is and has been for a long time in a piteous condition, wading through a series of sorrows of various kinds. I have been so crushed down sometimes with a sense of my meanness and infinite unworthiness, that I have been ashamed that any, even the meanest of my fellow-creatures, should so much as spend a thought about me; and have wished sometimes when I travelled among the thick brakes, as one of them to drop into everlasting oblivion. In this case, sometimes I have almost resolved never again to see any of my acquaintance, and really thought I could not do it and hold up my face; and have longed for the remotest region for a retreat from all my friends, that I might not be seen or heard of any more. Sometimes the consideration of my ignorance has been a means of my great distress and anxiety. And especially, my soul has been in anguish with fear, guilt, and shame, that ever I had preached, or had any thought that way. Sometimes my soul has been in distress, on feeling some particular corruptions rise, and swell like a mighty torrent with present violence; having, at the same time, ten thousand sins and follies presented to view, in all their blackness and aggravations. These things, attended with such external circumstances as mine at present are:—destitute of most of the conveniences of life, and, I may say, of all its pleasures; without a friend to communicate any of my sorrows to; and sometimes without any place of retirement, where I may unburden my soul before God, have greatly contributed to my distress. Of late more especially, my great difficulty has been a sort of carelessness, a kind of regardless temper of mind, whence I have been disposed to indolence and trifling. And this temper of mind has constantly been attended with guilt and shame, so that sometimes I have been in a kind of horror, to find myself so unlike the blessed God; and have thought I grew worse under all my trials; and nothing has cut and wounded my soul more than this. Oh! if I am one of God's chosen, as I trust through infinite grace I am, I find of a truth that 'the righteous scarcely are saved.'"[1]

The place where Mr Brainerd lodged being at some distance from the Indians, he found this extremely inconvenient, as it obliged him to travel backward and forward, almost daily, on foot; and notwithstanding his utmost endeavours, he could not be with them in the morning and evening, the seasons when they were most generally at home, and when they were most at liberty to attend to instruction. He, therefore, took up his residence among them, and lodged at first in one of their wigwams, until he succeeded in building a small cottage for himself. Here he lived quite alone, and though his situation was far from agreeable, yet it was much more comfortable than before. He blessed God that he had given him a little cottage where he might live alone and enjoy a happy retirement, free from noise and disturbance, and could at any hour of the day lay aside all his studies and lift up his soul in prayer to God for spiritual blessings. He one day thus writes in his diary: "Was enabled in secret prayer to raise my soul to God with desire and delight. It was indeed a blessed season to my soul. I found the comfort of being a Christian. I counted the sufferings of the present time not worthy to be compared with the glory of divine enjoyments even in this world. All my past sorrows seemed kindly to disappear, and I 'remembered no more the sorrow for joy.' O how kindly and with what filial tenderness the soul hangs on, and confides in the Rock of Ages at such a season, that he 'will never leave it nor forsake it,' that he will 'cause all things work together for its good.' I longed that others should know how good a God the Lord is. My soul was full of tenderness and love even to the most inveterate of my enemies: I longed they should share in the same mercy. I loved and longed that God should do just as he pleased with me and every thing else. I felt exceeding serious, calm, and peaceful, and encouraged to press after holiness, as long as I live, whatever difficulties and trials may be in the way. May the Lord always help me so to do! Amen and amen."[2]

Mr Brainerd was often in a poor state of health, and this was probably greatly aggravated by the toils and privations which he underwent. Two days after he thus writes: "Spent most of

[1] Brainerd's Life, Edinburgh 1798, p. 89, 294, 550. [2] Ibid. p. 91, 92, 550.

the day in labour to procure something to keep my horse on in the winter. Enjoyed not much sweetness in the morning. Was very weak in body through the day, and thought this frail body would soon drop into the dust: had some very realizing apprehensions of a speedy entrance into another world. And in this weak state of body, was not a little distressed for want of suitable food. Had no bread, nor could I get any. I am forced to go or send ten or fifteen miles for all the bread I eat; and if I get any considerable quantity, it is sometimes sour and mouldy before I eat it; and then, again, I have none for some days together for want of an opportunity to send for it, and cannot find my horse in the woods to go myself. This was my case now; but, through Divine goodness, I had some Indian meal, of which I made little cakes and fried them. Yet felt contented with my circumstances, and sweetly resigned to God. In prayer I enjoyed great freedom; and blessed God as much for my present circumstances, as if I had been a king, and thought I found a disposition to be contented in any circumstances: blessed be God."[1]

Of Mr Brainerd's deadness to the world, and of his spiritual enjoyments, we have many interesting examples. One day he writes: "In the morning, felt exceedingly dead to the world and all its enjoyments. I thought I was ready and willing to give up life and all its comforts as soon as called to it; and yet then had as much comfort of life as almost ever I had. Life itself now appeared but an empty bubble; the riches, honours, and common enjoyments of life appeared extremely tasteless. I longed to be perpetually and entirely crucified to all things here below by the cross of Christ. My soul was sweetly resigned to God's disposal of me, in every regard; and I saw there had nothing happened to me but what was best for me. I confided in God that he would 'never leave me,' though I should 'walk through the valley of the shadow of death.' It was then 'my meat and drink' to be holy, 'to live to the Lord, and to die to the Lord.' And I thought that I then enjoyed such a heaven, as far exceeded the most sublime conceptions of an unregenerate soul; and even unspeakably beyond what I myself could conceive of at another time. I did not wonder that Peter

[1] Brainerd's Life, p. 93.

said, 'Lord, it is good to be here,' when thus refreshed with Divine glories.

"My soul was full of love and tenderness in the duty of intercession; felt especially a most sweet affection to some precious godly ministers of my acquaintance. I prayed earnestly for dear Christians, and for those I have reason to fear are my enemies; and could not have uttered a word of bitterness, or entertained a bitter thought against the vilest man living. I had a sense of my own great unworthiness. My soul seemed to breathe forth love and praise to God afresh, when I thought he would let his children love and receive me as one of their brethren and fellow-citizens; and when I thought of their treating me in that manner, I longed to lie at their feet, and could think of no way to express the sincerity and simplicity of my love and esteem of them, as being much better than myself."[1]

In labouring among the Indians, Mr Brainerd studied to instruct them chiefly in those principles of religion which he deemed most important, and most calculated to promote their conversion to the Redeemer, endeavouring, at the same time, to make them level to the comprehension of the weakest and most ignorant of them. The knowledge of Christianity which some of them acquired, was far from contemptible; and there were even several on whose consciences the word appeared to make a serious impression. Some of them came to Mr Brainerd of their own accord, to converse with him about the things which belonged to their eternal peace; several inquired with tears in their eyes, "What they should do to be saved?" He could not, indeed, say that he had satisfactory evidence of the conversion of any of them, but there was a considerable reformation of manners among them. Their idolatrous sacrifices were entirely abolished; their heathenish dances were, in a great degree, abandoned; their habits of drunkenness were, in some measure, corrected; and the observation of the Sabbath was established among them and their children. By his advice, most of them, after he had spent about a year among them, removed to Stockbridge, which was only about twenty miles distant, and placed themselves under the care of the excellent Mr Sergeant.[2]

[1] Brainerd's Life, p. 123. [2] Ibid. p. 551.

In May 1744, Mr Brainerd, who was now at liberty to pursue his labours among the Indians in some other quarter, proceeded to the Forks of Delaware, in the province of Pennsylvania. Here the number of his hearers was at first very small, often not exceeding twenty-five, and even afterwards, they seldom amounted to more than forty. The Indians in this quarter were now greatly diminished, most of them being either dispersed, or removed further back into the country. There were not more than ten houses which continued to be inhabited, and some of these were several miles distant from the others, so that it was very difficult for his little congregation to assemble together as often as he wished.[1]

Among these Indians Mr Brainerd pursued his labours with unwearied diligence and zeal; but, as he was deeply sensible that no human exertions could command success, he combined with his endeavours earnest and constant supplications for the divine blessing upon them. Of his importunity in prayer, we have an interesting example in the exercises of his mind, one day soon after his arrival in this part of this country. "This morning," says he, "I was greatly oppressed with guilt and shame, from a sense of my inward vileness and pollution. About nine o'clock, I withdrew to the woods for prayer, but had not much comfort. I appeared to myself the meanest, vilest creature upon earth, and could scarcely live with myself; so mean and vile I appeared, that I thought I should never be able to hold up my face in heaven, if God, of his infinite grace, should bring me thither. Towards night, my burden respecting my work among the Indians began to increase much; and was aggravated by hearing sundry things that looked very discouraging; in particular, that they intended to meet together the next day for an idolatrous feast and dance. Then I began to be in anguish. I thought I must in conscience go and endeavour to break them up; and knew not how to attempt such a thing. However, I withdrew for prayer, hoping for strength from above. And in prayer, I was exceedingly enlarged: my soul was as much drawn out as I almost ever remember it to have been in my life. I was in such anguish, and pleaded with so much earnestness and importunity, that when I rose from my knees, I felt extremely weak

[1] Brainerd's Life, p. 129, 555.

and overcome; I could scarcely walk straight; my joints were loosed; the sweat ran down my face and body; and nature seemed as if it would dissolve. So far as I could judge, I was wholly free from selfish ends in my fervent supplications for the poor Indians. I knew they were met together to worship devils and not God, and this made me cry earnestly that God would now appear and help me in my attempts to break up this idolatrous meeting. My soul pleaded long; and I thought God would hear, and would go with me to vindicate his own cause. I seemed to confide in God for his presence and assistance. And thus I spent the evening, praying incessantly for Divine assistance, and that I might not be self-dependent, but still have my whole dependence upon God. What I passed through was remarkable, and indeed inexpressible. All things here below vanished, and there appeared to be nothing of any considerable importance to me, but holiness of heart and life, and the conversion of the heathen to God. All my cares, fears, and desires, which might be said to be of a worldly nature, disappeared, and were in my esteem of little more importance than a puff of wind. I longed exceedingly that God would get to himself a name among the heathen; and I appealed to him with the greatest freedom, that he knew I preferred him 'above my chief joy.' Indeed, I had no notion of joy from this world: I cared not where or how I lived, or what hardships I went through, so that I could but gain souls to Christ."[1]

On another occasion he thus writes: "In the evening God was pleased to help me in prayer, beyond what I have experienced for some time; my soul was especially drawn out for the enlargement of Christ's kingdom, and for the conversion of my poor people; and my soul relied on God for the accomplishment of that great work.

"Oh, how sweet were the thoughts of death to me at this time! Oh, how I longed to be with Christ, to be employed in the glorious work of angels, and with an angel's freedom, vigour, and delight! And yet how willing was I to stay a while on earth, that I might do something, if the Lord pleased, for his interest in the world! My soul, my very soul, longed for the ingathering of the poor heathen; and I cried to God for them

[1] Brainerd's Life, p. 143.

most willingly and heartily; and yet because I could not but cry. This was a sweet season; for I had some lively taste of heaven, and a temper of mind suited, in some measure, to the employments and entertainments of it. My soul was grieved to leave the place; but my body was weak and worn out, and it was near nine o'clock. Oh, I longed that the remaining part of my life might be filled up with more fervency and activity in the things of God! Oh, the inward peace, composure, and God-like serenity of such a frame! Heaven must needs differ from this only in degree, not in kind. Lord, ever give me this bread of life." [1]

Though Mr Brainerd was now settled at the Forks of Delaware, he did not confine his labours to the Indians in that part of the country. Having heard of some of these poor people at a place about thirty miles distant, he proceeded to visit them; but as they were then on the point of removing to the river Susquehannah, he had an opportunity of preaching only twice to them. In general, they appeared sober, friendly, and attentive. Two or three of them, indeed, suspected he had some ill design upon them, urging that the White people had maltreated them, and taken their lands from them: it was not reasonable, therefore, to think they were now concerned for their happiness, but rather that they designed to make them slaves, or to carry them on board their ships, and cause them fight with the people over the water, meaning the French and Spaniards. But notwithstanding these insinuations, most of them appeared to entertain no jealousy of Mr Brainerd's design, and invited him to visit them after their return home, and to instruct them in the principles of religion.[2]

Encouraged by this invitation, Mr Brainerd proceeded shortly after to visit these Indians on the Susquehannah, accompanied by the Rev. Mr Byram, a neighbouring minister, his interpreter, and two of his principal people from the Forks of Delaware. After the first day's journey, they had nothing before them but a vast and dreary wilderness. Here they had by far the most difficult and dangerous travelling any of them had ever experienced, having to make their way over lofty mountains, through deep valleys, and among hideous rocks. One evening Mr

[1] Brainerd's Life, p. 185. [2] Ibid. p. 557.

Brainerd's horse hung one of its legs in the rocks, and fell under him ; but through the kindness of Providence he escaped without injury. The poor animal, however, broke its leg ; aud being in such a dreadful place, near thirty miles from any house, nothing could be done to preserve its life : He was, therefore, obliged to kill it, and to prosecute his journey on foot. At night they kindled a fire, cut up a few bushes, and placed them over their heads as a shelter from the frost ; and after commending themselves to God in prayer, they lay down on the ground and slept till morning. On the fourth day, they arrived at an Indian town on the banks of the Susquehannah, called Opeholhaupung, where were about seventy people, including men, women, and children. Mr Brainerd remained among them several days, preaching regularly when they were at home, while they, in order to hear him, delayed their general hunting match, which they were just about to begin. Before leaving them, he gave them to understand, that he would visit them again the following spring ; a proposal to which they readily assented.[1]

Many were the fatigues, the dangers, and the distresses which Mr Brainerd experienced in the course of his frequent journeys among the Indians ; and no less singular were the faith, the patience, and the self-denial he manifested under trials of this description. One day in travelling from the place of Mr Byram's residence to the Forks of Delaware, a distance of about forty miles, he lost his way in the wilderness, wandered over rocks and mountains, down hideous steeps, through swamps, and other dangerous places. The night was dark and cold, and, to add to his misfortune, he was troubled with a pain in his head, accompanied with sickness at stomach, which rendered every step he took distressing to him. He had little or no expectation for several hours but that he would have to lie out all night in the woods in this melancholy condition. Providentially, however, about nine o'clock, he found a house, and was kindly entertained by the people. Yet trying as was his situation, no expression of discontent, no murmur of complaint, dropt from his lips. His reflections on this occasion are not unworthy of an apostle. "Thus," says he, "I have been frequently exposed, and sometimes have lain out the whole night ; but

[1] Brainerd's Life, p. 149, 558.

hitherto God has preserved me, and blessed be his name. Such fatigues and hardships serve to wean me more from the earth, and, I trust, will make heaven the sweeter. Formerly, when I was thus exposed to cold, rain, &c., I was ready to please myself with the thoughts of enjoying a comfortable house, a warm fire, and other outward comforts; but now, through the grace of God, these have less place in my heart, and my eye is more to God for comfort. In this world, I expect tribulation; and it does not now as formerly appear strange to me. I do not in such seasons of difficulty flatter myself that it will be better hereafter, but rather think how much worse it might be; how much greater trials others of God's children have endured; how much greater, perhaps, are yet reserved for me. Blessed be God, that he makes the thoughts of my journey's end and of my dissolution a great comfort to me under my sharpest trials; and scarce ever lets these thoughts be attended with terror or melancholy; but they are attended frequently with great joy."[1]

In May 1745, Mr Brainerd, agreeably to his promise, renewed his visit to the Indians on the river Susquehannah, accompanied by his interpreter from the Forks of Delaware. In travelling through the wilderness, he suffered, as usual, great fatigues and hardships. After lodging one night in the woods, he was overtaken by a north-easterly storm, in which he was in danger of losing his life. Having no kind of shelter, and not being able to kindle a fire on account of the rain, he resolved to prosecute his journey in the hope of finding some place of refuge, without which, he thought it was impossible he could survive the night. But, unfortunately, the horses, both of Mr Brainerd and of his interpreter, having eaten poison for want of other food, now became so sick, that they could neither ride nor lead them, but were obliged to drive them on before, and to walk themselves on foot. Providentially, however, in the evening, they came to a bark hut, where they took up their lodgings for the night. Having at length reached the Susquehannah, Mr Brainerd travelled about a hundred miles along that river, visited many of the Indian towns, and preached the gospel to some of different tribes through the medium of interpreters. He was sometimes greatly disheartened by the opposition which they made to

[1] Brainerd's Life, p. 156.

Christianity; and sometimes he was much encouraged by the disposition which some of them manifested to hear the word. He spent about a fortnight among the Indians in this part of the country, and suffered considerable hardships, frequently sleeping on the cold ground, and sometimes in the open air. He was at last taken very ill as he was riding in the wilderness, being attacked with an ague, accompanied with violent pains in his head and bowels, and with a great evacuation of blood, so that he thought he would have perished by the way. Having reached, however, the hut of an Indian trader, he obtained liberty to stop there; and though without medicine or food proper for one in his situation, he so far recovered, that after about a week's illness, he was able to resume his journey homeward.[1]

After his return from the Susquehannah, Mr Brainerd was ready to sink into the depths of despair. As his body was extremely feeble, in consequence of his late illness, so his hopes of the conversion of the Indians were scarcely ever so low. He even began to entertain serious thoughts of relinquishing the undertaking, not that he was weary of the toils and trials of a missionary life, nor because he had freedom in his own mind to settle among the White people, but simply on account of the little hope he had of success among the Indians. But as the night is often darkest before the dawn, so it was from the midst of this thick cloud that the prospect began to brighten around him. Having heard of a number of Indians at a place called Crosweeksung, in New Jersey, about eighty miles from the Forks of Delaware, he proceeded to visit them; but, on his arrival, he found them scattered in small settlements, at a considerable distance from each other, and not more than two or three families residing in the same place. He preached, however, to the few he found, consisting of only four women and some children. So inconsiderable was the congregation, and so inauspicious the spot which was soon to be the scene of a most remarkable work of divine grace. After hearing Mr Brainerd, these poor people set off and travelled ten or fifteen miles to give notice to their friends that a minister had arrived among them, by which means their little company was in a few days increased to between forty and fifty, including both old and young. No objections, no opposition was

[1] Brainerd's Life, p. 177.

heard among them, though in time past they had manifested as strong a dislike to the gospel as any Indians whatever, and even lately several of them had been much enraged at his interpreter for telling them something about Christianity. Now, however, they were very anxious to obtain instruction; they asked Mr Brainerd to preach to them twice a day, that so they might learn as much as possible during his stay; and they appeared to listen to his instructions with the utmost seriousness and attention. This favourable disposition in these Indians he attributed to the exertions of one or two of their own people, who having heard him some time before at the Forks of Delaware, had on their return endeavoured to shew their friends the evil of idolatry, and of other practices common among them: a circumstance which may afford the Christian missionary some consolation under the greatest of all his trials, the want of success; for though no success should, for a season, crown his labours in his own neighbourhood, yet, perhaps, some who have heard the gospel from his lips, may, in the mean while, be instrumental in preparing the way for its introduction even among distant tribes.[1]

After spending about a fortnight at Crosweeksung, Mr Brainerd returned to the Forks of Delaware, and from this period these two places were alternately the principal scene of his labours. Soon after his arrival, he had the pleasure of baptizing his interpreter, together with his wife, the first of the Indians whom he received into the bosom of the church. When Mr Brainerd first employed him as his interpreter, he was in some respects well qualified for the office, as he was not only acquainted with the Indian and the English languages, but had a strong desire that his countrymen should abandon their heathenish notions and practices, and should adopt the manners and customs of the White people, particularly as to their mode of living. But he had little or no impression of religion on his mind, and on this account was very unfit for his work, being incapable of communicating to others many truths of the first importance, for want of an experimental, as well as a more doctrinal knowledge of the gospel. Now, however, there was a material improvement in his performances as interpreter.

[1] Brainerd's Life, p. 180, 363, 405.

Though it might naturally be supposed that a discourse, in passing to the audience through the medium of a second person, would lose much of its force and meaning, yet Mr Brainerd's sermons did not ordinarily lose any thing of their original energy, unless it was sometimes owing to the want of suitable expressions in the Indian language, a defect which his own knowledge of it could not have supplied. His interpreter addressed the Indians with admirable fervency; he scarce knew when to give over; and sometimes when Mr Brainerd had concluded his discourse, and was returning home, he would stay behind to repeat and enforce what had been spoken; nor did this appear to arise from spiritual pride, or from an affectation of being a public teacher; but from a spirit of faithfulness, and an honest concern for their souls. As his indifference to religion was formerly a source of great distress to Mr Brainerd, so now his zeal for the salvation of his countrymen was no small comfort to him.[1]

On visiting the Indians at Crosweeksung a second time, Mr Brainerd was happy to find them not only still favourably disposed toward Christianity, but a number of them under serious concern for their souls, their convictions of their sinfulness and misery having been much promoted by the labours of the Rev. William Tennant, to whom he had advised them to make application. Scarcely had he returned among them, when these impressions increased and spread in a surprising manner. In two or three days, the inquiry was general among them, "What they should do to be saved." Such was their sensibility of heart, that a few words concerning their souls would make the tears flow in streams down their cheeks; in their public assemblies, a dry eye was often scarcely to be seen; it was astonishing how they were melted with the love of the Redeemer, and with the invitations of the gospel, when not a word of terror was spoken to them.[2]

It must not, however, be supposed that Mr Brainerd neglected to instruct the Indians concerning their sinfulness and misery: this he at first inculcated in almost every discourse, as he knew well that no sinner will come to the Saviour unless he feel his need of him. Still, however, the awakening among the Indians

[1] Brainerd's Life, p. 367, 407, 510. [2] Ibid. p. 378.

was not produced by the terrors of the law; but by the grace of the gospel. Christ crucified was the grand theme of his preaching; this was the point in which all his sermons centred. It was often matter of wonder to himself, that whatever was the subject of discourse, he was naturally led, after having explained it, to speak of Christ Jesus, and of its relation to him. If he treated of the existence and attributes of God, he took occasion to represent Christ as the only way to the Father. If he illustrated the sinfulness and misery of man, he proceeded to shew the need we had of Christ, to atone for our guilt, and to save us from everlasting woe. If he discoursed of the law of God, he did not forget to recommend Christ as "the end of the law for righteousness to every one that believeth." Sometimes when he designed to say only a few words on a subject, he was insensibly led, by the view of its connection with Christ, to speak of his incarnation or satisfaction, of his qualifications as a Saviour, or of the gracious invitations which he addresses to sinners, to "come to him, and take of the water of life freely." The awakening, in short, was always most remarkable when he discoursed of the condescension and love of a dying Redeemer; of the ample provision he has made for the salvation of man, and of the free offers of mercy, which he makes to guilty, miserable creatures.[1]

This was strikingly displayed one day, when Mr Brainerd, in preaching on the parable of the Great Supper, exhibited to the Indians, with uncommon fervour and freedom, the unsearchable riches of divine grace. During the sermon a deep concern was visible among them, and afterwards, when he was speaking with such individuals as were under concern about their souls, the Spirit of God appeared to descend on the whole assembly, and, with astonishing energy, overpowered all opposition like a mighty torrent, which, with irresistible force, sweeps before it whatever comes in its way. Almost the whole congregation, the old, the middle-aged, and the young, were overwhelmed with its influence. Even the most stubborn hearts were made to bow. One of the principal Indians, who previously had felt secure in the armour of self-righteousness, because he possessed more knowledge than most of his countrymen, and who, only

[1] Brainerd's Life, p. 408, 472.

the day before, had asserted, with the utmost assurance, that he had been a Christian for upwards of ten years, was now impressed with deep concern on account of his sinful, miserable state; his tears flowed in streams down his cheeks; his self-confidence vanished like a vision of the night. There was also a young woman who was so thoughtless and ignorant, that she seemed scarcely to know she had a soul, but who having heard of something strange among the Indians, came to see what was the matter. As she called at Mr Brainerd's lodgings by the way, he informed her of his design to preach immediately, at which she laughed and seemed to mock. She came, however, to hear him, and before he had concluded his discourse, not only felt she had a soul, but was so impressed with her sinfulness and misery, that she seemed like one pierced through with a dart; she could neither walk, nor sit, nor stand, without being supported. When public worship was over, she lay prostrate on the ground, praying in the most fervent manner, and neither took notice of others, nor returned them any answer when they spoke to her. The burden of her cry was, "Have mercy on me, O God, and help me to give thee my heart." In this manner she continued most importunate in supplication for several hours together; thus she who came to mock, returned to pray.

The whole assembly, indeed, appeared as it were transfixed to the heart with concern for their souls. Almost all of them were crying for mercy, either within or without the house. So overwhelmed were they with a sense of sin, so absorbed in serious thought, that none appeared to observe another; but each prayed as freely, and probably, in his own apprehension, as secretly, as if he had been in the midst of a desert, far removed from every human eye. Such as had been awakened for some time, it was observed, complained chiefly of the corruption of their heart; those who were newly impressed, of the wickedness of their life. It is also worthy of notice, that they who had lately obtained relief, appeared, on this occasion, calm and composed, rejoicing in Christ Jesus as their God and Saviour. Some of them took their weeping friends by the hand, telling them of the love of Christ, and of the comfort which is enjoyed in him; and on this ground invited them to come and give him their hearts. The whole scene, in short, presented a striking and interesting illustration of that prediction of the prophet Zechariah, "I will pour upon the house of David, and upon the inhabitants of Jerusalem, the spirit of grace and of supplications; and they shall look on me whom they have pierced, and they shall mourn for him, as one mourneth for his only son, and shall be in bitterness for him, as one that is in bitterness for his first-born. And the land shall mourn, every family apart; and their wives apart."

This was not merely a transient scene, but lasted, in a greater or less degree, for a considerable time. Every sermon seemed now productive of good; some were newly awakened, some further impressed, or some comforted. No sooner did any come from remote places, than they were seized with concern about their souls. It was common for strangers, before they had remained a day, to be convinced of their sinfulness and misery, and to inquire, with the utmost solicitude, "What they should do to be saved." Others, who previously had experienced only some slight emotion of their passions, were now wounded to the heart; their tears and sighs and groans, bore witness to the inward anguish of their souls. On the other hand, such as had obtained comfort, appeared humble, serious, and devout, endowed with remarkable tenderness of conscience, and concerned to regulate their life by the laws of Christ. Observing a woman one morning very sorrowful, Mr Brainerd inquired into the cause of her grief, and found she had been angry with her child the evening before, and was now afraid lest her anger had been immoderate and sinful. This had so vexed her, that she awoke before daylight, and continued weeping for several hours. A man, who some time before had put away his wife, and taken another woman, a practice common among the Indians, was now much concerned about this circumstance in particular, being fully convinced of the evil of his conduct, and anxious to know what was his duty. Inquiry being made into the cause of his leaving his wife, it appeared she had given him no just occasion to desert her; and, as it was found that she was willing to forgive his past misconduct, and to live peaceably with him in future, he was told it was his indispensable duty to renounce the woman he had last taken, and to receive back the other, who was properly his wife, and to cleave to her alone as long as she lived. With this advice he readily complied, a striking proof of the power of religion on his mind; for it is likely, a few weeks before, the whole world would not have induced him to conform to the law of Christianity on the subject of marriage. Mr Brainerd was apprehensive lest this decision should prejudice some of the Indians against the gospel, when they saw the strictness it enjoined, and the sacrifices it required; but so far was it from having any bad effect in this respect, that most of them acknowledged the reasonableness of the regulation.[1]

As there was now a considerable number of the Indians, who gave satisfactory evidence of the sincerity of their conversion, Mr Brainerd, after explaining to them the nature of baptism, administered that ordinance to twenty-five of them in one day, namely, fifteen adults, and ten children, in the presence of a large congregation of White people. After the crowd of spectators had retired, he called the baptized together, and discoursed to them in particular. He warned them of the evil and danger of indifference in religion, after making so public a profession of it; he reminded them of the solemn obligations under which they had come, to live devoted to God; he gave them some directions respecting their conduct in life; encouraged them to watchfulness, stedfastness, and devotion; and set before them the comfort on earth, and the glory in heaven, which await the faithful followers of the Lamb. To all of them, this was a most interesting and delightful season. The baptized Indians appeared to rejoice in the solemn dedication they had that day made of themselves to the service of God; love reigned among them, and displayed itself in the most simple unaffected manner. Several of the other Indians, when they saw and heard these things, were much affected, weeping most bitterly, and longing to be partakers of that comfort and happiness, which their Christian countrymen appeared to enjoy.

On the following day, Mr Brainerd, after discoursing some time to the Indians, addressed himself to those in particular, who hoped they were partakers of divine grace, representing to them the happiness which Christ confers on his people on

[1] Brainerd's Life, p. 376, 405.

earth, and the glory he prepares for them in heaven. Scarcely had he begun to speak in this strain, when the Christian Indians appeared to dissolve in love to the Redeemer, mingled with desire after the full enjoyment of Him, and of a state of perfect holiness of heart and life. They wept abundantly, yet joyfully. Their tears, and sobs, and sighs, were accompanied with inward peace and comfort; a circumstance which seemed to manifest, that the whole was the effect of a spirit of adoption, not of that spirit of bondage, under which many of them had so lately groaned. The sacred influence spread over the whole assembly, which now consisted of nearly one hundred Indians, including both old and young, almost all of whom were either animated with joy in Christ Jesus, or impressed with concern for an interest in Him.

Having now been nearly a month in this quarter, Mr Brainerd proposed undertaking a new journey to the Susquehannah, as this was the best season of the year for finding the Indians at home. After informing his congregation of his design to leave them for the present, and to go to their countrymen far remote, to preach among them the glad tidings of salvation, he asked them, Whether they would not employ the remainder of the day in prayer for him, that God would crown the attempt with his blessing, and render it effectual for the conversion of their brethren? Having cheerfully agreed to this proposal, they soon after began the exercise, and continued praying the whole night till near the dawn of day, never apprehending it was past their usual bedtime, until having gone out and viewed the heavens, they beheld the morning star a considerable height in the horizon; so earnest and unwearied were they in their devotions.

In his way to the Susquehannah, Mr Brainerd visited the Forks of Delaware, where he now found the Indians much more impressed with religion, and more deeply affected in hearing the word than before. Some of them had been at Crosweeksung, and had there beheld, and, it was hoped, felt the power of divine truth. In this part of the country, however, there were several Indians who had always refused to hear Mr Brainerd preach, and even manifested an inveterate hatred to those who attended his ministry. These now became more violent in their opposition than ever, scoffing at religion, and asking the converts insulting questions, as, "How often they had cried? Whether they had not cried enough to do the turn?" Thus the Christian Indians soon began to have "trial of cruel mockings," the uniform reward of serious piety in every age, and in every part of the world.[1]

Leaving the Forks of Delaware, Mr Brainerd proceeded on his journey to the Susquehannah, directing his course toward an Indian town named Shomokin, about a hundred and twenty miles to the westward. Here there were upwards of fifty houses, and, it was said, about three hundred inhabitants, though he never saw much above the half of that number. They were reckoned a most worthless, drunken, mischievous race, but yet they received him kindly, listened to the gospel with great attention, and expressed a desire for further instruction. Leaving this place, Mr Brainerd travelled down the river to Juneauta, an Indian town through which he had passed in his last journey. At that time the inhabitants appeared extremely friendly, and less under the influence of prejudice against Christianity than most of their countrymen, but now they seemed quite rooted in their Pagan notions, and strongly averse to the gospel. They were at this time busy making preparations for celebrating a great idolatrous feast on the following day. Having provided no fewer than ten fat deer for this purpose, about a hundred of them assembled in the evening, and danced round a large fire which they had previously kindled. During the dance, they threw the fat into the fire, which sometimes raised the flame to a prodigious height, while, at the same time, they yelled and shouted in a most hideous manner. After continuing this exercise nearly the whole night, they devoured the flesh of the animals, and then retired to their huts. Such a scene was extremely distressing to Mr Brainerd; it pierced him like a dagger to the heart. After walking about till he was almost overwhelmed with grief and fatigue, he crept into a little crib made for corn, laid himself down on the poles, and slept in this situation. As soon as the Indians rose next morning, he attempted to collect them together, with the view of instructing them in the truths

[1] Brainerd's Life, p. 380.

of religion; but he soon found they had other business to pursue. About noon, they assembled all their powaws, in order to discover, by their charms and incantations, the cause of the sickness which at that time raged among them, many of them being attacked with flux, attended with fever. In this exercise, they made all the wild, ridiculous, frantic motions it is almost possible to imagine; sometimes singing; sometimes howling; sometimes extending their arms to the utmost, spreading their fingers, and seeming to push with them; sometimes stroking their faces with their hands, then spurting water as fine as mist; sometimes sitting flat on the earth, then bowing their faces to the ground, wringing their sides as if in the utmost anguish, distorting their faces, turning up their eyes, puffing, grunting, &c. Some of them appeared much more earnest in these exercises than others; they chanted, peeped, and muttered with such ardour and such energy, as if they were determined to awaken the infernal powers, and extort the secret from them. After continuing these hideous charms and incantations, with some intervals, for upwards of three hours, they were completely exhausted, and broke up the meeting without appearing to have received any satisfaction on the subject of their inquiry.

In this quarter of the country, Mr Brainerd met with a zealous reformer of the Indian religion, or rather a restorer of what he considered the ancient mode of worship. But of all the spectacles he ever saw, none appeared so horrible, none excited such images of terror in his mind, none corresponded so nearly with the common idea of the infernal powers. He presented himself to Mr Brainerd in his pontifical garb, consisting of a coat of bearskins hanging down to his toes, a bearskin cap on his head, and a pair of bearskin stockings on his feet; a large wooden face, the one half painted black, the other of a tawny colour like the Indians, with an extravagant mouth, cut extremely awry. In his hand was the instrument he employed for music in his idolatrous worship: it was a tortoise shell with some corn in it, fixed on a piece of wood for a handle. As he came forward he beat to time with his rattle, and danced with all his might; but allowed no part of his body, not even his fingers, to be seen. His appearance and gestures were so unlike all that was human, that when he came near, Mr Brainerd could not help shrinking back with horror, though it was then noonday, and he knew perfectly who it was. It appears he had a house consecrated to religion; in it were several images, and the ground was beaten as hard as a rock by his frequent and violent dancing. Mr Brainerd conversed with him about the principles of Christianity; some of them he liked; others he disliked. "God," he said, "had taught him his religion; and he never would turn from it. He was anxious, however, to find some who would cordially join with him in it, for the Indians were grown very degenerate and corrupt. He had thoughts, therefore, of leaving all his friends, travelling abroad, and searching for some who would join with him; for he believed God had some good people in the world, who viewed things in the same light as himself. He had not always felt as he now did: formerly he was like other Indians: but about four or five years before, he became greatly distressed in his mind: he could no longer dwell among his countrymen, but retired into the woods, and lived there alone for some months. At length God comforted his heart, and shewed him what he should do: since that time he had known God, and endeavoured to serve him; he also loved all men, whoever they were, in a manner he never did before." It further appeared from the accounts of the Indians themselves, that he was a great enemy to their drinking spirituous liquors, and when he could not dissuade them from that ruinous practice, he used to leave them and go crying into the woods. Some of his sentiments, indeed, were rational and just; Mr Brainerd even informs us, there was something in his temper and disposition more like true religion than any thing he ever beheld in a Pagan. He appeared to be sincere, honest, and conscientious in his own way; and on this account, was derided by his countrymen as a precise zealot, who made a needless noise about religion.[1]

Having again failed in his attempts to introduce Christianity on the Susquehannah, Mr Brainerd returned to Crosweeksung; and, on his arrival, was much struck with the vast difference between the Indians in that quarter, and his congregation at

[1] Brainerd's Life, p. 396.

this place. To dwell with the one was like being banished from God and all his saints; to live with the other, like being received into his presence and his family. Yet only a few months before, these were as thoughtless, as barbarous, as averse to Christianity, as those on the Susquehannah; but now, instead of engaging in idolatrous feasts and drunken revels, they worshipped the God of heaven, received his word, and lived devoted to his glory. Such is the power of divine grace! Such the transforming influence of the gospel!

On resuming his labours at Crosweeksung, Mr Brainerd beheld the same powerful and happy effects attend his ministry as before. He was often wonderfully assisted in his public discourses, being enabled to accommodate his sentiments and his expressions to the understanding of the Indians, in such a way as he never could have done by the most careful study; yet he spoke with as much ease and freedom, as if he had been addressing an ordinary congregation, who had been instructed in the principles of Christianity from their early years. A dry eye was often scarcely to be seen in their assemblies; yet there was no disturbance of the public worship. A deep impression was made on their hearts; but there was no boisterous agitation of their passions. All was powerful and efficacious; yet calm and peaceful. One day, after a sermon on the Transfiguration of Christ, Mr Brainerd asked a woman, whom he observed weeping most affectionately, What she now wanted. To this she replied: "Oh! to be with Christ: She knew not how to stay." On another occasion, when a number of them were assembled in Mr Brainerd's house, a woman burst forth in prayer and praises to God before them all, with many tears, crying sometimes in English, and sometimes in Indian, "O blessed Lord, do come, do come! O do take me away; do let me die and go to Jesus Christ. I am afraid, if I live I shall sin again! O do let me die now; do come! I cannot stay, I cannot stay! O how can I live in this world! do take my soul away from this sinful place! O let me never sin any more! O what shall I do, what shall I do!" In this ecstacy she continued for some time, incessantly uttering these and similar expressions, and employing as her grand argument with God to enforce her prayer, that if she lived she would sin against him. When she had recovered a little, Mr Brainerd asked her, If Christ was now sweet to her soul. Turning to him, she replied, with tears in her eyes, and with the deepest tokens of humility, "I have often heard you speak of the goodness and the sweetness of Christ; that he was better than all the world. But, O, I knew nothing of what you meant; I never believed you; I never believed you. But now I know it is true." Mr Brainerd then asked her, If she saw enough in Christ for the greatest of sinners. "O, enough, enough!" she replied, "for all the sinners in the world, if they would but come." On hearing something of the glory of heaven, particularly that there was no sin there, she again fell into the same kind of ecstacy, and employed similar expressions as before: "O dear Lord, do let me go! O what shall I do! what shall I do! I want to go to Christ! I cannot live! O do let me die." In this pleasing frame she continued more than two hours, before she was well able to go home.[1]

One day after a sermon on the New Birth, by which a general and deep impression was made on the minds of the Indians, many of them followed Mr Brainerd to his lodgings, and begged to be further instructed in the way of salvation; but he had not spoken long, when they were so affected with what he said, that the house was filled with their cries and groans. Almost all whom he apprehended to be still in an unconverted state, were seized with concern for their souls; it seemed as if none, whether old or young, would now be left. No pen can describe the interesting scene. Numbers might be seen rejoicing that God had not taken his Holy Spirit from them, and delighted to behold so many of their countrymen "striving to enter in at the strait gate." Others, both men and women, both old and young, might be seen dissolved in tears, some of them so overwhelmed with anguish, that they seemed like malefactors on the way to execution. The whole scene exhibited a striking emblem of the day of judgment; of heaven and hell; of infinite joy and of inexpressible misery.[2]

Here it may not be improper to remark, that the concern of the Indians about their souls, was not only very great, but perfectly scriptural and rational. Though some, like the jailor,

[1] Brainerd's Life, p. 399, 417, 443. [2] Ibid, p. 427.

were made to tremble under a sense of their sinfulness; though others were forced to cry out from a view of their perishing condition; though many were for a time deprived in a great measure of their bodily strength, through the anguish of their minds; yet the awakening among them was singularly free from those disorders, corporeal and mental, which often accompany remarkable revivals of religion. For a considerable time there was no appearance of convulsions, screamings, swoonings; no pretences to visions, trances, revelations; no symptoms of censoriousness, ostentation, or spiritual pride; no tendency, in short, to any thing like display. Afterwards, indeed, when the awakening became so general, and acquired such universal credit among the Indians, that Satan could have little hope of counteracting it, in the garb of the spirit of darkness, he transformed himself into an angel of light, and made some vigorous efforts to introduce turbulent commotions of the passions, in the room of genuine convictions of sin, and imaginary notions of Christ appearing to the mental eye in particular forms and postures, instead of spiritual discoveries of his glory and excellence. Some individuals, who had been deeply impressed with divine things, wished on that account to be thought truly converted, and manifested considerable resentment against Mr Brainerd, when he expressed his doubts and apprehensions about their spiritual state. There were one or two persons whose concern seemed in a great measure affected; and there were one or two more, who discovered an undue disposition to become teachers of others. But though some disagreeable things of this kind made their appearance, they never acquired any footing among the Indians. Mr Brainerd, than whom few men were ever more free of enthusiasm, was careful to observe the first symptoms of these evils, and to check them in their commencement.[1]

With the view of improving the Indians in Christian knowledge, Mr Brainerd now began a catechetical exercise among them. Sometimes he examined them on some important point of divinity; sometimes on the discourses he had delivered to them; but most commonly on the Assembly's Shorter Catechism. In these catechetical exercises, he had much satisfac-

[1] Brainerd's Life, p. 409, 483.

tion. It was truly surprising to see how readily and scripturally the Indians answered the questions proposed to them: their knowledge of the principles of religion was found on trial far more extensive and correct, than could reasonably have been expected. When Mr Brainerd began this exercise, he was apprehensive it would necessarily prove of so doctrinal a nature, as merely to enlighten the understanding, without impressing the conscience or affecting the heart. But in this he was mistaken, for it was remarkably blessed for promoting their progress in experimental as well as in theoretical knowledge. The serious attention, the tender affection, the many tears which often appeared at these catechetical meetings, would have been deemed very extraordinary, had not these things been now so common that they ceased to excite surprise.[1]

In February 1746, a school was opened for instructing the Indians in the English language, and other useful acquirements, under the care of an excellent schoolmaster, whom Mr Brainerd had procured for this purpose. About thirty children immediately entered it, and made such surprising progress, that the teacher remarked, he never had English scholars who, taking them in general, learned so rapidly. Though some of them were very young, there were not more than two or three who failed in making themselves master of all the letters of the alphabet within three days after the opening of the school; several in that short time even made some progress in spelling, and in less than five months were able to read the New Testament. Besides the children, there were about fifteen or twenty of the old people, who attended the school at night, when the length of the evenings would admit of it.[2]

Besides attending to the religious and moral improvement of the Indians, Mr Brainerd was anxious to obtain for them a fixed settlement, and to form them to habits of industry. Many of them having in time past run themselves in debt by their excessive drinking, and several of them having been arrested by the White people on this account, he was apprehensive they might be deprived of a great part of their lands; and being convinced that they could not remain in that quarter of the country, nor maintain the order of a Christian congregation,

[1] Brainerd's Life, p. 421, 427, 432, 448, 452, 494. [2] Ibid. p. 436, 483.

should their grounds be taken from them, he prevailed on the gentlemen who had the superintendence of the mission, to expend a considerable sum of money in discharging the debts of the Indians, and thus averted the danger which threatened them. Having by this means secured their lands to them, he was anxious to excite and to cultivate in them a spirit of industry. By his advice they fixed on a spot at Cranberry, about fifteen miles from the place of their present residence, and proceeded to form a regular settlement upon it. Here they began to clear and to plant their lands; and in little more than a twelvemonth, they had upwards of forty acres of English grain in the ground, and nearly as many of Indian corn. In general, they followed their secular occupations as well as could be expected, considering that during the whole of their life, they had been habituated to idleness and sloth. Much of the burden, however, of their temporal affairs devolved on Mr Brainerd, as they were utterly incapable of arranging and managing them without the constant care and advice of others.[1]

Apprehending that a number of the Indians were now qualified to become partakers of the Lord's Supper, Mr Brainerd, after instructing them more particularly in the nature and design of that holy ordinance, resolved to administer it to them. He accordingly appointed a day of fasting and prayer, for the purpose of humbling themselves on account of the partial withdrawment of that spiritual influence which had of late been so prevalent among them, and on account of the appearance of carelessness, vanity, and vice, among some who not long before seemed impressed with a sense of their sinfulness and misery, as well as for imploring the presence and blessing of God in the sacred service which they had in prospect. On the following Sabbath he administered the Lord's Supper to twenty-three of the Indians; and there were several absent, who would otherwise have been admitted along with them. The exercise was attended with great solemnity, with singular devotion, and with a sweet, yet powerful melting of their affections. During the administration of the ordinance, especially in the distribution

[1] Brainerd's Life, p. 434, 450, 452, 461, 482; Account of the Society in Scotland for Propagating Christian Knowledge, prefixed to a Sermon by Robert Walker, 1748, p. 74.

of the bread, they were affected in so lively a manner, that it seemed as if "Christ Jesus had been set forth crucified among them." Mr Brainerd afterwards walked from house to house to converse with the communicants; and he was happy to find that almost all of them had been refreshed "as with new wine." Never did he witness such an appearance of Christian love among any people. It was so remarkable, that one might justly have exclaimed, "Behold how these Indians love one another!" Even among the primitive Christians, there could scarcely be greater tokens of mutual affection, than what appeared among these poor people. In the evening, he preached on the design of Christ's death, "that he might redeem his people from all iniquity." On this occasion, many of the Indians were much refreshed. So delightful was their frame of mind; so full were they of love, and peace, and joy; so ardently did they long to be delivered from the power of sin, that some of them declared they had never felt the like before. It seemed almost grievous to them to conclude the exercise; and even when it was closed, they appeared loath to leave a place which had been so endeared to them by the sacred services of that day.[1]

A few days after the administration of the Lord's Supper, Mr Brainerd baptized a man, who had been a most notorious sinner, a drunkard, a murderer, a conjurer; but who now appeared to be an illustrious trophy of the power and the riches of divine grace. He lived near the Forks of Delaware, and occasionally attended Mr Brainerd's ministry, but, like many others of the Indians, was nowise reformed by the means of instruction which he enjoyed. About that very time, he murdered a promising young Indian, and he still followed his old trade of conjuration, being held in high reputation among his countrymen. Hence, when Mr Brainerd told them of the miracles of Christ, and represented these as a proof of his divine mission, and of the truth of his religion, they immediately mentioned the wonders of the same kind which this man had wrought by his magical charms. As he was, in this way, a powerful obstruction to the progress of the gospel among the Indians, Mr Brainerd often thought it would be a great mercy if God would remove him out of the

[1] Brainerd's Life, p. 455.

world, for he had little or no hope that such a wretch would ever himself be converted; but He "whose thoughts are not as man's thoughts," was pleased to take a more gracious and a more effectual method with him.

Having been impressed, by witnessing the baptism of Mr Brainerd's interpreter, he followed him to Crosweeksung shortly after, and continued there several weeks, during the season of the most remarkable and powerful awakening of the Indians. He was now brought under deep concern for his soul, and, "upon feeling the word of God in his heart," as he expressed it, his spirit of conjuration entirely left him; and from that time, he had no more power of that description than any other man; and he afterwards declared, that he no longer even knew how he used to charm and conjure, and that he could not do any thing of that kind though he were ever so desirous of it. These circumstances we simply state; how they are to be accounted for we do not pretend to explain.

His convictions of his sinfulness and misery became by degrees more deep, and the anguish of his mind was so increased, that he knew not what to do, nor whither to turn. One day he was in such extreme distress, that he trembled for several hours together, and apprehended he was ready to drop into hell, without any power to escape or help himself. Soon after this, indeed, he became quite calm and tranquil, his trembling ceased, his burden vanished; but yet, in his own apprehension, he had little or no hope of mercy. Observing him so remarkably composed, Mr Brainerd asked him, "How he did?" To this he replied, "It is done, it is done, it is all done now." On being asked what he meant, he answered, "I can do no more to save myself; it is all done for ever, I can do no more." "But," said Mr Brainerd, "can you not do a little more, rather than go to hell?" "My heart," he replied, "is dead; I can never help myself." Being asked if he thought it right that God should send him to hell, he answered, "Yes, it is right. The devil has been in me ever since I was born. My heart has no goodness in it now, but is as bad as ever." Mr Brainerd says he scarcely ever saw a person more completely weaned from dependence on his own endeavours for salvation, or lying more humbly at the foot of sovereign mercy, than this poor Indian conjurer.

He continued in this frame of mind for several days, pronouncing sentence of condemnation upon himself, and acknowledging the justice of his punishment; yet it was evident he had a secret hope of mercy, though probably it was imperceptible to himself. During this time, he repeatedly inquired at Mr Brainerd when he would preach again, and seemed desirous of hearing the gospel every day. On being asked why he wished to hear the word, seeing, according to his own account, "his heart was dead, and all was done for ever." He replied, "Notwithstanding that, I love to hear about Christ." "But," said Mr Brainerd, "what good can that do you, if you must go to hell at last?" "I would have others," replied he, "come to Christ, if I must go to hell myself." It is not unworthy of notice, that, at this very time, he appeared to have a great love to the people of God, and nothing affected him so much as the thought of being for ever separated from them; this seemed a very dreadful ingredient in the hell to which he considered himself as doomed. He was likewise exceedingly diligent in the use of the outward means of grace, though he had at the same time the clearest views of their insufficiency to afford him help. "All he did," he would frequently say, "signified nothing;" yet never was he more constant in attending to the ordinances of religion, not excepting even secret and family prayer.

After continuing in this state of mind upwards of a week, he obtained, one day as Mr Brainerd was preaching, such a lively and delightful view of the excellency of Christ, and of the way of salvation through him, that he burst into tears, and was dissolved in admiration, and gratitude, and praise. From that time he appeared an humble, devout, affectionate Christian; serious and exemplary in his behaviour; often complaining of his barrenness and his want of spiritual life; yet frequently favoured with the quickening and refreshing influences of the Holy Spirit. In short, he appeared, in all respects, to possess the character and the disposition of one who was "created anew in Christ Jesus unto good works."[1]

Many as were the difficulties which Mr Brainerd had to encounter, and great as were the hardships he had often to endure, yet so far was he from being weary of the life of a missionary,

[1] Brainerd's Life, p. 376, 436, 462.

that now when he had the prospect of settling as the pastor of the Indian flock which he had collected in the wilderness, he looked forward to it with apprehension, and considered it as a kind of trial. So ardent, so unabated was his zeal for the conversion of the heathen, that it was still his desire to spend his life in preaching the gospel from place to place, and in gathering souls afar off to the Redeemer. We envy not that man, however distinguished he may be for birth, or talents, or learning, who can read the exercises of his mind on this occasion, without admiration, mingled with self-abasement; they display a disinterestedness, a zeal, a deadness to the world, which perhaps have scarcely a parallel in modern times. "Had apprehended for several days before, that it was the design of Providence I should settle among my people here, and had in my own mind begun to make provision for it, and to contrive means to hasten it. My heart was somewhat engaged in it, hoping I might then enjoy in several respects more agreeable circumstances of life; and yet was never fully determined, never quite satisfied with the thought of being confined to one place. Nevertheless, I seemed to have some freedom in that respect, because the congregation I thought of settling with, was one which God had enabled me to gather from amongst Pagans; for never since I began to preach, could I feel any freedom to 'enter into other men's labours,' and settle down in the ministry where the gospel was preached before; I never could make that appear to be my providence. When I felt any disposition to consult my ease and worldly comfort, God has never given me any liberty in that respect, either since or for some years before I began to preach; but he having succeeded my labours, and made me instrumental in gathering a church for him among the Indians, I was ready to think it might be his design, to give me a quiet settlement and a stated home of my own. And this, considering the late frequent sinking and failure of my spirits, and the need I stood in of some agreeable society, and my great desire of enjoying conveniences and opportunities for profitable studies, was not altogether disagreeable to me; and though I still wanted to go about far and wide, in order to spread the blessed gospel among benighted souls far remote, yet I never had been so willing to settle in any one place for more than five years past, as I was within the last few days. But now these thoughts seemed to be wholly dashed in pieces, not by necessity but of choice; for it appeared to me, that God's dealings towards me had fitted me for a life of solitariness and hardship; it appeared to me I had nothing to lose, nothing to do with earth, and consequently nothing to sacrifice by a total renunciation of it; and it appeared just right, that I should be destitute of house and home, and many comforts of life, which I rejoiced to see others of God's people enjoy. And, at the same time, I saw so much of the excellency of Christ's kingdom, and the infinite desirableness of its advancement in the world, that it swallowed up all my other thoughts, and made me willing, yea even rejoice, to be made a pilgrim or a hermit in the wilderness to my dying moment, if I might thereby promote the blessed interest of the great Redeemer. And if ever my soul presented itself to God for his service, without any reserve of any kind, it did so now. The language of my thoughts and disposition (although I spoke no words) now were, 'Here am I, Lord, send me; send me to the ends of the earth; send me to the rough, the savage Pagans of the wilderness; send me from all that is called comfort on earth; send me even to death itself, if it be but in thy service, and to promote thy kingdom.' At the same time, I had as quick and lively a sense of the value of worldly comforts as ever I had, only I saw them infinitely overmatched by the worth of Christ's kingdom, and the propagation of his blessed gospel. The quiet settlement, the certain place of abode, the tender friendship I had the prospect of enjoying, appeared as valuable to me as ever before, considered absolutely and in themselves; but, considered comparatively, they appeared nothing; compared with the enlargement of Christ's kingdom, they vanished like the stars before the rising sun. And sure I am, that although the comfortable accommodations of life appeared valuable and dear to me, yet I did surrender and resign myself, soul and body, to the service of God and promotion of Christ's kingdom; though it should be in the loss of them all. And I could not do any other, because I could not will or choose any other. I was constrained, and yet chose to say, 'Farewell, friends and earthly comforts, the dearest of them all, the very dearest, if the Lord calls for it. Adieu, adieu! I'll spend my life to my latest moments in caves and dens of the earth, if the kingdom of Christ may thereby be advanced.'—Oh! with what reluctance did I find myself obliged to consume time in sleep! I longed to be a flame of fire, continually glowing in the service of God, preaching and building up Christ's kingdom to my latest, my dying moment."[1]

With Mr Brainerd, these were not empty words. Though his constitution was now broken by the toils and hardships he had endured; though he already harboured in his breast the seeds of a disease which would certainly soon prove mortal; and though his journeys to the Susquehannah had hitherto been attended with little success, yet he shortly after proceeded on a new visit to the Indians in that quarter, accompanied by several of his congregation, whom he judged best qualified to assist him in his labours. In the course of this journey, he suffered not a little from a cough, cold night sweats, and spitting of blood; yet, alarming as were these symptoms, he was often obliged to sleep in the woods. One evening he was so extremely faint, that he was apprehensive that should he lie out in the open air, it would prove fatal to him; and yet as some of his companions were absent, and the others had not an axe, he had no resource but to climb up a young pine-tree, to lop the branches with his knife, and so make some kind of shelter from the dew. Exposed, however, as he was to all the coldness of the night, he perspired so profusely, that his linen was completely drenched with sweat. He was now, indeed, so extremely feeble, that he was scarcely able to ride: sometimes he felt as if he would fall from his horse, and have to lie in the woods. With this remarkable weakness of body, was combined uncommon depression of spirits, which, as it unfitted him for exertion among the Indians, gave rise to the most humbling reflections upon himself. "I was scarcely," says he, "ever more ashamed and confounded in myself than now. I was sensible that there were numbers of God's people who knew I was then out on a design (or at least a pretence) of doing something for God and his cause, among the poor Indians; and that they were ready to suppose I was fervent in spirit; but, oh, the heartless frame of

[1] Brainerd's Life, p. 211.

mind I felt, filled me with confusion. Oh, methought, if they knew me, as God knows me, they would not think so highly of my zeal and resolution, as perhaps they now do. I could not but desire they should see how heartless and irresolute I was, that they might be undeceived, and 'not think of me above what they ought to think.' And yet I thought, if they saw the utmost of my flatness and unfaithfulness, the smallness of my courage and resolution for God, they would be ready to shut me out of their houses, as unworthy of the company or friendship of Christians."[1]

After being absent upwards of a month, Mr Brainerd again arrived among his own people, and though very ill, resumed his labours among them, as far as his exhausted strength would permit, often discoursing to them even from his bed. His disorder now rapidly increased, and he was at length obliged to leave them altogether. Being recommended to ride about for his health, the loss of time which this occasioned was a severe trial to him, and often contributed, with other circumstances, to inspire him with very gloomy reflections. But though he was at first troubled with melancholy, he afterwards became more cheerful, especially as the prospect of death drew near. One evening, when he was attacked with a slight degree of diarrhœa, which he rightly considered as a symptom of the fatal progress of his disorder, he exclaimed, "Oh, the glorious time is now coming! I have longed to serve God perfectly; now he will gratify these desires." As new symptoms of approaching dissolution made their appearance, he became still more animated and cheerful. When he spoke of the period of his death, he used to call it "that glorious day;" nor was this because he should then be delivered from sorrow and pain, and raised to dignity and honour, for he thought that a comparatively low and ignoble consideration, but because he should then be able to glorify God with a pure and perfect heart. One evening, when he was attempting to walk a little, he writes in his diary, he thought with himself, "How infinitely sweet is it to love God, and to be all for him. Upon which it occurred to me: 'You are not an angel, not lively and active.' To this my whole soul immediately replied: 'I as sincerely desire to

[1] Brainerd's Life, p. 226, 231.

love and glorify God, as any angel in heaven.' Upon which it was suggested again, 'But you are filthy, not fit for heaven.' Hereupon instantly appeared the blessed robes of Christ's righteousness, which I could not but exult and triumph in, and I viewed the infinite excellency of God, and my soul even broke with longings that God should be glorified. I thought of dignity in heaven; but instantly the thought returned, 'I do not go to heaven to get honour, but to give all possible glory and praise.' Oh, how I longed that God should be glorified on earth also. Bodily pains I cared not for; though I was then in extremity, I never felt easier. I felt willing to glorify God in that state of bodily distress, as long as he was pleased to continue me in it. The grave appeared really sweet, and I longed to lodge my weary bones in it; but oh that God might be glorified! This was the burden of all my cry." The extraordinary frame of mind he was in that evening could not be hid. Among many remarkable expressions which he then uttered were such as the following:—"My heaven is to please God, to give all to him, to be wholly devoted to his glory. That is the heaven I long for; that is my religion; that is my happiness, and always was, ever since, I suppose, I had any true religion.—I do not go to heaven to be advanced, but to give honour to God. It is no matter where I shall be stationed in heaven, whether I have a high or a low seat there; but to love, and please, and glorify God is all. Had I a thousand souls, if they were worth any thing, I would give them all to him; but I have nothing to give when all is done. I long to be in heaven, praising and glorifying God with the holy angels; all my desire is to glorify God.—My heart goes out to the burying ground; it seems to me a desirable place; but, Oh, to glorify God! that is it, that is above all.—It is a great comfort to me to think, that I have done a little for God in the world. Oh! it is but a very small matter; yet I have done a little, and I lament I have not done more for him. There is nothing in the world worth living for but doing good, and finishing God's work,—doing the work that Christ did. I see nothing else in the world that can yield any satisfaction besides living to God, pleasing him, and doing his whole will.[1]

[1] Brainerd's Life, p. 235, 243, 255, 272.

Mr Brainerd was now daily growing worse ; yet ill as he was, he eagerly employed the little strength which still remained, in some attempts to promote the glory of the Redeemer and the salvation of souls. It greatly refreshed him amidst all his bodily sickness and pain, that he was enabled to contribute a little towards these important objects. Nature, however, was, at length, exhausted. He gradually sunk under the ravages of his disorder, and after a severe struggle, breathed his last, 9th October 1747, in the thirtieth year of his age.[1]

Thus died David Brainerd, a young man, whose extraordinary worth and piety entitle him to the warmest admiration and respect of the Christian world, and whose memory deserves to be embalmed to the latest generations. He possessed, according to President Edwards, uncommon natural talents, a quick perception, a ready invention, a strong memory, a clear, correct, penetrating judgment, a sound and vigorous understanding, much natural eloquence, and a peculiar facility of communicating his ideas to others. He had an extraordinary knowledge of men, as well as things, and a happy faculty of accommodating himself to the capacities, tempers, and circumstances of those whom he wished to instruct. His gift in prayer was almost inimitable: there was such a propriety in his petitions, such a weight in his expressions, such an appearance of sincerity, reverence, and solemnity in his manner. His learning was very considerable: he excelled in knowledge, in general, but, particularly, in the knowledge of theology. He was truly, for one of his age, an extraordinary divine, especially in all matters relating to experimental religion. Grace in him appears to have been, with scarcely any interruption, in sensible and vigorous operation. He was distinguished by the purest and most ardent love to God ; by a most abasing sense of his own vileness, particularly of the depravity of his heart; by deep contrition of spirit, on account of his small attainments in piety, and fervent longings after perfection in holiness ; by intense desires to promote the glory of God, and the extension of the kingdom of Christ in the world ; by singular spirituality of mind, and entire deadness to earthly things ; by clear and impressive views of eternity, as if he were actually out of the

[1] Brainerd's Life, p. 258, 270, 285.

body, and beheld with his eyes the grand realities of the other world.[1] The chief defect in his character, perhaps, was a disposition to melancholy; but this was, no doubt, much increased by the unfavourable circumstances in which he was placed.

In his labours among the Indians, Mr Brainerd, as we have seen, was most unwearied, and his success on the whole was considerable. The whole number whom he collected together amounted to about a hundred and fifty, though, when he first visited that part of the country, they did not amount to ten. Of these, near ninety were baptized, about one-half of whom were adults, and near forty were communicants. It is proper, however, to observe, that he baptized no adults, but such as gave satisfactory evidence of their sincere conversion to Christ. There were many others of the Indians who possessed considerable knowledge of the principles of Christianity, and manifested deep concern about their souls; but as they appeared to be merely under convictions of their sinfulness and misery, and did not give sufficient evidence of a change of heart, he very properly delayed their baptism.[2]

After this excellent man was obliged to leave his Indian flock, he was succeeded in the charge of it by his younger brother, Mr John Brainerd. Under him the mission continued for some years to flourish in a pleasing manner. The number of the Indians increased to about two hundred, including old and young, notwithstanding there was for some time a considerable mortality among them. Most of those who appeared to have been converted under the ministry of his excellent brother, not only persevered in the profession of religion, but adorned it by a holy and exemplary conversation, though several, as might be expected, were guilty of grievous backsliding. Some of those who had lately joined the settlement were brought under serious concern for their souls; and others of the congregation appeared to be made partakers of divine grace. Besides, they made considerable progress in civilization, and in the arts of life. The men cultivated the ground; the women learned to spin; and both, in a great measure, abandoned that idle slothful course of life which is so habitual to all the tribes of Indians.

[1] Edwards' Sermon on the Death of Mr Brainerd, p. 27.

[2] Brainerd's Life, p. 450, 481, 225, 240.

The school also was in a flourishing state; even the old people were so anxious to learn to read and understand the Scriptures, that many of them attended it in the evening, among whom were some of forty or fifty years of age. Several of the boys were put out to trades, and it was proposed to erect a working-school for the girls.[1]

Besides labouring among his own congregation, Mr John Brainerd occasionally made journeys among the Indians in distant parts of the country, though with no other material effect than inducing some of them to come and settle with his people. In one of his visits to the Susquehannah, he had to encounter a difficulty of rather an extraordinary nature. On his arrival, the Indians pretended they had just received a revelation from heaven, which, after representing the evil of some particular vices, and recommending the sacrifice of a deer, and certain other superstitious practices, concluded by telling them, that God made two worlds, one for the White people, the other for the Indians; that the White people had no business to come into the Indian country, much less to persuade them to embrace their religion, for that he had commanded them to worship him in their own way, and their Red brethren to worship him in another; that though the White people made some pretences of instructing them, yet they had no design of doing them good, but merely to put money into their own pockets. In consequence of this revelation, the production, probably, of some interested Indian, Mr Brainerd was able to do little amongst these poor people, though in other respects they seemed more civilized than any he had hitherto seen.[2]

In 1759, Mr John Brainerd settled with his congregation upon a tract of land, which was purchased on their account by the government of New Jersey. Among the many difficulties attending the christianizing and civilization of the Indians, their living in small villages, scattered through the wilderness,

[1] Brainerd's Life, p. 249, 283, 341; Edward's Works, vol. i. p. cxlvi, cxlviii, clxxii.; Letter from Mr John Brainerd, London 1753, p. 4, 12; Account of the Soc. in Scotland for Prop. Christ. Know., prefixed to a Sermon by Robert Walker, p. 71; Blair's Sermon before the Soc. in Scotland for Prop. Christ. Know. p. 44; Plenderleath's Sermon, ditto, p. 75.

[2] Letter from Mr John Brainerd, p. 5, 9.—Bonar's Sermon before the Soc. in Scotland for Prop. Christ. Know. p. 50.

was none of the least. Hitherto this evil had been only partially corrected; but it was now proposed to collect them together in one place, and to fix them in regular habitations. The extent of country under Mr Brainerd's charge was a hundred miles east and west, and near eighty north and south. The land for the use of the Indians consisted of about four thousand acres, and was situated near the centre of the country, between the river Delaware and the Atlantic Ocean. The soil was suitable for Indian corn, rice, beans, potatoes, clover, and various kinds of fruit-trees, and wanted nothing but cultivation, to supply the Indians with plenty of vegetables.[1] It does not appear, however, that this new arrangement was attended with that success which was expected or desired.

In 1774, Mr Thomas Rankin, a methodist preacher, met with Mr John Brainerd, and received from him a very unfavourable statement with respect to the Indians under his care. "What an unpleasing account," says he, "did he give me of the remains of his excellent brother's labours, as well as of his own, among the Indians! When his brother died, there was a large company of Indians who regularly attended the preaching of the word, and above sixty who were communicants. The number, however, who attended his ministry, was now small, and there were not above ten or twelve who were qualified for admission to the Lord's Supper. On asking him the reason of this declension, he observed, that some were dead, and died happy in the Lord; others had grown careless and lukewarm; and many had wandered back among their Pagan countrymen, several of whom had even returned to their idolatrous customs. Some, also, had yielded to the love of spirituous liquors, from which they seemed once completely weaned. Thus 'the gold had become dim, and the most fine gold was changed.'" We have given Mr Rankin's account at large, but do not pledge ourselves for its accuracy. It is obvious he was mistaken with regard to the number of communicants at the time of Mr David Brainerd's death, for, instead of being upwards of sixty, they did not amount to forty; and it appears from an official statement pub-

[1] Macqueen's Sermon before the Society in Scotland for Prop. Christ. Know. p. 67. —Account of the Society in Scotland for Prop. Christ. Know., 1774, p. 15, 18.

lished about this very period, that the number of Indians under the pastoral care of Mr John Brainerd, instead of being small, amounted to about 150 or 160, which is equal to what they were when he succeeded his brother; and it is stated by the same authority, that, "as to their morals, they were in general rather reformed, and many of them even supported an unblemished character." Perhaps, therefore, Mr Rankin, in the picture he has drawn, may undesignedly have overcharged the colouring in some other particulars; yet still, we fear, his representation was by no means without foundation.[1]

During the American War, Mr John Brainerd's correspondence with the Society in Scotland for Propagating Christian Knowledge was suspended, and toward the close of it he died. In 1783, he was succeeded in the charge of his congregation, by Mr Daniel Simon, an Indian, who had been ordained to the ministry; but it was soon found necessary to suspend him from his office, on account of drunkenness and other irregularities. No missionary was appointed to succeed him; but the congregation was occasionally supplied by the neighbouring ministers.[2]

In July 1802, some Commissioners from New Jersey conducted eighty-five Delaware Indians, the remains of Mr John Brainerd's congregation, to New Stockbridge, to place them under the ministry of Mr Sergeant, the missionary in that town. For many years past they had been left entirely to themselves, having no spiritual shepherd to watch over them, no meetings for divine worship on the Sabbath, and no school for their children. Hence, they in general grew very wicked, and had been long in a very miserable state, scattered through the country, and excessively addicted to drinking. To this, however, there might be some exceptions: mention, at least, is made of one old woman dying after they removed to Stockbridge, who dated her conversion from the time of the great awakening under Mr David Brainerd, and who was distinguished for her piety to the day of her death.[3]

Such a result of those bright and pleasing prospects, which

[1] Methodist Magazine, vol. xxxiv. p. 445; Account of the Soc. in Scotland for Prop. Christ. Know. 1774, p. 18.

[2] American Correspondence, among the Records of the Society in Scotland for Propagating Christian Knowledge, MS. vol. i. p. 48, 49, 72, 122, 123.

[3] Religious Monitor, vol. i. p. 189; Massachussets Missionary Magazine, vol. iii. p. 387.

once dawned on this tribe of Indians, is truly deplorable. Few of these individuals, however, could have belonged to Mr David Brainerd's congregation, and such as did, must, in general, have been little more than children at that time. Indeed, though there certainly was an extraordinary work of grace among his people, yet it was never supposed they were all converted.[1] Of adults, he baptized only between forty and fifty, and though there were many others, as we have already mentioned, under deep concern for their souls, yet as they did not give satisfactory evidence of a saving change, he judged it expedient to delay their baptism. Now, as the Christian Indians, in general, continued for several years at least to adorn their profession by a holy and exemplary conversation; as some of them died happy in the Lord; as twenty-seven years after Mr Brainerd's death, there were still, even according to the most unfavourable accounts, ten or twelve who were considered as fit for admission to the Lord's Supper, it is probable there were as many, or even a greater number than he ever supposed, who were truly converted to Christ, maintained a Christian deportment to the last, and now join with him in heaven, in celebrating the praises of God and of the Lamb. It gives us much pleasure to state, that the late Dr Witherspoon, president of New Jersey College, in referring to these Indians, assures us that it was fully attested, that they had persevered, with scarcely any exceptions, in their profession of religion, and even adorned it by their exemplary conversation.[2] Still, however, it is melancholy to think, that our hopes with respect to so many others of the Indians, as well as with regard to the extension and the permanence of the mission, have been so miserably disappointed. Let us learn not to be too sanguine in our expectations, even when appearances are of the most promising nature; and especially, not to be so intoxicated by the most promising appearances, as to cease to "watch unto prayer."

[1] Brainerd's Life, p. 340.

[2] American Correspondence, MS. vol. i. p. 171.

SECT. VI.—ONEIDA.

In November 1764, Mr Samuel Kirkland proceeded, under the auspices of the Rev. E. Wheelock of Lebanon in Connecticut, to the country of the Seneca Indians, with the view of learning their language, in order to qualify himself for labouring as a missionary among them. It was considered at that time as a bold and perilous adventure, for the distance was great, and no missionary had before penetrated their forests, and there being room for the imagination to work, they were pictured as a wild and ferocious race. After a long and toilsome journey, he, under the guidance of two of the Indians, reached their principal town, Kanadasega, near Seneca Lake, and met with a very friendly reception from them, having been strongly recommended to them by Sir William Johnson, the General Agent for Indian affairs. Within a few weeks after his arrival, he was, by authority of the council, formally adopted as a member of the family of the head Sachem; but the chief's house being much exposed to company, it was arranged that he should live in a neighbouring house, occupied by a small family; the man was "one of the best in all the town, sober, temperate, industrious, honest, and telling no lies." Here he was treated very kindly; every thing, in fact, appeared exceedingly promising. The scene, however, was soon changed. He was but a short time in his new abode, when his host died suddenly in the night, having been in perfect health the day before, and never "sick in his life." Early in the morning, the whole village was aroused; crowds came pouring in to look at the corpse; their countenances as they turned towards Mr Kirkland were "very forbidding;" and messengers were despatched to six or seven villages to communicate the tidings and to summon a council. The head Sachem came in at a later hour in the morning, and addressed a few words of consolation to the bereaved widow, and then said to Mr Kirkland, "A dark morning, my son; but possess your mind in peace. It may be we shall see good by and by. You must know that the Great Spirit, in very deed, must do as he pleases."

The next day at noon, great numbers having assembled, they began to hold a council. It soon appeared that a large party were disposed to charge the sudden death of the Indian upon Mr Kirkland, maintaining that either he wrought it by magic, or that it was an intimation of the displeasure of the Great Spirit at his visit and residence among them, and that he must be put to death. "My adopted father," he says, "came out of the council before night to speak to me. He wished me to possess my mind in peace; assured me that he would not quit the council till all was settled and done well. He smiled and appeared cheerful, or at least tried to do so; but I plainly saw that he had a weight upon his mind."

On the third day, about an hour before sunset, the corpse was interred. The funeral, however, did not interrupt the sitting of the council. About one hundred and fifty women and girls followed the body to the grave; but no male person except Mr Kirkland, and one other, the grave-digger. The deceased was neatly dressed in a clean white shirt, black shroud blanket, scarlet leggins, a pair of new moccasons, his face curiously painted. His pipe, tomahawk, tobacco pouch, flint, steel and punk, were put into the coffin, and placed on both sides of his head. While carrying the body to the grave, "they sang the most mournful strain of music ever heard, interspersed with the most savage yells and screams." The night of the funeral, Mr Kirkland slept with "his elder brother" (for the children of the head Sachem were reckoned his brothers and sisters), in a blockhouse formerly erected by Sir William Johnson, with the design of stationing a company of soldiers in it, which however the Senecas would not permit. Here "one of his sisters" brought him a bit of venison, and a dish of samp-pottage, which was very acceptable to him, as he had been fasting for thirty-six hours. He saw plainly that the family into which he had been adopted, and all his friends, felt great anxiety for his safety, which increased and became more apparent the next day, when "his youngest brother" put a gun into his hand, and took another himself, and under the pretext of shooting partridges, invited him to take a walk into the woods, and led him by a circuitous course a considerable distance from the village, to a solitary sugar hut, where they remained for several days "one of his sisters bringing him food at night, about ten o'clock."

After passing several days in this concealment, during which he was not allowed to leave the hut, or to speak but in a very low voice, he returned to the village, the council having broken up and the members dispersed. He was received by the whole family with marks of joy, and was saluted by them and others who came to see him, with the welcome words, "All is now only peace." From this time, he took up his residence in the blockhouse, his elder brother and his family living there with him. He was of course very anxious to learn the proceedings of the council; but from policy, he suppressed his curiosity, manifested no anxiety, and asked no questions, hoping that some information would be given to him. Several weeks, however, passed before he learned any particulars of its proceedings, and he finally obtained them, not from any of the Indians, but from a Dutch trader who passed several days at the village, and who, through his long acquaintance with several of the chiefs, easily gained the desired information. It appears that while the head Sachem earnestly pleaded the cause of Mr Kirkland, another famous chief of great influence among the Indians, proposed that he should be put to death; but the advice of the former prevailed, being assented to by all except a small minority of fifteen, and after a general shout of applause, which made the council-house ring, the meeting broke up.[1]

Mr Kirkland, however, was soon subjected to severe sufferings from another source. Provisions were exceedingly scarce in that part of the country. There was little Indian corn left. White oak acorns suitable for food, could not easily be found. Game too was not plentiful at that season of the year, and the little they killed, they were obliged to husband very carefully. It was often kept till it "almost came to life again," and what was worse, had to be eaten in that state. Two months he lived without bread, flesh, or salt, except once that he eat part of a bear, though in a most unpalatable condition. His chief food was small fish, roots, acorns, and a handful of pounded corn boiled in a large quantity of water. His peace too was again

[1] Lothrop's Life of Samuel Kirkland *in* Spark's Lib. Amer. Biog. vol. xxv. p. 151, 155, 157, 165, 168, 169, 182, 282.

disturbed by his old enemy in the council, who came to the village to induce some of the young warriors to join him in an expedition against the Cherokees. But as they generally declined his proposal, he attributed this to the influence of Mr Kirkland, who he said had poisoned the minds of the young warriors with White men's notions; and he gave it out as his fixed purpose to kill him if he did not go away. One day shortly after, as Mr Kirkland was riding home in the evening, an Indian, a sort of lieutenant in the troop of this chief, attempted to shoot him; but he set off his horse at full speed, and happily made his escape.[1]

In May 1766, Mr Kirkland left the Seneca country, and after being ordained in New England to the office of the ministry, he set off for Kanonwarohare, the chief town of the Oneida Indians, about fifteen miles south of the east end of Oneida lake. A school had already been established in that village; the children who attended it made great progress in learning; and the inhabitants in general were very anxious to have a minister settled among them. Taking advantage of this circumstance, Mr Kirkland, soon after his arrival, assembled them together, and told them, that if they would all solemnly engage to abandon drinking, and enable him to carry their determination into execution, by appointing six or eight of their principal men to assist him, with full power to seize all spirituous liquors, and destroy them, or dispose of them as he should think fit, he then would remain with them; but if they would not agree to this, he would then leave them. After four days' consideration, they unanimously appointed eight persons, whom Mr Kirkland nominated, as his assistants, who proved very active and faithful in carrying the measure into effect. Such, indeed, was its success, that though in a short time about eighty casks of rum were carried through the town, and offered to the Indians for sale, and even in some cases as a present, yet in no instance were they prevailed on to accept of it. For about three months, only two were guilty of intoxication; and one of these was the only person in the town who opposed Mr Kirkland's measures.[2]

[1] Lothrop's Life of Kirkland *in* Spark's Lib. Amer. Biog. vol. xv. p. 183, 193; Narrative of the Indian Charity School at Lebanon, Connecticut, p. 53.

[2] Lothrop's Life of Kirkland *in* Spark's Lib. Amer. Biog. vol. xxv. p. 199, 200, 202, 206. Narrative of the Indian Charity School, p. 35, 38, 43, 55.

In the summer of 1767, Mr Kirkland, and the Indians under his care, suffered much distress from the scarcity of provisions. For two years past the frost had destroyed their corn, and this season the worms threatened to lay waste at least one-half of the crop which was then in the ground. "From week to week," says Mr Kirkland, "I am obliged to go with the Indians to Oneida lake, to catch eels for my subsistence. I have lodged and slept with them till I am as lousy as a dog. Flour and milk, and a few eels, have been my only living. Such diet, with my hard labour abroad, is not sufficient to support nature; my strength, indeed, begins to fail. My poor people are almost starved to death. There is one family, consisting of four persons, whom I must support in the best way I can, or they would certainly perish. Indeed, I would myself be glad of an opportunity to fall upon my knees for such a bone as I have often seen cast to the dogs. Without relief I shall soon perish. My constitution is almost broken; my spirits sink: yet my heart still bleeds for these poor creatures. I had rather die than leave them alone in their present miserable condition."

Mr Kirkland's necessities were no sooner known than they were relieved by his friends. But he had not long escaped from danger of perishing by hunger, when he was in no small hazard of his life from one of the Indians, in consequence of his endeavours to execute the law regarding spirituous liquors. Having learned that two or three women were drinking near the town, and that they had a great quantity of rum, he went immediately to them; and though they had concealed the liquor for fear of him, yet he soon discovered it, and destroyed it without further ceremony. One of the poor creatures afterwards fell upon her knees, and with bitter cries and tears mourned over the loss of her beloved liquor, and even licked up what was not soaked into the earth, uttering many imprecations against him for his cruelty. The husband of the woman to whom the spirits belonged, (a man who, by his own confession, had murdered no fewer than fourteen persons,) was so enraged, that he threatened to kill Mr Kirkland, and even brought some Indians, from a neighbouring town, to assist him in executing his bloody design. "The matter," said he, "is now settled; the minister shall never see another rising sun." Being apprized of his danger, Mr Kirkland was persuaded to leave the village that night, and to retire to a sugar-house about a mile and a half distant. He returned, however, to the town the next morning; and though some of the Indians were still much enraged against him, yet most of them seemed more than ever attached to him, and expressed the utmost concern for his safety. One of them even offered three times to die in his stead.

Soon after this event, Mr Kirkland visited the neighbouring town of Old Oneida, the inhabitants of which had manifested the utmost aversion to the gospel, and were so violent against the new regulations regarding spirituous liquors, that they employed every artifice to check the progress of the reformation; and even near relations, such as brothers and sisters, would not visit each other after the agreement was made. Now, however, they were much impressed by the word; and the inhabitants of the two villages not only came to hear the gospel with each other, but their mutual differences were completely removed, and a formal reconciliation was effected between them. The people of Old Oneida even expressed their determination to enter into the same engagement as their brethren with regard to spirituous liquors; and it was agreed among them, that Mr Kirkland should preach at the two places every alternate Sabbath. * This change in the temper of the inhabitants of that town was the more extraordinary, as only a few months before they were loading Mr Kirkland with imprecations, and wishing he was dead. The whole transaction was remarkably solemn. The tears flowed from many an eye which formerly was seldom known to weep.

The mission among the Oneidas now assumed a most promising aspect; it seemed as if "the wilderness would soon rejoice and blossom as the rose." The Lord's day was observed by the Indians with the utmost strictness; drunkenness was in a great measure banished from among them; and there were a number who appeared to be sincere converts to the faith of Christ. Even the poor wretch who had lately sought Mr Kirkland's life was under deep convictions of sin, and made a public confession of his guilt in a most humble manner.[1]

In June 1773, the Society in Scotland for propagating Christian Knowledge took Mr Kirkland under its patronage, and

[1] Continuation of the Narrative of the Indian Charity School, p. 1, 3, 11, 17, &c.

agreed to pay his salary in conjunction with the Corporation of Harvard College in New England.[1] During the American war, which began not long after, Mr Kirkland was much interrupted in his labours among the Indians, as the country was in a very distracted state.[2] His mission, indeed, though not absolutely abandoned, was virtually discontinued, as he was often and for a long time absent, and at a great distance from Oneida, serving as a chaplain in the American army, or acting as an agent for Congress, in negociations with the Indians, for the purpose of securing their friendship, and maintaining their neutrality in the war which was then carrying on between England and the Colonies. With this view, he took long journeys among the Indian tribes in all directions, attended several councils that were held at the German Flats, Albany, Oneida, and Onondaga, and put forth all his personal influence with them. He had at first great hopes of success; but the machinations of the agents of England prevailed in drawing these bloodhounds of war into the contest, and ultimately some were ranged on the side of the British, and others on that of the Colonies.

Mr Kirkland took a warm interest in the cause of his country, and, even when at his post among the Oneidas, was much employed in procuring, through friendly Indian scouts, intelligence from Niagara and the lake frontier, of the plans and purposes of the enemy in that quarter.[3]

During the war, the Oneidas were severe sufferers. A few of them joined the British; but the greater part adhered to the Americans. Many of their warriors were killed in battle; and after the destruction of their villages and churches by the English, they removed to the plains of Schenectady, or wandered among the neighbouring towns, till the cessation of hostilities permitted them to return to their own settlements.[4]

After the conclusion of the war, the Oneidas made a grant of land to a considerable number of other Indians of different tribes, that they might come and settle in their neighbourhood; and they expected that in a short time there would be upwards

[1] Account of the Soc. in Scotland for prop. Christ. Know. 1774, p. 17.
[2] Fraser's Sermon before the Soc. in Scotland for prop. Christ. Know. p. 43.
[3] Lothrop's Life of Kirkland *in* Spark's Lib. Amer. Biog. vol. xxv. p. 238, 246.
[4] Mass. Hist. Coll. vol. iv. p. 69; vol. v. p. 16.

of a thousand of their countrymen in their vicinity disposed to listen to the Word of God, and to cultivate the arts of civilized life. Having now the prospect of being again settled in their own country, they earnestly invited Mr Kirkland to return and take up his residence among them. "We have been attending," said they, "for many years to the vast difference between White people and Indians. We have laboured much to investigate the cause; for the one are in prosperous circumstances, the other are indigent and wretched. The one appear to be the favourites of heaven, and honourable in the sight of men; the other are despised and rejected of both. We Indians, therefore, must alter our conduct. We must give up our Pagan customs. We must unite with all our wisdom and strength, to cultivate the manners and civilization of the White people, who are thus distinguished by the favour and protection of the Great Spirit above, and embrace the religion of Christ, or we shall, before many years, be not only despised by the nations of the earth, but utterly rejected by the Lord Jesus, the Saviour of the White people.

"We entreat our Father to make one trial more for christianizing the Indians, at least for one, if not for two years; and if there be no encouragement after this that we shall be built up as a people and embrace the religion of Christ, he may leave us, and we shall expect nothing but ruin."

About the same time, the Indians addressed a letter to the Commissioners in Boston, who were invested by the Society in Scotland with the superintendence of the mission; and in this letter, they beseech them to send Mr Kirkland among them, in the following energetic language:

"Fathers, attend to our words!

"It is a long time since we heard your voice. We hope you have not forgotten us. The Great Spirit above hath preserved us, and led us back to our country, and rekindled our fire in peace, which we hope he will preserve to warm and refresh us and our children to the latest posterity.

"Fathers, we have been distressed by the black cloud that so long overspread our country. The cloud is now blown over. Let all thank the Great Spirit, and praise Christ Jesus. By means of his servants, the good news of salvation have been published to us. We have received them. Some of us love the Lord Jesus, who hath preserved us through the late storm. Fathers, our fire just begins to burn again. Our hearts rejoice to see it. We hope it will burn brighter and brighter than ever, and that it will enlighten the Indian nations around us.

"Fathers, we doubt not but your hearts will rejoice in our prosperity; and as the Great Spirit above hath given us the light of peace once more, we hope he will, by your means, send to us the light of his holy word; and that you will think of our father Mr Kirkland, and enable him to eat his bread by our fire-side. He hath for several years laboured among us, and done every thing in his power for our good. Our father Mr Kirkland loves us, and we love him. He hath long had the charge of us, hath long watched over us, and explained the Word of God to us. Fathers, we repeat our request, that you will continue our father to sit by our fire-side, to watch over us, to instruct us, and to lead us in the way to heaven."[1]

In the autumn of 1785, Mr Kirkland, agreeably to the request of the Indians, returned and settled among them. In several villages, particularly Kanonwarohare, Old Oneida, and Kanadesko, he found the people so desirous of religious instruction, with the exception of only two or three who were professed Pagans, that they would assemble for that purpose at almost any time of the day. On the Sabbath, he generally performed divine service at Kanonwarohare, as it was not only the principal village, but the most central of the whole. Here the Indians collected in such numbers from the other towns, which were four, six, ten, and even near thirty miles distant, that there was no house sufficiently large to contain them, and therefore they were often obliged to assemble for public worship under the trees in the open air. The order, attention, and solemnity which appeared in their meetings, were often truly delightful. They never seemed tired of hearing the Word of God; their applications for instruction were frequently so incessant, that Mr Kirkland had scarcely leisure to take his food. Upwards of seventy appeared to be under serious impressions of religion. Their views of divine truth were, in general, scriptural and rational, though some appeared to have a tincture of

[1] Fraser's Sermon before the Soc. in Scotland for Prop. Christ. Know. p. 46.

†

enthusiasm. Their convictions of sin were deep and pungent; and in many instances, the sense of its evil seemed to rise higher than the fear of punishment. There was, at the same time, a remarkable reformation of manners among them. Many who had been guilty of the foulest crimes, and had led an extremely dissipated life, now became sober, regular, and industrious: for some months there was not a single instance of intoxication in two of the villages;[1] but this fair prospect was afterwards overcast; religion declined among them, and even sunk to a very low ebb.

In the summer of 1796, the Rev. Drs Morse and Belknap proceeded, by desire of the Society in Scotland for Propagating Christian Knowledge, to the Oneida country, in order to inquire into the state of the mission among the Indians. By their report, it appears, that the number of Indians, including men, women, and children, under the care of Mr Kirkland, amounted to six hundred and twenty-eight. For some years past, however, there had been no pure Oneidas. There was scarcely, indeed, an individual among them who was not descended on one side or other from English, Scotch, Irish, French, German, or Dutch parents, and some also from Negroes. Among them there were only eight persons who were professed Pagans; but though the others called themselves Christians, the greater part of them appeared to have nothing of Christianity but the name. Of the women, there were thirty-six who were reputed sober, and among these Mr Kirkland reckoned twenty-four to be serious Christians. Of the men, there were only three or four who were of a sober character; and at the last communion only one attended. Mr Kirkland baptized no children except those whose parents, or at least one of them, were members of the church. But the others were at little loss on this account, as they carried their children thirty or forty miles to the Dutch or German plantations, where, on paying the usual fee of half a dollar, they found no difficulty in obtaining baptism for them, and then they were perfectly easy about their salvation.

Though the number of professed Pagans was small, yet the whole nation, notwithstanding their opportunities for religious improvement, were still influenced in a great degree by their

[1] Rippon's Baptist Register, vol. ii. p. 233.

ancient mythology. They were all firm believers in witchcraft and the agency of invisible beings; they paid great regard to dreams and omens, and attributed the most common events to causes with which they could not have the most distant connection. Some time before, an Indian was drowned in one of the Oneida creeks, which were annually visited by salmon. When the fishing season returned, they imagined that no salmon would be found in that stream, until a gentleman from Albany, who happened to be in the neighbourhood, persuaded them that he had put something into the water to purify it; upon which, they resorted to the creek, caught the fish as formerly, and thought themselves much indebted to the gentleman for his kindness.

In the savage state, it was usual for the men to attach themselves to no particular woman, but to rove at large among the females till they had passed the vigour of youth, and then they confined themselves to one as their wife. The Oneidas now married young, and were said to be more continent than formerly.

Murders were said to be less frequent than formerly; but still they were by no means uncommon. A melancholy instance of this kind, which happened a few days before the arrival of Drs Morse and Belknap, exhibits a striking proof of the relaxed state of society amongst them. Two young Oneidas having had a quarrel, the one shot the other dead. The father of the deceased immediately went and despatched the murderer, and no further notice was taken of the matter.[1]

With respect to drinking spirituous liquors to excess, they were generally addicted to it, when they had them in their power, except the few individuals already mentioned. The chiefs, indeed, had frequently attempted to prohibit the introduction and sale of that pernicious article; but from the small degree of power they possess, and the unquenchable thirst of the people for ardent spirits, these efforts had hitherto proved ineffectual.[2]

As to agriculture, it was yet in its infancy among the Oneidas, and the labour of cultivating the fields was still performed chiefly by the women. Idleness was the sin that easily beset them, and was the natural parent of many other of their vices.

[1] Mass. Hist. Coll. vol. v. p. 12, 15, 17. [2] Ibid. vol. v. p. 20, 21.

"Indians cannot work," was a saying often in their mouths. They had an idea, that to labour in cultivating the ground is degrading to the character of a man, who, they say, "was made for war and hunting, and holding councils; and that women and hedgehogs were made to scratch the earth." It was also a proverbial tradition among them, that "the Great Spirit gave the White man a plough, and the Red man a bow and arrow, and sent them into the world by different paths, each to get a living in his own way." Among the Oneidas the land was still held in common, which necessarily proved a powerful obstacle to its improvement. Not more than two or three families procured a subsistence entirely by agriculture; and these had little encouragement to proceed, as their neighbours used to live upon them as long as they could find any thing to eat. The Oneidas, in general, procured a miserable subsistence, by fishing and fowling; by raising a little corn, beans, and potatoes; and by means of an annuity of 3552 dollars from the Legislature of New York, as the price of lands purchased from them; but this money, instead of proving an incitement, was a check to industry; for as long as an Indian can procure a living in any other way, he will not work.[1]

Such was the very unfavourable account which Drs Morse and Belknap gave of the mission among the Oneidas. The zeal and perseverance, the piety, faithfulness, and benevolence, which Mr Kirkland displayed in promoting Christianity and civilization among the Indians, had afforded the highest gratification to the Society in Scotland for Propagating Christian Knowledge; but after receiving this Report, the Directors felt much dissatisfied with him, and came to a resolution dissolving his connection with it.[2] It appears that after the restoration of peace with England, he was a good deal engaged in assisting in conferences and negotiations with, or relative to, the Indians; and his biographer states that he rendered them various and important services in settling their affairs with the United States. His health at length began to fail, and the infirmities of age to come upon him, and he was no longer equal to his former exer-

[1] Mass. Hist. Coll. vol. v. p. 19, 22, 26, 28.

[2] American Correspondence among the Records of the Society for Propagating Christian Knowledge, vol. i. p. 259, 279, 316, 317, 327, 349, 378, 385.

tions. In consequence, too, of the failure of his youngest son, who was extensively engaged in business speculations, and for whom he was in several instances security, he was stripped of nearly all his property, and was involved in pecuniary embarrassments, from which, during the remainder of his life, he had to struggle to relieve himself. At length, after having been engaged for upwards of forty years as a missionary among the Indians, he died, after a brief but severe illness, February 28. 1808.[1]

In 1825, the Oneida Indians consisted of about 1150 persons. A few years before this, the Pagan party of the Oneidas addressed a letter to the Governor of New York, containing a formal renunciation of heathenism and a solemn profession of Christianity. Through the benevolent exertions of the Quakers, or Friends, this branch of the Oneida tribe had made considerable improvement as regards industry and sobriety. With a few exceptions, they appeared to be weaned from the use of spirituous liqours, and they were making considerable progress in agriculture. A few of them had enclosed large farms, and so improved them as to produce plentiful crops. But notwithstanding their professed renunciation of heathenism, there was little appearance of true religion among them. Part of the Oneida Indians removed some years ago from the State of New York to near Green Bay, on the western shore of Lake Michigan. The Rev. Eleazar Williams, the son of an Indian chief, laboured among them as a missionary of the Board of Missions of the Episcopal Church in the United States.[2]

[1] Lothrop's Life of Kirkland in Sparks' Lib. Amer. Biog. vol. xxv. p. 257, 260, 287, 290, 297, 301, 305, 316, 321, 331, 339, 350, 362.

[2] New York Christian Herald, vol. ii. p. 361, vol. iv. p. 148, vol. v. p. 461; Report American Board for Foreign Missions 1829, p. 88; Account of Measures pursued by the Friends of New York for the Civilization of the Indians, p. 7, 10, 14, 20, 25.

CHAPTER V.

PROPAGATION OF CHRISTIANITY BY THE DANES.

SECT. I.—EAST INDIES.

Soon after the commencement of the eighteenth century, Frederick the Fourth, King of Denmark, in consequence of the recommendation of the Rev. Dr Lutkens, one of his chaplains, resolved to make an attempt for the conversion of the heathen on the coast of Coromandel in the East Indies. In November 1705, Bartholomew Ziegenbalg and Henry Plutcho, two young men who were educated for the ministry at the University of Halle in Upper Saxony, and whom he had engaged with this view, embarked at Copenhagen; and, after an agreeable voyage of seven months, they arrived in safety at Tranquebar, the principal town belonging to the Danes in that quarter of the world.[1]

In commencing their labours among the heathen, the missionaries were anxious to lose no time. As a corrupt dialect of Portuguese, which had been introduced into India about two centuries before, was now spoken and understood by great numbers of the natives, they had begun to learn that language during the voyage, and on their arrival they proceeded to study with unwearied diligence, the Tamil, which is the vernacular language of that part of the country. Impressed with the importance of instructing the young, they early opened charity schools, in which the children were not only educated, but fed and clothed. With the natives, they had frequent conversations on the subject of religion, and in a short time, they baptized a number of them.[2]

[1] Niecampii Historia Missionis Evangelicæ in India Orientali, p. 2.
[2] Ibid. p. 126, 128, 129, 133, 139; Hough's Hist. vol. iii, p. 113.

While the missionaries prosecuted their labours with much diligence and zeal, they were not without their difficulties and discouragements. Besides meeting with many powerful obstacles from the prejudices of the natives, they experienced great opposition from the Europeans resident in the country, who, instead of being their friends and supporters, proved their enemies and persecutors. The hostility they manifested, was not only keen, but of long continuance; nor was all the authority of the King of Denmark, able for some years to suppress it. Order followed order in favour of the missionaries; but their enemies, among whom was the Danish Governor of Tranquebar, disregarded the commands of His Majesty, and continued to molest them in their labours. Ziegenbalg was even at one time arrested, and kept in confinement for four months.[1]

The missionaries at the same time suffered great embarrassments from the want of pecuniary support. The first subsidy of two thousand Imperial pieces which was sent to them from Europe, was lost in the sea near Tranquebar. The mission was now so enlarged, that forty or fifty Imperial pieces were required monthly for its support; but where to raise so large a sum, the missionaries could not tell. They were ready to endure the greatest privations themselves; but they could not bear the thought of their children and domestics suffering want. While they were harassed with these painful apprehensions, they providentially obtained a supply of money. A person from whom they could have little expected it, offered them forty Imperial pieces to keep in trust for him until the arrival of the ships from Europe; and when this sum was expended, others offered them two hundred Imperial pieces on similar conditions. At length, when they had scarcely two oboli left, a ship arrived from Europe which brought them a large supply of money, together with three assistants in their work, John Ernest Grundler, John G. Bœving, and Polycarp Jordan.[2]

In 1710, the Society for Promoting Christian Knowledge, which was established a few years before in London, began to patronize the mission on the coast of Coromandel, and from that time, it was a chief instrument of supporting and extend-

[1] Niecampii Hist. p. 96, 141, 154; Propagation of the Gospel in the East, part i. p. 32, part iii. p. 18.

[2] Neicampii Hist. p. 140, 143.

ing the undertaking. As the missionaries had often complained of the great trouble and expense they were at, in getting books transcribed for the schools, and for distribution among the natives, the Directors of that Society, not only printed an edition of the Portuguese New Testament, chiefly for their use, but sent them a printing press, a fount of Roman and Italic characters, and a quantity of paper. A fount of Tamil types was afterwards cast at Halle in Saxony, according to a specimen sent home by the missionaries, and was forwarded to them. But as it was very inconvenient for them to depend on Europe for all their printing materials, they at length erected a type foundry at Tranquebar, and built a paper-mill to supply themselves with paper.[1]

Having now a press of their own, the missionaries began to employ that powerful engine for the spread of Christian Knowledge through the country. From this period, great quantities of books were every year printed by them, and widely circulated among the natives, who not only received them with great eagerness, but read them to their neighbours, and held conversations concerning them, both among themselves and with the missionaries, so that a general stir was excited in the country about religion. Some malicious persons, indeed, endeavoured to stop this important part of their operations, under the pretence that, according to law, the missionaries had no right to print any work until it had passed through the hands of the censor. But His Majesty the King of Denmark soon settled this point, by transmitting orders to the governor and council at Tranquebar, to allow the missionaries to publish whatever books they should judge necessary, for promoting Christianity among the natives.[2]

In 1715, the New Testament, translated into Tamil, by Ziegenbalg, issued from the press at Tranquebar. The translation of the Holy Scriptures into the language of the natives, was an object on which the heart of this indefatigable man had been early fixed; but, lest he should produce an inaccurate version, he delayed entering on this important undertaking, until he was able to write the language with perspicuity and

[1] Niecampii Hist. p. 155, 158, 163, 171, 199; Propagation of the Gospel, part i. p. xxxvi, part iii. p. 33. [2] Niecampii Hist. p. 163, 170.

correctness. Upwards of two years, therefore, elapsed after his arrival in India, before he began this work ; and notwithstanding the many difficulties which attended the attempt, he finished the translation of the New Testament in about two years and a half. Various circumstances, however, combined to delay the publication of it for several years longer, among which was the advice of his friends in Europe to review it carefully before he put it to the press; an advice, which, no doubt, contributed materially to the correctness of the version.[1]

In February 1719, Bartholomew Ziegenbalg, who had the honour of originally establishing the mission, and who possessed, in no ordinary degree, those qualifications, which exalt and adorn the character of a Christian missionary, died in the thirty-sixth year of his age. In the mean while, Benjamin Schultze, Nicholas Dal, and John H. Kistenmacher, three new missionaries, had embarked for India, and though on landing they were deeply affected to hear of the death of Ziegenbalg, yet their arrival was a source of no small consolation to Grundler. After the loss of his excellent colleague, he was for two months in so weak a state of health, that in conducting public worship, he was obliged to sit in the pulpit. It was truly affecting to hear him supplicating God with many tears, not to afflict the little flock which they had gathered from among the heathen, by depriving them of both their pastors, before other missionaries should arrive in the country and be prepared for the work. His prayers were heard and answered. Accordingly, upon the arrival of the new missionaries, he was at particular pains to prepare them for entering upon their labours among the heathen; and having gained so far the object of his wishes, he was soon called to follow his departed colleague to the grave.[2]

Thus, within little more than a twelvemonth, the mission lost its two principal pillars in the eastern world. Both Ziegenbalg and Grundler were men admirably qualified for the important station in which Providence had placed them ; yet they were taken away at a time when their continuance seemed of peculiar importance, and promised the most extensive usefulness. These severe and successive blows threatened the very extinction of the mission, and afforded the enemies of the under-

[1] Niecampii Hist. p. 141, 153, 182.

[2] Ibid. p. 213, 217, 222.

taking a temporary triumph. The Roman Catholics in India pleased themselves with the hope, that the Danish mission was now at an end; and even among the Protestants in Europe, there were not wanting some who held similar language. By the false reports which they industriously circulated concerning the failure of the undertaking, they even succeeded, to a certain extent, in diminishing its pecuniary resources, and by this means involved it in considerable difficulties.

Meanwhile, Schultze and his fellow missionaries endeavoured to encourage themselves by faith in God; and though the circumstances under which they commenced their labours were so very unfavourable, yet the mission, instead of declining in their hands, was not only continued, but extended by them. On account of the smallness of their number, they were at first under the necessity of giving up the practice of making journeys into different parts of the country, and preaching the gospel to the inhabitants, but after some time, they were again able to resume this important part of their work.[1]

With the view of paving the way for the progress of Christianity among the natives, they resolved to augment the number of schools for the education of children; and the governor, about the same time, issued an order that all the inhabitants of the Danish territory, should have their children instructed in reading, writing, and arithmetic. The schools, in consequence of this, were increased from five to twenty-one; and though only four of them contained Christian children, while the other seventeen consisted of Pagan and Mahomedan children, yet they were all under the inspection of the missionaries, who appointed two catechists to visit them regularly. The whole number of youth attending these schools, amounted at one period to no fewer than 575; but the management of them was attended with so many difficulties, that after some time, it was found necessary to withdraw the salary of several of the teachers.[2]

In 1727, the Old Testament in Tamil issued from the press, thus completing the translation of the Holy Scriptures in that language. To this, it is to be regretted, was shortly after added the Apocrypha. Previous to his death, Ziegenbalg had pro-

[1] Niecampii Hist. p. 223, 231. [2] Ibid. p. 253, 285.

ceeded in the translation of the Old Testament, as far as Ruth: the remaining books were completed by Schultze. Besides consulting the Hebrew original, and the German translation of Luther, he was able to make use of the Spanish, Italian, French, Danish, and Dutch versions, and other useful works; he likewise enjoyed the assistance of a learned Brahman and of others of the natives, some of whom understood the German and Portuguese languages. To this work he usually devoted six hours a day; and at length, after about two years' assiduous study, he was so happy as to finish it. The joy which the converts expressed at having the whole Bible in their own language, amply compensated him for all the labour and toil he had employed upon it. Indeed, while he was engaged in this work, he enjoyed so much pleasure in studying the Holy Scriptures, that his soul daily fed, as it were, in green pastures.[1]

In 1728, Schultze, who had removed two years before from Tranquebar to Madras, was taken under the patronage of the Society for Promoting Christian Knowledge, which was anxious to establish a mission in that city. The attempt was attended with many difficulties; but yet, it was not long before he succeeded in forming a church at this place. Numbers of the converts had previously been Roman Catholics, a circumstance which mightily enraged the Popish priests against the mission. Some, who resided at St Thomas' Mount, proceeded to such extremities, that they rushed violently on one of the congregation, and after beating him severely, designed to carry him bound to Goa, and deliver him into the hands of the Inquisition. But the governor of the place, though a Mahomedan, took the part of the poor man, and ordered his persecutors to be punished. On another occasion, some of the Catholics beat one of the converts most unmercifully, assigning this ridiculous reason for their conduct, that he was of the religion of the Turks. The missionaries advised the catechists not to enter into disputes with the Papists on controverted points of religion, but to content themselves with stating the simple truths of the gospel, that so they might afford them as little occasion as possible for their enmity. But though the catechists acted, in this respect, with

[1] Niecampii Hist. p. 234, 255, 287, 311.

great prudence and moderation, the Papists continued to manifest the same rancour as ever against them.[1]

Besides preaching four times on the Lord's day, in the Tamil, the Telinga, and the Portuguese languages, Schultze translated the whole of the Old and New Testament, and the Apocrypha, into Telinga; but though he was anxious to have them printed, it does not appear that this was ever accomplished. He also wrote a Grammar of that language, and translated into it several works on the subject of religion. He afterwards translated into Hindustani, the New Testament, the first four chapters of Genesis, the Psalms of David, the Prophecy of Daniel, and some books of the Apocrypha. He likewise compiled a Grammar of that language. The whole of these, with the exception of the Apocryphal books, were printed at Halle, in Saxony, after his return to Europe.[2]

In August 1737, John A. Sartorius, and John E. Geister, who had been labouring for several years at Madras, proceeded from that city to Cuddalore with the view of establishing a branch of the mission in that place, under the auspices of the Society for Promoting Christian Knowledge. Here the inhabitants at first shewed little or no inclination to hear the word; but afterwards, numbers of them not only heard, but embraced the gospel.[3]

In the course of their labours among the Heathen, the missionaries had many difficulties to encounter. To reason with them was scarcely possible, as there were so few common principles admitted by them: or the force of them was evaded by the grossest subterfuges. The Brahman imagined himself insulted, when told that he was a sinner; other persons of high caste, thought their present rank in life was a token of their future happiness. The inferior orders, on the contrary, considered their miserable condition in this world, as a proof of their entire reprobation, and would not be persuaded it was possible for them ever to be happy. Nothing was more common, than

[1] Niecampii Hist. p. 276, 312, 321.

[2] Niecampii Hist. p. 296, 365; Meier Missions Geschichte oder Auszug der Evangelischen Missions-Berichte aus Ostindien, von 1737, bis 1767, p. 63, 74, 109, 140, 160, 478; Bibliographical Dictionary, vol. i. p. 285, vol. vi. p. 222.

[3] Meier Missions-Geschichte, p. 45, 65, 165; Abstract of the Reports of the Society for Promoting Christian Knowledge, p. 70.

to hear them acknowledge that the doctrines taught by the missionaries were truth; that the representations of the Brahmans were lies; and, that the Hindu religion was nothing more than outward pomp and useless show. They even wished, they said, to embrace the gospel: but how could they? It was not so written in their forehead, meaning that it was not so determined in the book of fate. On some occasions, they would say, "It is all very right: but who can live so?" In this idea they were confirmed, by considering the example of their gods, to whom the most impure and unrighteous deeds are ascribed in their sacred books; and they naturally enough thought, that what was done by their gods could not be criminal in them. Many were so engrossed with the care of the body, that they were scarcely able to form any idea of the necessity of concern for the soul. Some would say, "What shall I do with my children? I shall get no wife for my sons, and no husband for my daughters: my relations and friends will cast me off, and your government will not protect me." Others raised objections to the truth of Christianity: "Who can tell," said they, "whether your religion will at last prove true? Who hath seen God? Who hath visited heaven or hell? You cannot shew us that the Christians have gone to heaven. Indeed, we see no difference in the lives of your own countrymen. They are wicked as well as we. Go and convert them first." Some insulted the missionaries in various forms, assailed them with nicknames, threatened to beat them, or made a jest of the most sacred truths of religion; others refused to listen to them, rose up, and went away.[1]

But notwithstanding the many obstacles which the missionaries had to encounter, they were encouraged in their labours, by witnessing, in many instances, the fruit of their exertions. Not a year passed without a considerable number of the natives, both Hindus and Mahomedans, embracing the gospel. Such of the converts as resided beyond the territory of Tranquebar, especially those who were Sudras, were under no small restraints in regard to the profession and exercise of their religion. Many of them were in the service of heathen masters, and were often obliged to work even on the Lord's day. Few of them, com-

[1] Neure Geschichte der Evangelischen Missions Anstalten in Ostindien, tom. i. p. 99, 123, 132, 243, 262, 264, 410.

paratively, were able to read, and hence they could derive no improvement from books. They lived dispersed through the country, and as there was a want of suitable labourers, they could not obtain that regular instruction which was so necessary to persons in their situation. The missionaries, indeed, visited them as often as possible, but they had not yet liberty to settle among them. The native pastors who were ordained over the country congregations, travelled regularly among them; the catechists, who were appointed to assist them, went each over his own district once or twice a month; and they so arranged matters among them, that on the Sabbath divine worship was performed in all the principal places.[1]

In September 1746, the French, under the command of M. Labourdonnais, captured Madras, after a short siege of six days. The new governor having ordered several streets of the Black Town to be razed to the ground, with the view of placing the city in a better state of defence, the house of the missionaries was demolished among others, and the church was converted into a magazine. As long as Madras remained in the hands of the French, Mr Fabricius, the missionary, carried on his labours at Palliacatta, a town in the neighbourhood, to which he had previously removed the children; but on the restoration of peace, he returned to that city, after an absence of near three years. In consequence of the destruction of the mission buildings, they were for some time very ill accommodated; but they at length obtained a grant from government of an excellent dwelling-house, a fine spacious church, a large garden, and a burying ground in the neighbouring village of Vepery, which had belonged to the Catholic missionaries, but which, on account of their treasonable practices, had been taken from them, and confiscated.[2]

In 1752, and several of the following years, the missionaries, particularly at Cuddadore, were materially hindered in their labours, as they were unable to perform their usual journeys through the country in consequence of the war which still raged between the French and English in India, and in which several of the native princes took an active part. The Marathis or Mahrattas, in particular, who sided with France, made frequent in-

[1] Niecampli Hist. p. 454. [2] Meier Missions-Geschichte, p. 249, :65, 353.

roads into the country, and spread terror and devastation wherever they came. The whole land, in fact, was ruined by them. With their fleet horses, they made sudden eruptions into the country, surprised the defenceless inhabitants, and cut them in pieces without distinction of age or sex. Terrified by their dreadful atrocities, the people on the first notice of their approach, abandoned their houses and fled. Parents sometimes killed their infant children when they would not hold their peace, lest their cries should discover them to the merciless foe. In some villages not a creature remained: all were either killed, or had fled, or were carried away prisoners. To these calamities, were, at length, added the horrors of famine. For several years the husbandman enjoyed little or no return for the corn which he sowed, as the enemy either destroyed the whole, or reaped it as soon as it was ripe. Besides, in one year, there was a deficiency of rain ; and afterwards, it fell in such torrents, and was accompanied with such violent winds, that it proved no less destructive than the previous drought. In these calamities the Christian converts deeply participated ; many of them were destitute not only of the comforts, but even of the necessaries of life. Cuddalore, at length, fell into the hands of the French and the missionaries retired with most of the congregation to Tranquebar. Madras was once more besieged by the enemy, and the missionaries in that quarter were completely plundered by them.[1]

In September 1758, Mr Kiernander, one of the missionaries who had lately retired from Cuddalore, proceeded to Calcutta, with the view of establishing a branch of the mission in that city, under the auspices of the Society for Promoting Christian Knowledge. Here he prosecuted his labours with great zeal, and with considerable success, among the descendants of the Portuguese, who were generally Roman Catholics, and also among the Hindus.

In May 1762, Christian Frederick Swartz visited Trichinopoly, and from this period, began to make it the principal place of his residence. This distinguished man, who for near half a century was one of the brightest ornaments of the cause of Christ in India, came to Tranquebar about twelve years before.

[1] Meier Missions-Geschichte, p. 361, 368, 379, 395, 445, 448, 451.

Entirely devoted to the work in which he had embarked, he early resolved on a life of celibacy, that he might not be encumbered with domestic cares, and might direct his sole attention to the duties of his office. He appears, indeed, to have been decidedly hostile to the marriage of missionaries, especially during the first years of their ministry, as being likely to interfere with the acquisition of the language, and with the diligent performance of the duties of their office; and though we know that in this sentiment Mr Swartz stands somewhat alone, yet assuredly, the opinion of such a man is well deserving of the serious consideration of candidates for missionary labours, especially when viewed in connection with the doctrine of the Apostle Paul (1 Corinthians vii.) on the subject of marriage.[1]

In November 1768, Manuel Jotze da Costa, a friar of the Dominican order, was received into the congregation at Madras, after making a public recantation of the errors of Popery, and a solemn profession of the Protestant faith. He was a native of Portugal, and after spending near seven years at Goa, he proceeded to Diu on the coast of Gujarat, where he was invested with the authority of an inquisitor. Having been afterwards sent to Siam, he began to entertain doubts respecting some of the dogmas of the Church of Rome, particularly the prohibition to read the Word of God. Here he became acquainted with Antonio Rodrigues, a Father of the Jesuit order, who felt a similar dissatisfaction with the faith in which he had been educated. He now for the first time in his life, got into his hands a copy of the Bible in Latin; and after some time, he procured among other books, a Catechism published at Tranquebar, which afforded him much light relative to the agreement of the doctrines of the Reformation with the Word of God.

Meanwhile, Father Rodrigues was so convinced of the errors of the Church of Rome, that he withdrew from her communion, and placed himself under the protection of the Dutch, who at that time had a factory in Siam. In consequence of this, he was excommunicated by his brethren, and an order was received from Goa to deliver him up to the Inquisition. This commission was addressed to Father Costa; but as his friend was now

[1] Meier Missions-Geschichte, p. 318; Missionary Register, vol. i. p. 305, 346.

connected with the Dutch, he had a plausible apology for not carrying it into execution. Afterwards, when Rodrigues was dying, one of the Jesuits visited him, and promised him the removal of the sentence of excommunication, and plenary absolution, if he would return to the Church of Rome, and submit to extreme unction. This offer, it was reported, he rejected; nevertheless the Fathers pretended that he had returned to the bosom of the church, and buried him with great pomp.

Hitherto, Father Costa had carefully concealed the change in his sentiments, but notwithstanding all his caution, it was discovered by his brethren. One day as he lay sick in bed, another friar of the Dominican order came upon him by surprise, and opening his writing table, found a paper, in which were noted many of the errors of the Church of Rome. This manuscript he took with him, together with his heretical books; and as in the absence of a bishop, every Father is invested with authority to deliver up an apostate brother to the Inquisition, he sent him on board a vessel bound to Goa. Father Costa, however, found means to leave the ship, and afterwards came to the coast of Coromandel; but though he wished to join the Protestant Church, he wanted the decision of mind necessary for so important a step. His intercourse with the missionaries was only occasional, and was long carried on in a covert manner. After many struggles, however, he broke through all difficulties, and joined the congregation at Madras. He was now anxious to return to Siam, with the view of taking charge of a number of Portuguese whom he had secretly instructed in the principles of evangelical religion, and in the hope of extending still farther the light of divine truth in that heathen country. In consequence, however, of the infirm state of his health, he was unable to prosecute his design, and after a lingering illness of near a twelvemonth, he died at Calcutta.

Besides Father Costa, there were three other Catholic priests, who about this period renounced the errors of Popery, and joined the congregation at Calcutta. One of them had been upwards of fifteen years a missionary in Bengal, and another about four years at Bussora.[1] These facts are the more worthy of notice, because they induce a hope, that among the mission-

[1] Neure Geschichte, tom. i. 65, 299, 771, 1074, 1363.

†

aries of the Church of Rome, there may have been numbers of others, who by reading the Scriptures, amidst the privations and trials which they suffered in a heathen land, and at a distance from the pernicious influence and example of their brethren, may have acquired somewhat correct views of the fundamental doctrines of Christianity, and may have disseminated among the inhabitants, not the fooleries of Popery, but the principles of evangelical religion.

To shew the extensive scale on which the mission was now carried on, it may not be improper to give in this place, a general view of the different stations about this period.

In 1775, there were in the TRANQUEBAR station, six missionaries, three native preachers, twenty-four catechists and assistants, ten schoolmasters, and three schoolmistresses. In the town and neighbourhood there were three churches, and in the country six places of worship. The different congregations were this year increased with 421 new members, including the children of the converts, and proselytes from the Church of Rome. The number of schools was ten, in which were 355 boys and girls, who were not only educated but clothed and supported by the missionaries, besides other children, who were maintained by their friends, and merely enjoyed the benefit of instruction.

At MADRAS there were two missionaries, who had under their care two congregations, the Tamil and the Portuguese. In the course of this year, they were augmented with 141 new members. In the school there were 40 children, who were not only educated, but supported at the expense of the mission.

At CUDDALORE there were two missionaries: the congregation was this year increased with 74 new members; and in the school there were 64 children.

At CALCUTTA there were two missionaries, who had under their care two congregations, the English and the Portuguese. In the course of this year, they were augmented with 67 new members. In the schools there were 104 children, many of whom were maintained as well as educated at the expense of the mission.

At TRICHINOPOLY there was only one missionary; but with him were associated no fewer than eleven catechists, schoolmasters and other assistants, two of whom were Europeans. The congregation was this year increased with 206 new members. In the English and Tamil schools, there were 70 children.

At TANJORE no missionary as yet resided; but there had long been a congregation in that city. It was frequently visited by Mr Swartz and his catechists; and within a few years, it became the principal place of his residence.

From this statement, it appears that the mission consisted of five principal branches; that in the different stations, there were thirteen missionaries, and upwards of fifty native assistants; that the several congregations were in one year augmented with no fewer than 909 new members, and that in the schools there were 633 children.[1]

In 1779, Mr Swartz received an unexpected summons to repair immediately to Madras, and on his arrival, he was informed by Sir Thomas Rumbold, the governor, that the British government were anxious to maintain peace with Hyder Ali; but that he, from misconceiving their views, appeared to entertain hostile designs toward them; that it was their wish he would proceed in a private manner to Seringapatam, and undeceive him by a fair declaration of their pacific sentiments, while at the same time, he should endeavour to ascertain what were his intentions. Mr Swartz was surprised at this proposal, and begged some time for consideration and prayer. As the only object of it appeared to be the preservation of peace, he, after some reflection, acceded to it, especially as he hoped, in travelling through the country, to have an opportunity of making known the gospel to multitudes who had never before heard of the Saviour.

Having proceeded to Seringapatam, Mr Swartz was received by Hyder Ali in a friendly manner. Agreeably to his instructions, he stated to him the pacific views of the Madras government. The usurper in return, explained his own sentiments with apparent frankness, complained of the treachery of the English, and charged them with having broken their most solemn engagements; but declared that he was still willing to maintain peace with them. After Mr Swartz had

[1] Neure Geschichte, tom. ii. p. 3, 256, 329, 461, 470.

taken leave of him, Hyder sent to his palanquin, a bag containing three hundred rupees to pay the expenses of his journey; but as he had been provided with whatever was necessary by the Board at Madras, he delivered it to them, and when they urged him to keep it, he asked their permission to employ it as the commencement of a fund for an English charity school at Tanjore, in the hope that some benevolent individuals might increase it with their contributions.[1]

But though Mr Swartz had undertaken this journey to the court of Hyder with the view of averting from the country the calamities of war, he soon perceived from the conduct of the governor of Madras, that peace would be of short continuance,[2] a circumstance which shews with what extreme caution a Christian missionary should interfere in political affairs, lest, while he flatters himself that he is the instrument of promoting the happiness of nations, he should prove merely the tool of unprincipled designing men.

In July 1780, Hyder Ali, provoked by the perfidy and aggressions of the Madras government, invaded the Carnatic at the head of an army of a hundred thousand men. In the course of the conflict which ensued, the most dreadful atrocities were committed by both the belligerent powers. The whole country was laid waste: the towns and villages were burnt to ashes; the inhabitants plundered and put to the sword. To the calamities of war, were, in a short time, added the horrors of famine. As the sluices which supply the country with water were destroyed by Hyder's troops; and as the inhabitants had no security for the crop, they did not sow their fields, and of course they could reap no harvest. The people, indeed, forsook the country, and fled to the larger towns, particularly to Tranquebar, which was so full of strangers, that a moderate lodging for a family, cost a thousand rix-dollars a year. Here the scarcity rose at length to such a height, that people died daily of hunger in the streets; the government was obliged to appoint some persons to carry the dead bodies out of the town and bury them. Before the doors and windows of the inhabitants, stood crowds of people famishing for want, and crying for rice. To alleviate

[1] Neure Geschichte, tom. iii. p. 283; Rep. Christ. Know. Soc. p. 224.
[2] Neure Geschichte, tom. iii. p. 515.

the general distress, the missionaries and other benevolent individuals, distributed provisions among them. The whole street, on such occasions, was filled with hundreds of these miserable victims of famine, whose impetuosity could be restrained only by a guard of sepoys, laying about them with blows: in the confusion they threw one another to the ground, and seized the rice out of each other's hands. No individual benevolence, however, could relieve the general distress. A subscription was therefore raised among the more wealthy inhabitants for the relief of the poor: one of the missionaries was appointed to receive the contributions: two of the native Christians were chosen to oversee the distribution of the rice; and some sepoys were present to maintain order. At one time, the number of poor amounted to twelve hundred, many of whom were little better than skeletons, covered only with a slender skin. Scarcely able to stand on their feet, and to preserve their balance, they tottered like children along the street. Many sunk down from absolute weakness, remained under the rays of a burning sun, or lay in the rain and died. Some were led or carried to the spot where the provisions were distributed: the sick and weary lay at the place, and received their miserable pittance twice a day. It was truly deplorable, to behold the bodies of the dead lying in the streets, many of which were devoured by dogs, and birds of prey, and other ravenous animals, before they were found and buried by those appointed to collect them. One day, one of the missionaries saw within about two hundred feet, no fewer than sixteen dead bodies lying in the streets. More died of unwholesome food, than even of absolute hunger. Here and there might be seen some of these wretched creatures, sitting on dunghills, picking up any little particles of food they could discover. Others might be seen devouring bones, shells, horns of young animals, the leather of palanquins, the leaves of trees, grass, roots, and even pure earth. In Pondicherry and Negapatnam, there were examples of mothers eating their own children: others, scarcely less cruel, abandoned them in the streets, and left them to perish, without ever inquiring after them, or allowing them a particle of that food which they procured for themselves. In this season of universal distress, even the distinction of castes was little regarded. The Brahmans mingled with the Pariars: persons of all religions flocked together to the same spot, Christians, Mahomedans, and heathens. Many begged to be taken as slaves: parents of the highest classes, offered to sell their children for a mere trifle, but offered them in vain.

These horrid scenes were general over the whole country, particularly in all the larger towns, to which the people flocked for safety. All business was at an end: whole families perished; it seemed as if the country would be entirely depopulated by disease, by famine, and by war.[1]

In April 1782, the town of Cuddalore capitulated to the enemy; and on this occasion, Mr Gericke, the missionary at that place, rendered some essential services to the cause of humanity. He prevailed with the French General not to deliver up the town to the troops of Hyder Ali, and thus was instrumental in preserving it from the devastations of these infernal marauders. He concealed in his own house seven of the English officers, whom Admiral Suffrein had engaged to surrender to the tyrant, and by this means saved them from imprisonment, and from all that horrid train of miseries, in which many others were involved who fell into his hands. The Admiral's secretary, who had been severely wounded in a late naval engagement, he kept for a considerable time in his own house, and took care of him, at great expense to himself, as if he had been his friend or brother. In the mean while, however, the church was converted into a magazine, and the mission-garden was entirely destroyed. Mr Gericke, therefore, performed divine worship in the school, or in his own house; but after a few months he proceeded to Madras; and though he wished to return, yet for the present he could find no opportunity. From that period, Cuddalore ceased to be one of the principal branches of the mission: there was still a small congregation at that place; but it was only occasionally the residence of a missionary.[2]

These were not the only instances in which the missionaries were useful in alleviating the calamities of this dreadful period. The services of Mr Swartz in this respect, place the utility of

[1] Memoirs of the late War in Asia, vol. i. p. 134, 138, 172, 413; Neure Geschichte, tom iii. p. 59, 76, 118, 130, 258, 320, 406, 423, 453.

[2] Neure Geschichte, tom. iii. p. 384, 409, 698.

the mission, even in a political view, in a very striking light, and furnish a fine example of the influence of Christian integrity in commanding the respect and confidence of mankind.

Soon after the commencement of hostilities, the fort of Tanjore was reduced to the greatest distress. A powerful enemy was at hand, the people in the fort numerous, and not provisions even for the garrison. The sepoys dropped down dead emaciated with hunger; the streets were every morning lined with corpses; the condition of the place was truly deplorable. There was grain enough in the country; but the inhabitants would neither bring it themselves, nor send in their bullocks, as when they formerly brought paddy into the fort, the rapacious dubashes denied them full payment. In vain did the Rajah order; in vain did he entreat them to come to his assistance. They had no confidence in either him or his courtiers. He at last said to one of the principal English gentlemen who were with him: "We have all lost our credit with the people: let us try whether they will trust Mr Swartz." Being empowered by the Rajah to treat with the people, Mr Swartz immediately sent letters to the whole of the surrounding district, promising to pay every man with his own hands, who should come to the relief of the fort, and to indemnify them for any bullock that might be taken by the enemy. Having in the course of one or two days obtained upwards of a thousand bullocks, he sent some of the Christian converts into the neighbouring country to purchase corn. It was at the risk of their lives that they went, yet such were their exertions, that in a short time they brought into the fort 80,000 kalams. By this means, the place was saved, and the miseries of the inhabitants relieved for the present. Having accomplished this important object, Mr Swartz, agreeably to his promise, paid the people with his own hands, made them a small present, and sent them to their homes.

The following year, the fort of Tanjore was reduced a second time to the same miserable condition, as the enemy always invaded the country when the harvest was nigh at hand. Mr Swartz was desired to repeat the experiment, and succeeded as before. Knowing they would be regularly paid, the people came with their cattle; and though the danger was now greater than formerly, as the enemy was just at hand, yet the Christians conducted the inhabitants of the country to proper stations, and in this manner supplied the fort with grain.[1]

It is a circumstance not unworthy of notice, that even Hyder Ali, in the midst of this cruel and vindictive war, gave orders to his officers "to permit the venerable Father Swartz to pass unmolested, and to shew him respect and kindness, for he is a holy man, and means no harm to my government."[2] Such, indeed, was the estimation in which he was held, that Colonel Fullarton assures us, "the knowledge and integrity of this irreproachable missionary had retrieved the character of Europeans from the imputation of general depravity."[3] These testimonies from a Mahomedan prince, and from a military officer, given under circumstances which preclude every idea of partiality or prepossession, convey a eulogium on the character of Mr Swartz, which far exceeds the highest panegyric we could bestow.

In 1784, several of the native assistants were sent by the the missionaries to Palamcotta, with the view of spreading Christianity in the southern part of the peninsula of India. Several years before, when Mr Swartz was in that quarter of the country, the widow of a Brahman applied to him for baptism; but as she then lived as the concubine of an English officer, he informed her, that as long as she maintained that criminal connection, he could not comply with her request. It appears, however, that the officer had privately promised to marry her; and in the mean while, he instructed her in the English language, and even in the principles of Christianity. After his death, she renewed her application to Mr Swartz, and as her conduct was now perfectly correct, he baptized her by the name of Clarinda. She continued to reside in the South of India; but about the time of the conclusion of the war, she and two Roman Catholic Christians from the same quarter of the country, came to Tanjore to visit Mr Swartz. One of these persons had obtained a copy of the New Testament, and of the Ecclesiastical History published by the missionaries, which he read with so much effect, that he was not only convinced himself of

[1] Rep. Christ. Know. Soc. p. 402.
[2] Buchanan's Apology for promoting Christianity in India, p. 196,
[3] Fullarton's View of English interests in India, p. 183.

the errors of the Church of Rome, but testified against them so strongly among his neighbours and acquaintances, that many of them were much impressed by his representations. He and his fellow-traveller now visited Tanjore, in order to beg, in the name of these poor people, that a missionary, or one of the country priests, might come and instruct them more perfectly in the principles of religion. In consequence of this application, several of the native assistants successively proceeded to that part of the country, and in the course of a short time, they received into the church, upwards of a hundred people in the neighbourhood of Palamcotta, some of whom were previously heathens, others Roman Catholics. Such was the commencement of the congregations in the South of India, which since that period have become so numerous.[1]

Though peace was now restored to the country, the kingdom of Tanjore was still doomed to suffer fresh calamities. The inhabitants were so terribly oppressed by their rulers, that they emigrated from the country in great numbers: whole towns and villages were left desolate; few people remained to cultivate the land. The operations of agriculture should commence in the month of June; but nothing was done, even in the beginning of September. Sir Archibald Campbell, the governor of Madras, dreading that this emigration would end in a famine, appointed a Committee of four gentlemen to examine into the management of the country, and requested Mr Swartz to act as one of the members. This excellent man had already manifested his anxiety for the welfare of the people by entreating the Rajah to take pity upon them; and though his entreaties were disregarded, he now shewed an equal concern for the interests of the prince. Perceiving that if the Committee proceeded to issue orders in their own name, the authority of the Rajah in the country would be lessened, he begged them not to enter on business, until he should represent to him the absolute necessity of administering justice to his people, and of removing those oppressions under which they groaned. The Rajah was now alarmed, and yielded to Mr Swartz's representations, though it was evidently with extreme reluctance. He himself had sent notice to the people, that justice would be done them; but

[1] Neure Geschichte, tom. iii. p. 756, 773, 789, 1025, 1028.

they placed no confidence in his promises. He therefore engaged to Mr Swartz to treat his subjects with kindness, and begged him to invite them back, not in the name of the Committee, but in his own name, as one who was the common friend of the prince and the people. With this request Mr Swartz was happy to comply, and such was the confidence of the people in his integrity, that they returned immediately: seven thousand men came back in one day, and others in a short time followed their example. When he exhorted them to make the utmost exertions in cultivating their lands as the season was almost lost, they replied, "As you have shewn kindness to us, you shall not have reason to repent of it: We intend to work night and day to manifest our regard to you." They accordingly exerted themselves to such a degree, that, though the season was now so far advanced, they had a more abundant crop than the year before.[1]

In January 1787, the Rajah of Tanjore, who had lost all his own children, adopted as his successor a youth of a noble family, who was only nine or ten years of age. A few days before his death, he called for Mr Swartz, and pointing to the prince, said, "My adopted son, I deliver up to you: I appoint you to be his guardian." Such an appointment an ambitious man would have accepted with joy; but Mr Swartz, with his usual disinterestedness, replied, "You know, Sir, my willingness to serve you, according to my small ability; but to comply with this, your last request, is beyond my power. You have adopted a child of nine years of age, and you now leave him as a garden without a fence. You know there are different parties in your palace, who aspire to the government of the country. The boy will be in danger of his life, and the kingdom will be involved in confusion. I may see him once or twice in a month; and may give him my best advice; but I can scarcely do more. What poor guardianship will this be! It is necessary you adopt some other plan." By the advice of Mr Swartz, the dying prince accordingly appointed his own brother the guardian of the child; but this arrangement was overruled by the British government. Ameer Sing himself, the brother of the Rajah, was for the present invested with the sovereign authority; but his government

[1] Rep. Christ. Know. Soc. p. 254, 405; Neure Geschichte, tom. iii. p. 1154, 1157.

having proved very oppressive, he was, after some years, removed, and Serfogee, the young prince, was raised to the throne.[1]

In 1793, when a bill for the renewal of the East India Company's charter was under the consideration of the British Parliament, Mr Wilberforce brought forward a series of resolutions in the House of Commons, with a special view to the promotion of Christianity among the natives of India. These were agreed to in Committee; and Mr Dundas, who was then President of the Board of Control, promised to give them his official support. But the Directors of the East India Company, and the Court of Proprietors being found strongly opposed to them, the whole of the clauses were, with his consent, struck out on the third reading of the bill.[2] In the course of a debate on this

[1] Neure Geschichte, tom. iii. p. 1101, 1390; Rep. Christ. Know. Soc. p. 258.

Though Mr Swartz declined the request of the late Rajah to be the guardian of Serfogee, his adopted son, yet the government of Madras afterwards appointed him guardian to the youth, in order to protect him from the oppressive treatment which he met with from Ameer Sing. Mr Swartz was even much consulted by the Madras government in regard to the affairs of the Tanjore country, and he laid before it his views on various points, such as the administration of justice, the collection of the revenue, the treatment of Serfogee, &c. Indeed, it was chiefly through his efforts, that the right of the latter to the throne was cleared up, and that he was, at length, raised to the Rajahship in 1798.—*Pearson's Memoirs of Swartz*, vol. ii. p. 177, 179, 189, 201, 205, 211, 213, 221, 249, 315, 379; *Memoir of the Rev. Joseph D. Jænicke*, p. 51.

[2] Calcutta Review, vol. iii. p. 219, 222.

Considering the opposition which was long manifested by the Government of India to missionaries, it is not unworthy of mention, that by the charter granted by William III. in 1698 to the East India Company, it was expressly provided that the Company "shall maintain one minister in every garrison and superior factory" which they may have; and "that all such ministers shall be obliged to learn, within one year after their arrival, the Portuguese language, and shall apply themselves to learn the native language of the country where they shall reside, the better to enable them to instruct the Gentoos that shall be the servants or slaves of the Company, or of their agents in the Protestant religion."—*Calcutta Review*, vol. iii. p. 225. The records of the Company, both before and after that time, furnish various instances of the countenance which they gave to efforts for the spread of the Christian faith in India.—*Auber's Rise and Progress of the British Power in India*, vol. ii. p. 491.

Though we have no sympathy with the views of the men who opposed Mr Wilberforce's proposals, yet it was well for the cause of pure and scriptural Christianity that they were rejected. They were no doubt well-meant; but it is impossible now to read them without astonishment, mingled with shame. The following were the clauses of the bill before the House of Commons, which were struck out on the third reading:

"And whereas such measures ought to be adopted for the interest and happiness of the native inhabitants of the British Dominions in India, as may gradually tend to their advancement in useful knowledge, and to their religious and moral improvement:

Be it therefore further enacted, that the said Court of Directors shall be, and are hereby empowered and required to appoint and send out from time to time, a sufficient subject, Mr Montgomery Campbell threw out some severe reflections on the character of the converts on the coast of Coromandel, and even reprobated the idea of converting the Hindus Missionaries, he said, had made proselytes of the Pariars; but they were the lowest order of the people, and had degraded the religion they professed to embrace. Mr Swartz, whose character

number of fit and proper persons for carrying into effect the purposes aforesaid, by acting as schoolmasters, missionaries, or otherwise; every such person, before he is so appointed, or sent out, having produced to the said Court of Directors a satisfactory testimonial or certificate from the Archbishop of Canterbury or the Bishop of London for the time being, or from the Society in London for the Promotion of Christian Knowledge, or from the Society in Scotland for Propagating Christian Knowledge, of his sufficiency for these purposes.

"And be it further enacted, that the said Court of Directors are hereby empowered and required to give directions to the Governments of the respective Presidencies in India, to settle the designation, and to provide for the necessary and decent maintenance of the persons so to be sent out as aforesaid; and also to direct the said Governments to consider of and adopt such other measures, according to their discretion, as may appear to them most conducive to the ends aforesaid.

"Provided always, and be it further enacted, that if any person so sent out as aforesaid, shall at any time prove to be of immoral life and conversation, or shall be grossly negligent or remiss in the discharge of the duties of the station to which he shall have been so appointed, or shall engage, directly or indirectly, in any trade whatsoever, or shall accept of and hold any office, or employment, public or private, other than that to which he shall have been so appointed, the Governments of the respective Presidencies shall be empowered, and they are hereby required to remove him from his employment, and send him back to Great Britain; and the act of Government in so doing shall be final and conclusive, and shall not be examinable in any court of law whatsoever.

"And that due means of religious worship and instruction may also be provided for all persons of the Protestant communion in the service or under the protection of the said Company, be it enacted, that the said Court of Directors shall be, and are hereby empowered and required, from time to time, to send out and maintain in their several principal garrisons and factories, a sufficient number and supply of fit and proper ministers; and also to take and maintain a chaplain on board every ship in the service or employment of the said Company, being of the burthen of 700 tons or upwards: and that every charter-party to be entered into by the said Company for any ship of the burthen aforesaid, or any greater burthen, shall contain an express stipulation for the said Company to nominate and send on board such ship a chaplain, for the purposes aforesaid, at their nomination and expense. Provided always, that no such minister or chaplain shall be so appointed or sent out, until he shall first have been approved of by the Archbishop of Canterbury or the Bishop of London for the time being."—*Calcutta Review*, vol. iii. p. 222.

This was truly strange legislation—to turn the Court of Directors of the East India Company virtually into a Missionary Society; and the Governments at the three Presidencies into its Corresponding committees. Sad work they would have made of it! The generality of them were men indifferent to, and some of them were violently opposed to, efforts for the conversion of the natives of India. In the hands of such propagators, what success could Christianity be expected to have? It was vain to think that an Act of Parliament would inspire them with holy zeal. To say nothing of the important part which the Archbishop of Canterbury and the Bishop of London were was so deservedly high, had no reason to boast of the purity of his followers: they were proverbial for their profligacy. An example occurred to his recollection perfectly in point. Mr Swartz had been preaching for many hours to some of his proselytes on the heinousness of theft; and in the heat of his discourse had taken off his stock, when it and his gold buckle were stolen by one of his virtuous and enlightened congregation. Such was the description of natives who embraced Christianity. Men of high caste would spurn at the idea of renouncing the religion of their ancestors.

This story we should scarcely have thought worth noticing, unless as an example of the little dependence which is to be placed on the accounts given of missionaries, by persons who are indifferent or opposed to the propagation of Christianity among the heathen. There was not a word of truth in the whole statement. It may not, therefore, be improper to give a correct version of the story which Mr Campbell considered as so perfectly in point, but which he so grievously misrepresented.

Early one morning as Mr Swartz was travelling to Tanjore, he arrived at a village called Pudaloor, which was inhabited by Collaries, a set of men so infamous for stealing, that the name Collary, signifies a thief. They were even a kind of licensed robbers, as they paid annually 750 pagodas to the Rajah as a compensation for the outrages they committed. Having taken off his stock, and laid it on a sand-bank, he advanced a short way to look for the man who carried his clothes. In the mean while, the stock disappeared; it was stolen by some boys

ex officio, without regard to the personal character of the men, to act in the matter, it is plain that the Church of England, then in a lamentably low condition, was to be the main, probably the sole, instrument employed. The Church of Scotland might possibly furnish agents; but all other denominations of Christians were passed over as of no account; there was not so much as provision of liberty to them to go out to convert the Hindus, not even if some Bunyan, or Baxter, or Doddridge had been ready to embark on this errand of mercy.

Here we may mention, that in 1796, Robert Haldane, Esq., a gentleman of considerable property in Scotland, projected a mission to India on a large scale, and engaged, among other associates, the Rev. David Bogue of Gosport, the Rev. Greville Ewing of Edinburgh, and the Rev. William Innes of Stirling, to take part in it. Mr Haldane undertook to bear the whole expense of the mission, and with this view, he sold his beautiful estate of Airthrey, near Stirling; but the Directors of the East India Company refused to grant them permission to go out, and so the scheme was broken up.—*Memoirs of Robert Haldane, and of James A. Haldane*, p. 97, 113.

belonging to the village. The elder inhabitants had no concern in the theft, and on hearing of it, they even desired Mr Swartz to confine all the boys, and to punish them as severely as he pleased; but he did not think the trifle he had lost worth so much trouble. It is surely not wonderful, that boys, whose fathers were professed robbers, should commit a paltry theft of this description. There was not one Christian family in the whole village: all the inhabitants were heathens. The trifle of a buckle, therefore, Mr Swartz did not lose by any of the Christian converts, as Mr Campbell asserted, but by some heathen boys. Neither did he preach at that time, though that gentleman alleged, he preached many hours, and that too, on the heinousness of theft. He did not so much as converse with any man on the subject of religion. Mr Campbell, on finding that Mr Swartz had so completely confuted his misrepresentations, wrote an apology to him, and excused himself by saying, that his speech had been erroneously reported in the newspapers![1]

It is not unworthy of observation, that only a few months before Mr Campbell brought forward these charges against the converts on the coast of Coromandel, a considerable reformation had been effected through the instrumentality of Mr Swartz, among that very class of people whom he had stigmatized as Christian thieves. As the Collaries had of late committed terrible outrages in their plundering expeditions, government, after sending among them a number of sepoys without effect, applied to Mr Swartz to inquire into their thievish transactions. By his desire, the chiefs of the robbers appeared before him, and not only agreed to make restitution of the stolen property, but promised in writing to steal no more. This engagement they kept faithfully for eight months; but they then commenced their old trade, though not to the same extent as before. By desire of some of them, Mr Swartz at last began to instruct them; and when they had acquired a tolerable knowledge of the principles of Christianity, he baptized them. He now exhorted them to steal no more, but to work with their own hands; and when he afterwards visited them, he was happy to find their fields under excellent cultivation. "Now," said he, "one thing remains to be done: You must pay your tribute

[1] Rep. Christ. Know. Soc. p. 396, 464.

readily, and not wait till it is exacted by military force." Such had hitherto been their ordinary practice; but now they paid it without compulsion. The only complaint against them was that they refused to go on plundering expeditions, as they had done before. The Pagan Colleries even assembled together, and formed an encampment, threatening to extirpate Christianity out of the country; but after this commotion had lasted four months, they returned to their homes in peace, and began to cultivate their fields with more diligence than ever. As the water-courses in that part of the country had not been cleansed for fifteen years, in consequence of which, the cultivation of the land was impeded, and the crop diminished, Mr Swartz had of late proposed that the collector should advance money to clear them, and promised to send people to inspect the work. This was attended with so much success, that the inhabitants, instead of one kalam of corn, reaped four. In that district alone, the people raised near a hundred thousand kalams more than they had done before.[1]

In February 1798, died the venerable Christian Frederick Swartz, in the seventy-second year of his age, and the forty-eighth of his labours as a missionary in India. Hitherto, he had enjoyed almost an uninterrupted state of good health; but of late, his strength had been visibly on the decline, and he at length sunk into such a state of debility, that he was obliged to be lifted and carried about like a child. Though the pain he suffered was very severe, yet no murmuring word escaped from his lips; and at length, after exhibiting an interesting example of Christian faith, and hope, and joy, he expired without a struggle or a groan.

On the following day, the remains of this venerable man were interred in the chapel erected by him in the garden near his house. Serfogee, the young prince of Tanjore, came to see his corpse before the coffin was nailed down. He even bedewed it with his tears, covered it with a piece of gold cloth, and accompanied it to the grave. His fellow-missionaries designed that a funeral hymn should be sung on the way to the chapel; but the lamentations of the multitude, who had crowded into the garden, prevented it. At the funeral, the servant of Mr Swartz,

[1] Rep. Christ. Know. Soc. p. 386, 406.

in a deep tone of sorrow and despondency, exclaimed, "Now all our hopes are gone." Nor was this the sentiment of a solitary individual; it was the feeling of multitudes, both Christians and heathens, both great and small. On examining Mr Swartz's will, it was found that, with his usual benevolence, he had appointed the mission at Tanjore, the poor, and the establishments belonging to it, the principal heirs of his property. Though he had spent large sums on the mission during his life, yet he now left to it not less than between eight and ten thousand pounds.[1]

To mark their high sense of Mr Swartz's worth, and of the important services which he had rendered the country, the East India Company erected in Madras a monument to his memory, executed by the celebrated Mr Bacon. As the apostolic labours of this illustrious man were already well known in India, it was thought unnecessary to represent him, as that distinguished artist first intended, in his official character as a missionary. It was judged more expedient to represent the correspondence of his dying moments with the general tenor of his life.

The PRINCIPAL compartment of the monument is occupied with an alto-relievo representation of Mr Swartz, in the closing scene of his life. He is surrounded by a group of his infant pupils, to whom he afforded an asylum in his house, and by several of his fellow-labourers, who attended him in his last moments. One of the children is embracing his dying hand, and one of the missionaries is supporting his head; but the eyes of Mr Swartz are directed, and his hand is raised, toward an object in the upper part of the bas-relief, namely, the cross, which is borne by a descending angel, implying, that the death of Christ, the grand subject of his ministry, was now the chief support of his soul, "when flesh and heart were ready to faint and fail."

OVER the bas-relief, is the ark of the covenant, which was peculiarly the charge of the priests, and was a striking emblem of the constant theme of his preaching.

UNDER the bas-relief, are further emblems of the pastoral office, namely, the crosier; the gospel trumpet, with the banner

[1] Rep. Christ. Know. Soc. p. 473; Neure Geschichte, tom. v. p. 640, 790; Pearson's Mem. of Swartz, vol. ii. p. 412.

of the cross attached to it; and an open Bible, on which is inscribed our Lord's commission to his disciples, "Go ye into all the world, and preach the gospel to every creature."[1]

On this beautiful monument was engraved the following honourable yet characteristic inscription:

SACRED
To the Memory
of the REVEREND FREDERICK CHRISTIAN SWARTZ,
Whose life was one continued effort to imitate the example of his
BLESSED MASTER.
Employed as a Protestant Missionary from the Government of
Denmark,
And in the same character by the Society in England for the
Promotion of Christian Knowledge,
He, during a period of Fifty Years, "went about doing Good,"
Manifesting, in respect to himself, the most entire abstraction
from temporal views,
But embracing every opportunity of promoting both the temporal
and eternal welfare of others.
In him Religion appeared not with a gloomy aspect
or forbidding mien,
But with a graceful form and placid dignity.
Among the many fruits of his indefatigable labours,
was the erection of the Church at Tanjore.
The savings from a small Salary were, for many years, devoted
to the pious work,
And the remainder of the Expense supplied by Individuals
at his solicitation.
The Christian Seminaries at Ramnadporam and in the
Tinevelly province were established by him.
Beloved and honoured by Europeans,
He was, if possible, held in still deeper reverence by the Natives
of this country, of every degree and every sect:
And their unbounded confidence in his Integrity and Truth
Was, on many occasions, rendered highly beneficial
to the public service.
The Poor and the Injured
Looked up to him as an unfailing friend and advocate;
The Great and Powerful
Concurred in yielding him the highest homage ever paid in this
Quarter of the Globe to European virtue.
The late HYDER ALI CAWN,
In the midst of a bloody and vindictive war with the Carnatic,

[1] Evan. Mag. vol. xv. p. 8.

Sent orders to his officers "to permit the venerable Father SWARTZ
to pass unmolested, and shew him respect and kindness,
For he is a Holy Man, and means no harm to my Government."
The late TULJAJA, Rajah of Tanjore,
When on his deathbed, desired to entrust to his protecting care
His adopted Son, SERFOJEE, the present Rajah,
With the administration of all affairs of his Country.
On a spot of ground granted to him by the same Prince,
Two Miles east of Tanjore,
He built a House for his Residence, and made it an
Orphan Asylum.
Here the last 20 years of his life were spent in the Education
and Religious instruction of Children,
Particularly those of indigent parents, whom he gratuitously
maintained and instructed;
And here, on the 13th of February 1798,
Surrounded by his infant flock, and in the presence of several of
his disconsolate Brethren,
Entreating them to continue to make Religion
the first object of their care,
And imploring, with his last breath, the Divine Blessing
on their labours,
He closed his truly Christian Career, in the 72d year of his Age.
THE EAST INDIA COMPANY,
Anxious to perpetuate the Memory of such transcendent worth,
And gratefully sensible of the Public Benefits which resulted
from its influence,
Caused this Monument to be erected, Ann. Dom. 1807.[1]

Such testimonies of respect to the memory of Mr Swartz were not confined to Europeans, or even to Christians. The Rajah of Tanjore placed his portrait among the pictures of the princes of that country, in his principal hall of audience.[2] No son, indeed, could have a greater veneration for his father, than Serfogee had for Mr Swartz. In token of his respect for him, he ordered from England a monument of marble, which he erected in his capital, in the church where the good man preached, with a view, he said, to perpetuate the memory of Father Swartz, and to manifest the high esteem he had for the character of that great and good man, and the gratitude he owed him, as his

[1] Buchanan's Apology for promoting Christianity in India, p. 196.
[2] Buchanan's Researches, 3d edition, p. 63; Relig. Mon. vol. v. p. 278.

father, and his friend, the protector and guardian of his youth.[1] The Rajah, at the same time, gave proofs of his respect and attachment for Mr Swartz of a more substantial nature, and which, to the generous soul of that excellent man, would have afforded far higher satisfaction. Having erected a Charitable Institution for the maintenance and education of Hindu children of different castes, his affectionate regard for the memory of his late guardian induced him to form a similar establishment for the benefit of fifty Christian children; and, besides them, there were thirty poor Christians maintained and clothed in this Institution. He also gave orders that his Christian servants, civil and military, should not be denied liberty by their officers, of attending divine worship on the Sabbath, or on festival days, and that they should be excused from all other duty on these occasions.[2]

In May 1799, died at Calcutta the Rev. Mr Kiernander, aged eighty-eight years, nearly sixty of which he had passed in India. He was twice married, and by both his wives he came into the possession of large property, but with that disinterestedness which formed a striking feature of his character, he employed his wealth in supporting and extending the mission, which had hitherto struggled with considerable pecuniary difficulties. Besides exercising great liberality to the poor and needy, he built a dwelling-house for two missionaries, a church for the congregation, and a school-house for the children. On these and other objects of a missionary and benevolent nature he expended upwards of a hundred thousand rupees of his private fortune. But when old age came upon him, he was overtaken by worldly calamity. His son, who had also married a lady with a considerable fortune, lived in high style, and as a

[1] The inscription on the monument may be found in *Le Bas' Life of Bishop Middleton*, vol. ii. p. 399. Over the stone which covers the grave of Swartz, there is also an inscription in *English verse*, which is the more curious and interesting as it was the composition of the Rajah himself.—*Ibid.* vol. i. p. 215.

[2] Rep. Christ. Know. Soc. p. 496, 499, 504, 561, 565.

We regret to find the following statement by Mr Winslow, one of the American Missionaries, who visited Tanjore in 1828: "The Rajah has become very unfriendly to missionaries. He has yielded himself up to dissipation, and given immense sums to the Brahmans and to the temples, to make himself a Brahman. His only son is growing up in ignorance, making no steady application to any study or science."—(*Amer.*) *Miss. Herald*, vol. xxv. p. 140.

means of supporting it, was drawn by various parties, in accordance with the prevailing spirit of the times, into schemes for making money. He began especially to speculate in building houses, which was then a very lucrative way of employing money. Ready cash, however, was necessary to a considerable amount, and this was raised by means of bonds. To these bonds Mr Kiernander put his name as security, and thus the safety of his own property was risked upon the success of his son's projects. He had in his hands 80,000 rupees belonging to a lady who was his ward, and she having married a worthless attorney, he at once demanded her fortune, and would not wait for it. It was shewn distinctly, that if he waited three months, all the houses, finished and unfinished, with the materials, could be sold, and that after paying the sum due to his wife, and all other debts, Mr Kiernander would have remaining a surplus of two and a half lakhs of rupees. He still refused; and others of the creditors having taken the alarm, the whole property was attached by the Sheriff, and was sold at a ruinous loss. The mission property, which cost 100,000 rupees, was valued at only 10,000; a house which cost 30,000, was sold for 5000; and so of the rest.[1] No writ was issued against the person of Mr Kiernander or his son; but as it was expected, they left the whole of their property in the hands of their creditors, and retired to the Dutch settlement of Chinsurah.

Here Mr Kiernander was received very kindly by an excellent lady, and lived in her house. The Dutch Governor appointed him chaplain to the settlement, on a small salary of 60 rupees a month. In the wreck of the family fortunes, young Mrs Kiernander's dowry, which had been settled on her and her children, was invested profitably; and on the proceeds of it, the whole family lived very comfortably. Mr Kiernander was fond of botany, and at Chinsurah he had two gardens in which he delighted to cultivate his favourite science. The son having died, his family returned to Calcutta; but the good old man remained behind, provided with many comforts, suitable to his age, by his affectionate daughter-in-law. Notwithstanding his

[1] The Church, School, and Burying-ground were purchased by Charles Grant, Esq., and were invested by him in trust for the use of the Mission, and given over to the Society for Promoting Christian Knowledge.—*Calcutta Review*, vol. vii. p. 175.

fallen condition, he still retained his friends, and both visited and was visited by them. Finding himself, when eighty-five years of age, unable to discharge his duties as chaplain, he resigned the office, and retired to Calcutta, where he was welcomed most affectionately by his daughter-in-law's family. Such was the quiet and even course of his days in the evening of life. His spirit, chastened by affliction, had greatly profited by it. His character was just such as we love to see an old man exhibit, and which none display but they whose treasure is laid up in heaven. His heart was full of gratitude, and overflowing with love. His fortune was gone; he had had many trials, but he was full of peace. Even previous to his removing to Chinsurah, the mission in Calcutta had sunk into a languishing state; and, though various attempts were made to maintain it in existence, it was at length abandoned about the period of his death.[1]

In July 1802, Mr Gericke proceeded on a visit to Palamcotta, and the other southern districts, with the view of collecting and comforting the converts in that quarter of the country, who had of late suffered great distress in consequence of the rebellion of the Polygars. On arriving near the extremity of the peninsula, he found whole villages of heathens anxiously waiting for his arrival, in order to be further instructed and baptized by him. They had got acquainted with the native Priests, the Catechists, and the Christians, in that part of the country, and had already learned from them the Catechism. On hearing of Mr Gericke's arrival, they broke their idols to pieces, and converted their temples into churches, in which he instructed and baptized them by hundreds in a day. He afterwards formed them into regular congregations, procured for them catechists and schoolmasters, and made them choose, in each place, four elders. These examples awakened the whole country, and when he was about to leave it, the inhabitants of many other villages sent messages to him, requesting him to remain some time longer among them, and perform in their towns the same good work which he had executed in those of their neighbours. With this request it was not in his power to comply; but he recommended them to the care of the native priests and catechists. In the

[1] Neure Geschichte, tom. v.; Rep. Christ. Know. Soc. p. 278, 445.; Calcutta Review, vol. vii. p. 136, 155, 164, 167, 172, 177, 184.

course of this journey, Mr Gericke baptized about thirteen hundred persons; and after he left the country, the native teachers formed eighteen new congregations, and baptized two thousand seven hundred people, so that the whole number amounted to no fewer than four thousand.[1]

Highly as we respect the character of Mr Gericke, we cannot but express our deep regret at the course he pursued on this occasion. Had the most of these people afforded such evidence of their sincere conversion to the Christian faith as to warrant their baptism, this might have ranked among the most extraordinary events in the history of the church in ancient or modern times. But there are no grounds for forming such an exalted idea of it. Most of these people, indeed, possessed little knowledge of Christianity, and still less of its spirit: their chief inducement for professing themselves Christians, was a hope which they foolishly entertained, that they would then be exempted from the public burdens, or gain other worldly ends.[2]

In 1806, the Rev. Dr Buchanan visited the principal missionary stations on the coast of Coromandel, and has presented us with an interesting account of his journey, and a general view of their state at that period.

"Tranquebar," says he, "was the scene of the first Protestant mission in India. There are at present three missionaries here superintending the Hindu congregations. Yesterday I visited the church built by Ziegenbalg. His body lies on one side of the altar, and that of his fellow-missionary Grundler on the other. They laid the foundation for evangelizing India, and then departed, 'having finished the work which was given them to do.' I saw also the dwelling-house of Ziegenbalg, in the lower apartment of which the registers of the church are still kept. In these I found the name of the first heathen baptized by him, and recorded in his own handwriting in the year 1707. The missionaries told me that religion had suffered much at Tranquebar of late years from European infidelity. French principles had corrupted the Danes, and rendered them indifferent to their own religion, and consequently hostile to the conversion

[1] Relig. Mon. vol. i. p. 236.; Rep. Christ. Know. Soc. p. 514: Neure Geschichte, tom. vi. p. 6.

[2] Miss. Trans. vol. iii. p. 100, 101, 105, 118, 133, 140, &c.

of the Hindus. 'Religion,' said they, 'flourishes more among the natives of Tanjore, and in other provinces where there are few Europeans, than here or at Madras; for we find that European example in the large towns, is the bane of Christian instruction.'

"On the day after my arrival at Tanjore, I visited the Rajah in company with Major Blackburne, the British resident. When the first ceremonial was over, his highness conducted us to the grand saloon, which was adorned with the portraits of the kings of Tanjore. All around there was a display of gold, and silver, and mirrors, English paintings, musical instruments, orreries, portfolios of oriental drawings, and many other curiosities both of nature and art. Finding that I wished to hear the music of the vina, he ordered up the chief musician. He has a band of twenty performers, twelve of whom play on the vina, and one on the harp.

"My visit to the Rajah was very long. Our chief conversation related to Mr Swartz. When I first mentioned his name, his highness led me up to the picture of the reverend apostle, which is placed among the portraits of his predecessors. I smiled to see Swartz's picture among these Hindu kings, and thought with myself many would consider such a combination scarcely possible. While the harp and the vina played, I conversed with the Rajah about that good man, and of his present happiness in the heavenly state. I afterwards thanked him in the name of the Society in England for Promoting Christian Knowledge, and of all Mr Swartz's friends in India, for his kindness to that excellent man, and to his successors, and particularly for his recent acts of benevolence to the Christians within his dominions. Before my departure, a servant came up with four pieces of gold cloth of different kinds, which the Rajah presented to me. He then, agreeably to the usual etiquette, put a chaplet of flowers around my head, and a bracelet of flowers on my arms, and leading me and the resident, one in each hand, to the steps of the hall, he bowed and retired.

"Last Sunday was an interesting day at Tanjore. It being rumoured that a friend of Mr Swartz had arrived, the people assembled from all quarters. Three sermons were preached that day in three different languages. At eight o'clock in the morning we proceeded to the church built by Mr Swartz within the fort. From the pulpit of that venerable man I preached in English from these words, 'And the gospel must first be published among all nations.' The English gentlemen attended, civil and military, with the missionaries, catechists, and British soldiers. When this service was ended, the congregation of Hindus assembled in the same church, and filled the aisles and porches. The Tamil service commenced with some forms of prayer, in which all the congregation joined with great fervour. A chapter of the Bible was then read, and a hymn of Luther's sung. After a short extempore prayer, during which the whole congregation knelt on the floor, Dr John delivered an animated discourse in the Tamil language, from these words, 'Jesus stood and cried, saying, If any man thirst, let him come unto me and drink." As Mr Whitfield, on his first going to Scotland, was surprised at the rustling of the leaves of the Bible, which took place immediately on his pronouncing his text, (so different from any thing he had seen in his own country) so I was here surprised at the sound of the iron pen engraving the palmyra leaf. Many persons had olas in their hands writing the sermon in Tamil short-hand. Mr Kolhoff assured me that some of the elder students and catechists will not lose a word of the preacher, if he speak deliberately. It is an old regulation of the mission, that the sermon of the morning should be read to the schools in the evening, by the catechist, from his palmyra leaf.

"There is another custom among them which greatly pleased me. In the midst of the discourse the preacher sometimes puts a question to the congregation, who answer it, without hesitation, in one voice. The object is to keep their attention awake, and the minister generally prompts the answer himself. Thus, suppose he is saying, 'My brethren, it is true that your profession of the faith of Christ is attended with some reproach, and that you have lost your caste with the Brahmans. But be of good cheer and say, Though we have lost our caste and inheritance amongst men, we shall receive in heaven a new name and a better inheritance, through Jesus Christ our Lord.' He then adds, 'What, my beloved brethren, shall you obtain in heaven?' They answer, 'A new name and a better inheritance, through Jesus Christ our Lord.' It is impossible for a stranger not to be affected with this scene. Children of tender years inquire of each other, and attempt the responses. This custom was introduced by Ziegenbalg, who proved its use by long experience.

"After the sermon, I returned with the missionaries into the vestry or library of the church. Here I was introduced to the elders and catechists of the congregation. Among others came Sattianaden, the Hindu preacher. He is now advanced in years, and his black locks have grown grey. As I returned from the church, I saw the Christian families going back in crowds to the country, and the boys looking at their olas. What a contrast, thought I, is this to the scene at Jagganath![1] Here there is becoming dress, humane affections, and rational discourse. Here I see no skulls, no self-torture, no self-murder, no dogs and vultures tearing human flesh! Here the Christian virtues are found in exercise by the feeble-minded Hindu, in a vigour and purity which will surprise those who have never known the native character but under the greatest disadvantages, as in Bengal. It certainly surprised myself; and when I reflected on the moral conduct, upright dealing, decent dress, and decorous manners of the native Christians of Tanjore, I found in my breast a new evidence of the peculiar excellence and benign influence of the Christian faith.

"At four o'clock in the afternoon, we attended divine service at the chapel in the Mission Garden, out of the fort. Mr Horst preached in the Portuguese language. The organ here accompanied the voice in singing. I sat on a granite stone which covered the grave of Swartz. In the evening Mr Kolhoff presided at the exercise in the schools: on which occasion the Tamil sermon was repeated; and the boys' olas examined.

"In consequence of my having expressed a wish to hear Sattianaden preach, Mr Kolhoff had given notice that there would be divine service on the Monday. The chapel accordingly was crowded at an early hour. Sattianaden delivered a discourse full of fire in the Tamil language, with much natural eloquence, and with visible effect. In quoting a passage from Scripture, he desired a lower minister to read it, listening to it as to a record;

[1] Dr Buchanan had visited the temple of Jagganath in Orissa, on his way to the South of India, and had witnessed the horrid scenes which are connected with the worship of that celebrated idol.

and then proceeded to the illustration. The responses by the audience were more frequently called for than in the former discourse. After the sermon, I went up to Sattianaden, and addressed him in a few words, expressive of my hope that he would be faithful unto death. The aged Christians crowded around us and shed tears. He said he was unworthy to preach before his teachers.

"I had long conversations with the missionaries relative to the present circumstances of the Tanjore mission. It is in a languishing state at this moment, in consequence of the war on the Continent of Europe. Two of its sources have dried up, the Royal College at Copenhagen, and the Orphan-house at Halle, in Germany. Their remaining resource from Europe is the stipend of the Society for Promoting Christian Knowledge, whom they never mention but with emotions of gratitude and affection. But this supply is by no means commensurate with the increasing number of their churches and schools. The chief support of the mission is derived from itself. Mr Swartz had in his lifetime acquired considerable property, through the kindness of the English government and of the native princes. When he was dying, he said, 'Let the cause of Christ be my heir.' When his colleague, the pious Mr Gericke, was departing, he also bequeathed his property to the mission.[1] And now Mr Kolhoff gives from his private funds upwards of a thousand pagodas a year; not that he can well afford so large a sum, but the mission is so extended, that he gives it, he told me, to preserve the new and remote congregations in existence.

"Leaving Tanjore, I passed through the woods inhabited by the Collaries, many of whom are now humanized by Christianity, and proceeded to Trichinopoly. The first church built by Swartz is at this place. It is a large building, capable of containing perhaps two thousand people. The aged missionary, Mr Pohle, presides over this church, and over the native congregations at this place. Christianity flourishes; but I found that here, as at other places, there is a famine of Bibles."[2]

[1] Mr Gericke left to the Vepery Mission 15,000 Star Pagodas, besides the reversion of a considerable sum and a large dwelling-house, on the demise of his widow.

[2] Buchanan's Researches, p. 61; Pearson's Memoirs of Dr Buchanan, vol. ii. p. 28, 32; Christian Observer, vol. vi. p. 335.

In 1825, the missions at Madras or Vepery, Trichinopoly, and Tanjore, which had hitherto been supported chiefly by the Society in London for Promoting Christian Knowledge, were transferred to the Society for the Propagation of the Gospel in Foreign Parts.[1] These stations, and also that at Tranquebar, had for many years been in a state of lamentable and increasing decay. In consequence of the decline of doctrinal purity, and of vital piety in the churches of Germany during the latter part of the eighteenth century, few or no successors worthy of Swartz and Gericke were to be found. Of the small number of missionaries who were sent out, some, by their unworthy conduct, helped to injure and destroy what they were employed to preserve and extend. Others, more recently, fell early victims of the climate, or of the opposition which they encountered in their earnest endeavours to repair the mischiefs which, from this and other causes, had been so long in unresisted operation; while the few venerable survivors of the ancient German School were quite unequal to the burdens of their situation, and to the care of the several missions. Great numbers of the native Christians in the Tinnevelly district, relapsed into heathenism; and, indeed, all accounts agree in representing the state of morals and religion, even at the principal stations, as exceedingly low. Much of this melancholy state of things may, we doubt not, be traced to the laxity of the missionaries in the admission of the natives into the church, under the common but mistaken idea, that if they were once brought to an outward profession of Christianity, they would be more likely to be afterwards brought to the saving knowledge of the gospel.[2]

Such was the state of these missions when they were transferred to the Society for the Propagation of the Gospel in Foreign Parts. Under its auspices, they were much extended, and were carried on with greatly increased vigour. New missionaries, chiefly belonging to the Church of England, were provided; numerous stations were formed in various parts of the

[1] Miss. Reg. 1825, p. 199, 327.

[2] Pearson's Memoirs of Dr Buchanan, vol. ii. p. 26, 43; Strachan's Examination of Mr Grove's Brief Account of the Tinnevelly Mission, p. 50; Hoole's Personal Narrative of a Mission to the South of India, p. 229; Memoir of the Rev. C. T. E. Rhenius, p. 197, 219, 242, 280. Quarterly Chronicle of London Miss. Soc. vol. iii. p. 503, 504; Hough's Hist. vol. iii. p. 469, 502, 506; vol. iv. 217, 219, 223.

country, and great numbers of converts were made from among the natives, both Hindus and Roman Catholics; but we fear that the fallacious principle to which we have just adverted, was now acted on more largely than ever. Many villages in the south of India, entered into an agreement to renounce their idols, and to place themselves under Christian instruction. The inhabitants of a village often came over in a body, and in some instances, they gave up their temples and their idols.[1] In such wholesale conversions, we confess, we have no confidence. They arise generally not from knowledge or conviction, but from worldly views and motives. Such converts, instead of adorning their Christian profession, often bring disgrace upon it, and prove a main hinderance to the conversion of others.

In July 1833, Dr Wilson, Bishop of Calcutta, addressed a pastoral letter to the missionaries in his diocese, and to the congregations under their care, requiring them to give up the distinction of castes, so far as it affected religious practice, with particular reference to the Tanjore and other missions in the south of India, in which it had been tolerated ever since their commencement. The means employed by his predecessors to abate the evil having proved unavailing, he felt himself constrained, "as the pastor and bishop of souls in that diocese, to prescribe to them what seemed to him essential to the preservation of the purity of the Christian faith." "The distinction of castes," he wrote, "must be abandoned decidedly, immediately, finally; and those who profess to belong to Christ, must give this proof of their having really 'put off, concerning the former conversation, the old, and having put on the new man in Christ Jesus.'" In issuing this order, the Bishop referred simply to usages arising out of caste in the church, so far as religious ordinances were concerned. Civil and domestic relations he exempted from express censure, trusting that these would be corrected by degrees, or find their proper level. The evils referred to by him were unquestionably very great;[2] they had been far too

[1] Miss. Reg. 1844, p. 176; Ibid. 1845, p. 141, 152; Ibid. 1846, p. 138.

[2] The following list of evils which arose out of the toleration of caste in the missions in the south of India, was given by the Bishop of Calcutta:—

"As to *religious services*, (1.) The different castes sat on different mats, and (2.) on different sides of the church, (3.) to which they entered by different doors. (4.) They approached the Lord's table at different times; and (5.) had different cups, or managed long tolerated, and called loudly for a remedy. The authority assumed by the Bishop, was, we doubt not, in perfect confor-

to get the catechists to change the cup before the lower caste began to communicate. (6.) Even the missionary clergyman was persuaded to receive the Holy Supper last. (7.) They would allow no sponsors at baptism of an inferior caste. (8.) They had separate divisions in the burial grounds; and (9.) none of inferior castes could perform the service; (10.) after which they were all compelled to bathe as being unclean; and (11.) for eight days the howling women continued their heathen custom of mourning. (12.) The country priest or catechist would not reside in a village of Pariars; nor (13.) receive them into his house for instruction; nor (14.) would a Sudra congregation receive a Pariar teacher; and (15.) when a congregation was convened, the inferior classes were all excluded. (16.) Separation between the children after eight years of age was insisted on.

"In the *domestic circle*, (17.) The wife was not allowed to sit or eat with her husband, but was treated as his slave, or rather as part of his goods and chattels. Nor (18.) was she permitted to sit with her husband at church. (19.) No intermarriages were allowed between different castes; but (20.) illicit connections, intemperate feasts, &c., were connived at fast enough; and the Christian married his daughter to a heathen of his own caste rather than to a Christian of a lower one. (21.) The widows of Sudras were not allowed to marry again; (22.) Virgin-widows of betrothed husbands were subject to the same law. (23.) Brahmans were consulted as to the lucky time for marrying. (24.) The Christian put away a Christian wife he did not like, and took a second heathen one. (25.) The ill effects of their going to a Christian church to be married were removed by charms, and (26.) by the custom of Tom-Toms and heathen processions after they left the church. (27.) Ceremonies of purifications as to females were retained as among the heathen. (28.) The children were marked with various heathen insignia; (29.) These marks they wore when among heathens, and obliterated them in Christian society. (30.) So they had Christian names, but also heathen ones, for passing current in the world, often after heathen gods.

"As to *general society*, (31.) they considered themselves as of a superior race; and (32.) the Pariars born to be their slaves. (33.) They would not drink of the same well; nor (34) live in the same street; nor (35.) take food from the same vessel. But (36.) broke all the earthen vessels a Pariar had touched as being defiled; (37.) they would not receive from him even the sacred waters of the Ganges to save their own lives. (38.) The touch of a Pariar made them unclean. (39.) Christians who retained caste were admitted to the festivities, often indecent, of the heathens, (40.) paid reverence to their gods, (41.) made vows at the Pagodas, (42.) and called for the Brahmans to exorcise the sick.

"As to the *laws of caste*, they proceeded (43.) from the Shasters or pretended Sacred Books; (44.) the initiation was according to the Shasters; (45.) the determination of offences was according to the Shasters; (46.) the caste tribunals judged according to the Shasters. (47.) These tribunals were sometimes held in Christian churches; and (48.) upon their decision the condemned Christian was forbidden to partake of the Lord's Supper.

"Finally, as to the due *order of society*, (49.) the lowest vagabond, a filthy, drunken beggar or thief, might contemn the most pious, learned, respectable man, a possessor of land and property, attired in the most becoming manner, and sustaining the office of a catechist perhaps, if of an inferior rank; and (50.) all this was unchangeable from age to age, from generation to generation."—*Two Charges delivered to the Clergy in the Diocese of Calcutta*, by D. Wilson, *Bishop of Calcutta*, in *Christian Intelligencer*, vol. v. p. 270.

mity with episcopal claims and usage; and though he expresses himself with greater moderation in some of the details into which he enters for the abolition of particular practices, than is manifested in the general order, yet it may be questioned whether the attempt to destroy the usages arising out of the distinction of castes with so high a hand, was an advisable measure, or likely to prove effectual in accomplishing the end in view. At the same time, it is probable that the exercise of somewhat of authority was necessary in order to put down the evil.[1]

This question of the abolition of caste proved an occasion of much trouble. Some of the natives addressed the Governor of Madras on the subject. Much misapprehension and misrepresentation appear to have been excited in regard to it. In Tanjore and the out-stations, upwards of 1200 persons, including two of the native priests, seceded, rather than submit to the new regulations; but the latter, after some time, submitted. Years passed away without the opposition being subdued; nor is it yet at an end. In Madras, there was still a large class of professed Christians who were determined to uphold caste, and who sought to stir up the converts in other missions to maintain it. It would almost seem as if the efforts to put it down had infused new vitality into it. On this subject, the converts manifested a resolution and perseverance quite unusual with Hindus. Still, however, the measures adopted for putting down caste, were attended with considerable success. Though some refused to receive the communion, except on condition of being protected from the contact of Pariars, and on this not being yielded to them, walked out of the church when it was administered, yet persons of different castes might now be seen receiving the Lord's Supper together. Even, however, of those who yielded, some acted more from submission to the authority of man, or with a view to retaining or regaining their situations, than from conviction of duty, or the exercise of the spirit of the gospel. Though legislation may regulate outward acts, it cannot change the inward feelings, and these will ever be ready to shew themselves when it can be done with impunity. We accordingly find that in private life, and in all that regarded social intercourse, caste still maintained its influence among

[1] Miss. Reg. 1834, p. 178; Ibid. 1835, p. 459.

the congregations in Southern India. The spirit and power of caste were still to be found among native Christians, who yet had professedly renounced it.[1]

With regard to the total numbers received into the congregations connected with the several missions, we are not able to state them up to a recent date; but we find that up to 1802 (exclusive of a few years, for which we have not the returns), they amounted to about 34,824.[2] This includes not only converts from heathenism, but many Romanists, who came over to the Protestant faith, and children baptized in their infancy, many of whom, it is to be feared, by their conduct in after life, forfeited all title to the name of Christians. In the course of the

[1] Miss. Reg. 1836, p. 207; Ibid. 1837, p. 131; (Amer.) Miss. Her. vol. xlii. p. 20, 131; Ibid. vol. xliv. p. 260; Sum. Orient. Christ. Spect. vol. i. p. 272, 280; Bp. Corrie's Memoirs, p. 579; Cal. Christ. Observer, vol. xiii. p. 6; vol. xix. p. 203.

[2] In 1802, the whole numbers received in the Tranquebar Mission from its commencement, including converts from Romanism and children baptized in their infancy (exclusive of those in the year 1799, for which we have not the returns,) amounted to 20,126.—*Neure Geschichte*, tom. v. p. 157; *Hough*, vol. iii. p. 355.

In 1802, the whole numbers received in the Madras or Vepery Mission from its commencement (exclusive of those for 1780, 1782, and 1787), amounted to 4,838.—*Neure Geschichte*, tom. i. p. 1181; *Hough*, vol. iii. p. 444, 450, 460, 473.

In 1802, the whole numbers received in the Trichinopoly Mission (exclusive of those for 1780, 1781, 1782, 1783, and 1798), amounted to 2343.—*Hough*, vol. iii. p. 514, 530, 535, 541, 548.

In 1802, the whole number of persons received into the congregation at Tanjore from 1778 (excepting those for 1777, which were wanting in the church books), amounted to 3775, namely,

Pagans, ...	2225
Roman Catholics, ...	863
Children born in the Congregation, . . .	687

—*Neure Geschichte*, tom. v. p. 944; *Rep. Christ. Know. Soc.*

Up to about 1804, the number of baptisms at Negapatam, amounted to 435.—*Hough*, vol. iii. p. 506.

In 1806, the whole numbers received in the Cuddalore Mission from its commencement (exclusive of those for 1753, 1757, 1758, 1759, and 1768), amounted to 2105.—*Hough*, vol. iii. p. 480, 486, 494, 499, 508.

In 1786, the whole numbers received in the Calcutta Mission from its commencement was 1202, *Hough*, vol. iii. p. 17, 34, 39; but in this number there were probably included many English, who formed what was called the English congregation. "On a careful examination," says a well-informed writer in the Calcutta Review, "we find that Mr Kiernander baptized at least 209 adult heathens, and received into the congregation 300 papists.—*Cal. Rev.* vol. vii. p. 172.

The above numbers amount in all to 34,824. Several of the years for which we have not the returns, were years of war and of great distress in the country; and the numbers received in them were probably small. In the above-mentioned number the 4000 baptized by Mr Gericke and his assistants in 1802, are not included. See p. 164.

present century great numbers were added to these; but we are not able to make even an approximation to the amount.

In June 1846, the following were the numbers connected with the congregations of the Propagation Society in the south of India :—

	Men.	Women.	Children.	TOTAL.
Baptized, . .	4158	5129	7330	16617
Catechumens,[1]	2035	2099	3010	7144
	6193	7228	10340	23761

The congregations and the numbers of the baptized have greatly increased of late years. They are scattered over a large extent of country; but the greatest numbers are found in Tinnevelly.[2]

The external establishment of the Tanjore Mission, its churches, mission-houses, schools, and Christian villages, has been pronounced superior to every thing of the kind connected with any Mission or any Society in the country. Yet Tanjore

[1] Unbaptized persons under Christian instruction.

[2] Sum. Orient. Christ. Spect. vol. i. p. 440.

The numbers connected with the Tranquebar Mission are not included in the above table. It was all along a Danish Mission, but during the present century it was in a very declining condition, and it, at length, became extinct or nearly so.—*Malcolm's Travels in South-Eastern Asia*, vol. ii. p. 68. In 1841, the Royal Danish College of Missions formed a connection with the Dresden Missionary Society for the express purpose of reviving it. But when in 1845 Tranquebar was ceded to the East India Company, that connection was dissolved, and the mission is now carried on exclusively by the Dresden Society, which has also stations at Vepery, Mayaveram, and Puthucotta. The missionaries of the Dresden Society are now the only missionary body which is favourable to the maintenance of caste. This may partly be accounted for by the peculiar character of that Society. It is supported chiefly by what is known as the *Old Lutheran* party in Germany, which was called into being in its present form by the ill-judged and arbitrary proceedings of Frederick William III. King of Prussia, who laboured to form a union between the Lutheran and the Reformed Churches in his dominions. One effect of these proceedings was to produce in the minds of multitudes a powerful re-action in favour of Lutheranism, including its doctrines of the ubiquity of the body of Christ and of the real presence in the Lord's Supper, and its semi-popish ceremonies, such as placing a crucifix and burning tapers on the altar. They sympathize extensively with the Tractarian movement in England, though they would not perhaps be found willing to return to Rome.—*Calcutta Christian Observer*, vol. xix. p. 198, 203. It is probably this spirit of the *olden* times which leads them to look with a favourable eye upon caste.

is from many causes an unfavourable soil for the growth and progress of Christianity. Hinduism and Mahomedanism are under the special patronage of the Court. Temples and sacred structures of various kinds are seen rising in every street. A continual round of festivals, processions, and spectacles, occupy the heathen mind and exclude all serious thought. Every one almost whom you meet is directly or indirectly connected with the court or employed in its service; and being in some way or other dependent upon it, they are, like all dependents of native courts, of the court religion. No one who is unacquainted with Tanjore, can conceive how powerful, and apparently how youthful, heathenism is in that city, and how difficult it is, in the face of opposition and scorn from every caste and every quarter, there to propagate or to embrace Christianity.[1]

Before we conclude our account of this important mission, we cannot help noticing the remarkable fact of the longevity of many of the missionaries, especially as compared with the early death or return home of English and American missionaries. Though some died soon after their arrival, while others did not live longer than is common in other missions, yet there was a much larger proportion than is usual in India, who attained to a good old age. Whether this is to be ascribed to original constitution, or to a more simple style of living, or to any other special cause, we are not able to say; but the subject is not unworthy of inquiry.[2]

[1] Sum. Orient. Christ. Spect. vol. i. p. 280.

[2] Of the missionaries who came out in the course of the eighteenth century, we have taken down the principal names, fifty in number; and we find that of these sixteen, or nearly one-third, attained to old age, some of them indeed to extreme old age, as will be seen by the following list:—

Names.	Period of Service.	Names.	Period of Service.
Huttemann, .	31 years.	Caemmerer, .	46 years.
Cnoll, .	35	Swartz, .	48
Breithaupt, .	36	Fabricius, .	50
Gericke, .	36	Kolhoff (Father),	53
Zeglin, .	40	Kolhoff (Son, born in India), .	57
*Pohle, .	41	*Rottler, .	58
John, .	43	Kiernander, .	59
Klein, .	44		

Those marked * were still living at the age we have given.

Schultze after being twenty-four years in India returned to Halle, and it appears he lived till 1799, when he must probably have been upwards of 100 years of age, as he came out to India in 1719.—*Niecamp. Meier, Hough*, and *Miss. Reg.* passim, *Grinfield's Sketches of the Danish Mission*, p. 138.

SECT. II.—GREENLAND.

In 1708, Mr Hans Egede, soon after he was settled in the ministry at a place called Vogen, in Norway, recollected having read of Christians, and churches, and other monuments of our holy religion, in Greenland.[1] Anxious to learn the present state of that country, he applied for information to a friend in Bergen, who had been engaged in the whale-fishery, and in consequence of the accounts he received, he began to feel a deep concern for the inhabitants, who, he apprehended, must now, from want of Christian instructors, have relapsed into a state of absolute heathenism. He thought his countrymen were bound in a particular manner to carry the gospel to them, as they were not only descended from Christian ancestors, but were of the same extraction as themselves, and were considered as subjects of the same government. He himself had a strong desire to go and make known the gospel to them; but on reflecting upon the subject, he was exceedingly perplexed. On the one hand, the concern which he felt for the glory of God, and the salvation of the Greenlanders, urged him forward to the work; on the other, the consideration that he was already settled in the ministry, the necessity of providing for his family, and the difficulties and dangers of the attempt, deterred him from it. He, therefore, prayed to God, that he would deliver him from this temptation, and preserve him from plunging himself and his family, by any rash project, in misfortune and ruin.

In 1710, Mr Egede, with the view of relieving his mind, resolved to address an humble memorial concerning the conversion of the Greenlanders, to His Majesty the King of Denmark,

[1] The Norwegians or Icelanders settled in Greenland early in the eleventh century. We have accounts of their bishops for about three hundred years afterwards; but since the beginning of the fifteenth century, little or nothing has been heard of them; and for a considerable time, Greenland itself was almost entirely forgotten. Many ruins of churches and other buildings, however, are still found in the country.—*Crantz's History of Greenland*, vol. i. 249, 252, 264; *Cranz Fortsetzung der Historie von Gronland*, p. 342; *Egede (Hans) Nachricht der Gronlandischen Mission*, p. 67, 88; *Graah's Narrative of an Expedition to the East Coast of Greenland in search of the Lost Colonies*, p. 1, 7, 36, 38, 43.

in the hope that the work would be undertaken by some others, who might engage in it more conveniently than himself. He was afraid, however, that such a proposal from so obscure an individual would meet with little attention, and that, as it would require a considerable sum of money to carry it into effect, there was little hope of its being done while the war lasted in which Denmark was then engaged with Sweden. He forwarded, however, a copy of his memorial to the Bishop of Bergen, the port from which the trade to Greenland was chiefly carried on, and to the Bishop of Drontheim, to whose diocese he belonged, entreating them, at the same time, to recommend to government his proposal for the conversion of the Greenlanders. The bishops, in reply, commended his zeal, and promised to forward his memorial to court with the view of its being laid before His Majesty. The mind of Mr Egede was now in some measure set at rest: he committed the whole affair into the hands of God, in the hope that he would overrule every thing for his own glory.

Hitherto the whole plan had lain concealed in his own bosom; he had not mentioned it even to his wife, as he was apprehensive she would be completely adverse to it. It could now, however, be no longer concealed. Some of their friends who about this time visited Bergen, having heard of his proposal, wrote to him on their return, censuring in the strongest terms his fool-hardy project. His own, and his wife's mother, now endeavoured to divert him from his purpose, representing to him in the most affecting manner the dangers and distress into which he would plunge himself and his family. Mrs Egede was confounded by their representations, and even he himself was so overcome by the entreaties and the tears of his friends, that he repented of his rashness in ever proposing to go to Greenland, and promised to remain at home in the situation in which he had been already placed by Providence. He thought he had now done his utmost for the conversion of the Greenlanders, and that God could not require from him more, as he was withheld from the attempt chiefly by his relations, and in such an undertaking it was impossible for him to act and suffer alone. He even became quite easy in his mind, and thanked God that, through these circumstances, he had delivered him from this temptation. His tranquillity, however, was of short duration: that solemn declaration of the Redeemer struck his conscience, and destroyed all his peace: "He that loveth father or mother more than me, is not worthy of me; and he that loveth son or daughter more than me, is not worthy of me." His mind was now thrown into a state of terrible perturbation: he had no rest night or day. His wife observed his deep distress, and did her best to comfort him; but all in vain. Growing at length impatient, she called herself unfortunate in having given her heart, and been united in marriage, to a man who wished to plunge himself and her in all manner of misfortunes. These circumstances drove him almost desperate; he now desired death rather than life. In the mean while, various little occurrences, particularly the hatred and envy, the lies and calumnies of some wicked people, rendered their situation at Vogen very uncomfortable. Mr Egede submitted it to the serious consideration of his wife, whether they might not view this as a punishment on account of their unwillingness to deny themselves, and to endure hardships for the sake of Christ. By his advice, she referred the matter to God in humble prayer, and she at length so completely changed her views, that instead of a rooted aversion, she felt a strong desire to go to Greenland.

Having gained the consent of his wife, Mr Egede thought he had vanquished all his difficulties. He again sent an humble memorial respecting the conversion of the Greenlanders, to the College of Missions at Copenhagen, and to the new Bishop of Bergen. He also wrote letters to him and to the Bishop of Drontheim, entreating them to recommend his proposals as far as lay in their power; but they, in reply, informed him that he must wait with patience until the return of peace, as in the present distressed state of the country, nothing of importance could be undertaken by the court. In this manner, Mr Egede was disappointed, year after year; yet such was his zeal for a mission to Greenland, that nothing could divert him from his purpose.

As, however, there was little appearance of the return of peace, Mr Egede's patience was at last exhausted. He therefore resolved to go and prosecute the object of his memorial in person, especially as he was doubtful whether the individuals to whom he had entrusted it were zealous and active in promoting it. Meanwhile a report was circulated that a ship from Bergen had been wrecked in the Greenland seas, and that the crew, on escaping to land, were not only murdered, but devoured by the savages. Mr Egede was at first considerably alarmed by this account, particularly as many people took occasion from it to represent the Greenlanders in a most frightful light, and to rouse the fears of his wife. They both, however, consoled themselves with the thought, that God is able to preserve his people under all circumstances when in the path of duty. Before proceeding on his journey, Mr Egede had wished to resign his charge, on condition that his successor would grant him a small annuity until he was provided for in Greenland or in some other quarter; but as the bishop wrote him that no person would accept of so inconsiderable a benefice on such terms, he relinquished it without any provision of the kind.

In July 1718, Mr Egede set off with his family for Bergen, and on his arrival was viewed by the inhabitants of that town as a kind of wonder. Many alleged he must have had visions and revelations to induce him to embark in so wild an enterprise; yet some, when they understood his design, regarded him in a more favourable light. With the view of carrying his plan into effect, he endeavoured to find persons who would embark in the trade to Greenland; but as the traffic of the Norwegians with that country had of late been destroyed by the Dutch, nobody would hear a syllable from him on that subject, at least while the war lasted. Some, however, said that if peace were restored, and if government would assist them, they might perhaps make the attempt. As the unexpected fall of Charles the Twelfth, at the siege of Fredeickshall in Norway, gave rise to hopes of a speedy peace, Mr Egede seized the opportunity, repaired to Copenhagen in person, and presented to the College of Missions various propositions relative to a mission to Greenland. His Majesty Frederick the Fourth, who appears to have taken a special interest in the propagation of Christianity among the heathen, was friendly to the design; and even did Mr Egede the honour of conversing with him on the subject of his proposals.

In consequence of these communications, orders were transmitted from His Majesty to the magistrates of Bergen to make inquiry, Whether the trade to Greenland could be carried on with advantage from that port, and whether any of the inhabitants were disposed to embark in it? In obedience to these orders, the captains and pilots who had been engaged in the whale-fishery, were assembled in the council-house, to give their opinions concerning the state of the country, and the prospects of the trade: but as they were afraid that if their testimony were favourable, they might be required to go thither, and even to remain for some time, they deviated entirely from the representations which they had previously given to Mr Egede, describing the country as most inhospitable, and the navigation as most dangerous. His hopes of assistance from man now vanished, and his heart even began to murmur against God, who had for so many years cherished in his breast an unquenchable desire to make known the gospel in Greenland, while yet he blasted all his schemes for carrying it into effect. Depressed as he sometimes was with such distressing thoughts, he still poured out his heart to God in prayer, in the hope that he might yet crown his endeavours with success.

He now applied to individuals of some property, and urged them by all the arguments he could devise, to risk a portion of it on the trade to Greenland. Influenced by his earnest representations, several of them began to listen to him, and about the same time, a gentleman from Hamburg, who had heard of the proposal, offered to invest a considerable capital in a company for trading to that country. Mr Egede now flattered himself with the expectation of seeing his plans effected at last; but scarcely had he begun to indulge this hope when the gentleman in Hamburg withdrew his engagement, and information was at the same time received from the College of Missions, that the privileges asked by the company could not be granted by the Crown. In consequence of this the merchants were dispirited; and every thing was once more thrown into confusion.

But notwithstanding these difficulties and disappointments, which must have damped the ardour of any ordinary mind, Mr Egede did not desist from his purpose. Having renewed his applications to the merchants without success, he at last persuaded several piously-disposed persons in Bergen to meet together, that he might lay before them some propositions relative to Greenland. Moved by his indomitable zeal and his unwearied exertions, they promised, that if he could prevail with others, they would assist him to the utmost of their power in carrying his plans into effect. With the view of making a beginning, Mr Egede subscribed as his share three hundred rix-dollars; some of those who were present contributed two hundred; and others one hundred. Having presented this document to the bishop and clergy of Bergen, and various of the merchants, he now obtained subscriptions from them, notwithstanding the little success which had attended his previous applications. In this manner a capital of between eight and ten thousand rix-dollars was raised, and though it was not equal to the expense of the undertaking, Mr Egede determined to make the attempt without further delay. With this view a ship was purchased to carry him and the other settlers to Greenland, and to remain in that country during the winter. Two other vessels were freighted, one for the whale-fishery, the other to bring back an account of the colony. Meanwhile he was informed by the College of Missions, that His Majesty most graciously approved of the undertaking, and had appointed him a salary of three hundred rix-dollars a year, and a present of other two hundred to assist in his equipment. Thus, after an arduous struggle of no less than thirteen years, Mr Egede had now the prospect of carrying his plans into execution.[1]

In May 1721, Mr Egede sailed from Bergen, with his wife and four children, and a number of other persons as settlers. On reaching the Greenland seas, they met with so much ice, which not only floated around them in frightful forms, but stretched along the whole coast, that the captain in despair of finding a passage was almost induced to return. After sailing about for nearly three weeks, they one morning discovered an opening, and ventured into it; but they had not proceeded far, when their progress was checked by the ice encompassing the shore. They, therefore, endeavoured to escape from amongst it, and to run out into the open sea; but the attempt was vain, for the wind was contrary as well as stormy. Nothing seemed

[1] Egede (Hans) Nachricht vom Anfange und Fortgange der Gronlandischen Mission, p. 1.

now before them but inevitable destruction. The ship which accompanied them struck on the ice and sprung a leak; and, though the crew stopped it with clothes and whatever else was most at hand, it was apprehended that both the vessels would soon be dashed to pieces. The captain sprung into the place where Mrs Egede and her children were, and told them to prepare for death, as there was now no hope of escape. The feelings of Mr Egede on this occasion, it is more easy to conceive than describe, when he saw before his eyes that very event of which he had been so often warned in vain, the destruction of himself, his wife, and his children. To increase their alarm there was such a thick fog during the whole day, that they could see nothing before them; but yet they were surprised to find, that the ship gradually gained more and more room; and when the mist disappeared after midnight, the quantity of ice was so inconsiderable, that they could scarcely believe they had been in such imminent danger. The same storm which threatened them with destruction had rid them of the ice; but this circumstance had escaped their notice owing to the thickness of the fog.[1]

After a voyage of about eight weeks, they landed in Greenland, at Balls River, in 64° North Latitude, and immediately on their arrival began to erect a house of turf and stone on one of the islands. The Greenlanders appeared at first very friendly to them, and even assisted the workmen in their operations, imagining that it was a ship they meant to build; but when they discovered it was a house, they made signs that the vessel would be crushed to pieces by the ice, and the house buried in the snow; they pointed to the sun and to the horizon, shivered, closed their eyes, and laid their hands under their head, intimating by all this, that when the winter came, they would be frozen to death, and therefore they had better take their departure without delay. But as the colonists shewed no disposition to follow their advice, the savages began to manifest considerable dread of them. They could not conceive for what purpose the Kablunaks, as they call Europeans, had come to their land, unless it were to revenge the death of their countrymen, whom the ancient Greenlanders were said to have murdered. They therefore em-

[1] Egede (H) Nachricht Gronlandisch. Mission, p. 20.

ployed their Angekoks to harass and destroy them by their incantations; but as the conjurors found that all their arts were of no avail, they reported that the strangers would do them no harm, and that the priest himself was an Angekok. In a short time the fears of the savages subsided; they readily received the colonists into their houses when they went among them; and they were not backward to visit them in return. They frequently applied to Mr Egede to heal their sick by blowing on them like their Angekoks; and on one occasion, they even conducted him to a grave and entreated him to raise the dead.[1]

Anxious to enter on his work of instructing the Greenlanders, Mr Egede, as he was still unable to speak their language, employed his eldest son to draw pictures of various Scripture facts, such as the creation of the world, the fall of man, the deluge, the miracles, death, and ascension of Christ, the resurrection of the dead, and the last judgment. These drawings he shewed to the Greenlanders who visited him, and explained to them, as well as he was able, what they were intended to signify. The figures, however, were so extremely rude, that even the savages used to laugh every time they were catechised upon them.[2]

The aspect of the trade was at first very unpromising. The Greenlanders possessed few articles of traffic, and what little they had, they did not choose to barter with the Danes, as they had been accustomed for many years to dispose of it to the Dutch, who knew the commodities most acceptable in Greenland, and could afford them at a cheaper rate. A ship from Holland, which ran into Balls River, bought more in half an hour than the colonists had been able to buy during the whole winter.[3]

In May 1722, the colonists, as there was no appearance of any vessel from Norway with supplies, resolved to leave the country in the ship which had wintered with them, alleging, that with only the provisions which remained, they would soon be reduced to want. Mr Egede was now involved in fresh perplexity. On the one hand, he could not think of deserting a

[1] Egede (Paul) Nachrichten von Gronland von 1721, bis 1788, p. 18; Egede (H.) Nachricht Gronlandisch. Mission, p. 23, 25, 28, 32, 36, 44, 48, 50, 81.

[2] Egede (H.) Nach. Gron. Miss. p. 36; Egede (P.) Nachrichten von Gronland, p. 25.

[3] Egede (H.) Nach. Gron. Miss. p. 27, 34, 37.

post which be had attained with so much difficulty, and after the labour of so many years; on the other, he could not stay alone with his wife and children only to see them perish of hunger or murdered by the savages. He endeavoured to persuade the colonists to wait till the end of summer for the arrival of the ship; but though they were under no necessity of departing sooner, they would not listen to his proposal. He was obliged to agree to be ready to sail within fourteen days. Still he hoped a vessel might arrive to their assistance; yet his hopes were mingled with many fears. The colonists were happy at the prospect of leaving so inhospitable a country, and returning to their own land; but to him the thought was bitter as wormwood and gall. Amidst these trying circumstances, Mrs Egede was wonderfully composed. She not only would make no preparations for the voyage; but when the colonists were packing up their goods, she told them they were giving themselves unnecessary trouble; God would yet put them to shame for their distrust of his gracious providence. Three weeks however elapsed, and still there was no appearancc of any vessel. At last when all hope had nearly vanished, two ships arrived; and brought them not only a supply of provisions and other necessary articles, but intelligence that the Company at Bergen was resolved to prosecute the trade and His Majesty to support the mission.[1]

Encouraged by these assurances, Mr Egede resolved to spare no pains in prosecuting the great object of his settlement in the country. With the view of acquiring the language, he made frequent visits to the Greenlanders in the neighbourhood; and though the stench and dirtiness of their houses were extremely noisome, yet to this and other inconveniences he cheerfully submitted, in the hope of ultimately being useful to them. Two or three of the young Greenlanders were at length induced to take up their residence with him, which saved him the trouble of going to live with the savages, as he endeavoured, by conversing with them, to acquire a knowledge of the language. He at the same time instructed them in reading and in the principles of religion. At first, they did tolerably well, and even strove with each other who should be the best scholar, as they had a fish-hook for every letter they learned; but they

[1] Egede (H.) Nach. Gron. Miss. p. 38, 40.

soon grew weary of the employment, and said, They knew not the use of sitting every day, looking at a piece of paper, and crying A, B, C; whereas to go to sea, to hunt seals, and to shoot birds, was attended with both profit and pleasure. On the return of summer, they accordingly stole away, one after another, so that all the pains he had taken with them proved of no avail.[1]

In July 1723, Mr Albert Top arrived in Greenland as an assistant to Mr Egede in his labours among the savages; but neither of them met with much encouragement in their attempts to instruct them. Though the Greenlanders listened to them with wonderful attention, yet from their extreme stupidity they understood little of what was told them; though they approved of all they heard, yet they felt no personal interest in it. They were so credulous, that they were ready to believe any thing; they never questioned nor contradicted what they were taught; they seldom offered any objections, or desired any explanation of difficulties; but at the same time, the truths of religion made no impression on their hearts; they heard them with perfect coldness and indifference. It is, however, not unworthy of notice, that the immortality of man was a favourite doctrine with the Greenlanders. It pleased them to hear that the spirit did not die with the body; that even the body would be restored to life at the last day; that friends would meet together in another and a better world; and that they would be no more subject to sickness and sorrow.[2]

Much as we admire the zeal of Mr Egede, it must be acknowledged that in some instances he employed means for influencing the minds of the savages which were inconsistent not only with the spirit of Christianity, but even with common veracity. Having one day found that some of the Greenlanders in the neighbourhood, had in a great measure forgotten his instructions, he gave them to understand that unless they were more attentive, the king of the country from which he came, would take them away in ships and carry them to that distant land, and instruct them there. On another occasion he told

[1] Egede (H.) Nach. Gron. Miss. p. 51, 53, 66, 72.

[2] Egede (H.) Nach. Gron. Miss. p. 53, 62, 73, 86, 92, 153, 213; Egede's Description of Greenland, Edit. 1818, p. 214.

them, that if they would not pay attention to his instructions, more people would come to the country and punish them for their stubbornness, and even put them to death. Mr Egede was not content with mere threatenings; he sometimes proceeded to inflict corporal punishment on such of the Greenlanders as offended him. Being told that one of the Angekoks had been saying, it would be an easy thing to root the Kablunaks out of the country and to seize on their property, he proceeded with seven or eight armed men to the place of his residence, seized him, and brought him to the colony, where he gave him some corporal chastisement, with which the poor man seemed happy to escape, as he anticipated nothing less than death. Into these errors the good man was probably betrayed by considering the Greenlanders in the light of children, like many a parent who not only administers correction to his offspring, but endeavours to keep them in awe by threatenings which he never means to execute.[1]

In 1726 the colonists were reduced to great distress for want of the necessaries of life. Their food had of late consisted chiefly of seals' flesh; but as this affords only slender nourishment, they became so extremely weak, that in rowing they were almost ready to drop the oars from their hands. One evening several of them came to some Greenlanders, who treated them with flesh and eggs, which proved a most seasonable repast to them, as they had eaten nothing since the day before, and in the meanwhile had been exposed in the country to the storm. On another occasion, they obtained from them two tons of the spermaceti of a Caschalot whale, the train of which they used instead of butter to their seal flesh, and with it and a little meal they baked pancakes. Mr Egede, on whom the care of the temporal as well as the spiritual interests of the colony chiefly devolved, set off on a dangerous voyage to a place about two hundred and fifty miles distant, in the hope of finding the Dutch ships employed in the whale-fishery, and of procuring a supply of provisions from them. There he found twelve Dutch vessels; but necessitous as were the circumstances of the colony, he obtained from them very scanty relief. Eight men had now

[1] Egede (H.) Nach. Gron. Miss. p. 95, 106, 116, 120, 128, 142, 184, 209; Egede (P) Nach. von Gron. p. 37.

to live on the portion of bread which would have been needed by one. These circumstances were a severe trial to Mr Egede. As to himself, he had learned with the Apostle Paul, "in whatsoever state he was therewith to be content;" but to see his wife and children suffering the miseries of want, wrung his heart with anguish; while at the same time, the daily murmurs and impatience of the colonists contributed still further to embitter his situation. In the midst of these trying circumstances, a ship arrived from Norway with a supply of those articles which they so much needed. Still, however, Mr Egede was much distressed to learn that another vessel had sailed from Bergen; but as she had not been heard of, he felt serious apprehensions for her safety; and the event shewed that his fears were not without foundation.[1]

Besides labouring for the conversion of the Greenlanders, Mr Egede exerted himself to the utmost of his power in promoting the temporal interests of the colony, being sensible that the existence of the mission might ultimately depend on the success of the trade. With this view he undertook many long and hazardous voyages, in the course of which he suffered no small hardships, and was even in danger of his life. But notwithstanding all his exertions, the trade proved so unsuccessful, that the Company at Bergen relinquished the undertaking.[2]

In 1728, Frederick the Fourth, who had now taken upon himself the whole concern, adopted new and more vigorous measures for extending both the trade and the mission. With this view he sent out several ships, one of which was an armed vessel, with materials for the erection of a fort, and a small garrison of soldiers for the protection of the colony. Major Paars was appointed governor, and Captain Landorp commandant. Besides the military, there were a number of artificers, masons, carpenters, and smiths, some of whom came voluntarily, others were taken out of confinement, and were married to females from the house of correction, with the view of peopling the country and establishing a permanent colony. There came also two new missionaries, Messrs Ohle Lange, and Henry Miltzoug, to assist Mr Egede in instructing the Greenlanders. As the

[1] Egede (P.) Nach. von Gron. p. 49; Egede (H.) Nach. Gron. Miss. p. 146.
[2] Egede (H.) Nach. Gron. Miss. p. 65, 71, 78, 89, 95, 123, 127, 134, 163.

colony was in an unfavourable situation, it was now removed from the island on which it had hitherto been established, to a place on the mainland, some miles distant. This new settlement was called Good Hope. A second colony, which had been begun at Nepisene, about two hundred miles to the northward, and which was afterwards abandoned, was again established by the new settlers.[1]

Scarcely had the winter commenced, when many of the colonists were taken ill, partly, it was supposed, in consequence of the wetness of the summer, when they were obliged to live in tents, and partly from the dampness of their new dwellings. So general was disease that there was often scarcely a sufficient number well to attend the sick and to manage the household affairs. The soldiers and artificers died rapidly one after another: in the course of the winter no fewer than forty were laid in the grave. As a natural consequence of this, great discontents arose among the colonists, particularly against Mr Egede, whom they considered as the principal cause of their being sent to so inhospitable a region. The conduct of many of them, especially of the women, was so reprehensible, that even the Greenlanders were offended by it.[2]

In 1731, the ministry of Christian the Sixth, who had now ascended the throne of Denmark, thinking there was no probability that the money expended for so many years on this undertaking would ever be reimbursed by the trade, sent orders to Greenland that the colonies should be abandoned, and that all the settlers should return home. This was like a thunderbolt to Mr Egede. It was left, indeed, to his own choice to return with the others, or to remain in the country; and in the latter case, he was allowed to retain as many of the colonists as were willing to stay, and as much provisions as would be sufficient for a year; but he was expressly informed that he had no further assistance to expect from government. Some of the Greenlanders having been told as a reason for the recall of the colonists, that the King had heard they were little the better of all the instructions they received, and that they would not seek

[1] Egede (H.) Nach. Gron. Miss. p. 108, 126, 163, 175, 197; Egede (P.) Nach. von Gron. 53.

[2] Egede (H.) Nach. Gron. Miss. p. 179, 182, 194; Egede (P.) Nach. von Gron. p. 53.

after God, but still followed their old courses, they alleged that whoever had said so to his Majesty was a great liar; and they, at the same time, entreated Mr Egede not to leave them, but to let the King know what a well-behaved people they were. As, however, it was impossible for him to remain in the country alone, and as none of the colonists were willing to stay, he petitioned the governor and the other officers who constituted the council, to appoint eight or ten men to stop with him during the winter in order to preserve the buildings, and other property of the colony which the ships could not carry away that season, and which would otherwise be seized by the Greenlanders, or by foreigners in the spring. With this request, the council, after some difficulty, complied. Mr Egede now beheld the governor, the officers, the rest of the colonists, and even his two colleagues, take their departure, while he himself, with a few sailors, remained behind in a cold inhospitable country, suspended for a whole year between the hope of assistance, and the fear of being abandoned for ever.[1]

In 1732, His Majesty Christian the Sixth, in consequence of Mr Egede's urgent representations, was pleased to send a ship with supplies to Greenland; but without giving him any assurance of further assistance or support. Meanwhile, the blubber trade was more successful than usual, and a larger cargo was sent home this season than in any of the preceding years, when it was carried on with so much trouble and expense. Encouraged, probably by this circumstance, His Majesty resolved to renew the trade to Greenland, and to prosecute it with more vigour than ever, and he was graciously pleased to order the sum of two thousand rix-dollars to be devoted to the support of the mission. After so many disappointments, this intelligence afforded Mr Egede some gleam of hope, but the prospect was quickly overcast, and even became darker than ever.[2]

In 1733, two of the Greenlanders who had been taken to Denmark by the colonists when they left the country, were sent back to their native land, as they did not keep their health in Europe. One of them, a girl, died at sea; the other, a boy, came home to all appearance perfectly well. It was not long, however, before he was seized with an eruptive disorder, and

[1] Egede (H.) Nach. Gron. Miss. p. 221. [2] Ibid. p. 235, 243.

after wandering up and down among his countrymen, he fell a victim to it. One of the next who was taken ill was the Greenland youth, Frederick Christian, who was a particular favourite of Mr Egede's, whom he employed as a kind of catechist among the children. Nobody at first knew the nature of the disease, nor any remedy for it; but at length Mr Egede discovered that it was the small-pox. With the view of checking its progress, he sent intelligence to different parts of the country, warning the Greenlanders of the danger, desiring them to remain in their own habitations, as those who were already infected could not escape, and advising those among whom the disease had not made its appearance, to allow no strangers to visit them, lest they should bring the contagion with them. To these friendly admonitions, however, they lent a deaf ear. Such as had caught the disease, but were not yet confined by it, fled to other parts of the country, and as the Greenlanders never refuse to receive strangers, it spread among them with amazing rapidity.

As this was the first time the small-pox had made its appearance in Greenland, the inhabitants were entirely ignorant of the way of treating it; and as it was at the same time under a very malignant form, it committed terrible ravages among them.[1] Few of those who were attacked by it lived beyond the third day. Some, in despair, stabbed themselves, or plunged into the sea to put an end to their sufferings. One man whose son and daughter died of it, stabbed his wife's sister, and threw her into the sea, under the idea that she had bewitched them to death. Such, indeed, was the general consternation and distress, that the living did not as usual bewail the dead, not even their nearest and dearest relations.

The distress of the Greenlanders deeply affected Mr Egede, and notwithstanding the feeble state of his own health, he went about from place to place, sometimes alone, and sometimes in company with the Moravian missionaries who had lately come from Germany, or he sent his son among them in order to instruct and comfort the poor dying creatures. In many places,

[1] It has been observed that when diseases of an infectious nature are first introduced into a country, they are often of a peculiarly virulent type, and commit fearful ravages among the inhabitants.

they found nothing but empty houses and unburied corpses, some within and some without doors, lying in the snow. Besides travelling among them, Mr Egede and the new missionaries kindly lodged all the sick who fled to them. They laid as many of them in their own houses, and even in their bedrooms, as the places would hold; and attended and nursed them as well as they were able, though the stench of the sick and the dying was so insufferable, and the toil they had with them was so great, as materially to affect their own health. Many of the Greenlanders were sensibly touched with these acts of kindness; and among others, one who when in health had often derided Mr Egede, said to him as he was dying: "Thou hast done for us what our own countrymen would not have done; thou hast fed us when we had nothing to eat; thou hast buried our dead, who would otherwise have been devoured by the dogs, the foxes, and the ravens; thou hast instructed us in the knowledge of God, and told us of a better life to come." On the other hand, as Mr Egede had often informed the savages, that if they prayed to God, he would grant them the good things they asked, some of them now alleged that God did not hear them; that though they cried to him for help, yet he answered them not; and therefore they would pray to him no longer, a circumstance which should teach the Christian missionary not to speak in too general or too absolute terms with respect to the efficacy of prayer, as an ignorant untutored heathen is apt to interpret that of temporal which is true only of spiritual blessings; and even, as to them, the answer is often not immediate, nor in that form which we desire.

In this manner did this virulent disorder rage among the poor Greenlanders for about twelve months, if not even still longer, spreading its devastations at least forty leagues northward, and nearly as far to the south. When the traders afterwards went into the country, they found all the houses empty for thirty leagues north. Mr Egede calculated that in the neighbourhood of the colony, upwards of two thousand persons fell victims to this malignant disease, an immense number, considering the small population of the country.[1]

[1] Egede (H.) Nach. Gron. Miss. p. 243, 246, 253, 255, 258, 261, 263; Crantz's History of Greenland, vol. i. p. 333; Egede's Description of Greenland, p. 120.

In 1734, Mr Martin Ohnsorg, Mr Andrew Bing, and Mr Paul Egede, our excellent missionary's eldest son, who had been at Copenhagen prosecuting his studies, were sent to Greenland, together with materials for erecting a new colony in Disco Bay. Mr Egede had been greatly rejoiced on receiving His Majesty's promise that the undertaking would be carried on with fresh vigour; but when only three missionaries arrived, he felt extremely disappointed, as he considered so small a reinforcement as totally inadequate for the accomplishment of this design. He himself was now so much enfeebled, both in body and mind, by the exertions he had made, and the anxieties and hardships he had suffered, that he was no longer able to discharge the duties of a missionary with his former vigour and alacrity. He considered himself, indeed, as bound before God to promote, as long as he lived, the interests of religion in Greenland; but this he apprehended he could do more effectually by leaving the country than by remaining in it. He, therefore, resolved on returning to Europe, with the view of communicating full information as to the state of the mission, and of explaining the means by which it might be prosecuted with the greatest prospect of success.[1]

In December 1735, died Mrs Egede, a woman who well deserves to hold an honourable place among those "daughters who have done virtuously." Notwithstanding the entreaties of her friends and the scorn of the world, she magnanimously accompanied her husband to the inhospitable shores of Greenland, and though the difficulties and trials which befel them in that country were so many and so great, yet she not only endured them with patience and cheerfulness, but often supported and comforted him when ready to give way to discouragement and disappointment.[2]

After the death of his wife, Mr Egede's health, which had of late been on the decline, was still further impaired, and his spirits were at the same time so depressed, that he was sometimes like a man on the brink of despair. One Sabbath in particular, he tells us, he felt such hatred of God in his heart, and

[1] Egede (H.) Nach. Gron. Miss. p. 266, 287.
[2] Ibid. p. 278.

such dislike to hear his word,[1] that he absented himself from public worship the whole day, spending it in private, in deep distress, without making known his situation to any. In the evening as he was going to bed, he was struck with great horror of mind. His body began to shake; his tongue he could not move; he felt as if he were beset with the bands of death, and encompassed with the pains of hell. After he had so far recovered as to be able to speak, he burst forth in expressions of despair, as if the Lord had forsaken him. His children and his fellow-labourers, on hearing his moanings, came to his assistance and sought to console him; but he refused to be comforted. His own conscience condemned him, and he thought there was no help for him in God. His mind, indeed, became at length more calm; but yet for some time he was more or less subject to these paroxysms of despondency.[2]

He now prepared to take his departure from a country where he had laboured upwards of fifteen years, amidst innumerable privations, hardships, and dangers, yet apparently with little or no success. He preached his farewell sermon from these solemn and affecting words: "I said, I have laboured in vain, I have spent my strength for nought, and in vain; yet surely my judgment is with the Lord, and my work with my God."[3]

In August 1736, Mr Egede sailed from Greenland with his youngest son and two daughters; and after a voyage of about seven weeks, he arrived at Copenhagen. He had soon afterwards an interview with His Majesty, to whom he gave a representation of the state of the mission in Greenland. By his recommendation, a seminary was instituted for the education of catechists and missionaries for Greenland, in which they might acquire the language, as well as other branches of learning, that so they might enter on the work of instructing the natives immediately on their arrival in the country, whereas hitherto, they had been obliged to pass several years, amidst great trials and privations, before they were able to commence their labours. Of this seminary Mr Egede was appointed the superintendent, with a salary of 500 rix-dollars a year.[4]

[1] Here I literally translate his own words: "Ich fuhlte erstlich solchen hass gegen Gott in meinem hertzen, und solchen abscheu, sein wort zu horen."

[2] Egede (H.) Nach. Gron. Miss. p. 280, 282.

[3] Ibid. p. 287.

[4] Ibid. p. 288; Egede (P.) Nach. von Gron. p. 257.

In August 1740, Mr Paul Egede, who had remained in Greenland after the departure of his father, sailed from that country for Denmark. He appears to have possesssd the entire confidence of the Greenlanders, and to have been greatly beloved by them. Previous to his departure, he translated the first three books of Moses into the Greenland language; but as Ulphilas, bishop of the Goths, when he translated the Bible into German, omitted the books of Kings, lest they should foster in his countrymen their disposition to war, so the two Greenlanders who assisted Mr Egede in this undertaking, expressed many objections to the book of Genesis; apprehending it would be better to leave their countrymen ignorant of some of the facts mentioned in it, such as the murder of Abel by his brother Cain; the imposition practised by Jacob on his father and brother; the polygamy of the patriarchs; and particularly, the perfidy of Simeon and Levi in massacring the inhabitants of Shechem. A selection of the most important passages, they thought, would be more useful to their countrymen. Mr Egede himself appears to have formed a similar opinion as his native assistants, and regretted that he had spent so much time in translating the books of Moses. He, therefore, began a version of the New Testament a short time before he left Greenland, and after his return to Europe he completed the work.[1]

In 1750, Mr Paul Egede published a dictionary of the Greenland language, with an explanation of the words in Danish and Latin. Ten years after, he printed a Greenland grammar: he also published his translation of the New Testament. It was not, however, approved of by the missionaries who were settled in Greenland. After his death, Mr Fabricius, who had also left the country a great many years, made another translation of the New Testament into the Greenland language. This, however, was no better than the other: it was exceedingly incorrect, and was not even understood by the people. Besides these works, the Danish missionaries printed one or two spelling-books, a catechism, a hymn book, and various other small pieces in the Greenland language.[2]

[1] Egede (P.) Nach. von Gron. p. 146, 166, 180, 196, 213, 246, 258.

[2] Edinburgh Encyclopædia, vol. x. p. 502; (Moravian) Periodical Accounts, vol. xv. p. 271; MS. Accounts *penes me*.

New Colonies were established from time to time at various places on the western coast of Greenland, from the 59° to the 73° of North Latitude, for the purposes of trade, and missionaries or catechists were settled in most of them. They were divided into two Inspectorships, the northern and the southern. The following were the chief of these establishments, commencing with the most northerly:—

Founded.		Founded.	
	NORTHERN.		SOUTHERN.
	Upernavick.	1756	Holsteinburg.
1758	Umanak.		Kirgurtursuk.
1755	Rittenbenk.		Omanarsuk.
	Klokkerhuk.	1755	Zukkertop.
1773	Good Haven.	1721	Good Hope.
1778	Crown Prince Island.	1754	Fisher Point.
	Dog Island.	1742	Frederick's Hope.
1759	Egede's Memorial.	1775	Juliana's Hope.
1741	Jacob's Haven.	1797	Nennortalik.[1]
1752	Claus Haven.		
1734	Christian's Hope.		

Formerly there were ten missionaries in the Danish colonies in Greenland, and double that number of catechists and schoolmasters. But since 1792 the number of missionaries has been reduced to about one-half, in consequence of which one missionary had to serve several colonies. The most populous among them was generally the place of his residence; from whence he paid visits in the summer to the other settlements, administered the Lord's Supper to the inhabitants, baptized their children, and performed the other duties attached to his office. On the whole coast there were five churches, namely, at Good Hope, Jacob's Haven, Frederick's Hope, Claus Haven, and Holsteinburg. The missionaries appear to go out for a term of years, as a stage in their professional course, and, on

[1] Crantz's Hist. Green. vol. i. p. 4; Egede (P.) Nach. von. Gron. 272, 282; Edin. Encyclop. vol. x. 482; Period. Accounts, vol. viii. p. 84; Hans Egede Saabye's Green. p. 68.

It is a curious geological fact, that coal is found both at Umanak and at Good Haven, on Disco Island. The vein of coal on Disco Island is said to extend far into the sea.—*Saabye's Greenland*, p. 69, 72.

completing it, they return to Denmark to enter on what is called a *living*. The catechists are generally natives of the country, sometimes of a mixed race; but they appear to be very imperfectly qualified for their office. Indeed, it may be questioned, whether either the missionaries or the catechists feel much interest in their work.[1]

The number of Greenlanders who are connected with the Danish colonies, and who are said to be under Christian instruction, has been estimated at about 4000. There are scarcely any heathens to be found in them: the people generally are baptized; but most of them, we fear, are Christians only in name. Many of them, however, have obtained some knowledge of the gospel; and its beneficial influence is obvious in promoting civilization among them; there is a marked difference between their manners and customs, and those of their heathen countrymen. They are said to be almost all able to read and write; but here as in other countries, the conduct of the colonists is a great hinderance to their improvement. Many of these carry moral corruption along with them, and Greenlanders are like children, who readily follow the examples which are set before them. With regard to the arts of life, it is necessary to leave them to the occupations of the country, as the catching of seals, the chase of birds, and the hunting of the reindeer, by which means they not only provide for the subsistence of themselves and their families, but are able to sell seal-bacon, seal-skins, and other articles to the colonists, for which they receive in return implements for seal-fishing, and other kinds of European goods.[2]

[1] Egede (P.) Nach. von Gron. p. 316; Saabye's Green. p. 53, 59, 107; Edin. Encyclop. vol. x. p. 482; MS. Accounts *penes me*.

[2] Saabye's Green. p. 50, 52, 64; Period. Accounts, vol. xii. p. 480; MS. Accounts *penes me*.

CHAPTER VI.

PROPAGATION OF CHRISTIANITY BY THE UNITED BRETHREN.

THE United Brethren, or, as they are more commonly called, the Moravians, are generally supposed to have taken their rise from Nicholas Lewis, Count Zinzendorf, a German nobleman, soon after the commencement of the eighteenth century. They themselves, however, trace their origin to the churches of Bohemia, which, even previous to the Reformation, maintained the principles of Christianity in considerable purity, and were distinguished by giving birth to those two well-known martyrs, John Huss and Jerome of Prague.[1]

Early in the seventeenth century, the churches of Bohemia were reduced to the brink of ruin, through the oppressions and persecutions of their enemies. Multitudes of the people were driven into exile, and took refuge in other countries, where they were soon lost in the mass of the population. In the beginning of the eighteenth century, a number of the Ancient Brethren were still to be found in Moravia; and some of them having been awakened by the conversation and exhortations of Christian David, a native of that country and a carpenter by trade, they besought him to direct them to a place inhabited by Christian people, where they would not, as in their own land, be exposed to persecution, and would enjoy the means of religious instruction. Having failed in his first attempts for this purpose, he applied to Count Zinzendorf, who, on learning the circumstances of these poor oppressed people in Moravia, offered to grant them a place to dwell in, upon an estate which he had lately purchased in Upper Lusatia. Little did the Count then imagine the various consequences which were to result from this simple incident, or the important part which he himself

[1] Crantz's History of the Brethren, p. 13, 22.

was to act in the new and manifold undertakings to which it was destined to gave rise.[1]

In the summer of 1722, Christian David returned from Moravia, with two families of the name of Neisser, consisting of ten persons, one half of whom were children. Upon their arrival on Count Zinzendorf's estate in Upper Lusatia, they proceeded to build a house for themselves, and in this way commenced the village of Herrnhut. Christian David afterwards returned a number of times to Moravia with the view of stirring up his countrymen to attend to religion. They often held meetings during the night; but being discovered, some were thrown into prison, and others suffered severe corporal punishment. Harassed by the outrageous proceedings of their enemies, many determined to leave the country, and after encountering many difficulties and dangers, they happily effected their purpose. Some of them afterwards returned, and sought an opportunity of bringing away their husbands or wives, their parents or children, their brothers or sisters; and though their enemies watched them very narrowly, they often succeeded in their dangerous enterprises beyond expectation.[2]

Count Zinzendorf had at first imagined that only a few persecuted families would settle on his domains, to whom therefore he could not refuse an asylum. As, however, a considerable number of these refugees were now collected at Herrnhut, he endeavoured to persuade them to unite themselves with the Lutheran church. But they resolved that a constitution of nearly three hundred years' standing, on account of which many of their ancestors had suffered and bled and died, and which they had handed down to them as a most precious inheritance, should on no account be abandoned by them. They agreed, however, not to separate from the Lutheran church, but still to hold communion with it; while, at the same time, they maintained among themselves the Bohemian constitution and discipline. In this decision, the Count at last acquiesced: he afterwards became the head of the whole body, and was consecrated one of their bishops.[3]

[1] Crantz's Hist. Breth. p. 66, 82, 91; Periodical Accounts relating to the Missions of the United Brethren, vol. xvi. p. 166.

[2] Crantz's Hist. Breth. p. 97, 103, 108; Period. Accounts, vol. xvi. p. 167.

[3] Crantz's Hist. Breth. p. 109, 123, 136, 169, 215, 291; Spangenberg's Life of Count Zinzendorf, p. 50, 58, 80.

The Count had, even at an early period of his life, turned his thoughts to the state of the heathen world, and within a few years after the building of Herrnhut, the Brethren were led to direct their views to the same important object. In 1731, when the Count attended the coronation of Christian the Sixth, the King of Denmark, at Copenhagen, he saw two of the natives of Greenland who had been baptized by Mr Egede, and he learned with regret that the Danish Government had resolved to abandon the mission in that country. About the same time, a Negro, called Anthony, who had become acquainted with some of his servants, told them that he had a sister in the island of St Thomas in the West Indies, who earnestly desired to be instructed in the principles of religion; but as she had neither time nor opportunity for it, she often besought the Great God to send some one to shew her the way of salvation. On returning to Herrnhut, the Count spoke to the congregation concerning the Negro slaves and their wretched condition. His account made such an impression on John Leonard Dober and Tobias Leupold, both of them young men, that they felt an impulse to go to St Thomas and tell them of the way of salvation, and they communicated their desire to the Count, who made it known to the congregation. A few days after, Anthony came to Herrnhut, and in a meeting of the congregation, he gave an account of the lamentable condition of the poor Negroes in the West Indies; but he said that no one could have an opportunity of teaching them unless he was himself a slave, and instructed them in the midst of their daily labours. The two brethren were no way shaken in their views by this representation, but were rather the more confirmed in their desire. Their proposal, however, was but coldly received by the congregation in general, with the exception of Count Zinzendorf; most of the Brethren considered it as merely a momentary effusion of youthful zeal, but that were the experiment made, it would be found attended with insuperable difficulties. More than a twelvemonth elapsed before any thing was done; but the matter was at last referred to the lot, a method of learning the will of God, which is very common among the Brethren. As to Dober, the lot proved favourable, but unfavourable as to Leupold. Such were the interesting circumstances which gave rise to the exertions of the United Brethren for the conversion of the heathen.[1]

It is not unworthy of notice, that when the Brethren sent forth their first missionaries, the congregation consisted of only about six hundred persons, most of them poor despised exiles; yet this inconsiderable company, in the short space of eight or nine years, sent missionaries to Greenland, to St Thomas, to St Croix, to Surinam, to Berbice, to the Indians of North America, to the Negroes of South Carolina, to Lapland, to Tartary, to Guinea, to the Cape of Good Hope, and to the Island of Ceylon.

It is right, however, to state, that the early missions of the Brethren were a very simple affair, compared with the missions of modern times, involving neither much preparation nor much expense, the missionaries often not even knowing how they were to get to the place of their destination, yet trusting that the way would be opened up to them by God, to whose care and guidance they committed themselves, and intending generally to support themselves by the labour of their hands. Of these important undertakings, we shall now proceed to give some account, beginning with the mission to Greenland.[2]

[1] Spangenberg's Life of Zinzendorf, p. 9, 143; Crantz's History of Greenland, vol. i. p. 317; Oldendorp Geschichte der Mission auf St Thomas, St Croix, und St Jan, tom. ii. p. 453; Period. Accounts relating to the Missions of the United Breth. vol. xii. p. 242.

[2] Crantz's Hist. Breth. p. 169, 184; Period. Accounts, vol. xiv. p. viii.

We feel great difficulty in forming an estimate of the early Moravians; yet it is of much importance to pass a right judgment concerning them, in order to our obtaining a correct idea of the character of their missions. It is well known that they were long the object of general obloquy in Germany, in Holland, and other parts of the Continent, in England, and in America; and that they were viewed in an unfavourable light not only by men of the world, and such as made no pretensions to piety, but by many religious people, some of them eminently distinguished for both learning and piety. Among these we may mention in Germany the celebrated Bengelius, *Burk's Memoirs of John Albert Bengel*, p. 399; in England, Dr Doddridge, *Orton's Memoirs of Doddridge*, p. 126; John Wesley, *Moore's Life of the Rev. John Wesley*, vol. i. p. 476, 481; Whitfield, *Philip's Life and Times of Whitfield*, p. 434; the Countess of Huntingdon, *Life and Times of the Countess of Huntingdon*, vol. i. p. 36, 41, 58, 64, 102, 203, 454; in America, David Brainerd, *Brainerd's Life*, p. 189; and Dickenson, President of New Jersey College, *Dickenson's Familiar Letters*, p. 169. Most of these were persons whom one would not have expected to take up readily an evil report or mere prejudices against a body of fellow-Christians. Some of them were distinguished for their candour and moderation; others were likely to be indulgent to piety, even though it did run somewhat wild; yet these very persons, some of them after being for a time favourably disposed toward the Brethren, became quite opposed to them, and speak of them in terms of utter reprobation.

The charges brought against them by their opponents had reference to important

SECT. I.—GREENLAND.

In January 1733, Matthew Stach and Christian Stach, accompanied by Christian David, set off from Herrnhut in Upper

points of doctrine, to their phraseology and modes of speaking, and to various practices prevailing among them. They were charged, for example, with crude, gross, mystical notions in religion; with contemning the Holy Scriptures; with, though not perhaps the denial of the doctrine of the Trinity, yet with too exclusive a regard to the Son, and with an unscriptural and unwarranted way of speaking of the Father and of the Holy Spirit; with a familiar, light, unhallowed manner of speaking of the Saviour, with Antinomian views, and even with indecent and impure sentiments and language.—See *Rimius' Narrative of the Rise and Progress of the Herrnhuters*, London 1753, p. 32; *Stinstra's Essay on Fanaticism*, p. lxxii. 197.

We cannot, indeed, avoid coming to the conclusion, that there was much that was imperfect, and much that was wrong, about the Brethren in the early part of their career. Count Zinzendorf, who wielded nearly absolute authority in their Church, and who, especially in his later years, regulated all its concerns, even to the minutest points, appears, from his Life by Spangenberg, to have been essentially a wrong-headed, though a pious man. There was a great deal of singularity about him and his proceedings. He was much guided by impulses, emotions, and impressions; and his views and feelings were often characterised by enthusiasm, not to say fanaticism. He spoke in a familiar way of the Saviour and of his intercourse with him; and as if he knew his mind and will with certainty, and was under his immediate direction, and understood the causes and designs of his procedure, and that in regard even to very trivial matters. He was fitful, changeable, ready to take up fancies and new notions, to run into extravagancies and frivolities, and to magnify trifles, as if they were matters of great importance. His language was vague, mystical, and often not very intelligible; he employed much of a novel, strange, unscriptural phraseology. With him the religion of the heart was every thing; and he was very restricted in his views of Christian doctrine. The incarnation, the life, sufferings, and death of the Saviour, and the atonement which he made for sin, were the topics on which he chiefly dwelt, and these he often spoke of in a very exceptionable manner. His fancy and his feelings had more influence in forming his opinions and his language than either Scripture or sound reason. He appears, like most men of his temperament, to have been very easy of belief as to a blessing resting on his labours, and on those of his brethren. The institutions or order which he introduced into the Church of the Brethren, were, generally speaking, without any authority from Scripture, and ill-accorded with the simplicity of Christianity. Every thing was artificial; every thing was reduced to regulation. Much importance was often attached to mere forms and trifles. There was in the whole system much which may be called emphatically, "Will-worship." It was founded neither on Scripture nor reason, but was the pure devising of man's wisdom or rather of man's folly.

But while there was much in the character and course of Count Zinzendorf which we cannot but deeply regret, there was also much in him to admire. He appears to have possessed a heart flowing with love to the Saviour and to his fellow-men. He devoted himself with singleness of mind to the service of Christ, and he prosecuted it with great perseverance and unwearied diligence, with much self-denial and disinterestedness, and with an humble and simple trust in God for his counsel and blessing. Where there

Lusatia, on a mission to the inhospitable shores of Greenland.[1] "There was no need," says one of them, "of much time or expense for our equipment. The congregation consisted chiefly of poor exiles, who had not much to give us, and we ourselves had nothing but the clothes on our backs. Being accustomed to make a shift with little, we did not trouble our heads how

was so much good, it is sad to find so muth evil.—See *Spangenberg's Life of Count Zinzendorf*, passim. See also *Exposition de L'Origine, de la Doctrine, des Constitutions, Usages, et Ceremonies Ecclesiastiques de L'Eglise de L' Unité des Freres*, 1758, and the Plates annexed to it.

It is acknowledged on the part of the Brethren themselves, that at one period, particularly from 1747 to 1753, great extravagancies, both in doctrine and practice, made their appearance among the congregation at Herrnhaag, a settlement belonging to them in the county of Buedingen, now uninhabited and in ruins. Count Zinzendorf having, in an ode on the birth-day of his son, employed some puerile unintelligible expressions relative to the believer's love to the Redeemer, others of the Brethren following his example, indulged in language which, if possible, was still more foolish and trifling. In their discourses, hymns, and other writings, they employed the strangest expressions and the wildest allusions when speakiug of the most sacred truths of religion, particularly of the sufferings of Christ and the experience of his people. Each strove to surpass another in this senseless, miserable jargon; and the evil which first made its appearance at Herrnhaag, spread like a contagious disease among the other congregations of the Brethren. A great part of the members were contaminated with these silly reveries; others finding themselves unable to check the malady, wept over it in secret; while some who considered it as utterly incurable, left the Society.

Though Count Zinzendorf had set the example of these extravagancies, yet on learning the excesses into which many of the Brethren were running, he set himself to counteract the evil. Most of those who had fallen into these fooleries were convinced of their error, and acknowledged it with grief and shame. After a short time, the hymns, and other writings which contained their reveries, were formally disavowed and cancelled by a Synod of the Church of the Brethren.—*Spangenberg's Exposition of Christian Doctrine as taught in the Church of the Brethren*, preface, p. iii. *Crantz's History of the Brethren*, p. 218, 244, 298, 367. *Christian Observer*, vol. vii. p. 196.

Count Zinzendorf himself published a Declaration (we suppose in 1748) that "he could from that time no longer authorise his own writings hitherto published, till they had been reprinted with his amendments, remarks, and explanations." He assigned as his reason for this, that "it had been his own case, like many other writers, to publish thoughts which he was quite taken with at first, but which he was afterwards ashamed of and retracted; and that it was not in his power to correct the whole so entirely at the first revisal as he would have done." He condemned and destroyed all the copies which he could collect of the 12th Supplement to the Hymns; and gave this public testimony in relation to the doctrine of the Trinity, that from the moment he saw how his expressions relative to the Father, the Son, and the Holy Ghost were taken, he was shocked at it, and abandoned every expression of the sort. He desired that wherever such were found in his writings, they might be erased, and that no one in future would repeat them. That he abhorred unscriptural speculations upon the mys-

[1] Christian David merely accompanied the two missionaries to Greenland with the view of seeing them settled in the country, and was then to return.

we should get to Greenland, or how we should live in that country. Some money having come from a friend at Venice the day before our departure, we received part of it to pay the expense of our journey to Copenhagen; and as we considered ourselves as richly provided for, we would take nothing of any person on the road, believing that He who had sent a supply for

tery of the Godhead, and was thankful to the Saviour of all men, that he had escaped the fire uninjured."—*Burk's Memoir of Bengel*, p. 419.

These statements may assist us materially in forming an estimate of the early missions of the Moravians. It is natural to conclude that they would participate in no inconsiderable degree of the faults and imperfections of the general body and of its head. In tracing their history (especially where we have access to original documents) we accordingly find not unfrequently indications of some of the evils we have mentioned, for example, the influence of impulses, impressions, and feelings on the missionaries, and their easy belief of a blessing resting on their labours. It is also of importance to state, that most of them were plain unlettered men, and that they must consequently have been, generally speaking, but imperfectly qualified to be the instructors of others, and especially of heathens and savages, to whose minds it is so exceedingly difficult to convey clear and simple ideas of the truths of religion. "All the early missionaries," we are told, "were either artisans or husbandmen, men of simple manners, few wants, and for the most part inured to toil and hardships. It gave them little concern whether they would have to perform a long or a short journey, whether that journey was to be undertaken by sea or by land, and would lead them to the frigid or a sultry zone. They were not able to form extensive plans; their whole mind was exclusively bent upon winning souls for Christ: the salvation of but one soul they esteemed so inestimable a prize, that they were willing to give their liberty, yea their life, in exchange for it."—*Period. Accounts*, vol. xii. p. 225.

Since the period to which we have referred, we have no doubt that a considerable improvement has taken place in the Church of the Brethren. It would appear from *Spangenberg's Exposition of Christian Doctrine as taught in the Church of the Brethren*, that their views as regards the fundamental principles of Christianity are essentially in unison with those of evangelical Christians of other denominations. They still retain, indeed, in a greater or less degree, many of their old peculiarities, in regard to which we are by no means disposed to vindicate their sentiments and practices. In short, though in the course of the last century they materially improved their phraseology, we apprehend there is still considerable room for improvement in their manner of expression, as well as in their mode of thinking on many points of Christian theology.

Before concluding this note, we cannot forbear adducing the following testimonies to the Christian character of the Brethren. "I feel myself bound," says Dr Haweis, "from near forty years' acquaintance with the Brethren, to speak of those whom I have known, as men full of faith and of the Holy Ghost, and truly devoted to the work and service of our crucified Lord. With peculiarities, some of them perhaps exceptionable, yet admitting of no such impure ideas as have been imputed to them, the more the principles of the Brethren are truly known, and the more intimately their lives are scrutinized, the more will they be acknowledged among the few faithful who follow the Lamb of God."—*Haweis' Church History*, vol. iii. p. 177.

"The Moravians," says the late Mr Cecil, "have very nearly hit on Christianity. They appear to have found out what sort of a thing it is,—its quietness—meekness—patience—spirituality—heavenliness—and order." —*Cecil's Remains*, 6th Edit. p. 243.

After alluding to the improprieties of expression with which the early Moravians our journey at the critical moment, would take care for every thing that was necessary for carrying our purpose into execution as soon as we should want it. Neither could any one give us much information on the subject of our work, or any instructions how we should proceed: for the congregation had as yet no experience in the management of missions. It was, therefore, left to ourselves to act in all circumstances as the Lord should lead us. In short, we neither knew nor imagined how it would be with us."

Such were the circumstances in which these simple unlettered men set out on their journey. On their arrival at Copenhagen, Christian David obtained access to various persons of distinction in that city. He was even introduced to several members of the Royal family, and other persons at Court, who,

were chargeable, Mr Wilberforce bears a no less honourable testimony to the general excellence of the Brethren. "This body of Christians," says he, "have since reclaimed their character, and have perhaps excelled all mankind in solid and unequivocal proofs of the love of Christ, and of the most ardent, and active, and patient zeal in his service. It is a zeal tempered with prudence, softened with meekness, soberly aiming at great ends by the gradual operation of well-adapted means, supported by a courage which no danger can intimidate, and a quiet constancy which no hardships can exhaust."—*Wilberforce's Practical View of Christianity*, 9th Edit. p. 51.

To these testimonies we may add Cowper's beautiful eulogium on the Missionaries in Greenland:—

"See Germany send forth
Her sons to pour it on the farthest North:
Fired with a zeal peculiar, they defy
The rage and rigour of a Polar sky;
And plant successfully sweet Sharon's rose
On icy plains, and in eternal snows."

&c., &c., &c.—*Cowper's Poetical Works*, vol. i. p. 108, Edit. London 1830.

To these statements we cannot but add, that the missions of the Brethren furnish a striking example of how much may be effected by patience and perseverance combined with humility and simple piety. Intellectually the missionaries were generally but indifferently qualified for their work; the fields selected were often ill-chosen, in unhospitable climates, with a small population, low in the scale of civilization, and presenting peculiar difficulties in the way of their evangelization; yet most of their present missions have now existed for a considerable length of time, some of them for upwards of a century, and they are at this day, with few exceptions, if we may judge by the numbers composing the congregations, in a more flourishing state than at any former period. In reading the accounts of the missions of the Brethren, we are greatly charmed with their childlike simplicity, their lowliness of mind, their freedom from self-complacency and self-confidence, their simple trust in God, their meekness, patience, and inoffensiveness; though, it must also be acknowledged, that these excellencies are accompanied with a degree of feebleness and passiveness of character which unfits them for attempting great, and even in some instances, generous designs.

it is stated, conversed with him in the most affable and unaffected manner. The King himself renewed the expression of his desire to promote the conversion of the Greenlanders, and gave them a passage on board a ship which was then going out to Greenland. The Lord Chamberlain, Von Pless, asked him one day, "How they meant to provide for themselves in Greenland." "By the labour of our hands, and the blessing of God," Christian David replied, "we will cultivate the ground, and live upon the produce. For this purpose," he added, "they would take seeds with them, plant a garden, build a house, and be burdensome to no one." The Chamberlain, in reply, observed, "There was no timber in the country, and how could they build a house?" "Then," said Christian David, "we will dig a hole in the ground, and live there." "No," replied he, "take timber with you, and build a wooden house, towards which I will contribute," and he immediately gave him fifty dollars. With this and the contributions which they received from other friends, the Brethren purchased materials for building, various articles of household furniture, some implements of husbandry, clothes, provisions, and other useful articles.[1]

Having at length sailed from Copenhagen, the Brethren after an agreeable voyage of about six weeks, landed in Greenland. Immediately on their arrival, they repaired to Mr Egede, who gave them, as might be expected, a very cordial welcome, and promised them his best assistance in learning the language. Having fixed on a spot for a settlement near the colony of Good Hope, they built themselves a house; but, for the present, they had little opportunity of conversing with the Greenlanders, or of holding any kind of intercourse with them. Though the savages were at that time very numerous in Balls River, yet during the summer they were so dispersed among the islands and the hills, catching seals or hunting reindeer; and towards winter they were so accustomed to go sixty, a hundred, and even two hundred leagues to the north or to the south, that the missionaries seldom saw them. Some, indeed, called on them occasionally as they passed, but it was merely from curiosity to see their buildings, or to beg for fish-hooks, knives, and other similar articles, or even to carry them off by stealth.

[1] Crantz's Hist. Green. vol. i. p. 322; Period. Accounts, vol. xii. p. 390.

When the Brethren went to visit them on the islands, they seldom found any who would entertain them, even though they offered to pay them; and instead of entering into conversation with them, the savages were continually asking them, whether they would not soon go away.

These were not the only trials which the Brethren had to endure at the commencement of their missionary career. It was only a few months after their arrival, that the small-pox made its appearance in Greenland, and committed such terrible ravages among the inhabitants, as to threaten to depopulate the whole country. The Brethren, as we have already mentioned, assisted Mr Egede in visiting the sick and the dying; but they themselves were, at length, successively attacked with an eruptive disorder, which so increased during the winter, that they were often confined to bed, and were scarcely able to move their limbs. Happily, however, they were not all ill at the same time, but one of them was always able to help the others, and even to go with the colony's boat to visit the savages. During the indisposition of the Brethren, Mr Egede shewed them all the kindness of a father and a friend; and his excellent wife never omitted sending them some refreshment or cordial, when she had any herself. They were, indeed, so generous to them, that the missionaries often felt scrupulous in accepting the many favours with which they loaded them.[1]

In such inauspicious circumstances did the Brethren pass the first year in Greenland. Indeed, Christian David and Christian Stach began to think of returning home by the first opportunity, as they did not see what good they could do in a country so completely depopulated by the late dreadful ravages of the small-pox, while the few inhabitants who remained appeared totally averse to the gospel.

In March 1734, two other missionaries, Frederick Boehnish and John Beck were sent by the congregation to the assistance of the Brethren in Greenland, with the strongest assurances of their design to support the mission. This raised the drooping spirits of the missionaries, and inspired them with fresh courage. Rough as was their post, they resolved to remain by it, in the hope that God would crown their labours with success. They

[1] Crantz's Hist. Green. vol. i. p. 326, 328, 331, 332, 338.

now applied to the study of the language with new diligence and alacrity; but the further they proceeded, the more difficult they found it, especially as they were no longer satisfied with such expressions as were applicable merely to the common affairs of life, but began to translate into it the language of Scripture, and other phrases relative to experimental religion. They were told, indeed, that it was impossible to translate into it any but historical pieces, as the Greenlanders had no terms in their language to express the peculiar doctrines of the gospel, and could not even form the most distant idea of spiritual things. The Brethren, however, were not discouraged by these accounts; and in the course of a few years they made further progress in the language than they could ever have imagined, especially after some of the natives embraced Christianity, and found words themselves to express the views and feelings of their hearts.[1]

With the view of observing the state of the country, and learning the condition, customs, and language of the inhabitants, as well as of sowing "the good seed of the word" among them, the Brethren made frequent voyages to the islands and other places. One day as they were preparing for an excursion of this kind, the only woman's boat[2] they possessed, was raised from the ground by a violent tempest, carried some hundred paces in the air, and dashed to pieces on a rock. This reduced them to a sad dilemma; but Mr Egede was so kind as give them an old European boat, and materials to repair it; and when they had not hands to man it, he sometimes lent them a small boat to follow their occupation in the neighbourhood; he likewise frequently took them with him to visit the heathen. They also occasionally went in company with the traders; but as the Greenlanders saw that they readily put their hands to any kind of work, they at first imagined they were the factor's servants, and on that account slighted and despised them. But when they understood that they came not to trade with them, but to make known their Creator to them; and observed at the same time, that they were distinguished from the other Europeans by the meekness and modesty of their behaviour, they formed a higher opinion of them. By degrees, indeed, their

[1] Crantz's Hist. Groen. vol. i. p. 345.

[2] The large boat of the Greenlanders.

friendly deportment towards them, untainted with jesting or licentiousness, yet unsoured with harshness or austerity, so won their affection and confidence, that they sought their conversation, constrained them to go into their houses, begged them often to come and see them, and promised to visit them in return.

Agreeably to their promises, numbers of the Greenlanders returned the visits which the Brethren made them in the course of their voyages. The selfishness of their design, however, was obvious. Sometimes they wanted shelter or victuals; sometimes they wished to have a couple of needles or some other trifle; sometimes they even bluntly declared, that if the Brethren would give them no more stock-fish, they would no longer listen to their words; for the savages imagined that they conferred a favour on the missionaries by listening to their instructions, and that they were entitled to payment for condescending to hear and believe them. The Brethren, indeed, could not in conscience send them away empty, as the cold was so intense that the poor creatures were unable to procure sufficient food for themselves, and many of them had often scarcely a morsel to eat for several days together. Afterwards, on the return of summer, when they caught plenty of game, and had danced perhaps during the whole night at a revel, they still occasionally visited the Brethren; but they were generally so sleepy, that it was impossible to carry on any serious conversation with them; or they were merely curious to hear some news, to see what was strange, or to obtain such things as happened to suit their fancy; and if the missionaries found it necessary to deny their request, they were obliged to watch them narrowly, lest they should secretly carry off the articles which they coveted. This often rendered their visits extremely troublesome; but yet the Brethren did not choose to treat them harshly, lest it should frighten them away altogether. Indifferent as were the motives of the savages, they were obliged to be satisfied for the present with their willingness to visit them; and they even drew encouragement from this of more propitious days.[1]

In 1735, the Brethren had to endure a more terrible calamity than any which had yet befallen them, the fearful horrors of

[1] Crantz's Hist. Green. vol. i. p. 348.

famine. They had been supplied the year before with the necessaries of life, by an eminent benefactor at the Court of Denmark ; but this season they were entirely forgotten, and even some articles which could not come with the last missionaries for want of room, were neglected to be sent to them. Their only remaining provisions for the ensuing year were a barrel and a half of oatmeal, most of which they bartered at the colony for a little malt, half a barrel of pease, and a small quantity of ship biscuit. Hitherto, indeed, they had been pretty successful both in fishing and hunting ; but this season they were able to catch little or nothing, as there was a great scarcity of beasts, birds, and fishes. They had, therefore, scarcely any resource except to buy seals from the Greenlanders ; but no sooner did the savages learn that they were in want, than they raised their articles very high ; and even most of them, particularly those with whom they were best acquainted, and to whom they had lately shewn much kindness, refused to sell them provisions at any price. Often, after rowing among them for two or three days together, the missionaries by their utmost entreaties, could obtain scarcely more than half a seal, and as that was soon consumed, they were glad to pacify the cravings of nature by eating shell-fish or raw sea-weed. The Greenlanders, indeed, would be rioting in plenty, while they were starving with hunger. At one banquet, which lasted the whole night, the Brethren saw eleven seals devoured by the gluttons, while they, with all their entreaties, could not move the unfeeling wretches to sell them a single morsel.

Besides suffering the horrors of famine, the missionaries had now to increase their labours, and were thus exposed to further dangers. Urged by the cravings of hunger, they could not always wait for settled weather to embark on the ocean ; but were often compelled to trust themselves to the mercy of the waves, even when the day was stormy, in an old crazy boat, and that to the distance of several leagues. Once, when they had nearly got to land, they were hurried two leagues back by a sudden squall, and were completely wet by the breakers ; and in this state they were obliged to remain on an island till the fourth day, exposed to all the inclemency of the weather. On another occasion, after being completely fatigued at their oars, they stopped all night in an uninhabited spot, and were obliged to rest satisfied with a little seal's flesh which they procured from a Greenlander at a feast, but, in fact, they could scarcely eat any of it for weariness and cold. As they had no tent, they lay down in a hole in the snow, and as that was at length closed up by the drift, they had to rise from their retreat and warm themselves by running. Sometimes they ventured in serene weather to embark in a kajak,[1] and to angle for fish. But one of them was once overset by a sudden squall of wind, and would certainly have been drowned had not two Greenlanders, who were near at hand, come to his assistance, bound him fast between their boats, and towed him safe to land.

In the midst of all these trials, the providence of God was often remarkably displayed in their behalf. He who sent a raven to feed the prophet Elijah disposed a Greenlander, called Ippegau, to come forty leagues from the south, and to sell them, from time to time, whatever he could spare. One day the boatmen found a dead whale, and gave them a couple of meals of it. Another time a Greenlander left them a porpoise taken out of the belly of the dam, which served them for a meal after they had eaten nothing but shell-fish for five days. As they were returning home on another occasion quite empty, they were driven by a contrary wind on a desolate island, and were obliged to remain there all night. Here they spied an eagle on her nest, and shot her. They had, indeed, to climb up a steep and dangerous precipice to reach the place; but the prize they obtained they considered as an ample reward for their trouble.

Impelled by necessity, the Brethren had inured themselves to the eating of seal's flesh, mixing up the little oatmeal they had left with the train oil; yet disagreeable as this was, it was a perfect delicacy in comparison of the old tallow candles which they were obliged to use when they had no train oil. As long, indeed, as they could procure any seals, they retained their health and strength tolerably well; but in the following spring, when they could obtain no more of this kind of food, and were obliged to subsist on shell-fish and sea-weed, their strength declined so much, that they could scarcely manage their boat. Once, when they had not drawn it far enough on land owing

[1] The small boat of the Greenlanders.

to their extreme weakness, it was very much damaged by a high tide and storm.[1]

In May 1736, after a long continued train of sufferings, they very unexpectedly received a supply of provisions from Holland, with a promise of future assistance from that country. They had just returned from a toilsome excursion in which they could get nothing, and were therefore the more struck with the wonderful interposition of Providence in their behalf. This supply, so extremely seasonable, was the more remarkable as neither they nor any of the congregation had expressed the least desire of that kind to their friends in Holland; but the Lord had put it into the heart of a Mr Le Long to make an experiment whether he could not send some stores to them by the ships from that country. He was also so kind as promise that, if they received them, he would solicit the aid of some other friends, and send them further supplies the following season. This generous offer the missionaries gladly accepted, and requested that in case he could convey them nothing else, he would at least send them a strong durable boat, an article they stood much in need of for gaining a livelihood, and for rendering them less dependent on supplies from abroad.[2]

Hitherto, the Brethren had seen no fruit of their labours in Greenland. The savages who came from a distance were stupid, ignorant, and thoughtless. The little they could learn in a short visit, even if it made some slight impression at the time, was soon forgotten by them in the midst of their constant wanderings from place to place. On the other hand, those who resided in the neighbourhood were not disposed to receive instruction. At one time they would not hear them because they had some business, or perhaps a dance, in view. At another, if they were told any kind of news, they readily listened to them; they would even bear to hear some little histories out of the Bible, particularly of the miracles of our Lord and his Apostles. But if the Brethren began to speak to them of the nature and attributes of God, of the fall and wickedness of man, of the wrath of God against sinners, of the necessity of an atonement, of faith in Jesus Christ, of the sanctification of the heart, of the happiness of heaven, or the misery of hell, they quickly became

[1] Crantz's Hist. Green. vol. i. p. 356, 360. [2] Ibid. vol. i. p. 361.

sleepy, said 'Yes' to all, and slunk away. At other times they avowed their dislike of such discourse, and began to talk of their seal-catching, or they excused themselves saying they could not understand it. If the missionaries on their visits tarried with them more than one night, they employed every kind of art to entice them to their wanton dissolute practices ; and when they failed in this, they endeavoured to weary and provoke them by mocking and mimicking their reading, singing, and praying, or by accompanying these exercises with their hideous howling or the beat of their drums. They took occasion from their poverty to ridicule them ; and if the Brethren alleged that they did not come to Greenland for the sake of outward advantages, as good eating and drinking, but to teach them the will of God and the way to heaven, they taunted them saying, "Fine fellows indeed, to be our teachers ! We know very well ye yourselves are ignorant, and must learn your lesson from others." All this rudeness the Brethren bore with patience and serenity : but the savages, instead of being softened by their meek and gentle behaviour, were only encouraged to abuse them the more. They pelted them with stones, climbed on their shoulders, seized their goods and broke them to pieces ; they even attempted to spoil their boat and to drive it out to sea, which would have deprived them of their chief means of subsistence.[1]

Five years had now elapsed since the Brethren landed in Greenland ; yet hitherto they had toiled and laboured in vain, but now they began, at last, to see some fruit of their exertions.

In June 1738, a number of Southlanders happening to visit them, at a time when one of the Brethren was writing out a fair copy of a translation of part of the Gospels, they were curious to know what the book contained, a wish which he was very ready to gratify. After reading a portion of it to them, he told them of the creation of the world, of the fall of man, of our misery in consequence of sin, and of our redemption through Jesus Christ. In speaking on the latter subject, he was enabled to describe the sufferings and death of the Redeemer with more than ordinary force and feeling ; and he, at the same time, read to them from the New Testament, the history of his agony in

[1] Crantz's Hist. Green. vol. i. p. 367, 376.

the garden. Upon this, one of the Greenlanders, named Kaiarnak, stepped up to the table, and in an earnest manner said, "How was that? Tell me it once more; for I also would fain be saved!" These words so affected the missionary, that the tears ran down his cheeks while he gave them some account of the life and death of Christ, and of the plan of salvation through him. Meanwhile, the other brethren came home from their labours, and began to speak to them still further concerning the way of salvation. Some of the savages laid their hands on their mouth, as is their custom when they hear anything which strikes them with surprise or wonder. Several, indeed, who had no relish for these things, slipped away secretly; but others requested they might be taught to pray; and when the missionaries did pray with them, they frequently repeated their expressions, in order that they might not forget them. In short, there appeared among them such an interest in divine things as the Brethren had never beheld before among the Greenlanders. At taking leave, they promised soon to call again and hear of these things; and they further engaged to speak to their countrymen concerning them.

From that time, Kaiarnak made frequent visits to the missionaries, and he at length took up his abode with them. "When we speak to him," they say, "he is often so affected, that the tears roll down his cheeks. He is, indeed, a very singular man. We cannot but wonder at him, when we consider that the Greenlanders, in general, are so extremely stupid, that they can comprehend almost nothing except those things with which they are daily conversant. But this man scarcely hears a thing twice before he understands it, and retains it in his memory. He at the same time shews an uncommon attachment to us, and a constant desire for further instruction, so that he seems to drink in every word which drops from our lips, a thing we never before observed in any Greenlander." Besides Kaiarnak, there were about twenty others of the savages who took up their abode this winter in the neighbourhood of the missionaries.[1]

In March 1739, the Brethren had the pleasure of baptizing Kaiarnak and his family as the first-fruits of their labours in

[1] Crantz's Hist. Green. vol. i. p. 385.

Greenland; but their prospects, which had of late begun to brighten, quickly threatened to set in darkness. Scarcely had a month elapsed, when a band of murderers killed his brother-in-law, who also lived with the missionaries, under the pretence that he had conjured the ringleader's son to death; and as they likewise threatened to murder Kaiarnak and his other brother-in-law, he resolved to fly with his family to the south. Against this proposal the Brethren remonstrated in the strongest manner. They expressed their fears that so young a convert, and especially his two children, would adopt the manners of the heathen, should they again live among the savages; they reminded him of the solemn promises he had lately made at baptism; they offered to maintain both him and his family, that they might have no occasion to go to a distance so long as the murderers remained in the neighbourhood. By the representations made to him by the missionaries he was much affected, but yet he could not resolve to stay. Before he left them, they once more exhorted him to faithfulness and good conduct among the heathen, and commended him in prayer to the protection of the Shepherd of Israel. In the course of two weeks, they beheld, with sorrow, the country stripped of most of their Greenlanders, and were forced to bear this new reproach, that though they could baptize heathens, they could not make them Christians, nor even wean them from their roving habits.[1]

In the year 1740, a remarkable change took place in the Brethren's method of instructing the Greenlanders, and it was followed by such remarkable effects as to merit particular notice. Hitherto they had been accustomed, in the first instance, to direct the attention of the heathen to such preliminary truths as the existence of God, the creation of the world, the fall of man; a mode of instruction which appears *a priori*, not merely the most rational, but the only plan that could be adopted with any prospect of success. It is worthy of observation, however, that reduced to practice, it had proved not only almost entirely ineffectual, but even seemed a bar to the conversion of the heathen. They now adopted a different method, and directed the attention of the savages, in the first instance, to Christ Jesus, to his incarnation, his life, and especially to his sufferings and

[1] Crantz's Hist. Green. vol. i. p. 400.

death. In discoursing of these things, the Brethren themselves were often so much impressed, that they spoke in a manner entirely new; the subject so warmed and animated their own hearts, that the words flowed from their lips with wonderful fervour and affection; they were even astonished at each other's powers of utterance. Happily, this was attended with corresponding effects on the Greenlanders. Their darkened understandings were enlightened, their stubborn hearts melted, and in their cold icy breasts was kindled the flame of spiritual life. This, therefore, may be considered as a new era in the history of the Greenland mission.[1]

Of late, indeed, the missionaries had beheld some little fruit of their labours. The conversion of Kaiarnak and his family, they would have reckoned a rich reward for all their toils, had not his sudden flight dashed their hopes, and pierced them with new sorrows. Of his return, they entertained little or no expectation. How great then was their joy, when, after about a year's absence, he suddenly stepped in among them, while they were celebrating the marriage dinner of Frederick Boehnish and Anna Stach! He brought with him his brother and his family, to gain whom, it appears, was one principal object of his expedition. Of late, he said, he had longed exceedingly to return to the Brethren; and now, he should never leave them more, for even during his absence he had felt how much they loved both him and his children.[2]

Besides Kaiarnak's family, there were several others of the Greenlanders who now manifested some concern for their souls; but no sooner did this appear, than they were exposed to the contempt and ridicule of their neighbours. Their exhortations and example, however, produced very salutary effects on many of their countrymen. The missionaries sometimes took them with them in their visits to the heathen, in order to exhibit them as living monuments of the power and pleasure of religion. By this means they were furnished with an answer to an observation which the heathen often made as an apology for their neglect of the gospel: "You," said they, "are a different kind of people from us: It is your profession: You have both time and ability to think of these things." But now they beheld examples of

[1] Crantz's Hist. Green. vol. ii. p. 2, 27, 424. [2] Ibid. vol. ii. p. 2, 6.

their own countrymen, who originally were no better than themselves, and yet had embraced the gospel, were transformed by its influence, and exhibited its happy effects in their life. The testimony which the converts bore on these occasions to the love and grace of the Saviour, was often so fervent and striking, that numbers of the savages were filled with astonishment, and deeply impressed with a sense of their need of salvation. They were particularly surprised at the prayers of the converts. In token of their wonder, they used to lay their hand on their mouth; and imagining that the converts had merely committed them to memory, they were eager to learn them also: but they were told, they must first feel their misery, and then a sense of distress would teach them how to express themselves in prayer.[1]

The Brethren now derived essential help from the young converts. Having begun to translate a Harmony of the Gospels into the Greenland language, they were much assisted by them in this important work. The missionaries often remarked, that the converts used expressions, especially in prayer, which it would have been impossible for them ever to have discovered from their intercourse with the other Greenlanders, or by any rules of grammar. They therefore took particular notice of such words and phrases, and learned to speak from the young converts after the latter had learned to think from them. They now saw the propriety of a resolution which they had early taken, not to converse with the Greenlanders on the subject of religion while their knowledge of the language was imperfect, for such equivocal expressions were even still pointed out to them by an upright mind, as the crafty savages might have taken occasion to pervert to the worst of purposes.[2]

But though the Christian Greenlanders afforded the Brethren much satisfaction, they were not without their imperfections. Several of them, for example, began to betray a spirit of pride, arrogance, and self-conceit. No sooner had they obtained some knowledge of the gospel, and were able to speak of it to others, than they set themselves up for teachers, and entertained high notions of their own acquirements. The missionaries now found that one of the chief lessons they would have to inculcate on them was not to "think of themselves more highly than they

[1] Crantz's Hist. Green. vol. ii. p. 6, 9, 29. [2] Ibid. vol. i. p. 399; vol. ii. p. 11.

ought to think,"[1] a circumstance which shews that vanity and pride of intellect are to be found among the lowest and most degraded portions of the human family, as well as among civilized nations and cultivated minds.

In October 1742, the number of Greenlanders who took up their winter quarters in the neighbourhood of the Brethren amounted to thirty. These they endeavoured to reduce into some kind of order, with regard both to their temporal and their spiritual concerns. At the catechetical exercises, and the other meetings, they regularly read to them the Harmony of the Gospels, which was now finished; they also taught them some hymns, which the poor creatures learned with great eagerness, and which seemed to afford them peculiar pleasure, for they sung them perpetually, both at home and abroad. In their meetings such powerful impressions were often made, both on the speaker and the hearers, that they mingled their tears together, and were scarcely able to proceed with the exercise. The missionaries also now began to form them into little classes, in which four or five individuals of the same sex conversed freely with each other concerning the state of their hearts, and their progress in the knowledge of religion.[2]

The prospects of the missionaries now became brighter than ever: the effects of the gospel were so remarkable, that it seemed as if a general awakening of the Greenlanders was about to take place in that part of the country. Most of them, indeed, had not resolution enough to forsake their usual places of hunting and fishing, and to fix their residence with the Brethren for the purpose of enjoying regular instruction. But though, in consequence of this, many of them for a season lost their serious impressions, and some wandered to distant parts of the country, yet most of them afterwards returned, became concerned about their souls, and were admitted as members of the congregation; or they went to the Danish colonies, and were there baptized. From this period, the whole Greenland nation manifested a new and improved temper toward foreigners, whom they at first had so hated, dreaded, or despised. Many who formerly derided and maltreated the Brethren, now came and asked their pardon; and even those who once were the most untractable, stood along

[1] Crantz's Hist. Green. vol. ii. p. 29. [2] Ibid. vol. ii. p. 31.

the shore as the missionaries sailed by, entreated them to land, and tell them the words of God.[1]

As it was impossible for the Brethren to make so frequent or so extensive visits among the heathen as the urgency of the call demanded, they were obliged, in many cases, to rest satisfied with the simple testimony of the young converts, when they went abroad in search of provisions. But though the scattering of their little flock in summer ultimately promoted the spread of the gospel, the missionaries often felt great solicitude at the prospect of their departure, lest any evil should befal them, through the numerous snares and temptations to which they would be exposed. On one of these occasions, they sent for all the baptized, both men and women, and spoke with them separately, before parting with them. They entreated them with tears in their eyes, not to forget the Lord Jesus, who was crucified for them, and to watch over their own hearts, while surrounded with temptations among the heathen. They then blessed them and kissed them, and went down with them to the strand. There they once more addressed them, from these words of the apostle, "And now, brethren, I commend you to God, and to the word of his grace, which is able to build you up, and to give you an inheritance among all them which are sanctified." The Greenlanders then set off in their boats, and the missionaries, in the mean while, sung a hymn on the shore. In the course of the summer, some of the converts frequently returned, and informed them of whatever circumstances occurred among them. In those cases where several were together in the same place, it was pleasing to witness the brotherly love they shewed toward each other; even the heathen bore testimony to their exemplary behaviour. There were, however, some instances of misconduct among them; and therefore, on their return, the Brethren spoke with them, one by one, in order to remove every kind of misunderstanding between them, before restoring them to their separate meetings, and the kiss of charity as a token of their closer fellowship. On this occasion, most of them displayed remarkable ingenuousness, acknowledging their faults with readiness, and begging each other's pardon with tears.[2]

[1] Crantz's Hist. Green. vol. ii. p. 34, 38. [2] Ibid. vol. ii. p. 38, 45.

In 1746, this general awakening, after it had lasted about three years, began to subside among the Greenlanders. Many of those who had heard the gospel and been impressed by it were still undecided, and sought to get rid of their convictions, and even to deter others by force or fraud from joining the congregation. The Angekoks, in particular, afraid of losing their standing, and the gains of their impostures, laboured to terrify the poor people by the most ridiculous tales. One of these deceivers brought heavy charges against the Christians, alleging that their new doctrine and way of life frightened away the sea fowl, after he, by his art, had released them from the subterranean regions. Another of them warned his countrymen not to listen to the believers, as he had performed a journey to heaven with the view of ascertaining how it went with the souls of the deceased Greenlanders, and that he there found all the baptized in a most deplorable condition, without food and clothing; while those who had not received the gospel were blessed with plenty. A frightful report was circulated about a Christian Greenlander, who had died at the northern colony and appeared again perfectly naked, saying, he had been thrust into a dark dismal hole, where he endured the greatest misery. Such of the savages as sought an apology for neglecting the gospel, readily credited these foolish stories, alleging that the Europeans inflicted these punishments upon their deceased countrymen, because the Greenlanders had murdered their ancestors; and though such as were now in the country did no harm to their bodies, yet they endeavoured to ruin their souls hereafter. Most of them, however, paid little regard to these idle tales, and as soon as the first impressions of them were effaced, they came in great numbers to visit the Brethren, and to hear the word, especially if they understood that any of the converts were to be baptized.[1]

Meanwhile the little flock of Christian Greenlanders increased both in numbers and in grace. Many painful circumstances, indeed, occasionally occurred among them; but nothing else could be expected in a congregation collected from among savage heathens, since the church of Christ on earth, even in its best state, is only an hospital of sick people, who have begun to re-

[1] Crantz's Hist. Green. vol. ii. p. 78.

cover, but have yet the seeds of disease in their constitution, and are still liable to partial relapses. Their intercourse with their heathen countrymen was attended with no small danger to their spiritual interests; yet it could not be altogether avoided, as they were obliged to be often from home in search of provisions. The more indeed they experienced the advantages of daily instruction, and the many inconveniences attending their being scattered abroad, the more they endeavoured to live together under the inspection of their teachers, and the more readily did they submit to the external rules of the congregation, which they saw aimed at their spiritual prosperity, not at their temporal subjection. When, therefore, they were under the necessity of going to the fishing among the islands, they went almost all to one place, that they might hold their meetings together; and as soon as they obtained an adequate supply of their wants, they hastened back to their teachers. They were now more and more sensible of the love of the missionaries towards them, since, notwithstanding their own accumulated manual labours, one or other of them always devoted his time to their service, either going to sea with them, or frequently visiting them; and when none of them could be with them, the converts followed the advice of the helpers and class-keepers, who informed the Brethren from time to time of whatever occurred among them.[1]

Hitherto the missionaries had been afraid to admit any of the Greenland converts to the Lord's Supper, lest they should afterwards apostatize and dishonour their Christian profession; but they now resolved to admit three of them to that holy ordinance. On being informed of this, and having the nature of the institution explained to them, the candidates were filled with the liveliest joy, mingled with emotions of shame. When they afterwards partook of the ordinance, a solemn awe overpowered their hearts, and a flood of tears rolled down their cheeks. "It was," they said, "as if their body had sunk into the dust, and their spirit taken its flight to heaven. All their thoughts centred in this. Oh! how is it possible our Saviour should so dearly love poor sinful men." Such were the pleasing effects of the first Greenland communion.[2]

[1] Crantz's Hist. Green. vol. ii. p. 69, 80, 93, 95. [2] Ibid. vol. ii. p. 94, 102.

In the course of their labours among the Greenlanders, the Brethren had often to encounter no small hardships and dangers; but yet, in the midst of all, the Lord appeared as their deliverer. Once, when two of them had sailed to the distance of about six leagues, in search of wood, they were obliged to remain no less than eight days on an uninhabited island, exposed to all the violence of three dreadful storms, without either a house or a tent to shelter them. During the last four or five days, they had nothing to eat but shell-fish, and even of these they could scarcely procure enough to satisfy the cravings of hunger. At length, they ventured to return homewards; but scarcely had they set foot on shore, when there arose such a terrible storm, that it was with difficulty they secured and sheltered their boat. About the same time, John Beck and two new assistants from Europe were in imminent danger of their lives, on arriving on the shores of Greenland. After reaching the latitude of Good Hope, they durst not approach the land, on account of the violence of the storms; but were obliged to proceed about eighty leagues to the north, before they could venture to leave the ship. Even then the captain advised them to wait another opportunity, as he was afraid they might be murdered by the savages who inhabited that part of the country, and who had an exceedingly bad character. They resolved, however, to make the attempt. The day was calm and serene when they set off in their boat; but in the evening, as they were attempting to cross a broad inlet, the wind arose all of a sudden, and threatened to drive them into the wide ocean. After long and severe rowing, they at length reached a lonely uninhabited island. Here they were obliged to remain, without either house or tent, for two days and three nights; and to aggravate their distress, they had, in lightening the boat during the storm, thrown into the sea, among other articles, their implements for striking fire, so that they now suffered very severely both from wet and cold. They had, however, a small quantity of bread and cheese, as also some bottles of wine, but these had frozen and burst, owing to the severity of the cold. At night, they lay in a hole dug in the snow, and covered themselves with the sail of the boat. On leaving this place, on the third day, they came to the first Greenland house in Omenak, and were received by the inhabitants in a friendly manner; but as that quarter of the country was notorious for the murder of several navigators, they kept a strict watch during the whole of the night. After sailing in their boat for six days longer, in the course of which they suffered a variety of other hardships and dangers, they at length arrived in safety at New Herrnhut, as the missionary settlement was now called.[1]

In 1750, when the Greenlanders who resided with the Brethren removed from their tents into their winter houses, they amounted to upwards of three hundred. In that part of the country, it was formerly deemed impossible for two families to find subsistence; yet this great number of persons not only subsisted, but were able to afford relief to those who were in need, though there had been such famines in other places, almost every year, that even where provisions used to be most plentiful many had died of want. Some of the savages from Kangek had lately buried an old man alive, and when they were called to an account for their conduct, they pleaded, in excuse, that it was done at his daughter's request, because he had an ulcerated hand and could do nothing for his own support! The Christian Greenlanders had never been reduced to such extremity, for they had learned to work as well as to pray, and even to be good economists. They now, indeed, enjoyed great advantages for the preservation of their provisions, in consequence of their connection with the missionaries. Formerly they used to conceal their dried meat, fish, capelins, and other articles under heaps of stones, where they were often half-devoured by the foxes and ravens, or reduced to a state of putrefaction; but now they had a large storehouse in which they could lay them up in safety.[2]

In the beginning of 1752, there was one of the most dreadful winters in Greenland that ever was known; and in this, as well as several of the following years, the inhabitants suffered all the horrors of famine, in consequence of the extreme severity of the weather. From February to Easter the cold was perfectly horrible. The inlets were so frozen and blocked up with ice, that frequently not a kajak could stir in the water. The weather was so unsettled and so tempestuous, that the people

[1] Crantz's Hist. Green. vol. ii. p. 90. [2] Ibid. vol. ii. p. 124, 129, 133, 138.

could seldom go abroad, and when they made the attempt, it was not only at the risk of their life, but was attended with little or no advantage, as they rarely caught even a single bird. Imminent, however, as was the danger, only one of the congregation was lost. He was carried away in a violent tempest, by the impetuosity of the waves, and was not found until three months after, when he was discovered in his kajak, half-devoured by the ravens and foxes. One day, the storm was so awfully tremendous, that nothing like it was remembered by any of the Greenlanders. The new and largest boat of the missionaries, though it was drawn up on the shore and tied to a post, was shattered by the waves. A few days after, there was such a dreadful hurricane, attended with lightning, that their dwelling-house and chapel were nearly thrown down; they tottered and cracked like a ship in a storm. In consequence of the severity of the weather, the Greenlanders were reduced to the utmost extremity, being in danger of perishing either by cold or hunger. The Brethren constantly allowed one company after another to come into their rooms to warm themselves. They also distributed dried capelins among such of the families as were poor; and when these were exhausted, they supplied them with pease. They at the same time exhorted the more wealthy Greenlanders not to shut up their bowels of compassion against their indigent brethren; but to impart provisions to them as long as they had any remaining, without taking thought for the morrow. This had so good an effect, that, among the communicants at least, it needed no repetition. Some at last made their way to the islands; but most of them soon came back, as they were able to do less there than even at home, owing to the storminess of the weather. The return of the others was prevented, partly by the intense cold which soon after ensued and froze the sea as far as the eye could reach, partly by a tempest which shattered most of their boats to pieces.[1]

But dreadful as was the famine this season, instead of being alleviated, it appears to have been aggravated the following year. The islands were so enclosed with ice, that it was impossible for the Greenlanders to go in quest of food; and such a

[1] Crantz's Hist. Groon. vol. ii. p. 157.

terrible scarcity ensued as no European in the country had ever witnessed. Frequent accounts were received of children perishing of hunger in one part of the country, and of old helpless people being buried alive in another. In a visit which two of the missionaries paid to Kangek, they found, in one place, fifteen persons nearly starved to death. They were lying in a house so small and so low, that it was impossible to stand upright in it; and the only way of entering it was by creeping in on the belly. They had no fire, but lay one upon another, in all directions, in order to keep themselves warm. Neither had they a morsel to eat; and such was their extreme weakness, that when the missionaries entered, they did not care to raise themselves, or even to speak to them. At length, a man brought a couple of fishes from the sea. A girl seized one of them, raw as it was, tore it in pieces with her teeth, and gorged it down with the utmost voracity. She looked as pale as death. Four of the children of these poor creatures, indeed, had already died of hunger. The Brethren distributed among them a part of their own provisions, and advised them to remove to New Herrnhut. They accordingly came thither soon after; but, at first, it was scarcely possible to satisfy their hunger. Their appetite was so keen, that they went to the very dust heaps in search of fish-bones, already sufficiently chewed, and even of pieces of old shoes. To these and many others of their destitute countrymen, the Christian Greenlanders communicated supplies with the utmost cheerfulness, though they had often to make a hard enough shift for themselves.[1]

But though numbers of the savages were driven to New Herrnhut by the severity of the famine, yet neither the afflictions of life, nor the kindness of the Brethren, made any serious impression on their minds. The aversion which they had to their Christian countrymen was so rooted, that it was with great reluctance, that even the half-starving people now mentioned resolved to apply to them for assistance; and though they came and obtained relief, yet not one of them remained, not even such as had relations in the place, who spared no pains to induce them to stay. The same was the case with others of the savages. No sooner was their hunger satisfied, than they

[1] Crantz's Hist. Green. vol. ii. p. 258, 260.

hastened away as from a place infected by the plague. It was evident the judgment of many of them was convinced of the excellence of Christianity, but yet their heart was opposed to the purity of its precepts. They admired the fine order of the converts; they could not but acknowledge that they led a happier life, and suffered less from external want than other Greenlanders, yet such was their dislike of religion, that they would not stay among them, and many of them even ran away as soon as the name of the Saviour was mentioned.[1]

Famine, however, was not the only calamity which now visited this ill-fated country. In 1754, several Dutch ships having run into Ball's River to avoid the ice, numbers of the Greenlanders went on board, and were treated with foreign victuals, particularly pease, which they ate to the greater excess, as hunger had for some months past whetted their appetites. It was at length discovered, though too late, that a contagious distemper prevailed in at least one of these vessels; and it was not long before it broke out, first among the heathen, and then among the Christian Greenlanders, and carried off great numbers of them, for at least fourteen leagues round the colony. During the time that it raged, which was about three months, scarcely a day passed at New Herrnhut without either a death or a funeral; and, in one instance, four corpses were laid in the grave on the same day, namely, two brothers, their nephew, and a child. Some also died in other places, who could not be brought thither for burial, as at least one-half of the people were sick. The case of these was the more deplorable, as they were not only in great want of the necessaries of life, but were also at such a distance, and so dispersed among the islands, that it was impossible they could be duly attended to, especially as the weather was extremely stormy. Had suitable remedies been early administered to them, it is probable many of them might have recovered. The whole number of Christian Greenlanders who died this year was fifty-seven, and of these thirty-five were supposed to have been carried off by this contagious disorder. Many of them, on their deathbed, exhibited pleasing proofs of the power of religion on their hearts. No people on earth, perhaps, have such a horror of death as the Greenland-

[1] Crantz's Hist. Greon. vol. ii. p. 263.

ers; yet many of the Christian converts not only exercised patience and resignation to the will of God under their affliction, but were full of peace, tranquillity, and joy.[1]

As among the Greenlanders who died there were some of the principal heads of families, the number of widows and orphans, which was large before, was by this means greatly increased. On the return of the congregation to their winter quarters, it was therefore necessary to make arrangements for the support of such as were left destitute. In those cases where there was a son who was able to maintain his mother and the rest of the family, this duty was of course assigned to him. Such children as were only rising to manhood, were distributed in other families, with the view of being trained up to the usual occupations of the country. Those who were not yet able to engage in manual employments were left with their mothers; or if they were bereaved of them also, they were placed under the care of some of the Greenland Sisters; and if they were only infants at the breast, such of the women as were then nursing were obliged to suckle them by turns. In these arrangements most of the Greenlanders acted in a manner highly becoming their Christian profession; and some who were not rich, put to shame others who were more wealthy. It may easily, however, be conceived, that the missionaries must have had no small difficulty in making such arrangements as were satisfactory to all parties. They at the same time took their own share of the burden, being at the expense of clothing some of the poor children, and of furnishing many of the boys with boats and other utensils, that they might learn to provide for themselves and their relations; for they were determined to afford them no excuse for indolence or idleness, but chose rather to spend a little upon them in early life, to enable them to work with their own hands, than by neglecting them in their youth, to allow them to remain a burden on the community. It is not unworthy of observation, that the women nursing the infants which were deprived of their mothers, was an interesting proof of the power of religion on their hearts. There is nothing, perhaps, to which the Greenland females have so rooted an aversion, as suckling the children of another, lest their own child

[1] Crantz's Hist. Green. vol. p. 215, 217, 219, 221, 223.

should have a rival in their affections. Hence, among the savages, when a woman dies, and leaves an infant behind her, the unfortunate father has no other resource but to bury it alive immediately, that so he may not behold his little babe lingering to death before his eyes. In such cases, a Greenland woman has no feeling of compassion; yet the gospel, by its transforming influence, overcame this barbarous prejudice.[1]

Of the power of Christianity in expanding the heart and exciting the principle of benevolence in the breast even of the most brutish and degraded savages, we may here notice another striking example. It was customary with the Brethren at some of their meetings, to read to their Greenland flock the accounts which they received from their congregations in Europe, and particularly from the missions among the heathen. By these a very lively impression was often produced on the converts; but nothing of this kind ever touched them so sensibly, as the account of the destruction of the Indian settlement at Gnadenhuetten, in Pennsylvania, by some of the savages in the interest of France.[2] When they were told that most of the missionaries were either shot or burnt to death; but that the Christian Indians had escaped to the Brethren's settlement at Bethlehem, they were so impressed with the relation, that they burst into tears, and immediately offered to make a contribution for the relief of the unfortunate sufferers. "I," said one, "have a fine reindeer skin, which I will give."—"I," cried a second, "have a new pair of reindeer boots, which I will send them."—"And I," said a third, "will send them a seal, that they may have something to eat and to burn." The whole scene was extremely interesting, affording a fine display of the simplicity and benevolence of their hearts. Their contributions, indeed, when turned into money, were of little value; yet the missionaries did not choose to reject them, but directed the amount of the whole to be transmitted by their Brethren in Europe to the sufferers in America.[3]

New Herrnhut had now become a pleasant little village. The country originally consisted entirely of bald rocks, thinly inter-

[1] Crantz's Hist. Green. vol. ii. p. 226.

[2] See Section III.

[3] Crantz's Hist. Green. vol. ii. p. 266.

spersed with spots and veins of earth, or rather sand. But the missionary house and chapel, the area and the garden, were laid out in neat and regular order; and all the adjacent land, where once not a blade of grass grew, was now enrobed with the richest and most beautiful verdure, so that the settlement might justly be considered as a garden of the Lord, in the midst of a horrible wilderness. The Brethren even introduced sheep into Greenland, and the attempt succeeded beyond their most sanguine expectations. The grass was so nutritious, that the ewes brought forth two, and even three lambs a year; and though there were so many lambs from the same mother, yet they were larger in autumn than sheep of a year old in Germany. This little flock of sheep was of great use to the missionaries, especially as the number of reindeer was daily decreasing.[1]

As the Brethren had now collected a numerous congregation at New Herrnhut, they were anxious to establish another settlement in a part of the country more convenient for the Southlanders, many of whom had often invited them to come and reside among them. Besides other difficulties, however, there were not missionaries enough to carry such a design into execution. Matthew Stach, one of the original founders of the mission, had lately returned to Europe, and was now thinking of taking some rest in fellowship with the congregation at home, after the many toils and hardships he had endured abroad. Such, however, was his attachment to the Greenlanders, that he never could speak or hear of them without earnestly wishing to be again among them. When, therefore, it was proposed to him to undertake the establishment of a second settlement, he cheerfully agreed to make the attempt, notwithstanding the new toils and dangers to which it would necessarily expose him.

In May 1758, Matthew Stach sailed from Europe, accompanied by two other of the Brethren as his assistants. In the course of the voyage, they did not meet with a single storm, and what was still more wonderful, they were treated with kindness and civility by the ship's company. In this respect there had been a remarkable change for some years past, especially

[1] Crantz's Hist. Green. vol. i. p. 74; vol. ii. p. 162, 399.

after the trade to Greenland was consigned by His Majesty to the Incorporated Company of Merchants, and the Brethren, instead of being allowed a free passage, were required to pay a moderate sum for the transport of themselves and their goods, a circumstance which proved both for their interest and their comfort. Formerly, the ship's company used to make it their study to vex and annoy them by their words and actions, mocking them on account of their religion, and even denying them such external accommodations as were really necessary. But on this occasion, Matthew Stach and his companions were treated not only with civility, but with kindness by the captain and the whole of the crew. After visiting New Herrnhut, they proceeded with four of the Greenland families in search of a suitable situation for a new settlement. Having examined different places, they fixed on a small island near the coast, about a hundred miles to the south of New Herrnhut. Here they pitched their tents, and called the name of the settlement Lichtenfels.[1]

In building the houses necessary for their accommodation, the new settlers had to encounter considerable difficulties, owing to the want of suitable materials; but this inconvenience they overcame by their usual patience and perseverance. There was, at the same time, such a scarcity of provisions, that it was with difficulty they maintained themselves. Nor was this merely a temporary calamity. It lasted, in a greater or less degree for two or three years, and towards the end of that period was little short of famine. The Greenlanders at Lichtenfels, indeed, suffered less than the savages, many of whom died of hunger; but yet they had often to make a miserable shift with a few crowberries left on the ground during the winter, or some small meagre fishes. The missionaries themselves were often reduced to the greatest straits, and were able to afford but little assistance to the poor heathen in their neighbourhood.[2]

In June 1774, John Soerensen and G. Grillich, two of the Brethren, commenced a third settlement in the South of Greenland, which they called Lichtenau. It was about 400 miles from Lichtenfels, and within sight of Cape Farewell.[3]

[1] Crantz's Hist. Green. vol. ii. p. 131, 273; Period. Accounts vol. v. p. 238.
[2] Crantz's Hist. Green. vol. ii. p. 279, 309, 356.
[3] Fortsetzung Bruder Historie tom. i. p. 122; Period. Accounts, vol. v. p. 238.

During the first winter of the Brethren's residence in this quarter of the country, near a hundred of the savages took up their abode with them. This part of Greenland appears to have been more than ordinarily populous. Within the circuit of a few miles, it was supposed there were about a thousand inhabitants. Here, therefore, the Brethren had an ample field for labour, and after some years, they collected a larger congregation at this place than in either of their other settlements in Greenland.[1]

Though the Brethren, in the admission of the Greenlanders to baptism, paid greater regard to the state of their hearts than to their intellectual attainments, yet most of the converts were not defective in the doctrinal knowledge of the gospel. There was, indeed, a material difference between those who were baptized in their infancy, and trained up under the eye of the missionaries, and such as were not connected with them until they were advanced in life. The young people enjoyed not only the advantage of the daily catechetical exercises, which the adults had not leisure to attend, but most of them learned to read, and were able to understand more fully, and to retain more perfectly, what they were taught. Many of the old people, however, by their diligence made wonderful progress in Christian knowledge. It was often observed, that such as possessed more grace than knowledge at the time of their baptism, soon outstripped, even in understanding, others who, in this respect, were in advance of them; while, on the other hand, those who, after baptism, made little progress in grace, remained at the same time defective in knowledge.[2]

In 1804, C. F. Rudolph, one of the missionaries, in returning to Europe after labouring twenty-six years in Greenland, experienced a very remarkable deliverance at sea. Having embarked on board a vessel bound for Copenhagen, he was detained a number of weeks in the harbour; but the captain at length resolved to set sail, as he understood there was no ice about Nunarsoak. Three days after, however, a storm arose from the south-west, and drove the fields and mountains of ice close upon the ship. The scene was awfully tremendous and

[1] Fortsetzung Bruder Hist. tom. i. p. 124, 330.
[2] Crantz's Hist. Green. vol. ii. p. 426, 431.

sublime. The vessel, with her sails close-reefed, drove among the ice before the wind, and it seemed as if she would every moment be crushed to pieces. She, at length, struck with great violence against a large field of ice: several planks started at once; the water rushed into her; and in a very short time, only the larboard gunwale appeared above the surface. The captain and the sailors immediately took to their boats, and carried off one party after another to a neighbouring field of ice. Rudolph and his wife were the last who were taken off: by this time they were above the knees in the water, holding fast by the shrouds. Being only about a league from land, they now made towards the shore; but the large boat was so heavily laden, it had already taken in so much water, and the wind was so high, that they were afraid it would sink, and therefore they were obliged to sail to the nearest island they could reach. It proved to be a rough, pointed, naked rock. Here they endeavoured to land the provisions which they had saved from the wreck; but in making the attempt, the boats, with eight of the crew on board, were carried away by the storm, driven to the opposite shore, and appeared to be dashed to pieces among the rocks. The others being thus left destitude of provisions, had nothing before them but the prospect of perishing of hunger on this uninhabited island. It was a heavy rain the whole day, and in the evening they lay down to sleep close to each other, without either tent or covering. Here they were completely wet, lying as it were in a pool of water; for, besides the incessant rain, the water flowed in streams from the top of the rock upon their resting place.

After two days, the captain and most of the crew endeavoured to gain the shore, by walking across the ice. The attempt was extremely hazardous, as they had to leap from one piece of ice to another, and might readily have fallen into the sea between them. Rudolph and his wife would willingly have joined them; but as they had now been without food for two days, they did not think they had strength remaining to undergo the fatigue. The crew, however, promised that should they reach the shore in safety, they would send off a boat to rescue them. Besides them, there remained on the island the ship's cook; and on an adjoining rock, there were two others of the crew who came over the ice several times to see them.

In this dismal situation, they remained till the ninth day. When the sun shone, they employed themselves in drying the few articles they had saved from the wreck ; but they were at last so enfeebled with cold and hunger, that they were scarcely able for even this small service ; for during all this time they had no support, except the fresh water collected in the chinks and holes of the rocks, of which they every now and then drank a little. All day long they looked with eager eyes towards the land in the hope of descrying some Greenlander coming to their relief ; but as they looked from day to day in vain, they began to fear that the crew had perished in attempting to reach the shore. There now, therefore, seemed no prospect before them, but that of ending their lives on this barren rock ; of lying unburied under the canopy of heaven ; and of becoming food to the ravens, and the other birds of prey, which were continually hovering around them. Painful, however, as was their situation, they felt perfectly resigned to the will of God, and united in singing hymns relative to their departure into the world of spirits.

At length, however, on the evening of the ninth day, Rudolph's wife, happening to raise herself up, as they were lying down to rest, espied two Greenlanders, in their kajaks, making towards the island, and hailing them. Their enfeebled limbs having now collected new strength, they immediately climbed to the top of the rock, and called to their deliverers to let them know where they were. On landing, the Greenlanders told them, that they had been in search of them the whole day, and at last concluded that they must be dead. On reaching the shore the following evening, they found that the whole crew, with the exception of one man, had escaped in safety, after suffering great hardships in the attempt. On their way to Lichtenau, which was about twenty-eight miles distant, they met a boat, in which was one of the Danish missionaries, who was astonished to see them alive, as he concluded they must have perished, and had come thus far, with the view of carrying their corpses to that place for interment. Having spent the following winter with their brethren at that settlement, they again set off for Europe the ensuing year ; and after encountering many hardships and dangers in sailing along the icy shores of Greenland, they arrived in safety at Copenhagen.[1]

In July 1824, John C. Kleinschmidt, J. A. De Fries, and J. F. Baus, three of the Brethren, began a new settlement in the South of Greenland near Staatenhuk, which was called Fredericksthal. The heathen Greenlanders, on hearing of their arrival, came thither in great numbers, and in little more than twelve months upwards of a hundred of them were baptized. It is well known that the Greenlanders are commonly of small stature; but among those from the East coast, who constituted the majority of the congregation, which, after some years, was collected at this place, many were of tall stature, and of European features. They were probably descendants of the ancient Normans or North-men, who once inhabited these coasts, but who it is supposed, were at last entirely amalgamated with the natives.[2]

In 1852, the number of persons belonging to the Brethren's congregations in Greenland was as follows :—

Begun.	Stations.	Communicants.	Baptized Adults.	Baptized Children.	TOTAL.
1733	New Herrnhut,	199	62	133	394
1758	Lichtenfels,	163	121	104	388
1774	Lichtenau,	267	130	263	660
1824	Fredericksthal,	236	68	166	470
		865	381	666	1912[3]

To some these numbers may appear inconsiderable; but it should be remembered that they form a large proportion of the Greenland nation. In 1850, the native population of Western Greenland was estimated at 9200,[4] so that if this calculation be correct, the congregations of the Brethren form upwards of one-fifth of the whole inhabitants of the country. There is in fact no longer any body of heathen Greenlanders residing within reach of any of the Brethren's settlements, with the exception of Fredericksthal, near Staatenhuk. As one result of the

[1] Period. Accounts, vol. iv. p. 341.

[2] Ibid. vol. ix. p. 253, 414, 421; vol. xix. p. 286. 287.

[3] Ibid. vol. xxi. p. xxvi.

[4] Johnston's Physical Atlas.

Danish and Moravian Missions in Greenland, there are now scarcely any unbaptized Greenlanders along the whole of the West Coast to the 72° North Latitude; and the people generally make a profession of Christianity, though with many it is nothing more than a profession. On the east coast, the inhabitants are still heathen ; but their number is small, and they are nearly inaccessible by Europeans.[1]

The prosperity of the mission in Greenland was greatly hindered by the necessity under which the people were of engaging in hunting and fishing, in order to obtain the means of subsistence, and of dispersing themselves far and wide for this purpose during the summer months. This evil was greatly aggravated of late years by the regulations made by the Danish authorities with a view to the promotion of trade, according to which a considerable part of the people belonging to the Brethren's congregations were obliged to remain during the winter also at a distance from the settlements. In consequence of this, the instructions which they received, and any good impressions made upon them, were apt to be obliterated from their minds, while they were at the same time exposed to many temptations in their wanderings.[2]

The missionaries established schools at all the stations ; and it is worthy of remark, that the Greenland youth, when at school, did not appear to be at all inferior to European children of the same age ; but there is no chance of their equalling them in their attainments, unless the year were one perpetual winter, so strong and irresistible are the attractions of a roving life, even on the inhospitable coasts of Greenland, the sea being the element on which they must seek their subsistence, the land yielding little or nothing that can support life. Indeed, the education of the young is now greatly interrupted by the regulations of the Danish authorities, requiring the people to live at a distance from the missionary stations even during the winter, and many of them are growing up without being able to read.[3]

Besides the Harmony of the Gospels, which the Brethren prepared a few years after their arrival in Greenland, they

[1] Period. Accounts, vol. iii. p. 219 ; vol. xvii. p. 370, 380.
[2] Ibid. vol. xii. p. 293, 301 ; vol. xvii. p. 212, 321 ; vol. xviii. p. 23 ; vol. xx. p. 129.
[3] Ibid. vol. xviii. p. 23, 119.

translated the whole of the New Testament, and such portions of the Old Testament into the Greenland language as they judged most necessary for the Christian converts. They likewise printed a hymn-book, a spelling-book, and a catechism or summary of Christian doctrine for the use of their congregations, and a short compendium of the Bible for the children; and they compiled, with great pains, a grammar and dictionary of that singular dialect.[1]

SECT. II.—WEST INDIES.

PART I.—DANISH ISLANDS.

ART. 1.—ST THOMAS.

IN August 1732, John Leonard Dober and David Nitschman, left Herrnhut, in Upper Lusatia, for Copenhagen, intending to proceed from thence to St Thomas, for the purpose of instructing the negroes on that island. Dober was one of the two Brethren who originally offered themselves for this service. Nitschman was merely to accompany him and see him settled, and was afterwards to return to the congregation. The Brethren being then little acquainted with missionary undertakings, gave them, instead of all other instructions, only this general direction, "In all things to follow the guidance of the Spirit of Christ." Count Zinzendorf gave each of them a ducat for their journey, in addition to about a pound sterling which each of them had of his own. With this scanty sum in each of their purses, and with staff in hand, they set out on their journey to Copenhagen, a distance of about 600 miles from Herrnhut. On the road they called on some pious friends; but these, instead of giving them any encouragement, sought to dissuade them from their design, representing it as altogether impracticable. The Brethren did not attempt to answer their objections; but trusting in God, they resolved to follow their own convictions of

[1] MS. Accounts *penes me*; Fortsetzung Brud. Hist. tom. i. p. 328; Period. Accounts, vol. v. p. 379; vol. vii. p. 22; vol. viii. p. 81.

duty, and to act agreeably to what they considered as his will. The Countess of Stollberg was the only individual who endeavoured to confirm them in their purpose: she encouraged and animated them to make every sacrifice for the cause of the Redeemer, saying, he was well worthy that we should even die for his sake. The sentiments of the Countess were so much the more cheering to them, as, except Count Zinzendorf, nó one had hitherto spoken to them in the way of comfort and encouragement.

On their arrival at Copenhagen, the Brethren had many difficulties to encounter. They were told that no ship would take them to St Thomas; and that should they even get there, it was very doubtful whether they would be allowed to instruct the slaves. But notwithstanding every discouragement, Dober and Nitschman remained firm to their purpose; the less help there appeared for them in man, the more they looked to God for assistance. Struck with their stedfastness, several persons in Copenhagen began to view their design with a favourable eye: among these were His Majesty's two chaplains, several of the councillors of state, and some members of the Royal Family, who were so condescending as to befriend and assist them.[1]

Having sailed from Copenhagen, the two Brethren reached St Thomas after a voyage of about ten weeks. Neither of them, however, remained long on the island. Nitschman, as was originally designed, soon returned to Europe. Dober found great difficulties in the way of supporting himself, and lived for sometime in great poverty. He had not, however, been more than twenty months on the island when he also returned to Germany, having, though but a young man, been chosen by the congregation at Herrnhut to the office of general or superintending elder among them. It does not appear that the two Brethren while on the island did much for the instruction of the negroes. This was probably not in their power. They do not appear to have assembled them for public worship, but confined themselves entirely to efforts of a private nature, speaking to individuals as they had opportunity, of Jesus Christ and of redemption through his blood.[1]

[1] Oldendorp's Geschichte der Mission der Evangelischen Bruder auf St Thomas, St Croix and St Jan, tom. ii. p. 456; Mission of the Church of the United Brethren to the Danish West India Islands, London 1832, p. 7.

[2] Oldendorp's Geschichte, tom. ii. p. 460, 474, 492; Period. Accounts, vol. xvi. p. vi.

In December 1735, Frederick Martin, accompanied by John A. Bonike, and T. W. Grothaus, sailed for St Thomas, with the view of renewing the mission on that island. Immediately after his arrival, Martin met with the few negroes whom Dober used to visit. He did not, however, content himself with holding meetings with the slaves in the town of Tappus and the neighbourhood, but extended his labours to some of the plantations in the country. The negroes attended on his instructions in considerable numbers, and listened to him with great attention. In his intercourse with them he won their affections wonderfully, by his kind and condescending manners. He used to shake hands with them, sit down beside them, and converse with them, as if they had been his friends and his equals. These little acts of condescension made a strong impression on the hearts of the negroes, who had never been accustomed to such treatment from a White man, and convinced them more effectually than any other means he could have employed of the sincerity of his regard for them. He, at the same time, divided his own scanty supplies with such of them as were poor and needy. The cripple, the lame, and other miserable creatures who crawled to his door, found in him a friend and benefactor.[1]

Hitherto the mission had been favoured by many of the inhabitants, and had met with serious opposition from none; but when religion began to spread among the negroes, its enemies endeavoured to check its progress. Many of the White people prohibited their slaves from attending the meetings for divine worship; and ordered such as were guilty of this high crime to be beaten and whipped. Some endeavoured to excite the government to suppress the mission by its authority. Others sought to check its progress by seducing the converts to sin. The negro women, in particular, who would no longer submit to the criminal desires of their masters, had much to endure: but they in general bore their trials with patience, and were even excited by them to seek with more earnestness the salvation of their souls.[2]

In September 1737, died John A. Bonike, under circumstances of a very distressing nature. This young man came to

[1] Oldendorp's Geschichte, tom. ii. p. 506, 514, 522, 525, 537.
[2] Ibid. tom. ii. p. 511, 527, 535.

St Thomas with the view of working at his trade for the support of Martin, as well as of himself, that the former might give more undivided attention to the instruction of the negroes. He had not, however, been long on the island when he grew conceited of his own gifts, conceived prejudices against the other Brethren, and at last separated himself from them. He retired to Mosquito Bay, and began to instruct the negroes in that quarter; but the instructions he gave them, were strongly tinctured with enthusiasm. A few weeks after, when he called on the Brethren at Tappus, they entreated him in an affectionate manner to humble himself before God and to acknowledge his error; but he persisted in maintaining his own opinion, and on going away, called on God to judge between them. Soon after his departure, they heard a very loud thunderclap, and in a short time, they received the painful intelligence that Bonike had been struck from his horse and killed on the spot. After he was struck, according to the account of a young negro who accompanied him, he made some fruitless attempts to stand, but before medical aid was procured, he was dead. His lifeless corpse was brought to the Brethren at Tappus, and on the following day was committed by them with sorrow to the grave.[1]

In October 1738, Frederick Martin and Matthew Freundlich his assistant, together with the wife of the latter, were thrown into prison under circumstances of a somewhat extraordinary nature. Timothy Fredler, who was originally sent to St Croix,[2] and afterwards withdrew from the congregation, had of late come to St Thomas; but seemed now to have no object in view except the improvement of his own worldly circumstances. The difference between him and the two missionaries was so marked, that the Christian negroes no longer considered him as a brother. Martin, however, did not entirely withdraw from him; but sought to recover him from the snare into which he had fallen. Fredler had soon after the misfortune to be accused and imprisoned as a thief. The inspector of the plantations of the Lord Chamberlaine Von Pless, alleged that in his chest he had found various articles belonging to that nobleman, to the value of about fifteen rix-dollars. In consequence of this charge, Fredler was thrown into prison, and the two Brethren, who, it

[1] Oldendorp's Geschichte, tom. ii. p. 507, 551. [2] See Article II.

was supposed, must at least have known of his crime, were summoned before a court of justice, and required to give evidence upon oath; but as this was inconsistent with their principles, they refused, though, at the same time, they promised to answer such questions as might be proposed to them in strict accordance with truth, and as in the presence of God. As nothing would induce them to violate the dictates of their consciences, they were fined in thirty rix-dollars; and though they declared they had not as much in their possession, yet on failing of payment, they were all three committed to prison. They still expressed the utmost readiness to answer whatever questions might be proposed to them relative to Fredler's affair, of which they in fact knew nothing; but as they refused to do it upon oath, the fine which was already more than they could pay, was increased to sixty, and afterwards to ninety rix-dollars.[1]

Previous to these events, the prejudices against the Brethren which at this period prevailed in Europe, had reached the island of St Thomas, and furnished the enemies of the missionaries with a specious pretext for putting a stop to their labours among the negroes. Mr Borm, the minister of the Reformed Church, presented, in the name of the consistory, a representation to Government calling in question the validity of Frederick Martin's ordination, and of the ordinances administered by him, particularly the marriage he had celebrated between Freundlich his assistant, and a mulatto woman, one of the converts. In consequence of this petition, the governor had prohibited Martin from administering the sacraments until he should obtain instructions on this point from Copenhagen. Thus the matter appeared for the present to be settled; but while the missionaries were in prison, the accusation of Borm was revived, particularly with respect to the marriage of Freundlich. Without waiting for an answer from the Court of Denmark, their enemies determined not only that it was invalid; but that he should pay within twenty-four hours a fine of one hundred rix-dollars; that he should be imprisoned during life; that his wife should be sold as a slave, and the proceeds devoted to the hospital! This cruel sentence, the judges founded on the punishment which the Danish laws inflict on such as

[1] Oldendorp's Geschichte, tom. ii. p. 564.

live together as man and wife, without being regularly married by a priest.[1]

In January 1739, Count Zinzendorf landed on the island of St Thomas, accompanied by two others of the Brethren who came to assist in the mission. Until his arrival, he knew nothing of the situation of the missionaries, so that his coming at this particular crisis appeared singularly providential. Previous to this Martin had been liberated from prison on bail, on account of the state of his health, which had suffered materially from his confinement. Freundlich and his wife, however, were still prisoners; but on the application of Count Zinzendorf for liberty to them for a few days, they were not only released for a short period, but were not again required to return to jail. Here it may not be improper to add, that Fredler also was at length liberated from his confinement; that there appears to have been no foundation for the foul charge that was brought against him; and that to the close of his life he maintained an affectionate respect for the Brethren, and at his death left part of his property to the missions.[2]

The hostility to the Brethren, however, had not ceased. Their enemies still insisted that they should be banished from the island, and in a petition to the government, desired that they should be entirely prohibited from instructing the negroes. On the day before the Count's departure, when the baptized were assembling to a farewell meeting at Tappus, some of the White people attacked them with sticks and swords. After maltreating the poor defenceless slaves, who, under the worst usage, durst not lift their hand to a White man, the rioters hastened to Posaunenberg, a small plantation which the missionaries had lately purchased, and where they now resided. There they fell on the few negroes who remained, beat them, and wounded them, and put them to flight. They then broke the chairs, the glasses, the dishes, and other articles of furniture: every thing, in short, was destroyed, or dashed to pieces, or thrown out of the house.[3]

The Governor, indeed, offered to the Count to obtain satisfaction for this outrage, and even promised to be in future a father to the missionaries; yet scarcely had Zinzendorf taken

[1] Oldendorp's Geschichte, tom. ii. p. 560, 572.

[2] Ibid. tom. ii. p. 574, 583, 597, 617, 748.

[3] Ibid. tom. ii. p. 557, 587, 596.

his departure, when, in compliance with the demands of some of the planters, he issued an order that no negro should appear after sunset beyond the estate of his master; that a watch of four men should be appointed in every quarter to go about and disperse any slaves whom they might find assembled; and that every offender should on the following day be called before the court, and punished with thirty lashes, and pay all costs. This order the Brethren, in the simplicity of their hearts, imagined was merely a renewed declaration of the law common throughout the West India islands, which prohibits nocturnal assemblies of the slaves as dangerous to the peace of the community, and supposed that it could have no reference to those meetings which they held for instructing them in the principles of religion, as that would be a complete infringement of the toleration granted them by the Court of Denmark. They, therefore, proceeded in their ordinary course, and on the following Sabbath held their meeting after sunset as usual. Next night about eight o'clock, six White people completely armed came to Posaunenberg: by the way they had seized two of the negroes, beaten them, and bound them. On hearing the noise, the missionaries went out and entreated them not to disturb the meeting; but the ruffians appealed to the order of the governor, and boisterously insisted on searching the house. In vain did Martin represent to them the toleration granted to them by the Crown: three of them, armed with naked swords and loaded pistols, burst into the house, where were assembled twenty-four of the negroes. Martin still endeavoured to appease them; but as he could obtain no mercy from men, he sought protection from God, and, with the whole of the little assembly, fell down on his knees in the presence of the White people. In the midst of this scene, the three others entered the house, and instigated by their leader, attacked the defenceless negroes in the most outrageous manner. The Brethren with their characteristic disinterestedness placed themselves before their unoffending people, and received the blows which were aimed at them. Meanwhile, the negroes sprang out of the house, one after another, most of them without sustaining any material injury. Enraged at their escape, the drunken leader of the band required the missionaries to bring them back, a demand which it is needless to say he made in vain. His wrath being still unsatiated, he attempted to stab the Brethren with his sword, but was prevented by his companions. Though none died in consequence of this brutal attack, yet several were severely injured. One of the Brethren received a wound in the shoulder and some cuts through his coat. His wife was stabbed in the breast through her handkerchief. The wife of another of the missionaries was wounded in the shoulder, and a woman who had a child in her arms was cut in the head.

Two days after, five White men came to the house of the Brethren, and on finding no negroes with them, assailed them with mockery and threatenings, brandished about their naked swords and pistols, and one led his horse into their apartment. Before their departure, they read the order of the governor concerning the watchers, and with many threatenings, gave them to understand that no negro would in future be allowed to attend their meetings.

The White people, however, soon grew tired of maintaining so strict a watch on the plantations, and after a few days some hundreds of the negroes came again in the evening to Posaunenberg. As the missionaries could not think of refusing instruction to those who manifested so much desire for it, they retired with them among the brushwood, appointing some to watch and give notice if any White people appeared in the neighbourhood. In no instance, however, did they meet with any interruption, and after a short time they were again allowed to hold their assemblies without disturbance.

By desire of the governor, the Brethren drew up an account of the wanton assault which had been committed upon them. In this statement they asked no satisfaction for themselves, nor any punishment of the offenders, but merely protection in future; yet simple as was their representation, it nearly involved them in new troubles. With the effrontery of consummate villains, two of the rioters denied the whole, purged themselves upon oath, and demanded that the missionaries should be punished as calumniators. After some weeks, however, they dropped their complaint, through the interposition of Mr Carstens, one of the most respectable planters on the island, who, under all the trials of the Brethren, had uniformly been their kind and stedfast friend. An order was soon after received from the Court of Copenhagen, in answer to the appeal which had been made to it, sanctioning the ordination of Martin, and authorizing him to preach, to administer the sacraments, and to celebrate marriage, a circumstance which happily put an end to the violent opposition which they had of late experienced.[1]

In January 1740, Albinus T. Feder and Christian G. Israel, two missionaries destined to St Thomas, were shipwrecked near that island. Feder appears to have been a man of some learning, having studied at the universities of Jena, Leipsic, and Halle. Israel was lame, of a weakly constitution, and walked mostly with a crutch ; but was at the same time full of zeal to make known the Saviour among the heathen. Having sailed from Holland, they landed at St Eustatius, and proceeded from thence in an English vessel for St Thomas. As the voyage, though short, was dangerous on account of the numerous rocks and islets which infest the course, the captain, afraid to sail in the dark, anchored one night under a small island called Skrop, near Tortola. In the morning there arose a terrible storm, which drove the vessel on a rock within a short distance of the island. The sailors instantly took to the boat, but when the missionaries begged to be admitted, it was either carried away by the waves, or there was no room. Anxious to leave the ship, they, together with three negroes who were on board, crept along the bowsprit to the rock against which she had struck ; but still their situation was far from safe, as the place was so small, that they had to lie one upon another, while at the same time, the rigging of the vessel, which hung over them, threatened to thrust them into the sea, as often as it heaved from one side to the other. At that moment, they had no resource, but suddenly to seize the sail and shove it past them.

As between the rock and the neighbouring island there appeared a number of stones at a small distance from one another, Feder resolved to attempt escaping across them to the shore. With this view he dropped down from the rock by means of a rope ; but just as he was setting his feet on one of the stones, he lost his balance, was seized by the waves, and dashed among the rocks. Beholding him rise again to the surface, apparently

[1] Oldendorp's Geschichte, tom. ii. p. 471, 602, 616.

motionless, Israel gave him his parting blessing: "Go in peace," said he, "my dear brother." Instantly the body was swallowed up by the waves and was seen no more. Amidst this trying scene his companion in tribulation felt perfectly resigned to the will of God should he also be doomed to perish in the tempestuous ocean; the calm within his breast forming a striking contrast to the storm which raged without.

Meanwhile the stern of the vessel drove nearer the stones by which Feder had attempted to reach the shore. One of the persons who still remained on board, immediately threw out a plank, and by means of it got safe to land. Israel, as well as some others, wished to follow his example; but he found a difficulty in climbing again upon the bowsprit in order to go on board. This, however, proved his safety. The stern of the vessel was immediately overwhelmed by the waves, and five or six persons who remained on it were drowned.

As the ship was no longer in the way, the waves which had before broke against it, now beat over the rock without obstruction. Poor Israel was liable every moment to be washed into the sea, or to be wounded by the broken pieces of the vessel which were dashed about by the surf. He perceived three boats on shore, but none of them could approach the rock without imminent danger of destruction. At length, in the after noon, some people succeeded in throwing a rope to him and to a negro who still remained on the rock, and hauled them both ashore.

Having lost the whole of his little property in the wreck, Israel scarcely knew how he should get to St Thomas; but in this extremity friends were unexpectedly raised up to assist him. He at length surmounted all his difficulties, and on reaching that island, was received by his brethren in the most affectionate manner.[1]

In the course of a few years, the mission to St Thomas assumed a very promising aspect, through the indefatigable exertions of Frederick Martin and his fellow-labourers. The negroes flocked to them for instruction in great numbers; and many of them appeared to be impressed with the word. Often the church would not contain the crowds who came to it: it was

[1] Oldendorp's Geschichte, tom. ii. p. 623; Crantz's Hist. Breth. p. 312.

therefore necessary to hold divine worship under the canopy of heaven. For several years, indeed, the Brethren, from, it is alleged, the mistaken views of some of them, baptized few of the converts; but afterwards they received great numbers, generally upwards of a hundred in the course of a year. Many of the baptized, however, afterwards fell away, and some fell into grievous sins. This occasioned the missionaries much distress; but yet they exercised singular patience and tenderness toward the wanderers, and in many instances succeeded in bringing them back to the fold of the Redeemer.[1]

In June 1750, the law was renewed that no negro should pass through the town of Tappus, or appear in the streets, after ten o'clock at night. This, however, was not as formerly designed as a covert attack on the Brethren, or as a check to their labours among the slaves: it was occasioned by intelligence of an insurrection of the negroes in Surinam. There was now a great change in the public sentiment in St Thomas with regard to the labours of the missionaries. Most of the White people were convinced that they were attended with beneficial effects on the slaves. On this occasion an exception highly honourable to the Brethren was made in favour of the negroes under their care. As it was not always possible to close the evening meetings in time for the slaves to be home before the appointed hour, the governor ordered that those who were furnished with a certificate by one of the missionaries, should be allowed to pass unmolested by the watch.[2]

Though the Brethren now met with no public persecution, and even enjoyed the approbation of the White people in general; yet they were not without frequent instances of private opposition. Some of the planters and overseers prohibited the negroes from attending on their instructions, and punished them on this account in the severest manner. Others, to prevent their slaves from frequenting the meetings, oppressed them with heavy work, and did not allow them even the Sabbath to themselves, as was customary in the West India Islands. In general, however, the poor creatures chose rather to submit to punishment, than absent themselves from the house of God.[3]

[1] Oldendorp's Geschichte, tom. ii. p. 622, 676, 681, 684, 738, 765, 799, 827, 934, 952, 971.

[2] Ibid. tom. ii. p. 787.

[3] Ibid. tom. ii. p. 694, 788, 818, 983, 942.

In 1782, no fewer than one hundred and twenty-seven of the Brethren, including members of their families, had died on this and the two other Danish islands, St Croix and St Jan, since the commencement of the mission, a period of only half a century.[1] The ravages of disease among them were truly deplorable. New missionaries often scarcely arrived, when they or some of their family sickened and died: sometimes they followed each other in rapid succession to the grave. Even those who survived, had such severe and frequent attacks of sickness as materially interrupted their labours among the negroes: sometimes most of them were so ill at the same time, that one could scarcely help another.[2] The mortality among the missionaries in the Danish West India Islands is the more striking, when contrasted with the small number of deaths in Greenland. Of sixty-four Brethren and sisters who proceeded to that country during the first fifty years of the mission, forty-two were still living: seven only died while resident in that cold inhospitable region, and fifteen after their return from it.[3] But, though the mortality in the Danish West India Islands was so great, it is surprising with what cheerfulness others came forward to fill the ranks of those who had so prematurely fallen. On one occasion when it was made known to the congregation at Bethlehem in North America, that five persons had died within a short time on the island of St Thomas, no fewer than eight Brethren voluntarily offered that very day to go thither and supply their place.[4]

In 1789, this and the other Danish islands were visited with an extraordinary drought, which lasted about three years, and occasioned an universal failure of the crops. Numbers of the negroes died of hunger, as their masters were not in circumstances to support them. Many of the planters were driven by necessity to sell their slaves to foreign islands, particularly to

[1] Fortsetzung Brud. Hist. tom. i. p. 279.

[2] Oldendorp's Geschichte, tom. ii. p. 650, 674, 766, 810, 900, 903.

[3] Risler Erzahlungen aus der Geschichte der Bruderkirche, tom. iii. p. 177.
The longevity of some of the missionaries in Greenland is remarkable. Of between sixty and seventy Brethren employed in that mission during the first century, there were no fewer than six who were engaged in it between forty and fifty years, and one not less than fifty-two.—*Period. Accounts*, vol. xii. p. 301, 480.

[4] Spangenberg's Account, p. 37.

those belonging to France and Spain. Some of the helpers were hindered from fulfilling the duties of their office, as they were appointed to watch and oversee the plantations, particularly on the Sabbath, being found to be persons in whom confidence might be placed at a period when the temptation to unfaithfulness was peculiarly strong. Many of the negroes could not come to church in consequence of their extreme weakness, and an idea spread very widely among them, that in their present trying circumstances, stealing could be no great sin. Some, even of the members of the congregation, adopting this pernicious notion, were guilty of theft: but others withstood the temptation with the utmost firmness, and chose rather to die than commit so great a crime.[1]

With regard to the marriage of those negroes who embraced Christianity, the missionaries had at first considerable difficulties. It often happened that a man at the time of his conversion had more than one wife, a case with respect to which it was not very evident from Scripture what course should be pursued. In one place the Apostle Paul says, "If any brother hath a wife that believeth not, and she be pleased to dwell with him, let him not put her away." In another place he says, "A bishop must be blameless, the husband of one wife." As nothing further is said in the New Testament on this subject, the Brethren laid down the following principles for the regulation of their conduct in cases of this description:

First, That they would not oblige a man who, previous to his conversion, had taken more than one wife, to put the others away without their consent.

Secondly, That notwithstanding this, they would not appoint such a man a helper in the congregation.

Lastly, That they would allow no one who had already embraced Christianity to take more than one wife; and that he was to be considered as bound to her as long as she lived.

But notwithstanding these regulations, the Brethren had often great difficulties with regard to the marriage of slaves, even after their baptism. When a planter in the West Indies, for instance, died in debt, his slaves and other property were liable to be sold by auction; and in these cases, part of the negroes

[1] Fortsetzung Brud. Hist. tom. ii. p. 270; tom. iii. p. 365.

were frequently purchased by proprietors from other islands, by which means it often happened, that not only parents and children, but husbands and wives, were for ever parted from each other.[1] How to act in such circumstances, the Brethren were at first quite at a loss; and they appear for some time to have prohibited the converts from contracting another marriage, apprehending this to be contrary to the principles of Christianity.[2] Now, however, though they do not advise, yet neither do they hinder, a regular marriage with another person, especially if a family of children, or other circumstances, seem to render a helpmate necessary.[3]

Art. 2.—St Croix.

In August 1733, Tobias Leupold, Martin Schenk, and twelve others of the Brethren, set off from Herrnhut, with the view of proceeding chiefly to St Croix. This island, which had been almost entirely forsaken for thirty-seven years, had lately been purchased from the crown of France by the Danish West India Company. The Lord Chamberlain Von Pless, who had bought six plantations, induced by the favourable opinion which he had formed of the Brethren, applied to the congregation at Herrnhut for some of their number to go out as overseers of his estates, and, at the same time, to employ themselves in instructing the slaves. In consequence of this, a number of the Brethren offered to go to St Croix; but though they went out partly in the character of colonists, the spread of the gospel among the negroes was the object they had specially in view.[4]

Having sailed from Copenhagen with near a hundred other persons, chiefly soldiers and labourers, they at length reached the West Indies after a very tedious and unpleasant voyage. As the Island of St Croix had been so long forsaken, it was now completely overgrown with trees and brushwood, the consequences of which soon appeared among the new settlers. Though most of the Brethren were weak and sickly at the time of their arrival, yet, partly from ignorance of the precautions necessary

[1] Spangenberg's Account, p. 99.
[2] Crantz's Hist. Breth. p. 542.
[3] Period. Accounts, vol. i. p. 14.
[4] Oldendorp's Geschichte, tom. ii. p. 482.

in a warm climate, and partly from laudable but mistaken principles, they denied themselves that rest and refreshment which were requisite to recruit their enfeebled health; they made exertions in clearing the land, and in other manual operations beyond their strength; they were at the same time ill accommodated in respect of lodgings, being much exposed to wet, and to the noxious vapours arising from the newly cleared land. In consequence of these combined circumstances, they were soon attacked with fever and dysentery, which carried them one after another in rapid succession to the grave.[1]

To aggravate these outward distresses some misunderstanding had arisen among them during the voyage, nor was harmony restored after their arrival in the West Indies. Some now appeared to be actuated by worldly motives, manifesting more concern for their own temporal interests than for the glory of Christ and the salvation of souls. Engaged in labouring for their own support, they made little or no exertion for instructing the negroes; and they even omitted, for a considerable time, the daily meetings for prayer.[2]

In February 1735, a second company of eleven persons set off from Herrnhut for the Island of St Croix; but they were scarcely more fortunate than their predecessors. On their arrival, indeed, they succeeded in rekindling among such as still survived, a zeal for the conversion of the negroes and in restoring the meetings for prayer. Scarcely, however, had they begun to settle on the island, when they fell a prey one after another to those diseases which had already proved fatal to so many of their brethren. The few who survived soon afterwards left the island, and the colony itself was for the present abandoned.[3]

In October 1740, Martin, Israel, and Weber, three of the Brethren in St Thomas, sailed to St Croix with the design of renewing the mission on that island, where a colony had again been settled. Not being able to procure lodgings in Christianstadt, they accepted of a small house on the plantations of the Lord Chamberlain Pless. It was at a considerable distance from the town, in a low uncultivated spot, surrounded by thick

[1] Oldendorp's Geschichte, tom. ii. p. 494.
[2] Ibid. tom. ii. p. 495, 500.
[3] Ibid. tom. ii. p. 502.

bushes which hindered the free circulation of air, a circumstance extremely prejudicial to health in a warm climate. In a short time the missionaries, with the exception of Martin, who had returned to St Thomas, were all taken ill; and, indeed, so long as they remained at this place, they never enjoyed perfect health. Notwithstanding their frequent indisposition, they did not, however, neglect the chief object of their residence on the island. Even when unable to visit the negroes, they spoke from their sickbed to such as called upon them. After labouring upwards of a year in St Croix, they were recalled to St Thomas in consequence of the urgent need of assistance on that island. The Brethren, however, did not entirely abandon St Croix. They occasionally came thither from St Thomas, baptized several of the negroes, appointed some of them as helpers and assistants, who, in the interval of these visits, maintained in some degree the influence of religion among their sable countrymen.[1]

In April 1751, George Ohneberg, accompanied by two others of the Brethren, proceeded from St Thomas to St Croix with the view of settling on that island. He was received with much joy by the Christian negroes; but for a considerable time both he and the slaves in the neighbourhood were kept in constant alarm by the frequent attempts which were made to burn their houses. This was the work, it was supposed, of some pagan negroes who were hostile to the instruction of their countrymen, and who sought by this means to put an end to it. In many instances the fire was discovered and quenched before it did much mischief; but in others the huts of the negroes fell a prey to the flames. The poor creatures were afraid lest Ohneberg should leave them, as the attempts appeared to be made chiefly on his account; but he assured them that he would not forsake them, though he should lose his little all. His house was at length burned; but through the exertions of the Christian negroes the furniture was saved.[2]

In the course of a few years, the mission on the island of St Croix assumed a very flourishing aspect. The Brethren were not, indeed, without their trials, but yet, amidst them all, they were cheered by witnessing the success of their labours. Mul-

[1] Oldendorp's Geschichte, tom. ii. p. 645, 699, 703, 707, 748, 846.
[2] Ibid. tom. ii. p. 846.

titudes of the negroes attended on their instructions, and many of them gave pleasing evidence of the power of religion on their hearts. Some, so far from regretting the loss of their freedom, viewed it as a distinguished mercy, considering themselves inexpressibly more happy in a state of slavery with an opportunity of hearing the gospel, than if they had been at liberty in their native land, without that inestimable privilege.[1]

Art. 3.—St Jan.

In November 1754, John Brucker proceeded from St Thomas to St Jan, with the view of establishing a settlement on that island. For many years past the Brethren in St Thomas had paid frequent visits to St Jan, and were attended by considerable numbers of the negroes; but as the poor creatures were in the interval left in a great measure without instruction, religion made little progress among them. There were, however, a few who were baptized, and who formed the beginning of a Christian congregation on the island.[2]

Even now, the progress of the mission in St Jan was extremely slow. The negroes shewed little desire for instruction, grew negligent in attending the meetings for divine worship, and lost, in a great measure, any impressions they might have had of religion. Even the helpers in the congregation, who should have been examples to the flock, were chargeable with similar faults, and entirely neglected the duties of their office. After a few years, however, the mission experienced a considerable revival. The number of converts in St Jan was not, indeed, so great as in some of the other West India islands; but in proportion to the population, it was greater, perhaps, than in any other mission in the world.[3]

In August 1793, there was a tremendous hurricane in the West Indies. It was felt in various islands, but it appears to have raged with peculiar violence in St Jan. Of the Brethren's two settlements, Emmaus and Bethany, the latter was most ex-

[1] Oldendorp's Geschichte, tom. ii. p. 856, 860, 877, 880, 981, 994, 1003, 1014.
[2] Ibid. tom. ii. p. 664, 708, 714, 733, 754, 769, 772, 890, 892.
[3] Ibid. tom. ii. p. 1029, 1031, 1037, 1046, 1054.

posed to its fury. It began in the evening, and before morning, the missionaries, and many White and Black people, who had fled to them from the neighbourhood, could scarcely find shelter in any of the buildings. About eight in the morning, the wind changed to the south, and all the negro houses were swept away in a moment. Shortly after, the church fell with a dreadful crash, and was broken into a thousand pieces. Beams, shingles, rafters, boards, were carried to a great distance in the air; and no person durst venture out of the house but at the risk of his life. The sea-water being driven by the violence of the wind upon the roof of the dwelling-house, ran in streams in the apartments. The whole building trembled, and cracked, and threatened every moment to bury the inhabitants in its ruins. Meanwhile, they were assisted by the negroes in fastening the roof with ropes, and in nailing up the doors, windows, and every crevice; but they were at last quite overcome with fatigue and hunger, for they had only a loaf and a half to divide among twenty-six persons, while a little water, sweetened with molasses, was their only drink. In other parts of the island, the planters had their dwelling-houses, sugar-works, stores, and other property destroyed. The thickest trees in the woods were broken in the middle; the cassibi plantations were all torn up, and the garden crops totally laid waste. Numbers of vessels were wrecked on the coast, and many people lost their lives. At Emmaus, the other settlement of the Brethren, the church and dwelling-house were safe; all the other buildings were destroyed.[1]

To these accounts of the individual missions in St Thomas, St Croix, and St Jan, we shall here add a few general statements.

In August 1832, the Brethren in the Danish West India Islands celebrated the centenary of the mission; and, on this occasion, there was exhibited a striking proof of the change which had taken place in the public mind in regard to them and their labours. For some years after the commencement of the mission, the utmost hostility, as we have already seen, was manifested toward them; but now the Colonial authorities, as

[1] Period. Accounts, vol. i. p. 229.

well as the Danish Government, afforded them every protection and encouragement in their labours. His Excellency the Governor-General and the Lieutenant-Governor attended the Centenary Jubilee in St Croix. They were preceded by a detachment of cavalry and artillery, and followed by forty-three coaches, containing the first authorities of the island. The Governor had even issued a proclamation to the planters to grant to the negroes connected with the Brethren's congregations throughout the island that day and the half of the preceding to themselves, that they might have an opportunity of being present on so interesting an occasion. The numbers assembled in St Croix alone amounted to upwards of 7000 persons, being at least one-third of the population of the island; but there was not the smallest disturbance either before or after the festival, and his Excellency remarked, that however large a number of persons belonging to the Brethren's congregations might be assembled together, no detachment of police was found necessary to maintain order.[1]

The whole number of persons who were employed in St Thomas and the other two Danish islands, St Croix and St Jan, during the first hundred years of the mission, was 307 Brethren and sisters.[2]

The following table exhibits the numbers who were baptized, &c., during the same period:—

	Baptized.	Received into Church Fellowship.	Admitted to the Communion.	Died.
Adults,	18,503	5413	13,333	17,042
Children,	12,807	......	......	4963
	31,310	5413	13,333	22,005[3]

In January 1841 a commencement was made in the work of negro education in the Danish West India Islands. For up-

[1] Period. Accounts, vol. xii. p. 274.
[2] Mission to Danish West India Islands, p. 30.
[3] Period. Accounts, vol. xii. p. 275.

wards of a century the Brethren had little or no opportunity of giving instruction to the children and youth; they were not even at liberty to open a single school, in which they might teach them to read the Word of God. In consequence of this want of early tuition, it was very difficult, nay, almost impossible, to communicate even the most simple truths to minds which had never been taught to think; and when sinful habits were once formed, it was no easy matter for the poor creatures, even if brought under the influence of religion, to resist and to overcome them. But a number of school-houses now began to be erected by order of Christian VIII., the King of Denmark, with a view to the education of the children of negroes of every religious denomination, and the conduct of them was entrusted to the Brethren. The school-houses were built at the expense of the Colonial Treasury, and grants were also made from it for the maintenance of the teachers. The hopes which were formed of these schools were, in the first instance, but very imperfectly realized: yet we trust that, under an improved system, they may ultimately produce more abundant fruit.[1]

In July 1847, the King of Denmark issued an ordinance, that, after the lapse of twelve years, all rights of proprietorship claimed previously by the masters of slaves, should cease absolutely and for ever, and that all children born after the date of the decree should be free, it being, however, provided, that they should remain with their mothers on their respective plantations, and be maintained by the parties to whom their mothers belonged. It is probable that the emancipation of the slaves had been in contemplation for some years, and that it was with a view to it that His Majesty adopted the measures already mentioned for the education of the negro children. He now also issued an ordinance abolishing the Sunday markets, and prohibiting the negroes working for hire on that day without the permission of the authorities, which was to be granted only in cases of absolute necessity; but though these laws relative to Sunday markets, and Sunday labour, with other measures which were in contemplation, were no doubt designed to promote the amelioration of the condition of the slaves, and to

[1] Period. Accounts, vol. xvi. p. 428. 483; vol. xvii. p. 357, 402; vol. xviii. p. 315, 365; vol. xix. p. 74.

prepare them for their future emancipation, yet they were in general but indifferently observed. The period of emancipation, however, was hastened on by events which were probably but little anticipated.[1]

In July 1848, the slaves in different parts of St Croix rose in arms and demanded their freedom, being resolved, if necessary, to obtain it by force. The White people appear to have been panic struck; and the Governor-General Von Scholten, yielding to the demands of the insurgents, declared them free. The emancipation was of course not confined to St Croix, but was extended also to the other two islands, St Thomas and St Jan.[2] Whether the convulsions of so many of the nations of Europe in the early part of that year, and the emancipation by the new Government of France of the slaves in the West India Islands belonging to that country, had any influence in stirring up the negroes in St Croix to demand their own immediate emancipation, we do not know; but if they had intelligence of these events, as they no doubt would, it is not unlikely they might be an exciting cause of their rising, and also of the Governor yielding so readily to their demands.

In 1852, the congregations of the Brethren in the Danish West India Islands, consisted of the following numbers:—

Begun.	Stations.	Communicants.	Baptized Adults.	Baptized Children.	Total.
1732	ST THOMAS—				
1738	New Herrnhut. . .	270	113	292	675
1753	Niesky.	473	160	431	1064
1843	Town of St Thomas.	104	30	123	257
1734	ST CROIX—				
1751	Friedensthal. . . .	628	136	416	1180
1771	Friedensberg. . . .	460	102	411	973
1805	Friedensfeld. . . .	702	205	580	1487
	ST JAN—				
1754	Bethany. . . .	192	58	208	458
1782	Emmaus.	288	127	477	890
		3117	931	2938	6986[3]

[1] Period. Accounts, vol. xvi. p. 484; vol. xviii. p. 316.
[2] Ibid. vol. xix. p. 51.
[3] Ibid. vol. xxi. p. xxvi.

The congregations of the Brethren in the Danish West India Islands constitute a considerable proportion of the whole Black and Coloured population; but within the last forty years they have materially diminished in numbers, and their tendency appears to be still to decrease. At nearly all the stations, the missionaries had much cause to complain of the carelessness and indifference on the part of their negro flocks to the things that belong to their everlasting peace. The majority of them had grown up in heathenism, and many of them were still under the influence of old customs and habits, of evil example, and of depraved propensities and feelings. Under such circumstances, it was no wonder though there should be frequent instances of backsliding and transgression of the pure and holy law of God. Too many there were who found their way into the porch of the temple, and who were content to remain there, though invited into the sanctuary. It was painful to see how many of them, not excepting such as had for years attended on the preaching of the gospel, were still strangers to its power. There were not a few who were desirous of joining a Christian church, merely that they may be decently and respectably interred. Indeed, it was disheartening to witness the extreme ignorance, stupidity, and indifference of the older generation, and the waywardness, licentiousness, and impatience of all salutary restraint which prevailed among the young.[1]

PART II.—ENGLISH ISLANDS.

IN October 1754, Z. G. Caries was sent to Jamaica with two others of the Brethren as his assistants, in compliance with the request of some gentlemen who possessed considerable estates in that island. Missionaries were afterwards at different periods sent to Antigua, Barbadoes, St Christophers, and Tobago. On some of these islands, particularly where they were countenanced by the planters, the negroes attended at first on their instructions in considerable numbers; but after a time they for the

[1] Period. Accounts, vol. v. p. 368; vol. xvi. p. 256, 428; vol. xviii. p. 208; vol. xix. p. 101; vol. xx. p. 477.

most part, gave over attending, and were utterly indifferent about religious instruction. Nor was this confined to such as had been merely hearers; a great part even of the baptized shewed little or no disposition to attend divine worship. There appears ground to apprehend that the whole work was of a very superficial kind. The people probably attended at first chiefly from curiosity and the novelty of the thing; and most of those who were received into the church were baptized, it is to be feared, without giving proper evidence of piety.[1]

But though the Brethren saw for many years but little fruit of their labours, the missions in Antigua, St Christophers, and Jamaica, assumed at length a more encouraging aspect. The congregations increased, new stations were formed, and great numbers of the negroes were baptized. The extension of the mission in Jamaica has taken place chiefly in the course of the present century, and particularly since the abolition of slavery in 1834. Since then, greatly increased efforts have also been made for the education of the young; and two Normal schools, one in Jamaica, the other in Antigua, were established for the training of schoolmasters, and other assistants in the missions.

Though, since the abolition of slavery, the numbers connected with the Brethren's congregations in Jamaica have been more than doubled, the character of many of those who compose them is far from being satisfactory. In the days of slavery, such as joined them generally shewed some interest in religion, and did not care for reproach or even persecution; but now every one thought it a disgrace not to belong to some church, and therefore sought to be received into them, though they gave no evidence of piety. In like manner, the children of many parents who belonged to the Brethren's congregations, joined them for no other reason than that they were born and baptized in them. Hence there were great numbers connected with them who were mere professors of religion, having "a name to live while they were dead." A stranger might easily be deceived when he heard them uttering the language of piety which they had been taught from their youth; but those who looked not so much to the beautiful foliage of the tree as to the fruit which it produced, often found themselves sadly disappointed.

[1] Crantz's Hist. Breth. p. 430, 481, 602, 604; Period. Accounts, vol. i. p. 67.

In the young of both sexes, the missionaries had much wickedness, a roving disposition, and a false spirit of independence to contend with; in those of mature years, much deceit, instability, and worldliness; and in the aged, much ignorance and stupidity, with "ears dull of hearing," and hearts indifferent to the great truths of religion. It was found necessary to exclude considerable numbers from the fellowship of the church, while others withdrew quietly of their own accord. Even the best friends of the negroes were now ready to acknowledge that they had been somewhat blinded to their faults by their sympathy in behalf of the wronged and oppressed. Yet, on the other hand, there was a danger of forgetting the ignorance and degradation in which they were formerly held, and the permanent baneful influence which this could not fail to have on their character, and of not making due allowances for them on this account. Multitudes of professors there were, and too many who "held the truth in unrighteousness;" yet there were also not a few whose "life and conversation were such as becometh the gospel."[1]

In 1852, the numbers connected with the Brethren's congregations in the English West India Islands, were as follows:—

	Communicants.	Baptized Adults.	Baptized Children.	Total.
Jamaica, . . .	4,349	964	5,277	10,590
Antigua, . . .	4,000	675	2,632	7,307
Barbadoes, . .	1,132	246	1,746	3,124
St Christophers,	1,570	536	1,417	3,523
Tobago, . . .	689	298	739	1,726
	11,740	2,719	11,811	26,270[2]

SECT. III.—NORTH AMERICA.

In November 1734, a number of the United Brethren proceeded to North America, and settled in Georgia, with a special view to the instruction of some of the neighbouring tribes of Indians. Soon after their arrival, they began to make known

[1] Period. Accounts, vol. xiii. p. 96, 300; vol. xvi. p. 302; vol. xvii. p. 31, 86; vol. xviii. p. 350; vol. xix. p. 382, 386.

[2] Ibid. vol. xx. p. 518, 523, 526; vol. xxi. p. xxvi.

the gospel to the Creek nation, many of whom lived on an island called Irene, about five miles above the town of Savannah; and they likewise established a school for their children. The prosperity of this little colony, however, was of short duration. The neighbouring Spaniards having endeavoured to expel the English from the country, the Brethren were called upon to take up arms against the enemy; and though, on representing the declaration which they had made to the trustees of Georgia before they left Europe, that they would on no account carry arms, they were exempted from all personal interference in the war, yet, as many of the other inhabitants were dissatisfied on that account, and as an application of the same kind was again made to them on the renewal of the dispute, they left their flourishing plantations, and retired into Pennsylvania, where they were allowed to live in peace.[1]

Meanwhile, the Rev. Mr Spangenberg, who had accompanied the colony to Georgia, returned to Germany; and the picture which he drew of the miserable condition of the Indians made so deep an impression on many of the Brethren, that several of them offered to go and make known the gospel to them, even though it should be at the expense of their life.

In 1739, Christian Henry Rauch was sent to New York to commence a mission among some of the neighbouring tribes. Shortly after his arrival, he heard that an embassy of Indians had come to that city to treat with government. He accordingly went in search of them, and though they were much intoxicated when he first found them, yet he waited till they were sober, and then asked two of them, named Tschoop and Shabash, Whether they would not like a teacher to settle among them, and shew them the way to heaven. As they readily agreed to this proposal, he proceeded to Shekomeko, the place of their residence, about twenty-five miles to the east of North River.

On arriving at this place, Rauch was received by the Indians with much kindness; but when he spoke to them next day on the subject of religion, they quite disregarded his instructions, and set him at nought. Not discouraged, however, by this, he visited them daily in their huts; he also travelled to

[1] Loskiel's History of the Mission of the United Brethren in North America, part ii. p. 2.

the neighbouring towns, though, as he had neither the means to keep a horse nor money to hire a boat, he often suffered extremely from heat and fatigue in the woods; and even on his arrival, he was frequently refused admission into their houses. But he soon forgot all his trials when he began to observe some favourable symptoms in the two Indians, to whom he had originally made the proposal to come amongst them. Though amongst the most abandoned of the whole tribe, their eyes now overflowed with tears, whenever he described to them the sufferings and death of our Redeemer. They often lamented their past blindness and their ignorance of the true God, who loved them so much that he sent his Son to die for them.

Scarcely, however, had he begun to see the fruit of his labours, when some White people in the neighbourhood took the alarm, and endeavoured to thwart his further usefulness. Apprehensive that, if the Indians embraced Christianity, it would prove injurious to their interests by promoting sobriety among them, they laboured to rouse the indignation of the savages against their teacher, by spreading the basest reports concerning him, particularly that he designed to seize their young people, carry them beyond the sea, and sell them for slaves. As the Indians are extremely tenacious of their personal liberty, nothing was better calculated to excite their jealousy than such a rumour, especially as they had too often experienced the baseness and fraudulence of the White people. Irritated by these reports, the savages threatened to shoot him unless he left the place without delay. He therefore thought it prudent to withdraw for a season, and took shelter with a farmer in the neighbourhood. Still, however, he daily visited the Indians at Shekomeko, though often at the risk of his life. Several of the White people sought occasion to beat and abuse him, but this he was careful not to afford them, uniformly conducting himself in the mildest and most inoffensive manner. Some threatened to hang him up in the woods; others sought to intoxicate the savages, in the hope they might murder him in a drunken frolic. An Indian once ran after him with his hatchet, and would probably have killed him had he not accidentally stumbled and fallen into the water. Even Tschoop, who had shewn some concern about his soul, was so incensed against him, that he sought an opportunity to shoot him; and Shabash, though he did not threaten his life, was always careful to avoid his company. Rauch, however, was not deterred by these various difficulties and dangers, but persevered in his labours in the hope they would at length be crowned with success.[1]

By degrees, the Indians began to admire his patience, courage, and perseverance, combined, as they were, with so much meekness, gentleness, and humility. He often spent half a day in their huts, ate and drank with them in a friendly manner, and even lay down to sleep in the midst of them with the utmost composure. This circumstance made a strong impression on the minds of the Indians, particularly on Tschoop. One day when Rauch was lying in his hut fast asleep, he was struck at the sight, and thought with himself: "This cannot be a bad man: he fears no evil, not even from us who are so savage. Here he sleeps comfortably, and places his life in our hands." On further reflection, he was convinced that the reports circulated by the White people concerning him were entirely without foundation, and proceeded purely from their own wickedness and malice. He now endeavoured to persuade his countrymen of the missionary's innocence; and, notwithstanding their violent jealousy, he succeeded in removing their prejudices, and re-establishing confidence between them.

Having now regained the friendship of the Indians, Rauch had soon the pleasure of witnessing the fruit of his labours among them. Several of them were much impressed with the love of Christ to sinners, as manifested in his sufferings and death. The change which took place on Tschoop in particular was remarkably striking. Formerly he was one of the greatest drunkards in the whole town: now he had learned to be sober. He afterwards gave the Brethren the following simple, yet interesting account of his conversion: "I," said he, "have been a heathen, and have grown old among the heathen; therefore I know how the heathen think. Once a preacher came and began to tell us that there was a God. We answered him saying, 'Dost thou think us so ignorant as not to know that? Go back to the place from whence thou camest.' Then another preacher came to us and began to say: 'You must not steal,

[1] Loskiel, part ii. p. 7.

nor lie, nor get drunk.' To him we answered: 'Thou fool, dost thou think we do not know that? Go learn first thyself, and then teach thy own people to leave off these practices. For who are greater drunkards, or thieves, or liars than thine own people?' Thus we dismissed him. After some time, Brother Rauch came into my hut, and sat down by me. He then spoke to me as follows: 'I am come to you in the name of the Lord of heaven and earth. He sends to inform you that he will make you happy, and deliver you from that misery in which you at present lie. For this purpose he became a man, gave his life a ransom, and shed his blood for us.' When he had finished his discourse, he lay down upon a board fatigued by his journey, and fell sound asleep. I then thought with myself, What kind of a man is this? There he sleeps. I might kill him and throw him out into the woods; and who would regard it? But this gives him no care or concern. At the same time, I could not forget his words. They constantly recurred to my mind. Even when I slept, I dreamed of that blood which Christ shed for us. I found this to be something different from what I had ever heard before; and I interpreted Christian Henry's words to the other Indians. Thus, through the grace of God, an awakening began among us. I say, therefore, brethren, preach Christ our Saviour, and his sufferings and death, if you would have your words to gain entrance among the heathen."[1]

In the spring of 1742, several of the Indians were baptized, among whom were Tschoop and Shabash. The gospel now made rapid progress, not only in Shekomeko, but in some of the neighbouring towns, particularly Pachpatgoch, and Wechquatnach. It was truly delightful to see the Indians coming from distant places to hear the new preacher, who, as they expressed it, spoke of God who became man, and loved the Indians so much, that he gave his life to save them from the devil and the service of sin. The doctrine of the atonement, as preached by the missionary and confirmed by the converts, so touched and melted the hearts of the savages, that the fields seemed, as it were, "white for the harvest."[2]

[1] Loskiel, part ii. p. 13; Spangenberg's Account, p. 62.
[2] Loskiel, part ii. p. 19.

Encouraged by the prospect of success, several of the Brethren now joined Rauch in his labours; and it was not long before they shewed themselves to be men of the same stamp, endowed with a like zeal, and possessed of a similar disinterested spirit. Such was their humility, that they earned their livelihood chiefly by working for the Indians; though the savages, as may easily be conceived, were able to pay them but little for their labour. They lived and dressed in the Indian manner; so that in travelling through the country, they were often taken for natives. They now extended their labours to some of the neighbouring towns; and though they were by no means without their trials, yet, in general, they met with a kind reception from the people. Some Brethren who resided at Bethlehem, a settlement they had lately formed in Pennsylvania, and others who came merely on a visit to North America, among whom was Count Zinzendorf himself, likewise made journeys among the Indians in various parts of the country, and preached the gospel to them; and though this was not productive of any immediate good effects, yet the kindness with which they uniformly treated the savages, made a strong impression on their minds, and prepared them for the reception of the gospel.[1]

Meanwhile, the Indian congregation at Shekomeko continued to flourish and increase. When some of the converts were admitted for the first time to the Lord's Supper, there was a most delightful season among them. "During the meeting for adoration and praise," says one of the Brethren, "we were overcome with weeping; and whilst I live I shall never forget the impression which this first communion with the North American Indians made upon me." About this time, the congregation made a number of statutes for the regulation of their affairs; and in order that these laws might be strictly executed, they chose Cornelius, one of the converts, who had formerly been a captain among the savages, to be the overseer, an office which he exercised with great faithfulness, and to the general satisfaction of his countrymen. One day, however, after the administration of the Lord's Supper, he came and begged to be dismissed from that post, alleging that he had felt such happiness during the service, that he resolved to retire from all pub-

[1] Loskiel, part ii. p. 24, 45, 51.

lic business, and to devote his whole time to uninterrupted communion with the Saviour. He was easily persuaded, indeed, to retain his office until one should be found to succeed him; but it was on this condition that he should no longer be styled captain, "for," said he, "I am the least among my brethren." On many occasions, the remarks which the converts made were simple yet striking. A trader having endeavoured to persuade Shabash that the Brethren were not privileged teachers, the Indian sagely replied, "It may be so; but I know what they have told me, and what God has wrought within me. Look at my poor countrymen there lying drunk before your door. Why do you not send privileged teachers to convert them? Four years ago I also lived like a beast, and not one of you troubled himself about me. But when the Brethren came, they preached the cross of Christ, and I have experienced the power of his blood, so that sin has no longer dominion over me. Such are the teachers we want."[1]

In the spring of 1744, a violent and unmerited persecution was begun against the Brethren by some White people in the neighbourhood. These miscreants had never ceased to employ every means in their power to thwart the labours of the missionaries, and to seduce the Indians from them, not only by circulating the basest and most unfounded reports, but by trying to promote intemperance and other vices among them. Having failed in poisoning the minds of the Indians by these insidious arts, they now endeavoured to rouse the fears of their own countrymen, by representing the Brethren as in league with the French in Canada, and as employed to furnish the savages with arms to fight and murder the English. This report they spread far and wide; and asserted it with so much confidence, that the whole country at last believed it, and were struck with terror, and inflamed with rage. The inhabitants of Sharon, a neighbouring town, remained under arms for a whole week together, and some even forsook their plantations. The Brethren were now, with singular consistency, called upon to serve in the militia; but they represented that, as ministers of the gospel, they ought to be exempted from military service; and, accordingly, after a variety of vexatious proceedings, the proposi-

[1] Loskiel, part ii. p. 46, 55.

tion appears to have been relinquished. They were afterwards, however, dragged from court to court, and even before the governor of New York; but notwithstanding the violence of their enemies, they were honourably acquitted, many of the people, and even some of the most distinguished magistrates, candidly acknowledging the purity of their intentions and the utility of their labours. Being thus baffled in these various attempts, their enemies changed their mode of attack. Knowing the aversion of many of the Brethren to the taking of oaths, they procured an Act of Assembly, ordaining that all suspicious persons should take the oath of allegiance, or be expelled from the province; and they had even the influence to procure another Act, expressly prohibiting the missionaries from instructing the Indians, under the old pretence that they were in league with the French, and forbidding them under a heavy penalty to appear again among them without having first taken the oath required.

Being in this way obliged to leave the province of New York, the missionaries retired to Bethlehem, in Pennsylvania. The grief they felt at parting with their beloved congregation is beyond description; but they resolved to wait with patience, till God should manifest their innocence and dispel the storm. The Indians, in the mean while, continued to keep up their usual meetings; and some of the Brethren occasionally went from Bethlehem, and held conferences with them, though at the risk of persecution to themselves. Two of them, Frederic Post, and David Zeisberger, a man of whom we shall often have occasion to make honourable mention, when on a journey to the Iroquois Indians, or, as they are commonly called, the Six Nations, were unexpectedly arrested at Albany, and after suffering many indignities, were carried to New York, and imprisoned for seven weeks.[1]

But though a mutual intercourse was kept up between Shekomeko and Bethlehem, it was evident that the suspension of the regular services of the missionaries could not fail to be ultimately injurious to the interests of the congregation. The Brethren, therefore, proposed, that the Indians should remove from the province of New York, and settle upon some eligible

[1] Loskiel, part ii. p. 57, 68, 69.

spot in Pennsylvania; and, in order that no difficulty might remain on the part of the Iroquois, to whom that part of the country belonged, which they had ultimately in view, they sent an embassy to the great council at Onondago, to ask permission for the congregation to take up their residence upon it. To this proposal, the Iroquois readily agreed; but, contrary to all expectation, the Indians at Shekomeko refused to accede to it. They alleged that the governor of New York had particularly commanded them to remain in their own town, and had promised them his protection; that, on this account, they could not leave the country without giving rise to further suspicion, and exposing the missionaries to new persecution; and that if they should emigrate, their unbaptized friends and relations would still remain in the town, and probably return to their old sinful courses, a circumstance which would give them the greatest uneasiness.

It was not long, however, before a circumstance occurred which obliged the congregation to follow the advice of the Brethren; for the White people came to a resolution to drive the Christian Indians from Shekomeko, under the pretence that the ground on which the town was built did not belong to them, and that the rightful owners would soon come and take possession of it. They accordingly seized upon the land, and appointed a watch to prevent the visits of the Brethren from Bethlehem. Besides, it was reported that a thousand French troops were on their march to the province, and that the Indians of Shekomeko were to join them, and then to ravage the country with fire and sword. This rumour excited such rage and terror among the White people, particularly at Reinbeck, that the inhabitants of that town demanded a warrant from a magistrate, to go and kill all the Indians at Shekomeko. The warrant, indeed, was not granted; but yet the oppression of these poor unoffending creatures arose, at length, to such a height, that though they were strongly attached to their own village, a number of them left it and came to Bethlehem, where they erected some temporary huts for themselves and their families.

As, however, it was soon found that an Indian town could not be conveniently supported so near to Bethlehem, the Brethren purchased a piece of land about thirty miles from that place, near the junction of the rivers Mahony and Lecha, where they might build, plant, and live in their own way. Having here marked out a new town, which they called Gnadenhuetten, or *Tents of Grace*, numbers of the Indians immediately repaired thither, and began to clear the land and to build themselves houses. When the news of this settlement reached Shekomeko, many of the converts, who still remained in that place, resolved to leave it; but their enemies, though determined to expel them from the town, having seen, with regret, that all the others had emigrated to the Brethren, now endeavoured to frighten the remainder from going to them, by circulating a false and malicious report, that the last party had been attacked and murdered on the road. The Indians, however, who were then preparing for the journey, disregarded the rumour, and set forward without fear. The emigration of the converts was attended by other embarrassing circumstances. Many of them were deep in debt, contracted by them in their unconverted state, and increased not a little by the base impositions of their creditors. As soon, therefore, as a family proposed to remove, the traders brought in bills against them, demanded immediate payment, and threatened to cast them into prison. The converts not being able to pay their debts, and not being willing to run away, had no resource but to apply to the congregation at Bethlehem to assist them, who accordingly did it with the greatest readiness. The settling of the Indians at Gnadenhuetten was, in other respects, attended with no small trouble and expense. As the land was covered with trees and shrubs, it required to be cleared and planted. The Brethren joined the Indians in these operations, and had their meals in common with them; but as the converts were unacquainted with husbandry, and unable to bear much fatigue, the missionaries had the heaviest part of the work, which they cheerfully performed, considering it as done in the service of Christ.[1]

Meanwhile, the situation of the Christian converts who remained at Shekomeko and the neighbouring towns became every day more embarrassing. The French Indians having made an inroad into the neighbouring country, setting fire to

[1] Loskiel, part ii. p. 78, 82.

the houses, and murdering the inhabitants, the English called upon all who were able to carry arms, to rise in their own defence. This message being sent to the Christian Indians, as well as others, several of them joined the army, while the rest lived in a state of continual apprehension and alarm. By this means, however, some of them were convinced of their error, in neglecting the advice of the Brethren; and several of them sent very penitential letters to the congregation. "I am like a child," said one, "whose father loves him dearly, clothes him, and gives him all he stands in need of. Afterwards, the child becomes refractory, deserts his parents, and despises his counsel. At length, through folly, he loses all the good things he possessed; his clothes become ragged; nakedness and want follow. Then remembering how well he fared, he weeps night and day, yet scarcely presumes to return. This is precisely my situation." Such is a specimen of the figurative language in which the Indians clothed their penitential expressions of sorrow. But there were others who suffered themselves to be prejudiced against the missionaries; many disorderly proceedings took place among them, and years elapsed before they returned to the congregation of the faithful.[1]

The temporal support of the Indian congregation at Gnadenhuetten, was a principal object of the care and attention of the Brethren. It was a striking and interesting proof of the influence of religion upon the converts, that they laboured diligently at their work, and planted the fields allotted to each of their families. But as, owing to the increase of their numbers, the land was not large enough for them, the Brethren bought a neighbouring plantation for their use, a circumstance which afforded them much satisfaction. Besides, a saw-mill was erected in the settlement, and many of them had an opportunity of earning a little money, by cutting timber, and conveying it to Bethlehem in floats down the river Lecha. Hunting, however, continued to be their chief support, and from fifteen to twenty deers or bears were frequently shot in a day. When provisions were scarce, they gathered wild honey, chestnuts, and bilberries, in the woods.

Still, however, a constant supply of provisions was required

[1] Loskiel, part ii. p. 86, 88.

from Bethlehem; for the congregation at Gnadenhuetten were frequently visited by companies of Indians belonging to various tribes, whom they not only received with kindness, but entertained free of expense, rejoicing that by this means, their Pagan countrymen had an opportunity of hearing the gospel. In the course of these visits, nothing made so deep an impression on the savages as the peace and harmony which prevailed among the Christian Indians, and the patience and resignation which they manifested in the midst of trouble, circumstances so diametrically opposite to their national character. These visits of the savages were also very agreeable to the missionaries, as they hoped some of them might by this means be brought to the knowledge of Christ; but, in some instances, they were extremely troublesome by their wild disorderly conduct. It was, therefore, necessary to act with great circumspection in the treatment of them. By severity they might be deterred from repeating their visits; and yet disorder was not to be tolerated in the town, lest it should prove injurious to the Christian Indians, particularly to the young people. The Brethren, therefore, introduced some salutary regulations, with the view of preventing these different evils.[1]

Besides labouring with unwearied diligence at Gnadenhuetten, the missionaries and others of the Brethren made frequent journeys among the Indians in other parts of the country; and in various instances attempted to establish settlements among them. The Iroquois were the principal object of their benevolent exertions. Some of the Brethren visited Shomokin, and various other places on the River Susquehannah; and though the Indians in that quarter were amongst the most savage, drunken wretches in the whole country, yet several of the missionaries took up their residence among them. This establishment was attended with great expense, as all the necessaries of life had to be sent to them from Bethlehem; and, indeed, the missionaries were not unfrequently in danger of their lives from the violence of the savages, particularly in their drunken fits.[2] Besides making frequent journeys to Wajomick, and other places in the neighbourhood, the Brethren visited Onondago, the chief town of the Iroquois, and the seat of their

[1] Loskiel, part ii. p. 104. [2] Ibid. part ii. p. 91, 101, 106, 148.

great Council, from which they received permission for two of the missionaries to settle in that place, for the purpose of learning the language; and accordingly, when two of them went thither, they were received by the Indians with the utmost cordiality; but yet they often suffered much from want, and were obliged to hunt for their subsistence, or seek roots in the forest.[1] The Brethren likewise made various journeys to Shekomeko, Pachpatgoch, and Wechquatnach, the scene of their early labours. In the first of these places, every thing was now destroyed except the burying-ground; but there were still a number of the Indians who had wandered from the paths of religion, some of whom they persuaded to return to the congregation. In the other two places, the Christian Indians were formed into a regular congregation, and had missionaries settled among them, and for several years proceeded in a very pleasing manner.[2] Meniolagomekah, a town about one day's journey from Bethlehem, was likewise often visited by the Brethren; a regular establishment of Christian Indians was formed at that place, and a missionary was settled among them.[3] So various and so extended were the labours of these excellent men.

In the mean while, the course of the Indian congregation at Gnadenhuetten, was peaceful, prosperous, and happy; but there at length arose a succession of troubles, of the most unpleasant kind, and which were followed by very tragical consequences.

In March 1753, an embassy of Nantikoks and Shawanoes arrived at Bethlehem, with a proposal that the congregation should remove from Gnadenhuetten to Wajomick, in the Indian country. For this change, they assigned no particular reason; but it afterwards appeared that they had secretly resolved to join the French in hostilities against the English; but that they wished, in the first instance, to provide a safe retreat for their countrymen, the Christian Indians, that so they might attack, the more easily, the White people in that part of the country. Most of the congregation, however, were averse to leave their present settlement, especially after they discovered the design of the proposal; but yet there was a party in favour of it, and, at last, upwards of eighty retired to Wajomick and the neigh-

[1] Loskiel, part ii. p. 120, 140, 147, 155. [2] Ibid. part ii. p. 101, 113, 115, 181, 183.
[3] Ibid. part. ii. p. 116, 142.

bourhood. They had scarcely, however, left the town, when their loss was in some degree made up by the arrival of about fifty Christian Indians from Meniolagomekah, who were ordered by the proprietor to leave that place.[1]

It was not long, however, before the tranquillity of the congregation of Gnadenhuetten was again disturbed. They were not only charged with a kind of tribute, as an acknowledgment of their dependence on the Iroquois, but a new message was sent to them to the following effect, "The Great Head, that is, the Council of the Iroquois in Onondago, speak the truth and lie not. They rejoice that some of the believing Indians have removed to Wajomick; but now they lift up the remaining Mohegans and Delawares, and set them down also in that place; for there a fire is kindled for them; there they may plant and think on God: but if they will not hearken, the Great Council will come and clean their ears with a red-hot iron;" meaning, that they would burn their houses, and shoot musket-balls through their heads. This threatening, especially at first, was not entirely without effect. Some of the congregation thought it best to remove to Wajomick; others again refused to emigrate. It was discovered, indeed, that the plan of removing them did not originate in the Great Council of the Iroquois, but only with the Oneida tribe, and the warlike Delawares and Mohegans, who falsely ascribed it to the Six Nations in general. The Brethren used no authority with their people to make them remain in their present residence; but they employed the most gentle and affectionate representations, and that with so good an effect, that almost all of them resolved to stay. One of them said, "What can the Chief Captain of the Six Nations give me in exchange for my soul? He does not consider how that will fare at last." "God," said another, "who made me and saved me, is able also to protect me. I am not afraid of the anger of men, for not a hair of my head can fall to the ground without his will."[2]

Hostilities having commenced between the French and the English, the Indian war at length began. The whole country was now involved in disorder and bloodshed. Every day disclosed new atrocities committed by the savages. The inhabi-

[1] Loskiel, part ii. p. 143, 149. [2] Ibid. part ii. p. 157.

tants of the country knew not what to do, nor whither to go. Some fled to the east; some to the west; some sought safety in places which others had just forsaken. The Christian Indians at Gnadenhuetten being considered as the friends of the British government, were in imminent danger of being destroyed by the French Indians; and as the most dreadful reports were daily multiplying from all quarters, some were so much intimidated that they took refuge in the woods. But the greater part of the congregation remained in the town, and the missionaries resolved to stand by their post, notwithstanding the dangers to which they were exposed. This, however, was a fatal resolution, and in a short time was followed by the most tragical consequences.[1]

In November 1755, a party of French Indians arrived in the neighbourhood of Gnadenhuetten, and attacked the house of the missionaries, which was situated on the Mahony, about half a mile from that place. As the family were sitting at supper, they heard an unusual barking of dogs, upon which Gottlob Senseman, one of the Brethren, went out at the back door to see what was the matter. On hearing the report of a gun, several others ran to open the house door. Here stood a number of Indians, with their pieces pointed to it, and no sooner was it opened than they instantly fired and killed Martin Nitschman on the spot. His wife and some others were wounded, but they flew up stairs to the garret with the utmost precipitation, and barricaded the door with bedsteads. Partsch, one of the Brethren, jumped out at a back window; another of them named Worbas, who was lying ill in bed in an adjoining house, escaped in a similar manner, though the enemy had placed a guard at his door. Meanwhile the savages pursued those who had taken refuge in the garret, and endeavoured to burst open the door; but being baffled in the attempt, they set the house on fire. A boy named Joseph Sturges, having got on the flaming roof, leapt down and made his escape; though, on the opening of the back door, a ball had grazed his cheek, and one side of his head was severely burnt. Encouraged by this, the wife of the missionary Partsch, followed his example, and having come down unhurt, fled unobserved by the enemy, and hid herself behind a tree

[1] Loskiel, part ii. p. 164.

upon a hill near the house. Christian Fabricius, one of the Brethren, was the next who made the attempt; but before he could escape, he was perceived by the savages, and instantly wounded with two balls: he was the only one whom they seized alive; and after despatching him with their hatchets, they cut off his scalp, and left him dead on the ground. All the others who fled to the garret were burnt to death. Senseman, the missionary who went out at the back door, had the inexpressible pain of beholding his wife perish in this frightful manner. When surrounded by the flames, she was seen standing with folded hands, and in the spirit of a martyr was heard to exclaim, "'Tis all well, Dear Saviour!" The whole number who perished in this terrible catastrophe was eleven, namely, Martin Nitschman, the first who was killed, and Susanna his wife; Gottlieb Anders, his wife and daughter, an infant only fifteen months old; Anna Catherine Senseman, Christian Fabricius, Leonard Gattermeyer, George Shweigert, Martin Presser, and John Frederic Lesly. Five only made their escape. Besides burning the house, the savages set fire to the barns and stables, and thus destroyed all the corn, hay, and cattle. They then divided the spoil, soaked some bread in milk, and, after making a hearty meal, departed from the place.[1]

On this occasion, the Brethren were the only sufferers; the Indian congregation at Gnadenhuetten providentially escaped. As soon as they heard the report of the guns, and saw the house of the missionaries in flames, and learned the cause of the sad catastrophe, they offered to go and attack the enemy; but being advised to the contrary by one of the Brethren, they all fled into the neighbouring woods, by which means the town was cleared of them in a few minutes, though some of them were already in bed, and had scarcely time to dress themselves. But though they escaped with their life, they lost their property; for some of the savages afterwards came and set fire to the town, destroyed the mill, and laid waste all their plantations. Thus the Indian congregation was reduced to the utmost poverty.[2]

[1] Loskiel, part ii. p. 166; Heckewelder's Narrative of the Mission of the United Brethren among the Delaware and Mohegan Indians, p. 44; Succinct Account of the Missions of the Brethren, 1771, p. 9.

[2] Loskiel, part ii. p. 167, 171.

These were disastrous events; but yet they proved the means of averting still greater calamities. About this very time there was a design on foot to destroy the whole establishments of the Brethren in North America. Some base villain had forged a letter, purporting to be written by a French officer at Quebec, in which it was stated, "That his countrymen were certain of soon conquering the English, as the Indians had not only taken their part, but the Moravians also were their good friends, and would afford them every assistance in their power." This letter being published in the newspapers, excited general suspicion of the Brethren; and this suspicion, instead of being diminished, was increased by their calm, patient, steady behaviour. That cheerfulness which sprung from a consciousness of their own innocence, as well as from resignation to the will of God, was considered by the deluded multitude as a certain indication of their guilt. As the common people were exceedingly exasperated against them, the Brethren were under continual apprehensions of being attacked by a mob; nor could Government probably have protected them, though convinced of the purity of their intentions, and the utility of their labours. In the Jerseys, a declaration was publicly made with beat of drum, that Bethlehem should be destroyed; and the most dreadful threatenings were added, that in the several settlements of the Brethren such a carnage should be made, as had never before been heard of in North America. It afterwards appeared, from the best authority, that a party of a hundred men who came to Bethlehem, were sent for the express purpose of raising a disturbance; but the friendly and hospitable manner in which they were treated by the inhabitants, who knew nothing of their intentions, disarmed them of their malice, and made them alter their design. Thus the Brethren were, in general, considered as the secret friends and allies of the French; and these suspicions were daily on the increase, when the attack on their missionary settlement on the Mahony convinced the deluded people of their error, since they were among the first in the country against whom the enemy had directed their rage. Such, indeed, was the revolution in the public sentiment, that Bethlehem, and the other settlements of the Brethren, soon became a common asylum for the White people, who fled from the murderous ravages of the Indians. Hundreds of men, women, and children, came even from distant places, begging for shelter, some of them almost entirely destitute, as they had left their all behind them, and fled in the night. These the Brethren supplied with food and clothes, and other necessaries, to the utmost of their ability, notwithstanding they themselves had suffered considerable losses by the inroads of the savages, while, at the same time, their resources were materially diminished by the troubles of the war.[1]

Meanwhile, the Indian congregation had likewise retired from Gnadenhuetten to Bethlehem, a circumstance which contributed to render the situation of that place still more dangerous. On the one hand, the savages insisted on their Indian brethren rising in arms against the English, and threatened to come and murder them all in case of a refusal. On the other, there arose among the White people a set of fanatics, who demanded the total extirpation of the Indian tribes, lest the vengeance of God should fall upon the Christians for not destroying them, as on the Israelites of old for not exterminating the Canaanites; and, as might be expected, they were mightily incensed against the Brethren, on account of the protection and assistance which they afforded to a race of beings, whom they, in their wisdom, deemed accursed of God. The Governor, indeed, promised to protect the Christian converts; but, as a reward of one hundred and thirty pieces of eight was offered for the head of every hostile Indian, they durst not go abroad, either to hunt, or to pursue other necessary avocations, lest they should be killed by mistake, or for the sake of so large a recompense, or even simply through the malice of those who thirsted for their blood. Exposed as the Brethren were to the wrath of the White people, they were no less an object of indignation to the enemy. Four soldiers, who had deserted from their regiment and fled to the savages, told them, that at Bethlehem they saw the Brethren cut off the heads of all the Indians in that town, put them into bags, and send them to Philadelphia, where they received fifty dollars for each; and that they had left only two alive, with the view of employing them as spies. On hearing this report, the savages were so

[1] Loskiel, part ii. p. 169, 175.

enraged, that, though they had no great regard for the Indian congregation, a large party of them set off to murder all the Brethren, and to burn their settlements. By the interference, however, of a chief who was friendly to the missionaries, most of them were induced to return, while the few who still persisted in their design, not judging themselves a match for the enterprise, thought proper to disperse. Sometimes, too, well-disposed Indians, on hearing of a plot against them by the warriors, would travel all night to warn the Brethren of it, and thus frustrated the schemes of the enemy.

Being, in this manner, continually exposed to the rage of both parties, the inhabitants of Bethlehem considered themselves as sheep ready for slaughter. At night when they lay down to sleep, they knew not whether they should behold the morning; in the morning when they rose, they knew not whether they should see the evening. In general, however, they displayed wonderful resignation to the will of God. Not an individual left the place; each seemed chiefly concerned to be prepared to die. At the same time, they neglected no means that might contribute to their safety. They surrounded the town with palisadoes, and maintained a constant watch both night and day: even those who were at work in the plantations had a guard to attend them. This office was committed chiefly to the Indians, who considered it as a high honour to be thus employed. "Who am I," said one of them, "that I should watch over children of God? I, poor man, am not worthy of this grace. Nor can I guard them aright: therefore, watch thou over them, gracious Saviour, for thou alone canst protect them."

By such means as these, the settlement was happily preserved from several attacks which the savages meditated against it. They still continued to lay waste the neighbouring country, and everywhere committed the greatest barbarities. They plundered and destroyed several villages so near to Bethlehem, that the flames of the houses were distinctly seen from that place. They even approached the town itself, lurking about with torches, and endeavouring to shoot burning wadding upon the roofs, in order to set the place on fire. They attempted several times in the night, to make a sudden attack upon this and some other settlements of the Brethren; but when the spies observed that the inhabitants were upon their guard, they were afraid, and were glad to withdraw. One day, a party of them were on their way to a field, where about forty Sisters were picking flax, whom they intended to seize and carry off as prisoners. They were already close to it, creeping on their bellies in the Indian manner; but on perceiving a strong guard of Indian Brethren, with their pieces loaded, they were glad to retire. Thus an engagement was happily avoided; for though the converts were very unwilling to shed the blood of their enemies, yet they were determined to defend the women and children intrusted to their care, and consequently had an attack been made, they would have fired upon the assailants, and probably have killed some of them, a circumstance which would have occasioned both them and the missionaries deep regret.[1]

By degrees, the Indian congregation began to enjoy peace and rest, dwelling in safety under the wings of the Brethren at Bethlehem. Some few, indeed, seduced by the arts of their countrymen, forsook the place, and relapsed into heathenism; but, in general, they remained stedfast to their Christian profession, and exhibited many pleasing proofs of the influence of religion on their heart and life. As, however, the residence of the Indians in Bethlehem was attended with some disadvantages, the Brethren obtained for them a grant of land from government, at a place about a mile distant. Here they erected a settlement which they called Nain. In a short time, most of the baptized, who, at the invitation of the savages, had moved to Wajomick, or who had fled to the Susquehannah after the murder of the missionaries, returned and obtained permission to reside in the town. They were lodged at first beyond the river Lehi, until they afforded full proof of their repentance; but as soon as they gave evidence of this, they were received with joy into the fellowship of the congregation. The inhabitants of Nain, indeed, increased so rapidly, chiefly by the return of those who had wandered during the late troubles, that it soon became necessary to divide them, and form a second settlement. With this view, the Brethren at Bethlehem purchased a tract of land behind the Blue Mountains, consisting of

[1] Loskiel, part ii. p. 168, 172, 174; Crantz's Hist. Breth. p. 474.

about fourteen hundred acres. Thither a number of the Indians repaired under the inspection of one of the missionaries; and having erected a new town, which they called Wechquetank, they introduced into it the same regulations as at Nain.[1]

For a considerable time, both the congregations enjoyed peace, prosperity, and rest; and even the external appearance of the settlements excited the most pleasing emotions in every pious and benevolent mind. Hostilities were long suspended in this part of the country; and for several years, the congregation experienced no disturbance from the savages; but at length they broke forth with fresh violence, and involved the Christian Indians in new calamities.[2]

In 1763, the Brethren received intelligence that the Indians had commenced hostilities near the lakes of Canada and on the river Ohio, where they had murdered several hundred of the White people. They had even begun to make incursions into Pennsylvania; and there was every reason to dread a repetition of those melancholy scenes, which had been exhibited a few years before on the banks of the Mahony. Besides, some persons revived the old foolish doctrine, that this new war was a punishment from God on the White people, because they had neglected to extirpate the savages; and therefore they asserted that all the Indians, without exception, should be put to the sword. A party of Irish freebooters, in particular, declared, that no Indian should appear in the woods under pain of being shot immediately; and that if only one White man were murdered in that neighbourhood, the whole Irish settlement would rise in arms, and kill all the inhabitants of Nain and Wechquetank, without waiting for an order from government, or even a warrant from a justice of the peace. In consequence of these threatenings, the congregation were often harassed by false alarms; and, at length, a messenger arrived one forenoon, with the painful intelligence, that at the break of day that morning, the house of Mr John Stinton, at an Irish settlement about eight miles from Bethlehem, had been attacked by the Indians, and that he himself, together with Captain Wetterhold, his lieutenant, and several soldiers, who had been lodging in the house, were either killed or mortally wounded. His wife nar-

[1] Loskiel, part ii. p. 177, 182, 189, 193.

[2] Ibid. part ii. p. 190, 202.

rowly escaped, though she was the cause of the whole disaster, by dropping some inconsiderate words against a company of Indians who lodged in that quarter.[1] This sad catastrophe naturally excited the utmost alarm in the two missionary settlements; and it soon appeared that their apprehensions were not without foundation. The very next day, about fifty White people assembled on the opposite side of the river, with the view of surprising Nain in the course of the night, and of murdering the inhabitants. But a person in the neighbourhood having represented to them the difficulty and danger of the enterprise, they were diverted from their purpose for the present, and returned home in peace. On the same day, a party of the Irish freebooters came to Wechquetank, with the design of murdering the whole of the Indians; but the missionary, after he had employed reasoning and expostulation in vain, at last succeeded in pacifying them by means of presents, and by giving them plenty to eat and drink. On taking their departure, however, they were heard to say, that if the Indians did not soon quit the place, they would return and destroy them all. During the night, all the men were upon the watch; several spies were discovered lurking about the settlement, and a fire at some distance betrayed a neighbouring encampment. A sudden attack, it was supposed, was intended; but this was prevented, probably by a violent rain which fell during the night.[2]

It would now have been the height of temerity for the congregation at Wechquetank to have postponed their flight any longer; and therefore they resolved to abandon a place where they were in such imminent danger; especially as they received an express from Bethlehem, with the most pressing solicitations, to break up immediately, and to retire to the Brethren's settlement at Nazareth. Just, however, as they were preparing to depart, several musket shots were heard in the neighbourhood. Alarmed by the report, the Indians, who supposed that the savages had attacked the English, resolved to go to the defence of the White people. The missionary, however, urged them not to quit the place, but merely to repel any attack that might

[1] Captain Wetterhold's party of soldiers had a few weeks before, in a state of intoxication, murdered four Indians who had come to a store for the purpose of exchanging their pelfrey.—*Heckewelder*, p. 69. Perhaps this might be one cause of the attack now made upon them.

[2] Loskiel, part ii. p. 207; Heckewelder, p. 71.

be made upon it; and he exhorted them, at the same time, to stand by each other, and to expect deliverance from God: "Very true," answered one of the converts, "only don't you stand before me, but go behind, for I will be shot first." The party, however, from whom the attack was dreaded, suddenly marched off with the Indian war-whoop; but it afterwards appeared, that it was a band of soldiers who wished to draw the Indians into the field, in order to fight them. Having happily escaped this snare, the whole congregation immediately set off for the Brethren's settlement at Nazareth. It was not, indeed, without extreme regret that they left so pleasant a place, where they possessed excellent houses and large plantations; especially as they had to leave their crop on the ground, and a great part of their cattle behind them.

Meanwhile the congregation at Nain was in a state of close blockade. The savages continued to lay waste the neighbouring country with fire and sword, and to murder as many of the inhabitants as fell into their hands. By this means the White people were so enraged against the Indians in general, that the inhabitants of Nain durst not go even to Bethlehem on business, as the fugitives, who had resorted thither from various quarters, abused, insulted, and maltreated them. Even at home they had to maintain a strict watch both by night and by day, in order that they might hold their meetings, and that the women might gather the crops in safety. Having made such arrangements as that the enemy could not attack them without danger, they began to hope, that government would support them with more energy, and secure them rest in their own dwellings. These expectations, however, were soon disappointed. A member of the congregation, named Renatus, was unexpectedly seized as the murderer of Mr Stinton, one of the Irish settlers, and as his person was sworn to by the widow, he was carried to Philadelphia and committed to prison. Innocent as he was of the charge, the report of his apprehension flew like lightning through the country, and kindled the fury of the White people against the Indians into a violent flame. The danger of the two congregations now became greater than ever; but in this emergency, an express arrived from Philadelphia, with an order from the chief magistrates, that they should all deliver up their arms and repair to that city, where they would be protected from their enemies: To the Indians the idea of a removal was extremely painful; but they resolved to resign themselves to the will of God, and to obey the order of government. As soon, therefore, as the sheriff arrived, they delivered up their arms to him with a cheerfulness and composure which strikingly illustrated the influence of the gospel upon their minds, for a Pagan Indian would sooner part with his head than with his gun. They now set forward on their journey; and it was truly an affecting sight to behold these poor unoffending creatures, travelling patiently along, ignorant of what might be their future destiny. On the road, they suffered much from the malice of some White people, who abused and loaded them with curses. In passing through German-town, they were not only insulted as usual, but the population talked of nothing but burning and hanging them, and other similar punishments.[1]

Having at length arrived in Philadelphia, they were ordered to be lodged in the barracks; but the soldiers quartered there refused them admittance, notwithstanding the positive command of the governor. The Indians were by this means detained in the street from ten o'clock in the morning, till three in the afternoon. Here a mob collected around them, who derided, reviled, and charged them with all the horrid outrages committed by the savages, and even threatened to murder them on the spot. The soldiers having peremptorily persisted in refusing them admittance into the barracks, the magistrates ordered them to proceed to Province Island, about six miles distant, in the river Delaware. As they passed through the city, thousands followed them with tumultuous clamour, so that they seemed like sheep in the midst of wolves. At length, they reached the place of their destination, where they were safely lodged in some large buildings, and kindly provided by government with whatever they needed.

Soon after their arrival at this place, the settlement at Wechquetank was burnt by the White people; and some incendiaries likewise endeavoured to set fire to Bethlehem. The oil-mill was consumed, and the flames raged with such fury, that it was

[1] Loskiel, part. ii. p. 211; Heckewelder, p. 72, 74.

with great difficulty the adjoining water-works were saved from destruction. Besides committing these outrages on the Brethren's settlements, a party of White people attacked a number of Indians in the small village of Canestoga, near Lancaster, and though they were perfectly inoffensive, and had long lived quietly among the English, butchered fourteen of them, men, women, and children. The rest having fled to Lancaster, the magistrates of that town took them under their protection, and lodged them in the jail or workhouse, a strong and secure building. Thither, however, the murderers followed them. They marched into the town at noonday, broke into the place where they were lodged for security, and though the poor defenceless Indians begged for life on their knees, the ruffians massacred them all in cold blood, and threw their mangled bodies into the street. They then departed with a diabolical shout of triumph, threatening that the Indians in Province Island should soon share a similar fate.[1]

Against these outrages, government immediately issued a proclamation, forbidding any one to molest the Indians in Province Island under the severest penalties, and offering a reward of two hundred pounds to any person who should discover the two ringleaders of the party; and bring them to justice. It soon appeared, however, that an incredible number of people, including many of the inhabitants of Philadelphia, were connected with them; none of the conspirators were taken up, though they walked publicly in the streets; and some even stood before the governor's house and bade him defiance. The rioters became at length so numerous and daring, that many hundreds of them agreed to march to that city, and never to rest till all the Indians taken under the protection of government were massacred.

Apprehensive of the consequences of these villainous combinations, government resolved to send the Christian Indians to the English army by the way of New York, and to place them under its protection. In January 1764, the congregation having received an order to this effect, set off on their journey; and on their arrival at Philadelphia, they were provided with waggons

[1] Loskiel, part ii. p. 216; Heckewelder, p. 77; Franklin's Works, 18mo. Edit. 1803, vol. i. p. 168.

for the aged, the sick, the children, and the heavy baggage. On leaving that city, they were accompanied by so great a crowd of people, that they were scarcely able to proceed. The mob cursed and reviled them in a dreadful manner; but no one ventured to lay hands on them. In all places, indeed, through which they passed, the populace insulted them; but after about a week's journey, they arrived in safety at Amboy, where two sloops were ready to convey them to New York. Just, however, as they were about to embark, a messenger unexpectedly arrived from the governor of New York, with strict orders that not an Indian should set foot in that province; and even the ferrymen were prohibited, under a severe penalty, from crossing the river with them.

Information of this being sent to Philadelphia, the Christian Indians were ordered to return to that city; and on their arrival they were, for their better security, lodged in the barracks, and attended by a military guard night and day. But as the number and violence of the mob still increased, the first guard was not sufficient for their protection; it was therefore doubled, and the magistrates were even under the necessity of preparing to repel force by force. By their orders, eight heavy pieces of cannon were planted in the front of the barracks, and a rampart was thrown up in the middle of the square. An association of the citizens, including even many of the young Quakers, was formed by the celebrated Benjamin Franklin at the desire of the governor, and repaired to the barracks to assist the soldiers in defending the Indians. On the following day, intelligence was received of the approach of the conspirators. The whole city was now in an uproar; yet every body prepared to receive them with manly firmness. The eighteen pounders being discharged, the poor Indians, who had never before heard the report of such large cannon, were terribly frightened; the guns, indeed, stood so near the building, that several of the windows were broken by the firing. Understanding that such vigorous preparations were made to repel them, the rioters did not venture to enter the city; and accordingly the citizens returned to their homes in peace. Two nights after, however, a report was circulated, that the conspirators were again approaching the city. The whole town was now in motion; the church bells were rung, the streets illuminated, and the inhabitants being waked out of their sleep, were summoned to attend at the townhouse, where arms and cartridges were distributed among them. Two companies of armed citizens repaired to the barracks, and four other cannon were mounted. The following day was spent in hourly expectation of the arrival of the conspirators; but information was at length received, that being dismayed by the preparations made to repel them, they had desisted from the attempt. Some gentlemen were then deputed by government to inquire what complaints they had to make. After behaving in a very insolent manner, they asserted that several of the Indians were murderers whom they had seen at Pittsburg, and demanded that they should be delivered up. In order to pacify them, one of the ringleaders was invited to enter the barracks, and to point out the culprits. He accordingly came and examined the whole of them; but he did not find an individual whom he could charge with the smallest crime. They then asserted that the Quakers had conveyed away six of them out of the barracks, and concealed them in some other place. But when this allegation was investigated, it also was proved a falsehood; upon which the rioters marched off, and relinquished their design for the present.[1]

During the residence of the Indians in the barracks, the missionaries kept up the usual meetings and exercises of the congregation, as far as their peculiar circumstances would allow. They met with them regularly every morning and evening; they administered the Lord's Supper to them at stated intervals; they even opened a school for instructing the youth in the English language. People of all descriptions came to see the Indians: and though this was attended with various inconveniences, yet many who previously were ill-disposed towards them, were, by this means, convinced of their innocence. The public worship of the congregation, especially on the Lord's day, was attended by such crowds of people, that the chapel could not contain them; and it was hoped that to some of them the preaching of the word was not in vain. Meanwhile, the Indians had no care as to their temporal support; for the English Government generously supplied all their wants; and, indeed,

[1] Loskiel, part ii. p. 218; Woodhouselee's Memoirs of Lord Kames, vol. ii. p. 19.

the attention which it uniformly paid to their safety and comfort deserves our warmest encomium.

But notwithstanding these circumstances, the Indians felt their present situation to be very trying; some of them were even more distressed by it than by all the dangers and hardships they had hitherto experienced. Their situation, though rendered as agreeable as possible, they viewed as little short of imprisonment, and by degrees it became quite insupportable. As they were no longer at liberty to range and hunt in the forests, a spirit of insubordination broke out among them, particularly among the young people, some of whom grew melancholy, and others refractory. At the same time, the excellent quality of their victuals was as ill adapted to the state of their stomachs, as the want of freedom was to their minds. Besides, as the summer advanced, the small-pox and fever broke out among them, and filled them with such alarm, that many of them meditated their escape from the barracks. These diseases cut off nearly sixty of them, many of whom died in the blessed hope of glory, honour, and immortality beyond the grave.

In March 1765, the Indians, to their inexpressible joy, were set at liberty, after a confinement of about sixteen months; but as there was reason to apprehend they could not live in the neighbourhood of the White people without being greatly molested by them, it was agreed that they should settle in the Indian country on the banks of the river Susquehannah. In their journey thither they had new and almost incredible difficulties to encounter. Though peace was now restored, yet the enmity of many of the White people against the Indians was still so violent, that to avoid danger, they were under the necessity of taking a very tedious and circuitous route. Such parts of their baggage as were not sent by waggons, they had often to carry over high, steep, and rocky hills, in small parcels, by which means they had to travel the same road several times over. In some places they had to cut their way through the woods; in one instance, for no less than five miles together. Through the brooks and rivers the men were obliged to wade; and for the women and children they had to construct rafts, a work of considerable difficulty, as the violent currents often carried away the trees they had cut down for this purpose before they could be fixed together; some rivers were so broad and deep that they were obliged to encamp on their banks, and to build canoes in which to cross them. As for lodging, they had to sleep chiefly in the open woods; and in some instances they were under the necessity of stopping all night in swamps, there being no dry ground near at hand. The greatest difficulty of all, however, was the want of provisions. Hunting was their chief support; but in some places neither game nor fish could be found. When their whole stock of flour was exhausted, it was truly affecting to see them receive their last portion. They were now glad to find wild potatoes in the woods, though nothing but hunger could have rendered them palatable. To satisfy the children who cried for want, they peeled the chestnut-trees and made them suck the juices under the bark, and even the old people were under the necessity of resorting to the same expedient. As for drink, they had often nothing but the muddy water found in swampy puddles. One night they were terribly alarmed by the woods being on fire, and burning most furiously around their encampment, from ten o'clock till one in the morning. After a tedious and irksome journey of five weeks, they at length arrived at the place of their destination; and as a mariner after a storm rejoices to enter the haven, so the Indian congregation, after the many trials and hardships they had of late endured, were happy to reach their new abode, where they hoped to enjoy peace, tranquillity, and rest.[1]

Having pitched on a convenient spot on the banks of the Susquehannah for a settlement, they here began to build a regular town, which they called Friedenshuetten, or *Tents of Peace*. It was pleasing to see how judiciously the Indians planned, and how diligently they executed, the work of each day. The town when completed consisted of thirteen Indian huts and upwards of forty houses, built of wood, in the European fashion, lighted with windows, covered with shingles, and provided with chimneys. The street was eighty feet broad; and in the middle of it stood the chapel, a neat and spacious building. The ground next the houses was laid out in gardens; and between the settlement and the river about two hundred and fifty acres were divided into regular plantations of Indian corn. The burying-

[1] Loskiel, part ii. p. 225.

ground was situated at some distance at the back of the buildings.[1]

After the erection of this settlement, great numbers of the Indians came to it from every quarter, and were much delighted with the external appearance of the place. It was, they said, the most beautiful Indian town they had ever seen. But what was of more importance, many of them were deeply impressed by the gospel, and were filled with serious concern for their souls. Frequently the whole assembly was so affected, that the missionaries were obliged to stop, and mingle their tears with those of their people. This may not unjustly be viewed as a striking proof of the powerful efficacy of the gospel on their hearts, considering the contempt in which the savage Indians hold the person who, according to them, is so weak as to weep. "Whenever I saw a man shed tears," said one of the converts, "I used to doubt whether he was a man. I would not have wept, though my enemies had cut the flesh from my bones: that I now weep is of God, who has softened the hardness of my heart." Besides holding the daily meetings with the congregation, the missionaries were often called upon, on other occasions, to make known the gospel; for their Indian visitors came into their houses, begging to hear more of "these sweet and comfortable words." It seemed, indeed, as if they would never be satisfied, so that frequently the Brethren had scarcely time to eat or to rest. Many of those also who, during the troubles of the war, had wandered from the congregation, now returned and were received with affection and joy.[2]

The town increased so rapidly, and the number of hearers was so great, that in less than two years it was necessary to build a larger place of worship. Among their visitors, were Indians of various tribes, particularly Mohawks, Cajugus, Senekas, Tutelas, Delawares, Mohegans, Wampanose, Nantikoks, and Tuscaroras. Many of these were driven to Friedenshuetten, by a famine which prevailed in the country; others preferred this road on their way to different parts of the Indian territory, wishing to see a place so renowned for its hospitality. At one time, for instance, seventy-five Tuscaroras from Carolina, and at another, fifty-seven Nantikoks from Maryland, impelled

[1] Loskiel, part iii. p. 1.

[2] Ibid. part iii. p. 4, 11, 38.

by hunger, came and stopped for several weeks. Induced by the hope of being useful to them, the Christian Indians cheerfully fed the hungry, and even overlooked the impositions of some, who, abusing their generosity, ate up their provisions, and led an idle profligate life, without ever attending to the word of God.[1]

For several years, the course of the Indian congregation at this place was of the most pleasing nature. The Christian converts appeared to grow both in knowledge and in grace; many of their heathen visitors were awakened to a sense of their sin and danger; and even several who had once been robbers and murderers, seemed now to "hunger and thirst after righteousness," and by their simple unaffected declarations, afforded the missionaries no small satisfaction. The Brethren had likewise much pleasure in the young people, among whom the symptoms of religion were of the most pleasing nature; and for whose use two new and spacious schools were erected in the settlement. Besides, a powerful awakening began in a town about thirty miles up the river; and a missionary was at length settled in that place, and maintained regular meetings for public worship, so that it might be considered as a kind of chapel of ease to Friedenshuetten. For some time, indeed, it appeared as if all the Indians in that town and neighbourhood would embrace the gospel.[2]

In September 1767, David Zeisberger set off on a journey to the river Ohio, accompanied by two of the Indian assistants, as he had heard that some of the inhabitants of that part of the country were desirous of hearing the gospel. His design was to visit Goshgoshuenk, though in every town through which he passed, he received the most unfavourable accounts of the people of that place. He was not intimidated, however, by these reports; but proceeded on his journey, in the course of which he and his companions endured many and grievous hardships. They had often to travel across extensive plains, overgrown with such high grass that a man on horseback was entirely covered by it; and when either dew or rain had fallen, they were completely drenched to the skin. The further they proceeded, the more horrible did the wilderness become;

[1] Loskiel, part iii. p. 18.

[2] Ibid. part iii. 36, 51.

they had often by day to work a path through the thickets, and at night to sleep in the open air, exposed to the cold and all the inclemency of the weather.[1]

Having arrived at Goshgoshuenk, Zeisberger soon discovered that the accounts he had received of the inhabitants of that town were but too well founded. Never had he seen the abominations of heathenism practised in so horrid a manner; never had he beheld sin assume so hideous and unblushing a form, as at this place.

But notwithstanding the wickedness of the place, the people were highly pleased with his visit, owing no doubt to the novelty of the circumstance. Many of them could never hear enough of the great fundamental principle of the gospel, that "Christ Jesus came into the world to save sinners;" and as the language in which the truths of religion were expressed was not very intelligible to them, the two Indian assistants were often employed till past midnight, in repeating and explaining "the great words" uttered by the missionary.

After a short stay, Zeisberger left Goshgoshuenk; but he returned the following summer accompanied by another of the Brethren and several of the converts, with the view of establishing a mission in this place. On their arrival, they preached every day, and held meetings with the people morning and evening, for the purpose of instructing them in the principles of the Christian faith. On these occasions, the Indians attended in great numbers; and it was not a little curious to see so many assembled to hear the gospel, with their faces painted black and vermillion, and their heads decorated with clusters of feathers and foxes' tails. At first, they heard the word with great attention; but afterwards many of them opposed it violently. Instigated by the chiefs, who became jealous of their own authority, the old women went about publicly complaining, that the Indian corn was blasted, or devoured by the worms; that the deer and other game already retired from the woods; that chestnuts and bilberries would no longer grow in the country, because the White men brought strange things to their ears, and the Indians began to change their manner of life. To appease the wrath of the offended spirits, the sorcerers appointed solemn

[1] Loskiel, part iii. p. 20.

sacrifices, and offered up hogs by way of atonement. A report was circulated by others, that some New England Indians had been on the other side of the great ocean, and brought a letter from King George of England to all the Indians in North America, warning them against the Moravians who lived at Bethlehem, as they would lead them straight to hell. Some of the neighbouring chiefs and tribes likewise sent messages to them, expressing their displeasure that they should have allowed White men to settle among them, and urging them either to banish or kill them without delay. By these means, the whole town was thrown into the utmost confusion. The enemies of the missionaries became daily more violent than ever; and even many of those who expressed joy at their arrival, were now the most bitter against them. Some openly advised to kill them; others insisted, that not only the missionaries, but all the Christian Indians should be murdered, and thrown into the Ohio. Two of them even entered into an agreement to assassinate the Brethren; and one evening several disagreeable visitors made their appearance at a late hour, with an intent to murder them; but their hearts failed them, so that they did not carry their design into execution.[1]

Notwithstanding these difficulties and dangers, the Brethren resolved to stand firm by their post. With this view, they built a small winter-house at a little distance from the town, where they might have an opportunity of administering the Lord's Supper to their own people, and of holding other meetings with them and such of the inhabitants of the place as chose to attend. Several, dreading the reproach of their countrymen, stayed away, or came only by night to escape observation. Young people were prohibited by their parents from visiting the missionaries; and some parents were prevented by their children. Such as came boldly to the meetings were abused and persecuted by their neighbours, who branded them with the most opprobrious names, as Sunday Indians, Shwonnaks, that is, White people, an appellation which, in the view of an Indian, is the most intolerable in the world. Some were even driven from their houses, and took refuge among the Brethren,

[1] Loskiel, part iii. p. 20, 28.

by whose intercession an aged chief, who was extremely friendly to the cause, took them under his protection.

The inhabitants of the town were now divided into two parties, one of which was violently opposed to the gospel, while the other was so much attached to it, as to declare they would sooner quit the place, and build a town in some other quarter, than be deprived of it. The opposition at length rose to such a height that the Brethren, and such of the people as were friendly to them, retired to a place about fifteen miles distant, on the opposite side of the river. Here they built a new settlement; and the missionaries had soon the pleasure of baptizing several of the Indians, among whom was the aged chief now mentioned, who had lost his sight. The inhabitants of Goshgoshuenk at length ceased in their opposition; and the council of that town, convinced of the disinterestedness of the missionaries, begged them to forget all that was past, and adopted them as members of the Delaware nation, that so, in case of war, they should not be treated as other White people, but be considered as native Delawares.[1]

Hostilities having commenced between the Seneka and the Cherokee Indians, the Brethren judged it prudent to retire from this part of the country, on account of its vicinity to the seat of war, especially as the number of those who came to hear the gospel increased so rapidly, that they began to be in want of room, and as an offer had lately been made them by some distant chiefs of land in their neighbourhood.

In April 1770, the congregation embarked on the river Ohio in sixteen canoes, and sailed by Pittsburg to the mouth of the Beaver Creek. Having entered this river, they proceeded up to the falls, where they had to unload, and transport their goods and canoes by land. After a journey of upwards of a fortnight, they arrived in that part of the country where they designed to take up their abode, and immediately proceeded to build a new settlement, which they called Friedenstadt, or the *Town of Peace.*[2]

The Indians in the neighbouring country were at first astonished to see a people settle among them so different in manners and customs from themselves, and to hear a doctrine

[1] Loskiel, part iii. p. 33, 42, 53, 59.
[2] Ibid. part. iii. p. 55.

so novel and so opposite to the views they had been accustomed to entertain. In some, however, this astonishment soon degenerated into opposition, especially after one of the chiefs manifested a decided attachment to the gospel. They harassed the Brethren by incessantly propagating the most daring falsehoods, and even counterfeiting messages and letters from the chiefs to them. In consequence of a very peremptory message of this kind from the chief and council of a distant town, requiring that an Indian woman, who had lately been baptized, should immediately be sent back, Zeisberger, dreading the pernicious consequences of such an order, set off for that place, and, after a tedious journey, reached it in safety. Having requested a meeting of the council, he read the letter to them, when it was discovered that neither the chief nor the council knew any thing about it; but that one of the councillors present had written it of his own accord, and signed it with two fictitious names. Being in this manner detected, he was publicly confounded before the whole assembly, who expressed great indignation at his conduct, and agreed that as the Brethren never detained any in their settlements contrary to their inclination, so none should be compelled to leave them, for the Indians were a free people, at perfect liberty to act in all things according to their own will. Zeisberger having embraced the opportunity of his visit to this town to preach the gospel to the inhabitants, numbers of them heard it with much attention; but others opposed it with no less violence, in consequence chiefly of the insinuations of some Pagan teachers, who had strenuously recommended the use of emetics, as a speedy and infallible method of cleansing from sin, so that here this singular practice was quite general. In vain, therefore, did he attempt to shew them, that though an emetic may cleanse the stomach, it can never cleanse the soul; and that this could be effected only by the application of the blood of Christ to their guilty consciences.[1]

Indeed, Zeisberger, who was now well known among various of the Indian tribes, was a marked object of their malice, and was frequently in danger of his life. One night some malicious people came to Friedenstadt, and insisted on compelling the inhabitants to get drunk; but having failed in the attempt,

[1] Loskiel, part iii. p. 57. 69.

they threatened to murder first the missionaries, and afterwards the whole congregation, and raised such a hideous uproar in the town, that the Indian sisters fled to the woods, and the men were obliged to keep a strict watch around the dwelling of their teachers.

Meanwhile, notwithstanding these and other trials, the congregation at Friedenstadt continued to flourish and increase. The number of hearers was daily augmented, among whom was a man who belonged to the party which murdered the Brethren at the settlement on the Mahony some years before. He was often so much affected in hearing the word that he shed floods of tears. The first person who was baptized at this place, was the wife of the blind and aged chief already mentioned, who formerly opposed his embracing the gospel with the utmost violence, but who now herself submitted to the yoke of the Redeemer. A chief named Glikkikan, when he first visited the Brethren, came with the express purpose of disputing with them, and confounding them by his arguments; but now he took a decided part with the congregation, notwithstanding the contempt and obloquy to which this exposed him. One day, after hearing a discourse, he wept aloud on his way home. The Pagans wondered to behold such a noted and valiant captain weep in the presence of his old acquaintances; but the Brethren were delighted to see this proof of the power of the gospel in melting the proud and stubborn heart, even of a wild Indian chief. He and another of their captains were at length baptized together, and both of them afterwards proved ornaments of the Christian name.[1]

Meanwhile, the congregation at Friedenshuetten resolved to leave that place and to retire, at least for the present, to the settlement of Friedenstadt. The Iroquois Indians had secretly sold the land on which their town was built to the English, notwithstanding the grant they had previously made of it to them; the number of European settlers in the neighbourhood was daily increasing, a circumstance which exposed the young people to numerous and powerful temptations; the Senekas, by their mischievous conduct, occasioned them no small trouble, as the White people were very apt to suspect the Christian Indians as

[1] Loskiel, part iii. p. 46, 57, 60, 62, 71.

accomplices with them in their wicked deeds. For these reasons, the Brethren resolved to leave the place; but as this subjected them to very considerable loss, and as it could be proved that they were compelled to go away in consequence of the sale of the land to the English, they applied to the governor of Philadelphia for redress, which was afterwards granted them, though not to the whole extent of their loss.[1]

In June 1772, the Indian congregation at Friedenshuetten, consisting of two hundred and forty-one persons, left that place, and set off on their journey, some of them proceeding by land, and a still greater number by water. The toil and trouble attending the emigration of such a number of people, with all their goods and cattle, in so wild and woody a country as North America then was, can scarcely be conceived by a person who was not an eye-witness of the journey. Those who went by land had about seventy oxen, and a still greater number of horses, to take care of. In the course of the journey they suffered incredible hardships, in working a way for themselves and their beasts, through the woods and swamps where they were directed merely by a small path, which, in some places, was scarcely discernible, so that it seemed almost impossible even for a single individual to mark a path and force a passage, the thickets were so close and the woods so immense, one of them being computed to be about sixty miles in length. Through these, indeed, they had often rather to creep than to walk; and in one part of the country, they were obliged to wade no fewer than thirty-six times over the windings of the river Munsy. But notwithstanding the difficulties and hardships of the journey, they kept up their daily worship as regularly as possible; and they had frequently strangers among them, both Indians and White people, who attended their meetings, a circumstance which served greatly to lighten their toils and sorrows. The party which went by water had likewise their troubles and difficulties. Soon after their departure, the measles broke out among them, and many fell sick, especially the children, a circumstance which was not a little trying to them. Every night they were obliged to seek a lodging on shore, and they suffered much from the cold. In some places they were annoyed by inquisitive, in

[1] Loskiel. part iii. p. 41, 64, 76.

others by drunken people ; and the many falls and dangerous currents in the river Susquehannah occasioned them many difficulties and frequent delays. The two parties having at length met, they united together and proceeded the rest of the way by land. In crossing the mountains, they had great difficulties to encounter ; for as they had not horses enough to carry all their baggage, most ofthem were obliged to take part of it on their backs or in their hands. They were also in continual alarm on account of the rattle-snakes, which were very numerous during a considerable part of the journey. Ettwein, one of the Brethren who accompanied them, happening to tread on one of these reptiles, was so frightened that for many days after he durst hardly venture to step forward ; every rustling of a leaf made him dread the approach of a snake. But the greatest plague both to man and beast, especially in passing through the woods, was an insect called by the Indians Ponk or *Living ashes*, from its being so small that it was scarcely visible, and its bite like the burning of red-hot ashes. As soon as the evening fires were kindled, the cattle, in order to get rid of these troublesome creatures, ran furiously towards them, crowding into the smoke, and thus greatly annoyed the people, both in their sleep and at their meals. Besides, our travellers were sometimes under the necessity of stopping a day or two in one place to supply themselves with the necessaries of life. In the course of the journey, they shot upwards of a hundred and fifty deer, and caught great quantities of fish in the brooks and rivers. After a tedious and irksome journey of eight weeks, they at length arrived at Friedenstadt, and met with a hearty welcome from the whole congregation in that town.[1]

When the Indians of Friedenshuetten came to that place, it was not with the view of settling in it. Both the congregations had lately received an invitation from the chief and council of a town on the river Muskingum, to come and reside in that part of the country, on whatever tract of land they might choose. Zeisberger, accordingly, had undertaken a journey thither, in order to fix on a suitable spot for a settlement. Here he pitched on a place about seventy miles to the southward of Lake Erie, with an excellent spring, good planting grounds, plenty of

[1] Loskiel, part iii. p. 77.

game, and various other conveniences for an Indian town; and on his requesting a grant of this tract of land from the council to the congregation, they not only informed him that this was the very spot which the chiefs had destined for them, but they in a solemn manner granted them all the lands within certain bounds, including a very considerable territory; they determined that no other Indians should settle upon them, and they directed that all Indians dwelling on the borders of that district should behave peaceably to the missionaries and their people, that they should neither disturb their worship nor hinder their countrymen from going to hear the gospel. Zeisberger, returned to this quarter soon after with five families, consisting of twenty-eight persons, and began to erect a new town, which he called Schoenbrunn, or *the Beautiful Spring*. Not long after, a great part of the Indian congregation removed from Friedenstadt to the Muskingum, and built a settlement about ten miles below that place, which they called Gnadenhuetten.[1]

Meanwhile, the situation of the congregation at Friedenstadt became more trying than ever. The daily encroachments of their Indian neighbours occasioned them much perplexity, and the pernicious consequences of the rum trade were altogether intolerable. Sometimes the savages brought a quantity of spirits close to the town, and there they drank, and danced, and raved like so many maniacs. After getting intoxicated, they frequently entered the settlement, rambled through the town, and broke every window that happened to be open, so that the inhabitants were at last under the necessity of fastening their shutters and burning candles even by day. Nothing, indeed, but the providence of God preserved the settlement from destruction. In several instances, when they entered the town intent on mischief, they quarrelled among themselves, and instead of injuring the missionaries or the Christian Indians, they attacked and mangled one another with their knives in the most brutal manner. Some, however, burst open the doors of several houses, and rushed forward, brandishing their arms, and threatening to murder every one of the family. These outrages rose at length to such a height, that the Christian Indians, much against their inclination, were under the necessity of seizing

[1] Loskiel, part iii. p. 73, 82.

several of the rioters and keeping them bound till they became sober, lest they should proceed to still greater excesses. One day a savage came running into the settlement, exclaiming he would kill the White man. Having proceeded at full speed to the house of the missionary, he burst open the door and entered the room with all the fury of a wild beast. Terrified at his appearance, the missionary's wife snatched up her child, and instantly fled; but the missionary himself, who was confined by sickness, sat up in bed and looked at him with the utmost composure. Disconcerted by this, the man suddenly stopped short, and the Indian Brethren hastening to the assistance of their teacher, seized and bound him with ease. These circumstances, however, were so extremely troublesome, that the remainder of the congregation at length removed from this disagreeable neighbourhood, and proceeded to join their friends on the banks of the Muskingum.[1]

Meanwhile, the congregation in that quarter was not without its vicissitudes and trials. Not only did the petty wars of the Indians still continue, but hostilities at length broke out between some of them and the inhabitants of Virginia, which created such trouble and confusion throughout the whole country, that for a considerable time neither of the Brethren's settlements enjoyed almost a single day of rest; and, in consequence of the rage of the savages against the White people, the missionaries, in particular, were often in danger of their life. Numerous troops of warriors marched through the settlements, some upon murdering expeditions, others returning with scalps and prisoners, uttering dreadful threatenings that both places should soon be surprised and burnt to the ground. Reports were perpetually flying through the country, that they were actually on their way to destroy the towns, and to murder the inhabitants. Canoes were always kept in readiness for any sudden emergency, as the congregation were frequently so terrified, even in the night, by frightful rumours, that all were on the point of taking flight; the women were repeatedly driven from their plantations at noonday; and all the people were confined to their houses for days and even for weeks together, as several parties appeared in the neighbourhood with the view

[1] Loskiel, part iii. p. 87.

of seizing on stragglers. When the Virginians first flew to arms, they had no authority from those in power; but government was at length obliged to interfere in the quarrel, and to march troops into the field; and as the Indians were completely defeated, peace was soon re-established.[1]

In the midst of these external trials, the settlements of the Brethren were not only preserved in safety, but enjoyed internal prosperity. The chapel at Schoenbrunn, though it held about five hundred people, became too small for the number of hearers. Multitudes of strangers visited the settlement, and heard the gospel; many of the warriors were impressed by the word, and several even of the chiefs were at length baptized. A man, who about this time was dismissed from Gnadenhuetten on account of his ill behaviour, was so exasperated at his expulsion, that he entered the house of Schmick, one of the missionaries, armed with a large knife, and intent on revenge. Not finding him at home he came away, and having afterwards repented of his conduct, he earnestly begged to be readmitted into the congregation, and was baptized by the very man whom he had so lately intended to murder. Another Indian, who had been appointed successor to a neighbouring chief, declined the offer, choosing rather to be an humble follower of Christ, than to occupy the most honourable place among his countrymen.[2]

During the war, there was such a marked contrast between the conduct of the Christian and the Pagan Indians, as places in a striking and interesting light the beneficial influence of the gospel in ameliorating the temper, views, and manners of the wildest and most uncultivated savages. The former, notwithstanding the frequent interruptions to which they were exposed, laboured diligently at their ordinary employments, sowing their fields, planting their gardens, boiling sugar, &c.; while the latter neglected work of every kind, and would, at length, have been reduced to absolute starvation, had not their Christian countrymen relieved their wants as long as this was in their power. Indeed, they not only supplied the needy, but provided many of the warriors who marched through their settlements with food and other necessaries, a circumstance which surprised the Pagan Indians, and had a happy effect in lessen-

[1] Loskiel, part iii. p. 89, 93, 96.

[2] Ibid. part iii. p. 97, 99, 104, 108.

ing their prejudices against their Christian countrymen. "I have found," said a captain on one of these occasions, "I have found your people to be very different from what I heard of them in our towns. There, it is said, that when an Indian comes to you, he is sent to make his fire in the wood, and can get nothing to eat; but it is false, for we have been all fed and lodged by you. In the neighbouring town, the inhabitants made wry faces at us; but here all the men, women, and even the children, made us welcome." Such was the success with which the Brethren had infused their own mild benevolent spirit into the Indians under their care.[1]

Indeed, the Indians who had originally invited the Brethren into this part of the country, were now so much impressed in their favour, that they not only ratified their former acts, but sent an embassy to them, requesting that a third settlement might be established in their neighbourhood. Their address on this occasion was to the following effect: "Brothers and friends! You told us, upon your arrival, that you intended to build two or three towns for the believing Indians. Two are erected, and we perceive that they are already filled with inhabitants. We, therefore, having long ago resolved to receive the gospel, have thought, upon mature deliberation, that it is now time to build the third town, that those of our people who believe may have a place of refuge. We, therefore, desire you to begin as soon as possible. We wish particularly to see our children instructed in reading the Holy Scriptures, that they may never forget them. Our eyes look towards you, for we are not able to accomplish it ourselves." Encouraged by this message, the Brethren proceeded to form a third station, which they called Lichtenau, and they had soon the satisfaction to find that a better situation could not have been chosen for the purpose. In the neighbouring town, and in other places, many of the Indians became concerned about their souls; and as all who appeared truly in earnest were permitted to reside in the settlement, it was not long before it increased both in numbers and extent.[2]

But while the mission was, in this manner, extending its boundaries, its progress was suddenly checked by the war which

[1] Loskiel, part iii. p. 98.

[2] Ibid. part iii. p. 102, 110.

had now commenced between England and the Colonies. The dispute had already risen so high, that the disturbances occasioned by it reached even to the Ohio and the Muskingum. The Brethren were placed in extremely embarrassing circumstances; and though they resolved to take no part in the war, yet it was scarcely possible for them to act with such circumspection as to offend neither the English nor the Americans, nor the several tribes of Indians who sided with the one or the other party. They saw that they would be placed, as it were, between three fires; that each of the contending powers would be dissatisfied with their neutrality, and that they would all view them with suspicion and dislike.

The Brethren, agreeably to the resolution they had taken, cautiously avoided interfering with the messages which the Delawares sent, either to the English, the Americans, or the neighbouring tribes, or with any thing relative to political affairs. There was one circumstance, however, which was very perplexing to them. The Delaware Indians occasionally received letters from Pittsburg and other places; and as they could not read them, they generally applied to the missionaries to know their contents, and sometimes desired them to answer them in the name of the chiefs. To have refused their request, would not only have been ungrateful but dangerous; yet, innocent as their compliance was, the Brethren anxiously wished to have been excused this office, as they were afraid that people, who knew not the nature of the business, might suspect that they themselves were carrying on a correspondence with one of the contending powers.

While several of the Indian tribes joined either the English or the Americans, and committed the most shocking outrages on their enemies, the chiefs of the Delaware nation determined to maintain a strict neutrality, both with the White people and their own countrymen. The Monsys, indeed, one of the Delaware tribes, secretly resolved to separate from the body of the nation, and to join the Mingoes, a gang of thieves and murderers. Before, however, they avowed their design, they endeavoured to form a party among the enemies of the mission; and they even ventured into the settlements, and sought to decoy some of the congregation to join them, a measure in which they were too successful. In the midst of Schoenbrunn, they found a party of apostates who seemed resolved to relinquish Christianity, and to return to their old heathenish practices. The Brethren had never before met with so severe a trial; in comparison of this, all their past difficulties and hardships were light and trivial. To recover the backsliders, they spared no labour or pains, employing every means which reason could suggest, or love could dictate. The attempt, however, was vain. It even appeared that the Monsys and the apostate party had nothing less in view, than either to murder the missionaries, or to convey them to Fort Detroit, as it was supposed that it was through their influence the Delaware chiefs were so firm in maintaining peace. The Brethren, therefore, resolved to continue no longer in a place, where not only themselves but the faithful part of the congregation were exposed to so many and so great dangers. It was, therefore, resolved to abandon Schoenbrunn, though this was not without deep regret, as it was the largest and most beautiful town which the Indians had hitherto built, and they had also there made considerable advances in agricultural pursuits. After pulling down the chapel, they accordingly retired with their people to the other two settlements.[1]

In August 1777, the Brethren received information that two hundred Huron warriors, under a chief called Half-king, were on their march to the settlement of Lichtenau. This intelligence occasioned them at first much alarm; but after mature deliberation, they resolved to shew no symptoms of fear, but rather to gain the savages by hospitality and kindness. They accordingly lost no time in killing oxen and pigs, and preparing other kinds of provisions for them; and it may be remarked to the honour of the Christian Indians, that their liberality on this occasion was truly remarkable, as they considered this the only means of saving their teachers. The warriors, on their arrival at a neighbouring town about two miles distant, were no less pleased than surprised at meeting a number of the congregation from Lichtenau with provisions for them; and as this put them in good humour, an embassy was sent to the Half-king, and the other chiefs of the Hurons, when the Christian Indian, Glikkikan, addressed them in the following manner:

[1] Loskiel, part iii. p. 109, 113, 119; Heckewelder, p. 157.

"Uncle! We, your cousins,[1] the congregation of believing Indians at Lichtenau and Gnadenhuetten, rejoice at this opportunity to see and to speak with you. We cleanse your eyes from all the dust, and whatever the wind may have carried into them, that you may see your cousin with clear eyes and a serene countenance. We cleanse your ears and hearts from all evil reports, which an evil wind may have conveyed into them on the journey, that our words may find entrance into your ears, and a place in your hearts." Here he delivered a string of wampum, and then proceeded: "Uncle, hear the words of the believing Indians, your cousins, at Lichtenau and Gnadenhuetten. We wish you to know that we have received and believed the Word of God for upwards of thirty years, and meet daily to hear it, morning and evening. You must also know that we have our teachers dwelling amongst us, who instruct us and our children. By this Word of God preached unto us by our teachers, we are taught to keep peace with all men, and to consider them as friends; for thus God has commanded us, and therefore we are lovers of peace. These, our teachers, are not only our friends; but we consider and love them as our flesh and blood. Now, as we are your cousin, we most earnestly beg of you, uncle, that you would also consider them as your own body, and as your cousin. We and they make but one body, and therefore cannot be separated; and whatever you do unto them, you do unto us, whether it be good or evil." Here he delivered a second string of wampum, several fathoms in length, when the Half-king of the Hurons replied, that these words had entered his heart, and that he would immediately consult with his warriors concerning them. Having done this, he returned the following answer to the deputies:

"Cousins! I am very glad, and feel great satisfaction that you have cleansed my eyes, ears, and heart from all evil, conveyed into me by the wind on this journey. I am upon an expedition of an unusual kind; for I am a warrior, and am going to war; and therefore many evil things and evil thoughts enter into my head, and even into my heart. But thanks to my cousin, my eyes are now clear, so that I can behold him with a serene countenance. I rejoice that I can hear my cousins with

[1] The several tribes of Indians consider themselves as standing in certain relations to each other, as grandfather, uncles, brothers, &c.

open ears, and take their words to heart." Having here delivered a string of wampum, and repeated all the words of the deputies relative to the missionaries, he expressed his approbation of them, and then added, "Go on as hitherto, and suffer no one to molest you. Obey your teachers, who speak nothing but good unto you, and instruct you in the ways of God, and be not afraid that any harm shall be done unto them. No creature shall hurt them. Attend to your worship, and never mind other affairs. Indeed, you see us going to war; but you may remain quiet and easy."

During these negotiations, the Brethren at Lichtenau were under strong apprehensions as to the issue of this embassy. It had indeed been agreed, that should the Half-king speak in a rough angry tone, the deputies should instantly send a messenger at full speed to that place, that so the congregation might have an opportunity of taking flight before he concluded his speech. As their apprehensions were so strong, their joy was proportionally great when the negotiation took so favourable a turn. Every heart was filled with gratitude and praise to God, who had so graciously heard the prayers which were presented to him at this critical juncture.

The Half-king and his warriors came the same day to Lichtenau, and behaved in a very friendly manner. He was joined by a great number of other Indians, Hurons, Iroquois, Ottawas, Chippeways, Shawanoes, Wampanoes, Pitawontakas, and some Frenchmen; but yet he maintained good order, and would allow of no excesses among them. He was particularly careful to prevent all drunkenness, knowing that it would soon be followed by murder and bloodshed, and other evils. Sometimes two hundred of the warriors lay all night in the neighbourhood of Lichtenau; and though they behaved with wonderful quietness, considering they were savages, yet the maintenance of such a number of people, many of whom came dancing before the houses, asking for bread and tobacco, proved extremely troublesome. The inhabitants were therefore glad when they took their departure, especially as so much rum had lately been imported from Pittsburg into that part of the country, that the whole neighbourhood became one scene of drunkenness and riot.

†

The dangers to which the missionaries in particular were now exposed, were so many and so great, that it was judged expedient that most of them should, for the present, leave the Indian country and retire to Bethlehem. Two only remained behind, Zeisberger at Lichtenau, and Edwards at Gnadenhuetten; places twenty miles distant from each other. They, however, paid mutual visits to one another, participating cordially in each other's joys and sorrows; and though they saw nothing before them but troubles, and hardships, and dangers, they resolved to remain with their beloved Indian congregation, even though it should cost the sacrifice of their life. Both they and their people, indeed, were kept in continual alarm by the rumours which were daily circulated through the country. One day they heard that an American general had arrived at Pittsburg, who would give no quarter to the Indians, whether friends or foes, being resolved to root them all out of the country; and it was said that several plans were formed for destroying Lichtenau and Gnadenhuetten, and other Delaware towns. One rumour after another proclaimed the approach of the Americans; and as the Christian Indians were resolved to take no part in the war, they had no other resource but to prepare for flight. A spot of ground on the banks of a neighbouring river was pitched on as a place of rendezvous for the two congregations; and every family packed up their goods to be ready to fly on the first emergency. One night an express arrived at both the settlements with an account of the approach of the enemy. The two congregations immediately fled with their teachers in canoes; and, indeed, it was with such precipitation, that they left the greater part of their goods behind them. They met at the place appointed, and there encamped, expecting every hour to hear of a bloody engagement in the neighbourhood of Lichtenau. Happily, however, before daybreak they received intelligence, that what had been taken for an American army was nothing more than a great number of horses in the woods. Soon after, indeed, a troop of American freebooters set off, contrary to the express orders of the governor of Pittsburg, to destroy the Delaware towns, and of course the missionary settlements among the rest; but being met by the Half-king of the Hurons and his warriors, they were entirely defeated, and the greater part of them slain.[1]

The Hurons, who were in the interest of England, continued to carry on hostilities against the Americans; and the most frightful accounts were received from time to time of the ravages and murders committed by them and other Indians in the plantations of the White settlers. The missionaries were often shocked to behold the savage warriors, on their return from their murderous expeditions, leading captive men, women, and children; or what was still more distressing, carrying their dead bodies and scalps through the town. The Christian Indians shewed great compassion to the unfortunate prisoners, supplied them with food, and would never suffer them to be scourged or abused in any form in the settlement, as is the Indian custom whenever warriors pass through a town with captives. The savages were often mightily incensed at this compassionate prohibition, yet nevertheless they had to yield. Among the prisoners, there was an old man of a venerable appearance, together with two youths. The Christian Indians greatly commiserated his situation, and offered a large sum to the warriors for his ransom, but all was of no avail. When the savages arrived in their own town, the two youths were tortured and burnt alive, according to the custom of the Indians towards their unfortunate prisoners. The old man was doomed to a similar fate; but being warned of this by a girl, a prisoner like himself, who had overheard their deliberations, he made his escape; and though pursued by the savages, he succeeded in eluding them, and was accidentally found by two boys in the woods, eight miles from Lichtenau, quite exhausted with fatigue and hunger, having, it is said, eaten nothing but grass for ten days. Being brought, though with much difficulty, to the settlement, the poor man was there taken care of, and after his recovery, was conveyed in safety to Pittsburg.[2]

During this period many troops of warriors were prevailed on, by the friendly persuasions of the Christian Indians, to relinquish their murderous designs and to return to their homes, by which means much bloodshed was happily prevented. By the influence of the missionaries and the congregation, the Delaware chiefs were confirmed in their resolution to take no part in the

[1] Loskiel, part iii. p. 123, 127. [2] Ibid. part iii. p. 132; Heckewelder, p. 167.

war, notwithstanding the threats as well as entreaties of the governor of Detroit; and by the neutrality and efforts of the Delawares, many other Indian tribes were kept at peace, being unwilling to offend their grandfather, as they called that powerful nation. The government at Pittsburg acknowledged the deportment of the Indian congregation to be a benefit to the whole country; and Colonel Morgan observed with gratitude, that the fury of the Indian warriors was, upon the whole, greatly mitigated by the influence of their Christian countrymen.

The Delaware Indians, notwithstanding they had been greatly urged to join the English, had long maintained their neutrality, a policy which had been recommended to them by the American government; but, being now called on by it to make war on the Indians in the interest of England, the chiefs, who had previously been divided on the subject, began to waver; and they at length resolved to join the English, and take up arms against the Colonies. Now they not only ceased to be the friends of the missionaries and the congregation, but, by degrees, they became their enemies, considering them as a check on their proceedings, and a hinderance to the accomplishment of their designs. As the Indians in league with England had resolved in a council held at Detroit, that the hatchet should fall on the head of every one who refused to accept of it, and as those in the interest of the Colonies had taken a similar resolution, the Christian Indians were now placed between two cruel and inexorable enemies, so that there seemed nothing before them but inevitable destruction. According to their late resolution, the Delaware chiefs sent messages to the young men to take up arms; but as they refused to do so, the missionaries were in the utmost danger, the refusal being ascribed solely to their influence and authority. The savages threatened either to kill the Brethren, or to carry them off prisoners, hoping that if they were removed, the Indian congregation would then comply with all their demands.

In consequence of the confusion and distress which prevailed throughout the whole country, considerable changes had taken place in the settlements of the Brethren. Not only was Schoenbrunn deserted by the faithful part of the congregation, but it was afterwards judged necessary to abandon Gnadenhuetten also, and to concentrate the whole mission in Lichtenau. As this place, however, was soon overcrowded with inhabitants, it was agreed that part of them should return to Gnadenhuetten, and that Schoenbrunn should be rebuilt, though not on the same spot as before, but on the opposite side of the river. Lichtenau, which had hitherto been the safest place of residence for the Christian Indians, became so exposed to the outrages of the savages, that it was at length judged necessary to leave it also, and to build a new settlement, which they called Salem, about five miles below Gnadenhuetten.[1]

In the midst of these external trials, the internal state of the congregation was of the most pleasing nature. Notwithstanding the disturbances occasioned by the daily marching of the warriors through their settlements, the Christian Indians never lost their confidence in God, but were led by their various trials to cleave more closely to him, and to unite more cordially in the bonds of brotherly affection. It was peculiarly pleasing to witness the spirit of forgiveness which they displayed towards their enemies, particularly to the apostates in the congregation of Schoenbrunn. Notwithstanding the hatred and malice which these unhappy people manifested towards them, yet they would never consider them as enemies, but as brethren who had wandered from the paths of purity and peace. Nor were their prayers in behalf of them in vain. Most of the wanderers, especially the young people, returned like the prodigal son, acknowledged their guilt, and earnestly begged for admission into the bosom of the congregation. Their request was granted in the presence of the whole assembly, whose manifestations of compassion, gratitude, and joy, on such occasions, furnished an interesting example of that brotherly love which characterizes and ennobles the followers of Christ.[2]

For some time, the Christian Indians enjoyed peace and rest in their new settlements, scarcely seeing any thing of the horrors of war, except that the warriors occasionally passed through their towns. But this period of tranquillity was of short duration. The missionaries had long been obnoxious to the warlike Indians in the interest of England, and plans were repeatedly

[1] Loskiel, part iii. p. 133, 137; Heckewelder, p. 170, 173.

[2] Loskiel, part iii. p. 129, 139, 145.

formed to murder them. But they had no greater or more active enemies than three miscreants of the name of Elliot, M'Kee, and Girty, who had long sought to stir up the Indians and also the commandant of Fort Detroit against them and the congregations under their care. Imposed on by the representations which were made to him, Colonel de Peyster, the new governor of Fort Detroit, was led to believe that the Christian Indians were partisans of the Americans, and that the missionaries were spies who carried on a secret correspondence with them; and he therefore resolved to rid himself of such troublesome and dangerous neighbours. With this view, a proposal was made to several of the Indian tribes to carry off the missionaries and the congregation; but the service not being to their liking was declined by them. At length, however, the Half-king of the Hurons suffered himself to be persuaded by Elliot and Captain Pipe, one of the Delaware chiefs, and a violent enemy of the mission, to make the attempt, though even he declared that he did it to save the Christian Indians from destruction.

In August 1781, the Half-king came to the neighbourhood of the Brethren's settlements, accompanied by Elliot, and by Pipe the Delaware chief, and upwards of three hundred warriors. They all behaved at first in a friendly manner; Elliot acted like a thorough hypocrite. The Half-king having intimated his wish to have a meeting of the chief men of the three settlements, they accordingly met at Gnadenhuetten, when he delivered to them the following speech:—"Cousins, ye believing Indians in Gnadenhuetten, Schoenbrunn, and Salem, I am much concerned on your account, perceiving that you live in a very dangerous spot. Two powerful, angry, and merciless gods stand ready, opening their jaws wide against each other; you are sitting down between both, and are thus in danger of being devoured and ground to powder by the teeth of either the one or the other, or of both. It is therefore not advisable for you to stay here any longer. Consider your young people, your wives, and your children, and preserve their lives, for here they must all perish. I therefore take you by the hand, lift you up, and place you in or near my dwelling, where you will be safe and dwell in peace. Do not stand looking at your plantations and houses; but arise and follow me. Take also your teachers with you, and worship God in the place to which I shall lead you, as you have been accustomed to do. You shall likewise find provisions, and our father beyond the lake[1] will care for you. This is my message, and I have come hither purposely to deliver it." He then delivered to them a string of wampum; and the missionaries and Indian assistants having met in conference to consider this unexpected message, the latter on the next day returned the following answer to the Half-king:— "Uncle, and ye Captains of the Delawares and Monsys, our friends and countrymen! Ye Shawanoes, our nephews, and all ye other people here assembled! We have heard your words; but have not yet seen the danger so great, that we might not stay here. We keep peace with all men, and have nothing to do with the war, nor do we wish or desire any thing, but to be permitted to enjoy rest and peace. You see yourselves that we cannot rise immediately and go with you, for we are heavy, and time is required to prepare for it. But we will keep and consider your words, and let you, Uncle, know our answer next winter, after the harvest. Upon this you may rely."

With this answer not only the Half-king, but the greater part of the warriors, appeared to be satisfied, declaring that it would be wrong to compel their cousins to move from a favourite spot, where they had in abundance every thing they could wish, and where they lived so contented and happy. Elliot, however, continued to urge Captain Pipe and the Half-king not to give up their design, but to have recourse to other and more severe measures. Accordingly, the latter, in a meeting held a few days after, sought to frighten the Indians into his proposals, by representing to them in strong terms the dangers to which they would be exposed from the hostile Indians, and also from the Virginians or Long Knives, as he called them. But the Indians still persisted in expressing their wish to remain where they were. Meanwhile, the common warriors sought to decoy them, by describing the country to which they proposed to carry them as a perfect paradise, and, unfortunately, they were too successful in making an impression on the minds of some who were not up to their artifice and cunning. Thus a division

[1] The Governor of Fort Detroit.

arose among the Indians. Some advised to rise and go with the Half-king, without considering the consequences: others, and that by far the greater number, opposed this measure, declaring that they would rather die on the spot. This division among the Indians occasioned the Brethren great perplexity and distress, but yet they resolved not to follow the savages unless by compulsion, that so, if the congregation were involved in ruin, they might not have to reproach themselves on account of it.

The Half-king of the Hurons, it is probable, would not have urged the proposal further, had he not been pressed by Elliot to employ coercive and even violent measures, alleging that, if he returned to Detroit without the missionaries, the governor would be highly dissatisfied. Besides, some of the congregation proved unfaithful, and even insinuated to the savages that if they only seized the Brethren and carried them off, the rest of the people would quickly follow. Others were so simple, that when asked, Whether they would go with the Half-king? they replied: "We look to our teachers; what they do, we will do likewise." Thus the whole blame fell upon the missionaries, who, in consequence of this, became the chief object of the resentment of the savages. The heads of the party had several consultations, in which, as some of them afterwards related, they resolved to murder all the White Brethren and Sisters, and likewise the Indian assistants. Before, however, carrying their bloody purpose into execution, they wished to know the opinion of a common warrior, who was much esteemed among them as a sorcerer; and as he was decidedly against the proposal, and even threatened them with his displeasure if they persisted in it, they laid aside the design for the present.

The savages, however, now became more bold and outrageous in their behaviour than before. Though they were supplied by the congregation with as much meat as they could eat, and nothing in fact was denied them, yet they wantonly shot the cattle and pigs on the road, and would not even suffer the carcasses to be taken away, so that the place was soon filled with an intolerable stench. Small parties of them likewise made inroads into the neighbouring country, and brought their prisoners to Gnadenhuetten, thus converting that seat of industry and peace into a theatre of pillage and war.

The chiefs now called once more on the Indian assistants to come with their teachers and hear what they had to say to them. On their appearing before the Council, the Half-king asked them whether they would go with him, and required of them an immediate answer in the affirmative or negative, without even allowing them to retire and consult about it. To this they replied, they would abide by the reply given at the last meeting, upon which they were immediately dismissed.

Next day, shortly after dinner, as the Brethren Zeisberger, Senseman, and Heckewelder, were walking behind the garden, they were seized by a small party of Huron warriors and marched off towards the camp, which was about a hundred yards distant. On the way thither, an ugly-looking Huron aimed a blow at Senseman's head with his tomahawk; but the missionary fortunately eluded the stroke. On reaching the line which divided the Huron and Delaware camps, their captors raised what is called the Scalp-whoop, each of them raising a yell for his man, this being the way in which the Indians indicate the number of prisoners who have fallen into their hands. Several others of the Hurons now came up and stripped them of their clothes, watches, and other articles. The missionaries were then placed in two huts, which however were merely roofs of bark raised on poles to keep off the rain from above, the sides and ends being open.

About half an hour after, the Brethren all of a sudden heard the word given to start, and immediately about thirty armed Hurons set off for Salem. To Heckewelder this was a peculiarly trying circumstance, as he concluded that they would take his wife and children together with Michael Young prisoners, and rob his house.

Gnadenhuetten and Salem being situated on the Muskingum, the bells and barking of dogs in the one place could be distinctly heard at the other in calm weather, particularly at Gnadenhuetten which stood on somewhat elevated ground. "This," says Heckewelder, "being a very close and calm night, we in our camps, although the distance was between five and six miles, heard distinctly the scalp-yell sounded at Salem by the party who had gone thither, and who had effected their object; and every time they, while returning in triumph from this expedition, renewed the scalp-whoop, it was heard by those who remained at our station, and who sounded theirs in reply, by which means both parties, although distant from each other, were in a manner conveying intelligence and congratulating each other on their triumphs. The nearer those coming from Salem approached the camp, the more terrible their yells sounded in my ears. The three yells they gave each time shewed that three persons had fallen into their hands at Salem, but whether they were alive or had been murdered by them, could not be known until their arrival." At length, near midnight, the party arrived with Michael Young, who informed Heckewelder that his wife and child were safe, and that the Indian Sisters having begged the warriors to place them under their care for the night, they consented, under a promise that they would bring them to Gnadenhuetten next day. The savages, however, had broken open the house with their war hatchets, and plundered or destroyed its contents.

The missionaries passed a long and anxious night, lying on the bare sod, with their eyes directed toward the east that they might catch the first glimpse of the morning light, when at length the sound of the scalp-yell was heard to the north in the direction of Schoenbrunn, though at a great distance, which not only damped their hopes, but set the whole body of the savages in motion. That something had taken place at Schoenbrunn was certain. There it was that the wives of Zeisberger and Senseman were left, together with the missionary Jungman and his wife. The nearer the party drew, the greater was the commotion among the warriors in the camp, the scalp-yell being sounded and re-sounded on both sides. At length the warriors arrived by water with the missionary Jungman and his wife, and the Sisters Zeisberger and Senseman, the last of whom was particularly to be pitied, as she had been delivered of a child only three days before, yet was she now hurried from home by the savages with the infant at her breast in a dark and rainy night. It appears that late on the preceding evening, some Hurons came to Schoenbrunn after they had gone to bed, and under the pretence of protecting them, plundered the house, and brought them off as prisoners.

On the following day the prisoners obtained permission to visit each other. The Sisters, who under all their trials shewed wonderful composure and resignation, were allowed to go and lodge in the house of one of the Brethren, named Shebosh, who had not been taken prisoner, being considered as an Indian, as he had completely adopted the Indian mode of life, and had married an Indian wife. Here the prisoners were occasionally allowed to see their friends, and they had also liberty to visit them in return. Meanwhile, the savages were strutting about in the clothes which they had taken from the missionaries, and they even compelled their wives to make them shirts of the linen of which they had robbed them.

At the commencement of these disasters, the conduct of the Christian Indians was like that of the disciples of Christ; they forsook their teachers and fled. On arriving in the woods, they lifted up their voices and wept so loud, that the air resounded with their lamentations. They soon, indeed, recovered from the panic which had seized them on the first appearance of danger. Having collected their courage, they returned and recovered many articles belonging to the missionaries out of the hands of the robbers, or they generously paid for them, in order to restore them to their rightful owners. They used to carry victuals to the prisoners, and late in the evening blankets to cover them during the night, and early in the morning they brought them away again, lest they should be stolen by the savages in the course of the day. Some had even the courage to enter the camp by day, to seize the booty taken by the savages, and to carry it off by main force.

After keeping the Brethren prisoners for several days, the leaders of the savages perceived that the Christian Indians would never be persuaded to forsake their settlements, unless they were conducted by their teachers; and, therefore, they called the missionaries before them, and set them at liberty, on the understanding that they would encourage the congregation to go with them to Sandusky. The missionaries now returned to their beloved Indians, and as they saw that there was no alternative left them but to emigrate, they proposed it to them, and they being of the same mind, acquiesced in the measure.[1]

Never, however, did they forsake any country with so much regret. They were now obliged to leave three beautiful settlements, and the greater part of their property behind them. They had already lost upwards of two hundred black cattle, and four hundred hogs; but, besides this, they had to abandon great quantities of Indian corn in their stores, upwards of three hundred acres of land, where the crop was just ripening, together with potatoes, cabbages, and other garden stuffs in the ground. Their losses, according to a moderate calculation, amounted to not less than 12,000 dollars, a large sum certainly to belong chiefly to Indians, and a striking proof of the improvements which the missionaries had introduced among them. But what gave them special concern, was the total loss of the books and manuscripts which they had compiled, with great labour, for the instruction of the Indian youth, all of which were now burnt by the savages. Besides, they had nothing before them but the prospect of trials and disappointments, of hardships, difficulties, and dangers. But there was no help for this. They could only possess their souls in patience, and commit their way to God, in the hope that he would command deliverance for them.

On leaving their settlements on the Muskingum, they were escorted by a troop of savages, who enclosed them on all hands, at the distance of some miles. They went partly by land, partly by water. Some of the canoes sunk, and those who were in them lost all their provisions, and whatever else they carried with them. Those who went by land, drove their cattle before them, having collected a considerable herd of these animals from two of the settlements. The Brethren and their wives usually travelled in the midst of their beloved people. One morning, however, when the Christian Indians could not set off so expeditiously as their conductors thought proper, the savages attacked the missionaries, and forced them away alone, whipped their horses forward till the animals became quite unmanageable, and would not even allow the women to suckle their infant children. The road too was extremely bad, being

[1] Loskiel, part iii. p. 149; Heckewelder, p. 170, 185, 203, 229, 232, 238, 241, 244, 251, 254, 256.

through one continued swamp. Zeisberger's wife fell twice from her horse, and in one of these instances, was dragged for some time, hanging in the stirrup; but through the kindness of Providence she was mercifully preserved. Some of the Christian Indians followed them as hard as they could, but with all their exertions they did not overtake them till night; and hence the missionaries and their families were not delivered out of the hands of the savages till next morning. But though the journey was extremely irksome, they all travelled along with the utmost resignation and patience. Not one left the congregation, not one laid the blame of their troubles and losses upon others; no dissatisfaction, no disunion arose among them. They adhered to each other as brethren and friends, rejoicing in God their Saviour, and even held their daily meetings upon the road.

Having arrived at Sandusky Creek, after a journey of upwards of four weeks, the Half-king of the Hurons and his warriors left them, and marched into their own country, leaving them to shift for themselves in the best way they were able. Thus, they were abandoned in a wilderness where there was neither game nor provisions of any description; for such was the place to which the savages had led them, notwithstanding they had represented it as a perfect paradise. After wandering to and fro for some, they resolved to spend the winter in Upper Sandusky; and having pitched on the most convenient spot they could find in this dreary region, they erected small huts of logs and bark to shelter themselves from the rain and the cold. They were now, however, so poor, that they had neither beds nor blankets; for, on the journey, the savages had stolen every thing from them, except their utensils for manufacturing maple sugar. But nothing distressed them so much as the want of provisions. Some had long spent their all, and now depended on the charity of their neighbours for a morsel to eat. Even the missionaries, who hitherto had uniformly gained a livelihood by the labour of their hands, were now reduced to the necessity of receiving support from the congregation. As their wants were so urgent, Shebosh the missionary, and several of the Christian Indians, returned as soon as possible to their settlements on the Muskingum, in order to fetch the Indian corn which they had left growing in the fields.

Scarcely had the congregation begun to settle in this place, when the missionaries were ordered to come and appear before the governor of Fort Detroit. Four of them, Zeisberger, Senseman, Heckewelder, and Edwards, accompanied by several of the Indian assistants, accordingly set off without delay, while the other two remained with their little flock. It was with a heavy heart they took their departure, partly, as they knew not what might be the issue of the journey, and partly, as they were obliged to leave their families in want of the common necessaries of life. As they travelled chiefly by land along the banks of Lake Erie, they had to pass through numerous swamps, across deep creeks, and through thick forests. Besides, a report reached them by the way, that Shebosh and some of the Indians who had gone to the Muskingum to fetch corn, had been murdered by the Americans, and that a large body of them were marching to Sandusky to surprise the new settlement. This report, indeed, was not correct. The commander of the party, on finding that they were not the enemy but Christian Indians, did not suffer one of them to be molested, but he took Shebosh, the missionary, and five of the Indians to Pittsburg, where they were kindly treated, and left to return to their homes when they pleased. The others came back safe to Sandusky, with about four hundred bushels of Indian corn, which they had gathered in the fields. But as our travellers did not hear a correct account of these circumstances until afterwards, the report, in the mean while, occasioned them much anxiety and distress.

Having arrived at Detroit, they appeared before the governor, in order to answer to the accusations brought against them of holding a correspondence with the Americans to the prejudice of the English. The investigation, however, was delayed till Captain Pike, their chief accuser, should arrive, a circumstance which could not but give them much uneasiness, as he had hitherto shewn himself their bitter and determined enemy. They had no friend on earth to interpose in their behalf; but they had a friend in heaven in whom they put their trust. Nor was their confidence in Him in vain. On the day of trial, Captain Pipe, after some ceremonies had passed between him and Colonel de Peyster, respecting the scalps and prisoners which he had brought from the United States, rose and addressed the governor as follows: "Father, you commanded us to bring the believing Indians and their teachers from the Muskingum. This has been done. When we had brought them to Sandusky, you ordered us to bring their teachers and some of their chiefs unto you. Here you see them before you. Now you may speak with them yourself as you have desired. But I hope you will speak good words unto them: Yea, I tell you, speak good words unto them, for they are my friends, and I should be sorry to see them ill-used." These last words he repeated two or three times. In reply to this speech, the governor reminded him of the various complaints he had made against the Brethren, and called upon him to prove that they had actually corresponded with the Americans to the prejudice of the English. To this the chief replied, that such a thing might have happened; but they would do it no more, as they were now at Detroit. The governor, justly dissatisfied with this answer, peremptorily demanded that he should give a direct reply to his question. Pipe was now greatly embarrassed, began to shift and shuffle, and, bending to his councillors, asked them, What he should say? But they all hung down their heads in silence. On a sudden, however, he rose, and thus addressed the governor: "I said before that such a thing might have happened: Now I will tell you the truth. The missionaries are innocent. They have done nothing of themselves. What they did, they were compelled to do." Then smiting his breast, he added: "I am to blame, and the chiefs who were with me. We forced them to do it when they refused;" alluding to the correspondence between the Delaware chiefs and the Americans, of which the missionaries were the innocent medium. Thus the Brethren found an advocate and a friend in their accuser and their enemy.

After making some further inquiries concerning them, the Governor declared before the whole court, that the Brethren were innocent of all the charges alleged against them; that he felt great satisfaction in their endeavours to civilize and christianize the Indians; and that he would permit them to return to their congregation without delay. He treated them in the most friendly manner; and as they had been plundered contrary to his express command, he ordered them to be supplied with clothes and various other articles of which they stood in need. He even bought them four watches which the savages had taken from them, and which they had sold to a trader. After experiencing various other acts of kindness from him, they returned to Sandusky, and were received with inexpressible joy by their families and the whole congregation, who had been under strong apprehensions that they would be detained prisoners at Detroit.[1]

The congregation at Sandusky were still in extreme want of provisions, and at length famine with all its horrors appeared among them. Often they knew not to-day what they should eat to-morrow. At Christmas, they could not as usual observe the Lord's Supper, as they had neither bread nor wine. The cattle, of which they possessed considerable herds, had no forage, so that such of them as were not killed for food perished of hunger. Provisions were not to be had even for money; or if any were bought in other places, it was at a most exorbitant price. Many of the poor lived on wild potatoes; and at last their want was so extreme, that they greedily devoured the carcasses of the horses and cattle which died of starvation.

Impelled by the severity of the famine, several parties of the Christian Indians went from Sandusky to the settlements on the Muskingum to fetch provisions, as it was reported there was now no danger in that quarter of the country. They had been there already several weeks gathering the corn and burying it in the woods, whence they proposed fetching it as it should be needed. Having secured as much as they thought would serve them for the season, they intended setting off the following day on their return to Sandusky. They were still without any apprehensions of danger; but in this they were wofully mistaken. That quarter now became the scene of a catastrophe, which has few parallels in the annals of treachery and murder. Having heard that many of the Christian Indians came occasionally from Sandusky to the Muskingum for provisions, a party of Americans, about one hundred and sixty in number, determined to murder these poor people, to destroy their settlements, and then to march to Sandusky and cut off the rest of the congregation. Colonel Gibson at Pittsburg having heard of this bar-

[1] Loskiel, part iii. p. 161; Heckewelder, p. 298.

barous plot, sent messengers to the Christian Indians on the Muskingum to apprize them of their danger, but it was too late before they arrived. The Indians, however, received information of the approach of the White people, from a different quarter, in time enough to have saved themselves by flight; but though on other occasions they used to manifest the utmost caution and timidity, yet at this time they shewed no signs of fear, apprehending that they had nothing to dread from the Americans, but only from the savages.[1]

In March 1782, the conspirators, headed by a man of the name of Williamson, arrived at Gnadenhuetten. When within about a mile of the settlement, they fell in with Joseph Shebosh, a son of the missionary of that name, and murdered him in a barbarous manner, notwithstanding he told them he was a White man's son, and entreated them to spare his life. They then came to the Indians, most of whom were working in their corn-fields, accosted them in a kindly manner, and spoke of themselves as their friends and brothers who had come to relieve them from the distress brought on them by the enemy on account of their being friends to the American people. The simple Indians believed every word, returned with them to the town, and treated them in the most hospitable manner. Having informed their visitors that a small barrel of wine, which was found among their goods, was designed for the Lord's Supper, and that they were to carry it with them to Sandusky, the ruffians told them that they should not return thither but go with them to Pittsburg, where they would be in no danger either from the English or the savages. This proposal the Indians heard with resignation, hoping that God might by this means put an end to their present sufferings, which were so many and severe. Under this idea, they cheerfully delivered up their guns, their hatchets, and their other weapons to the conspirators, who promised to take care of them, and on their arrival at Pittsburg to return every article to its rightful owner. The poor unsuspecting creatures even shewed them all those articles which they had secreted in the woods, assisted in packing them up, and thus emptied all their stores into the hands of this band of miscreants.

[1] Loskiel, part iii. p. 169, 170, 175; Heckewelder, p. 302, 311.

Meanwhile, John Martin, one of the Indian assistants, went to Salem, with the news of the arrival of the White people, to his Christian countrymen in that town, and assured them they need not be afraid to go with them, as they were come to conduct them to a place of safety. The Indians at Salem did not hesitate to accept of the proposal, believing that God had sent the Americans to release them from their present disagreeable situation at Sandusky, and imagining that when they arrived at Pittsburg, they might soon find a place where to build a new settlement, and easily procure assistance from Bethlehem. John Martin accordingly returned to Gnadenhuetten, accompanied by two of them, to acquaint both their Brethren and the White people with their resolution. The ruffians having expressed a desire to see Salem, a party of them were conducted thither, and received with the utmost hospitality. Here they professed the same attachment to the Indians as at Gnadenhuetten, and easily persuaded the poor creatures to go with them to that place.

Having by such hypocritical arts completely deceived the unsuspecting Indians, the bloodthirsty villains at length threw off the mask, and displayed their character in its true colours. In the mean while, they had seized the poor defenceless inhabitants of Gnadenhuetten, and bound them without resistance. The Indians from Salem now shared a similar fate. Before they entered the town, they were suddenly surprised by their conductors, robbed of their guns, and even of their pocket-knives, and brought bound into the settlement.

The White people, having consulted together what they would now do with them, resolved, by a majority of votes, to put them all to death. Some were for setting fire to the houses and burning them alive. Others wished to carry their scalps home with them as a signal of victory; whilst others remonstrated against both these proposals, declaring that they would never be guilty of murdering a harmless innocent people, and proposed setting them at liberty, or, if that would not be agreed to, taking them as prisoners, and delivering them up to the proper authorities; but, finding that they could not prevail on the others to spare their lives, they wrung their hands, and calling God to witness that they were innocent of the blood of these Christian Indians, they withdrew to some distance from the scene of slaughter.

One of the conspirators was sent to the prisoners to tell them, that as they were Christian Indians, they might prepare themselves for death in a Christian manner, for that they must all die on the morrow.

The Indians, on hearing their frightful doom, could scarcely fail to be struck with terror; but they soon recollected themselves, and became patient and resigned. Their last night on earth they spent in prayer, and in exhorting each other to remain faithful unto death; and, as the morning approached, they employed themselves in singing the praises of God their Saviour, in the joyful hope of soon joining in the songs of the redeemed in heaven.

When the day of execution arrived, the murderers fixed on two houses, one for the men, the other for the women and children, to which they wantonly gave the name of slaughter-houses. Some of them even came to the prisoners manifesting great impatience that the execution was not yet begun. No time, however, was now lost. The poor innocent creatures, men, women, and children, were bound with ropes, two and two together. They were then led into the slaughter-houses appointed for them. There they were scalped and murdered in cold blood by these demons in human form. In this horrid manner perished no fewer than ninety-six persons, among whom were five of the most valuable assistants, and thirty-four children! According to the testimony of the murderers themselves, they behaved with wonderful patience, and met death with cheerful resignation. They even acknowledged that they were good Indians: "for," said they, "they sung and prayed to their latest breath."

Of the whole number of Indians at Gnadenhuetten and Salem, only two youths escaped; and their escape was little less than miraculous. One of them was so fortunate as to disengage himself from his bonds; then slipping unobserved from the crowd, he crept through a narrow window into the cellar of the house where the women and children were slaughtered. He had not been long there when their blood penetrated through the floor, and, according to his account, ran in streams into the cellar. Here he lurked till night, no one coming down to search the cellar; and then, though with much difficulty, he climbed up the wall to the window, and fled into a neighbouring thicket. The escape of the other youth was still more singular. The murderers gave him only one blow on the head, cut off his scalp, and then left him. After some time he recovered his senses, and beheld himself surrounded by bleeding corpses. In the midst of these, he observed one of the converts named Abel, moving and attempting to raise himself up. But he lay perfectly still as though he had been dead, a caution which proved the means of his deliverance; for, shortly after, one of the murderers came in, and perceiving Abel's motions, killed him outright with two or three blows. Our youth lay quiet till the dusk of the evening, though suffering exquisite pain from his wounds. He then ventured to creep to the door, and having observed nobody in the neighbourhood, he escaped into the wood, where he lay concealed during the night. Here the two lads met with each other; and before they left their retreat, they saw the murderers, with a ferocious insensibility, making merry after the accomplishment of their diabolical enterprise· and at last they set fire to the two slaughter-houses filled with the corpses of their innocent victims.

While the Christian Indians at Gnadenhuetten and Salem were in this manner inhumanly butchered, those at Schoenbrunn providentially escaped. As they had occasion to send a message to Gnadenhuetten, the bearer of it, before he reached that place, found young Shebosh lying dead on the ground; and looking forward, he saw a number of White people about the town. Alarmed by this discovery, he fled back to Schoenbrunn in haste, and told the Indians what he had seen. Upon this they all took flight and ran into the woods, so that when the conspirators came to the town they found nobody in it; and though the Indians lay concealed in the neighbourhood, yet happily they escaped undiscovered. Having, therefore, set fire to the three settlements, they marched off with the scalps of their innocent victims, about fifty horses, and such other parts of their property as they chose to carry with them.[1]

In the mean while, the missionaries at Sandusky were not without their trials. In the congregation itself, there arose some false brethren, who, having relapsed into the paths of sin,

[1] Loskiel, part iii. p. 177; Heckewelder, p. 319.

endeavoured to introduce their heathenish practices among their Christian countrymen. They would not even leave the settlement, but stopped in defiance of all remonstrances, were enraged when kindly reproved, and went among the neighbouring Pagans, trying to exasperate them against the missionaries. Besides, though the governor of Detroit had promised that the Brethren should not be molested in their labours, yet this was an engagement he was not able to fulfil. Soon after their return to Sandusky, some of the principal Delaware chiefs expressed their surprise that he should have permitted them to depart, and thus disappointed their hopes of getting rid of persons whom they deemed so troublesome. Hitherto, however, the governor had found means to pacify them by the wisdom and firmness of his conduct. But now the Half-king of the Hurons again took part against them. Two of his sons, who had lately gone on a murdering expedition, having both been killed, he foolishly ascribed their death to the intrigues of the Brethren, and determined to be revenged upon them. Besides, with the dread natural to a guilty conscience, he lived in continual apprehension that the Christian Indians, if they were suffered to remain in a body, might revenge on him the many injuries which they and their teachers had lately suffered. To disperse them, therefore, was a great object with him; and he knew nothing so likely to accomplish this as to take their instructors from them. Influenced in part, perhaps, by his insidious representations, the governor of Detroit now sent an order to their old enemy Girty, to bring all the missionaries and their families to that place, but with strict charges not to plunder or abuse them.[1]

This order was like a thunderbolt to the missionaries; death itself would not have been more terrible. To forsake their congregation, whom they loved as their own souls; to leave them exposed to all the fury of their enemies, or to be scattered in the wilderness among the heathen, wrung their hearts with anguish. It was vain, however, to resist. The slightest remonstrance might have subjected them to plunder and abuse, and could not be of the smallest service. When this order was communicated to the congregation, a most tender and affecting

[1] Loskiel, part iii. p. 171.

scene was exhibited among them. The poor Indians were dissolved in tears, and broke forth into the most bitter lamentations, exclaiming that they were left as sheep without a shepherd. This could not fail to aggravate greatly the distress of the missionaries. As yet they had heard nothing of the tragical catastrophe on the Muskingum; but, on the day before their departure, the report of it reached them. A warrior who came from that part of the country, related that all the Indians, who were found in the deserted settlements seeking provisions, had been taken prisoners by the Americans, carried off to Pittsburg, and some of them murdered. This report, though it by no means amounted to the whole extent of the evil, was yet frightful enough to aggravate the anxiety and distress of the missionaries. Thus overwhelmed with grief and sorrow, they took leave of their beloved Indian congregation. Zeisberger, after exhorting them with all the tenderness of a father to remain faithful unto death, kneeled down and gave thanks to God for all the spiritual mercies he had bestowed upon them in the midst of external misery, and commended them to his protection and love, till they should meet each other again, either here on earth, or before the throne in heaven. The Brethren now set off on their journey, believing one part of their congregation murdered, another part imprisoned, and the rest in danger of dispersion. They were accompanied a considerable way by a great number of their disconsolate people, weeping as they went; and by some as far as Lower Sandusky, where they arrived after suffering many hardships and inconveniences. Here they had to remain for some time, until the arrival of vessels to carry them forward. During their stay at this place, they were visited by Girty, who had employed a Frenchman to conduct them to Detroit; and being enraged at finding them still there, behaved toward them like a perfect madman, and, with horrid oaths, threatened to split their heads in two with his tomahawk. Two large flat-bottomed boats at length arrived, with a written order to treat the Brethren with all possible kindness; and, in case of stormy weather, not to endanger their life in crossing the lake; intimating at the same time, that, should any one do them the smallest injury, he would be called to account for his conduct.[1]

[1] Loskiel, part iii. p. 174, 185.

Having at length reached Detroit, they were soon after visited by the governor, who assured them, that though many new accusations had been brought against them, yet he was perfectly satisfied of their innocence; and had not sent for them on that account, but merely to provide for their safety, as he had received certain intelligence, that they were in the utmost danger of their life as long as they remained at Sandusky. He further left it entirely to themselves, either to stay at Detroit or to go to Bethlehem; and, in the mean while, he gave orders that they should be supplied with whatever they needed.

Meanwhile, the Indian congregation was reduced to the brink of ruin. After the departure of the missionaries, the assistants, indeed, continued to meet and exhort their countrymen in the usual and regular manner. But some false brethren now arose, who ascribed to the missionaries all the misfortunes of the congregation; attributing to them the massacre of their countrymen on the Muskingum; and even asserting, that, conscious of their guilt, they had now taken care to go off in safety. These absurd allegations, though condemned by the faithful part of the congregation, produced no small disquietude among them. Besides, the Half-king of the Hurons could not rest while the Christian Indians remained in a body in his neighbourhood. He therefore sent them a peremptory message to quit their present residence, and seek an asylum in some other part of the country. It seemed, indeed, as if no place were left where the poor Indians might have rest for the soles of their feet. They could expect no protection from the White people, and their own countrymen hunted them as partridges on the mountains. For the present, therefore, they resolved to separate, as it seemed vain to make further resistance. One part, accordingly, retired into the country of the Shawanoes, the rest stayed for some time in the neighbourhood of Pipetown, and then resolved to proceed nearer to the Miami river. Thus there was a period put for a season to the existence of the Indian congregation.[1]

Here we cannot but remark, that the removal of the congregation from the Muskingum, though a painful, was a very

[1] Loskiel, part iii. p. 187.

merciful circumstance. Had they remained in that part of the country, it is probable they would all have been massacred, whereas more than two-thirds of them escaped. A similar observation may be made as to the removal of the missionaries to Detroit, which, at the time, occasioned them so much distress. When they received the governor's orders to repair to that place, they immediately despatched a messenger to the Muskingum to call the Indians home, partly with the view of seeing them once more before their departure, partly for the purpose of getting horses from them for their journey. The bearer of these tidings reached Schoenbrunn the day before the arrival of the murderers at Gnadenhuetten, and when he had delivered his message to the Indians in that place, they sent another person with the news to Gnadenhuetten. It was this messenger, who, as we have already mentioned, found young Shebosh lying scalped on the ground. Struck with terror at the sight, he immediately fled back to Schoenbrunn, and gave the alarm to the Indians at that place, all of whom, by this means, escaped the fearful fate of their companions. But the results of the removal of the missionaries to Detroit did not stop here; it was the means of saving the Indians at Sandusky, as well as at Schoenbrunn. The gang of murderers, who committed the massacre on the Muskingum, had not relinquished their bloody designs against the rest of the congregation. In the course of a few weeks they marched to Sandusky, there to renew the same horrid catastrophe; but happily, on their arrival, they found nothing but empty huts. Had not the missionaries been called to Detroit, the congregation would have remained at Sandusky, and, in that case, would, in all probability, have fallen a sacrifice to the fury of this band of demons, who thirsted for their blood. Soon after this disappointment, these miscreants were attacked by a body of English and Indian warriors, and the greater part of them cut in pieces. Thus they met with that vengeance from the swords of their enemies, which would probably never have been inflicted on them by the laws of their country; a circumstance in which every heart would exult, were it not for the awful consideration that persons whose hands were still reeking with the blood of their murdered victims, were but ill prepared to appear before the tribunal of the Great

Judge of all, who has threatened to avenge the death of the innocent.[1]

Notwithstanding the dispersion of the congregation was the means of their preservation from the hands of these bloodthirsty villains, the missionaries could not but feel the utmost anxiety concerning them, now that they were scattered among the heathen. Instead, therefore, of availing themselves of the liberty which the governor gave them of retiring to Bethlehem, they resolved to stay in the country, and endeavour to collect the remains of their wandering flock. In this design they were kindly assisted by the governor, and through his friendly interposition they obtained a grant of land from the Chippeways, about thirty miles to the northward of Detroit, on the banks of the river Huron. He likewise furnished them with provisions, boats, planks, and such other utensils as were necessary, from the royal stores, and his lady presented them with a valuable assortment of seeds and roots. Having received these seasonable supplies, the missionaries set off for that place, accompanied by a number of the Indians, who had already collected to them. Here they marked out the ground for a new settlement, which they called Gnadenhuetten, built themselves houses, and laid out gardens and plantations. At first they were so tormented by the stings of various kinds of insects, particularly mosquitoes, that they were constantly obliged to keep up a thick smoke, and to lie in the midst of it, a situation certainly not very agreeable. But the more they cleared the ground of the brushwood with which it was covered, the more the insects decreased in number. They likewise employed themselves in hunting, and bartered the venison and skins for Indian corn and other necessaries. They made canoes, baskets, and other articles, for which they found a good market at Detroit. By degrees, more of the dispersed Indians collected to them. Whenever any of them passed through Detroit, the governor generously supplied them with food, and, if necessary, with clothing also. Even when the inhabitants of Gnadenhuetten occasionally went thither to fetch provisions, he ordered them to be given to them free of expense until their own crops were ready. Indeed, we may observe, in general, that the British government uniformly shewed particular kindness to the missionaries and their people.

[1] Loskiel, part iii. p. 181, 184, 188.

Still, however, the greater part of the congregation remained scattered among the heathen, particularly in the country of the Twichtwees, about two hundred and fifty miles to the south-west of the new settlement. The missionaries lost no opportunity of sending them verbal messages, inviting them to come and join them; but it often happened that the bearers perverted these messages, and employed every means in their power to prevent their return. Some of the chiefs even commanded them in an authoritative manner to be resigned to their fate, and to resume the pagan mode of life: "For now," said they, "not a word of the gospel shall any more be heard in the Indian country." But notwithstanding the means which the savages employed to hinder their return, many of them came back the following spring. Some of these, however, had cause to mourn over the injury they had sustained in their spiritual interests by living among the heathen. They were all, however, received with open arms, and treated with the love and compassion due to brethren. Others through fear continued to reside among the savages, and some even relapsed into heathenism.[1]

In the beginning of 1784, there was a very severe frost, attended with a deep fall of snow, extending over the whole of the neighbouring country. As no one expected such a winter, no provision was made for either man or beast. The extraordinary and early night-frosts in the preceding autumn had destroyed a great part of the promising crop of Indian corn, so that it was not long before the people began to be in want. They were therefore obliged to disperse and seek a livelihood wherever they could find it; some of them, indeed, lived on nothing but wild herbs. A general famine at length ensued; the hollow eyes and emaciated countenances of the poor people were now sad indications of their distress. Still, however, they appeared cheerful and resigned to the will of God; and at last it pleased him to relieve their wants. A large herd of deer having strayed into the neighbourhood of Gnadenhuetten, the Indians shot upwards of a hundred of them, though the cold was then so intense that several of them returned with frozen feet, owing chiefly to their wearing snow-shoes. As soon as the snow melted, they went in search of wild potatoes, and came home loaded with

[1] Loskiel, part iii. p. 189, 194.

them. When the ice was gone, they caught vast numbers of fishes. Bilberries were their next resource, and of these they found great quantities in the woods. Soon after they reaped their Indian corn, of which happily they had an abundant crop.

By the industry of the Christian Indians, Gnadenhuetten became, in a short time, a very neat regular town, and was much admired by the White people, many of whom came to see it from the reports they heard concerning it. The houses were remarkably well built, and the country around, which was lately a wilderness, was now cultivated to a considerable extent. The whole neighbourhood acknowledged, that they were an industrious, sober, honest people, insomuch that the traders at Detroit never refused them credit, being certain of full and punctual payment. Some of the converts, however, were not sufficiently cautious in this respect, especially during the famine, when necessity obliged them to run in debt. One trader alone had a claim of two hundred pounds sterling upon them, a circumstance which the missionaries were afraid might give rise to some unpleasant consequences. But their apprehensions proved groundless, for the Indians began to work hard, and it was not long before they paid all their debts. There was only one poor man who, having a large family to support, was not able to discharge his accounts, and, therefore, he came to the missionaries to make his distress known to them. On account of the peculiarity of his circumstances, they readily agreed to assist him; but, in the mean while, his wife, as she was walking with her children in the fields, accidentally found a guinea. She supposed it to be only a piece of brass, till the missionaries informed her of its value; and then her husband went and paid his debt, which was so small, that, after discharging it, he had a few shillings over.[1]

But the congregation were not allowed to remain long in this place, where they were just beginning to be comfortably settled. The Chippeways, who had originally given them permission to settle on the land until peace should be restored, complained of their remaining upon it now that peace was concluded, this part of the country being one of their chief hunting-grounds.

[1] Loskiel, part iii. p. 199, 207.

They accordingly urged the Christian Indians to leave it, and employed threatening language to make them remove. The Brethren, therefore, found it necessary to leave this part of the country; but whither to go they were for some time at a loss. The Congress of the United States, after the conclusion of the war with England, had expressly ordered that the district belonging to the three congregations on the Muskingum should be reserved for them, with as much land as the Surveyor-General should think proper. An Indian has commonly a strong aversion to live on a spot where any of his relations have been killed; but the Christian Indians had laid aside this remnant of superstition, and longed to return to the place of their former abode. Though peace had been concluded between the English and the Americans, yet the Indian tribes felt great dissatisfaction with the manner in which they had been dealt with by the United States, and manifested a very hostile disposition towards them, particularly on account of the claims which they made to their lands. In a great council, held by them at Sandusky, they resolved to commence a war with the States, and that if the Christian Indians would not give up the idea of returning to the Muskingum, they would compel them to do so by force. Notwithstanding their threats, the Brethren resolved to emigrate from Gnadenhuetten; and, should they not be able at present to take possession of their land on the Muskingum, to settle in the first convenient place they could find. The new governor of Fort Detroit, Major Ancrum, approved of their determination, and sent a formal message to the Indian tribes, that they should not molest their Christian countrymen. He likewise so managed the business, that they received a compensation of two hundred dollars for their houses and plantations on the river Huron, as it was resolved that the town should be inhabited by White people. Besides, he was so generous as to offer them vessels to carry the whole congregation across Lake Erie to Cayahaga, and to supply them with provisions on their arrival.[1]

In April 1786, the missionaries and their people left Gnadenhuetten, and embarked on board of two vessels belonging to the North-West Company. One of the partners kindly offered them

[1] Loskiel, part iii. p. 201, 203, 204, 205.

for the service of the congregation, and gave orders to the captains to treat their passengers with all possible kindness, and not to run any kind of risk in case of danger. They had a good voyage till they arrived at one of the islands, where they were obliged to stop, and had their patience tried for no less than four weeks, the wind being contrary all that time. They pitched their camp upon the island, and followed the vessels whenever they shifted their station, in order to be ready to start with the first fair breeze. As often as there appeared the least prospect of proceeding, they all went on board; but to their great disappointment, they had several times to return on shore. Having once, however, a brisk gale, they sailed in good earnest, and made such rapid progress, that they saw the coast of Cayahaga before them; but suddenly the wind shifted, and drove them back to their former station on the island. During the gale, most of the Indians were so sick, that they lay on deck senseless and almost half dead. To prevent them rolling overboard, the captains ordered them to be fastened to the vessels.

One of the vessels being ordered to return to Detroit, owing to their long detention in this quarter, it was agreed by the captains to land the congregation in two divisions in Sandusky Bay, and then to proceed with the baggage to Cayahaga. The first division accordingly sailed the following day under the care of David Zeisberger, but, being unable to reach Sandusky, they went on shore at Rocky Point, about eighty miles from the Bay. Here they had to ascend very high and steep rocks, and to cut their way through a thicket to the summit of them. Scarcely had they pitched their camp, when a party of Ottawas, who were hunting in the neighbourhood, came upon them, and expressed great astonishment to find such a number of people encamped in this pathless desert. On the following day they all set out on foot, and every one, Zeisberger and his wife not excepted, was loaded with a part of the provisions. Such as formed the van had the greatest difficulties to encounter, being obliged to cut and force their way through the thickets. Having arrived at a large brook, running through a swamp, all the Indians, both men and women, waded through it, some of them up to the armpits in the water. After several days, the second division of the congregation overtook them, in canoes, made hastily of bark, and at length they all arrived in safety at Cayahaga. From thence they proceeded up the river till they came to an old town, which had been forsaken by the Ottawas. This was the first spot they discovered fit for a settlement, for from the mouth of the river to this place it was nothing but one continued forest. As they were entire strangers to the state of the neighbouring country, they resolved to spend the summer here; and accordingly, they encamped on the east side of the river, upon an elevated plain, built themselves huts, and having with much difficulty, cleared the ground for plantations, they ventured to sow Indian corn, though it was then so late in the season. This place was called Pilgerruh, or Pilgrim's Rest.[1]

Soon after their arrival at this place, the congregation received a very acceptable supply of various necessary articles from the Brethren at Bethlehem. There were also some traders who were so kind as to furnish them with provisions, and to trust them for a great part of the payment. The Congress of the United States was likewise so generous as to order them a supply of Indian corn and blankets; and they even sent a written message to them, informing them that it gave them much satisfaction to hear of their return into the territory of the United States; that they might rest assured of the friendship and protection of government; and that upon their going to the Muskingum, they should receive five hundred bushels of Indian corn from the public magazines on the river Ohio, with other necessaries; a promise which was fulfilled to its utmost extent, even though the congregation remained in this part of the country.[2]

Meanwhile, however, the congregation was not without its trials and difficulties. One evening, a messenger arrived from Captain Pipe, the Delaware chief, with an account that the Americans had surprised the towns of the Shawanoes, pillaged and burnt them, murdered a number of the people, and carried others away prisoners; and that an army had arrived from Pittsburg at Tuscarawi; and therefore he advised the inhabitants of Pilgerruh to fly immediately, lest they also should be surprised and murdered by the enemy. This report seemed so incredible to the missionaries, that they endeavoured to per-

[1] Loskiel, part iii. p. 207. [2] Ibid. part iii. p. 211, 215, 219.

suade the Indians of its falsehood. But here arguments were of no avail. The massacre on the Muskingum immediately presented itself to their troubled imagination; and the women and children fled the same night into the thickest recesses of the wood. Messengers, however, being sent to Tuscarawi, and on the road to Pittsburg, it was soon discovered that their dread of an American army was entirely without foundation. The alarm was renewed a few evenings after, in consequence of a great noise, and the sound of many horse-bells being heard in the neighbourhood. The missionaries supposed, that the whole proceeded from a convoy of flour which they expected, and this, indeed, proved to be the case; but the Indians, ever fearful and suspicious, would not so much as listen to their representations. Imagining that this was the army which was to surprise and murder them, they fled into the woods, and left their teachers quite alone in the settlement. By degrees, however, they recovered from their panic, and returned to their dwellings.

The Indian congregation were still extremely desirous to return to the Muskingum; but this the savages were as determined to oppose. Neither would they allow them to remain in their present situation; but insisted on their removing to some other part of the country. Thus, the Brethren were placed in very embarrassing circumstances; but, after mature deliberation, they resolved to give up all thoughts of returning to the Muskingum for the present, and to settle on some spot between the river Cayahaga and Pettquotting, where they might enjoy a calm and safe retreat.[1]

In April 1787, the congregation left Pilgerruh, and proceeded, partly by land and partly by water, to the place they had fixed on for a new settlement; and on their arrival, they were much delighted with its appearance. Unlike the rest of the wilderness, it seemed like a fruitful orchard. Here and there grew apple and plum trees. The country abounded with wild potatoes, an article of food now much esteemed by the Indians; and the lake afforded them a plentiful supply of fish. Never, indeed, had the Brethren settled in so pleasant and fertile a spot; and now they rejoiced in the prospect of establishing a settlement

[1] Loskiel, part iii. p. 216.

in so agreeable a situation, especially as it was not frequented by any of the savages who had hitherto been such troublesome neighbours to them.

Their joy, however, was of short duration. Scarcely had they begun to indulge these pleasing hopes, when a Delaware captain arrived in the camp, and informed them that they must not settle in that place, but come and reside at Sandusky; adding, at the same time, that they were not to consider this as a matter about which they were to deliberate, but as a thing that was positively determined. As usual he made them the most solemn promises of protection and safety; and he assured them, that the place appointed for their residence was not in the vicinity of any Indian town, the nearest being ten miles distant. Nothing could be more disagreeable to the congregation than this message; and though they represented to the captain the malice and treachery of the Delaware chiefs to them for the last six or seven years, yet they resolved to submit, lest their opposition should involve them in still greater calamities. Nothing, it is worthy of remark, appeared so dreadful to them in this proposal, as the prospect of being again subject to heathen government. They, however, set forward on their journey, but before they had proceeded far, they learned that the greater part of the message was false; for the place fixed on for their residence was not above two miles from the savages. They, therefore, resolved to go no further for the present; but to remain in that quarter of the country near Pettquotting, let the consequences be what they might, and even to maintain their post in opposition to the will of the savages. Having sent a message to the chiefs to this effect, they obtained permission from them to stay at least one year in that place without molestation. Here, therefore, they proceeded to erect a settlement, which they called New Salem.[1]

Many of the Indians who had wandered astray during the late troubles of the congregation, continued to return from time to time, and were received by their brethren with open arms; though, with regard to such of them as, through persuasion or fear, had been drawn aside into heathenish practices, the missionaries exercised much caution and care, before they admitted

[1] Loskiel, part iii. p. 220; Heckewelder, p. 392.

them to the full privileges of members. They were also visited by great numbers of strangers; for as there was then a famine in the country, the savages knew that they would find provisions more readily with their Christian countrymen than among their heathen neighbours. Some of these were forcibly struck with the order and comfort which they observed among the converts; and one of them said, "You are truly a happy people. You live cheerfully and peaceably together. This is to be found nowhere but with you." In no place, indeed, where the Brethren had resided, were they visited by so many strangers as at New Salem. The town was sometimes so full, that there was not room for them; but though their visitors were so numerous, the best order was preserved in the settlement; no riots, no disturbances were occasioned by them. When any of them wished to take up their residence in the town, the Christian converts built a house for them. This was done, not with the view of enticing them to join the congregation, but, merely, that in case any of them should not conduct themselves with propriety, and it should be found necessary to desire them to leave the place, there might be no obstacle to their removal, by their having the smallest claim to their houses. It is also worthy of notice, that when the cattle of the congregation had injured the fields of the neighbouring Chippewas, who had no fences, the Christian Indians, in order to prevent a similar occurrence for the future, gave them trees and shrubs, and even planted hedges round their lands to their entire satisfaction. Such was the wisdom displayed by the Brethren in their labours among these savages; and such the success with which they had infused the principles of justice and benevolence into the minds of their converts, thus affording a fine practical illustration of the precept of their divine Master: "Be ye wise as serpents and harmless as doves."[1]

In April 1791, the whole congregation, consisting of about two hundred persons, moved across Lake Erie, and settled in a place about eighteen miles from Detroit. Of late, they had been not a little molested by the dealers in rum, and other noisy visitors. Hostilities which had again commenced between the Indians and the Americans, now threatened to extend to

[1] Loskiel, part iii. p. 224; Period. Accounts, vol. i. p. 20, 22, 24, 43.

this part of the country. The savages in returning from their predatory expeditions often took the road by Salem, in consequence of which, the congregation at that place not only suffered from their irregularities, but were exposed to the attack of the American militia who were in pursuit of them. Such were the circumstances which gave rise to the emigration of the congregation into the British territory, where they hoped to enjoy peace and quietness. But neither were they without difficulties in their new settlement. Some of their White neighbours, who were ill affected towards them, greatly molested them; and one of them more bitter than the rest, drove his cattle into their plantations, by which the corn and other produce in their fields were totally destroyed. The congregation were at the same time much harassed with messages from the savages, requiring them to take up the hatchet against the White men, and to fight for the land of their fathers; and threatening in case of a refusal, that when the war was ended, they would come and plunder them, and carry them off as prisoners. The representation of a struggle for the common interests of the Indian tribes, combined as it was with this terrible threatening, made so powerful an impression on some of the young men, that, notwithstanding the earnest entreaties of the missionaries, they left the congregation and repaired to the war.[1]

In April 1792, the congregation left this temporary residence on Lake Erie, and proceeded, some by land and others by water, to Upper Canada, where the British government had assigned them a piece of ground, consisting of twenty-five thousand acres, on the river Thames, which falls into Lake St Clair. Here they began to build a new town, which they called Fairfield. The settlement was afterwards declared to be a regular township, containing twelve miles in length and six in breadth; and in a short time, the Indians so improved it by cultivating the ground, and planting gardens, that the wilderness was literally changed into a fruitful field.[2]

It is well known that White people, with the exception of traders, commonly avoid settling near an Indian town, as they

[1] Period. Accounts, vol. i. p. 108, 127, 136, 139; Fortsetzung Brud. Hist. tom. iii. p. 493, 499, 510.

[2] Period. Accounts, vol. i. p. 175, 315; vol. iii. p. 269.

are afraid of their horses being stolen, their cattle killed, their persons molested, and their improvements marred. Nothing, therefore, could be a more decisive and unequivocal proof of the favourable opinion which was generally entertained of the Christian Indians than this circumstance, that no sooner was it known that they were to establish themselves in this quarter, than the White people were eager to take lands in the vicinity of the settlement. When the congregation settled in this place, there were neither White people nor Indians nearer than thirty miles; but, in the course of a few years, the inhabitants increased so rapidly, that they were continually passing up and down, both by land and water, and the missionary settlement came to be on the great road to Niagara. Among others, the rum traders came frequently to the place, and notwithstanding the sale of that pernicious article was prohibited in the town, they often contrived to furnish one or other of the Indians with it, that they might take advantage of them in their dealings, and by this means they produced no small disorder among them. Besides the Monsy tribe, the offscouring of the Indian nations, lived higher up the river, and not only refused to receive the gospel themselves, but delighted in disturbing the peace of the congregation, and endeavoured to seduce them to drunkenness, whoredom, and all manner of vice.[1]

In August 1798, the venerable David Zeisberger, now near eighty years of age, left the settlement of Fairfield, where he was beloved and revered as a father by the whole congregation, and set off for the river Muskingum, accompanied by Benjamin Mortimer, another of the Brethren, and upwards of thirty of the Indians, in order to renew the mission in that part of the country, where Congress had made them a grant of the three towns they formerly possessed in that quarter, with four thousand acres of land attached to each of them, making in all twelve thousand acres. The Brethren who previously went to survey the country, found the whole land covered with long dry grass, to which, on the day after their arrival, they set fire, in order to defend themselves from the numerous snakes and serpents which had taken possession of it. All the ground where Gnadenhuetten stood was covered with briars, hazle-bushes, plum

[1] Period. Accounts, vol. ii. p. 150, 333; Fortsetzung Brud. Hist. tom. iii. p. 546.

and thorn trees, like a low impenetrable forest, excepting where the bears, deer, and other wild animals had made themselves a path. Some of the chimneys appeared in their rows. The place where the Indians were massacred was strongly marked. Part of their bones were still to be seen among the coals and ashes, and in every quarter the ground was covered with the bones of the cattle slaughtered by the enemy.[1]

Having arrived in this part of the country, Zeisberger and his companions began immediately to build a new town, which they called Goshen. Here the Brethren enjoyed peace and quietness, and proceeded in their labours with their usual diligence and zeal; but, we regret to add, with little success. There was now, indeed, no great number of Indians in that part of the country, so that they could not expect any considerable accession to the congregation from among the savages. Over such, however, as lived in the settlement they had no small cause of joy, as amidst numerous and powerful temptations to vice, particularly to drunkenness, the besetting sin of the Indians, the converts remained faithful to their Christian profession; though at a place about three miles distant there was an English village, which might be considered as a kind of Sodom for wickedness.[2]

In February 1801, John P. Kluge and Abraham Luckenbach, in consequence of an invitation from the Delaware Indians at Woapikamikunk, on the river Wabash, proceeded to that part of the country. On their arrival they obtained from the chief a grant of a piece of land for a settlement, situated between nine Indian towns, though some miles distant from the nearest of them; and it was agreed that no rum traders or drunken people should be allowed to molest them, and that no persons should be hindered from joining them. Here they for some time enjoyed peace and tranquillity, and they had the satisfaction to see their instructions attended by considerable numbers of the Indians. Afterwards, however, the aspect of things changed, and the situation of the Brethren became truly alarming. One chief, who was their protector, having died, and another, who was friendly to them, having been deposed, the savages became perfectly ungovernable, threatened to murder the

[1] Period. Accounts, vol. i. p. 40; vol. ii. p. 145, 269, 333.
[2] Ibid. vol. ii. p. 340, 354; vol. v. p. 43.

missionaries, and even killed their cattle before their eyes. These evils were materially promoted by the rum trade, which was now carried on to a greater extent than ever throughout the whole country, and was rapidly proving the ruin of all the Indian tribes.[1] The settlement on the Wabash was at length broken up by one of those tragical occurrences, which have been but too frequent in this eventful mission.

In February 1806, all the Indians in this quarter were summoned by their teachers or prophets to assemble on the Woapikamikunk, to hear the foolish stories which these emissaries of Satan had fabricated, and to be instructed in the revelations which they pretended to have received from heaven. Among these teachers was a Shawanoe Indian, an arch-impostor, who gave out that he was able to discover the most secret mysteries. The Delaware tribe received him with the utmost cordiality, and resolved to hold a grand council, in order to root out the arts of witchcraft and mixing poison, and to extort a confession from all such as the Shawanoe should accuse; and that whoever would not confess, should be hewn in pieces with their hatchets and burnt. With a view to the execution of this horrid design, the young Indians met together, chose the most ferocious characters to be their leaders, deposed all the old chiefs, and guarded the whole assembly, as if they were prisoners of war, particularly the aged of both sexes. The venerable old chief Tettepachsit was the first whom they accused of possessing poison, and of destroying many of the Indians by his pernicious art. As he would not, however, acknowledge the charge, they bound him with cords to two posts, and began to roast him over a slow fire. Unable to endure such torture, the poor old man declared that he kept poison in the house of the Christian Indian Joshua. Nothing could be more agreeable to the savages than this accusation, as they wished to deprive the missionaries of the assistance of this man, who was the only convert residing with them. Seven of them accordingly came to the settlement of the Brethren, and carried him away by force.

When Joshua was presented to Tettepachsit, the old chief frankly acknowleged that he had accused him merely to escape

[1] Fortsetzung Brud. Hist. tom. iii. p. 566; Period. Accounts, vol. iii. p. 69, 71, 123, 272, 471.

from the torture. The savages therefore pronounced him not guilty, but yet they would not set him at liberty till the Shawanoe should arrive. Having come the same day, the impostor ordered all the Indians of both sexes to sit down in a circle, when he would declare who had poison in their possession. The two old chiefs, Tettepachsit and Hackinpomska, he now accused of mixing poison, and he charged the former in particular with the untimely death of many of the Indians. When he was asked about Joshua, he declared that he had no poison, but yet he possessed an evil spirit, by which he was able to destroy the other Indians. Pleased with this verdict, the savages seized all the accused, and set a watch over them as condemned criminals. An old woman named Caritas, who had been baptized by the Brethren in former times, was the first whom they devoted to the flames; and two or three days after, ten of the savages, with their faces painted black, came to the missionary settlement, conducting Tettepachsit, the aged chief. Upon their arrival they kindled a large fire close to the Brethren's dwelling, and after giving the venerable old man a blow on the head with a hatchet, they threw him into the flames, and diverted themselves with his miserable cries. After committing this horrid murder, they came boldly into the house of the missionaries, boasted of the atrocious deed, and demanded some refreshment, which it was of course necessary to give them. The Brethren, however, took courage, and asked them what would be the fate of Joshua, vindicated him from the charges which had been alleged against him, and obtained a promise from them that he should not be put to death. Though they understood that they themselves were suspected by the savages of keeping poison for the purpose of making those Indians sick who would not do as they desired, or even of killing them; yet they resolved to go to the assembly, and try what could be done for the preservation of Joshua, or at least to afford him comfort and advice in the hour of trial. As the missionary Kluge, however, could not leave his wife and children under these alarming circumstances, Luckenbach was so bold as go alone; but he had scarcely advanced half way when he heard, to his astonishment and grief, that Joshua had been murdered by the savages the preceding day. It appears they first struck him on the head with a hatchet, and then threw him into a large fire. With these frightful tidings, Luckenbach hastened back to his fellow-labourers; and though for some days past they had suffered the utmost anxiety and distress, yet this now crowned their misery. Overwhelmed with grief and terror, they lost the power of speech and reflection, and could do nothing but utter cries of lamentation and woe. On the following days, others of the Indians were accused by their countrymen, and shared a similar fate; and as the missionaries continued to be in imminent danger of their lives, they at length abandoned the settlement.[1]

Besides these settlements, the Brethren formed others among the Chippeway Indians in Canada, among the Monsys near Lake Erie, among the Wyondats and Mingoes in Upper Sandusky, among the Creeks on the river Flint, and among the Cherokees in Georgia; but these various stations, with the exception of the last, they were obliged to abandon one after another.[2]

In October 1813, in consequence of the unhappy and unnatural war which was then carried on between England and America, the settlement at Fairfield, which lay near the confines of the British territory, was involved in new calamities. Immediately after the occupation of Malden and Detroit by the American army under General Harrison, the congregation had several consultations about a place to which they might flee for safety. The houses of the missionaries and of the Indians, had been occupied for some time by fugitives from the surrounding country; and there were about seventy sick soldiers in the church and schoolhouse. General Proctor, the English commander, intimated to the Brethren, that he intended to fortify Fairfield; but that he was willing to purchase their houses and all the Indian corn, garden stuffs, furniture, and whatever else they could spare, for the use of the army. He also promised that another tract of land should be assigned to the congregation, as a temporary residence during the war, and that they should be supplied with provisions and clothes from the royal stores. As under these circumstances, the stay of the Indians was no longer practicable, they resolved to quit the settlement.

[1] Period. Accounts, vol. iv. p. 1.

[2] Fortsetzung Brud. Hist. tom. iii. p. 565, 655; Period. Accounts, vol. iii. p. 350; vol. iv. p. 258, 491; vol. v. p. 203, 264; vol. vi. p. 253; vol. vii. p. 9.

Some of them had set off on their voyage as soon as the approach of the American army was known: others of them now followed, partly by land and partly by water. Previous to this, it was agreed that Christian F. Dencke, one of the missionaries, should accompany them in their flight; but that Schnall, who was sickly, and Michael Jung, who was old, should remain in the settlement with the view of retiring to Bethlehem.

Scarcely had the Indians left Fairfield, when an engagement took place between the American army and the English detachment, about a mile and a half from the settlement, in which the latter were completely defeated. In the evening, a great number of the victors entered the town, and professed at first to be friendly to the mission, promising to do the Brethren no harm, and expressing their regret that the Indians had fled. The same night, however, they began to treat the missionaries very harshly, accused them of secreting English officers and royal stores, and commanded them with great fierceness, to deliver them up without delay. The Brethren assured them of the contrary; but all in vain. Every room and corner was searched, particularly the roofs of the chapel and schoolhouse; each of the missionaries was ordered to open all his trunks and boxes for examination; nor was any person allowed to leave the house without a guard. Early next morning the soldiers began to plunder the settlement. The Brethren were now obliged to surrender their last morsel of bread: six hundred pounds of flour which they had just purchased for the winter, fifty bushels of potatoes, twelve of apples, and various kinds of kitchen stuffs, were all taken from them.

General Harrison and several other officers having arrived during the plundering, Schnall the missionary immediately waited on him, and recommended the settlement to his protection, requesting, at the same time, that some compensation might be made to them for the stores which had been taken from them. His request was refused; but he was told, that the missionaries had liberty to quit the place. Commodore Perry, who was one of the party, appeared more friendly to them, and several others of the officers, and even of the privates, expressed pity for their unmerited sufferings. Some even employed force to protect them from the wild and lawless soldiery, who all day long loaded them with the bitterest curses, and the most cruel mockeries. In the mean while, the Brethren found an opportunity to pack up their goods; but as they were about to load the waggon, they were once more obliged to submit their baggage to a thorough search. Nothing, however, was found, which could in the least degree impeach their character, as they very wisely never intermeddled with political matters. They were now obliged to leave behind them the whole of their household furniture, together with their cows, pigs, and other live stock, which, if time had been allowed them, might have been sold for several hundred dollars. After their departure, the settlement was set on fire, and all the buildings totally consumed: not even the smallest outhouse was spared.

In the mean while, nothing was heard of the fugitive congregation, nor of the missionary Dencke, who had fled with them, a circumstance which occasioned much anxiety to the friends of the mission. It afterwards appeared, that the Christian Indians, on leaving Fairfield, encamped with their cattle at a place about six Canadian miles up the river. The wife of the missionary Dencke followed them in a canoe to this spot; but, in the mean while, he himself remained at Fairfield, to see what would be the event. As soon, however, as the English soldiers entered the settlement on their retreat, he set off to join the congregation; but on arriving at the camp, he found his wife alone, for the Indians, frightened by the reports of the fugitives, had all fled into the woods. The mission was now to appearance broken up, for neither the Indians nor the missionaries knew where each other were.

Having learned that the other missionaries had not only left Fairfield, but that the settlement was burnt to ashes, Dencke was reduced to the greatest dilemma, not knowing what to do, nor whither to go. Happily, however, a man offered to convey him and his wife in a waggon to Delaware town, a proposal which they readily accepted. The journey proved extremely troublesome; but they received an ample compensation for all their toils, when on their arrival at that place, a number of the congregation came running to them, and with tears in their eyes, offered up thanks to God that they again beheld their teachers. They had heard that the missionaries were all taken prisoners, and that they would now be left without the means of instruction. As several of the women and children were still wandering in the woods, Dencke sent some of the young people to inform them that he would again settle with them, and to invite them to return. In a short time, the whole of them came back, except a single woman, who was murdered near Fairfield.

After wandering about from place to place for near two years, and suffering many inconveniences, the Indian congregation began to establish themselves in the neighbourhood of their old settlement on the river Thames. To this place they gave the name of New Fairfield. Here the congregation enjoyed for some years outward tranquillity; but the Brethren had few opportunities of usefulness among the heathen, and there was a want of spiritual life among the Indians, while at the same time the temptations to which they were exposed, particularly to intemperance, were more and more multiplied. The small congregation at Goshen, on the Muskingum, having been for several years on the decline, the few remaining Indians at that station removed to this place. It became, however, more and more difficult for the Indians, both here in Canada, and in the Cherokee country, to withstand the encroachments of the White people, who were set on obtaining possession of their lands.[1]

The mission among the Cherokees had never embraced any considerable number of that tribe, and at length, after it had existed for upwards of thirty years, the Government of Georgia, by a long series of most unjust and oppressive proceedings, seized on the territory of the Cherokee nation and other Indian tribes, and compelled them, in spite of their most solemn and earnest remonstrances, to emigrate to the West. They found refuge for a few years in the territory belonging to their tribe in the State of Tennessee; but they were forced to remove ultimately to the west of the Mississippi, to the Arkansas country, where new lands were assigned to them. The two small congregations of the Brethren were compelled to emigrate like the

[1] Period. Accounts, vol. v. p. 437, 471; vol. vi. p. 23, 117, 191, 252; vol. ix. p. 85, 454; vol. xx. p. 115.

rest of the nation, but several of the missionaries followed them to the Arkansas territory, and there formed two small stations, the one called New Spring Place, the other Canaan.[1]

In 1837, nearly two hundred of the inhabitants of New Fairfield, or more than two-thirds of the whole population, emigrated from that station in the hope of finding a more commodious place of abode on the Missouri. Vogler, one of the missionaries, accompanied them; and after a long journey, partly by land, and partly by water, they at length settled on the Konzas river, on the borders of the State of Missouri, near others of the Delaware Indians who had emigrated thither, and who gave them permission to settle on their lands. This place was called Westfield; but the neighbourhood of heathen Indians proved injurious to them, as many of them were led to take part in their heathenish practices and amusements.[2]

Though the inhabitants of New Fairfield were now much reduced in number, yet they enjoyed many advantages, and if they would only exercise more enterprise, and make a more judicious use of them, their outward condition would be much better than it is. They were still in possession of a tract of country consisting of more than 20,000 acres, a considerable part of which was good arable land, so that they might raise field and garden produce in as great abundance as they needed. Besides, when they ceded some years before the half of their land to government, they were promised an annuity of 600 dollars, and they also received from time to time, from the royal magazines, presents of various articles of clothing. They likewise drew their share of 400 dollars, which was granted to the congregation on the giving up of the land on the Muskingum, the other portion of it being paid to their brethren who removed to Westfield. It may, however, be doubted whether these various grants were of any benefit to the Indians. If rightly improved, they might have been of great advantage to them; but, instead of stimulating them to industry, they probably checked it; and thus they may in the end be in a worse con-

[1] Period. Accounts, vol. xi. p. 468; vol. xii. p. 46, 188, 387; vol. xiii. p. 41, 43, 296, 489; vol. xv. p. 43, 47, 143, 395, 417.

[2] Period. Accounts, vol. xiv. p. 349, 518, 518; vol. xv. p. 197; vol. xvi. p. 124; vol. xx. p. 109.

dition than if they had been left to depend more entirely on their own exertions.[1]

In 1842, the whole number of Indians, including children who had been baptized by the Brethren, since the commencement of the mission, amounted to about 1800. During the last fifty years, comparatively few adults had been received into the congregations: the baptized consisted chiefly of children born in the settlements.[2]

[1] Period. Accounts, vol. xv. p. 414.

[2] The following are accounts of the number baptized or received by the Brethren within particular periods:—

	Adults.	Children.	Total.
From .... 1734 to .... 1772, .	...	...	720
December 1769 to April 1792, .	266	217	483
.... 1792 to .... 1842, .	101	432	533

The total amount of these numbers is 1736; but, from this, we must make some deduction on account of the repetition of two or three of the years; and some additions must be made on account of the Cherokees, and perhaps others of the Indians who were baptized at other stations; but the number of these was not considerable. There were 130 who were baptized by others, and were received into the congregation.—*Loskiel*, part iii. p. 226; *Fortsetzung Brud. Hist.* tom. iii. p. 526; *Period. Accounts*, vol. xvii. p. 10.

Before leaving the history of this mission, we may mention that David Zeisberger, who died in 1808, having been upwards of sixty years a missionary among the Indians, possessed, in consequence of his long residence among, and his great intercourse with them, an extensive and intimate knowledge of different Indian dialects. Amongst other works, he compiled a grammar and a vocabulary of the Delaware language, and a dictionary of the Iroquois. Of these works, we have the following interesting notice in the Transactions of the Historical and Literary Committee of the American Philosophical Society held at Philadelphia:—

"In answer to the inquiries of your Committee," the Rev. John Heckewelder of Bethlehem, formerly one of the Moravian missionaries among the Indians, "laid open the stores of his knowledge, and his correspondence gives us a clear insight into that wonderful organization which distinguishes the languages of the aborigines of this country from all the other idioms of the known world. Through his means, your Committee obtained the communication of a MS. grammar of the Lenni Lenape or Delaware Indians, written in German by the late Rev. David Zeisberger, well known as the author of a copious vocabulary of the same language. This is the most complete grammar that we have ever seen of any of those languages, which are called *barbarous*. It gives a full, and, we believe, an accurate view of those comprehensive grammatical forms which appear to prevail with little variation among the aboriginal nations of America from Greenland to Cape Horn, and shews how little the world has yet advanced in that science, which is proudly called *Universal Grammar*. Through the same means, we are promised the communication of an excellent dictionary, by the same author, of the Iroquois language, explained in German, which is in the library o the Moravian Brethren at Bethlehem. Your Committee have procured a translation of Mr Zeisberger's grammar into English, and will endeavour to do the same with the dictionary when received."—*Transactions of the Historical and Literary Committee of the American Philosophical Society, held at Philadelphia for Promoting Useful Knowledge*, vol. i. p. 14.

In 1852, the following were the numbers connected with the congregations of the Brethren among the Indians:—

Stations.	Communicants.	Baptized Adults.	Baptized Children.	Total.
New Fairfield, .	38	50	80	168
Westfield, . . .	40	21	60	121
New Spring Place,	29	8	14	51
	107	79	154	340[1]

SECT. IV.—SOUTH AMERICA.

Art. 1.—Berbice.

In June 1738, Lewis Christopher Daehne and John Guettner sailed from Holland for Berbice in South America. Having on their arrival found no opportunity of instructing the negroes in the colony, they at length removed into the interior and formed a little settlement, which they called Pilgerhut, in the neighbourhood of the Indians. Here they were obliged to work, not merely for their own support, but in order to pay the passage of some other Brethren and Sisters who were sent to their assistance, as the congregation of Herrnhut was at that period so poor, that it could not furnish even the expenses of the voyage.[2]

As the Indians were widely scattered through an immense wilderness, the Brethren had many difficulties and hardships to encounter in visiting them. On these occasions they were obliged to carry with them a supply of bread or cassabi for five or six days, to take their hammocks on their shoulders, to sleep in them suspended on trees in the woods, to wade through brooks and rivers, and often to travel immense distances without meeting with a house or a human being. If they came to the huts of the Indians when the men happened to be absent,

[1] Period. Accounts, vol. xxi. p. 26.

[2] Risler Erzahlungen aus der Geschichte der Bruderkirche, tom. iv. p. 17, 28, 42; Period. Accounts, vol. i. p. 321.

the women fled with their children into the neighbouring thicket, uttering a frightful shriek. Having, by the help of a mulatto youth, translated into the Arawack language an Account of the Life of Christ, the Brethren, in the course of their visits to the Indians, read this compendium to them ; but though the savages listened to it with that attention which curiosity naturally excites, they were little affected by it. After some years, however, a number of them appeared to be impressed with the gospel, and were baptized by the missionaries as the first-fruits of their labours.[1]

Most of the converts, and some even of the unbaptized, now built themselves huts at Pilgerhut, that they might have an opportunity of daily enjoying Christian instruction. With the view of facilitating their settlement, the missionaries not only gave them permission to build on their land, but notwithstanding their own poverty, supplied them with provisions until the cassabi they had planted was ready. The more religion spread among the Indians, the more were the Brethren animated to prosecute their work with energy and zeal. No wilderness appeared to them too frightful, no road too dreary, no Indian hut too remote, if they might hope to find a soul ready to receive the gospel.[2]

In September 1749, soon after the mission had begun to assume a promising aspect, a storm arose which threatened its utter extinction. In consequence of letters from some gentlemen in Berbice, who were unfavourable to the Brethren and to their labours among the Indians, the Directors of the Company at Amsterdam had given orders to the new governor to require the missionaries to take the oath to government, with respect to which their enemies well knew they had conscientious scruples. The Brethren were accordingly summoned before the Council and required to take the oath, while at the same time a threatening was added, that should they refuse, they would all be sent home by the first ship to Europe. The Council, however, was so far satisfied with their representations, that it agreed to accept of their simple declaration until further orders were received from Holland. Disappointed in this stratagem, the enemies of the mission attempted to drive away the Indians

[1] Risler Erzahlungen. tom. iv. p. 33, 41. [2] Ibid. tom. iv. p. 38, 40, 43, 47.

from the Brethren, by circulating a report that they designed to make them slaves, a rumour well calculated to rouse the jealousy of the savages, as the idea of slavery is more frightful to them than death; but this report obtained no credit with the converts, as they had now the most perfect confidence in their teachers. In consequence, however, of new machinations of their enemies, the missionaries were ordered not to collect the Indians to Pilgerhut, but to allow them to live scattered through the country; to clothe the baptized, and to pay the poll-tax for them; to take the oath to government in the ordinary form, and to appear in arms in order to be exercised. The requisitions with respect to the Indians were given up, but not that which related to the Brethren swearing allegiance to government. In consequence of these vexatious proceedings, several of the missionaries left the country; but others took the oath, considering it not inconsistent with a good conscience to swear allegiance to government.[1]

In 1753, the number of Indians who resided with the Brethren amounted to upwards of two hundred and sixty. The savages, who came merely to visit them, spread the report of what they heard and saw to a vast extent through the surrounding country, in consequence of which numbers came to Pilgerhut from places at a great distance, were impressed with the gospel, and joined the congregation. Even from among the wildest of the Indian tribes there were several whose hearts appeared to be softened at the foot of the cross, and who became the followers of the Redeemer. But as the land of the Brethren was too small to support so great a number of inhabitants, many of them had constantly to be absent at the chase, or the fishery, or at their distant cassabi fields. There the native helpers held the daily meetings with them, and though some of the converts occasionally fell into their old sinful practices, yet, through the earnest and affectionate representations of the missionaries, they were, in general, soon brought to a sense of their guilt, and with many tears to seek forgiveness from the Redeemer.[2]

Such was the flourishing state of the mission, when the country was visited with a severe scarcity which lasted several years. The inhabitants of Pilgerhut, not only participated in

[1] Risler Erzahlungen, tom. iv. p. 48, 53, 56, 58. [2] Ibid. tom. iv. p. 50, 59, 68.

the general calamity, but were plundered of their crops by the soldiers and negroes from the colony, who, not content with seizing whatever was ripe in the fields, destroyed the rest in a most wanton manner. To scarcity, was at length added an epidemic disorder, which spread through the country, and cut off great numbers of the inhabitants, both Indians and Europeans. Near half of the inhabitants of the colony died, and among others, several of the missionaries. In consequence of these disastrous circumstances, most of the Indians forsook Pilgerhut, and retired into different parts of the country. The number whom the missionaries had baptized, was upwards of four hundred; but they were at length so completely scattered, that the congregation was reduced to about twenty. The Brethren, however, resolved to maintain their post, in the hope of the return of more auspicious times; but these hopes were never realized.[1]

In February 1763, the negroes in the colony rose in rebellion against their masters, murdered many of the White people, and laid waste the whole country. As the insurgents came at length into the neighbourhood of Pilgerhut, the Brethren were obliged to abandon the settlement and escape for their lives. One party of them proceeded immediately to Demerara; but, in the course of the journey, they suffered many privations and hardships, and were constantly in danger from parties of incendiaries and murderers who were strolling through the country. Happily, however, they escaped almost miraculously, by taking a road through woods and swamps, unknown even to the Indians themselves, and at length, after a journey of about four weeks, they reached the first plantation in that colony, to which they might have travelled in two days by the ordinary route. Another party remained for some weeks in the neighbouring woods, in the hope they might still retain possession of Pilgerhut; but they also were at length obliged to retire to Demerara. Several of the missionaries proceeded with the first ship to Europe. Two, who remained until they should receive instructions from home in regard to their future operations, died before the letters reached them. Such was the melancholy termination of the Brethren's labours in Berbice.[2]

[1] Risler Erzahlungen, tom. iv. p. 70, 83, 86, 90, 92.

[2] Ibid. tom. iv. p. 92; Period. Accounts, vol. iii. p. 214.

Art. 2.—Surinam.

PART I.—SHARON.

In 1739, John Hadwig, George Zeisberger, Henry G. Meiser, John H. Steiner, and Michael Tanneberger, sailed for South America, in consequence of an agreement which the Brethren had made with the Dutch Surinam Company, who were anxious to obtain settlers for that colony. After their arrival, they endeavoured to support themselves by working at their trades, and by cultivating some land which they purchased; but as they were so much engaged in labouring for their own maintenance, they had little time or opportunity for visiting the Indians, or learning their language. Their evening meetings, however, were attended by some Jews and Christians; but the government interfered, and prohibited them from admitting any strangers to their private worship. In consequence of this interruption of their labours, and of some dissensions among themselves, the Brethren, after a few years, left the country and withdrew, some of them to Pennsylvania, and others to the neighbouring mission in Berbice.[1]

In 1754, Lewis Christopher Daehne and Mark Ralfs proceeded to Surinam, with the design of renewing the mission in that colony. On their arrival, the governor appeared much prejudiced against them, in consequence of the unfavourable reports he had received from Holland concerning the Brethren; but through the representations of Mr Loesner, the late governor of Berbice, he so far changed his opinion, that he gave them permission to settle in the country, and even offered them land on which to establish a mission. Having pitched on two different pieces of ground for this purpose, the one on the river Sarameca, the other on the Corentyn, they received a grant of both from government, with a confirmation of all the privileges which the missionaries enjoyed, who were formerly settled in the colony.[2]

In January 1757, the Brethren began to build huts for them-

[1] Risler Erzahlungen, tom. iv. p. 21, 24; Crantz's Hist. Breth. p. 195.
[2] Risler Erzahlungen, tom. iv. p. 98.

selves on the river Sarameca, and called the name of their little settlement Sharon. Here they were joined by a number of the Indians, particularly from Pilgerhut in Berbice, so that in a short time, they had a small congregation collected around them. The settlement began to assume a very promising aspect; but it met with a powerful enemy in the free negroes. These people were originally slaves who had escaped from their masters, and taken refuge in the woods, where they maintained their independence, and whence they often committed depredations on the colony; but as the Indians received from government a reward of fifty florins for every runaway slave whom they carried back, the negroes were naturally dissatisfied with the collecting of so many of them to Sharon. They, therefore, resolved to destroy the settlement, and they at length carried their purpose into effect.[1]

In January 1761, a band of negroes came to the neighbourhood of Sharon one Lord's day when the congregation was met for divine worship. On the dismission of the assembly, they sallied forth from their retreat among the bushes, and commenced the attack. Such of the Indians as had dispersed after sermon to meditate on what they had heard, immediately took flight, some into the thicket, others to the house of the missionaries. The negroes, afraid to approach the house, as there were some within who were armed with guns, placed themselves behind the trees; and continuing the assault, wounded Odenwald, one of the Brethren, in the arm with a ball. As they at last set fire to the house, the missionaries, together with the Indians, fled into the thicket; but in the midst of their terror and confusion, they missed their way, and after rambling about till the evening, found themselves at no great distance from the settlement. The negroes having in the mean while taken their departure, the Brethren proceeded to the spot where Odenwald lay. He was still bleeding; but they dressed his wound, and having saved one hammock, put him into it, while they themselves lay down to sleep on the wet ground, as they durst not kindle a fire lest the enemy should discover their retreat. On the return of one of the missionaries next morning to the settlement, he found their house burnt to ashes, and all their

[1] Period. Accounts, vol. i. p. 326; Risler Erzahlungen, tom. iv. p. 107, 127, 161.

little property destroyed. Three of the Indians lay dead on the ground, and eleven others were carried away prisoners.[1]

Notwithstanding this terrible disaster, Schirmer and Cleve, two of the Brethren, returned soon afterwards to Sharon with a number of the Indians, and as they met with no further interruption from the negroes, they resolved to remain at that place. They had, indeed, a guard of fifteen men allowed them by the governor; but the neighbourhood of soldiers was often a burden to them, and proved a serious disadvantage to the Indians. Both of them at length fell sick: most of their time they lay in their hammocks without medical aid, and with no other food than cassabi and water. Sometimes, indeed, the one had a day's remission of the fever, and was able to afford a little assistance to the other. In the midst of these trials, they had the pleasure of welcoming some Brethren, who were sent from Europe to assist in this and the other missions in South America; but their joy was quickly turned into mourning, as one after another of the new missionaries sickened and died soon after their arrival.[2]

Hitherto the number of Indians who had settled with the Brethren was inconsiderable; and even those who had taken up their residence with them, were often so alarmed by false reports of a new attack from the negroes, that most of them fled into the wilderness. By degrees, indeed, many of them returned, and begged with tears to be again admitted into the congregation. When peace was at length restored between the negroes and the colonists, the missionaries hoped that such of the converts as were still scattered in the wilderness would return to them: but the dread which they had of their old enemy, instead of diminishing, seemed to increase after the termination of hostilities, as the negroes, when they came to Sharon, which they sometimes did in considerable numbers, treated them in a very unfriendly manner. The Indians, therefore, placed no confidence in the peace, especially as some malicious persons, with the view of scattering the congregation, circulated reports of the design of the negroes to make a new attack upon them.[3]

[1] Risler Erzahlungen, tom. iv. p. 127; Period. Accounts, vol. i. p. 333; Crantz's Hist. Breth. p. 546.

[2] Risler Erzahlungen, tom. iv. p. 130, 132, 136.

[3] Ibid. tom. iv. p. 142, 149.

In 1779, the Brethren relinquished the settlement at Sharon, as it appeared to serve no valuable purpose. The Indian congregation had of late years dwindled away, partly from dread of the negroes, partly from the land being so completely overrun by ants, that no cassabi would grow upon it; but chiefly from indifference to the gospel. The missionaries, therefore, retired from Sharon to Hope, on the river Corentyn, where a settlement had been established some years before.[1]

PART II.—HOPE.

In April 1757, Lewis Christopher Daehne took up his residence on the piece of ground which the Brethren had chosen for a settlement on the river Corentyn. On going thither, he was accompanied by some of the Indians, who assisted him in building a hut; but afterwards they all left him, except one, with whom he led a very solitary life. After some time his companion was taken ill, and the Indian doctors, who passed by, told him he would never recover if he continued to live with the White man, who was under the power of the devil, and would likewise soon turn sick. Influenced by these representations, the poor fellow, as soon as he got a little better, forsook his teacher, and retired among his own countrymen. But though Daehne was left alone, without either friend or companion, yet even in this wild solitude he was contented and happy. "Our Saviour," he says, "was always with me, and comforted me with his gracious presence, so that I can truly say, I spent my time in happiness and peace."

Some of the Indians at first entertained strong suspicions of his views, and even formed the design of putting him to death. The soldiers at the fort informed him of his danger, and invited him to come nearer them; but though he thanked them for their kindness, he determined to stand by his post, if he might be honoured to win only one soul to the Redeemer. One day, however, as he sat at dinner, about fifty of the Caribbee Indians landed from their canoes, and surrounded his hut with the view of carrying their threats into execution. Some of them were

[1] Risler Erzahlungen, tom. iv. p. 161; Fortsetzung Brud. Hist. tom. i. p. 300.

armed with swords; others with tomahawks. This was truly an alarming sight. Nevertheless he went out to them, and bade them welcome. They then asked him, through the medium of an interpreter, Who gave him liberty to build on their land? To this he replied, The governor. They next inquired, What design he had in coming thither? To which he answered: "I have brethren on the other side of the great ocean, who having heard that many of the Indians on this river were ignorant of God, have, from the great affection they felt towards you, sent me to tell you of the love of God, and what he has done to save you." The chief then said: "Have you never heard that the Indians intend to kill you?" "Yes," answered Daehne, "but I cannot believe it: You have among you some who have lived with me, and they can tell you that I am the friend of the Indians." To this the chief replied: "Yes, I have heard so: they say you are another sort of Christian than the White people in general." The missionary then said, "I am your friend: How is it that you come to kill me?" "We have done wrong," answered the chief. Every countenance now altered, and the Indians quickly dispersed. The chief, however, remained behind, and behaved in a very friendly manner. As Daehne was then in want of provisions, he gave him a supply of cassabi and other articles, and on taking his leave, promised that he would often come and see him. Thus our missionary, by his magnanimous, yet temperate conduct, warded off the blow that threatened his life, and even converted his enemies into friends.

During his stay in this solitary situation, Daehne was frequently in want of the common necessaries of life. Often he rose in the morning ignorant whether he should taste a morsel the whole day; yet Providence so ordered it, that repeatedly, when he could no longer bear the cravings of hunger, some Indians arrived, who divided with him their handful of cassabi. Often too, when, in clearing the ground, he was overcome with fatigue, the Indians who passed by were so kind as afford him assistance. He laboured, however, so hard, that he at length fell sick; and though one of the Brethren in Berbice set out immediately to visit him, yet for a considerable time he could get none of the Indians to carry him in their boats, for they were all afraid of going near a sick person, and particularly our missionary, as it was generally reported that the devil lived with him. They even did all they could to dissuade his brother from visiting so dangerous a person. He, at length, however, prevailed, and arrived to the assistance of his sick friend.

Besides suffering these various trials, Daehne was often in no small danger from wild beasts, serpents, and other venomous creatures. A tiger for a long time kept watch near his hut, seeking an opportunity, no doubt, to seize the poor solitary inhabitant. Every night it roared most hideously; and though he regularly kindled a large fire in the neighbourhood before he went to bed, yet as it often went out by the morning, it would have proved but a miserable defence had not the Lord protected him. The following circumstance is still more remarkable, and illustrates in a singular manner the care of God over his servants. Being one evening attacked with a paroxysm of fever, he resolved to go into his hut, and lie down in his hammock. Just, however, as he entered the door, he beheld a serpent descending from the roof upon him. In the scuffle which ensued, the creature stung or bit him in two or three different places; and, pursuing him closely, twined itself several times around his head and neck as tightly as possible. Expecting now to be stung or strangled to death, and being afraid lest his brethren should suspect the Indians had murdered him, he, with singular presence of mind, wrote with chalk on the table: "A serpent has killed me." Suddenly, however, that promise of the Redeemer darted into his mind: "They shall take up serpents, and shall not be hurt." Encouraged by this declaration, he seized the creature with great force, tore it loose from his body, and flung it out of the hut. He then lay down in his hammock in tranquillity and peace.[1]

After living about two years in this solitary situation, Daehne was relieved by the arrival of some others of the Brethren. Here they erected a little settlement which they called Ephraim. The Indians not only visited them in considerable numbers at this place; but many of them took up their residence with them. The missionaries, however, were often in great want of

[1] Period. Accounts, vol. i. p. 327; Risler Erzahlungen, tom. iv. p. 114.
This was probably one of that class of serpents whose bite is not venomous; but which destroy other animals by intwining themselves round their body.

the necessaries of life; they depended chiefly on what they could find in the thicket, and on what the Indians gave them.[1]

In February 1765, the Brethren removed from Ephraim to a place a number of miles further up the river Corentyn, and called their new settlement by the auspicious name of Hope. In that neighbourhood, a number of Indians who had fled from Pilgerhut in Berbice, now lived; but most of them had lost, in a great measure, any impressions of religion they might once have had. The missionaries were unwearied in visiting them and the other savages in that part of the country; but their labours were attended with little success. It was a great loss to the Indians, that they did not live under the immediate eye of their teachers. As the land in the neighbourhood of Hope was not adapted for raising cassabi, most of the congregation resided at a considerable distance: only a few families dwelt constantly in the neighbourhood. Such as lived at a distance used to come every four weeks to observe the Lord's Supper, and, as they were then obliged to leave their houses and plantations unprotected, and commonly remained about eight days at Hope, they often, on returning home, found their fields plundered of their crop. Many, in consequence of this, did not come oftener than once in two or three months. Such circumstances as these could not fail to prove very injurious to the spiritual interests of the congregation. They were not only deprived of the daily meetings for divine worship; but they forgot the instructions they had already received; they lost their relish for divine things, so that, even when the missionaries visited them, they did not like to hear them speak about vital religion; but endeavoured to turn the conversation to matters of an external nature; they, in short, mingled with the heathen, and learned of them their way.[2]

In July 1790, Fisher, one of the Brethren, with the view of preventing these evils, endeavoured to obtain from a neighbouring chief a piece of land where the congregation might raise cassabi for their subsistence. After presenting him, according to the custom of the country, with a basket of oranges

[1] Risler Erzahlungen, tom. iv. p. 117, 126, 134.

[2] Risler Erzahlungen, tom. iv. p. 146, 159; Fortsetzung Brud. Hist. tom. i. p. 93, 01; tom. ii. p. 305, 311.

and some bananas, he asked him whether he would grant the Christian Indians permission to plant in his neighbourhood. This request the old man immediately granted, and pointing out a considerable tract of forest land, said, "This ground God has given to me, as he gave that at Hope to thee. Thus I am the rightful owner of it. Now, as I have not created it, and thou canst use it, I deliver it over to thee freely. Thy people may come and clear it: the sooner the better." He then addressed the Indians in a very friendly manner, and expressed his satisfaction at their coming to plant in his neighbourhood; assuring them, at the same time, that no devil or evil spirit haunted the tract of land he had given them.[1]

In consequence of this new arrangement, the Indians began to build themselves huts, and to lay out plantations in the neighbourhood of Hope. The missionaries, however, had no small difficulties to encounter in forming them to habits of industry: at times, they even thought that all their plans would prove abortive. In the eyes of an Indian, the trench and the spade are the emblems of slavery. The young men, indeed, were above such prejudices, and performed their work with pleasure; but the old men were completely possessed with these foolish notions. By degrees, however, the Indians not only made considerable improvement in the cultivation of the land; but began to prepare all kinds of timber for building, and to convey it to Paramaribo and Berbice, from whence they received considerable orders. They also made a kind of hats from the leaves of a certain species of palm, which they sold to the Pagan Indians and negroes, as well as to the White people, who found them very useful, as they were much lighter, cooler, and stronger, than the common hats.[2]

In August 1795, Fisher and Kluge, two of the missionaries, together with four of the Indians, experienced a remarkable deliverance at sea, when in imminent danger of being drowned. In conveying the timber and other articles they had prepared to Berbice, they often ran great hazard in their small canoes, and therefore they at length purchased a large boat for this

[1] Fortsetzung Brud. Hist. tom. iii. p. 91; Period. Accounts, vol. i. p. 99.

[2] Fortsetzung Brud. Hist. tom. iii. p. 92, 96, 102, 105, 107; Period. Accounts, vol. i. p. 117, 153.

purpose. But on the very first voyage they made in her to the colony, she all of a sudden became leaky after they had proceeded a considerable way, and filled with water so rapidly, that before they could run her ashore she sunk to the bottom. At first they clung to a cask fastened to the boat, and then to the mast, part of which was above the surface of the water. In this perilous situation they remained for no less than eight hours, but at last, when it was after midnight, they contrived to get ashore, two and two at a time, in a small canoe they had providentially taken with them. In the morning, the missionaries and a little boy, (for the canoe would not hold more,) set out to return to Hope, and after rowing for about twenty-four hours in their wet clothes, without any covering for their heads, and even without food, they reached that place, to the great astonishment of their Brethren. It happened very providentially that all their efforts to get out to sea had been frustrated by contrary winds, which kept them near the shore; for as the boat sunk within less than five minutes after the leak was discovered, they must inevitably have perished had the accident happened at a distance from land.[1]

In December 1800, the inhabitants of the settlement at Hope amounted to two hundred and eight, of whom one hundred and sixty-nine were baptized, and eighty-four were communicants. Their number had of late been considerably diminished in consequence of the small-pox. Many had fled from dread of that frightful disorder, and others had died of it. Among the many advantages attending the introduction of the gospel and the arts of social life among them, it was none of the least, that in sickness they were much better taken care of than their heathen neighbours. It is a singular fact, that in epidemical diseases eight of the pagans died for one Christian.[2]

In August 1806, the whole settlement, including the church, the houses of the missionaries, and the habitations of the Indians, was burnt to the ground. The fire once kindled, ran along the roofs, which were thatched with leaves, with such prodigious fury, that there was no possibility of checking its progress. By this means, not only their houses, but all their garden tools, the stores of the Indians, the tackling and rigging

[1] Period. Accounts, vol. ii. p. 260. [2] Ibid. vol. ii. p. 259; vol. iii. p. 141.

of their boat, and various other useful implements, were totally destroyed. The fire began about two o'clock in the afternoon, while the missionaries were taking some refreshment, and there was much reason to suspect that it was kindled by incendiaries, as several attempts of the same kind had been made some days before, which being discovered were frustrated in time.[1]

In 1808, the mission among the Indians on the river Corentyn was relinquished by the Brethren. While the external circumstances of the settlement were so disastrous, its internal state was not more flourishing. Most, if not all, of the Indians belonging to the congregation, whose practice corresponded with their profession, had within a short time been seized with an epidemical disorder, and died rejoicing in the Redeemer. Such as still survived, so far from being truly religious, were disorderly, dissolute, and refractory, and even manifested a spirit of enmity to the gospel. Discouraged by these circumstances, the Brethren abandoned the settlement at Hope, which had hitherto but ill corresponded with its auspicious name. An attempt was afterwards made to renew the mission, but it was not successful, and after a few years it was again relinquished.[2]

PART III.—BAMBEY.

In 1765, Lewis Christopher Daehne, who had lately come to Europe, returned to Surinam, accompanied by Thomas Jones and Rudolph Stolle, in consequence of a request from the governor, who had now made peace with the free negroes on the river Sarameca, and wisely judging that the conversion of them and their children to Christianity would be the most effectual means of putting a period to those cruelties and depredations which they often committed on the colonists, made application to the church of the Brethren to establish a mission among them. Upon their arrival, the missionaries were presented by the agent of government to the captain of ten or twelve villages of the negroes, and were at first received by them with much friendship. Each of the chiefs wished to have one of them,

[1] Period. Accounts, vol. iv. p. 45.
[2] Ibid. vol. iv. p. 306; vol. v. p. 149, 242, 281; vol. vi. p. 376.

thinking it an honour perhaps to have a European residing with them; but the Brethren judged it best, at least for the present, to remain together. They promised, however, to visit them all, and with this view took up their abode in the centre of their villages. But though the negroes appeared friendly at first, yet when the missionaries explained to them the design of their coming, the poor creatures, particularly the old women, set up a most piteous howl, terrified lest their idols should be provoked if they had any thing to do with the great God; and a few days after, they appointed prayers and offerings to be made with the view of appeasing the wrath of their offended deities. Indeed, they in general considered themselves as very good people, and were angry with the Brethren when they exhorted them to seek redemption through the blood of Christ.[1]

In January 1771, Arabini, one of the chiefs, was baptized by the Brethren, as the first-fruits of their labours among the negroes. Though persecuted by his countrymen, and threatened with the vengeance of their gods, yet had he the fortitude to withstand the one and to depise the other. Having often heard the missionaries declare that the objects of their worship, which consisted chiefly of wooden images, large trees, heaps of sand, stones, crocodiles, and various kinds of serpents, could neither help nor hurt a man, he took his idol, which happened to be a staff curiously decorated with beads, and burnt it in the fire. He afterwards went one morning with his gun to the river, where the crocodile or alligator, which was said to be the god of the village, used to have its haunt; and on discovering the creature, he addressed it in the following manner: "I mean to shoot thee: Now, if thou art a god, my bullet will not hurt thee; but if thou art only a creature, it will kill thee." He accordingly fired his piece and killed the animal on the spot.[2]

In December 1773, the Brethren removed to a place which they called Bambey, two days' journey lower down the river, whither the negroes had gone a short time before. Here they had many difficulties to encounter. Their voyages to visit the negroes they had to make along the rivers, in an open boat,

[1] Risler Erzahlungen, tom. iv. p. 177, 185; Crantz's Hist. Breth. p. 488, 595; Period. Accounts, vol. i. p. 334; vol. ii. p. 414.

[2] Period. Accounts, vol. ii. p. 95.

exposed to the rays of a burning sun, or to violent rains, among precipitous rocks and waterfalls, of considerable height, which were at once troublesome and dangerous. They not only lived in a state of entire seclusion from the whole civilized world; but often laboured under severe attacks of sickness, which debilitated their frame, and incapacitated them for visiting the negroes in other villages so frequently as they could have wished. Indeed, they had often scarcely arrived, when they sickened and died, one following another in quick succession to the grave.[1]

In 1777, Christian L. Schuman, came to Bambey, and soon after his arrival he was left alone near a whole year at that place, in consequence of the death of one, and the return of another, of his fellow-missionaries. In this solitary situation, he was so debilitated by frequent attacks of fever, and painful abscesses over his whole body, that he was unable to walk or stand. He sometimes lay many days sick, destitute of all human help, as his own negro was afflicted with similar sores, and the inhabitants of the village were absent the whole week, working at their distant plantations. One night when he had fallen sound asleep, after a severe paroxysm of fever, an immense host of ants entered his chamber, and completely covered his whole body. On awaking, he hastened out of bed into another house as well as he was able. His pain, which was already very great, was dreadfully aggravated by the bites of the ants, and the means employed in removing them. But yet, amidst these heavy trials, he experienced, in a remarkable degree, the supporting and consoling grace of the Redeemer. He forgot all his sickness and pain, when the negroes came to hear from his lips the words of eternal life: sometimes, indeed, he was so weak, that he could not stand while he addressed them; but yet, he lay in his hammock, and from thence, spoke to them of the things which belonged to their everlasting peace.[2]

In October 1787, Andrew C. Randt, who had lately arrived at Bambey, was bit while asleep, in three places, by a species of bat which abounds in that quarter of the world, and on awakening, found himself bathed in blood. When a person is lying in

[1] Fortsetzung Brud. Hist. tom. i. p. 98; tom. iii. p, 70; Risler Erzahlungen, tom. iv. p. 195; Period. Accounts, vol. ii. p. 418.

[2] Risler Erzahlungen, tom. iv. p. 199.

his hammock, and his extremities accidentally uncovered, these animals insinuate their aculeated tongue into the veins of the feet, in so dexterous a manner as not to disturb him. They then suck the blood till they are satiated, fanning all the while with their enormous wings, and agitating the air in a manner so pleasing, in that hot climate, as to throw their victim into a still sounder sleep. After they are satisfied, they are obliged to disgorge: they then begin again, and continue sucking and disgorging till they are scarcely able to fly, and the sufferer has not unfrequently been known to sleep from time into eternity. They make similar attacks on other animals, and, it is said, that in some parts of South America, they have destroyed all the cattle introduced by the Roman Catholic missionaries.[1]

In May 1800, John Maehr, another of the missionaries, made a narrow escape from death under a form still more frightful He and several of the negroes having gone to a neighbouring creek, to prepare some cedar planks cut two months before, they carried with them a live tortoise, which they meant to kill and make a meal of in the wood. This creature they tied to one of the posts of their huts, while the negroes went to a place about a mile distant, to catch some fish. This they do by means of a certain species of wood, which being cut small, beaten to powder, and strewed on the water, stupifies the fish to the distance of a mile or more down the river. They are then pursued, and either pierced or shot with arrows by the negroes, who are placed along the banks, partly in boats, and partly standing in the water. Meanwhile Maehr was employed in preparing the cedar planks; but being at length overcome with fatigue, he lay down in the shade, near the tortoise, and slept about an hour. During this time a tiger came to the spot, tore the tortoise off the poll, and dragged it into the wood, while he was lying fast asleep near at hand. On awakening, and perceiving the danger he had been in, he was much struck with his merciful deliverance, and as the negroes returned soon after, and brought with them a large supply of fish, the tortoise was never missed.[2]

[1] Fortsetzung Brud. Hist. tom. ii. p. 382; Bingley's Animal Biography, vol. i. p. 96.

[2] Period. Accounts. vol. ii. p. 451; vol. iii. p. 144.

In January 1801, the whole number of negroes baptized by the Brethren since the commencement of the mission amounted only to fifty-nine; the congregation consisted then of forty-nine members, including baptized and candidates for baptism, of whom no more than seventeen were communicants.[1] Such had been the small success of the missionaries, notwithstanding the toils they had undergone, the sufferings they had endured, and the sacrifice which many of them had made of their lives.[2]

In 1813, the mission among the free negroes was relinquished by the Brethren. Of late it had assumed a very unpromising aspect, not only as regarded the Pagan negroes; but even as to many of the baptized: the expense of supporting it had become extremely burdensome, as the missionaries had resigned the office of agent for government, which one of them had held for many years, and which, though it had contributed to diminish the expense of the undertaking, had proved a very irksome and unpleasant charge. Maehr, the only missionary remaining in that quarter, was obliged to leave it on account of the state of his own and his wife's health, while, at the same time, there was none to supply his place.[3] These circumstances, combined with the small prospect of success, occasioned the suspension of this hitherto unfruitful mission.

In December 1840, the mission among the free negroes was again renewed, but in consequence of the sickness and death of the missionaries who were successively sent to carry it on, and the extreme unhealthiness of the country, it was after some years again given up.[4]

Such is a view of the rise, the progress, and the termination of the missions of the Brethren among the Indians and the free negroes in South America: none of them was attended with any remarkable success, and all of them it was at last found necessary to relinquish.

[1] Risler Erzahlungen, tom. iv. p. 207; Period. Accounts, vol. iii. p. 152.

[2] From the commencement of the mission to the year 1797, twenty-nine Brethren and Sisters were employed in this mission, and of these, no fewer than nineteen died either on the spot, or soon after their return. *Period Accounts*, vol. ii. p. 420.

[3] Period. Accounts, vol. v. p. 79, 151, 194, 243, 363; Holmes' Sketches, p. 287.

[4] Period. Accounts, vol. xv. p. 143, 427, 495; vol. xix. p. 281; vol. xx. p. 215.

PART IV.—PARAMARIBO.

In 1768, Christopher Kersten began to instruct a few negroes at Paramaribo, the chief town of Surinam. It was a part of the original design of the Brethren in coming to this country to make known the gospel among the slaves in the colony; but the planters and other inhabitants were so much prejudiced against them, in consequence of the unfavourable reports in circulation concerning them, that they would not allow them to carry their views into execution. Some of the Brethren, however, still resided at Paramaribo, where they wrought at their trades for the support of the missionaries in the interior, and by their excellent conduct, gradually acquired the confidence both of the government and of the people. As they employed some hired negroes to assist them in the way of their trade, Kersten now began to instruct three of them who manifested a desire after religious knowledge. Such was the commencement of the Brethren's labours at Paramaribo; but for several years their exertions were much interrupted, and did not extend beyond a few individuals.[1]

In 1776, the Brethren had the pleasure of baptizing several of the negroes at Paramaribo, who thus formed the beginning of a congregation in that place. The number of their hearers gradually increased, and they at length erected a church for their accommodation. Most of the White inhabitants of the colony viewed the labours of the Brethren with approbation; but there were a few who prohibited their slaves from attending on their instructions, and punished them on this account. Notwithstanding this opposition, however, the missionaries, in the course of a few years, collected a considerable negro congregation at Paramaribo.[2]

In April 1786, two of the Brethren took up their residence at a place called Sommelsdyke, where the governor had made them a grant of fifty acres of land for a settlement, with the view of instructing the slaves on the neighbouring plantations.

[1] Risler Erzahlungen, tom. iv. p. 208.

[2] Ibid. tom. iv. p. 213, 216, 219; Fortsetzung Brud. Hist. tom. i. p. 309; tom. ii. p. 314.

In the course of a few months both the missionaries died, in consequence, it was supposed, of the ground not being sufficiently drained; but they were soon succeeded by others who pursued their labours with considerable success. Some of the planters, however, considered the diffusion of Christianity among their slaves as useless: others, though they had no objection to their instruction, would not allow them to go to Sommelsdyke for that purpose, but wished the missionaries to visit them on the plantations, a circumstance which increased their labour without promoting their success.[1]

In 1826, the labours of the Brethren were still confined chiefly to Paramaribo, the station at Sommelsdyke having been given up many years before; but measures were adopted shortly after this for enabling them to extend their operations to other parts of the colony. The number of plantations on which they were allowed to make known the gospel increased from time to time until they at length amounted to nearly two hundred; but as they lay scattered throughout the colony, it was impossible for them to visit many of them oftener than once a month, and consequently the instruction communicated to the negroes must have been very imperfect. With the view of facilitating their labours, stations were occupied in different parts of the colony, and while some of them took charge of these stations, others were continually travelling about for the purpose of instructing the slaves on the various estates which they were allowed to visit.[2]

In 1852, the following were the numbers connected with the Brethren's congregation at Paramaribo, and on the plantations in the neighbouring country:—

Communicants.	Baptized Adults.	Baptized Children.	Candidates for Baptism, New People, and Excluded.	Total under Instruction.
2102	4787	2149	9934	18,972[3]

[1] Fortsetzung Brud. Hist. tom. ii. p. 316.

[2] Period. Accounts, vol. vii. p. 267; vol. x. p. 40, 336, 467; vol. xi. p. 135; vol. xiv. p. 155; vol. xviii. p. 274; vol. xix. p. 113; vol. xx. p. 460; vol. xxi. p. xi.

[3] Period. Accounts, vol. xxi. p. xxvii.

Before closing our account of the missions of the Brethren in South America, we

SECT. V.—TARTARY.

IN 1735, David Nitschman went to St Petersburg, the metropolis of Russia, with the view of proceeding among the Calmuck Tartars, and the descendants of the Bohemian Brethren, who, it was reported, still resided in the mountains of Caucasus. In this attempt, however, he failed; but yet he obtained some useful information by means of the visit, and formed a friendly acquaintance with a clergyman in that city, who was of great service to three missionaries destined for Lapland, who, three years after, were thrown into prison by the Russian government.

In 1742, Conrade Lange set off on a journey to China, together with two others of the Brethren, Zechariah Hirschel, and Michael Kund, who were designed as missionaries to the Calmuc Tartars. Having, however, applied for a passport on their arrival at St Petersburg, they met with the same treatment as their brethren destined to Lapland, being apprehended as suspicious persons, and thrown into prison. Here they were detained for several years; but at length they were dismissed, and returned to Germany. Still, however, the Brethren were not discouraged; and they at length found an opportunity of carrying their views into effect.[1]

In 1765, John E. Westmann and several others of the Brethren

shall add a few general notices which may not be altogether uninteresting to the reader.

From the commencement of these missions to the year 1800, there were 159 Brethren and Sisters employed in the different settlements at Pilgerhut, Sharon, Hope, Bambey, Paramaribo, and Sommelsdyke. Of these, 75 died in the country, many of them immediately after their arrival. The whole number of persons baptized by the missionaries until 1801, was as follows:

Indians	855
Free negroes,	59
Negroes and mulattoes,	731
	1645
Of these there had died in the faith of Christ,	658
Still under the care of the missionaries,	594
Forsaken the Congregation,	393

—*Risler Erzahlungen*, tom. iv. p. 221.

[1] Crantz's Hist. Breth. p. 189, 314, 394.

were sent to establish a colony in the province of Astrachan, with a particular view to the introduction of Christianity among the neighbouring Tartar tribes, the Empress of Russia having lately passed an edict granting the members of their church full permission to settle in her dominions, and promising them complete liberty of conscience. Having fixed on a place for a settlement, about twenty-four miles below Czaritzin, they began to erect the buildings necessary for their accommodation, to cultivate the ground, and to work at their respective trades. In the course of a few years, this place, which they called Sarepta, became a flourishing little town; but its history as a colony does not fall within our plan: it is only as it became a central point, from which attempts were made to extend Christianity among the neighbouring tribes, that we have to notice it.[1]

As this place was on the road from St Petersburg to Persia and the East Indies, the Brethren received frequent visits from travellers and other strangers who happened to pass in that direction. Among others, there was a merchant from Georgia, who, in conversing with them concerning the several tribes which inhabited the Mountains of Caucasus, mentioned one called the Tschecks, who, according to their own account, were some hundred years ago driven thither from Europe, and who still retained their own language, preserved their peculiar customs, and professed the Christian religion; but being no longer able to read the books of their forefathers, which were deposited in large strong-built churches, which now stood empty, they looked forward to a period when the use of them and their public worship would be restored. As the Bohemians call themselves Tschecks, the Brethren naturally conjectured that these were probably the descendants of their countrymen, who, about the end of the fifteenth century, were banished from Moravia on account of their religion, and were said to have gone to Moldavia, and from thence to the Mountains of Caucasus.[2]

In 1768, two of the Brethren, with the view of obtaining further information respecting these interesting people, set off for that part of the country which they were said to inhabit. Hav-

[1] Crantz's Hist. Breth. p. 525, 608. [2] Ibid. p. 611.

ing arrived at Astrachan, they procured from the governor letters of recommendation to the Russian commanders, with orders to give them some Cossacks as a guard, and a Tartar for their interpreter. On arriving, however, at Mosdok, the frontier fortress, where they were only four days' journey from the country which the Tschecks were said to inhabit, they were advised by the commandant of that place not to proceed further, as the Kabardian Tartars were approaching with an army of forty thousand men, who would in all probability take them prisoners, and carry them into slavery. In consequence of this intelligence, the Brethren had no alternative but to relinquish the enterprise for the present. They determined, however, to embrace the earliest opportunity of renewing the search; and, in the mean while, employed themselves in learning the Tartar language.

It was not long before the Brethren commenced an acquaintance with the Calmuck Tartars, who inhabit a vast tract of country on both sides of the Wolga. Soon after their arrival, a horde of these barbarians encamped on their land; and though this at first occasioned them considerable trouble, yet the colonists, by their kind and affable behaviour, quickly gained the confidence and friendship of their visitors. They were particularly happy when a physician arrived in the settlement. Many of them became his patients, among whom was one of their princes, who, with his train, pitched his winter quarters in the neighbourhood. He formed a particular attachment to two of the Brethren, who often visited him with the view of learning the language; and, on his departure, he offered, if they would go with him into the Great Steppe (an immense plain covered with long grass), to take them under his protection, and to furnish them with the means of acquiring the language. This offer the Brethren accepted with joy; and during the two following years, they resided among the Tartars, conforming to their manner of life, and accompanying them in their migrations from place to place with their tents and cattle. They neglected no opportunity of making known the gospel to them; but though they themselves were treated with civility and friendship, their message was not received by the barbarians. The great Derbet horde at length retired from that part of the country, and only a few straggling families remained in the neighbourhood of Sarepta.[1]

In November 1781, Gottfried Grabsch and George Gruhl, two of the Brethren, renewed the attempt to visit the Tschecks in the mountains of Caucasus. After passing through several Tartar towns, they arrived at Beregee, the place where Professor Gmelin was imprisoned and died. Here, had it not been for their guide, they would not have been received into any house, the inhabitants of the place being bigoted Mahomedans, and inveterate in their hatred of Christians; but at length one of them, to oblige their conductor, agreed to give them lodgings. Uzmei Khan, the prince of the country, happening to be in the town at this very time, could scarcely be persuaded that the account which Grabsch gave of himself was true, but suspected he was either a physician, a rich, or a learned man. One of the Tartar princes even told him very gravely, that he had heard that if a man's body were ripped up, he could heal him in a very short time. Uzmei Khan being at length satisfied with regard to their design, took them in his retinue to the place of his residence, and then sent them forward, under the care of a guide, to Kubascha, the principal seat of the Tschecks.

Here they arrived the same day; but their disappointment may be more easily conceived than described, when on entering the town, they heard the cry of the Mollahs on the turrets of the mosques, summoning the people to prayers, a plain proof that the inhabitants were Mahomedans. Grabsch, however, proceeded to make inquiry concerning their origin, their religion, their language, and their books; he visited every house in the town, and left no means untried, in order to ascertain whether any memorials of Christianity yet remained among them. He discovered the ruins of three churches, and an inscription over the door of one of them, cut in stone, which neither he nor any of the inhabitants were able fully to decipher; in the middle of it, the number 1215, in the usual Arabic figures, was still legible. Not far from this ruin stood a noble stately church, built of hewn stone, and decorated with a profusion of architectural ornaments, but now converted into dwelling-houses, and divided into five stories. On the top of this

[1] Crantz's Hist. Breth. p. 612; Period. Accounts, vol. ii. p. 191.

building, several inscriptions in stone were pointed out to him, but he could not discover in them the smallest resemblance to any letters with which he was acquainted.[1] It further appeared, that the inhabitants had no longer any books written in the characters used by their ancestors. They now employed the Arabic alphabet in writing their own language, as well as the Turkish and Tartar. Their ancestors, they acknowledged, were originally Christians; but upwards of three hundred years ago they embraced the religion of Mahommed; and now, they thanked God, that he had directed them in the right path to heaven. Some of them, however, expressed great regard for Grabsch; and Mahmud, his host, assured him, that whenever he came to Kubascha, he would consider him as his brother: "What," said Grabsch, "though I do not turn Mussulman?" "O, all that goes for nothing," replied Mahmud.

On arriving at Shamachy, on their way home, the Brethren were informed of a village three days' journey from that place, where there was a congregation of Christians, who were said to be the descendants of foreigners; and who, though the prince of the place had endeavoured, by threatenings and persecution, to compel them to embrace the Mahomedan faith, still maintained the profession of their own religion. Anxious as the Brethren were to visit these people, it was not in their power at present. They saw, however, a man from that village, who informed them that they came originally from Georgia, and were members partly of the Georgian, partly of the Armenian Church.

Having at length reached Tefflis, they were there received in the most friendly manner by the Prince or Czar, who expressed a strong desire that some of the Moravians would come and settle in his territories, and even wrote a letter to this effect to the Brethren in Europe. Our travellers intended, if possible,

[1] Some will, perhaps, be surprised to find the remains of Christian churches in the wilds of Tartary; but, it appears from our ordinary ecclesiastical historians, that the gospel was introduced into that country at least as early as the sixth century; that it was afterwards propagated over a great part of that extensive region, through the zeal of the Nestorians; and that metropolitan prelates, and a great number of inferior bishops, were established in those very districts which are now overrun with Mahomedanism and idolatry. It is chiefly since the fourteenth century, that Christianity has declined in this part of the world.—*Mosheim's Ecclesiastical History*, vol. ii. p. 95, 203, 372, 435; vol. iii. p. 9, 131; *Yeates' Indian Church History*, p. 97.

to proceed from this city across the mountains to visit the Tschegemzi, who reside on the banks of the river Tschegem, as the resemblance in sound to the name Tschecks, led them to suspect they might be the descendants of the Bohemians who had emigrated into Asia; but during their stay at Tefflis, Grabsch had an opportunity of conversing with some persons from that part of the country who spoke the Nogay language, and assured him, that their ancestors were descended from the Tartars in the neighbourhood of Astrachan, who had fled from the Russians into the mountains; but that the ruins of Christian churches in their neighbourhood, shewed that it had once been inhabited by a very different race of people. This account was confirmed by other persons, who ascribed these traces of Christianity to some colonies of Genoese who had formerly settled in that country. The Brethren, however, still wished to undertake the journey; but they were at present under the necessity of abandoning their design, and returned to Sarepta after an absence of about ten months.[1]

Besides embracing every opportunity of cultivating friendly intercourse with the Calmucks, the Brethren at different periods made attempts to introduce the gospel among them. With this view, several of them applied to the study of their language, and though they laboured under great disadvantages for want of an able teacher, yet they obtained possession of some of their books, which were of considerable assistance to them, for the Calmucks are not ignorant of the use of letters. Besides visiting the hordes which came into the neighbourhood of Sarepta, some of the Brethren occasionally accompanied them in their wanderings, in order to make known the gospel to them; but their labours were attended with little success. One poor blind Calmuck girl whom they saved from perishing on the road, and four Kirghisian children whom they ransomed from slavery, were the only individuals of the Tartar race whom they received into the church.[2]

In May 1815, John G. Schill and C. Hubner proceeded from Sarepta to the Choschut horde of Calmucks, with the view of renewing the attempts to convert them to the Christian faith;

[1] Period. Accounts, vol. iii. p. 363; Fortsetzung Brud, Hist. tom. i. p. 335.
[2] Period. Accounts, vol. i. p. 105; vol. ii. p. 115, 191, 196; vol. iv. p. 213; vol. v. p. xiv.; Edinburgh Review, vol. xxviii. p. 303, 315.

but they met with little or no encouragement in their labours. After some years, indeed, two or three families appeared disposed to receive the gospel; but they met with so much opposition from their countrymen, that they left the horde with their tents and cattle, and took up their abode on a small island in the river Wolga, near Sarepta. Thinking that there was no other way of protecting themselves from being compelled to return to their heathen countrymen, they applied for baptism to a Russian priest at Czaritzin, by whom they were baptized according to the rites of the Greek Church. Little was known of them afterwards; but there is too much reason to fear that they would suffer essentially in their spiritual interests, when deprived, as they now were, of the care and instruction of the missionaries, and left to mingle with an ignorant and superstitious people.[1]

In May 1823, the Brethren Schill and Zwick undertook a journey among the Calmucks, at the expense of the Russian Bible Society, and with recommendatory letters from the Russian minister, Count Nesselrode, for the purpose of circulating among them such portions of the Holy Scriptures as had been translated into their language; but under an express injunction from Prince Galitzin to confine themselves to the distribution of the sacred books, refraining from all comment upon them. In this journey, they visited five different hordes of Calmucks, and applied to the princes for permission to circulate the Scriptures among their people; but they commonly put them off with excuses, or positively refused their request. There were a few who accepted them, and who authorized their subjects to receive them, or undertook to distribute copies themselves; but it may be doubted whether the books thus circulated were preserved, and still more, if they were read. In visiting the horde in which the missionaries had resided previously for some years, they took occasion to inquire whether many of them had the copies of Matthew's Gospel, which were then distributed among them, and whether they wished for other books; but they found neither the Gospels nor any wish for other parts of Scripture; and some of the Calmucks told them that there was not by this

[1] Period. Accounts, vol. vi. p. 255; vol. viii. p. 289; vol. ix. p. 163, 288, 299; vol. xvii. p. 291.

time a book to be met with, results which, we fear, will very commonly be found to attend the distribution of the Scriptures among heathen and other unenlightened nations, if there are no missionaries to follow it up by personal instruction.[1]

This journey of Schill and Zwick among the Calmucks for the distribution of such parts of the Holy Scriptures as were printed in their language, was the conclusion of their labours among that people. The Brethren at Sarepta had applied to the Russian government for permission to carry on the mission in the manner usual among their body, and to instruct, baptize, and form into congregations such as through their instrumentality should embrace Christianity. But this application was refused, on the ground of its being a law of the Empire that no heathen, under the sway of Russia, should be converted to the Christian faith and baptized, except by the clergy of the Greek Church. As the labours of the Brethren were now restricted to the circulation of the Scriptures; as they had not even liberty to give oral instruction, and as, if converts should be made, they could not baptize them, nor receive them into their Church, nor afterwards watch over them, but must hand them over to the Russian priests to be baptized by them, and united to a Church grossly corrupt and superstitious, in which every spark of spiritual life was likely to be extinguished, they did not feel it to be their duty to prosecute the mission any longer.[2]

SECT. VI.—PERSIA.

In the spring of 1747, Christian F. W. Hocker, a physician, and J. Rueffer, a surgeon, set off for the East, with the view of visiting the Gaures, who resided in Persia, and were supposed by some to be the posterity of the Magi, or Wise men, who came to Bethlehem at the birth of our Saviour.[3] On arriving at

[1] Zwick and Schill's Journey from Sarepta to several Calmuck Hordes, p. 25, 61, 65, 69, 72, 83, 88, 103, 115, 178, 191, 194, 215, 245, 250.

[2] Period. Accounts, vol. viii. p. 342; vol. ix. p. 261.

[3] The Gaures, or Guebres, are the same as the Parsis, or worshippers of fire. They are descended from the ancient Persians, the followers of Zoroaster, to whose religious tenets and moral institutions, they still profess to adhere.—*Forbes' Oriental Memoirs*, vol. i. p. 109.

Aleppo, they were strongly dissuaded, by various European gentlemen in that city, from prosecuting their journey, on account of the anarchy and misery in which Persia was then plunged by Nadir Shah, who, amongst his other cruelties, had caused numbers of the Jews and Armenians to be burnt alive, because they would not satisfy his rapacious demands for money. But notwithstanding these representations, the Brethren resolved to follow out their original design. Afterwards, indeed, when they heard many new and frightful reports from Persia, particularly how the usurper had plundered Ispahan, the capital of the kingdom, and Kerman, the chief seat of the Gaures; that in the latter place he had been so inhuman as to erect three pyramids of men's heads; and that, in consequence of his unparallelled cruelties, the whole country was in a state of rebellion, Hocker was inclined to go to Bussora, and there wait a more convenient season for executing their design; but Rueffer rather proposed going to Bagdad, to which the other consented, on condition that should they find no opportunity of travelling from thence to Persia, they would then proceed to Bussora.

Having provided themselves with two camels, and a variety of other necessary articles, they left Aleppo with the caravan destined for the East, consisting of no fewer than fifteen hundred camels. In passing through the desert, they usually set off about sunrise, and travelled till noon, when they stopped for an hour, and prepared some coffee for dinner. They afterwards pursued their journey till sunset, when they again halted, and rested till a little after midnight. Their supper consisted of hard boiled rice, with melted butter; and though it was an unsavoury dish, yet hunger rendered it palatable, and even delicious. Their drink was muddy stinking water, which they were obliged to strain through a cloth before it was fit for use. After travelling about a fortnight in this manner, they arrived at Cowis, a place where the caravan usually divided into two, one part going to Bagdad, the other to Bussora; but to their great mortification, the whole, in this instance, proceeded to Bussora. They, therefore, went forward to Bagdad, in company with four Jews who were travelling thither; and, on their arrival in that city, they learned that a caravan was about to set off for Persia. Having joined it without delay, they proceeded a considerable way on their journey without molestation; but they were at length attacked by the Kurds, a race of robbers who infest that part of the country, to the great annoyance of travellers. Their way that day was first over a large hill, and then through a valley along the foot of the hills. The armed men, who were between fifty and sixty in number, stopped in the valley, to wait till the whole caravan had passed over the hill. Scarcely, however, had our travellers passed it, when they heard a hideous cry behind them on another hill, and on looking round, they perceived a numerous band of Kurds running straight toward them. A few of them were mounted, and armed with sabres and javelins; but most of them were on foot, and had chiefly clubs and javelins, so that if the people belonging to the caravan had possessed courage and a good leader, they might easily have repelled them, as there were only about two hundred of this undisciplined band. But as they retreated in full gallop over the hill, after firing only a few shots, those who had merely asses or mules were left an easy prey to the robbers. Before Hocker was aware, he was pierced in the back with a javelin, and while he turned and looked about, he received another stab in his right side; but as they both struck against his ribs, they did him no material injury. Such, however, was the violence of the latter, that he fell down the hill, upon which one of the robbers followed him, and before he had time to rise, aimed a stroke at his face, but though he received a pretty severe wound in the chin, he did not lose it, as some of the caravan did their ears, while others had their skulls fractured. When he rose, he suffered the robbers to take all his money and clothes, to his very shirt and breeches, which they did not offer to seize.

As soon as the robbers left him, he ran forward as fast as he could; but before he was aware, he received another violent stroke on the back of his neck from one of the banditti who lay in wait for him, so that for a time he lost all recollection, and fell almost lifeless to the ground. The ruffian, however, took nothing from him but the watch left in his pocket. Hocker then fell into the hands of a third, who stripped him of his boots and stockings. A fourth now came up and robbed him of his breeches, but yet he had the civility to leave him two pairs of old drawers. From the place where they were plundered to the nearest habitation was fifteen English miles, and toward this quarter each individual made the best of his way. As Hocker was naked and barefooted, his body was in a short time half roasted by the heat of the sun, and his feet were extremely sore from the hardness of the road; but yet the hope of reaching a place of safety supported his strength and courage. On his arrival he found many of his fellow-travellers naked like himself, and spent with fatigue, hunger and thirst. His first concern was to find his brother Rueffer, who was no less anxiously seeking for him, and if the Persians had not hindered him, would certainly have returned to the place where they were robbed. Hocker at last discovered him coming towards him, but for some time did not recognise him, stripped as he was of all his clothes. He was not, however, wounded, for as soon as he saw the robbers running up to him, brandishing their clubs, he made signs to them to take all he had, begging only his instrument for bleeding. Thus one after another stripped him till he was left perfectly naked. One of the Persians furnished him with a piece of cloth to bind round his waist; and Hocker, as soon as he saw him, gave him a pair of his drawers. Shach Ali Beg, who took them with him, and another Persian called Hassen Ali Beg, were so kind as supply him with an old waistcoat and sandals, and brought them to a house, where, as it was cold, they were glad to find a warm chamber, and some bread and grapes for their supper. Rueffer's body, however, was so full of sores and blisters, occasioned by the burning heat of the sun, that for many nights he could not shut his eyes for pain. In general, the Persians belonging to the caravan behaved toward them with great kindness. The two persons already mentioned would have purchased asses for them, but as they could not pay for them, they chose rather to walk.

On the following day, the Brethren set forward on their journey; but scarcely had a week elapsed, when they were again attacked by another gang of robbers, who rushed upon them with drawn sabres, and stripped them of the few articles they had left. Hocker saved only a pair of torn drawers; Rueffer, an old waistcoat. Their sufferings for some days were so great, that it is impossible to describe them. They had nothing for food but bread and water; and Hocker caught a violent flux from the difference of temperature between the night and the day. It was considered by them as a great mercy, that for a few nights they were permitted to sleep in a stable, though without either fire or covering. Hocker at last obtained some kind of dress for himself, but as it consisted of horse hair and cotton, it tore his skin, and was extremely painful. Happily, they at length reached Ispahan, and were received in a friendly manner by some fathers of the Roman Catholic Church who lived in that neighbourhood, and particularly by Mr Pierson, the English resident, who took them into his house, and supplied them with clothes, and such other articles as they needed.

On mentioning to this gentleman their design of visiting the Gaures, he dissuaded them in the strongest manner from making the attempt at that time, as the whole country was in a state of the greatest anarchy and distress. He told them that Nadir Shah, and after him the Affghans, had ransacked and plundered Kerman; that the Gaures in that quarter were a good, honest, industrious kind of people, but that most of them had either been massacred or expelled from the country; and that the roads to that place were still more dangerous, from the numerous gangs of robbers which infested them, than even those they had lately travelled. These representations of the English resident were confirmed from every quarter, and destroyed all the Brethren's hopes of being soon able to visit the Gaures. They might have settled at Ispahan in a medical capacity, with the fairest prospects of success, as the inhabitants of Persia have a very exalted idea of the learning and skill of physicians from Europe; but as they had no hope of being useful in their principal character as missionaries, they resolved to return to Cairo in Egypt, and there wait the advice of their Brethren.

In June 1748, the two missionaries left Ispahan; but they had not proceeded far on their journey, when the caravan was surprised and robbed by another gang of banditti. They now lost the third time every farthing they possessed, together with most of their clothes. In consequence of this, they came to Bender Buscher in rags and in debt; but here they found a friend in the Dutch agent, who took them under his care, kindly paid their debts, and forwarded them on their journey to Bussora. From thence they afterwards proceeded to Egypt; but while they were in that country, Rueffer died at Damietta, and was interred in the burying-ground of the Greeks.

In February 1750, Hocker, who was now deprived of his fellow-traveller, returned to Europe, after an absence of about three years. Thus terminated the plan of the Brethren for introducing the gospel among the Gaures in Persia.[1]

SECT. VII.—EGYPT.

In May 1752, Dr Hocker, who had returned from Persia two years before, proceeded to Egypt with the design of penetrating into Abyssinia. Among the various schemes of Count Zinzendorf, no one was more fondly cherished by him, or for a season more zealously prosecuted, than that of forming a spiritual connection or correspondence between the Church of the Brethren, and other sections of the Christian Church. His object in this was not so much to bring about a reformation of corrupt systems of faith, where these were found to exist, as to seek out and offer the right hand of fellowship to such among them, of whatever name or nation, as, while they kept connected with their respective churches, corrupt though they might be, adhered to the great doctrine of the Holy Scriptures, that salvation is to be obtained only through the merits of Christ, and that communion with him is the source of all true happiness. It was this wish that led him to entertain the idea of sending Brethren to open a communication with the Church of Abyssinia.

The plan of Hocker was to practise as a physician in Cairo, to seek to obtain the good-will of the Patriarch of the Copts, by whom the Abuna or metropolitan of Abyssinia is consecrated; and through him to form an acquaintance with the Abuna himself, and to offer him the services of the Church of the Brethren. Having presented to the Patriarch of the Copts a letter addressed to him by Count Zinzendorf, Hocker also

[1] Period. Accounts, vol. i. p. 381.

gave him a short account of the history and constitution of the Church of the Brethren, and of their wish to maintain friendly and brotherly intercourse with all the children of God, and so contribute to the fulfilment of the Saviour's prayer, that his followers might "all be one." He afterwards received from him an answer to Count Zinzendorf's letter, of which the following is an extract: "In the name of the merciful and gracious God. In God is salvation. From Mark,[1] the servant of the servants of the Lord. The peace of our Lord God, and the Captain of our salvation Jesus Christ, which he in an upper room at Zion poured forth upon the assembly of excellent disciples and apostles. May he pour out this peace upon the beloved, excellent, and experienced brother, the venerable Bishop our Father Aloysius,[2] the liturgist of the Unity of the Brethren. This is to testify, Beloved Brother, that the blessed son and venerable deacon, Irenæus[3] Hocker, has delivered unto us your letter, which was full of affectionate cordial love. We have read it; and it became unto us a taste of your love to all Christians. We, in like manner, pray God for you, and for all the Christian people, that he may exalt the glory of the Christians in the whole habitable world, through the nutrition of his life-giving cross."[4]

In December 1753, Dr Hocker proceeded to Constantinople with the view of providing himself with a firman or pass from the Grand Seignior, as there was no way of entering Abyssinia but by the Red Sea, the ports of which were all in the hands of the Turks, who would scarcely allow a European to enter them without orders from Court. Besides a firman from the Grand Seignior, he obtained recommendatory letters from the Grand Vizier to Ibrahim Kiaga, one of the most powerful Turkish officers in Egypt, and to the Pasha of Jidda, and likewise a letter of recommendation from the English Ambassador to the Prime Minister of Abyssinia; but before he was able to

[1] The Patriarchs of the Copts, who have also the title of Patriarchs of Alexandria, Jerusalem, Abyssinia, and Nubia, are all called after the Evangelist Mark, who is considered as the founder of the Church of Alexandria. This was Mark the hundred and sixth.

[2] Lewis, *i.e.* Count Zinzendorf.

[3] Frederic, or, in German, Freidrich, *i.e.* Rich in peace.

[4] Crantz's Hist. Breth. p. 433; Period. Accounts, vol. xii. p. 97.

carry his design into execution, both the Grand Seignior and Ibrahim Kisga died, in consequence of which the firman of the one, and the letter to the other, were of no use. Travelling was also rendered very unsafe by the banditti which infested the country; even in the neighbourhood of Cairo persons were in danger of being plundered. Egypt being in such a disturbed and unsettled state, Hocker resolved to return to Germany and receive instructions in regard to his future procedure.[1]

In May 1756, Dr Hocker set out again for Egypt, and was accompanied by George Pilder, who had been employed in the Theological Seminary of the Brethren, and was considered a man of learning. After their arrival in Cairo, they heard a report of great changes having taken place in Abyssinia; that the king was dead, and his son, who was only seven years old, had ascended the throne under the guardianship of his mother; that all the Roman Catholics and the Greeks who had been invited into the country by the former sovereign were expelled; and that the prime minister himself, to whom Hocker had received a letter of recommendation from the English ambassador at Constantinople, was disgraced, so that it could now be no longer of any use to him. In short, the country seemed shut against all foreigners; but yet the Brethren did not despair of being enabled to carry forward their design. They obtained from the Patriarch of the Copts a recommendation to the Abuna of Abyssinia, John the 137th. In this letter there occurs the following sentence, "Suffer me to recommend to you this blessed man, both for the sake of Him who said, 'I was a stranger and ye took me in,' and likewise out of love to me," language which appears to shew that in the Coptic, as in the Romish and other fallen churches, the phraseology of piety is retained while the spirit thereof is gone.

In September 1758, the Brethren, after many delays, set off for Abyssinia. Having crossed the country to Suez, they embarked on board a small Turkish vessel on the Red Sea, and after a tedious voyage of eleven days they anchored near the island of Hassane. On the following night there arose a violent storm from the south-east, which drove the vessel toward the coast; and the cable of one of the anchors having snapped, the

[1] Crantz's Hist. Breth. p. 435; Period. Accounts, vol. xii. p. 141.

Turkish boatmen who were employed to let down the largest anchor with a fresh cable, lowered two of the boats into the water and escaped to the island. About midnight the ship was stranded, and was expected every moment to upset. In a short time the main-mast broke and went overboard, carrying with it part of the deck. Meanwhile the sailors were continually calling to the Arabs on shore to bring out boats to save their lives; and at length, after sunrise, a boat did come out and conveyed all on board from the ship, but as it never approached nearer the shore than musket-shot, they were obliged to wade up to their shoulders in the water to reach the land. Besides their ship, there were other vessels wrecked on the island; indeed only two escaped. On the following days the unfortunate shipwrecked people endeavoured to get on board these two vessels that they might not be plundered or die of hunger on this barren and inhospitable island, as many others had done before them. The Brethren also endeavoured to get on board, but they were always refused admission. Nineteen days they had to remain on the island along with others, their companions in misfortune, and suffered much during that time from the treachery and rapacity of both the Greeks and the Arabs, as well as from the want of provisions and even of fresh water. Having found at length an opportunity of escaping from the island, they proceeded to the port of Jidda on the coast of Arabia. Here they received an unexpected visit from two Turkish merchants, who had been commissioned by the Regent of Abyssinia to search for a European physician, and to bring him to Gondar, with a view to the cure of the prime minister, who was labouring under a cutaneous affection of the face. They asked Dr Hocker to return with them; but, after taking the subject into consideration, he declined the proposal, chiefly on account of the loss of all his medicines by their late shipwreck, and the improbability of obtaining suitable remedies in Abyssinia. He stated, at the same time, that they did not give up their design of going thither next year, but begged that a written invitation, from the proper authority, might be sent to him to Cairo. They accordingly set out on their return to Egypt, and after passing through many dangers they arrived at Cairo. Pilder was obliged, on account of his health, to return to Europe;

and after some time,[1] Hocker followed him, without having carried into effect his purpose of penetrating into Abyssinia.[2]

Dr Hocker, however, was not discouraged by these repeated disappointments, and resolved not to abandon the undertaking. He hoped that, in the patient exercise of his medical profession, a door might at length be opened for promoting the interests of religion, if not in Abyssinia, at least in Egypt.

In September 1768, he accordingly set off again for Cairo, accompanied by John Henry Danke, another of the Brethren. On their arrival they found the whole country in a state of great confusion, in consequence of the attempt of Ali Bey to mount the throne of Egypt, and to erect it into an independent kingdom. They were not, however, long in the country, when they became acquainted, through the Coptic Patriarch, with the new Abuna of Abyssinia, John the 138th, who inquired whether they would not accompany him to that country; but Hocker excused himself on the ground of his age, requesting the Abuna's favour to his successors, which he promised to shew them.[3]

In October 1769, Mr John Antes, one of the Brethren, who was appointed to join the missionaries in Egypt, sailed from London; and after a voyage of about seven weeks, arrived at Larnica, in the island of Cyprus. Not being able to obtain a passage from that place to Egypt, he at length heard there was a vessel at Limasol, a port about fifteen leagues to the westward, bound for Alexandria; and though he was then very ill of an ague which he had caught immediately after his arrival, he crept out of bed, packed up his luggage during the paroxysm of the fever, and prepared to take his departure. As his conductor spoke no language but Greek, the English consul procured him a muleteer who understood Italian to carry his luggage and provisions. He cautioned him, however, against his very guides, telling him they would murder their own parents if they could make any thing by it. The muleteer, in particular, had so much the aspect of a villain, that Mr Antes charged a pair of pocket pistols before his eyes, and placed them in his belt, to shew the fellow he was perfectly on his guard.

[1] In 1761. [2] Period. Accounts, vol. xii. p. 189; vol. xx. p. 391.
[3] Crantz's Hist. Breth. p. 615; Period. Accounts, vol. xii. p. 196.

Thus equipped, he left Larnica in the dusk of the evening; but he had scarcely proceeded a mile, when it began to rain most furiously, attended with vivid flashes of lightning, and frequent peals of thunder. As he was but imperfectly sheltered from the storm in his Turkish dress, he threw a bed-quilt which he had in his saddle over his head, and was thus led in a manner blindfolded, entirely at the mercy of his guides. After they had travelled three or four hours through a desert country, the muleteer, who had the charge of the luggage and the greater part of the provisions, discovered among them a bottle of spirituous liquor, with which he made so very free, that he lost the command of his mule, and the animal, taking advantage of this circumstance, ran back to the place from which it came with the whole of its cargo. As the other guide endeavoured to assist him in catching it, he likewise forsook Mr Antes, who, from the manner in which he was covered, did not discover his solitary situation until after some time he no longer heard his companions following him. He then uncovered himself; but it was so extremely dark, that except at short intervals, by means of the flashes of lightning, he could see nothing even at the distance of a yard. He now dismounted, and tied his mule by the bridle to some brushwood near the path, which was only like a sheep's track, and began to walk back, in the hope of finding at least one of his guides; but reflecting on the little probability there was of success, he returned to the place where he left his mule, generally feeling the road, except when he obtained a glance of it by means of the lightning. When at last he got near the spot, the animal gave a sudden spring, broke loose from the brushwood, and ran away; but as it had come from Limasol, it of course followed the road to that place. After standing a considerable time, he perceived, by means of the lightning, a person coming towards him mounted on an ass; but he soon discovered with regret it was neither of his guides. The stranger, on approaching him, muttered something in Greek; but not finding himself understood, he proceeded on his journey. After Mr Antes had remained long in a state of painful suspense, his conductor returned; but as neither knew the language of the other, he could give him no information about his luggage. On learning, however, that his mule had run away, the poor fellow dismounted from his own beast, and made him get upon it, while he himself walked by his side, through deep mire, and under a constant rain. After some time, they discovered the runaway mule on the path before them, and were at length successful in catching it. About midnight, they reached a mud-built cottage, and knocked at the door. Never in his life was Mr Antes so happy to get under a roof; but on entering it, he found it was merely a shed, quite open on the other side. There was, however, a fire, and some men were lying on the ground around it. After he had taken a very hearty refreshment, the master of the house conducted him into a kind of room, furnished him with a great coat, and shewed him a place spread with a clean sheet, where he might take some rest. It was nothing but a large chest, yet hard as it was, he soon fell fast asleep, and rested most comfortably till about eight o'clock next morning, when his guide came in and made signs for him to rise and prepare for his journey.

The day was extremely cold and disagreeable. What had fallen in rain, the night before, in the valley, proved to be snow on Mount Olympus and the neighbouring hills. The sea also was still greatly agitated in consequence of the late storm, a circumstance which proved very harassing to our travellers. About three miles from the village where they had lodged, the road ran along the sands; and as the coast was perpendicular like a wall, and the waves rolled close on the shore, their legs were completely drenched in the water, which often reached even to the bellies of their mules. In this manner they travelled from morning till about four o'clock in the afternoon. Mr Antes was so distressed that he almost gave himself up for lost, not thinking he was able to stand the wet and cold any longer. He, at length, however, plucked up courage, in the hope of warming himself by walking, as soon as they got clear of the waves. The moment this was the case, he alighted from his mule, but he soon found that he had not taken the exhausted state of his body into account, for after walking two or three hundred yards, he felt himself unable to proceed further, and was obliged, with the assistance of his guide, to mount his mule again. About nine o'clock at night, they arrived at Limasol, at the house of a Greek who acted as English consul at that place.

Two days after, the muleteer likewise arrived, with the articles committed to his charge, except only a few trifles which he had purloined.

After waiting about a week at Limasol, Mr Antes embarked for Egypt, and in five days reached Alexandria; but as the plague had begun to make its appearance in that city, he hastened away as quickly as possible to Rosetta. The voyage from thence to Cairo is usually performed in three or four days; but in this instance, it occupied no fewer than eighteen. Besides, at that time, it happened to rain very heavily, as it often does in the lower parts of the Delta, in the winter season. The vessel in which Mr Antes had embarked was old and crazy, and as the deck was far from watertight, the rain penetrated freely through it, so that he could not sit dry even in the cabin. In a short time his very bed began to moulder under him, and he was obliged to suspend it with a cord, to allow the water to run off underneath. Even his provisions ran short. His janissary, or guide, had provided sufficient victuals for an ordinary voyage of five or six days, consisting of bread, fowls, and other articles; but as it was protracted so long, the bread by degrees became mouldy, and all the fowls were consumed. Besides, the wind was often so contrary and so boisterous, that they repeatedly lay at anchor before some paltry village for four or five days together. When the sailors were urged to exert themselves, they always exclaimed: "It is from God! It is so written in the book of fate!" At length they arrived before Bulac, the harbour of Grand Cairo, where, as if to complete their misfortunes, the vessel stranded on a sandbank in the middle of the river, nor were they, with all their efforts, able to move her. Mr Antes, however, got ashore in a boat, and proceeded to the house of his Brethren Hocker and Danke, who gave him a most cordial reception after all his toils.[1]

In January 1773, Mr Bruce, the celebrated traveller, who had penetrated into Abyssinia about four years before, returned safe to Cairo. As the Brethren were sent to Egypt chiefly with the view of visiting that country, they made various inquiries at him concerning the character of the inhabitants, their govern-

[1] Antes' Observations on the Manners and Customs of the Egyptians, p. 55; Period. Accounts, vol. v. p. 159.

ment, religion, manners, and customs ; but from the account he gave them, they perceived, that unless some great revolution took place, it would be vain to think of establishing a mission in a kingdom so bigoted to its own faith, and so torn by anarchy and intestine divisions. Mr Bruce informed them, that the hatred of the people to all Europeans, and especially to their priests, was so great, that they would stone a missionary to death the moment he opened his lips on the subject of religion; that though he himself had employed various means to avoid suspicion, it was with the utmost difficulty he had escaped persecution on account of his creed, and even this would have been altogether impracticable, had he not constantly resided at Court, and been protected by the king himself. These representations, which were afterwards confirmed by several Abyssinians themselves, destroyed all the hopes of the Brethren of being able to promote the interests of religion in that distracted country.[1]

In the mean while, the Brethren, as they had little prospect of penetrating into Abyssinia, endeavoured to render themselves useful in Egypt. With this view, Danke made repeated visits to the Copts in Upper Egypt, particularly in the town of Behnesse and the neighbouring villages. In his intercourse with them, he appears to have studied to insinuate himself into their good graces, by the mildness and kindness of his behaviour toward them ; and they, on the other hand, seem to have been so far won on by his gentle manners, as to treat him, or at least to make a shew of treating him, in a corresponding spirit. He did not directly attack their unscriptural dogmas and superstitious ceremonies ; but he endeavoured silently to undermine their confidence in them, by pointing them to the sufferings and death of Christ as the only foundation of hope for a guilty creature, and representing to them the happiness of living in daily communion with God. Though many of them entertained considerable suspicions of his orthodoxy, particularly on the subject of fasting, yet, in general, they heard him with attention, and some even professed to approve of his views ; but this arose partly from their inability to controvert the truth, and partly from their disposition to flattery. Danke was so far deceived by these appearances, that he formed favourable

[1] Period. Accounts, vol. v. p. 164.

hopes of many of them, and imagined that his instructions had been useful to them ; but he afterwards discovered with sorrow, that these expectations were without foundation.[1]

During the residence of the Brethren in Egypt, the country was in a state of the greatest anarchy and confusion: sometimes one party, sometimes another prevailed. In consequence of these frequent changes, there was nothing like the administration of justice in the land. The rulers themselves were guilty of the greatest oppressions, both toward their own people, and to such Europeans as were resident in the country.[2]

In November 1779, Mr Antes had the misfortune to fall into the hands of one of the Beys, who, in the hope of extorting money from him, treated him in a most barbarous manner. As his occupation was chiefly of a sedentary nature, he found it necessary, for the sake of his health, to take frequent exercise in the open air, especially as the place of his residence was in a close insalubrious part of the town. On this account he often went into the fields ; but the heat of the climate was so enervating, that when he had no particular object to call forth his activity, he was always inclined to sit down and rest himself under the shade of a tree, by which means the chief aim of his walk was frustrated. To remedy this, he sometimes took a fowling-piece with him, particularly in winter, when there was commonly plenty of game, which the inhabitants of every description are at perfect liberty to shoot, as the Turks are too indolent to fatigue themselves with that exercise. To meet the Beys, however, or other men in power, was dangerous, as they were always ready, under some pretext or other, to extort money, especially from Europeans, whom they generally supposed to be rich ; but as they commonly had a numerous train with them, it was easy from the flatness of the country, to observe them at a considerable distance, and to avoid them. In this way, Mr Antes had eluded them for many years ; but one day when he was out on this diversion, in company with the secretary of the Venetian consul, he and his companion were observed by some Mamelukes belonging to one Osman Bey, as they were returning home. The Bey himself and his train were

[1] Fortsetzung Brud. Hist. tom. i. p. 165; Period. Accounts, vol. xi. p. 296, 299, 307.

[2] Fortsetzung Brud. Hist. tom. i. p. 381.

near at hand; but they were concealed from their view by some hillocks of rubbish, which are very numerous all around Cairo, several of which are so high as to overlook almost the whole city. Two of the Mamelukes immediately rode up toward them at full gallop, with drawn swords in their hands, followed by others on foot. They instantly stripped them of their fur coats, shawls, and whatever else of value they had about them, and demanded, at the same time, one hundred maktubs, or Turkish zechins, each in value about seven shillings and sixpence, threatening to carry them before their master unless they immediately complied with their wishes. Mr Antes told them they had no such sum about them, and taking out his purse offered it to them. They at first took it, but finding it contained only about twenty-five shillings, in small silver pieces, they threw it back again with disdain, crying, "Da Sikab," that is, gold. As he knew he had nothing to expect from them but ill treatment, he told them he had no gold upon him, but if they would go home with him, he would give them some. Upon this they cursed and swore, not being at liberty to leave their master. Meanwhile ten more of the Mamelukes came up on horseback, and repeated the same demand of gold, enforcing it with the threat of carrying him before the Bey if he refused to comply. Mr Antes again answered, that he had none upon him, but he would give them some if they would go with him. At last the principal man among them said: "Go you home and fetch your gold; but we will keep your companion here, and if you do not speedily return, we will cut off his head." As the poor Venetian, who could not speak a word of Arabic, was overwhelmed with fear and trembling, Mr Antes could not think of leaving him in the hands of these merciless barbarians, and therefore he generously replied, that his friend might go and bring the money, but that he would remain with them. He had scarcely, however, advanced a few steps, when the servants fell upon him, and stripped him of the few clothes he had left, so that he was obliged to fly nearly naked into the city. By this time the sun had set, and as the Mamelukes durst not stay away from their master till the Venetian could return, one of them rode up to the Bey, and told him they had seized a European from whom some money might be obtained. As the fellow soon returned with an order to bring the prisoner before him, they placed him between their horses, and dragged him to the place where the Bey was sitting with his train about him. Mr Antes, on approaching the chief, addressed him with the usual salutation: "I am under your protection." To this, unless they are wickedly inclined, they commonly reply: "You are welcome." But the Bey, instead of answering him, stared furiously at him, and asked: "Who are you?" "I am an Englishman," replied Mr Antes. "What are you doing here in the night?" said the tyrant: "You must be a thief. Aye, aye, most likely the one who did such a thing the other day." To this Mr Antes answered: "I was entering the city half an hour before sunset, when I was seized by your Mamelukes, and detained till now, when, indeed, it is dark, but yet not an hour after sunset, the regular time for shutting the gates." Without making any reply, the Bey ordered one of his officers to carry him to the castle, a building at some distance from the town, situated in an extensive sandy plain, where most of the Beys had houses, and exercised their Mamelukes.

Every month, one of the Beys in rotation took his station at this place, in order to guard the city by night against the depredations of the wandering Arabs; and it so happened that this was the turn of Osman Bey. Before he was removed, Mr Antes wished to say a few words more in his own behalf; but he was prevented by a horde of servants, who are always glad of an opportunity to insult a European. One spat in his face, two others kicked him on the side, while another put a rope about his neck made of the filaments of the date-tree, which is much rougher than horse-hair. By this rope, a fellow in rags was ordered to drag him along, and another on horseback, armed with a sword and pistol, to guard him. In their way to the castle, they passed a gentle slope, with a large garden, surrounded by a mud-wall on the left; and as the garden here consisted chiefly of irregular plantations of orange, lemon, and other prickly trees, through which no horse can pass, it occurred to Mr Antes, that he might cut the rope by which he was held, and escape over the wall; but on searching for his knife, he found it was gone. Soon after, the fellow in rags advised him to give money to the guard, who would then let him escape. At the sound of the word *Money*, the guard instantly came galloping up to him, and asked, whether he had any left. Mr Antes replied that he would give him what he had if he would let him go; and accordingly he gave him the purse which the Mamelukes had refused. Having looked at it, the rascal put it into his pocket without saying a word, but still drove him forward to the castle. Here Mr Antes was thrown into a dungeon, half under ground; a large iron chain was put about his neck, secured at one end by a padlock, and fastened at the other to a piece of timber. In about half an hour the Bey himself arrived with his retinue, lighted flambeaux being carried before him. He alighted, walked up stairs into a room, sat down in a corner, while his people placed themselves in a circle round him. Mr Antes was then sent for, unchained, and led up to the chamber by two men. In going up stairs, he heard the rattling of the instruments used for the bastinado, and immediately guessed what was before him. On entering the room, he found a small neat Persian carpet spread for him, which was in fact a piece of civility, for the common people when about to receive the bastinado, are thrown on the bare ground. After asking him a question or two, the Bey exclaimed, "Throw him down." Mr Antes then inquired what he had done. "How, you dog," answered the tyrant, "dare you ask what you have done? Throw him down." The servants immediately threw him flat on his face, and with a strong staff, about six feet long, having a piece of an iron chain fixed to both ends, confined his feet above the ankles. Two of them, one on each side, then twisted the staff and chain together, so as to turn up the soles of his feet; and being provided with what is called a corbage, which consists of a strap of the skin of the hippopotamus, about a yard in length, somewhat thicker than a man's finger, and very tough and hard, they waited for the orders of their master. When they had placed him in this position, an officer came and whispered in his ear, "Do not suffer yourself to be beaten; give him a thousand dollars, and he will let you go." Mr Antes, however, reflected, that should he now offer any thing, the Bey would probably send one of his men with him to receive it, and that he would be obliged to open, in the presence of this officer, his strong chest, in which he kept not only his own money, but considerable sums belonging to others, which he had received in payment for goods belonging to different merchants, and that the whole of this would, in all probability, be taken from him. Being determined, therefore, not to involve others in his misfortunes, he said, "Mafish," that is, "No money;" upon which the Bey immediately ordered the servants to strike. They laid on at first pretty moderately; but yet Mr Antes gave himself up for lost, considering that his life was in the hands of a capricious tyrant, to whose unrelenting cruelty many others had fallen a sacrifice. Having therefore no other refuge, he commended his soul into the hands of his Heavenly Father, and he experienced his gracious support on this trying occasion, in so remarkable a manner, that the fear of death was entirely taken away. After they had beaten him for some time, the officer, probably supposing that he might now have become more tractable, again whispered in his ear the word money, but now the sum was doubled. Mr Antes again answered, "I have none here." They then laid on more roughly than before; every stroke was like the application of a red hot poker. At last the officer, thinking that, though he had no money, he might have some valuable goods, once more whispered in his ear something to that effect. As Mr Antes knew that English fire-arms often attract their fancy even more than money, he offered them an elegant blunderbuss, richly mounted with silver, which he could get without opening his strong chest. The Bey having inquired what he said, the officer answered with a sneer, "Only a blunderbuss." To this the tyrant replied, "Beat the dog." They now began to lay on with all their might. The pain was at first excruciating beyond conception, but after some time all sensation ceased; it seemed only like beating a bag of wool. When the Bey at length perceived that no money could be extorted from him, he probably thought that the prisoner might after all be a poor man, and therefore ordered them to take him away. Upon this they loosed his feet; but yet he was obliged to walk down to the dungeon with the chain about his neck. In about half an hour, a messenger came with orders to bring him up again. The servants now took off the chain, and after carrying him till he was near the door, told him to walk in or the Bey would beat him again. Mr Antes was afraid some one had told him, that with a little more beating, money might be obtained from him. There are instances, indeed, of the bastinado being repeated for three days successively, to the number of one or two thousand strokes. Persons of very vigorous constitutions may still perhaps survive; but in general, after five or six hundred strokes, the blood gushes from the mouth and nose, and the unhappy wretch dies either under the torture, or immediately after.

When Mr Antes entered the chamber, the Bey said to one of his officers, "Is this the man of whom you told me?" The fellow having stepped up to the prisoner, and stared him in the face, as if narrowly to inspect his features, on a sudden lifted up his hand, and exclaimed, "By Allah, it is! Why, this is the best man in all Cairo, and my particular friend. Oh! how sorry am I that I was not here before to tell you so," with other expressions of a similar kind. To this the Bey replied, "Then take him. I give him to you; and if he has lost any thing, see to get it restored." Mr Antes had never in his life seen the officer before; and he soon perceived that the whole was merely a trick to get rid of him in a decent manner, and to put a little money into the pocket of his pretended deliverer. He was obliged to walk once more till he was out of the Bey's sight, when the servants of his "particular friend" took him up and carried him to his house, which was at a considerable distance. Here the officer gave him something to eat, and made him a tolerably decent bed, which was the more welcome to him, as he had lost most of his clothes, and felt extremely cold. Mr Antes asked him, Whether what he had suffered was a proof of the boasted hospitality of his countrymen to strangers? but he got only the usual answer, "It is from God! It is so written in the book of fate, which cannot be altered!" After the officer had anointed his feet with balsam, and tied some rags about them, Mr Antes lay down to rest, but spent a very uncomfortable night, suffering, as might naturally be expected, most exquisite pain. In the morning, the artful fellow asked him, Whether he was acquainted with the master of the customs; and being answered in the affirmative, he offered to carry him to his house. Having set him on an ass, while he himself mounted a horse, they proceeded toward the city, accompanied by another soldier. On approaching the gate, the officer told him to take off his rags, as it would be a disgrace to him to ride into the town in that condition. "No disgrace to me," said Mr Antes, "but to him who has treated me so shamefully." "It is from God," was the answer of the officer. On arriving at the master of the customs' house, Mr Antes requested that person to settle every thing for him with his pretended deliverer; and on summing up the fees, it was found that he had about £20 to pay for this piece of service. Being then carried home, he was put to bed, and was confined to it for about six weeks, before he could walk even on crutches; and for more than three years after, his feet and ankles, which had been greatly hurt by the twisting of the chain, were very liable to swelling.[1]

In May 1783, the mission to Egypt, which the Brethren had prosecuted with so much patience and perseverance, was at length given up. Their residence in that country was attended with so much danger; their labours among the Copts were accompanied with so little success, and their prospect of being able to penetrate into Abyssinia was so small, that it was deemed inexpedient to persist any longer in so hopeless an undertaking.[2]

SECT. VIII.—LABRADOR.

In May 1771, Jens Haven, Christian L. Drachart, Stephen Jensen, and a number of other Brethren, sailed from England with the view of establishing a mission on the coast of Labrador. Within the last twenty years, the Brethren had made repeated attempts to commence a mission in that country, but it was not accomplished until now.[3] The place fixed on for a

[1] Antes' Observations, p. 115; Period. Accounts, vol. v. p. 169, 171, 174.

[2] Fortsetzung Brud. Hist. tom. i. p. 382.

[3] When on occasion of a previous visit, Drachart read to some of the Esquimaux a written declaration of friendship in the name of the governor of Newfoundland, they would on no account receive the paper into their hands, from an apprehension that there was something living in it, which might afterwards do them injury, since it communicated the thoughts of a man at a distance, which they imagined must be the effect of sorcery. The Esquimaux were not alone in their wonder at men communicating their thoughts by means of writing. Richard Baxter says, "When the Indians first

settlement was in the 57° North Latitude, and was called by them Nain. Having brought with them the materials of a framed house, they began immediately on their arrival to erect it; but with all their exertions, they had difficulty enough to finish it before the commencement of winter, which in Labrador is uncommonly severe. Though they kept large fires night and day, yet the windows and walls of their house were all the winter covered with ice, and their very bed-clothes froze to the wall. In this inhospitable region they were able to procure very little provisions, and as the ship with supplies did not arrive till near the beginning of winter the following year, their situation was exceedingly trying. Two pieces of meat were all they had left; and they could expect little or no help from the Esquimaux, as they were so improvident that they themselves were often reduced to the greatest straits. They had, however, collected a quantity of berries from the hills, dried them, and laid them up in store for the winter. Such was the situation of the Brethren when the arrival of the vessel with provisions relieved their distress. "Had you seen," said they, "the joy which reigned among us when we heard that the ship had arrived, you would certainly never forget it. We had given up all hope of her this season, and had devoted ourselves to extreme poverty; but yet we cannot say that a dejected spirit prevailed among us. We had resolved to surrender ourselves up to all circumstances, trusting that He who had sent us hither, who has counted the hairs of our head, and without whose permission none of them can fall to the ground, would preserve us." [1]

From their first arrival the Brethren were treated by the Esquimaux in a friendly manner, and in a short time the most perfect confidence was established between them. No European would formerly have ventured alone among the savages, or have passed a night with them on any consideration whatever; but the missionaries travelled over the ice notwithstanding the se-

saw the use of letters by our English, they thought there was surely some spirit in them, that men should converse together by a paper."—*Baxter's Saints' Everlasting Rest*, London 1688, p. 615. Most people little think what a wonderful thing written language is.

[1] Crantz's Hist. Breth. p. 404; Cranz Fortsetzung der Hist. von Gronland, p. 288, 291, 297; Fortsetzung Brud. Hist. vol. i. p. 125; Brief Account of the Mission of the Brethren in Labrador, 1774, p. 3, 11, 27; Period. Accounts, vol. xvii. p. 410.

verity of the season, visited them in their winter-houses, and slept among them many nights successively. These visits the Esquimaux were not backward to return. When the weather permitted, many of them came to Nain in their sledges over the frozen sea, and as soon as the ice was gone they came in still greater numbers in their kajaks. At one time there were no fewer than thirty-six tents pitched in the neighbourhood of the missionary settlement, which must have contained upwards of three hundred persons. Such, indeed, was the confidence of the savages in the Brethren, that when they set off for the islands, they committed to them their most valuable goods, and often left even their wives and children under their care.[1]

In the mean while, the missionaries did not neglect the main object of their settlement in the country. Scarcely had they arrived when they began to make known the gospel to the savages; but here they had many difficulties to encounter. The Esquimaux were ignorant in a great measure of the first principles even of natural religion, so that there was little the Brethren could lay hold of to impress their consciences. They appeared, indeed, to have some idea of a Supreme Being who made the heavens and the earth, yet so feeble was the impression, that no traces of religious worship were discovered among them. Even of their own guilt and depravity they seemed to have little consciousness, for though they were the slaves of the most brutal passions, and committed all manner of sin with greediness, yet they had always at hand some apology for their conduct. The liars consoled themselves that they were not thieves; the thieves that they were not murderers; the murderers that they were not Kablunats, *i. e.* Europeans and other foreigners, to whom, it seems, they assign the chief place in the scale of criminals. When the Brethren represented to them some of the great truths of the gospel, they often expressed their wonder at what was told them; at other times they would listen to nothing of a religious nature.[2]

In 1774, Haven, Brasen, Lister, and Lehmann, four of the Brethren, undertook a voyage to the north with the view of exploring the coast, and selecting a spot for a second settlement, as Nain was not found a convenient place for the Esquimaux

[1] Brief Account of the Mission to Labrador, p. 9, 13, 22, 24. [2] Ibid. p. 9, 13, 23.

obtaining provisions. They embarked in a small vessel which had been sent to them for this purpose from Newfoundland. In every place which they visited they were received by the savages with great kindness, and were even entreated by them to come and settle among them. But though they accomplished the chief object of their voyage, they met with disasters, of which, happily, we have not many examples in the history of missions. On their return they were shipwrecked, and two of them lost their lives. It had snowed the whole night and was very cold. A brisk gale sprung up from the north-east, which led them to hope that they would soon reach Nain; but all at once they found themselves in shoal-water, and their little vessel struck on a rocky bottom, which, as they afterwards found, was dry at spring tide. The wind roared furiously, every wave dashed over their little bark, and the raging of the sea was rendered yet more terrible by the darkness of the night. They expected every moment that their vessel would go to pieces. The two sailors entreated them to take to the boat; but the Brethren represented to them the danger of braving so tempestuous a sea in a small boat, and that they would inevitably perish among the breakers on the coast, which it would be impossible to avoid in the darkness of the night. They therefore begged them to stay by the ship as long as possible; perhaps they might be able to stand out till daybreak, and should it even come to the worst, they had still the boat to betake themselves to. By two o'clock in the morning, the sloop had shipped so much water, that though the waves were rolling mountain-high, all were now convinced that it was time to leave it. They therefore drew the boat astern, and descending one by one down the anchor shaft, they all, nine in number, succeeded in getting into it, and oars being useless in such a sea, they let it run before the wind, which it did with incredible celerity. They attempted, but in vain, to get under the lee of different islands, and, as no other resource appeared left, they resolved to run the boat ashore, which was only about twenty yards distant, but was begirt with cliffs on which the waves were dashing furiously. They darted rapidly through them, when it struck on a sunken rock with such violence that they were all thrown from their seats, and it instantly filled with water. The captain and the two sailors threw themselves into the sea and swam ashore, and thence reached out an oar to assist the others to land. Lister and Haven succeeded, though with great difficulty, in laying hold of it, and got ashore; but Brasen and Lehmann found a watery grave. Those who had reached the land found themselves on a bare rock, half-dead with cold, the night so dark that they could not see about them, without shelter, without food, without any prospect of being able to leave this desolate spot. In the morning as the tide ebbed, they were rejoiced to see first the prow and then the stern of their boat rising out of the water: the keel too was entire, and though the sides were completely shattered, they contrived to lash some blankets which had come ashore, over the open spaces, sewing to them all the seal skins they could muster from their upper and nether garments, including even their boots. Having spent three days in making these miserable repairs, they embarked in this frail conveyance for Nain, and with the help of an Esquimaux party which they met with, they reached it in the evening in safety.[1]

In September 1776, Jens Haven proceeded, with three others of the Brethren, to establish a new settlement on a small island called Okkak, about 150 miles to the north of Nain; and six years afterwards, a third station was begun at a place to the south of Nain, which they called Hopedale. Okkak appeared to be one of the most eligible places in Labrador for a settlement; but Hopedale proved so unfruitful a field that the Brethren had afterwards thoughts of abandoning that part of the country. However, they persevered, and it is still one of their stations in Labrador.[2]

In March 1782, two of the missionaries, Samuel Liebisch and William Turner, experienced a very remarkable deliverance at sea; and though the details are lengthened, they are too interesting to be here omitted.

One morning, these two Brethren set off from Nain for Okkak, in a sledge driven by one of the converts, and were accompanied by another sledge of Esquimaux, containing two men, one woman, and a child.[3] All were in good spirits; and as the

[1] Period. Accounts, vol, xvii. p. 458.

[2] Fortsetzung Brud. Hist. tom. ii. p. 59; Period. Accounts, vol. i. p. 50.

[3] In Labrador, sledges are drawn by a species of dogs, somewhat similar to the wolf in

weather was clear, and the track over the frozen sea in the best order, they travelled with ease at the rate of six or seven miles an hour, so that they hoped to reach Okkak in the course of two or three days. After passing the islands in the bay of Nain, they kept at a considerable distance from the shore, both to gain the smoothest part of the ice, and to avoid the high rocky promontory of Kiglapeit. About eight o'clock they met a sledge with Esquimaux turning in from the sea; and after the usual salutations, the strangers, in the course of conversation, threw out some hints, that it might be as well for them to return. As the missionaries, however, saw no cause of alarm, and suspected that the travellers merely wished to enjoy the company of their friends a little longer, they proceeded on their journey. After some time, their own Esquimaux hinted that there was a ground swell under the ice. It was then scarcely perceptible, except on lying down and applying the ear close to the ice, when a hollow disagreeable grating noise was heard, as if ascending from the abyss. The sky, however, was still clear, except towards the east, where a bank of light clouds appeared, interspersed with some dark streaks; but as the wind blew strong from the north-west, nothing was less expected than a sudden change of weather.

The Brethren continued to pursue their journey till the sun had reached its height in the horizon, and as yet there was

shape; and, like that animal, they never bark, but howl disagreeably. They are kept by the Esquimaux in greater or smaller packs, according to the wealth of the individual. They quietly submit to be harnessed to the yoke, and are treated with no great mercy by the savages, who make them do hard duty, and at the same time allow them little food. This consists chiefly of offals, old skins, rotten whale fins, entrails, &c.: or should their master not be provided with these or similar articles, he leaves them to go and seek dead fish or mussels on the beach. When pinched with hunger, they will eat almost any thing; and on a journey, it is necessary to secure the harness during the night, lest by devouring it they should render it impossible to proceed in the morning. In the evening, after being unharnessed, they are left to burrow in the snow wherever they please; and in the morning they are sure to return at the call of the driver, as they then receive some food. In the harness, they are not allowed to go abreast, but are tied by separate thongs of unequal length, to an horizontal bar on the fore part of the sledge. An old knowing one leads the way, running ten or twenty paces before the rest, directed by the driver's whip, which is very long, and can be properly managed only by an Esquimaux. The others follow like so many sheep. If one of them receives a lash, he generally bites his neighbour, and the bite then goes round. Their strength and speed, even with an hungry stomach, are truly astonishing. —*Period. Accounts*, vol. iii. p. 226.

†

little or no change in the aspect of the sky. But as the motion of the sea under the ice had grown more perceptible, they became rather alarmed, and began to think it prudent to keep close to the shore. The ice also had cracks and large chasms in many places, some of them one or two feet wide; but as these are not uncommon, even in its best state, and the dogs easily leap over them, they are frightful only to strangers.

As soon, however, as the sun declined toward the west, the wind increased to a storm, the bank of light clouds from the east began to ascend, and the dark streaks to put themselves in motion against the wind. The snow was violently driven about by partial whirlwinds, both on the ice and from off the peaks of the neighbouring mountains. The ground-swell had now increased so much, that its effects on the ice were very extraordinary, as well as alarming. The sledges, instead of gliding smoothly along as on an even surface, sometimes ran with violence after the dogs, and sometimes with difficulty as if ascending a rising hill; for though the ice was many leagues square, and in some places three or four yards thick, yet the swell of the sea underneath gave it an undulatory motion, not unlike that of a sheet of paper accommodating itself to the surface of a rippling stream. Noises, too, were now distinctly heard in many directions, like the report of cannon, owing to the bursting of the ice at a distance.

Alarmed by these phenomena, our travellers drove with all haste toward the shore; but as they approached it, the prospect before them was awfully tremendous. The ice, having burst loose from the rocks, was tossed to and fro, and broken in a thousand pieces against the precipices with a dreadful noise, which, added to the raging of the sea, the roaring of the wind, and the drifting of the snow, so completely overpowered them, as almost to deprive them of the use both of their eyes and ears. To make the land was now the only resource that remained; but it was with the utmost difficulty the frightened dogs could be driven forward; and as the whole body of ice frequently sunk below the surface of the rocks, and then rose above it, the only time for landing was the moment it gained the level of the coast, a circumstance which rendered the attempt extremely nice and hazardous. Through the kindness of Providence, however, it succeeded. Both sledges gained the shore, and were drawn up on the beach, though not without great difficulty.

Scarcely had they reached the land, when that part of the ice from which they had just escaped burst asunder, and the water rushing up from beneath, instantly precipitated it into the ocean. In a moment, as if by a signal, the whole mass of ice, for several miles along the coast, and as far as the eye could reach, began to break and to be overwhelmed with the waves. The spectacle was awfully grand. The immense fields of ice rising out of the ocean, dashing against each other, and then plunging into the deep with a violence which no language can express, and a noise like the discharge of a thousand cannon, was a sight which must have struck the most stupid and unreflecting mind with solemn awe. The Brethren were overwhelmed with amazement at their miraculous escape; and even the Pagan Esquimaux expressed gratitude to God on account of their deliverance.

The Esquimaux now began to build a snow-house about thirty paces from the beach; and about nine o'clock at night, all of them crept into it, thankful for such a place of refuge, wretched as it was. Before entering it, they once more turned their eyes to the sea, and beheld, with horror mingled with gratitude, the enormous waves driving furiously before the wind, like so many huge castles, and approaching the shore, where, with tremendous noise, they dashed against the rocks, foaming and filling the air with the spray. The whole company now took supper, and after singing a hymn, they lay down to rest about ten o'clock. The Esquimaux were soon fast asleep; but Liebisch the missionary could get no rest, partly on account of the dreadful roaring of the storm, and partly on account of a sore throat, which occasioned him severe pain. Both the Brethren, indeed, were much engaged in thinking of their late miraculous deliverance; and with their thanksgivings, they mingled prayer for still further relief.

The wakefulness of the missionaries proved the deliverance of the whole party from destruction. About two o'clock in the morning, Liebisch perceived some drops of salt water fall from the roof of the snow-house on his lips. Though rather alarmed on tasting it, he lay quiet till the dropping became more frequent, and then, just as he was about to give the alarm, a tremendous surf, all of a sudden, broke close to the house, and discharged a quantity of water into it; a second quickly followed, and carried away the slab of snow which was placed as a door before the entrance. The Brethren immediately cried to the Esquimaux to rise and quit the place. Alarmed at the call, they jumped up in an instant. One of them with a large knife cut a passage through the side of the house, and each seizing some part of the baggage, threw it out on a higher part of the beach. They all immediately retreated to a neighbouring eminence; but scarcely had they reached it, when an enormous wave carried away the whole of the house.

Thus were they a second time delivered from imminent danger of destruction; but yet they suffered great distress during the remaining part of the night, as it was scarcely possible to stand against the wind, the sleet, and the snow. Before the dawn of the day, the Esquimaux cut a hole in the snow to screen the two missionaries, the woman, and the child. Liebisch, however, could not bear the closeness of the air, and was obliged to sit at the entrance, where they covered him with skins to keep him warm, as the pain of his throat was extremely severe. As soon as it was light, they built another snow-house, about eight feet square, and six or seven feet high; yet still their situation was far from comfortable.

The Brethren had taken no more provisions with them than what was thought sufficient to carry them to Okkak, and the Esquimaux had nothing at all. It was therefore necessary to divide their little stock into daily portions, especially as there was no prospect of their being soon able to quit this dreary place, and to reach the dwellings of man. There were only two ways in which this could be effected: either to attempt the passage across the wild unfrequented mountain Kiglapeit, or to wait for a new ice-track over the sea, and when that might form it was impossible to say. They, therefore, resolved to serve out no more than a biscuit and a half daily to each individual; and though their allowance was so small, they were all preserved in good health. Liebisch very unexpectedly recovered, on the first day, from his sore throat, owing probably to the low diet on which he was obliged to subsist.

Meanwhile, the Brethren at Nain, and especially the wives of the two missionaries, were thrown into a state of the utmost anxiety and alarm on account of our travellers. During the storm, they had felt considerable apprehension for their safety, though it was by no means so violent in that quarter, as the coast is there protected by islands. The Esquimaux, however, who had met them, and had warned them of the ground-swell, now threw out hints in their obscure ambiguous manner of their inevitable destruction. One of them, to whom Liebisch or Turner was indebted for some article of dress, came to the wife of the missionary, and said he would be glad of payment for the work. "Wait a little," answered she; "when my husband returns, he will settle with you, for I am unacquainted with the bargain between you." "Samuel and William,"[1] replied the Esquimaux, "will return no more to Nain." "How, not return! What makes you say so?" After some pause, he replied in a low tone of voice: "Samuel and William are no more! All their bones are broken, and in the stomachs of the sharks." So sure was he of their destruction, that it was with difficulty he was prevailed on to wait their return. He could not believe it possible that they could have escaped the storm, considering the course they were pursuing.

Anxious as the two Brethren were to escape from their present dreary situation, yet of this there was little prospect. The weather had now cleared, and the sea, as far as the eye could reach, was so completely free of ice, that not a morsel was to be seen. One of the pagan Esquimaux, who was a sorcerer, suggested that it would be well to "try to make good weather;" but this was, of course, opposed by the missionaries, who told him that such heathenish arts were of no avail. They were now in such straits for provisions, that the Esquimaux one day ate an old sack made of fish-skin; and the next, they began to devour a filthy worn-out skin, which had served them for a mattress. Their spirits, too, began to sink; but they possess

[1] The names by which the two missionaries were known among the Esquimaux.

this convenient faculty, that they can go to rest whenever they please, and, if necessary, can sleep for days and nights together. Besides, as the temperature of the air was rather mild, this was a new source of uneasiness to them. The roof of the snow-house was melted by the warm exhalations of the inhabitants; and as this occasioned a continual dropping, every thing by degrees was so soaked with water, that there was not a dry thread about them, nor a dry place in which to lie.

Meanwhile, however, the sea had begun to freeze; and, in a short time, it acquired a considerable degree of solidity. The Esquimaux belonging to the other sledge now resolved to pursue their journey to Okkak; whilst the Brethren, after remaining six days in this miserable place, set off to return to Nain. Their Esquimaux driver ran all the way round the promontory of Kiglapeit, before the sledge, to find a good track; and, after travelling about three hours, they reached the bay, and so were out of danger. Here they made a meal of the remainder of their provisions; and then proceeded on their journey, without again stopping till about twelve o'clock at night, when they reached Nain, to the great joy of the whole settlement, and particularly of their own families.[1]

In December 1800, an event occurred, which, though less remarkable in its circumstances, was more disastrous in its consequences. One of the missionaries at Hopedale, named Reiman, who had gone out to procure some fresh provisions by shooting, never returned, nor was heard of more. In the evening his Brethren became much alarmed for his safety, particularly as the whole country was covered with ice, rain having fallen the day before upon the snow; and about seven o'clock they sent out four of the Esquimaux with muskets, to seek him, and to direct him toward them by the report of their guns; but they returned about break of day, without having seen or heard any thing of him. As soon, therefore, as it was light, the whole of the Brethren, together with all the Esquimaux, set off to renew the search. In several places, they discovered his footsteps in the snow, but these were soon lost on the ice; and though they persevered in the search for nine successive days,

[1] Period. Accounts, vol. iii. p. 226.

examining every place they could think of with the utmost anxiety, yet it was without success. On the approach of spring, they renewed the search, in order, if possible, to discover his remains; but this attempt also was of no avail. It was therefore impossible to determine in what manner he had perished, though of his death no doubt could remain.[1]

In June 1817, George Kmoch, J. Koerner, and J. C. Beck, embarked from London for Labrador. The two former had sailed the preceding year from Nain for Hopedale, but not being able to reach that settlement on account of the ice, they had come involuntarily to England, and were now returning to the scene of their labours. After a voyage of about a month, they met with large masses of ice, which were more than ordinarily abundant this season, and had a singularly picturesque appearance, especially when the atmosphere was clear, and the sun shone bright upon them. As the icebergs floated along, they assumed a great variety of forms, some resembling towers, castles, walls; others churches, waggons, and animals of various descriptions. When they or the ship changed positions, the same object acquired quite a new appearance: what before seemed a church, now looked like some huge monster of the deep. After sailing about for a fortnight amidst fields and mountains of ice, they encountered a furious storm from the north-east. Before them was an immense iceberg, to which they were driving with great velocity, without the power of avoiding it: there was at the same time a large field of ice near them to which they fastened their grapnels, so that they were in imminent danger of being crushed to pieces between them. Providentially, however, they passed the iceberg without sustaining any material injury: had they touched it they would have been wrecked in an instant. The following night was dreadfully dark: the heaven was covered with the blackest clouds; the sea was agitated by a furious wind; while the crashing of the fields and mountains of ice against each other, added to the terror of the scene. The storm, indeed, dispersed the ice, and made openings in several places; but this only rendered their situation more perilous, as when they got into

[1] Period. Accounts, vol. iii. p. 8.

clear water, the motion of the ship became more rapid, and the blows from the icebergs more violent. The shocks were repeated every five or ten minutes, and appeared continually increasing in violence. To describe all the terrors of this anxious night is impossible. As often as a field of ice was perceived through the gloom, they apprehended the vessel would be shattered to pieces, and themselves consigned to a watery grave. After remaining full ten hours in this dreadful situation, they found themselves in clear water not far from the coast. They could scarcely believe they had got rid of the ice: all seemed like a dream. But their difficulties and dangers were not yet at an end. Though at no great distance from Hopedale, they had to sail nearly three weeks longer amidst icebergs, rocks, and islands, now pleasing themselves with the hope of reaching that settlement, when they found an opening in the sea; then meeting with disappointment, when they discovered that the passage was still completely blocked up. At length, after a most difficult and dangerous voyage, they arrived at that place in safety.[1]

In April 1830, the Brethren commenced a fourth station, which they called Hebron, at a place about sixty miles to the north of Okkak. The frame-work of houses and other building materials, prepared partly in Europe and partly at Okkak, were transported to this place, which greatly facilitated the establishment of the settlement, though the Brethren who were engaged in the undertaking had a great deal of labour before the various houses and the church were finished. It is not unworthy of mention, that the sledges employed in conveying building materials and provisions from Okkak to Hebron performed no fewer than 105 journeys. Such is the inconvenience attending imperfect modes of conveyance. In England or America, the whole would probably have been carried at once in two or three waggons. The sledges travelled over the frozen sea; and it is worthy of notice, that they seldom spent more than one day on the road, though the distance was about eighty or ninety miles. The strength and perseverance of the Esquimaux dogs are truly admirable.[2]

[1] Period. Accounts, vol. vi. p. 270, 397.

[2] Ibid. vol. xi. p. 363, 375, 377; vol. xii. p. 311; vol. xvii. p. 177.

In 1852, the following were the numbers connected with the Brethren's congregations in Labrador:—

Begun.	Stations.	Communicants.	Baptized Adults.	Baptized Children.	TOTAL.
1771	Nain	92	85	118	295
1776	Okkak	178	67	168	413
1782	Hopedale . . .	60	56	99	215
1830	Hebron . . .	85	66	117	268
		415	274	502	1191[1]

The Brethren long laboured in Labrador amidst great difficulties and discouragements, and with little appearance of success. Numbers of the Esquimaux acquired some knowledge of the gospel, and were baptized and admitted to the Lord's Supper; but few of them, it was feared, were truly converted. Many a time were the missionaries grieved with their duplicity and hypocrisy; and, notwithstanding all the care and pains taken with them, they were ever ready to return to their old heathenish practices. About the beginning of the present century, there appeared something like a religious awakening among them; and from that period the gospel appeared to make evident progress among them, though that progress was often small, and at times seemed as if it were arrested by the temptations to which they were exposed, as well as through their own natural depravity. Among the circumstances which hindered the progress of religion among the Esquimaux, we may particularly mention the mode of life which they were constrained by the nature of their country to lead. As, like the Greenlanders, they depended chiefly on hunting and fishing for the means of subsistence, they were obliged to scatter themselves far and wide for this purpose during the summer months, and were thus removed for a considerable part of the year from under the watchful care of the missionaries, and from the daily means of grace.[2]

[1] Period. Accounts, vol. xxi. p. xxvi.

[2] Ibid. vol. iii. p. 332, 445, 451, 459; vol. xvi. p. 11; vol. xvii. p. 65, 67, 69, 212, 251; vol. xx. p. 121, 187.

The Esquimaux, particularly those in the two southern settlements, Nain and Hopedale, were also exposed to many evils from the Southlanders, both Europeans and natives, who have of late years been drawing nearer to the neighbourhood of these stations for the purposes of traffic. The traders from Europe and America not only circulated among them all manner of false and alarming reports, and endeavoured to destroy their confidence in the Brethren, but sought to shake their belief in the gospel itself, telling them there was no God and no Saviour, and acted as if they sought to be the patrons of murder, adultery, fornication, theft, intemperance, and every evil work.[1]

At all the stations schools were carried on, and the progress of the children in reading and writing was generally satisfactory. Some of their specimens of penmanship would have done no discredit to a European school. In arithmetic, however, they made little progress. In general, they were not able to proceed further than addition and subtraction. Few of them mastered the multiplication table. We suspect that savage tribes generally will be found defective in learning arithmetic. It appeared to be easy for Esquimaux children to commit any thing to memory; but where *thought* was required they were found wanting.[2]

Besides a spelling-book, a catechism, a summary of Christian doctrine, and a hymn-book,[3] the Brethren published a harmony of the four Gospels in the Esquimaux language; and a translation of the New Testament and of part of the Old has been printed at the expense of the British and Foreign Bible Society.

[1] Period. Accounts. vol. xii. p. 60, 67, 250, 257, 445, 449, 455; vol. xv. p. 104; vol. xviii. p. 14.

[2] Ibid. vol. xv. p. 114; vol. xvi. p. 226, 528.

[3] The last editions of the Esquimaux hymn-book contain about 700 hymns; a rare number in the language of a barbarous people.—*Period. Accounts*, vol. xv. p. 305.

SECT. IX.—NICOBAR ISLANDS.

IN 1756, a commercial establishment was begun by the Danes from Tranquebar on the Nicobar Islands, which are situated in the Bay of Bengal to the north of Sumatra, and it was intimated to the Brethren by a person of high rank at the Court of Denmark, that it would give His Majesty particular pleasure if some of them would settle as missionaries in that part of the world, and endeavour to convert the natives to the Christian faith. To this proposal they readily consented; and though intelligence was in the mean while received, that the attempt to establish a settlement on these islands had miscarried, and that almost all the colonists had died, yet they were not discouraged by these disastrous circumstances. It was judged proper, however, that they should have a settlement at Tranquebar, on the Coromandel coast, in order to carry on the mission in the Nicobar Islands from that quarter, as it did not appear advisable to establish a colony in so wild and distant a region, immediately from Europe. To this plan the Danish government readily gave its consent.

In November 1759, George J. Stahlman, Adam Voelcker, Christopher Butler, and eleven other Brethren of various occupations, sailed from Copenhagen for Tranquebar. Having on their arrival purchased a piece of ground about a mile from the town, they built themselves a house, together with some workshops and out-houses, wrought at their several trades, and met with good sale for the articles they made, at Tranquebar and the neighbouring Dutch and English settlements. This place they called *The Brethren's Garden*. For several years, however, they had no opportunity of making any attempt to introduce Christianity into the Nicobar Islands, as they were obliged to wait till the Danish East India Company should settle a colony on them.[1]

In 1768, the Danish government, after many delays, formed a new establishment on the Nicobar Islands, and six of the Brethren immediately went thither, and settled on one of them called Nancauwery. Several officers of the East India Company

[1] Crantz's Hist. Breth. vol. ii. p. 504, 507.

afterwards arrived from Tranquebar, with a party of soldiers and black servants, and brought with them a considerable quantity of merchandise. Most of them, however, died in a short time, so that at the end of eighteen months, only two European soldiers, and four Malabar servants, remained alive. This second failure deterred the Company from renewing the attempt; and thus the project of establishing a factory on the Nicobar Islands was abandoned. The four Brethren who still resided in the settlement were intrusted with the sale of such goods as remained; a commission from which they experienced no small inconvenience.[1]

In 1773, a vessel was sent from Tranquebar, which relieved them from this burden, by taking back such articles of trade as still remained on hand, the Company having resolved entirely to abandon the settlement. Though the Brethren at Tranquebar endeavoured to keep up intercourse with the missionaries in Nancauwery, and to send them supplies of the necessaries of life by ships sailing to the neighbouring coast, yet in their attempts for this end they were for the most part unsuccessful, it being often exceedingly difficult to make the Nicobar Islands on account of the contrary winds and currents. They were, therefore, obliged to charter vessels for this particular purpose, and in one or two instances succeeded in conveying supplies to them. But the difficulty of maintaining intercourse with them was never removed, as there was no regular trade with the Nicobar Islands, and even those ships which promised to touch at them, were seldom able to fulfil their engagement.[2]

In September 1778, John G. Haensel, and another of the Brethren named Wangeman, sailed from Tranquebar for the Nicobar Islands. Wangeman died not long after his arrival, and Haensel himself had not been three weeks on the island, when he was attacked by the seasoning fever, and was so ill that he was even thought to be dead, and preparations were made for burying him. He, however, recovered, but his recovery was extremely slow; and, indeed, during his residence on the Nicobar Islands he enjoyed but little health, never almost being

[1] Crantz's Hist. Breth. p. 614; Fortsetzung Brud. Hist. tom. i. p. 158.

[2] Fortsetzung Brud. Hist. tom. i. p. 356, 368, 372; tom. ii. p. 3; Haensel's Letters on the Nicobar Islands, p. 21.

free of ulcers in his legs; and to the end of his life, he had every fourth day a regular attack, in a greater or less degree, of intermittent fever, which no remedy nor any change of climate was ever able completely to remove.[1]

Besides clearing the land and planting it, in order to procure for themselves the necessaries of life, the Brethren endeavoured to lessen the expenses of the mission, by making collections of shells, serpents, and other natural curiosities, which they sent to Tranquebar for sale, as there was at that time a great demand for productions of this kind in various parts of Europe. Mr Haensel informs us, that whether he went into the woods or walked along the beach, whether he travelled by land or by water, he was accustomed to examine every object he saw, and acquired great facility in catching some of the most dangerous creatures, without any risk to himself. Far from being afraid of serpents, he went out purposely to discover their haunts in the jungles and among the rocks; and if he could only prevent them from slipping off into their holes, and irritate them so as to make them attempt to strike him, he was sure to gain his end. As a serpent in such circumstances bites whatever comes first in his way, he forthwith presented his hat to it, which the animal violently seized with its fangs; then instantly snatching it away, he seldom failed to extract them by the sudden jerk; for as they are curved, they cannot readily be withdrawn, and being loose in the gums, they are easily disengaged. He next laid hold on the creature, which was now in a great degree harmless, pinned down its head, and tied it up. It is necessary, however, to be very careful when preparing the heads and refixing the fangs of these reptiles, that you are not lacerated by their teeth, or injured in any other way; for it is a singular fact, that a wound inflicted in this manner, even long after their death, produces painful, and often fatal consequences.[2]

[1] Haensel's Letters, p. 18; Period. Accounts, vol. vi. p. 10.

[2] Haensel's Letters, p. 20, 35, 40.

At the Brethren's Garden near Tranquebar, Mr Haensel, after his return to that place, had a shop or work-room for the purpose of stuffing these and other animals, preserving them in spirits, or otherwise preparing them for sale; and he sometimes employed two or three Malabar boys to assist him. In the neighbourhood of that town there is a small serpent, called the Split-snake. It is black, with a white streak along its back, dividing the body longitudinally. Its bite is extremely venomous; and as it is a very slender creature, it can insinuate itself into the smallest hole or cranny. By

Mr Haensel, in his frequent excursions along the coast, was sometimes benighted, and could not conveniently return home; but in these circumstances he was never at a loss for a bed. The greater part of the beach consists of a remarkably fine white sand, which above the high-water mark is perfectly clean and dry. Into this he easily dug a hole large enough to contain his body, and he likewise formed a mound as a pillow for his head. He then lay down, and by collecting the sand over him, buried himself in it up to the neck. His faithful dog always lay across his body, ready to give the alarm in case of the smallest danger or disturbance. He was under no apprehension, however, from wild animals; crocodiles and kaymans never haunted the open coast, but confined themselves to creeks and lagoons, and there were no ravenous beasts on the island. He never suffered any annoyance unless from the nocturnal perambulations of an immense variety of crabs, the grating noise of whose armour

this means it often enters rooms and closets in quest of food, of which Mr Haensel gives the following example. "There was a door," says he, "in a dark part of my work-room, with a large clumsy lock upon it. One evening as I was attempting to open it, I suddenly felt a prick in my finger, and, at the same instant, a violent electrical shock, as if I were split asunder. Not thinking of a serpent, I at first imagined that my Malabar boys had, in their play, wound some wire about the handle, and that it was by this I was hurt; and therefore I asked them sharply what they had done to the door. They denied, however, that they had meddled with it; and when I made a second attempt to open it, I was attacked still more violently, and perceived the blood trickling down my finger. I then returned into my room and sucked the wound till I could draw no more blood from it; after which I applied to it some spirits of turpentine, and tied it up with a bandage; but being much hurried that evening with other business, I took no further notice of it. In the night, however, it swelled, and was extremely painful. In the morning, when I went into the workroom, I thought I felt an unpleasant musky smell; and on approaching the door already mentioned, the stench was altogether intolerable. I again asked the boys what nasty stuff they had brought into the room, for they were always playing themselves, but they still denied that they knew any thing about the matter. Having procured a candle, I then discovered the cause of all the mischief. About six inches of the body of a young split-snake hung out of the key-hole, perfectly dead; and on taking off the lock, I found the creature twisted into it, and so much wounded by the turn of the bolt, from my attempt to open the door, that it had died in consequence. It had been entering the room through the key-hole, when I thus accidentally stopped its progress and was bitten by it; and considering the deadly nature of the serpent's poison, I felt thankful to God, that, though ignorant of the cause of the wound, I applied proper remedies to it, in consequence of which my life was not endangered. I have been told that the bite of every serpent is accompanied, in a greater or less degree, by a sensation similar to an electrical shock. The name of split-snake which is given to this animal, we considered as descriptive not so much of its split appearance, as of the singular sensation occasioned by its bite."—*Haensel's Letters*, p. 40.

sometimes kept him awake. But they were well watched by his dog, and if any ventured to approach, they were sure to be seized by him and thrown to a more respectful distance; or if one of a larger size than ordinary deterred the dog from exposing his nose to its claws, he would bark and frighten it away. Haensel had many a comfortable sleep in these sepulchral dormitories, though in most parts of the East it would be exceedingly hazardous for a person to expose himself in this manner, on account of the number of wild beasts with which they abound.

Though the Brethren had little or nothing to dread from wild beasts on the Nicobar Islands, yet in their visits to other places they were sometimes in danger from them. On one of Mr Haensel's voyages, either to or from Queda, a Danish ship hailed the vessel, and approaching incautiously, ran foul of the stern and broke the flag-staff. Having put into a creek, some of the sailors landed near a wood to cut down a tree to make a new one. Mr Haensel accompanied them, armed with a double-barrelled gun, with the view of procuring some fresh meat for supper. While they were at work, he walked on the outside of the wood eagerly looking for some game, and soon discovered among the high grass an object which, by its motions, he mistook for the back of a hare. He immediately took aim, and was just going to fire, when the animal rose up and proved to be a tiger. Overcome with terror, his arm involuntarily sunk down; he stood perfectly motionless, expecting that the animal would instantly spring at him and tear him in pieces. Providentially, however, it seemed as much alarmed as himself, and after staring at him for a few seconds, turned slowly round, and began to creep away like a frightened cat with his belly close to the ground; then gradually quickening his pace, fled with precipitation into the distant recesses of the wood. It was some time before Mr Haensel recovered sufficient presence of mind to trace back his steps toward the beach, for his heart still trembled within him. As he approached the shore, there was a piece of jungle or low thicket before him, and he was turning to the left to pass round by the side opposite the boat, hoping he might yet find some game, when he observed the sailors labouring hard to drag the tree they had felled toward the water, and therefore he changed his course and went to their assistance.

No sooner had he entered the boat, than he discovered, on that side of the jungle to which he was first going, a large kayman watching their motions, and which he would certainly have met had he gone by the way he originally intended. Thankful as he was for this second deliverance, he could not help discharging his gun at the animal's head, and by the sudden plunge which it made into the water, and the appearance of blood on the surface as it was swimming to the opposite shore, it was evident the creature was wounded. He saw it reach the land and crawl through the mud into the jungle.[1]

After the officers and soldiers who had accompanied the Brethren to the Nicobar Islands were all dead, and it was known that the missionaries would not abandon their post, the government at Tranquebar required that one of them should act as the Royal Danish Resident. This office was frequently a source of much vexation, and even of danger, to them. The Danes, when they formed their first settlement on one of these islands, which they called New Denmark, had conveyed thither a considerable number of cannon; but after the death of all the soldiers, the carriages rotted to pieces, and the guns were suffered to lie on the ground. On one occasion, a *Nacata*, or general of the king of Queda, as he styled himself, arrived at Nancauwery with a large prow, and five of the guns on board. Mr Haensel

[1] Haensel's Letters, p. 36.

All the Nicobar Islands which have fresh-water lakes and streams are overrun with the crocodile or alligator. There are two species of this animal, the proper crocodile and the kayman. The former is said never to attack living creatures, but to devour only carrion, and therefore it is not considered as dangerous. "Of the correctness of this opinion," says Mr Haensel, "I had once ocular proof. I was walking at Queda, along the coast, and looking at a number of children swimming and playing in the water. On a sudden I observed a large crocodile proceed towards them from a creek. Terrified at the idea of their danger, I screamed out and made signs to some Chinese to run to their assistance; but they laughed me to scorn as an ignorant stranger. I afterwards saw the monster playing about among the children, while the young creatures diverted themselves by pretending to attack him and drive him away.

"The kayman is less in size than the crocodile. It is extremely fierce, and seizes upon every creature that has life; but it cannot lift any thing from the ground, on account of the projection of the lower jaw. Part of the flesh of this animal is good and wholesome when well cooked. It tastes somewhat like pork, for which I took it, and ate it with much relish when I first came to Nancauwery; till finding, on inquiry, that it was the flesh of a creature so disgusting in its appearance and habits, I felt a loathing for it which I could never overcome; but it is eaten by both the natives and Europeans."—*Haensel's Letters*, p. 31, 39.

being informed of this, considered it his duty as Resident to protest against the robbery, and spoke to him concerning it. The Nacata flew into a violent rage, and began to use threatening language, pleading the orders of his sovereign. Mr Haensel replied, with all the simplicity of truth, that his prince knew very well, that as he had laid nothing down there, he had no right to take any thing up, and that he would give notice of it to the king of Denmark. He then left him, but afterwards heard, that the Nacata threatened to kill him, and thus prevent him from reporting what he had done. The natives also assured Mr Haensel, that it was the general's intention to murder him; but that they would stay and defend him. They, accordingly, stopped till late in the night, when the Brethren desired them to return home, but could scarcely prevail on them to go away.

After they had gone, and just as the Brethren were preparing to retire to bed, they heard a noise without, and immediately after a violent knocking at the door. On opening it, Mr Haensel was surprised to see it surrounded by a great number of Malays; but though he was much afraid, he assumed an authoritative air, and kept his station at the entrance, as if determined not to let them in. The foremost, however, pushed by him, and then the Nacata himself came forward. The Malays immediately crowded into the room, and sat down on the chairs and on the floor, closely watching him, armed with their creeses or daggers. Though Mr Haensel preserved a firm undaunted look, yet it is impossible to describe his feelings on this occasion, as he expected every moment to fall a sacrifice to their fury. The Nacata then told him, that he had come to ask, Whose property the cannon were to be, the Resident's or his? To this question Mr Haensel replied to the following effect: "You have come to the wrong person to make that inquiry; for I am only a servant of the king of Denmark, as you, according to your own account, are the servant of the king of Queda. Neither of us, therefore, can determine who shall have the cannon. Our respective masters, and they only, can settle that point. You have told me that you have received orders to bring them; and I can assure you that I have orders to protest against it. We have both therefore only done our duty. All now depends on this point, whether my king or your king has the best right to give orders on these islands, and to claim the property in question." On receiving this answer, the Nacata became quite furious, and began to talk of the ease with which they could kill them all. Some of them even drew their daggers, and shewed the missionary how they were tipped with poison. On a sudden they all rose up, and to his imagination seemed to rush upon him ; but instead of this, they quitted the room, one by one, and left him standing alone in astonishment at their conduct. As soon as they were all gone, and he found himself in safety, he fell on his knees, and with tears in his eyes returned thanks to God Almighty, who had so graciously heard his prayers, and saved him from the hands of his enemies. His brethren, who had fled into the wood when the Malays first burst into the house, now returned, and they mutually wept for joy to see each other still in life.

After they had somewhat recovered from their fright, Mr Haensel went to the village, and told their old Nicobar captain what had happened, upon which he sent a message to all the neighbouring villages, and in a short time great numbers of the natives arrived, well armed, and watched at the landing-place all night. Had the Malays offered to return, not one of them, it is probable, would have escaped with his life. The Nacata, it seems, had said, that the Danish resident at Nancauwery was a very great sorcerer, for he had tied their hands that they could do nothing to him.[1]

With regard to religion, the inhabitants of the Nicobar Islands are in a most deplorable condition. Their notions of a Supreme Being are singularly perplexed; and it was even difficult to discover among them any fixed opinion regarding his existence or attributes. They are not professed idolaters, like most other Oriental nations. They have not even a particular word to express the name of God. They use the term *Knallen*, when they speak of him ; but it only signifies *above, on high*, and is applied to many other objects. They believe, however, that this unknown Being is good, and will not hurt them ; but wherein his goodness consists, they neither know nor care. But though the inhabitants of the Nicobar Islands pay little or no regard to a

[1] Haensel's Letters, p. 65.

Deity, they are firm believers in the doctrine of devils; and it is to them all their religious ceremonies appear to be directed. They even ascribe the creation of the world to the *Eewee*, or Evil Spirit. When they do any thing wrong, and are reproved for it, they commonly answer, "It was not I; it was the devil that did it." If you convict them of having done it with their own hands, they usually reply, "The Eewee did not make me perfect." They speak of a great many kinds of devils, all of them malicious and disposed to hurt them, if they had not among them such great and powerful sorcerers, who, by their superior ability, can catch and bring them into subjection. It is not wonderful that the conjurors should be able to impose on these poor ignorant creatures, for they really do possess astonishing dexterity. Every person who has been in the East Indies, knows with what curious sleight-of-hand tricks the jugglers amuse the people; but in the Nicobar Islands, where these arts are applied to what are considered religious exercises, the deception is so great, that an ordinary spectator is amazed, and is perfectly unable to account for them.[1]

The Brethren endeavoured to explain to the natives, in the best manner they were able, the love of God to man, and the way of salvation through a crucified Redeemer. These things the savages heard with silent attention; but that they themselves were interested in them, was more than they could comprehend. When the missionaries told them that they had come hither for no other purpose, but to make known to them their Creator and Redeemer, and begged them to reflect on what was taught them, they laughed in reply. Sometimes they even remarked, that they could not believe that the sufferings of one man could atone for the sins of another, and that, therefore, if they were wicked, what the Brethren told them concerning a crucified Saviour could do them no service; but they maintained that they were good by nature, and never did any wrong. When the missionaries replied, that they had but lately murdered some people, and afterwards abused the dead bodies, thrusting their spears into them, mutilating them in the most wanton manner, and at last cutting them to pieces; and asked them, Whether this was a proof of their natural goodness? their

[1] Haensel's Letters, p. 48, 51.

answer was, "You do not understand the matter: These people were not fit to live: They were cannibals."[1]

But though the inhabitants of the Nicobar Islands refused to embrace Christianity, they were always very friendly to the missionaries; and were not only forward, as we have already seen, to defend them against their enemies, but in some instances they behaved with a generosity which could scarcely have been expected of them. The Brethren used to buy from them such articles as they needed, and to pay them with tobacco at the current price. The natives, however, even when they had nothing to sell, would come for their portion of tobacco, which the missionaries never refused as long as they had any themselves, until, by the non-arrival of the ship, their stock was entirely exhausted. They then told the captain of the village, that as they had no more tobacco, the people need not bring them any more provisions, for they had nothing to give them in exchange. The chief did so; but yet on the very next day, the Brethren were more plentifully supplied than ever with the articles they wanted. The people would not even wait for payment; but hung up their fruit and meat about the house, and went away. The missionaries called after them and told them how they were situated, to which they generously replied, "When you had plenty of tobacco, you gave us as much as you could spare; now, though you have no more of it, we have provisions enough, and you shall have what you want, as long as we have any, till you get more tobacco." This promise they performed most faithfully. Indeed, though an ignorant, wicked, uncivilized race, yet in general they were kind and gentle in their dispositions, except when roused by jealousy or other provocations, and then their headstrong passions hurried them into the greatest excesses.[2]

The situation of the missionaries in the Nicobar Islands became more wretched and forlorn than ever. Here they lived destitute of every thing that renders life comfortable; surrounded by savages; separated from their brethren throughout the whole world; without any communications from their friends for years together. The island of Nancauwery was completely covered with trees, bushes, and plants; the climate was

[1] Haensel's Letters, p. 20, 48. [2] Ibid. p. 27, 48.

extremely moist and unhealthy; the house of the missionaries was so damp, that their very beds and mattresses rotted under them; they were obliged to go barefooted, as they had neither boots nor shoes, and their stock of other clothes was nearly exhausted: their supply of provisions was scarcely more abundant; rice, which was so putrid and so full of worms, that it was hardly fit for the lower animals, they were under the necessity of using themselves. In consequence of these combined circumstances, they were so sickly, that a month seldom passed, without their labouring under fever or some other disorder; and they became at length so feeble and emaciated, that they resembled creeping skeletons, covered with a thin pale skin, rather than living men.[1]

In August 1784, the government of Tranquebar, in consequence of orders from the Court of Denmark, sent a ship to the Nicobar Islands, for the purpose of conveying supplies to the missionaries, and of enabling them to maintain their post in that quarter. Difficult as it had always been to land at Nancauwery, the vessel made the island, not merely in this instance, but within a short period she performed the same voyage two other times with similar success. Encouraged by these circumstances, the Brethren applied to their work with new vigour; and they brought to Nancauwery a wooden house of two stories, which had been left on the neighbouring island of Sombreiro. by some European settlers. In this house, they hoped to enjoy better health than formerly, as they proposed residing in the upper story, a point worthy of the attention of all missionaries in a warm, and especially in a moist climate. But though the mission assumed a more promising aspect in its external circumstances, it was attended with no greater success than before.[2]

It must, however, be acknowledged that the Brethren can scarcely be said to have made a fair attempt to christianize the natives. Though they had an opportunity of conversing with some of the people in a corrupt dialect of Portuguese, yet, in order to preach the gospel to the inhabitants in general, it was necessary to acquire a knowledge of their own language. This,

[1] Fortsetzung Brud. Hist. tom. ii. p. 114.
[2] Ibid. tom. i. p. 369; tom. ii. p. 116.

however, was a task of extreme difficulty. Not only were they without the ordinary help of grammars, dictionaries, and written books, but it was no easy matter to get acquainted with it by intercourse with the natives themselves. The inhabitants of the Nicobar Islands are in general of so indolent a turn, that even talking seems a burden to them; and as long as they can express their meaning by signs, they are unwilling to open their lips. If a stranger enter their houses, they sit still and look at him; or, perhaps, pointing to some food, give him a sign to sit down and eat. There he may remain for hours, without hearing a syllable drop from their lips, unless he can begin himself, and then they will answer him in a friendly manner. Besides, both the men and women have always a large piece of the betel or areca nut in their mouths, which renders their speech so indistinct, that it is scarcely possible to distinguish between the sputtering sounds they make. Notwithstanding these and other difficulties, a few of the Brethren made some proficiency in the language, yet none of them acquired such a knowledge of it, as to be able to explain fully to the natives the way of salvation through Jesus Christ.[1]

Most of the missionaries, indeed, in consequence of the extreme unhealthiness of the climate, were cut off before they could learn the language, or just when they had advanced so far as to be able to converse with the natives; and thus their successors had to begin the work anew, and the prospect of accomplishing the chief design of the mission was suspended from year to year. During the comparatively short period of its existence, eleven valuable missionaries found an untimely grave in Nancauwery, and thirteen more died soon after their return to Tranquebar, in consequence of the malignant fevers, and the obstructions in the liver, which they had contracted on that island. Besides, these disorders, from which they were seldom entirely free, are accompanied with such pain in the head, such constant sickness, such dejection of spirits, that the mind is perfectly stupified, and is overwhelmed with such desponding views of the possibility of relief and of future usefulness, as renders a person altogether unfit for exercising that diligence,

[1] Haensel's Letters, p. 61, 64.

and making those exertions, which are necessary in the conduct of a mission.[1]

Indeed, the great exertions of the Brethren in clearing and planting the land, and in other laborious exercises which necessity imposed upon them, withdrew their attention from the great object of their settlement on the island. Men who are destitute of all external comfort, who have a daily struggle to obtain even the common necessaries of life, who in the morning scarcely know whether they shall have a morsel to eat through the day, are not in circumstances to make vigorous exertions for the conversion of the heathen. Besides, during some of the latter years of the mission, there was a want of that love among the Brethren, and of that union in the prosecution of their labours, which should ever prevail among Christian missionaries, and which are essentially necessary to their success.[2] In consequence of these and other circumstances, it was at length resolved to relinquish the mission.

In September 1787, Mr Haensel, who had returned before to Tranquebar, was sent to Nancauwery, to bring away the only missionary who now remained on the island. He was accompanied by a lieutenant, a corporal, and six private soldiers, who were sent by the governor to take possession of the premises, and to whom he delivered up every thing he could not carry away. No language can express the painful feelings of his mind while he was executing this disagreeable task, and bringing to a close the Brethren's labours in the Nicobar Islands. The sight of the burying-ground where so many of his fellow-missionaries lay, particularly affected him. He often visited this place, sat down, and wept over their graves. His last farewell with the natives, who flocked to him from all the neighbouring islands, was truly affecting. They wept and howled for grief, and begged that the Brethren would soon return.[3]

The mission on the continent of India, though not attended with such trying circumstances, was scarcely followed with greater success. Several Brethren went to Calcutta, Serampur, and Patna, and resided in these places for some time, in the hope of promoting the interests of religion among the Hindus; but their exertions were attended with little or no

[1] Haensel's Letters, p. 62. [2] Ibid. p. 22, 63. [3] Ibid. p. 26.

success. In Tranquebar the labours of the Brethren proved nearly equally fruitless: they did, indeed, baptize a few individuals; but most of these disappointed the favourable hopes they had formed of them.[1]

In 1795, the Brethren resolved to abandon the settlement at Tranquebar, as the maintenance of it was attended with great expense, while, at the same time, there appeared little hope of their being useful to the heathen in the neighbourhood, and no prospect of their being able to accomplish the original object of their settlement in India, the establishment of a mission on the Nicobar Islands. In consequence of this resolution, several of the Brethren returned at different periods to Europe; and at length, about 1803, the two last, who had been left to sell the houses and ground belonging to the settlement, took a final leave of the country.[2]

SECT. X.—SOUTH AFRICA.

In March 1737, George Schmidt sailed from Holland for the Cape of Good Hope, with a view to the religious instruction of the Hottentots. Having fixed on a spot for a settlement near Serjeant's river, he collected a number of them to that place; and in the course of a few years, he baptized several of them. As various impediments, however, were thrown in his way, he judged it expedient to return to Europe in 1744, in the hope of obtaining the removal of them, and of procuring some of the Brethren to assist him in his labours. He left his small congregation, consisting of forty-seven persons, under the care of a pious man; but on his arrival in Holland, the East India Company refused him permission to return, some persons having insinuated, that the conversion of the Hottentots would injure the interests of the colony. His little congregation, however, kept together for some time in expectation of the return of their teacher. They used to meet together, it is said, and read

[1] Fortsetzung Brud. Hist. tom. i. p. 158, 352; tom. ii. p. 109, 111, 121, 141, 143; tom. iii. p. 353.

[2] Ibid. tom. iii. p. 356; Period. Accounts, vol. iii. p. 221.

a Dutch Bible he had left among them. Even so late as 1787, some of the Brethren who touched at the Cape in their way from the East Indies, saw a Hottentot woman baptized by Schmidt, who had a Dutch Bible which she received from him, and who expressed a great desire for the renewal of the mission. A new application was now made to the East India Company for permission to send missionaries to the Cape of Good Hope; and though former petitions of the same kind had uniformly failed, the present, after meeting with much opposition, was at last granted.[1]

In July 1792, Hendrick Marsveld, Daniel Schwinn, and John C. Kuehnel, three of the Brethren, sailed from Holland for the Cape of Good Hope, with the view of renewing the mission in that colony. As on their arrival, they were recommended to fix their residence at Bavian's Kloof, about 120 miles from Cape Town, they proceeded to visit that part of the country without delay. It was the very place where George Schmidt had resided, and on their arrival the spot was pointed out to them where his house had stood. A large piece of the wall was still standing; in the garden were several fruit trees, and here and there appeared some ruins of walls, the remains of the huts of the Hottentots. Having obtained a grant of the land from the Dutch government, the Brethren here proceeded to build themselves a house for their accommodation, with the assistance of some of the neighbouring Hottentots, whom they engaged for this purpose.[2]

Even in the commencement of their labours, the Brethren had no small difficulties to encounter, chiefly from the hostility of the Dutch boors. As many of the Hottentots left them in order to come and hear the word of God, they were apprehensive they would no longer be able to obtain them as servants, or, at least, not on such easy terms as hitherto. Besides, as the Hottentots depended for subsistence chiefly on their cattle, and allowed them to pasture at large in a country where there are few or no enclosures, the animals sometimes wandered into the fields of the neighbouring farmers, an evil which the missionaries by all their exhortations were unable to prevent. Influenced by considerations of this kind, a man of the name of Teunis,

[1] Period. Accounts, vol. i. p. 122, 168; Fortsetzung Brud. Hist. tom. iii. p. 161.
[2] Period. Accounts, vol. i. p. 165, 273, 276, 282.

who, at first, had been a chief means of their settling at this place, now became their bitterest enemy, and sought in every possible way to check their progress. With this view he represented to government, that the cattle of the Hottentots were so numerous the country could not support them, and that there was a necessity for driving them back to the places whence they came. The statement was utterly false ; but yet the commissary was so far misled by it, that he empowered their accuser to order the Hottentots to drive back their cattle to their former places of abode. The Brethren were, at the same time, informed that they must receive no Hottentot into the settlement who had been in the service of a colonist, without a certificate that he had fulfilled the period of his service, and was now at liberty, an order which amounted nearly to a prohibition to admit any more Hottentots, as the farmers would rarely give such an attestation. Happily the triumph of their enemies was of short duration. A gentleman from the Cape, who visited the settlement soon after, informed the government, on his return, that the statement of the farmers was so far from being true, that at least five hundred head of cattle might be maintained on the ground. In consequence of this information, the commissary revoked the order for the removal of the Hottentots' cattle, and that gentleman purchased the land, chiefly, as he said, with a view to the security of the mission.[1]

In June 1795, upwards of a hundred of the boors rose in arms, determined to obtain by force a redress of their various grievances, among which the instruction of the Hottentots was not forgotten. For several weeks reports of the most frightful nature daily reached the missionaries, and kept them in a state of constant alarm. A troop of the Nationals, as the insurgents styled themselves, at length arrived in the neighbourhood of Bavian's Kloof, and sent notice to the Brethren that they were assembled at such a house, and that if they wished to know their determination concerning them they might come thither. Anxious to bring matters to an accommodation, or at least to learn with certainty the views of their enemies, one of the Brethren ventured to go to the place appointed, and on his ar-

[1] Fortsetzung Brud. Hist. tom. iii. 205 ; Period. Accounts, vol. ii. 5, 19.

rival he found that some of the articles of their Memorial to government were to the following effect:—

"That they would allow no Moravians to live in the country and instruct the Hottentots; for as there were many Christians in the colony who received no education, it was not proper that the Hottentots should be made wiser than they, but that they should remain in the same state as before.

"That the Hottentots should live among the farmers, and not collect together at Bavian's Kloof.

"That it was never meant the Moravians should be employed among the Hottentots, but among the Bushmen."[1]

Such were some of the demands of the insurgent boors. A troop of them were actually on their way to Bavian's Kloof to destroy the school, but being met on the road by a deputy from government with terms of accommodation, they returned to consult with their comrades, threatening, however, soon to renew the visit. A few days after, two horsemen brought an order to the missionaries from the commandant Pissani, to quit the place within three days, and to go either to Cape Town, or to some other part of the country inhabited by Dutch citizens, on pain of being severely punished in case of disobedience; they were further informed that Pissani himself was marching behind the mountains to the Cape, at the head of eight hundred men. These tidings flew like lightning among the Hottentots who still remained in the settlement, and filled them with the deepest sorrow. Resistance, however, was vain, and even delay might be dangerous.

Having employed the following day in loading two waggons with their goods, the missionaries prepared to follow in a cart drawn by ten oxen, into which they put such articles as might be necessary on the journey. They left their beloved congregation with a sorrowful heart, yet not without a secret hope of soon returning to them. In this expectation they were not disappointed. On their arrival at Cape Town they waited on the governor, and on informing him of what had happened, he expressed his astonishment at the presumption and arrogance of

[1] A savage people of the Hottentot race who inhabit the colony, and who from the circumstance of their lurking among the bushes, whence they shoot travellers with their poisoned arrows, are called Boschemen or Bushmen.

Pissani, but added, they had acted wisely in obeying his orders, for as the insurgents were exceedingly enraged, they might have proceeded to extremities in case of resistance. As, however, a British force had, in the mean while, arrived at the Cape of Good Hope, the principal party of the insurgents agreed to suspend their demands for the present, and to assist in repelling the common enemy. By the governor's permission, therefore, the missionaries returned immediately to Bavian's Kloof, where they were received by the poor Hottentots with gratitude and joy. The colony shortly after surrendered to the British, in whom the Brethren found powerful friends and protectors.[1]

In February 1796, the Brethren experienced a new instance of the watchful care of Providence over them. Some of the neighbouring farmers had collected together upwards of a hundred armed men, for the purpose of carrying their late resolution into execution by one bold decisive blow. Their rendezvous was in the vicinity, at the house of Baas Teunis, their old and artful enemy. They were already assembled at this place, when a message was delivered to them from the English general, who had received notice of their intention, that if any outrage were committed on the missionaries, the perpetrators of it would assuredly be brought to justice and punished in the severest manner. Finding their design discovered, and the government determined to punish them, the conspirators quitted their leader and dispersed to their homes without molesting the missionaries.[2]

By degrees the hostility of the farmers to the missionaries began to subside, not indeed from any satisfaction which they took in the instruction of the Hottentots, but merely from discovering that it might be turned to their own advantage. When the Brethren were erecting a smith's workshop in the settlement, some of the neighbouring boors were not only highly displeased, but agreed never to buy a single article from them, nor to give them any of their work; yet scarcely was the building finished, when several of these very persons came for knives and other articles; and some, when they had purchased them at a moderate price, carried them to Cape Town and other places, and sold them for more than double the sum. Similar

[1] Period. Accounts, vol. ii. p. 30, 33, 42, 44, 47. [2] Ibid. vol. ii. p. 82.

to this was their conduct with regard to provisions. Having failed in destroying the settlement by open violence, they threatened that they would starve the missionaries and their people out of the country. Accordingly, when the Brethren were building a mill, and required a considerable supply of corn, salt, wine, and other articles, on account of the number of hands they employed, the farmers carried their threats into execution for some time, and distressed them not a little for want of provisions. But at length these very persons brought them as large supplies as they needed; and even one of those who had conspired to destroy the place, sent a waggon with corn to the settlement at a season when it brought the highest price, and sold it cheaper than they expected to have found it in the country. Most of them, indeed, were convinced by experience that the gospel was beneficial to the temporal as well as to the spiritual interests of the colony, and now preferred employing Christian rather than heathen Hottentots in their service. This was so much the case, that it became a common practice with the Hottentots to represent themselves as inhabitants of Bavian's Kloof, though, perhaps, they had never seen the place; and as they often disgraced themselves by their ill conduct, the Brethren, in order to prevent such impositions, found it necessary to give certificates to their people when they went to labour with the farmers.[1]

The settlement of the Brethren at Bavian's Kloof was now an object of general curiosity, particularly to the inhabitants of Cape Town, many of whom came to see it, and were at once pleased and surprised to witness the great improvement which had been effected on the character and habits of the Hottentots, whom it was customary to consider as among the lowest and most degraded of the human family.[2] Among other visitors was John Barrow, Esq., who has given us the following interesting account of the settlement.

"Proceeding up the valley through which the Endless River meanders, we halted late in the evening at a place called Bavian's Kloof, where there is a small establishment of Moravian missionaries. Early next morning, I was awakened by some of the finest voices I had ever heard, and on looking out,

[1] Period. Accounts, vol. ii. p. 183, 188, 244; vol. iv. p. 38. [2] Ibid. vol. ii. p. 184.

saw a group of female Hottentots sitting on the ground. It was Sunday, and they had assembled thus early to chaunt the morning hymn. They were all neatly dressed in printed cotton gowns. A sight so very different from what we had hitherto been in the habit of observing with regard to this unhappy class of beings, could not fail of proving grateful, and at the same time it excited a degree of curiosity as to the nature of the establishment. The good fathers, who were three in number, were well disposed to satisfy every question put to them. They were men of the middle age, plain and decent in their dress, cleanly in their persons, of modest manners, meek and humble in their deportment, but intelligent and lively in conversation, zealous in the cause of their mission, yet free from bigotry or enthusiasm. Every thing in the place partook of that neatness and simplicity, which were the strongest features in the outline of their character. The church they had constructed was a plain neat building; their mill for grinding corn was superior to any in the colony; their garden was in high order, and produced abundance of vegetables for the use of the table. Almost every thing that had been done was by the labour of their own hands. Agreeably to the rules of the Society of which they were members, each of them had learned some useful profession. One was skilled in every branch of smith's work, the second was a shoemaker, and the third a tailor.

"These missionaries have succeeded in bringing together into one society upwards of six hundred Hottentots, and their numbers are daily increasing. These live in small huts dispersed over the valley, to each of which was attached a piece of ground for raising vegetables, and their houses and gardens were very neat and comfortable; numbers of the poor in England not so good, and few better. Those Hottentots who chose to learn the respective trades of the missionaries, were paid for their labour as soon as they could earn wages. Some hired themselves out by the week, month, or year, to the neighbouring peasantry; others made mats and brooms for sale; some bred poultry, and others found means to subsist by their cattle, sheep, and horses. Many of the women and children of soldiers belonging to the Hottentot corps reside at Bavian's Kloof, where they are much more likely to acquire industrious habits than by remaining in the camp.

"On Sundays they all regularly attend the performance of divine service, and it is astonishing how ambitious they are to appear at church neat and clean. Of about three hundred that composed the congregation, about half were dressed in coarse printed cottons, and the other half in the ancient sheep-skin dresses; and it appeared on inquiry, that the former were the first who had been brought within the pale of the church; a proof that their external circumstances at least had suffered nothing from their change of life. Persuasion and example had convinced them, that cleanliness in their persons not only added much to the comfort of life, but was one of the greatest preservatives of health, and that the little trifle of money they had to spare, was much better applied in procuring decent covering for the body, than in the purchase of spirits and tobacco, articles so far from being necessaries, that they might justly be considered as the most pernicious evils.

"The deportment of the Hottentot congregation during divine service was truly devout. The discourse delivered by one of the fathers was short, but full of good sense, pathetic, and well suited to the occasion. Tears flowed abundantly from the eyes of those to whom it was particularly addressed. The females sung in a style that was plaintive and affecting, and their voices were in general sweet and harmonious."[1]

In March 1808, the Brethren began a second settlement at a place called Gruenekloof, about forty miles from Cape Town, on the road to Saldanha Bay. Scarcely, however, had they settled in this part of the country, when a circumstance occurred which threatened to interrupt their peaceful labours. One night the slaves in a neighbouring district rose with a determination to burn Cape Town, to murder all the White men, and to reduce the women to slavery. They actually seized and bound several of their masters, carried off waggons, horses, arms, and committed various other depredations. One afternoon, a man came to Gruenekloof, pretending that he was an English naval officer, and that he had narrowly escaped from the rebel slaves. He shewed a certificate to that effect, containing a request to

[1] Barrow's Travels in Southern Africa, vol. i. p. 351.

all persons to furnish him with horses to prosecute his journey to Cape Town. This, however, was a mere forgery; and it turned out that he was one of the chiefs of the insurgents: but happily he was overtaken on the road to the Cape, and arrested as an impostor. Lord Caledon, the governor, on the discovery of the plot, sent dragoons through the country in every direction. Some of the colonists in the neighbourhood of Gruenekloof fled thither for safety; and the Brethren did every thing in their power to accommodate them and their slaves. They also distributed arms as directed by government, among their own Hottentots, and kept a strict watch during the night. Some hundreds of the insurgents were soon taken by the dragoons, and thus their evil designs were frustrated.[1]

In August 1811, the missionaries at this station were involved in great distress by an accident, which, though of a more private, was of a very distressing nature. As the neighbourhood had of late been much infested by wolves, which ventured even into their yard, and committed terrible havoc among their cattle, a day was appointed to hunt and destroy them, agreeably to the usual practice of the country. The Brethren Bonatz and Schmitt, with about thirty Hottentots, accordingly set out in the morning, armed with loaded guns. When about an hour's ride from the settlement, they discovered and wounded a wolf; but the animal made its escape among the bushes. They pursued it for some time, but not being able to discover its hiding-place, the two missionaries resolved to return home. They had already left the Hottentots a short distance, when the latter cried, they had discovered the wolf in a thicket near at hand. Schmitt immediately rode back to their assistance, but Bonatz remained behind, as he had not his gun with him. When they were in the midst of the thicket, the dog started the animal. Those within did not see what it was; but those without exclaimed it was a tiger, and ran off, leaving the missionary and one of the Hottentots in the middle of the bushes, and perfectly at a loss by what side to make their escape, lest they should come directly upon it. They therefore proceeded slowly with their guns pointed, designing to shoot the animal the moment it should make its appearance. On a sudden the tiger sprung

[1] Period. Accounts, vol. iv. p. 389, 441; Holmes' Sketches, p. 420.

upon the Hottentot, pulled him down, and began to bite his face. The distance of the place from whence the animal made his spring, to that on which the Hottentot stood, was full twenty feet, and over bushes from six to eight feet high, so that had it not been for the horror of the scene, it would have been very amusing to behold the enraged animal, flying like a bird through the air, with open jaw and lashing tail, and screaming with the greatest violence. Schmitt, who was close at hand, prepared to shoot the tiger; but the motions of the Hottentot, and of the animal in rolling about, and struggling together, were so rapid, that he was afraid to fire, lest he should kill or injure him whom he sought to save. Immediately, however, the tiger let go the Hottentot, and made a spring at himself. His gun being of no use at such close quarters, he threw it down, and in order to shield his face, held up his arm, which the animal instantly seized, close to the elbow, with his jaws. Schmitt, however, was still able, with the same hand, to lay hold of one of the tiger's fore feet; while, with the other paw, the animal continued striking his breasts, and tearing his clothes. Happily both fell in the struggle, in such a position, that the missionary's knee rested on the pit of the tiger's stomach. He, at the same time, grasped the animal's throat with his right hand, and kept him down with all his might. His face now lay directly over the tiger, whose open mouth, from the pressure of the windpipe, sent forth the most hideous, hoarse, convulsive cries, while his starting eyes seemed like live coals, to flash with fire. As his strength was fast failing, Schmitt called to his companions to come to his assistance; while, on the other hand, the rage and agony of the tiger supplied it with extraordinary energy. On hearing his cries, the Hottentots ran to his assistance, and one of them snatching up the loaded gun which lay on the ground, shot the tiger through the heart. His death was instantaneous. Had the spark of life not been completely extinguished, his dying struggles might have proved fatal to some of his assailants. As the case was of an extraordinary nature, the friends of Schmitt on his arrival at Gruenekloof were much at a loss how to treat him; and before it was possible to obtain medical advice from the Cape, the inflammation spread to an alarming extent. Every hour, indeed, he grew worse. He had seven or eight wounds from the elbow to the wrist; in some places they penetrated to the bone; and as the teeth and claws of a tiger are shaped like those of a cat, they had of course lacerated the parts. His brethren, after several days, procured a medical man from the Cape, who bled him very freely, and kindly promised not to leave him until he was out of danger. By degrees the inflammation abated; symptoms of a favourable nature began to appear; and to the astonishment of all his friends, he at length quite recovered.

The Hottentot, though severely wounded, did not suffer so much bodily pain as the missionary. It was the third instance in which he had encountered a tiger, and this time he would in all likelihood have lost his life, had not Schmitt risked his own to save him. After the tiger had thrown the Hottentot down, the missionary might easily have made his escape, as well as his companions, but he could not bear to see the poor man lose his life without at least endeavouring to save him.[1]

In February 1818, Schmitt and two others of the Brethren commenced a station which was called Enon, on the Witte river, near the borders of Kaffraria. In the course of years, other stations were formed in various parts of the country, as Elim, near Cape Aiguillas, Clarkson, near Plettenberg's bay, Shiloh, Mamre, and Goshen, the last three near the confines of Kaffraria. Several of these stations were begun by the desire of the British Government, which granted land for the purpose. The population which collected at some of them was of a very mixed character, Hottentots, Bushmen, Fingoes, Tambookies, Kafirs, &c.; but with the exception of Elim, none of them were attended with much success. The prosperity of Enon was greatly hindered by the severe and long-continued droughts which prevailed in some years, and in others by the violent inundations of the rivers, which overflowed their lands, and ruined the water-courses which they had made with great labour for the irrigation of their fields and gardens; and both it and the stations on the borders of Kaffraria suffered severely, or were even broken up, in the successive Kafir wars.

[1] Period. Accounts, vol. v. p. 118, 250; vol. xviii. p. 331; Latrobe's Journal of a Visit to South Africa, p. 306.

In 1852, the following were the numbers connected with the congregations of the Brethren in South Africa:—

Begun.	Stations.	Communicants.	Baptized Adults.	Baptized Children.	Total.
1792	Gnadenthal, . . .	910	421	1026	2357
1808	Grueneklöof, . . .	367	231	589	1187
1824	Elim, ...	343	191	414	948
1818	Enon, ...	92	66	120	278
1839	Clarkson, ...	85	34	114	233
1828	Shiloh, ...	86	60	152	298
		1883	1003	2415	5301[1]

Many of the Hottentots and others of the natives under the care of the Brethren shewed extreme ignorance of the great truths of Christianity. It was wonderful how slowly they in general learned any thing that required thought, and how soon they forgot it again, a remark which will probably be found to hold true as to barbarous tribes generally, especially in regard to topics of a religious and spiritual nature. In the older stations, where great numbers are now collected, there are many who give no evidence of conversion; and consisting as they do of a mixed multitude, it is not to be wondered at that cases of open immorality, and sometimes even of flagrant crimes, should occur. Many even of the baptized were seduced into sin, particularly drunkenness, an evil which has of late years been greatly on the increase among the Hottentots; and though some of these were brought to a sense of their guilt, and restored to the fellowship of the church, yet others were never recovered, but were plunged at once into temporal and spiritual ruin. Even among those who, on the whole, remained faithful to their Christian profession, many irregularities occurred; but yet it was pleasing to observe the spirit which in general prevailed among them; their desire for instruction, their ingenuousness in the confession of sin, their humiliation on account of it, their love to the Saviour, and their reliance on his atonement, as the only ground of their hope of salvation.[2]

It must, however, be acknowledged, that the Brethren learned

[1] Period. Accounts, vol. xxi. p. xxvii. [2] Ibid. vol. xvii. p. 382; vol. xix. p. 280.

by sad experience not to place implicit confidence in the professions of the Hottentots. To hear them speak was often very pleasing, yet sometimes it was nothing more than empty words.[1] This is an observation which may be extended to heathen nations in general, and claims particular attention from the Christian missionary. There is much of cunning in the character of Pagan, and especially of savage and uncivilized tribes. It is the weapon which the weak everywhere employ against the strong. They have penetration enough to see what pleases their instructors, and being under little or no restraint from moral or religious considerations, they will not hesitate, in order to gain some selfish and paltry end, to make those professions which they think will be agreeable to them. To no man is discrimination of character more necessary than to the Christian missionary, and even after all his care he will often be deceived.

SECT. XI.—GENERAL STATEMENTS.

We have now taken a view of the principal Missions of the United Brethren among the heathen. Of late years, they have been less eventful than at some former periods of their history; but they have been greatly extended, and if the numbers connected with their congregations could be held as a criterion of their usefulness, their success has been much increased.

In 1852, the following were the numbers connected with the congregations of the Brethren in the heathen world:—

Communicants.	Baptised Adults.	Baptised Children.	Total.
20,254	9871	20,639	50,764

Besides these, there appear to have been 19,306 whom the Brethren class under the head of candidates for baptism, new people, and excluded.[2]

[1] Period. Accounts, vol. iv. p. 393; Latrobe's Journal, p. 284.
[2] Period. Accounts, vol. xxi. p. xxvii.

In propagating the gospel among the heathen, the Brethren seek to imitate the example of the Apostle Paul, who "determined not to know any thing among them save Jesus Christ, and him crucified." Experience has shewn them, that little is effected by beginning with the principles of natural religion, as the existence of God, the perfections of his nature, or the duties of morality, in order to prepare them for receiving the gospel. After many years' trial in different countries, and under every variety of circumstances, they found that the simple testimony of the sufferings and death of Christ, delivered by a missionary who had an experimental sense of his love, was the most effectual means of converting the heathen. It is now, therefore, a rule with them, to enter into no discussions concerning the existence or attributes of God, the doctrine of the Trinity, and other similar truths, until their hearers appear to believe in Christ, and to feel the transforming influence of the gospel on their hearts. It is proper, however, to remark, that though the Brethren make the death of Christ the grand subject of their preaching among the heathen, they do not confine their instructions to this particular point, but endeavour, by degrees, to instil into the minds of the converts a knowledge of other parts of divine truth both doctrinal and practical.[1]

It is gratifying to find such numbers connected with the Brethren's congregations among the heathen; but the satisfaction which we feel on this account is materially diminished by the apprehension which we have, that their standard of qualifications for admission into the Church of Christ is much too low. They appear to baptize persons before they are duly instructed, and of whose conversion there is little or no evidence. They are much too simple in believing the professions of people; good words and fair speeches, the mere desire of baptism, or any outward manifestation of religious feeling, go a great way with them. We are not, indeed, without an apprehension that the Brethren give their hearers but an imperfect exhibition of Christianity, and that there is somewhat of formalism in their religion, as is very apt to be the case where every thing is so much a matter of prescribed form and order as it is with them. Though the atonement of Christ is unquestionably the grand

[1] Period. Accounts, vol. i. p. 7; vol. vii. p. xxvii.

and fundamental principle of the gospel, yet we fear they dwell too exclusively on his incarnation, sufferings, and death, and even on the mere historical circumstances regarding them, and that other parts of divine truth, both doctrinal and practical, have not that place in their instructions to which, by their importance, they are entitled. We accordingly suspect that the knowledge of the converts will generally be found to be very restricted, even after they have been years under instruction, and that it is not always of a scriptural character, and that to this imperfect foundation may perhaps be traced in part the great numbers who fall away, or in whose conduct at least there is much that is defective and blameworthy. If in these observations we wrong the Brethren, we shall feel deep regret, but they are the impressions made on our minds by their own accounts of their missions.

The General Synods of the Brethren's church, which consist of representatives from all the congregations, appoint a select number of bishops and elders to superintend the affairs of the whole church, till the next general synod, which, in times of peace, usually meets every seven or eight years. The Elders' Conference of the Unity, as they are called, is divided into four departments, one of which has the special care of the missions among the heathen. This committee, however, simply takes the affairs of the missions under consideration, and brings forward proposals concerning them: it neither forms resolutions, nor carries any measure into effect, until they are laid before the whole Elders' Conference of the Unity, and receive its concurrence. Societies for the furtherance of the gospel among the heathen were formed by the Brethren in England, Holland, and America; but it was simply with the view of assisting the missions, particularly such as were connected with these countries; they have no power to begin new missions, or even to send out missionaries. This, by the Synods of the Brethren's church, is vested solely in the Elders' Conference of the Unity.[1]

When any member of the Brethren's church feels disposed to go as a missionary among the heathen, he communicates his desire to that department of the Elders' Conference which has the superintendence of the missions committed to its care. If,

[1] Period. Accounts, vol. vii. p. xvi.; vol. xvi. p. 1.

on inquiry into his circumstances, there appears no objection to his proposal, he is considered as a candidate for missionary service in general, unless he has a predilection for any particular field, and then special attention is paid to his wishes. No person is ever urged, and still less compelled to become a missionary, or even to accept of a call to any particular station.

As to the qualifications of their missionaries, much erudition is not required by the Brethren. They have, they say, learned by experience, that a good understanding, a friendly disposition, unfeigned humility, fervent zeal for the salvation of souls, and a heart inflamed with the love of Christ, are the best and most essential qualifications of a missionary. In general, they think, the habits of a student are not so well calculated to form a person for the toils and hardships of a missionary life, as those of a mechanic. Yet men of learning are by no means rejected by them, and in various instances, their superior literary attainments have not been without their use, especially where translations of the Scriptures, or of other works, were to be made. When a new mission is to be undertaken, or a vacancy occurs in any of those already established, the list of candidates is examined, and such as are deemed most suitable are called upon, and accept or decline the invitation as they find themselves disposed.[1]

[1] Period. Accounts, vol. i. p. 6; vol. vii. p. iv.; Holmes' Sketches, p. 470; Panoplist, vol. ii. p. 436.

It may easily be supposed that the Brethren, in the course of their long experience, must have acquired much practical wisdom in the conduct of missions among the heathen. The following principles which we find stated in a letter from the Rev. C. J. La Trobe, long the Secretary of the Brethren in England, are, we think, well worthy of the attention of other missionary bodies :—

"It is of the greatest consequence, that we ourselves are intent upon doing whatsoever we do, in the name of God, and solely with a view to his glory, and not suffer ourselves to be swayed by our own spirit or prejudices. He will answer the prayers of his servants, if they are desirous to follow *his* directions in all things.

"In the choice of missionaries we ought to be very cautious, and well to examine the motives and character of the candidates.

"We think it a great mistake, after their appointment, *when they are held up to public notice and admiration, and much praise is bestowed upon their devotedness to the Lord, presenting them to the congregation as martyrs and confessors, before they have even entered upon their labours.* We rather advise them to be sent out quietly, recommended to the fervent prayers of the congregation, which is likewise most agreeable to their own feelings, if they are humble followers of Christ.

"As we wish above all things that brotherly love be maintained among fellow-

When the Brethren sent their first missionaries to the island of St Thomas and Greenland, they were, from their great poverty, scarcely able to furnish them with more than a few shillings to pay for what little they might need on their walk from Herrnhut to Copenhagen, leaving them to depend chiefly on friends by the way for a meal and a bed. Indeed, it would have been impossible for them to have carried on their missions among the heathen, had not Count Zinzendorf, with that liberality with which he devoted himself and all he possessed to the cause of Christ, provided for several years the necessary expenses. Though the Brethren, in the course of a few years, increased both in number and ability, yet finding that the most liberal contributions of their own body would not be adequate to the maintenance of the missions they had established, they formed a plan of rendering them as much as possible independent of such aid, by some of the missionaries working with their own hands for the support of themselves and their fellow-labourers, who were more particularly engaged in instructing the heathen. Thus some were sent to the Danish West India Islands, others to Surinam; some to Tranquebar and the Nicobar Islands, others to Egypt and the Cape of Good Hope, chiefly with the view of establishing trades, not for their own private advantage, but for the general support of the mission. They were, at the same time, willing, according to their ability, to assist in instructing the heathen, even as those Brethren on whom this more particularly devolved, were ready to help them in their secular concerns, whenever their assistance could be useful. In the Danish West India Islands, in Surinam, and in South Africa,

labourers, we do not advise to place two men of different religious opinions and habits, however worthy in other respects, under one yoke.

"When converts from among the heathen are established in grace, we would advise not immediately to use them as assistants in teaching, but to act herein with caution, and a reference to the general weakness of their minds, and consequent aptness to grow conceited.

"We also disapprove of bringing converts to Europe, under any pretence whatever, and think it would lead them into danger of injury to their own souls.

"Missionaries are no longer useful than as they are *with their whole heart* in their calling, and we advise to employ or retain none, but such as delight in their work.

"We advise that one of approved character and experience, be appointed first missionary to superintend the work, and that each prefer the other in love, and be willing to follow."—*Panoplist,* vol. ii. p. 437.

this plan succeeded so well, that the Brethren maintained themselves, and in some instances the benefits of it even extended to other stations, where a similar mode of support could not be adopted.[1]

Though the Brethren exercised remarkable economy in the conduct of their missions, yet during the war with France, their expenses in maintaining them were greatly increased, while their resources on the Continent of Europe were much diminished, and, towards the end of it, they found themselves deeply involved in debt on account of them. Averse to obtrude themselves on public notice, preferring retirement upon principle, and doing good without wishing that good to be known by any but its objects, they made no appeal for support to the Christian world at large, but struggled in secret with increasing difficulties, until, at length, the remonstrances of their friends, combined with the urgency of their wants, compelled them to come forward and make their embarrassments known. In consequence of the interest which was then excited in their behalf among the friends of missions, large sums were raised in aid of them; and since that time, they have continued to receive considerable contributions from Christians of other denominations, particularly in England.[2] There is, however, a danger that other churches, engrossed with their own missionary undertakings, may overlook the labours of the humble, modest, unobtrusive Moravians; and we cannot, therefore, conclude without expressing our earnest hope that the Christian world will not permit these excellent men to struggle with pecuniary difficulties; but will come forward with alacrity and zeal to aid them in carrying on those noble and important undertakings, in which they have been so long, so honourably, and so successfully engaged.

[1] Period. Accounts, vol. vii. p. 200; vol. xiii. p. 189; vol. xiv. p. viii.; vol. xix. p. 61; Spangenberg's Account, p. 56.

Of late years, the Brethren in the Danish West India Islands were not able nearly to meet the expenses of the mission, and they have now given up their former businesses.—*Period. Accounts*, vol. xvi. p. 269; vol. xvii. p. 148; vol. xix. p. 281.

[2] Concise Account of the Brethren's Missions, 1801, p. 14; Christian Guardian, vol. vi. p. 28, 141, 142; Period. Accounts, vol. vi. p. 383; vol. vii. Preface, p. iii., xxiv.; vol. viii. p. 165; vol. xiv. p. vii.; vol. xix. p. 120.

CHAPTER VII.

PROPAGATION OF CHRISTIANITY BY THE METHODIST MISSIONARY SOCIETY.[1]

SECT. I.—WEST INDIES.

IN September 1786, the Rev. Dr Coke, accompanied by Messrs William Warrener, John Clarke, and William Hammet, three other Methodist preachers, sailed from England for Nova Scotia; but after encountering a succession of tremendous storms, the ship proved so extremely leaky, that the captain thought it impossible to reach the port of Halifax that season, and he, therefore, resolved to direct his course for the West Indies. Having at length reached Antigua, Dr Coke and his companions met with so favourable a reception from many of the inhabitants, that after visiting some of the other islands, they resolved, instead of proceeding to the original place of their destination, to attempt the establishment of a mission in the West Indies.[2]

Such were the apparently accidental circumstances which led the Methodists to turn their attention to the heathen, and to adopt systematic measures for the diffusion of Christianity among them. Of the missions which they established, we shall now give some account, beginning with that to Antigua, as to which, however, it is necessary to go a few years further back.

[1] "The General Wesleyan Methodist Missionary Society" was not established till 1817. For many years the management of the Methodist Missions was intrusted chiefly to the Rev. Dr Coke, assisted by a committee of finance and advice, consisting of all the ministers of the connection resident in London.

[2] Coke's Journals of Five Visits to America, p. 49, 55.

Art. 1.—Antigua.

In 1760, Nathaniel Gilbert, Esq., Speaker of the House of Assembly in Antigua, began to make some efforts to promote the interests of religion on that island. Having, on a late visit to England, been himself impressed by the gospel, he endeavoured on his return to Antigua, to communicate to others the light of divine truth. His attempts were at first confined to a few persons, whom he collected together in his own house on the Lord's day; but afterwards he proceeded to preach in public, not only to the White people, but to the negro slaves. Conduct so singular and unexampled could scarcely fail to excite general notice, and to draw upon him the insults and slanders of the enemies of religion, notwithstanding the high station which he occupied in the island. He persevered, however, in his labours amidst much reproach; and he had at length the satisfaction of uniting about two hundred of his hearers into a Christian society, and continued to watch over them with all the affection and solicitude of a father. But in the midst of these disinterested labours, he was called away from this earthly scene, and his flock were left as sheep without a shepherd.

From the death of Mr Gilbert, near twenty years elapsed before one was found to supply his place. In 1778, Mr John Baxter, a member of the Methodist connection in England, embarked for Antigua, to work as a shipwright in the service of government; and, having on his arrival found religion at a very low ebb on the island, he immediately began to preach the gospel to as many as would hear him. Such of Mr Gilbert's hearers as had survived the ravages of death, and remained faithful amidst abounding iniquity, soon flocked to him. But as Mr Baxter was engaged in the employ of government during the day, he could devote only his leisure hours to their instruction. His ordinary practice was to travel in the evening to the plantations in the country, sometimes to the distance of ten miles; and after exhorting the slaves to flee from the wrath to come, he returned home under those heavy dews, which, in a tropical climate, are so injurious to health, that he might be ready for the labours of the ensuing day. In the course of a few years, Mr Baxter collected a society of near two thousand members; but unhappily, through a laxity of discipline, many were received into it whose conduct but ill corresponded with their profession.[1]

In January 1787, Mr Warrener, one of the preachers originally destined for Nova Scotia, was appointed to remain in Antigua; and Mr Baxter, in order to devote himself entirely to the work of the ministry, relinquished the situation he held under government, which was worth £400 a year currency. It was now found necessary to discard many of the members as unworthy of the profession they made, a circumstance which considerably reduced the number of the society. But the advantages which resulted from this step amply counterbalanced the loss. It rescued the gospel from disgrace, induced those who remained to walk with greater circumspection, and ultimately proved beneficial to the interests of religion.[2]

In 1795, the government of Antigua, dreading an attack from the French in Guadaloupe, applied to the Methodist and Moravian missionaries to raise a corps of the members of their societies to assist in defending the island. In compliance with this request they levied between them upwards of a thousand men. Sometime after, when Mr Warrener was riding into the country, a negro called to him and said, "Massa, when de fight to be?" "I hope never," answered Mr Warrener. "Well," he replied, "we hope so too, but if de French come, we'll fight dem." In order merely to try him, Mr Warrener said, "And, my negro, what would you fight for?" "Massa," replied he, "we fight for our wives, our children, our houses, and our chapel, massa." Happily the French never came, but had they landed, there is little doubt the negroes would have proved faithful. These facts may be considered as a proof at once of the loyalty of the Christian slaves, and of the confidence of government in them.[3]

[1] Coke's History of the West Indies, vol. ii. p. 427, 431, 438, 460; Account of the Rise, Progress, and Present State of the Methodist Missions, 1804, p. 8.

[2] Coke's Journals, p. 57; Minutes of the Methodist Conferences, from 1744, vol. ii. p. 326; Account of Methodist Missions, 1804.

[3] Coke's History, vol. iii. p. 64; Report of the Methodist Missions, 1816, p. 44.

In 1826, the mission in Antigua sustained a loss unexampled in the modern history of missions, the whole of the missionaries and part of their families, amounting in all to thirteen persons, having perished at sea. The sufferers were Mr White, his wife, and three children, Mr Truscott, his wife, and one child, Mr Jones, Mr Hillier, and Mr Oke, together with two servants. Of the whole party, one of the wives only, Mrs Jones, was saved.

The missionaries had gone to St Christopher's to attend what is called a district meeting, and when it was concluded, they sailed for Montserrat for the purpose of leaving there Mr Hyde and his family; and after having done this they proceeded on their voyage to Antigua, but such was the boisterous state of the weather, that after being twenty-four hours at sea, they put back again to Montserrat. After waiting there two or three days, they embarked on board the mail boat, by which they expected to reach home sooner than by the other vessel. The weather still continued exceedingly stormy; but towards sunset next day, they were fast approaching the island of Antigua, and were expressing their joy at the prospect of supping and sleeping ashore. The captain, however, was aware of the dangerous rocks and sands which lie in such numbers at the mouth of St John's harbour. About seven o'clock an alarm was raised by the cry of "breakers ahead;" and immediately after, the vessel struck on a reef to the leeward of Sandy Island. She fell on her side and filled directly. The sailors cut away her mast when she righted a little. They cast out the anchor and let out the chain cable which made her hang somewhat more securely on the rocks, whilst the sea beat over her in the most terrific manner. All the passengers and crew now hung upon the bulwarks and rails of the quarter-deck up to their middle in water. In this fearful situation they remained nearly an hour, when the waist of the vessel gave way and precipitated all who were clinging to the rails of the quarter-deck into the sea, namely, Mr and Mrs White with their three children, Mr and Mrs Truscott and child, Mrs Jones and two servants. Mr Jones being next to his wife, made a desperate effort to lay hold of her, and drew her up so far that she caught hold of part of the wreck on which he hung and was saved. The captain now exhorted all who were still on the vessel to come nearer to the head, as she was fast breaking up, and that part of her was likely to hold longest together; adding, "hold on if you possibly can till the morning, and then we shall be seen from Goat-hill battery and be rescued." With this advice they were enabled to comply, though not without considerable difficulty. The sea was tremendous and the night was dark. Wave followed wave in quick succession; and they had often only recovered their breath after one billow, when another struck them again. The long wished for morning at length dawned. They made the best signals of distress they were able, but these were not observed. They could see people walking on shore, but no one saw them, as they could not be distinguished from the reef amidst the dashing of the waves. Vessels and boats passed at some distance in the course of the day, and they endeavoured to hail them, but the beating of the sea on the rocks drowned their voices so that they were not heard. Notwithstanding all their disappointments, Mr and Mrs Jones were enabled to stay themselves on God, and to direct the captain and the sailors to "the Lamb of God which taketh away the sin of the world." Night again drew on apace, and enveloping them in darkness, rendered their situation at once more dreary and more perilous. Seated on a piece of the wreck up to their breasts in water, without a crumb of bread to eat or a drop of fresh water to drink, the sea rough, and the waves rolling over them, each billow threatening to swallow them up, they passed a fearful and an anxious night. If one ventured to sleep a little, another watched lest the waves should sweep him away. When morning dawned, it was welcomed with praise to God that their eyes were permitted once more to behold the light of day. Vessels and boats passed again, but they did not see them. Sometime after noon, Mr Hillier said he thought he could swim ashore, and might thus be instrumental in saving them all. Mr Jones and Mr Oke, as well as the captain, feared that he was too weak, in consequence of the want of food, to swim so far, the distance being about three miles. He, however, thought he could, and, in the spirit of prayer, committed himself to the deep, while they, after bidding him farewell, commended him to God. He struck off well; but in about ten minutes sunk to rise no more till "the sea shall give up the dead which are in it." One or two of the sailors also attempted to reach the shore on pieces of the wreck, but failed in the effort. Thus the survivors passed through another day of sorrows. The bodies of some of those who had perished were this day seen floating on the bosom of the deep. Night now approached once more, but with every appearance of its being their last, for the joints of the wreck began to open, and there was every likelihood of its being soon broken up. Contrary to expectation, however, they were spared to see another morning. The sea was now much calmer than it had been before; and about noon Mr Oke said he would endeavour to swim ashore; but he was drowned shortly after he got into the water, being too weak to swim far. Mr Jones now began to lose the use of his legs, and his wife called the captain to help her to raise them, if possible, out of the water. The captain made the attempt, but he was too weak to come to her assistance. Not long after, Mr Jones complained of a strange drowsiness. Feeling himself dying, he cried out, "Come, Lord Jesus, come quickly," and shortly after expired. Mrs Jones called to the captain but received no answer, for he too was dying. For a few minutes she held the body of her husband to her breast; but a wave soon washed it away from her enfeebled arms, and he fell at her feet. For a few seconds she saw it floating on the surge, and then sunk into a state of insensibility. In this condition she remained until rescued by Mr Kentish and Mr Ashford, two gentlemen who, on hearing of the wreck, through an American captain, who, it was said, passed by at noon, humanely came off without delay to render what help they could. When she was found, her face was so swelled that her head appeared almost a shapeless mass. On being touched, she came to herself, and asked, "What they were going to do with her?" They conveyed her ashore with all possible despatch, and at the house of Mr Kentish she received the utmost kindness and attention from him and his lady, as well as the best medical advice, which, through the blessing of God, were happily the means of restoring her. Only two others of the ship's company were saved, the mate and a black seaman, who, soon after the vessel struck, were carried away in the boat, and were picked up next day by a French sloop near the island of Nevis.[1]

[1] Meth. Mag. 1826, p. 349, 491.

In 1853, the number of church members in connection with the Methodist mission on this island amounted to 2472.[1]

Art. 2.—St Vincent's.

In January 1787, Dr Coke and three of his brethren visited St Vincent's, and were received with all that politeness and hospitality which distinguished the inhabitants of the West Indies. Mr Clarke, one of the missionaries, remained on the island, encouraged by the promise of several of the planters, that their houses should always be open to receive him, and their negroes ever ready to hear his instructions. Having commenced his labours, he proceeded in a calm peaceful course, without meeting with any thing remarkable, either to facilitate or to retard his operations. His congregations were large, and his exertions appeared to be crowned with considerable success.[2]

It must not, however, be supposed that opposition was entirely unknown; but for several years, it was confined to some lawless individuals, destitute alike of religion and humanity. One night, a number of rioters broke into the chapel, and after doing what mischief they could to the benches, they carried off the Bible, and hung it on the public gallows until the morning. Shocked at this gross act of impiety, the magistrates offered a reward of one hundred pounds for the discovery of the perpetrators; but though, in this instance, the arm of authority was exerted for the protection of religion, it was at length turned against her in a manner unknown in English legislation in modern times.[3]

In December 1792, the Assembly of St Vincent's, with the view of rooting the Methodists out of the island, passed a law, that no person except the rectors of parishes should preach without a licence; and that no individual should receive a licence until he had resided at least twelve months on the island, a clause admirably calculated to banish the Methodists from among them, as their preachers would never consent to lie idle a whole year, in order to have liberty of petitioning at the end

[1] Rep. Meth. Miss. Soc. 1853, p. 106.

[2] Coke's Journals, p. 59; Coke's History, vol. ii. p. 258.

[3] Coke and Moore's Life of John Wesley, p. 475; Coke's History, vol. ii. p. 270.

of that period for a licence, which, after all, would probably be refused, especially as, according to their system, they frequently change from one island to another. For the first offence, it was enacted that the culprit should be punished by a fine of £18, or by imprisonment for not more than ninety days, and not less than thirty; for the second, by such corporal punishment as the court should think proper, and by banishment from the island; and to crown the whole, if he returned from banishment, by DEATH! It is, however, but an act of justice to the people in general to state, that there is reason to believe they were decidedly hostile to this law; many of the most respectable inhabitants reprobated it in the most unequivocal terms. The act itself was hurried through the Assembly at the close of the session: many of the members had retired before it was passed, and though there remained only a very thin house, they were by no means unanimous.

Unappalled by this iniquitous law, Mr Lumb, the missionary in St Vincent's, preached as usual on the following Sabbath. In consequence of this, he was apprehended, and, on refusing to pay the fine, was thrown into prison. The magistrates, indeed, who committed him offered to lay down two-thirds of the penalty, and one of the merchants would have paid the whole, but Mr Lumb was determined to consent to nothing which might be construed as a voluntary submission to a law so execrable in itself, and so contrary to the spirit of the British constitution. When the period of his imprisonment had expired, he was released; but it was a release only to silence, or to voluntary banishment. He, of course, preferred the latter, and retired from St Vincent's, uncertain whether any missionary would ever again be allowed to settle on the island.

Happily the law was in force only for a short time, for as all the acts of the Colonial Assemblies had to be transmitted to His Majesty for his royal sanction, the King was graciously pleased to disallow it, as contrary to the principles of toleration, which were now an established part of the British constitution.[1]

In 1794, Messrs Thomas Owens and James Alexander were sent to renew the mission on the island of St Vincent's. Before the enactment of the late persecuting law, the members of the

[1] Coke's History, vol. ii. p. 271.

Methodist Society on this island, amounted to near a thousand, but scarcely was it passed, when the number was reduced more than one half. Multitudes who once appeared to run well, now wandered astray into the paths of error and of sin: so complete was their apostasy, that they threw aside even the form of godliness. Still, however, there were a few who, amidst the general declension, maintained their stedfastness, and continued to assemble in small companies for singing and prayer. To collect the scattered remains of the flock was among the first cares of the new missionaries. Many now returned from their wanderings; the congregations began to increase; no obstacles of any moment occurred, except those powerful moral impediments which exist in every country, and in every heart. A spirit of religious toleration breathed through the island. Many who were once the persecutors of the missionaries became their friends, and shewed them a degree of kindness and hospitality scarcely equalled in any other island. The prejudices of others, however, were rather smothered than subdued, and threatened to burst forth with renewed violence when any favourable opportunity presented itself.[1]

In March 1797, Mr H——, a magistrate and a member of the Council, who had been celebrating St Patrick's Day with other gentlemen of the island, proceeded at the head of some of his companions to the Methodist chapel, threw down the railing, burst open the door, broke nearly all the lamps, pulled down the communion rails, took the Bible, tore it in pieces and scattered them on the ground. The band of a regiment which accompanied them then struck up with their instruments of music, and after shouting and dancing like so many madmen, the rioters took their departure. Seeing Mr Pattison, the missionary, as they passed, Mr H—— the magistrate said to him with a shrug and a sarcastic smile, "Sir, I came here to keep the peace." His companions cursed, swore, and declared that if he said a word, they would take him to the market-place and give him a sound whipping. No disturbance of any consequence took place for another year, but when the celebration of St

[1] Coke's History, vol. ii. p. 277; Account of Methodist Missions, 1804; Watson's Defence of the Methodist Missions, p. 32; Missionary Notices relating to the Methodist Missions, vol. i. p. 73, 235.

Patrick's Day returned, Mr Pattison was apprehensive of a similar visit. He therefore proposed to Mr Hallet, his fellow-labourer, that they should sleep that night at the house of one of their friends who lived in the neighbourhood of the chapel. It was well they took this precaution, for in the dead of the night, some persons armed with swords or cutlasses broke into their house, entered the sleeping apartments, turned up the beds, and apparently searched for them in every corner. The friend at whose house they lodged that night having come out on hearing the noise, one of the ruffians struck her in the face with a bludgeon.[1]

In 1853, the number of church members in connection with the mission on this island amounted to 4813.[2]

Art. 3.—St Eustatius.

In January 1787, Dr Coke visited St Eustatius; but in consequence of the jealousy of the Dutch government, to which the island belonged, he was not allowed to preach to the negroes. During his stay, however, he employed himself in instructing small companies, from eight to twelve at a time, in the house of a free Black with whom he lodged. A poor slave from America, who endeavoured to instruct his countrymen, had shortly before been prohibited by the governor from preaching to them, and he was soon after whipped, imprisoned, and banished from the island, simply for continuing to pray with them. To prevent the commission of similar crimes for the future, the government issued an edict, that if any White person was found praying with his brethren, he should be fined for the first offence, fifty pieces of eight; for the second, a hundred pieces; and for the third, suffer whipping, confiscation of goods, and banishment from the island. But if the culprit was a coloured man, he should for the first offence receive thirty-nine lashes; for the second, he should, if a freeman, be whipped and banished; and if a slave, be whipped every time.[3]

[1] Watson's Defence, p. 80.
[2] Rep. Meth. Miss. Soc. 1853, p. 107.
[3] Coke's Journals, p. 64, 94; Account of Methodist Missions, 1804.

In December 1788, Dr Coke again visited St Eustatius, and notwithstanding the persecution under which the Methodist Society on this island had of late laboured, its numbers amounted before his departure to no fewer than two hundred and fifty-eight. He preached once; but next morning, he and two others of the company received a message from the governor and fiscal, requiring them to promise that they would not preach publicly or privately, by day or by night, to White or Black people, during their stay on the island, under the penalty of prosecution, arbitrary punishment, and banishment. Mr Brazier, a preacher who had been raised up in the West Indies, was not included in this message. He therefore remained on the island, but the governor soon discovered and dislodged him. In the mean while, Dr Coke left St Eustatius; and some days after, on visiting Saba, a small island in the neighbourhood, he was surprised to find Mr Brazier there before him. In compliance with the request of the governor and council, he appointed him to remain among them; but the governor of St Eustatius, who possessed the supreme authority in the Dutch possessions in that part of the West Indies, soon compelled them to part with their preacher.[1]

The Methodists in St Eustatius enjoyed some relaxation on the arrival of a new governor from Holland, but as the old governor was afterwards restored, the flames of persecution were again kindled. The poor slaves who met to sing and pray and speak about religion, were whipped, and many of them imprisoned. In consequence of these severities, the society was almost entirely broken up; but yet there were a few classes which kept together. They retired to some distance into the country that they might meet in quietness, and as often as circumstances allowed, they visited the neighbouring island of St Christopher's, that they might enjoy the ordinances of the gospel. Dr Coke went to Holland for the purpose of obtaining from the Dutch government toleration for the Methodists in St Eustatius, but his applications were not attended with success.[2]

In 1810, after a lapse of many years, two of the Methodist

[1] Coke's Journals, p. 95, 97, 99.

[2] Coke's Journals, p. 125, 167; Coke's History, vol. iii. p. 62; Drew's Life of the Rev. Dr Coke, p. 259.

missionaries waited on the governor of St Eustatius, which had lately been captured by the British, and obtained liberty from him to attempt the establishment of a mission on the island. The preachers who first went thither experienced considerable hostility, but they at length triumphed over all opposition. The tranquillity they enjoyed formed a striking contrast to the intolerance of former years. The congregations were in general large, and many of the White people, as well as the negroes, heard the word with great attention.[1]

In 1853, the number of church members in connection with the mission on this island amounted to 315.[2]

Art. 4.—Barbadoes.

In December 1788, Dr Coke, accompanied by Mr Benjamin Pearce, visited Barbadoes, and was received with the greatest politeness by different gentlemen on that island. Having obtained liberty to instruct the slaves on several plantations, Mr Pearce remained in Barbadoes, and immediately commenced his labours with great energy and zeal. It was not long, however, before he began to experience violent opposition from a number of the inhabitants. His enemies were many, and some of them men of rank and influence. A report was circulated, that, under the pretext of instructing the negroes in the principles of religion, the Methodists designed to disseminate among them notions incompatible with their condition as slaves, and with the interests of their masters. Repeated attempts were made by the mob to interrupt the meetings for divine worship. One Wednesday evening, near the close of the service, they broke forth with more than ordinary violence. All was confusion and disorder. They stamped, they whistled, they roared more like fiends than human beings. Leaving the chapel, they posted themselves at the door, and assailed it in a most outrageous manner. Here they shouted, threatened, swore, and discharged such vollies of stones, as if they intended to break

[1] Methodist Magazine, vol. xxxiv. p. 395, 396; Watson's Defence, p. 128; Rep. Meth. Miss. 1813, p. 8.

[2] Rep. Meth. Miss. Soc. 1853, p. 106.

it open. After taking ineffectual vengeance on the chapel, they retired amidst the noise of their own imprecations. In consequence of this attack, Mr Pearce applied to a magistrate for redress. He heard his statement with apparent indignation at the rioters, issued warrants against several of them, and promised to do him justice. On the day of trial, Mr Pearce appeared with several other respectable witnesses; but though the charges were proved by the most unquestionable evidence, the magistrate gave the following extraordinary decision: "The offence was committed against ALMIGHTY GOD: it therefore does not belong to me to punish it." Mr Pearce was left with all his expenses to pay, a prey to a lawless mob, at once the scorn and the pity of his foes.

Finding themselves sanctioned by those who ought to have checked them, the enemies of the Methodists increased in number and in violence. To preach at night was utterly impracticable: even to sing a hymn was almost a call to arms. The mob immediately surrounded the house, and assailing it with stones, compelled the few who had assembled to disperse. After some months, when tranquillity was in a considerable degree restored, Mr Pearce ventured again to preach in the evening; but in the course of a few weeks, a new disturbance was raised One night, several young men entered the chapel and endeavoured to interrupt the service. Mr Pearce bore with them for a considerable time without noticing their conduct; but the noise became at length so intolerable, as to overwhelm his voice. He then endeavoured to silence them by expostulation; but after making several ineffectual attempts, he was obliged to dismiss the congregation. On leaving the chapel, the rioters were joined by about a hundred others, who now constituted a formidable mob. Their first effort was to break open the door; but failing in the attempt, they demolished the window above it with stones. Mr Pearce now ventured out among them, with the view of endeavouring to make them desist, and of marking such as were most active in the assault. On beholding the chief object of their malice, several of the rioters attempted to strike him; but though encircled with danger, he escaped unhurt. They then surrounded his house, determined apparently to give some signal display of their prowess; but after wearying themselves with menacing parades, they retired without doing any particular mischief.

On reviewing this flagrant assault, Mr Pearce resolved to appeal once more to the justice of the island. The magistrates to whom he applied, issued their warrants with the utmost readiness against the rioters, and when brought before the court, five of them pleaded guilty. Previous to this, they had applied to Mr Pearce to have the matter accommodated without a trial, but the magistrates expressly prohibited any compromise with them. On pleading guilty, they received a severe reprimand from the bench, and were dismissed on condition of paying the whole expenses of that day's proceedings, and one-half of the sum paid by Mr Pearce to the lawyers whom he had consulted.

But notwithstanding this decision, some of the rioters soon afterwards, when Mr Pearce was in the country, attacked his house, and assailing it with stones, struck his wife very severely. As the delinquents were unknown, it was impossible to bring them to justice; nothing remained but to bear the injury with patience, and to watch with vigilance against any similar attempt in future.[1]

In 1791, Mr Pearce was succeeded in his missionary labours by Mr Lumb, who, on his arrival, found the prejudices of the planters, especially in the country, so far dispelled, that he had access to more estates than he was able to visit. There were no fewer than twenty-six plantations to which he went once a fortnight; but his visits were attended with little or no success. The Blacks, in general, were as indifferent to religion as the Whites. Many of them treated with contumely its sacred institutions, and poured contempt on such as professed themselves its friends. A very extraordinary name was given to them, Hallelujah. Even the little negroes learned the appellation, and called them by it, as they passed along the street.

The mission to Barbadoes continued in a very languishing state for many years. In Bridgetown, the capital, few attended the meetings for divine worship, and even among these, a want of reverence could not have been more conspicuous, had the chapel been a theatre, and the gospel a farce. Persecution was now nearly unknown, or at least, reared its head only occa-

[1] Coke's Journals, p. 75; Coke's History, vol. ii. p. 143.

sionally; but it had given place to a more deadly weapon, a settled contempt for divine things. In the country, a few doors still remained open; but the greater number were completely closed: the congregations were reduced to a shadow, seldom exceeding ten or twelve persons. In consequence of the death of several of the missionaries, and of the many discouragements they experienced, this island was repeatedly left without a preacher, a circumstance which contributed still further to retard the progress of the mission. Amidst these various trials, a few of the members maintained their stedfastness without wavering; but through abounding iniquity, the love of many waxed cold. Even some who once seemed pillars in the house of God, returned back to the world, and united with those whose chief delight it was to traduce the professors of religion.[1]

In October 1823, a storm burst forth on the mission which for the time threatened its entire extinction. Mr Shrewsbury, who had now been a missionary on the island for upwards of three years, had always had many enemies. He was the daily object of their scoffs and jeers, and even in the public streets he was frequently abused as a villain, and that not by the rabble merely, but by the great vulgar, by merchants from their stores, and by other persons in the garb of gentlemen. But there now occurred circumstances which raised the hostility of the Barbadians to a higher pitch than ever. Intelligence having been received of an insurrection of the slaves in Demerara, a notice was posted up in the Commercial Rooms, that "the Methodist clergymen of Demerara were both imprisoned, they being deeply implicated in the insurrection which had broken out in that colony." This falsehood[2] stated in so public a manner, set the people in a flame. Fresh stories were circulated every day. The island newspapers were filled with invectives against certain hypocritical characters, who, under the pretext of communicating religious instruction to the slaves, were introducing among them principles subversive of the foundations of civil

[1] Coke's History, vol. ii. p. 150; Coke's Journals, p. 119.

[2] The statement was false as regarded the Methodist missionaries; but it no doubt arose out of the fact that Mr Smith, one of the missionaries of the London Society in Demerara, was, as we shall afterwards have occasion to state, apprehended under a charge of being implicated in the insurrection of the slaves in that colony.

society, particularly as existing in the West Indies. The Methodist missionaries were represented as in correspondence with the African Institution; and it was said, that Mr Shrewsbury held private meetings with the slaves for the purpose of getting all the information he could from them in order to convey it to that society. Having in a letter, written three years before, spoken of the neglected and immoral state of the slave population, he was charged with having sent home to England the vilest calumnies against the Barbadians, and some even asserted, that he had therein stated that the slaves ought to take their liberty by force, if they could not otherwise obtain it. To crown the whole, the discussions in Parliament on the subject of slavery had of late been renewed with powerful effect, and Mr Canning, one of the Secretaries of State, had as an amendment on a motion by Mr Buxton, proposed a series of resolutions relative to measures for improving the condition of the slaves, preparatory to their being admitted to the rights and privileges of freemen. Official despatches had just reached the island containing His Majesty's recommendations of these reforms, and declaring, in terms the most express, the necessity of carrying them into effect with all possible despatch, and in the spirit of perfect and cordial co-operation with His Majesty's government; and that if any serious opposition should arise, the earliest opportunity would be taken of bringing the subject before Parliament again, and submitting to its consideration such measures as it might in consequence of this appear advisable to adopt. The arrival of these despatches raised still higher the angry passions of the colonists, and the Methodists were doomed to be the more immediate objects on whom they poured forth their wrath.

One Sabbath evening, some persons assembled at the chapel door and threw in among the congregation a number of thin glass bottles filled with a mixture of oil and assafœtida. Happily no one was seriously injured; but the confusion and uproar which ensued cannot easily be described. When this had subsided, Mr Shrewsbury proceeded with the service, though in the mean while, stones were rattling against the chapel from every quarter. Next day he offered a reward of £30 currency for the discovery of the offenders; but he soon found that whoever they were, many of the community were disposed to countenance and support them. Hence his offer of a reward was made sport of; and a person of low character was employed to go about the streets singing a ballad turning into ridicule his efforts to bring the offenders to justice. Meeting thus with general countenance, his enemies increased almost hourly both in number and in strength, and were emboldened for still further mischief.

On the following Saturday se'ennight, a handbill was circulated in Bridgetown, calling on the inhabitants to assemble next evening and pull down the Methodist chapel. Accordingly, on Sabbath evening by six o'clock, the rioters began to muster, bringing with them masons, carpenters, &c., armed with hammers, saws, hatchets, crows, and every other instrument necessary for the work of destruction. Having burst open the chapel gate and doors, they fell to work, demolishing the lamps, benches, pews, and pulpit, leaving nothing but the bare walls. They next went up stairs to the dwelling-house, broke open the doors and windows, chopped up tables, chairs, and every article of furniture, threw out the crockery ware, and proceeded to demolish the roof and to break down the walls. From 150 to 200 men were employed in the work of destruction, from seven in the evening till after one in the morning, it being full moon at the time, and though there was present an immense crowd of spectators, yet no attempt was made to stop their riotous proceedings either by the civil or military authorities. On the following evening the mob returned, and falling to work again, completely levelled the walls until not one stone was left upon another. As, in the exasperated state of the public mind, Mr Shrewsbury's life was considered as not safe, and every one, in fact, was afraid to harbour him, he and his wife, by the advice of their friends, betook themselves to places of concealment during the night, and next day they left the island and proceeded to St Vincent's.

Two days after Mr Shrewsbury's departure, the governor, Sir Henry Warde, issued a proclamation offering a reward of £100 to any person who should give such information, as should lead to the conviction of any who were concerned in these riotous proceedings. But so daring and outrageous were the rioters, that they issued next day a counter proclamation, threatening that if any person came forward to injure any individual, in any way, they should "receive that punishment which their crimes could justly deserve." This extraordinary and contumacious document, stated, at the same time, that as it might be supposed that the demolition of the chapel was the work of the rabble in order to create anarchy, riot, and insubordination, to trample upon the laws, and to subvert good order, it was "considered an imperative duty to repel the charge, and to state, First, That the majority of the persons assembled were of the first respectability, and were supported by the concurrence of nine-tenths of the community; Secondly, That their motives were patriotic and loyal, namely, to eradicate from the island the germ of Methodism which was spreading its baneful influence over a certain class, and which would ultimately injure both Church and State. With this view the chapel was demolished, and the villainous preacher who headed it and belied us, was compelled by a speedy flight to remove himself from the island." The proclamation concluded with an expression of their "fixed determination to put an end to Methodism in the island;" and "all Methodist preachers were warned not to approach its shores, as if they did, it would be at their own peril."[1]

This exasperated state of the public mind lasted for a considerable time, and it continued to be dangerous for any Methodist missionary to land on the island; but the proceedings in the case of Mr Shrewsbury having been brought before the House of Commons, and a resolution strongly condemnatory of them being passed, the Barbadians, though as hostile to the Methodists as ever, now changed their tactics. At a numerous meeting held in Bridgetown, it was resolved to present a petition to "His Majesty to protect the Colonies from the machinations of their enemies in England, and also to petition the Colonial legislature to go the utmost length in meeting the views and wishes of the Government and Parliament of England respecting the amelioration of the slaves, that may be consistent with the public peace, and with the real interests of all parties." With the view of furnishing their friends in England with the means of defending them, they, at the same time, issued a de-

[1] Miss. Not. vol. iv. p. 194, 209, 215, 517.

claration that, as many of the speakers in the debate in the House of Commons relative to the outrage committed on the Wesleyan chapel, endeavoured to throw the odium of it upon the community at large, by asserting that the demolition of the chapel was the act not of a mob but of persons who from their station and property must be supposed to belong to the most respectable classes of society, they felt themselves called on to declare that they cordially concurred in every sentiment of reprobation expressed by the House of Commons against that disgraceful act, and that they viewed, and ever did view, with indignation that scandalous and daring violation of the law. This declaration was signed by ninety-four persons, of whom eight were members of Council, three members of the House of Assembly, ten clergymen, and the rest planters, attorneys, and overseers, residing five, ten, and sixteen miles in the country: in fact, only about twelve of those who signed it could be said to live in Bridgetown. There were good reasons for believing the whole to be a piece of mere craft and hypocrisy.

In March 1826, Mr Rayner came from St Vincent's to Barbadoes with the view of renewing the mission. His landing was soon noised abroad, and a placard was posted up the same day, calling upon all the true friends of their country to prepare to tar and feather him. He did not immediately begin to preach, as the president refused to grant him a licence; but when he afterwards began to hold meetings, he was not interfered with. A new and spacious chapel was erected in Bridgetown; the prejudices of the inhabitants against the Methodists in some degree subsided; the congregations became large and more respectable than formerly; new openings were found in different parts of the island; many manifested much attention to the word, and numbers were admitted as members of Society. After some years, Methodism raised its head above the contumely of its enemies, and this became at length, as regards numbers, one of the most prosperous of the West India missions.[1]

In 1853, the number of church members in connection with the mission on this island, amounted to 3045.[2]

[1] Rep. Meth. Miss. Soc. 1824, p. 95, 100, 105; Ibid. 1825, p. 50. 56; Ibid. 1826, p. 58. Meth. Mag. 1826, p, 561, 566, 852; Ibid. 1829, p. 639. Miss. Not. vol. iv. p. 513, 524; vol. viii. 229.

[2] Rep. Meth. Miss. Soc. 1853, p. 107.

Art. 5.—Tortola and the other Virgin Islands.

In January 1789, Dr Coke, accompanied by others of his brethren, visited Tortola; and as a pleasing prospect of usefulness presented itself, Mr Hammet, one of the missionaries, remained on the island, and in a short time collected a large society. On the arrival of other preachers, they extended their labours to Spanish Town, and many of the other islets which are scattered up and down in the vicinity, and, like solitary rocks, lift up their heads above the waves. To several of these they paid frequent visits in open boats, to the prejudice of their health, and often at the risk of their life, in order to preach the glad tidings of salvation to the few forgotten families who inhabited them.[1]

As a proof of the importance of christianizing the negroes, even in a political point of view, it is worthy of notice, that not long after the commencement of the war with France, the president of the council received information, that the French inhabitants of Guadaloupe meditated a descent on the island. He immediately sent for Mr Turner, the superintendent of the mission in Tortola and the other Virgin Islands, and having informed him of this report, added, that there was no regular force in the colony to defend it against the enemy, and that they were afraid to arm the negroes, unless he would put himself at the head of them. Mr Turner was sensible that such a step was not properly within the line of the ministerial office; but yet considering that the island was in imminent danger, that if it were conquered by the French, the religious privileges of the negroes would probably be lost, and that the war on their part was entirely of a defensive nature, he consented to the governor's request, and was accordingly armed with the negroes. About a fortnight after, a French squadron made its appearance in the bay; but being informed, it is supposed, by some emissaries, of the armed force on the island, they abandoned their design, and retired.[2]

[1] Coke's Journals, p. 99; Coke's History, vol. iii. p. 112; Account of the Methodist Mission, 1804.

[2] Account of Methodist Missions, 1804.

In December 1805, a most brutal outrage was committed on Mr Brownell, one of the missionaries in Tortola. One day, as he was walking along the street, he was sternly accosted by a gentleman, who directed him to read a paper which he put into his hand. On stepping aside for that purpose, he was seized by the arm, and dragged to the middle of the street, by the person who had just given him the paper, and who now proceeded to bestow on him the epithets of rascal and scoundrel, and afterwards to strike him on the face, first with a stick, then with his fist, next to pull him by the nose, and then to kick him. He was instantly joined by another person, equally furious and foolish as himself, who, after pouring forth more abusive language, struck him a violent blow on the breast. Mr Brownell had scarcely time to turn round, before a third person struck him with the butt end of a whip, which cut his head very severely. His hand was raised to give a second blow; but providentially he did not strike, otherwise the consequences might have been fatal. A mob now collected around them, and while they were inquiring into the fray, Mr Brownell escaped to the house of a gentleman in the neighbourhood. No sooner did his assailants discover that he had fled, than they pursued him; but, happily, he eluded their notice by prostrating himself on the floor while they passed the window. In consequence, however, of the wound and bruises he had received, he was confined for some time, and was so ill, that he had to be attended by two physicians.

The cause of this brutal assault, was a letter written by Mr Brownell some time before, in which he said, "Fornication, adultery, and neglect of all religion, are reigning sins in this region." Of this letter, which had been published in England, an extract was transmitted to Tortola; and these gentlemen, from a conviction, no doubt, of the unspotted purity of their own characters, and of the perfect innocence of the community in general, took this incontrovertible method of demonstrating the falsehood of the charges.

Not convinced, however, by this kind of argument, Mr Brownell brought the affair before the Grand Sessions of the Virgin Islands; but though the deed was committed in the street, and in open day, the jury could find no bill. He was even checked their proceedings. Through the remonstrances of a gentleman of influence, some of the magistrates published an advertisement, which kept the mob from that time within tolerable bounds. One of the rioters was prosecuted, and three respectable White people gave the clearest evidence against him; but the oaths of the Methodists were considered as of no weight, and a midshipman being procured to swear an *alibi*, the fellow was acquitted of the charge. The grand jury, indeed, gave it as their opinion, that both Mr Hammet and the chapel ought to be prosecuted as nuisances. The newspapers were for several months full of letters for and against the Methodists. Every thing evil was said of Mr Hammet; every disgraceful epithet was heaped upon him. As to Dr Coke, a ridiculous story was published of his having been tried in England for horse-stealing, and flying to America to escape from justice.[1]

Harassed with opposition and fatigue, Mr Hammet was worn to a mere skeleton, and was obliged to remove to America on account of the state of his health; but previous to his departure, other two missionaries had arrived on the island. The violence of persecution now abated, and at length entirely ceased: a few stones were occasionally thrown at the chapel; but personal interruption seldom occurred. The missionaries by degrees extended their labours to Spanish Town, Montego Bay, and to various plantations in the country. Their exertions, were not, indeed, crowned with that extensive success which attended the labours of their brethren in some other islands; but yet they were not without fruit. In this peaceful course, they proceeded for a number of years; but at length the storm of persecution again burst forth, and raged with more violence than ever. Formerly it was the work of lawless individuals; now it was the deed of the Legislative Assembly.[2]

In April 1802, some of the local preachers visited Morant Bay, a place about thirty miles from Kingston, and in a short time a small society was collected in that village. The enemies of religion, however, did not view their progress with indifference or unconcern. Indignant at their proceedings, they presented the places in which their meetings were held, as nuisances

[1] Coke's Journals, p. 101, 135; Account of Methodist Missions, 1804.
[2] Coke's History, vol. i. p. 422, 431.

+

to the quarter-sessions of the parish; but being able to produce nothing against either the preachers or their hearers contrary to the laws of God or man, they were compelled, though with reluctance, to drop the prosecution. The meetings, therefore, were continued, as no legal opposition could be made to them, and they met with no interruption for some time, except from the lawless rabble, and a few disorderly people about the place. But here the matter did not long rest. The Assembly of Jamaica soon afterward passed an act, ordaining that no person, unless he was qualified by the laws of that island and of Great Britain, should preach or teach in meetings of negroes or people of colour; that persons offending against this law should be deemed rogues and vagabonds; that if the criminal was a freeman, he should be committed to the workhouse, and kept to hard labour, one month for the first offence, and six months for every repetition of it; that if the case were extraordinary, the assizes might inflict any punishment not extending to life they should think fit; that if the criminal was a slave, he should, for the first offence, be committed for hard labour to the nearest workhouse for one month, and for every subsequent offence be subjected to a public flogging, not exceeding thirty-nine lashes; and that any person who should knowingly permit such a meeting to be held on his premises, should be liable to a fine not exceeding £100, and be committed to the common jail until he should pay it, and give security for his future good behaviour.

As this act of the Legislature of Jamaica professed to prohibit only unqualified persons from preaching to the negroes and people of colour, the Methodist missionaries did not apprehend that they came within the meaning of the law, as they were possessed of regular licences, which they had obtained in England, and which would have been admitted as valid in any court of justice in Great Britain. Mr Campbell, therefore, continued to preach as usual in Kingston, and met with no kind of interruption; but when he proceeded to preach at Morant Bay, he was apprehended and taken before the magistrates, who committed him to prison, notwithstanding he produced to them a certificate of his being duly qualified according to the laws of England. When the month of his imprisonment expired, he returned to Kingston, and having applied to the quarter-sessions of that town for a licence, his request was immediately granted. After preaching there about two months, Mr Campbell, accompanied by his fellow-missionary Mr Fish, once more visited Morant Bay; but as this was a different parish, neither of them ventured to preach, though they had both qualified at Kingston under the new law, without asking leave of the magistrates in that quarter. They therefore respectfully petitioned them for permission to qualify before them also, if they required it; but the magistrates returned for answer, that they would grant no licences to preach, and as a punishment, it would seem, for even asking leave to qualify, they revived the old prosecution against Mr Campbell, though it had now been dropped for some time. Not content with his former imprisonment, they endeavoured to apprehend him for the penalty of £100, on account of the house in which he had performed divine worship, and resolved to make him give security that he would in effect never preach more; and unless he found such security, he was informed, he might be doomed to perpetual imprisonment. Mr Campbell, therefore, by the advice of his friends, made his escape from Jamaica and returned to England, leaving Mr Fish to take care of the flock at Kingston, where they still had the liberty of preaching. The serious people at Morant Bay, however, were now, in a great measure, deprived of the means of grace. One of them, a very sensible and respectable man, was imprisoned for a month, simply for singing and praying with a few friends, as the magistrates, with the wisdom and impartiality of judges, construed this to be the same as preaching or teaching. All social worship was now at an end; nor was the mischief confined to this place, for the new law was employed as an engine for putting a stop to the preaching of the gospel in various other parts of the island.[1]

But as, by the constitution of Jamaica, no act of Assembly is permanently established as a law, until it receive the royal assent, this bill had only a temporary operation. His Majesty, agreeably to the principles of toleration, which form an essential part of the British constitution, having refused his sanction

[1] Coke's History, vol. i. p. 443; Evan. Mag. vol. xii. p. 136.

to it, the pious people of Jamaica, after a lapse of two years, were again permitted to resume their meetings for the public worship of God. The missionaries now applied to their work with new energy: they extended their labours to other parts of the island; and their exertions appeared to be crowned with considerable success. But scarcely had the prospects of the Methodists begun to brighten, when a dark cloud again overcast them.[1]

Though the bill was disallowed by His Majesty, the Assembly of Jamaica endeavoured to elude, as far as possible, the effect of the royal negative, and to establish a system of persecution equally terrible, at least within the precincts of Kingston. An act of the legislature of the island having been procured for erecting a corporation in that town, an opportunity was taken of introducing into it a clause, by which that body was empowered, among a variety of other particulars, to impose on all who should violate their regulations, fine and imprisonment to a large extent. The design of this clause was probably not perceived by the Board of Trade, and accordingly the act obtained the sanction of His Majesty. As the proceedings of the Corporation of Kingston were not subjected to the revision of the king, this circumstance was soon improved as a means of reviving the old system of persecution.

In June 1807, the Common Council, under pretence of zeal for the purity of religion, passed an act by which any person not duly authorized by the laws of Jamaica and Great Britain, who should presume to preach or teach, or offer up public prayers, or sing psalms, in any meeting of negroes or people of colour, within the city or parish, should, if a free person, suffer punishment by a fine not exceeding £100, or by imprisonment in the common jail or workhouse for any period not exceeding three months; and, if a slave, by imprisonment and hard labour for a space not exceeding six months, or by whipping not exceeding thirty-nine lashes, or both; that a similar punishment should be inflicted on every person who permitted such an illegal meeting in his house or premises; and that even in a licensed place of worship, there should be no public wor-

[1] Coke's History, vol. i. p. 443; vol. ii. p. 3, 11; Evan. Mag. vol. xii. p. 136.

ship earlier than six in the morning, or later than sunset in the evening, under a like penalty.[1]

By this cruel law, the slaves in the parish of Kingston were completely hindered from attending divine worship, except on the Sabbath. Before the sun rises they had to be at their work, and they durst not leave it before it set. The Council of Kingston, therefore, did not restrict them from receiving instruction when they had no opportunity of getting it; they only prohibited them when they were at liberty! Such were the methods adopted "for preventing the profanation of religious rites and false worshipping of God." It is not unworthy of notice, that the French and Spanish priests, who either had chapels, or wished to erect them, were permitted to worship God according to the dictates of their consciences; while those who were not only Protestants, but the natural-born subjects of Britain, laboured exclusively under the prohibition.

It was reported by the advocates of this measure, that "the meetings of the slaves and others were held at unseasonable hours; that people could not pass through the streets without being annoyed with singing and praying; that the orderly inhabitants could not rest in their beds without being disturbed, as the new religionists were engaged in these exercises all night; and that there was nothing but singing and praying through all Kingston." Whatever may be thought of the other charges, the last of them was unquestionably erroneous; for rioting, dancing, billiards, theatrical amusements, and every species of dissipation, abounded in that town. Nobody was molested in the enjoyment of them, nor will any one suppose, that these nurseries of vice were closed at an early hour, or that those who frequented them were studiously careful not to interrupt the silence of the night. The professors of religion ought not, therefore, to have sustained alone the charge of disorder, while their accusers themselves were equally, or even more guilty.

It must, however, be acknowledged, that these allegations were not entirely without foundation. Among the Methodists and others who made a profession of religion, there were some whose zeal was greater than their knowledge, and hurried them

[1] Christian Observer, vol. vi. p. 686; Evan. Mag. vol. xv. p. 471; Coke's History, vol. ii. p. 15.

into extravagancies which the more sober-minded viewed with regret. Their enemies, at the same time, manifested a singular degree of sensibility with respect to improprieties of this kind, even the most inconsiderable. Previous to the enactment of the law, a man was put in confinement simply for praying too loudly in his own house between eight and nine o'clock at night, which, to say the least, was not a late hour!

Several months elapsed after the passing of this law before any of the Methodists fell under its iniquitous lash; but at length the missionaries in Kingston, by a piece of indiscretion which can admit of no apology, brought the weight of its vengeance on their head. One night there was a public dance in their neighbourhood, which was attended by some of the most powerful and opulent individuals in the island. It was Saturday, but yet the amusement was protracted to a late hour. Messrs Gilgrass and Knowlan, the two missionaries, apprehending an infringement of the Sabbath, availed themselves of the established law, and sent notice to the company to break up their amusement. Irritated by what they deemed an insult, the assembly refused to comply with the message, and probably protracted the entertainment longer than they otherwise might, purely from motives of defiance. The missionaries finding their notice slighted, and the laws trampled under foot by those very individuals who ought to have supported them by their example, insisted on the town guard going to disperse them. Mr Gilgrass himself accompanied the guard, and soon broke up the assembly. Such an imprudent step could not fail to embitter their enemies against them, and to render them more eager than ever to detect them in some breach of the law. Unfortunately it was not long before they found the desired opportunity. Mr Gilgrass was in the habit of teaching the young people to sing hymns between five and six o'clock in the evening. A few nights after the interruption of the dance, Mr Firth, a missionary who had just arrived from England, introduced a new tune, to which the others listened, he and his wife being excellent singers. At a quarter past six, the police-officer and a magistrate entered the house with a night guard, and were going to carry them to the cage, a place where vagabonds guilty of misdemeanours were confined; but they were satisfied for the present with taking their promise to appear in court. On appearing before the Corporation some days after, Mr Gilgrass was sentenced to be confined in the common jail for one month. Mr Knowlan's punishment was remitted in consequence of his indisposition, and even Mr Gilgrass was permitted to leave the prison after about a fortnight's confinement, a treatment more lenient than could have been expected, considering the temper of their enemies and the provocation they had of late received.[1]

The law of the Corporation of Kingston was necessarily confined in its operation to that parish; but, in the mean while, the Assembly of the island, under the pretence of exciting the proprietors of negroes to instruct them in the principles of religion, passed an act ordaining that the instruction of slaves should be confined to the doctrines of the Church of England; that no missionaries should presume to teach them, or receive them into their houses or assemblies, under the penalty of £20 for every slave proved to have been present; and if the offender refused payment, he should be committed to the county jail until the fine was discharged.

By this means a complete stop was put to the labours of the Methodists in Jamaica. Prohibited as they were from admitting slaves into their assemblies, they still wished to preach to people of free condition, but all their applications for a licence were refused in the most pointed manner. Frequently before the chapel was completely shut, while persons of free condition went in to attend divine worship, the slaves crowded around the door which the law forbade them to enter, with looks of the most expressive sorrow and words of the most melting eloquence. Some might be heard saying, "They would not make Massa go again to jail; me no go in a chapel, but me hear at door and window." Others were heard to exclaim, "Massa me no go to heaven now." "White man keep Black man from serving God." "Black man got no soul." "Nobody teach Black man now." The missionaries beheld them and wept, but durst say nothing. They were even obliged to appoint persons to stand at the door of the chapel, to prevent the slaves from entering and involving them in enormous fines.[2]

[1] Coke's History, vol. ii. p. 13, 21.

[2] Coke's History, vol. ii. p. 19, 23; Watson's Defence, p. 144; Rep. Meth. Miss. 1813, p. 11; Ibid. 1814, p. 11.

The Assembly knowing that such a measure would be disapproved of by His Majesty, resorted to the trick of ingrafting it upon an act to continue the general system of the Slave laws, which had been consolidated into a temporary act that was then about to expire. Their agent was of course instructed to represent, that if the act of continuation was disallowed, Jamaica would be left destitute of slave laws, a circumstance which could not fail to endanger the peace and safety of the island; but the Board of Trade found a way to frustrate this shameful artifice, by advising His Majesty to disallow both the act in question and the act of repeal, which had never expressly received the royal sanction, though it had been several years in force. The general slave laws, therefore, were by this means still established, and only the persecuting clauses of this new bill disannulled.

But as the legislature of Jamaica, by the stratagem of delaying to transmit the act for the royal sanction while it had its operation in the island under that of the governor, had for more than a year suspended the meetings of the negroes for public worship, His Majesty, to prevent the repetition of such shameful proceedings in that or any of the other islands, issued a general order to the governors in the West Indies, commanding them that they should, on no pretence whatever, give their assent to any law relative to religion, until they had first transmitted a draft of the bill to England and had received His Majesty's approbation of it, unless in the body of the act a clause was inserted suspending its operation until the pleasure of His Majesty should be known respecting it.

Enraged at this new disappointment, the Assembly of Jamaica came to various resolutions on the state of the island, in which they declared, that the prohibition of passing laws on the subject of religion was a violent infringement of the constitution of the colony; that until it was withdrawn, it was the duty of the house to exercise their privilege of withholding supplies; and that after a certain period, until this grievance was redressed, no money should be granted or raised within the island for the support of the military establishment. In consequence of these violent proceedings, the Duke of Manchester, the governor, immediately dissolved the Assembly.[1]

[1] Evan. Mag. vol. xvii. p. 296, 342; vol. xviii. p. 12

In November 1810, the Assembly, not discouraged by the decision of the government at home, passed a new act on the subject of religion, and introduced into it such regulations, relative to the licensing of preachers and places of worship, as plainly shewed that it was their design to prevent the instruction of the negroes by those who alone were willing to teach them. This law, indeed, was to continue in force only for twelve months; but this very circumstance, which might seem trivial, displayed the artfulness of the Assembly, being no doubt intended to elude His Majesty's disallowance of the bill, as by the time this could be notified, the law would have expired. How the governor, in direct opposition to an express command from His Majesty, should have given his assent to such a bill, it is not easy to explain.[1]

By these means, all preaching was for some time at an end; but as the restrictions did not extend to private assemblies, Mr Wiggins the missionary, employed himself in meeting classes, in administering the Lord's Supper, and in the discharge of other ministerial duties. After the expiration of the last act of Assembly, he ventured to preach in Kingston; but as the law of the Corporation of that town was still in force, he did not escape the vigilance of his enemies. Next day he was summoned before the magistrates, and was sentenced to one month's imprisonment in the common jail. It appeared indeed as if the enemies of religion were determined to put a period to the labours of missionaries on the island.[2]

[1] Christian Observer, vol. ix. p. 601; Evan. Mag. vol. xix. p. 395, 439.

[2] Buchanan on a Colonial Ecclesiastical Establishment, p. 86.

Though much of the hostility which the Methodists experienced in Jamaica, and some of the other West India Islands, arose, no doubt, in many cases from the natural enmity of the human heart against religion, and in other cases from ignorance and misapprehension of the nature and design of their labours, yet, in some instances, it was greatly increased by considerations of a private nature. We are often at a loss to account for the persecutions which broke out against them: no misconduct on the part of the missionaries; no conspiracies among the slaves; no rumour of the approaching attack, prepares us for any such event. The storm gathers and bursts before we are aware. Of this, however, we have an explanation in the following passages, in Mr Watson's able *Defence of the Methodist Missions in the West Indies.* "Other causes," says he, "which have produced many instances of individual opposition, and which, in some cases, have chiefly promoted acts of legislative oppression, could be adduced; but we do not seek occasion of crimination, though the causes of opposition we allude to would greatly explain and fix its character." "If it should appear that the real

In December 1815, Mr John Shipman began to preach again in Kingston, after the chapel had been shut, with one short interval, for upwards of eight years. After several unsuccessful applications, he had, to the astonishment and the joy of the friends of religion, obtained permission to take the oaths to government, and a licence to preach the gospel. This was so unexpected, and so improbable, that many of the leaders would scarcely believe it, even when assured of the fact on the best authority, and in the most positive terms. Others of the missionaries afterwards obtained similar licences, so that the pri-

offence given by missionaries is their preaching faithfully against certain reigning vices; that among the number of those 'turned to righteousness,' have been many females who were the objects of illicit attachment and licentious intercourse; that the personal ill treatment which the preachers of 'righteousness, temperance, and judgment to come,' have in many cases experienced, has been the consequence of violent resentment, produced by checks put upon vicious indulgence, by the introduction of a stronger principle of morality among the slaves and females of colour; and that restrictive laws, gravely proposed to legislatures, have been, in instances which might be given, mainly the work of men who had such injuries to complain of, then the whole controversy would be placed in a light in which that party are not, we are persuaded, disposed to have it viewed. On this subject evidence is not wanting; but the necessity of adducing it, shall be created only by the conduct of those who are most anxious to justify their zeal against missions on very different grounds."

Among the pretences under which the persecutors of the Methodists in Jamaica masked their opposition to them, was zeal for the purity of religion, and their dread of the pernicious principles taught by the missionaries. No doubt, they were admirable judges of orthodox doctrine, and of the language in which it ought to be expressed! We have an amusing instance of the proneness of some men to start at shadows, and of the strange construction which fear and jealousy may put on the most harmless matter, in the following extract from the Minutes of the Jamaica Common Council, containing questions put to Mr Bradnock, one of the missionaries:—

In Common Council, December 14th, 1807.

Question 6. Are you aware of a resolution of the Society of Wesleyan Methodists, entered into at the last Annual Conference to this effect: "That no person shall be permitted to retain any official situation, who holds opinions contrary to the total depravity of human nature?" If so, answer whether the term "official situation" does not include you as a preacher? and what, to the best of your knowledge and belief, is alluded to by the words, "total depravity of human nature?"

Answer. Does not know of such a resolution being enacted lately, but thinks it proper. Supposes the term "official," applies to his office among others. Thinks the words "total depravity," allude to our fallen nature.

Question 7. Do you *conscientiously* think that the resolution before mentioned, purports that no person should hold an official situation who has opinions against the fallen nature of man, as being born in sin, *and that it has no allusion whatever to the state of bondage as it exists in this country,* being the total depravity of human nature?

Answer. Answers particularly in the affirmative.

There were, it seems, some subtle divines in the Common Council in those days, men admirably qualified to judge of the doctrines taught by the missionaries.—*Watson's Defence*, p. 141.

vilege was not confined to Mr Shipman. Having divided the island into as many districts as there were principal societies, they proceeded in their labours with increased energy and zeal. They now received more invitations from planters to preach on their estates, than they had ever done before. Their congregations greatly increased, and their societies were augmented to an extent unknown in any other island. It is not unworthy of notice, as an indication of the change of opinion in Jamaica, that on the death of Mr Burgar, one of the missionaries, the magistrates and vestry of Morant Bay voted to his widow the sum of one hundred pounds sterling, as a testimony of their sense of his good conduct during his residence in that parish. In the mean while, the House of Assembly did not entirely lay aside its hostility to the Methodists; but though it passed some acts against them, the missionaries met with no serious interruption in their labours for a number of years. There, however, arose at length new and successive storms, at once violent and of long continuance.[1]

In 1824, the spirit of opposition again broke out against the Methodists. The more immediate cause of this, was the receipt in the island of the resolutions which had been lately passed by the House of Commons, for the amelioration of slavery in the West Indies, with a view to its ultimate extinction. Then it appeared that old prejudices had been smothered only, not extinguished, and that nothing was wanting but an occasion to kindle the latent spark into a flame. The missionaries were now, as in Barbadoes, accused of being the agents of the African Institution,[2] and every effort was made to blacken their characters and to send them off the island.

In December 1826, the House of Assembly passed what was called a Consolidated Slave Act, in which were inserted several clauses designed to restrict the labours of missionaries and others among the slave population. Under the pretext, that "the assembling of slaves and other persons after dark, at places of meeting belonging to Dissenters from the Established religion, had been found extremely dangerous, and great facili-

[1] Rep. Meth. Miss. 1815, p. 12; Ibid. 1816, p. 21; Ibid. 1817, p. 26; Miss. Notices, vol. i. p. 40, 66, 107, 163, 188; vol. iii. p. 372; Meth. Mag. vol. xli. p. 237; vol. xlii. p. 522.

[2] See p. 456.

ties were thereby given to the formation of plots and conspiracies, and the health of the slaves and other persons had been injured in travelling to and from such places of meeting at late hours in the night," it was enacted, "that any sectarian dissenting minister, or other person professing to be a teacher of religion, who should keep open any such places of meeting between sunset and sunrise, or permit any such nightly assembly of slaves therein, or be present thereat, should pay a sum not less than £20 nor exceeding £50 for each offence; and in default of payment thereof, the justices were required to commit such offender to the common jail, for any space of time not exceeding one month." To shew more precisely that it was the missionaries who were aimed at, exceptions were made in favour not only of the ministers of the Church of Scotland, but of persons of the Roman Catholic and Jewish persuasions. It was further provided, that "slaves found guilty of preaching and teaching without permission from their owner and the quarter-sessions for the parish, should be punished by whipping or imprisonment in the workhouse or hard labour;" and "that religious teachers taking money from slaves should pay a penalty of £20 for each offence, and in default of payment, be committed to the common jail for a month."[1]

This act was scarcely passed when an outrageous attack was made on the Methodist missionary Mr Ratcliffe and his family at St Ann's Bay. On Christmas-day, the Rev. Mr Bridges, the rector of the parish,[2] preached an inflammatory sermon, in which he professed to shew the evils of separation from the Church of England, and insinuated that the missionaries had political, not religious ends in view, and that their doctrines were artfully subversive of the civil institutions of the country, and dangerous in their effects on the minds of the slaves. About midnight a party of the light company of the St Ann's militia, which was stationed in the town as the Christmas guard, came and fired into the Methodist chapel, in which there were rooms partitioned off for the missionary's residence. Seven balls were afterwards extracted from the

[1] Meth. Mag. 1828, p. 134; (Baptist) Miss. Herald, 1827, p. 36.

[2] This person made himself notorious, as well by the part he acted as a slaveholder and as an advocate of slavery, as by his opposition to the cause of missions.—*Anti-slavery Reporter*, vol. iii. p. 174, 356, 358, 373, 440; vol. iv. p. 140, 246.

chapel; two were found on the floor, and one was sticking in the column nearest the pulpit. The ramrod of a pistol was also found not far from the window of the house; but happily none of the inmates were hurt. An inquiry was instituted by the magistrates as to the perpetrators of this outrage, and the vestry even offered a reward of £50 on their conviction; but the whole appears to have been little better than a farce for the purpose of vindicating the credit of the island. Several persons afterwards gave themselves up under the assurance probably that they were perfectly safe, and accordingly the grand jury, when the charge came before them, ignored the bill.

In May 1827, the act of Assembly came into operation in the island, under the sanction of the governor, and a few weeks after, Mr Grimsdall, who had lately come to St Ann's Bay, was committed to jail for ten days, by the quarter-sessions, for having held a meeting after sunset at which slaves were present, he having stated to the court that he would not pay any fine. Not long after, he was again thrown into prison on the alleged ground of his having preached in an unlicensed house. He had applied for a licence, but had been refused contrary to the judgment of the custos and of another magistrate who were present when the application was made. He was, however, liberated on bail, and a short time previous to the day on which he was to appear again before the court, he was delivered by death out of the hands of his persecutors.[2]

Though the act of Assembly had in the mean while come into operation in the island, yet when it was laid before His Majesty, it was, as might be expected, disallowed; the governor was informed that it was the settled purpose of His Majesty's government to sanction no colonial law which should needlessly infringe on the religious liberty of any class of His Majesty's subjects; and he was distinctly instructed not to give his assent to any bill imposing any restraint of that kind, unless there was a clause in it suspending its operation until His Majesty's pleasure should be known.[3] But notwithstanding the determination

[1] Meth. Mag. 1827, p. 567; Ibid. 1832, p. 670; Rep. Meth. Miss. Soc. 1829, App. p. 3; Duncan's Narrative of the Wesleyan Mission in Jamaica, p. 185, 190.
[2] Meth. Mag. 1827, p. 702; Ibid. 1828, p. 205.
[3] Meth. Mag. 1828, p. 134; Rep. Meth. Miss. Soc. 1829, App. p. 4.

manifested by the home government, the magistrates of St Ann's were not to be deterred from following out their persecuting course.

In August 1828, Mr Whitehouse, who had come to St Ann's Bay after the death of Mr Grimsdall, was thrown into prison on a charge of preaching without a licence for that parish. The cell where he was confined was exceedingly filthy, and the stench was intolerable. There was no bed provided for him, not even one of straw; a few benches, however, were allowed to be brought from the chapel on which to make up a bed. The jail, the hospital, and the workhouse, with their various miserable inmates, were all under one roof; no words, in short, can convey an adequate idea of the offensive and wretched nature of the place. Mr Orton, of Montego Bay, having been informed of the imprisonment of Mr Whitehouse, came to visit him, and having preached in the chapel, it being the evening of the weekly sermon, he also was next day thrown into prison, and orders were given that no persons should be allowed to see them, except their wives or other members of their family. Mr Watkis, a free person of colour, and one of the leaders of the Society, was on the following Sabbath committed to jail on the charge of "preaching and teaching," though he had done nothing more than sing and pray with the people; but he was liberated on bail two or three days after. Mr Orton now became seriously ill, while the heat was so oppressive, the stench so insufferable, and the almost incessant cracking of the whip, and the clamour of the various inmates so distracting, that he could not even get sleep. Application having been made for a writ of *Habeas Corpus* on an allegation of false imprisonment, the two missionaries were ordered to be removed to Kingston jail, that they might be brought before the chief justice for an examination of their case. On being transferred to that place and delivered up to the jailor, he begged them to remain with their friends, having perfect confidence that they would make their appearance when it was required. When they were brought before the chief justice, their legal adviser moved that they should be discharged, on the ground of illegal and false imprisonment, and the chief justice stated that having duly examined the case, he had no hesitation whatever in discharging them:

it was not his province to make laws, but to be regulated by them; and on this ground he ordered their full and unconditional discharge. Sir John Keane, the lieutenant-governor, shewed at the same time his determination to maintain religious toleration, by dismissing from His Majesty's commission the two magistrates, Messrs Rose and Hemming, who had committed them to prison. But even this did not put an end to the proceedings of their enemies. Rose, one of the magistrates who had been dismissed, now preferred an indictment against Mr Orton for wilful perjury, because he had stated in the affidavit for obtaining the writ of *Habeas Corpus* that bail had been offered for him, but that it had been refused unless he would give security that he would not preach again in the parish until he obtained a licence from the quarter-sessions, which would of course not be granted; but when the matter was brought to a trial, the jury brought in a verdict of Not guilty. Thus Mr Orton's persecutors, by the attempt which they made to ruin him, only covered themselves with disgrace. His health, however, was so much injured by his previous imprisonment, that after lingering for twelve months almost useless to society, and nearly falling a sacrifice to a constantly remittent fever, he was obliged to leave the field of his labours and return to England.[1]

Toward the close of the year, the Consolidated Slave Act was re-enacted by the House of Assembly, with the persecuting clauses which had previously occasioned its disallowance, and after some opposition in the council, it was tendered to Sir John Keane, the lieutenant-governor, for his assent, but this he refused to give, agreeably to the instructions of His Majesty's government. With the view of shewing the necessity of such restrictive laws, and of thus giving a colour to their contumacious proceedings in re-enacting the rejected bill, the House of Assembly had appointed a select committee "to inquire into the establishment and proceedings of the sectarians in the island," and this committee, in the report which they presented to the House, had gravely stated that the principal object of the sectarians was to extort money from their congregations under every possible pretext, and that to obtain it recourse had been had to the

[1] Meth. Mag. 1828, p. 845; Ibid. 1829, p. 59, 208; Rep. Meth. Miss. Soc. 1829, App. p. 6, 9.

most indecent expedients;[1] that in order to further this object, and to gain an ascendancy over the negro mind, they inculcated the doctrines of equality and the rights of man, preached and taught sedition even from the pulpit, and by misrepresentation and falsehood endeavoured to cast odium upon all the public authorities of the island, not excepting the representative of Majesty itself; that the consequences have been abject poverty, loss of comfort, and discontent among the slaves frequenting their chapels, and deterioration of the property of their masters; that their interference between the masters and slaves was dangerous and incompatible with the political state of society in the island; and they therefore recommended to the House of Assembly to adopt the most positive and exemplary enactments to restrain them. This report was not only adopted by the House, and extensively circulated in Jamaica, but it was resolved that a copy of it, and of the examinations on which it was founded, should be communicated to His Majesty's ministers, and large quantities of it were forwarded to the island agent in England, with a view to its circulation in the mother country; but he, not thinking it suited to the latitude of England, prudently withheld it from the public eye.[2]

In December 1829, the House of Assembly passed a new Slave act, in which the rejected clauses of the late bill were, with only a few alterations, again inserted. It is not unworthy of notice, however, that these clauses were carried in a way which shewed that the charges lately brought against the missionaries were scarcely believed by many even of the members themselves, for had they rested on such evidence as carried conviction to their minds, it might have been expected they would have been carried by a unanimous vote of the Assembly; whereas it was by majorities small beyond all former precedent on such questions; and in order to carry them, one of the members, who most strenuously and violently advocated them, found himself under the necessity of resorting to the artifice of using

[1] It was stated (we presume in evidence) that such was the desire of the missionaries for money, that they recommended females to prostitute themselves in order to obtain it for contribution.

[2] Anti-slavery Reporter, vol. ii. p 442; vol. iii. p. 24; (Bapt.) Miss. Herald, 1829, p. 20; Meth. Mag. 1829, p. 275; Rep. Meth. Miss. Soc. 1829, App. p. 12; Hinton's Memoir of the Rev. W. Knibb, 1st Edit. p. 94.

the name of His Majesty's ministers in a most unwarrantable manner to influence the division, asserting that he had high authority for stating, that if a few verbal alterations were made in the clauses, which had occasioned the rejection of the late act, they would receive the sanction of the government at home. It is further worthy of notice, that in the course of the debate on one of the clauses which aimed most directly at the suppression of missionary labours, by prohibiting assemblies of slaves before six o'clock in the morning and after six in the evening, an amendment was moved, which would have exempted all meetings of slaves for religious purposes from its operation, and that this amendment was lost by six votes only. Even this was not all. The amendment was moved by Mr Batty, the original framer of the clauses in the bill of 1826, and himself a member of the sectarian committee, as it was called, and it was seconded by Mr Marshall, the chairman of that committee, so that it is natural to conclude, that even they did not believe the statements of the report, nor the examinations on which it was founded. This act, strange to tell, was, notwithstanding the previous repeated instructions of His Majesty's government, passed by Earl Belmore, who had lately come out as governor of the island.[1]

When this act was laid before His Majesty in council, it was, as might have been foreseen, disallowed by him; and the House of Assembly, in its displeasure with the home government, resolved to take no step whatsoever to amend their slave law. It was proposed to enact the bill, with the exclusion simply of its persecuting clauses; but after long debates, which displayed not only an extraordinary degree of heat and asperity, but gross ignorance of all constitutional principles, and the most determined hostility to all missionary efforts, it was thrown out by a majority of 24 to 16.[2]

In December 1831, an insurrection broke out on the north side of the island, in the parish of St James', and quickly extended to Trelawney, Hanover, Westmoreland, St Elizabeth, and partially to Manchester, Portland, and St Thomas in the east. It does not appear to have been the design of the slaves to take

[1] Rep. Meth. Miss. Soc. 1829, App. p. 18; Duncan's Nar. p. 253, 260.
[2] Anti-slavery Report, vol. iv. p. 143.

the lives of the White people, grievously as they had been oppressed by them; their object was simply to obtain their freedom, which they erroneously supposed had been granted to them by the king, but that it was withheld from them by their masters and the local authorities. Accordingly, scarcely any blood was shed by them. At the outset, the most they did to their overseers was to put some of them in the stocks; but they injured them no further. In this respect, they displayed a moderation which has rarely been exemplified in the warfare of civilized nations. But they destroyed property to an immense amount. The flames might be seen bursting forth from one estate after another. A beautiful, rich, and highly cultivated country was in a few days laid waste. On many estates, the whole of the buildings were reduced to ashes. The White people fled to the towns, leaving all behind them: terror and dismay were depicted in their countenances.[1]

Immediately on the breaking forth of the insurrection, the military force of the island, including the militia, was called out; the disturbed districts were placed under martial law, and the most active measures were adopted to suppress it. The insurgents, ill armed, and altogether unorganized, and without proper leaders, were unable to withstand the military force sent against them. They fled before it; their confederacy was quickly broken. Many were killed, some in cold blood under circumstances of the most revolting barbarity; others took refuge in the woods and mountain fastnesses. Great numbers were taken prisoners; hundreds were tried by court-martial, and shot or hanged, often on very slender and even doubtful evidence. Many more were cruelly flogged, receiving 200, 300, and even 500 lashes. Others were condemned to be confined in workhouses, and to be worked in chains for life. Even many females were bound to the foot of the gallows and barbarously flogged: unable to move, they might be seen lying

[1] Meth. Mag. 1832, p. 296, 672; Rep. Bapt. Miss. Soc. 1832, p. 24; Rep. Scottish Miss. Soc. 1832, p. 23, 30.

The loss occasioned by the insurrection, according to a report of the House of Assembly, amounted to no less than £1,154,583 : 2 : 1. (*Anti-slavery Reporter*, vol. v. p. 253.) How far this estimate rested on adequate evidence, we do not know: it is not likely it would be under the truth. The reports of the House of Assembly were often worthy of little confidence.

about the sides of the roads, their lacerated bodies broiling under a scorching tropical sun. In fact, the cruelties exercised by the Whites on the poor negroes, even on the innocent and unoffending, baffles all description. They appear to have caught the spirit of bloodhounds, and were athirst for blood. No insurrection was ever more ferociously punished. On the other hand, it is worthy of notice, that many of the slaves who were executed, died exulting in suffering for the sake of freedom;[1] nor did they suffer in vain, for there can be no doubt that this insurrection of the negroes, and the cruelties exercised toward them by the Whites, contributed not a little to hasten on the general emancipation of the slaves throughout the British Colonies, and ultimately, it may be hoped, throughout the world.

Upon the breaking out of the insurrection, a violent outcry was raised against all missionaries, particularly the Baptist and the Methodist, as if they had been the cause of it. The island newspapers were filled with inflammatory articles against them. Nothing could be more false and calumnious, nothing more brutal and ferocious, than the attacks which were made upon them. At their door was laid all the blood which had been shed, the destruction of property, the incendiarism, the rapine, in short, all the evils of the insurrection. Without any trial, without even the least evidence, they were proclaimed guilty, and a loud and general outcry was raised for the most summary measures being taken with them.[2] Several of the Baptist and one of the Moravian missionaries were arrested and tried, or proposed to be tried, for their lives, and though every means was resorted to, not excepting subornation of perjury, in order to obtain their conviction, yet no charge could be established against them. Some of the Methodist missionaries were also arrested, but they were subsequently discharged. At meetings convened in different parishes throughout the island, it was gravely resolved, that the insurrection was attri-

[1] Facts and Documents connected with the late Insurrection in Jamaica, p. 22.

[2] "Shooting," writes the Editor of the Jamaica Courant, "is too honourable a death for men whose conduct has occasioned so much bloodshed, and the loss of so much property. There are fine hanging woods in St James' and Trelawney, and we do sincerely hope that the bodies of all the Methodist preachers who may be convicted of sedition, may diversify the scene."—*(Bapt.) Miss. Herald*, 1832, p. 22.

butable to the Wesleyans in common with the other sectarians, and petitions were prepared, praying the House of Assembly to banish them from the island. Even the committee appointed by the Assembly to inquire into the insurrection, did not hesitate, in the absence of all evidence, to represent the Methodist, the Moravian, and particularly the Baptist, missionaries, as one of the causes of it.[1]

It is scarcely necessary to express our conviction, that no missionaries of any denomination had any thing to do with the insurrection, or that they were in any degree the direct cause of it. Of their having instigated, promoted, or encouraged it, there never was even the shadow of evidence, notwithstanding the eagerness of their enemies to criminate them. Though as men and as Christians possessed of ordinary feelings of justice and benevolence, they could not but desire the downfal of the whole system of slavery, yet to imagine them capable of exciting the negroes to insurrection with a view to its overthrow, would be to suppose them without common understanding, the attempt being so utterly hopeless; while at the same time they could not but see that there was a spirit and a process in operation in England, and also in the Colonies, which could not fail to bring it to an end at no distant period, in a peaceful and bloodless manner. It is true the plot or combination originated among negroes connected with the Baptists; but it amounted to nothing more in the first instance, than to a resolution, confirmed in many cases by an oath, not to work after Christmas without wages, under the persuasion that an order for their freedom had come out from England; and there also appears no reason to doubt that many of them, as well as some of other denominations, took part in the rising. But while we apprehend this must be admitted, it is no less true that many of the Baptists and Methodists, as well as of other religious bodies, did all they could to persuade their fellow-slaves to go to their work after Christmas as usual; and after the insurrection did break out, when the Whites had all fled from the estates, or were engaged in the militia, there were many instances in which, at the risk of their own lives, they protected their master's

[1] Meth. Mag. 1832, p. 298, 672; Facts and Documents, p. 18; (Bapt.) Miss. Herald, 1832, p. 21; Anti-Slavery Reporter, vol. v. p. 234.

property against the insurgents; and when estates were fired, they exerted themselves to the utmost of their power to save what they could from the devouring flame.[1]

With respect to the causes of the insurrection, they are not far to seek. They lay with the White people themselves. The government of England having now fallen into the hands of that political party which many years before had carried the abolition of the slave trade, early shewed its determination to adopt effective measures for the amelioration of the condition of the slaves, with a view, it was obvious, to the ultimate abolition of slavery itself. No sooner was this known in Jamaica, than the White people rose nearly as one man, and vehemently protested against the violation of what they called their unprescriptible and unalienable rights. The clamour became loud and universal. Meetings were held in almost every parish of the island. Speeches were delivered and resolutions passed of the most violent and inflammatory description; resistance to the mother country and the renunciation of their allegiance to the sovereign were distinctly threatened; and similar language was held even within the walls of the House of Assembly. The proceedings of these meetings continued to fill the newspapers for several months together, and they could not fail to be known to the slaves, some of whom read the newspapers for themselves, while many more heard the news from others. Such, in fact, was their earnest desire to know what was going on in England as well as in the colony, that it was a common practice for pedlars, who went about from one estate to another with trinkets and other articles for sale, to take newspapers with them, by reading which they readily collected customers around them. The same topics were freely talked of at the tables of the White people in the presence of their household slaves. Thus the negroes saw their masters in a state of almost open rebellion against the supreme authorities of the empire, and that in reference to measures intimately connected with their interests and happiness. A report, in fact, was circulated among them that the king had sent out orders for their freedom; but that the White

[1] Facts and Documents, p. 10, 20; Knibb's Memoir, p. 117, 119; Meth. Mag. 1832, p. 296, 303, 381; Duncan's Nar. p. 289.

people withheld it from them. They were told it was in the newspapers, and they were confirmed in this by the unguarded language of some of their overseers. Hence some, as already stated, came to a resolution, and even took an oath, not to work after Christmas unless wages were paid to them; and some resolved to fight rather than remain any longer slaves, believing that in asserting their freedom, they might calculate on the neutrality of His Majesty's forces.[1]

But the more immediate cause of the insurrection, and what drew many into it who would not otherwise have risen against their masters, was a circumstance of a much more trivial kind, which occurring at so critical a time, was followed by the most disastrous consequences. It had always been the custom in Jamaica to allow the slaves three holidays at Christmas, during which no restriction was set on their amusements, provided they did not interfere with the public peace. These three days of complete relaxation of the ordinary restraints of slavery were of course greatly prized by the negroes. But Christmas having fallen this year on a Sunday, they were entitled to the three following days; and an attempt having been made in the parish of St James' and some of the neighbouring districts, to deprive them of the Wednesday, the great body of them refused to turn out to work on that morning. The disturbances began on those estates where this ancient custom was invaded, and which in the view of the slaves had passed into a right: on those properties where the usual relaxation was allowed, all was tranquil. The disturbances once begun quickly spread, and were no doubt greatly exasperated by the harsh measures adopted by the Whites for their suppression. Such were the chief causes of the insurrection; and though they could not be altogether unknown to the White people, even at the time, yet it was found convenient to avert the blame from themselves, by throwing it upon the sectarians, as all missionaries were called; at all events, the insurrection itself furnished a favourable occasion for rousing the popular indignation against them, and for organising a system of opposition to them which for a time

[1] Anti-slavery Reporter, vol. v. p. 83, 94, 234, 242; Facts and Documents, p. 9, 10, 13.

threatened the subversion of missionary operations throughout the island.[1]

In January 1832, immediately after the suppression of the insurrection, an association called the Colonial Church Union was established in St Ann's, the parish of which the Rev. Mr Bridges was rector; and similar associations were quickly formed throughout the whole island. The great object of these associations was the expulsion of all ministers from the country, except the clergy of the Established Churches of England and Scotland. The spirit of the Union seemed to fly like wild fire throughout the island; the utmost enthusiasm was every where manifested in its behalf; all classes of the Whites enrolled themselves as members, and those were held up as enemies to the country who refused to join it. At their meetings, resolutions of the most violent character were passed; they set all law and authority at defiance, and declared their determination to prosecute their great object, even at the hazard of their lives.[2]

Though the Colonial Unions greatly concentrated and exasperated the spirit of opposition to the missionaries, yet previous to their formation it had broken forth in acts of outrageous violence. Though the outcry was most vehement against the Baptists, and though they suffered to a far greater extent than the Methodists in the destruction of their chapels and other mission property, yet in St Ann's where the Colonial Union originated, the latter were equally, if not even more obnoxious than the former. The mob destroyed the chapel at St Ann's Bay, and three others in the same county. The St Ann's regiment of militia, which was quartered at Falmouth, before leaving that town destroyed both the Wesleyan and the Baptist chapels. It appears that magistrates, a member of assembly, captains of militia, the head constable, and the deputy-marshal of St Ann's, were present at the demolition of the chapels, encouraging the mob in their lawless proceedings; and though the rioters committed these outrages in open day, and persons who were witnesses of their deeds made affidavits to this effect,

[1] Anti-slavery Reporter, vol. v. p. 234, 242; Meth. Mag. 1832, p. 297, 678.

[2] Narrative of Recent Events connected with the Baptist Mission in Jamaica, Kingston 1833, App. p. 7; Meth. Mag. 1832, p. 673; West Indian Documents, p. 6; Facts and Documents, p. 7; (Bapt.) Miss. Herald, 1832, p. 75, 82.

yet the grand jury ignored the bills. Subsequently to the demolition of the chapels, Mr Whitehouse and Mr Wood, two of the Methodists, and Mr Nichols, one of the Baptist Missionaries, were hung in effigy in the market-place of St Ann's Bay. The custos having come into the town, ordered the whole to be taken down; but the mob were much enraged at this, and after he left the place, a Jew who was one of the leading men in destroying the chapels, caused the gallows to be erected on his own premises, where he could not be interfered with. There the effigies (two or three of the leaders being now added to them) dangled in the air for several days and nights, and volleys of musket-shots were fired at them; every morning a figure of Satan was affixed to the top of the gallows, and the following words in large characters were represented as proceeding out from his mouth: "These are my beloved, in whom I am well pleased." In Jamaica there are a considerable number of Jews, and some of them, as of old, were among the bitterest opposers of the missionaries.[1]

After the formation of the Colonial Unions, the anti-missionary spirit was not only excited to the highest pitch, but it pervaded nearly the whole island. At Falmouth, a band of ruffians forced an entrance one Saturday evening into the house of Mr Bleby the missionary, nearly all of them armed with bludgeons. Some of them seized him and held him fast, while others covered his head, face, and breast with tar, and one took the candle from the table and applying it to his clothes, attempted to set him on fire. Mrs Bleby seeing his danger, dashed the candle from the fellow's hand on the floor, by which means it was extinguished. An alarm being given by this time, several people came to Mr Bleby's assistance, and the ruffians who were up stairs hearing a scuffle below, left him and ultimately succeeded in making their escape. Mrs Bleby twice thrust herself between her husband and his assailants: the first time, one of them seized her and threw her violently on the floor; the second time, two of them dragged her away and attempted to lock her up in the pantry, but she clung to them and got out with them. Mr Bleby having made his way into the yard, the

[1] Facts and Documents, p. 14; Meth. Mag. 1832, p. 673, 756.

same man who had attempted to set him on fire rushed on him, and aimed a violent blow at his head; but he avoided it by stooping. He again ran up stairs, when one of the miscreants struck at him with a bludgeon, but missed his aim. He finally succeeded in making his escape over the fence at the back of the house, and took refuge in the house of a person of colour who offered him shelter and protection.'[1]

At Montego Bay, Mr Murray the missionary, was stopped preaching, on the allegation that neither the house nor himself was licensed. It appears that the old chapel, which was regularly licensed, had been pulled down, and as the new one was erected on the same site, it had not been thought necessary to apply for a new licence, that never having been the practice. Mr Murray, too, having taken the oaths in another parish, considered himself as duly qualified to preach in this. The magistrates, however, declared their determination to enforce the law, and at the same time refused an application which was made for a licence for the chapel, and for permission to him to take the oaths, and they also prohibited him from preaching. Notwithstanding this, Mr Murray would have preached; but he wisely yielded to the advice of some of his friends, who entreated him not to attempt it, as it was understood he would be apprehended in the pulpit, and as a large number of persons were determined he should not go to prison, a riot, perhaps bloodshed, might be the consequence. The chapel was therefore shut up, and all the services were for the present at an end. Mr Murray renewed his application at the next quarter-sessions, to have the restrictions laid on him removed; but he was told that the magistrates had come to the resolution not to allow any sectarians to preach in future, which they alleged they had a right to do, the toleration laws of England not being in force in Jamaica. Having, notwithstanding this, begun to preach, he was thrown into prison; but after eight days, he was released on bail, by an order from the chief justice. He immediately commenced preaching again, and the prosecutions which were raised against him, one at the quarter-sessions, another at the Assize Court, having completely failed, all proceedings were

[1] Anti-slavery Reporter, vol. iv. p. 537.

dropped, and he was thus left at liberty to carry on his labours without further interruption or molestation.[1]

At Manchioneal, Mr Rowden the missionary, was required to give up his house to the commanding officer of a party of soldiers which was sent to that place; but with this extraordinary demand he was not disposed to comply, more especially considering the manner and circumstances in which it was made. Inquiry was now made at him by two magistrates, as to his authority for preaching in the parish; and on his shewing them his credentials, they declared them insufficient, inasmuch as they alleged, there was a colonial law which required dissenting teachers to take out a licence in every parish in which they preached. Mr Rowden replied he was not aware of any such law; but at the same time expressed his readiness to take the oaths whenever called on to do so by any justice of the peace; and from a conviction that he was acting according to law, he felt himself bound to proceed in the discharge of his ministerial duties. Warrants were prepared by anticipation for apprehending him in the event of his preaching, and as he did preach on the Thursday evening, he was immediately arrested and committed to the common jail at Morant Bay. He was lodged in a damp cell, and the first night caught a severe cold, which was succeeded by so violent an attack of fever, that he was obliged to give bail to appear at the next quarter-sessions, himself for £100, and one of his brethren for £50. Though liberated from prison, his fever now increased, and brought him to the gates of death; but it afterwards abated, and ultimately left him. He was then ordered by his physician to go to Kingston for a change of air; but on arriving there, he had a relapse, which was equally, if not more severe than the first attack. His illness proved so protracted, that it was impossible for him to appear at the quarter-sessions.[2] We might mention other instances of the hostility of the colonists to the missionaries;[3] but this is scarcely necessary, after the examples we have already given.

During this period of persecution, the societies in various places

[1] Meth. Mag. 1832, p. 894; Miss. Not. vol. vii. p. 311; Rep. Meth. Miss. Soc. 1834, p. 75.

[2] Meth Mag. 1832, p. 826; Miss. Not. vol. vii. p. 177.

[3] Meth. Mag. 1832, p. 293, 673, 677, 760, 823, 896.

were left without pastoral care, and the congregations without public worship, the missionaries not being allowed to exercise their ministry, and some of them being even obliged to take refuge in Kingston or other places to escape personal violence. Even in those places where they continued to preach, not many of the negroes were able to be present. Numbers were prohibited by their attorneys and overseers from attending, and were consequently afraid to come; or if they did venture, it was by stealth, and often at the risk of punishment. To prevent their slaves from going to chapel, several of the planters made them work on those days which used to be allowed them for cultivating their provision grounds, and for the worship of God, and gave them other days in lieu of them. In order to neutralize the effects of the labours of the missionaries, the most strenuous efforts were made by some to revive the heathenish sports and amusements, which were formerly prevalent among the negroes, but which had now very generally fallen into disuse; and great preparations were made in many of the parishes to restore them in all their wonted vigour at the following Christmas. The efforts to corrupt the negroes were not altogether unsuccessful. The missionaries had to mourn over some who yielded to the temptation, while their enemies triumphed in their success. The member of Assembly for the parish of St Ann's, rose in his place and said, He was happy to inform the House that a great improvement had taken place in the manners and morals of the negroes in the parish which he had the honour to represent, since the sectarians had been expelled from it. Before, they were always melancholy, and nothing but religion, and singing, and praying, would do for them; but now, he was happy to say, they were returning to their old plays, dances, and other amusements, and were picking up all their old songs. Such was the improvement in manners and morals which pleased a Jamaica legislator.[1]

Meanwhile Earl Mulgrave[2] arrived as governor of the island, and he early shewed his determination to maintain the cause of religious liberty, and to protect the missionaries in the enjoyment of their rights and privileges. In January 1833, thirteen

[1] Rep. Meth. Miss. Soc. 1833, p. 76; Miss. Not. vol. vii. p. 245.
[2] Afterwards Marquis of Normanby.

months from the commencement of the disturbances, His Majesty's royal proclamation was issued in Jamaica, putting down the lawless and outrageous Colonial Church Unions, and declaring that he will maintain within the island the principles of religious toleration, and protect and defend all his subjects in the exercise of the public worship of God, according to their consciences. This proclamation was accompanied by a circular from his Excellency the governor, requiring the prompt obedience and co-operation of the magistrates in enforcing it. But the wild and daring contumacy of the planters was not to be easily and at once put down. A spirit of determined adherence to the great object of the Colonial Unions was manifested in several parts of the island. At what was called a numerous and respectable meeting of the Colonial Union, in St Thomas in the Vale, after laying it down as an indisputable principle that "Sectarian influence is Colonial ruin," and passing several resolutions in maintenance of this principle, it was further resolved: "That to carry into effect these resolutions, this meeting do earnestly call on the magistrates and vestry of this parish, and throughout the island generally, to resist every application made by sectarians for licences to preach to our slaves, or for licensing places of worship, which would only be licensing the strongholds of rebellion and secret dens for extorting the gains of our deluded slaves; that it be recommended that special constables be appointed from among the respectable members of our community, to attend at places where it may be reported that illegal meetings of slaves are held, and where unlicensed sectarians preach, for the purpose of dispersing such meetings; and the meeting will apply their funds, among other purposes, to the prosecution and conviction of such offenders." But these demonstrations of hostility were met by Lord Mulgrave with great firmness and decision. He early gave a very significant token of his determination to carry into effect the principles of His Majesty's proclamation, by depriving of their commissions two officers of the St John's troop of militia, for having signed their names to resolutions published by the Colonial Union, declaring their determination to prevent the "sectarian preachers" from exercising their ministry in that parish. The custos of the parish of St Ann's was also removed from his office, together with nine more of the magistrates; and the principal officers of the militia were publicly cashiered. Mr Barr, the missionary at Manchioneal, having been fined £20 for preaching, two magistrates had levied for that sum on the mission premises; but his Excellency having been appealed to, he ordered an investigation of the case, the result of which was, that he dismissed the two magistrates from the commission of the peace, and referred the matter to the Attorney-General for his opinion as to the best method of having the value of the furniture, which had been seized and sold by public auction, refunded to him. He even sent down a message to the House of Assembly, recommending that measures should be devised for refunding the losses which had been sustained by the destruction of the chapels by lawless mobs. After a stormy debate, however, it was resolved that the sectarians should not be refunded, but should be left to seek their redress at law. This was equivalent to saying, they should have no redress at all, for it had previously been sought at law, and denied.

It had often been alleged by the enemies of missions that the toleration laws of England were not applicable to Jamaica; but it was now decided in the Grand Court that the 1st of William and Mary was in force in Jamaica;[2] yet even this did not put a stop to the opposition of some of the magistrates. On this decision being given, Mr Greenwood attended the quarter-sessions in St Ann's for the purpose of qualifying according to the provisions of that act. This, however, was objected to by some of the magistrates, who acted in so violent a manner that the

[1] Miss. Not. vol. vii. p. 180, 246, 269, 311, 344; (Bapt.) Miss. Herald, 1833, p. 34. The estimate formed by the Methodists of the sums necessary for the restoration of the six chapels belonging to them which had been damaged or destroyed was £2090 sterling. From this it appears, that their losses were greatly less than those of the Baptists, which were estimated at the time at upwards of £12,000, and subsequently at £17,900. Application was afterwards made to the government at home for remuneration; and though His Majesty's Ministers, while they admitted the grievous hardship of the case, did not see it to be their duty to allow the claim to its full extent, yet they intimated to the Committee, that if the Society would provide one-half of the sum, they would recommend to Parliament to make up the other.—*Miss. Not.* vol. vii. p. 507.

[2] It was declared about the same time in England, that missionaries in the West Indies enjoyed the same ample religious privileges as the Act 52 George III. secures to all classes of His Majesty's subjects, who are not of the Established Church.—*Miss. Not.* vol. vii. p. 396.

custos unable to restore order, advised him to retire, to save himself from personal injury. A rush was made toward him by several persons; but he escaped through a private door, without sustaining any bodily harm. These circumstances having been represented to Earl Mulgrave, he promptly replied, that he was already taking the necessary measures which the emergency of the case required. In consequence, indeed, of the firm and vigorous course pursued by his Excellency, the enemies of religion were kept in check, and after some time, the missionaries were permitted to carry on their labours without molestation.[1]

On Friday the first of August 1834, slavery was abolished in the West Indies, in conformity with an act passed the preceding year by the newly reformed parliament of Great Britain. On that memorable day, about 700,000 immortal beings acquired (under certain limitations called an Apprenticeship) the mighty boon of civil liberty, and passed in the eye of the law from the state of goods and chattels into the rank and dignity of men. That boon had been eagerly and joyfully anticipated by the slaves, and when the day of jubilee came, it was welcomed by them with no ordinary feelings of exultation and gratitude. Throughout Jamaica, it was generally observed as a day of thanksgiving. 'The chapels of all denominations were crowded with attentive, devout, and deeply interested worshippers. Everywhere the people seemed to hasten spontaneously to the house of God to offer up praise and thanks for his mercy. In some places the chapels could not contain the multitudes who flocked to them. The day passed over very differently from what days of public rejoicing commonly do. Every countenance beamed with joy; every heart was filled with gladness; but there was little or nothing of those noisy ebullitions of mirth which are so common on days of public rejoicing, or if any thing of this description did occur, it was of a very harmless kind.[2]

On the following Monday, to which many looked forward with much anxiety, the newly liberated negroes, generally speaking, returned cheerfully to their work, and for a time peace and har-

[1] Miss. Not. vol. vii. p. 311, 376.

[2] Rep. Meth. Miss. Soc. 1835, p. 50; Miss. Not. vol. vii. p. 557; (Bapt.) Miss. Herald, 1834, p. 85; Anti-slavery Reporter, vol. ii. p. 11.

mony prevailed. After some weeks, however, considerable dissatisfaction arose among them, in consequence of the withdrawal on the part of many of the managers of estates of some of those allowances which had been enjoyed by them in a state of slavery, or of their refusal to pay them reasonable wages for working on their own time; or of imprudent, and in some instances, harsh measures adopted toward them by the Whites. Even, however, when things were at the worst, there was very little insubordination among them. Every offence, however, was magnified; there were persons who exaggerated the merest trifles into serious revolts, which had no existence save in their own imaginations. Those managers who met the new order of things in a fair and honourable way, and in whom the people had confidence, completely succeeded. At the same time, it must be acknowledged, that some of the negroes behaved very ill; and generally speaking, they performed less work than they might have accomplished with ordinary exertion. This, however, was the fault of the system rather than of the people. It afforded little motive to exertion. Formerly the fear of punishment was a strong incitement to labour; now that was in a manner done away with, while the hope of reward was not put in its place. The negroes had merely their houses, and some allowances of a few pounds value for their year's work; and consequently it is no way wonderful that even those who were under the influence of religious principles, and still more those who were not actuated by such motives, did not feel that they were bound to exert themselves in hard labour.[1]

The emancipation of the negroes was quickly followed, as might be expected, by some very important changes. Among its earliest fruits was the abolition of the Sunday markets, which had long been the curse of the West Indies, and one of the most powerful obstacles to the spread of religion among the slaves. It was truly surprising to see how entirely they ceased on the very first Sabbath after the abolition of slavery. In the towns the eye was no longer pained, nor the heart grieved in beholding the country people with their baskets of provisions on their heads for sale, or in seeing the stores open for the sale of all manner of commodities. All was now peace and quietness;

[1] Miss. Not. vol. viii. p. 28; Rep. Scot. Miss. Soc. 1835, p. 25.

nothing was to be seen but decently dressed people going to and from their respective places of worship.[1]

There was at the same time a greatly increased attendance of the negroes on public worship. Many whom persecution had "scattered in the dark and cloudy day" now returned to the house of God and to fellowship with their Christian brethren. Multitudes of others flocked to the preaching of the gospel, so that in many cases the chapels required to be enlarged to double their size, and in others, new congregations were raised, which were obliged, in the first instance, to worship in the open air.[2]

Education was also greatly extended among the negroes. In the days of slavery, the prejudices of the White people against schools were even stronger than against preaching; but now His Majesty's ministers having obtained from Parliament, for some years, an annual vote of money for the erection and support of schools in the West Indies, they made considerable grants to the Methodists as well as to other missionary bodies for these purposes, with the view of promoting the education of the negroes, particularly of the rising generation. Instruction was now no longer chiefly oral. Reading, writing, arithmetic, as well as the principles of religion and other useful branches, were taught in the schools, and could not fail to contribute greatly to the intellectual and moral improvement of the pupils, whether adults or children.

But while emancipation was productive of great and manifold benefits to the negroes, there was one grievous evil to which, in the first instance, it gave rise. The missionaries had always been in the practice of celebrating marriages among the slaves who attended on their ministry, and they admitted no persons as members of the Society while living in a state of concubinage, polygamy, or promiscuous intercourse, practices which were nearly universal in the West Indies. So long as the system of slavery continued, these marriages, though not formally recognised by law, were regarded by the negroes as morally binding, and were productive of the most salutary results. But on its abolition, a question was raised as to their validity, which introduced a painful and perplexing state of things. While the negroes were regarded by the law as merely "goods and chat-

[1] (Bapt.) Miss. Herald, 1834, p. 85, 87. [2] Rep. Meth. Miss. Soc. 1835, p. 51.

tels," the marriages celebrated by the missionaries were sufficient to answer the great moral ends of matrimony; but no sooner were they raised to the rank of persons and freemen, than they became capable of contracting legal marriages, and a question arose whether the marriages they had entered into as slaves were legally binding on them, and with this was combined another question as to the legitimacy of their children, the fruit of these marriages. The mass of the married negroes connected with the various missions in the West Indies were reduced to the painful alternative of either submitting to the unmerited reproach of living in a state of concubinage, or by being married according to the forms required by law, virtually to illegitimate their children and to render them incapable of inheriting their property. Besides, instances were not wanting of negroes taking advantage of the uncertainty which prevailed on the subject to desert their wives and children and to marry other females.

But the unsettling of past marriages was not the only evil which now arose: there were also difficulties attending the celebration of legal marriages. As only ministers of the Church of England were empowered by the laws of most of the colonies to marry free persons, the negroes belonging to other denominations could no longer be married by their own pastors. In these circumstances, owing to the fewness of the ministers of the Established Church, marriage could not, in many places, be celebrated at all; and in other places, where they were within reach, the expense and difficulty attending its celebration in the churches of the Establishment, were such as the people were not always prepared to encounter. The consequence was, that in numerous instances, negroes, who were attending on the ministrations of the missionaries, and were bidding fair to become respectable members of society, yielded to the pressure of circumstances, and forming illicit connections, settled down in the state of concubinage. These evils were greatly felt for several years; but an act was at length passed "to legalize, register, and confirm marriages by dissenters and other ministers not connected with the Established Church," which provided an effectual remedy for them.[1]

[1] Rep. Meth. Miss. Soc. 1837, p. 51, 92; Samuel's Wesleyan Methodist Mission in Jamaica and Honduras, p. 86.

On the 1st of August 1838, the system of apprenticeship, under which the negroes had been placed on the abolition of slavery, was terminated throughout the West Indies, by acts of the local legislatures, two years before it legally expired. It had all along worked so ill, been attended with so many grievances to the labourers, and with so little advantage to the masters, that all classes were heartily sick of it, and rejoiced on its being given up. The day was generally observed in Jamaica as a day of thanksgiving to God, in a way similar to that in which the day of emancipation was observed four years before. Many, as then, prognosticated that the negroes, on being completely liberated, would not work, but their predictions were falsified by the event. Such a change, however, in the whole frame of society could not fail, in the first instance, to give rise to many new questions, and to be attended with many difficulties. On the one hand, many of the White people, long accustomed to oppress and contemn the negroes, still sought to grind them to the dust, and offered them what were considered as unduly low wages. On the other hand, many of the Black people, estimating too highly the value of their labours, refused to work, except at a rate of wages which proprietors could not afford to pay. They also regarded their masters with fear and suspicion, a very natural result of the old system of slavery and its attendant oppressions. They were exceedingly jealous of their newly-acquired rights, guarded them with intense anxiety, and were prepared to resist to the very uttermost even the appearance of the slightest encroachment on them. Every proposal made by their employers was cautiously weighed by them, as if they were incapable of acting honestly, or of fulfilling their promises. The scarcity of silver money tended not a little to increase their distrust. It occasioned masters to allow the wages of the labourers to run on for weeks together, until the latter became dissatisfied, and, in some cases, they gave up work altogether, under the false impression that their employers were keeping back their wages intentionally. They could not understand "how Buckra no hab money; how him always hab plenty o money to buy negar; yet him no hab money to pay poor Negar when him work is done." They had also extravagant ideas of freedom. They conceived that a freeman could not be compelled to work nine hours a day; that he might come and go when he pleased; stop work, or proceed with work, as he chose; rise in the morning and go to work at seven o'clock or half-past seven, instead of six. They imagined that the queen had given them their houses and grounds, and that their masters had no right to take them from them; and, accordingly, many would neither work on the properties nor pay rent for their houses and grounds. On the other hand, some of the masters or managers made exorbitant demands of rent, and required it not only from the heads of families, but from all the children above a certain age. Processes of ejectment now became the order of the day; but these it was found exceedingly difficult to execute, and the negro often kept possession of his house and grounds in defiance of the proprietor. These and a thousand other things were constantly producing disagreement between masters and servants. Appeals were made to the magistrates, discontent followed their decisions on one or both sides, and obstinate refusal to work was often the consequence. The violence too of party spirit in Jamaica, and the opposition of the House of Assembly to the measures of the home government and of the governor, excited and cherished as they were by the newspaper press, contributed not a little to keep up agitation throughout the island, and to delay the adoption of those measures which might have allayed the general ferment, and brought matters to a fair and amicable arrangement.

Thus many things occurred to hinder the successful working of the new system; but this need be no cause of wonder. Considering the previous character, condition, and conduct of the two great parties who were practically the chief agents in carrying out the mighty change, the multiplied and opposite interests involved in it, and the consequent difficulties in bringing to a just and equitable settlement the many important questions to which it could not fail to give rise, it would have been little less than a miracle, if, in the first instance, there had been no differences of opinion, no jealousies, no excitement, no discontent, no disappointment in regard to its immediate results.[1]

Amidst the difficulties which attended the early working of

[1] Rep. Scot. Miss. Soc. 1839, p. 7, 11, 30, 39, 48, 52; Ibid. 1840, p. 13, 22; Ibid. 1841, p. 17, 22; Miss. Not. vol. i. (N. S.) p. 57.

freedom, it was amusing to witness the effect which it had on the bodies as well as on the minds of the people. Youths who, in the month of July, belonged to the second gang, were in August raised as if by magic to the first, and could manage a hoe with as much ease as many of their older and more athletic neighbours. The aged and infirm, who had done nothing for years, and were exempted from all labour, suddenly became young and strong. The sick also found freedom a sovereign medicine for most of their diseases, and left the hospitals to engage in the labours of the field. Whole hosts of the sick, diseased, and lame, were suddenly restored; and the tinkle of an English shilling wrought a cure more entire and lasting, than would ever have been effected by the doctor's skill.[1]

Meanwhile a great change took place in the public opinion of Jamaica regarding the Methodist missionaries. We have already seen how long and how grievously they were persecuted by the White people. Formerly no names were too vile, no treatment too bad for them; even their chapels were shut up or razed to the ground as public nuisances. Yet within five years of the late insurrection, the House of Assembly in Jamaica made a grant of £500 to aid in the erection of a Methodist chapel in Kingston, and in the course of the discussion which took place on that occasion, the highest eulogiums were pronounced on the usefulness of the Wesleyan missionaries. The common council of Kingston and several of the parochial vestries followed the example of the Assembly, and made grants for similar purposes.[2] We do not here inquire into the propriety of the civil authorities making grants of public money for religious purposes: we simply state the fact as a proof of the great change of opinion which had taken place in Jamaica regarding the missionaries. It is no doubt true that the state

[1] Miss. Not. vol. i. (N. S.) p. 60; Rep. Scot. Miss. Soc. 1839, p. 32.

The miraculous effects of freedom were not confined to Jamaica. The following statement refers to St Kitts:—One day as Mr Waymouth the missionary was passing by a large cane field, he was surprised to see the great and the small gangs blended together. Accosting them pleasantly, he asked why those small fellows had got among the men. "O," said one of them, "free make a we strong," and they were accordingly doing, as some stout boys might do, the work of men for men's wages. He also noticed among them some whose faces seemed to indicate they had but lately left the hospital. "O," said he, "are you turned out too?" "Yes, massa, free good physic," said they all.—*Miss. Not.* vol. i. (N. S.) p. 127.

[2] Rep. Meth. Miss. Soc. 1837, p. 48; Duncan's Narrative, p. 386, 391, 392.

and circumstances of the island were entirely changed. Formerly it was a slave, now it was a free, colony, and that might be deemed necessary for freemen which was thought dangerous for slaves; yet even this is a testimony to the innocence of the missionaries, and shews that the fault lay not with them, but with the White people and with the system of slavery, which it was foreseen could not long maintain its standing in opposition to the progress of knowledge.

After all, however, we apprehend it cannot be denied that the emancipation of the slaves has not as yet realized the hopes of the friends of justice and humanity; yet this need scarcely surprise us. It is rarely that we are able to point to any human schemes which have not to a considerable extent disappointed the expectations which were entertained of them, especially if the intellectual, moral, and social improvement of man was their object; or at all events it is only after a lengthened period when their results come to be somewhat fully developed, that the benefits arising from them are fully seen, and even then, they probably prove beneficial in ways which did not enter much, if at all, into the calculations of their original promoters, so little knowledge and foresight has man of futurity.

There is, indeed, no denying the fact that the abolition of slavery proved the abrogation of great and multiplied evils as regarded both the Black and the White people, and that multitudes of the slaves and of their children have reaped solid advantages from it, though there are probably still greater numbers who have participated but little in these advantages, and perhaps now suffer various evils to which they were not much liable in the days of slavery.

Besides the causes of the failure of emancipation in realizing the expectations formed of it, which arose out of the ill-working of the new order of things, there were others which contributed to the same end, particularly the continuance of the slave trade by Spain and Brazil, notwithstanding of the treaties they had entered into with England for its abolition, and the extensive cultivation by them, by means of slave labour, of the chief articles of our colonial produce, which so reduced its price, especially after the British Parliament removed the differential duties between the produce of slave and of free labour, that numerous plantations, particularly in Jamaica, were thrown out of cultivation, and the wages of labour sunk so low as to reduce the mass of the people to great poverty.

Though, after the emancipation of the negroes, the prospects of the mission appeared to brighten greatly, yet in the course of a few years the state of things changed much to the worse. Many of the Black and coloured people purchased small lots of land, sometimes in the mountains, on which they built themselves cottages, while they cultivated the ground for the maintenance of their families. Many left their old homes and sought employment elsewhere, often at such a distance from the house of God as to cut themselves off, to a great extent, from the ordinances of religion. Many in the days of slavery betook themselves to the missionaries as their best and only friends, and perhaps expected to find in religion something to comfort them under the many ills which they had to suffer; but now that they were free, they cared little about religion, and perhaps abandoned even the profession of it. Many grew worldly-minded, made money the great object of their pursuit, and sought for happiness in earthly things. Some of the evils of the olden times, which it was hoped had received a complete check, were revived, particularly among the young, as nocturnal dances, concubinage, the illicit connection of the sexes, and even obeahism and myalism.

As a consequence of all this, the congregations and the number of church members, though they were still great, were materially reduced as compared with what they were some years before; the contributions for the support of the missionaries and other religious objects were greatly diminished; the schools too fell off, and altogether the aspect of things was much less favourable than a few years before it had promised to be.[1]

In 1853, the number of church members in connection with the mission in Jamaica amounted to 19,478. The numbers are considerably less than they were some years ago. In 1844, they amounted to 26,585. The stations of the missionaries are now no longer confined to the chief towns as Kingston, Spanish Town, Falmouth, and Montego Bay; they are to be found in all parts of the island, both in the towns and in country places.[2]

[1] Rep. Meth. Miss. Soc. 1846, p. 105; Ibid. 1848, p. 111; Ibid. 1853, p. 68; Miss. Not. (N. S.) vol. vi. p. 15, vol. viii. p. 167.

[2] Rep. Meth. Miss. Soc. 1844, p. 99; Ibid. 1853, p. 108.

Art. 7.—Bermuda.

In 1799, Mr John Stephenson proceeded to Bermuda, with the view of commencing a mission in the Somers' Islands. On his arrival he had powerful prejudices to encounter; but in a short time, they abated in a considerable degree. His prospects having begun to brighten, the enemies of religion were roused to hostility; and finding themselves unable to check his progress, without the aid of law, they at last obtained the interference of the legislature.

In May 1800, the House of Assembly passed an act prohibiting all persons from preaching or exhorting, who were not ordained according to the forms of the Church of England or of Scotland, under a penalty of £50, and six months' imprisonment for every offence, and inflicting a similar punishment on the person in whose house the meeting was held. Mr Stephenson, considering this law as inconsistent with the principles of toleration, and therefore an infringement of the birthright of a British subject, continued his ministerial labours in nearly the same manner as before. He was allowed to go on without molestation for about a month; but he was at last apprehended, carried before the magistrates, and committed to jail to take his trial at the next assizes. With him was committed Mr Pallais, the person in whose house he preached.

After lying in prison a number of days, they were both liberated on bail. Mr Stephenson originally intended remaining in jail until the assizes, which did not meet for near six months; but on making the experiment for a short time, he found that confinement would not only impair his health, but prove exceedingly expensive, as the charges amounted to fifteen shillings a day. Besides, he was apprehensive that the society he had collected would be dispersed during his confinement, while, if he accepted of liberty, he would have an opportunity of visiting them privately, and might by this means keep them together until the storm blew over.

On the meeting of the assizes, Mr Stephenson appeared before them, was tried for the high crime of preaching the gospel, and condemned to six months' imprisonment in the common jail, to pay a fine of £50, and to discharge all the fees of the court. After he had lain five weeks in prison, the governor offered to liberate him on condition that he would quit the island within sixty days; but as he thought this dishonourable to the great cause for which he suffered, he declined the offer. He proposed, however, in case of his liberation, to find bail that he should not break the law while it continued in force; but this offer was refused.

In June 1801, Mr Stephenson, after lying in jail six months, was liberated agreeably to his sentence; but his constitution was so broken by his confinement, that he was disabled for those exertions which he had been accustomed to make. He continued on the island some months longer, languishing under a weight of bodily infirmities and the interdictions of law. The members of the Society had kept together better than might have been expected; but he could only visit them in their own houses, and converse with them privately. As there was so little prospect of his being useful, he was recalled from Bermuda, which was now left without a missionary.[1]

Applications were, in the mean while, made to the government in England to disallow the act of Assembly, but from various circumstances, near three years elapsed before its repeal was publicly announced. The spirit, however, which gave it birth did not expire with it. Many of the men in power still cherished their hostility to the Methodists, and exhibited a menacing aspect to any who should attempt to preach. On this account, a considerable time elapsed before any missionary could be induced to venture to Bermuda. Each saw before him an apparent certainty of persecution, and but little prospect of usefulness.[2]

In April 1808, Mr Joshua Marsden proceeded from New Brunswick to Bermuda, after that island had been without a missionary for about six years. He expected to find on his arrival a small society, the fruit of Mr Stephenson's labours, but in this he was disappointed. With the exception of Mr Pallais, who was now old, infirm, and poor, he did not find a single person who appeared to welcome his arrival. All to whom he spoke were of opinion that government would not allow him to

[1] Coke's History, vol. iii. p. 237. [2] Ibid. vol. iii. p. 243, 247.

preach, and their wishes seemed to be in unison with their sentiments.

Contrary to expectation, Mr Marsden obtained permission from the governor to preach, and was attended by considerable numbers of the inhabitants; but though he met with no violent opposition, he had to encounter great indifference. The prospects of the mission appeared indeed to brighten at times, but they were again greatly overclouded. Though many of the inhabitants, both rich and poor, attended the preaching of the gospel, comparatively few became members of the Society.[1]

In 1853, the number of church members in connection with the mission on this island amounted to 445.[2]

ART. 8.—BAHAMA ISLANDS.

IN October 1800, Mr William Turton arrived at New Providence, one of the Bahama Islands. Previous to this, Mr Hammet, who after retiring to America for the recovery of his health withdrew from the Methodist connection, had successively sent three missionaries to the Bahama Islands; but though they collected a small society, they were themselves chargeable with such gross misconduct, that they brought disgrace on the profession of religion. On the arrival of Mr Turton, the name of a Methodist, in consequence of this, was obnoxious in the ears of the inhabitants; but yet he obtained permission to preach, and though a law had previously been enacted prohibiting the instruction of the slaves, he was attended by considerable congregations, and succeeded in raising a small society. Other missionaries having afterwards arrived in New Providence, they extended their labours to Eleuthera, Harbour Island, Abaco, and others of the Bahama Islands. On some of these their prospects were highly encouraging; their congregations were large, attentive, and respectable, and their labours were productive of a great reformation among the inhabitants. In Harbour Island, drunkenness, swearing, fighting, and Sabbath-breaking prevailed in a

[1] Coke's History, vol. iii. p. 248; Rep. Meth. Miss. 1811, p. 13; Ibid. 1814, p. 13; Ibid. 1815, p. 14.

[2] Rep. Meth. Miss. Soc. 1853, p. 111.

very high degree when the missionaries first visited it, but after a few years these evils in a great measure disappeared. But though the utility of their labours was so apparent, they were not without their enemies, who were eager to oppose and to shackle them in their operations.[1]

In 1816, the legislature passed an act prohibiting, under a severe penalty, meetings for divine worship earlier than sunrise and later than sunset, a measure which not only deprived the slaves in general of the ordinary opportunities of instruction during the week, but many of them of all instruction whatsoever. On hearing of this iniquitous law, many of the negroes came to the missionaries in tears, lamenting the loss of their religious privileges. It was truly affecting on the Sabbath morning to see some of the oldest members ascending a neighbouring hill to see whether the sun was risen, before they durst begin to sing the praises of their Creator. After a few years, however, the legislature retraced its steps, and repealed the restrictions which it had laid upon the poor negroes.[2]

In 1853, the members of the Methodist Societies in the Bahama Islands, were as follows:—

New Providence,	816
Eleuthera,	804
Harbour Island,	538
Abaco, and Andros Island,	264
Turk's Island,	378
Total,	2800[3]

Art. 9.—St Domingo.

In November 1816, Messrs John Brown and James Catts sailed from England for Port-au-Prince, the capital of the republic of Hayti, in the island of St Domingo. A short time before, Captain Reynolds, a member of the Methodist body,

[1] Coke's History, vol. iii. p. 200; Rep. Meth. Miss. 1813, p. 13; Ibid. 1814, p. 12 Ibid. 1816, p. 23; Ibid. 1819, p. 50; Miss. Notices, vol. i. p. 32, 67, 193.
[2] Rep Meth. Miss. 1817, p. 27; Miss. Not. vol. i. p. 160; vol. iii. p. 94.
[3] Rep. Meth. Miss. Soc. 1853, p. 109.

when at Port-au-Prince, was informed by the Secretary of State, in reply to some inquiries which he had addressed to him, that Protestant missionaries would not only be tolerated, but welcomed by the government.

On their arrival, the missionaries began to preach in Port-au-Prince and other parts of the republic. In the capital, they had a numerous and attentive congregation: in the country, they were uniformly treated with kindness and respect. The inhabitants, indeed, were extremely ignorant, wicked, and superstitious; but yet, in a short time, a number of them appeared to be impressed with divine things, and were formed into a society.

In the whole of their intercourse with the government, the missionaries were treated with the greatest condescension and kindness. They were not merely tolerated; they experienced on all occasions the utmost readiness on the part of the President Boyer, to encourage and promote their plans, particularly in regard to the education of youth.[1]

But though the government was favourable to the missionaries, they were obliged, after a residence of about two years in St Domingo, to withdraw from the island in consequence of the tumultuous opposition of the populace. It is worthy of notice, that on their departure, the President Boyer not only expressed himself highly satisfied with their conduct, but transmitted a donation of five hundred pounds to the funds of the Methodist Missionary Society.[2]

By the constitution of Hayti, the Roman Catholic religion was declared to be the religion of the State; but there was an article providing that other religions should be tolerated. It may be questioned, however, whether the principle of toleration was at all understood; practically at least, the Methodists enjoyed nothing like religious freedom. The small society which the missionaries had collected were, after their departure, greatly persecuted, chiefly through the influence of the Catholic priests over the poor ignorant people, in which, however, they were too much seconded by some persons of higher rank. They

[1] Miss. Notices, vol. i. p. 93, 145, 217, 241; Rep. Meth. Miss. 1817, p. 33; Rep. Meth. Miss. Soc. 1818, p. 38.

[2] Rep. Meth. Miss. Soc. 1819, p. 63.

could meet only by stealth, and in small companies, and when assembled for divine worship, they were sometimes assaulted by the populace with stones and all kinds of violence. On one occasion a number of them were seized by the police, and carried to prison, and on being brought before the chief judge the following day, they were prohibited by him, in the name of the President, from meeting together again. "No one," said he, "can hinder you from worshipping God as you please; but let every one abide at home, for as often as you are found assembled, you shall be put in prison, and if you unhappily persist, I have received orders to disperse you every where." Several wished to reply; but he refused to hear them, saying, "It is not from me; it is not my fault; these orders are given to me." There is reason to apprehend that these were the orders of the President Boyer. But notwithstanding all this, the poor people continued to meet both on the Sabbath and on week evenings.[1]

In 1834, Mr John Tindall was sent to Hayti: other missionaries afterwards followed and settled at Port-au-Prince, Cape Haytien, and Samana. Their congregations were generally small, and they had no great encouragement in their labours. There was reason to believe that numbers saw the absurdities of the Romish Church, but ignorance, superstition, and vice, maintained their dominion over the great mass of the population.[2]

Though the successive revolutions which have of late years taken place in Hayti, the war which the Haytian government carried on with the Spanish part of the island, and the consequent agitated and unsettled state of the country, could not fail to have an unfavourable influence in regard to the state and progress of the mission; yet it is an interesting fact, that the principle of religious toleration has made marked progress with both the government and the people. Though the Romish priesthood did still in some instances seek to raise persecution, it was not with much success.[3]

In 1853, the number of church members in connection with the mission on this island amounted to 429.[4]

[1] Rep. Meth. Miss. Soc. 1824, p. 62. [2] Ibid. 1835, p. 62.
[3] Miss. Not. (N.S.) vol. i. p. 601; vol. viii. p. 137, 172, 174.
[4] Rep. Meth. Miss. Soc. 1853, p. 109.

Besides the Missions of which we have given an account, the Methodists established others in various other of the West India Islands,—in St Christopher's, in Nevis, in Grenada, in St Bartholomew, in St Thomas, in St Martin's and Anguilla, in Montserrat, in Tobago, and in Trinidad, and also in Demerara and Honduras.

In 1853, the number of church members in connection with the Methodist missions in the West Indies amounted to 48,589, the great body of whom were black and coloured people.[1]

Though in the preceding account of particular missions we have given many illustrations of the nature and difficulties of missionary labour in the West Indies in the days of slavery, we shall here add a few other statements illustrative of this subject.

It was a great disadvantage to the negroes, that the Lord's day was the season assigned them by their masters to cultivate the grounds allowed them in lieu of provisions, and that the regular market throughout the West Indies was on that sacred day when the chief towns exhibited all the noise and bustle of petty commerce. After breakfast, a driver with an overseer accompanied the slaves to the negro fields, where they spent the Sabbath toiling all day under a burning sun. On the following Lord's day, they went to market to sell the produce of their grounds, and to purchase such articles as were not allowed them by their masters; and they closed the day in drinking, dancing, and debauchery. Such was a Sabbath in the West Indies. The Christian slaves had to perform the same work as others, when their masters did not allow them the Saturday for that purpose. They went to market in the forenoon, and from thence to the chapel. It was no uncommon thing to see the chapel yard covered with baskets, whilst their owners were attending divine worship. The missionaries did not, however, as was insinuated, excite complaints among the slaves on this subject. They were no doubt grieved at the profanation of the Sabbath, and the beneficial effects of their labours were materially counteracted by it; but they accommodated themselves to the circumstances of the slaves, seized upon the broken frag-

[1] Rep. Meth. Miss. Soc. 1853, p. 114.

ments of their time, and made the best improvement of them they were able.[1]

There was in general no such thing as marriage, in the common sense of the word, among the slaves in the West Indies. They herded together like the beasts of the field, without any ceremony. Some lived together many years; others soon parted, and each chose a new mate. Promiscuous intercourse was extremely common; and the planters themselves, when they made the attempt, found themselves utterly unable to check it. Marriage, however, was uniformly introduced by the Methodist missionaries among the converts; but with respect to this they had many difficulties to encounter. They were frequently at a loss to determine which was the proper husband or wife. A female, for instance, wished to become a member of the society; but the man with whom she then cohabited, was not the first to whom she had been united. She had lived with many others, and the person with whom she was originally connected, had, in like manner, had many more women since he left her; and perhaps was living at that time with one by whom he had children. Sometimes the missionaries were content with an engagement on the part of the woman, that she would abide with the man with whom she lived when she joined the Society; at other times they acted to the best of their judgment, in selecting the person whom they thought most proper.[2]

[1] Watson's Defence, p. 55, 60.

[2] Ibid. p. 29.

Many of the White people were opposed to the marriage of the slaves. It would have been a standing reproof of their own licentious lives.—*Anti-slavery Reporter*, vol. v. p. 364. Among the many evils which resulted from their disregard of the marriage ties between their slaves, was the cruel practice of the separation by sale to different individuals, and sometimes to different islands, of husband and wife, parents and children. Many a tender scene did this produce; but one more heart-rending than the following, it is not easy to conceive. "A master of slaves," says Mr Gilgrass, who was for some time a missionary in Jamaica, "who lived near us in Kingston, exercised his barbarities on a Sabbath morning, while we were worshipping God in the chapel, and the cries of the female sufferers frequently interrupted us in our devotions. This man wanted money, and one of the female slaves having two fine children, he sold one of them, and the child was torn from her maternal affection. In the agony of her feelings she made a hideous howling; and for that crime was flogged. Soon after he sold her other child. This 'turned her heart within her,' and drove her to a kind of madness. She howled night and day in the yard, tore her hair, ran up and down the streets and the parade, rending the heavens with her cries, and literally watering the earth with her tears. Her constant cry was, 'Da wicked Massa Jew, he sell me children. Will no Buckra Massa pity Nega? What me do? Me no have one child.' As she stood before my window she said, 'My Massa,' (lifting up her hands

Though we have given many disgraceful instances of the hostility of the White inhabitants of the West Indies, to the labours of the Methodists, it would be an act of great injustice, both to the planters and to the missionaries, did we neglect to mention, that such feelings were by no means universal. In some of the colonies, there were not only no persecuting laws enacted against them; but they were greatly encouraged, both by the local government, and by the owners of slaves. Even in those islands where they met with persecution, they had many friends among the planters, and others of the White inhabitants. Some built chapels on their estates: others subscribed handsomely to their erection in the neighbourhood. There was scarcely a place of worship of any size, in the West Indies, in the building of which the gentlemen of the island did not assist by their contributions, or in some other form. Subscriptions of £10, £20, £50, and £100, for such purposes, indicate both the rank in life, and the sentiments of the contributors. Even in Jamaica, where the dark and dangerous fanaticism of the Methodists was detected with more than ordinary sagacity, the most liberal assistance was afforded. In other islands, planters, merchants, members of colonial assemblies, presidents, chief judges, governors, not only subscribed to the erection of chapels, but in some instances paid regular stipends to the missionaries, as a remuneration for their services in instructing their slaves. In several of the islands, indeed, the proprietors of estates, and the other inhabitants, were so fully satisfied with the conduct of the missionaries, and so sensible of the political as well as moral and religious advantages resulting from their labours, that they entirely supported the ordinary expenses of the missions.[1] Since the abolition of slavery, the views of the White people in the West Indies in reference to the Methodist missionaries have greatly changed; and it is probably now matter of wonder to many, that any hostility should ever have been manifested to so zealous, so laborious, so useful a body of men.

to heaven), 'Do me, Massa minister, pity me! me heart do so,' (shaking herself violently) 'me heart do so, because me have no child. Me go a Massa house, in Massa yard, and in me hut, and me no see em;' and then her cry went up to God. I durst not be seen looking at her."—*Watson's Defence*, p. 25.

[1] Watson's Defence, p. 74, 124; Coke's History, vol. ii. p. 286; Rep. Meth. Miss. Soc. 1820, p. 68; Ibid. 1821, p. 80.

SECT. II.—CEYLON.

In December 1813, Dr Coke sailed from Spithead with six missionaries, namely, Messrs William M. Harvard, Benjamin Clough, William Ault, George Erskine, Thomas H. Squance, and James Lynch. The heart of Dr Coke was particularly bent on a mission to Ceylon: neither his age, nor the length of the voyage, nor any other consideration, would divert him from his purpose. He had often met with much opposition from his Brethren in the Conference to other missions which he proposed, in consequence of the state of their finances; and as the missionary fund laboured at this time under considerable embarrassments, he was apprehensive that his favourite plan would be frustrated, unless he could obviate this difficulty. He, therefore, generously offered to bear out of his own private fortune, the whole expense of the outfit, to the extent of SIX THOUSAND POUNDS, should that sum be necessary. Awed into silence by this noble act of generosity, the Conference, while they were not without apprehensions of their ability to carry on so expensive an undertaking, agreed to extend their operations to the Eastern world.[1]

Anxious, however, as Dr Coke was to establish a mission in Ceylon, he was not destined to see it begun. During the first four months of the voyage, none on board enjoyed better health; but he at length felt himself rather indisposed for a day or two. His complaints, however, appeared of so trifling a nature, that neither he nor his companions felt the least alarm. He was still able to be present at table, walked on deck at his accustomed hour, and pursued his studies as usual. On the evening of the second day, when he was retiring to rest, Mr Clough, by his own request, gave him a little laxative medicine, and offered to sit up with him during the night. But the Doctor, not apprehending any danger, declined the offer with his usual sweetness of temper, and desired him to go to bed.

[1] The Conference do not appear to have accepted Dr Coke's generous offer, but only borrowed from him £3291. He expended, however, a considerable sum in the outfit of the mission beyond what was allowed for this purpose.

Thus terminated the intercourse of this venerable man with mortals. In the morning he was found lying on the floor, a cold and lifeless corpse. He died, it was supposed, of apoplexy, a disease to which he had a considerable pre-disposition. His mortal remains were consigned the same afternoon to the mighty deep, to be seen no more till that morning when "the trumpet shall sound, and the sea shall give up the dead which are in it."[1]

Among the advocates and promoters of Christian missions, Dr Coke is entitled to hold no ordinary place. During the last thirty years of his life, the diffusion of Christianity, particularly among the heathen, appears ever to have been uppermost in his thoughts. It was chiefly through his instrumentality that the missions of the Methodists were at first begun; and it was principally by his activity that they were for many years supported and carried on. With a view to the propagation of Christianity, he crossed the Atlantic not less than eighteen times. While in England, he was much employed in travelling through the country, soliciting subscriptions for missionary purposes. He stooped to the very drudgery of charity, and pleaded the cause of a perishing world from door to door. His unconquerable activity was attributed by the world to enthusiasm, and by his enemies to ambition; but by his friends, who knew him best, to zeal for the glory of God, and the salvation of men. He was not, however, without his faults. Of a warm sanguine temperament, he was frequently hurried into schemes without due consideration, was apt to be provoked by opposition, was improvident in his plans, profuse in his expenditure, and had, we suspect, no inconsiderable share of vanity. His many excellencies, however, more than counterbalanced his faults, and even threw a kind of lustre around them.[2]

In June 1814, the missionaries arrived in Ceylon, and though deprived of their venerable leader, were received in the most cordial manner by Sir Robert Brownrigg the governor, Sir Alexander Johnston the chief justice, and others of the principal inhabitants. This island, as we formerly mentioned, is

[1] Drew's Life of Dr Coke, p. 350, 352, 357; Meth. Mag. vol. xxxvii. p. 118, 473; vol. xxxviii. p. 30.

[2] Drew's Life of Dr Coke, p. 315, 344, 380, 383, 385, 387.

inhabited by two distinct races; the northern part by Hindus who speak the Tamil language, that of the opposite coast of India; the southern part by the Cingalese, who profess the religion of Budhu.[1]

The missionaries settled in the chief towns, both in the northern and southern parts of the island, as Jaffnapatnam, Batticaloa, and Trincomalee, Colombo, Negombo, and Galle; and after the conquest of the kingdom of Kandy by the British, they also entered the interior, and formed a station at Kornegalle, about twenty-two miles from Kandy, the capital.[2] They entered on their labours with great activity and zeal, but the propagation of Christianity in Ceylon was attended with many difficulties, some of them of a very singular nature.

It has been made a question whether a man can be an atheist; but it is a remarkable fact that the Budhist religion is a system of atheism. The priests and the more learned of the Cingalese argue against the existence of a Supreme Creator, and the superintendence of a Divine Providence. To explain the origin of all things they have recourse to an eternal succession of transmigrations, or to the doctrine of chance. One day, when an aged priest called on the missionaries at Colombo to converse with them on the subject of religion, Mr Harvard thought this a favourable opportunity of ascertaining, whether it was possible for a reasonable being to pass a number of years in the world without thinking of the existence of a Supreme Creator. To his inquiries the old man answered in the most unequivocal manner, that during the sixty years he had lived in the world, the idea of a First Cause, had never, to the best of his recollection, entered his mind until of late. Budhu is, perhaps, worshipped by the populace as a deity; but their sacred books represent him merely as a prophet or reformer, something like Mahomed, and incarnated simply to save mankind by the purity of his doctrines. The better informed reject with disdain the imputation of worshipping Budhu, and assert that they erect temples to his honour, present flowers to his images, and afford maintenance to his priests, merely as an expression of

[1] Meth. Mag. vol. xxxviii. p. 150, 357; vol. xxxix. p. 89; Miss. Notices, vol. i. p. 20, 25.

[2] Rep. Meth. Miss. Soc. 1824, p. 8, 11.

reverence for his memory, and of attachment to the doctrines he taught.[1]

As to the common people, they were sunk into a kind of mental torpor; they were not accustomed to think on any subject, and least of all upon religion. The ignorance, the apathy, the credulity, the superstition, the fickleness, and the flexibility of the lower orders, were enough to sink the hopes of the most zealous missionary. It was seldom they contradicted any thing; but then they took no interest or concern in what was said to them. The religion of the Christians they dismissed altogether as not necessary to be known by them, their own religion being superior to every other and quite adapted to them, though Christianity might be suited to the inhabitants of Europe.[2]

In Ceylon education is little known. With the exception of the Budhist priests and the families of the chiefs, few enjoy any thing like mental culture. Many even of the sacerdotal order are extremely ignorant, and some are unable to read correctly their own language.[3]

The missionaries commenced their labours in Ceylon with singular energy and zeal. To meet the low state of education in the island, they established numerous schools, in which large numbers of children, including some hundreds of girls, were educated. They preached to all classes of the inhabitants, and had considerable congregations; the school-houses served them as places of worship in the course of their journeys through the country. In Colombo, the capital of the island, they possessed a fine establishment, consisting of a chapel, a dwelling-house, school-rooms, a printing-office, and a type-foundry. From their printing press issued numerous works in the Cingalese, Tamil, Indo-Portuguese, and English languages. They also took part in the translation of the Scriptures into the languages of Ceylon. They early baptized a number of the natives, among whom were several Budhist priests. Nothing, in short, could exceed their sleepless activity and enterprize, and high hopes were for some years excited both in England and Ceylon of the success of the mission.[4]

[1] Miss. Notices, vol. i. p. 149. [2] Ibid. vol. i. p. 138, 151; Meth. Mag. 1831, p. 565.
[3] Rep. Meth. Miss. Soc. 1818, p. 111.
[4] Ibid. 1825, p. 13; Meth. Mag. 1832, p. 355; Miss. Not. vol. ix. p. 178.

But these hopes were far from being realized. The schools, which were so numerous and so numerously attended, were after some years found to be in a very inefficient state, and to have done little good. In some places the congregations continued good, but in Colombo and others of the principal stations they fell off greatly; they were small, fluctuating, and very discouraging. Even the children educated in the schools, when they grew up frequented the idol temples, and scarcely a youth was to be seen at chapel, unless he was still a scholar. Though a considerable number of the natives were baptized, there were comparatively few who gave evidence of genuine piety. Disappointment, in short, was felt in nearly every department of the mission, a result not unfrequent where high hopes have been excited in the beginning.[1]

In 1853, the following was the number of church members connected with the Methodist mission in Ceylon:—

Northern or Tamil district, . . .	293
Southern or Cingalese district, . . .	1416
Total,	1709[2]

SECT. III.—SOUTH AFRICA.

NAMAQUALAND.

IN December 1815, Mr Barnabas Shaw sailed for the Cape of Good Hope, but on his arrival, not being allowed by the governor to exercise his ministry at Cape Town, he set off for Namaqualand in the company of Mr Schmelen, of the London Missionary Society, who had settled in that country. By the way they met the captain of a Kraal in Little Namaqualand and some of his people, who were on their way to Cape Town, a journey of between four and five hundred miles, with the view of obtaining a missionary to come and live among them. Considering this as a call in providence, Mr Shaw, who previously had no

[1] Meth. Mag. 1826, p. 128; Miss. Not. (N. S.) vol. i. p. 597.
[2] Rep. Meth. Miss. Soc. 1853, p. 97.

particular place in view, agreed to accompany him to the Khamies mountain, where he and his people resided. Here he commenced a station at a place called Lily Fountain; and he had scarcely entered on his labours, when many of the people appeared to be deeply affected with what they heard. In the meetings for public worship, they sometimes fell down, and wept, and sighed to such a degree, that he could scarcely distintinguish his own voice; and after divine service, they might be seen retiring for prayer among the rocks, or they might be heard singing and praying in their huts. In a short time, he baptized a number of them; and he also instructed them in agriculture and other useful arts; but though some of them improved in industry, others were amazingly idle.[1]

In March 1820, Mr Shaw, accompanied by some of his people, undertook a journey into Great Namaqualand, to the north of the Orange River, with the view of exploring the country, and preparing the way for establishing missions in it. The country through which they travelled, was, for the most part, wild and desolate beyond description. Their route at first lay through defiles between the mountains, whose jagged summits resembled battlements and towers, or amidst enormous ridges of rocks, whose steep sides projected like so many lines of masonry, while the roads were so rugged that they were sometimes afraid their waggons might be dashed to pieces. After travelling some days, they entered on a barren sandy waste. No rain having fallen for some time, vegetation seemed at an end; scarcely any thing was visible but the shrivelled stems of dying bushes, with here and there a brown sickly heath, or a few succulent plants apparently struggling for life. Here were no traces of cultivation to relieve the eye, no tree or bush to invite the weary traveller to its friendly shade, no fountain or stream to refresh either him or his thirsty cattle.

Proceeding on their journey, our travellers saw before them an immense range of mountains rising in majestic grandeur to the skies, which appeared to present a barrier to their further advance. Their guide left them to try and discover a way by which they might pass over them; and on his return, he led

[1] Shaw's Memorials of South Africa, p. 57, 68; Miss. Not. vol. i. p. 92, 114, 125, 157, 197, 284.

them along the sloping side of a terrific steep, over which the wheel of waggon had probably never before rolled. The poor cattle dragged them along over shelved rocks and sharp stones, till worn out with fatigue, some of them fell to the ground. The large whip, which on account of its size requires both hands to wield it, was continually in motion, till at length they were so completely hemmed in amidst the shattered ridges, that the bullocks could proceed no further. To extricate their waggon from a situation so perplexing, they attempted to make a path for themselves, in the doing of which many a stone, which had lain at least for ages, was rolled from its ancient bed. The oxen being again yoked, our travellers still hoped to cross the mountainous chain; but after renewing the attempt, their guide, who had become quite bewildered as to the way, directed them to return to the place from which they came. Their waggon was almost shattered to pieces, their bullocks were beginning to fail, and the water they had to drink was very salt and exceedingly nauseous to the taste. Next day their guide succeeded in leading them across the mountainous heights, and before night they came in sight of the Orange River. The distant view of the water gladdened every heart, and fresh oxen being yoked, they hastened on in the hope of speedily reaching it; but it proved to be at a much greater distance than they imagined. The labouring oxen gave many a heavy groan; the relays bellowed around them, and the pedestrians who drove the loose cattle were weary with trudging in the sand. About midnight, they reached the banks of the river; but the Namaquas, unaccustomed to see such a mighty stream, or to hear its tremendous roar over the hidden rocks, hesitated to approach it. Some said, it was angry and the torrent might carry them away, others with more reason feared that wild beasts might be lurking amongst the trees and bushes on the banks, and might devour them in the dark; but notwithstanding the apprehensions of some, our travellers were not long of obtaining an abundant supply of water, which was the more cause of gladness, as the last they had drank was little better than that of a common sewer.

To cross the river was now the difficulty, and for this purpose they had to construct a raft consisting of poles fastened together with the bark of the thorn-tree. It had to be dragged over by persons swimming in the water, some before, some at each side, and some behind; and after much exertion on their part, accompanied with terrific shouting, it reached the northern bank of the river in safety with the first party; but it was of such a construction that it had to be loaded ten several times before the whole of them with their waggon and baggage were got over. They now proceeded on their journey and at length reached Bethany, the station of Mr Schmelen, about 250 miles to the north of the Orange River, who was almost overcome with joy at their arrival, having never before been visited by any fellow-missionary. Forty days had now elapsed since they left Steinkopff, a missionary station on the south side of the river, during which time they had not seen a single dwelling-house of any description, not even the hovel of a wandering Bushman. The country was a complete wilderness in every sense of the word, and, with the exception of a few Bushmen and Namaquas near the Orange River, was utterly without inhabitants.

From Bethany they proceeded in a north-easterly direction towards the Great Fish River, in the Damara country; but as the mountains were in many places impassable by waggons, and as they had no horses, they conformed to the custom of the country and mounted their horned cattle. About a dozen of Namaquas accompanied them, some as guides through the wilderness, some as marksmen to shoot animals for food, some as drivers of the bullocks which carried their baggage, and some merely from a disposition to wander through the desert and visit the adjacent tribes. Every one had a kaross or sheepskin, which served as a saddle by day and as a blanket by night.

The country through which they travelled was not so entirely destitute of inhabitants as that through which they had lately passed. Some of these were afraid to come near them, partly perhaps from being little accustomed to the sight of strangers, and partly from their having in former instances been plundered and barbarously treated by the Dutch boors, or as they called them, the hat-wearers, who had come into their country; but others received them in a friendly manner and attended on their worship. Some of the chiefs even expressed a strong desire that missionaries would come and settle among them.

After travelling about a fortnight, they reached the Great Fish River. Here there was plenty of land on both sides of the river, which exhibited every appearance of fertility. The majestic trees clothed with beautiful foliage afforded a delightful shade, and formed a striking contrast to the many sandy deserts through which they had lately toiled, and while regaling themselves with the cooling draughts of water from the river, they almost felt as if they were on enchanted ground.

Leaving the Fish River, they again pushed forth into the uninhabited wilderness on their return to Bethany. On the following night they became completely bewildered, having lost their way, and when the sun at length arose, it only disclosed to them fresh difficulties. The country before them was covered with large stones, and the high ridges of shattered rocks, confusedly thrown together, seemed to block up their path. The whole day was spent in crossing this rocky desolate region, nor could they lose time to make a single halt for the purpose of refreshing their oxen. Such a day as this they had never experienced before. Scorched by a tropical sun,. torn by the thorny bushes, jolted by their unruly bullocks, parched by a burning wind, faint for want of sustenance, tormented with indescribable thirst, their cattle weary, having travelled nearly thirty hours with but little interruption, their people lame, their tongues so parched that their voices were become harsh, and they began to speak with difficulty, it is not surprising that they grew impatient and dejected, and were almost ready to give up in despair. But whilst reflecting on their critical situation, and considering what methods it might be necessary to employ in order to extricate themselves out of it, one of their people proclaimed the joyful news of water. Having refreshed themselves and their cattle, their hopes revived, and they pushed on with fresh vigour, and at length about eight o'clock in the evening, they reached Bethany, the station of Mr Schmelen.

After resting themselves at Bethany, Mr Shaw and his companions resumed their journey, and at length, after an absence of fourteen weeks, reached Khamiesberg in safety.[1] We have

[1] Miss. Not. vol. iii. p. 68, 104, 119.

given these details of this long and toilsome journey, with the view of shewing what difficulties and hardships missionaries have to endure in travelling in this part of South Africa.

In October 1823, Mr Shaw, on returning to Lily Fountain from Cape Town after an absence of three years, gives the following account of the appearance of the station. "This institution," says he, "presents a pleasing contrast to the dreary wilds we have been crossing during the past week. Instead of a barren wilderness, exhibiting nothing but sterility as far as the eye can reach, here are fields waving with corn and ripening apace for the harvest. Instead of noxious water which the cattle often refuse to drink, here are numerous fountains ever sending forth their crystal streams. Instead of a parched desert destitute of verdure to relieve the languid eye, here are gardens producing vegetables in abundance, and trees richly laden with fruit. Instead of a lonesome Karroo which never used to hear 'the sound of the church-going bell,' these rocks and these dales now smile when the Sabbath returns, and a goodly company who dwell on high, join together in calling on the name of the Lord, and in shouting his praises from the tops of the mountains."[1] This picture is probably somewhat overcharged; the contrast between the wilderness through which Mr Shaw had lately travelled and the scene which he now beheld, may not unnaturally have excited his mind and given a colouring to his description. But whatever may have been the beauty of Lily Fountain, there appear to be grounds for concluding that it must have been indebted for it more to the bounty of Providence than to the industry of the people. Many years after, it is stated that the great evil which cramped all the energies of the mission was the destitution of the natives in their temporal circumstances, and that this was the fruit of their own negligence and indescribable idleness. Although there was abundance of garden ground, very few of them cultivated it, nor would they hire themselves to work with the farmers. The consequence was, that they depended for the most part upon the little wheat which they could raise, and as the produce of the land was small, not on an average more than fifteen fold, this was soon consumed, and the greatest wretchedness often prevailed

[1] Miss. Not. vol. iv. p. 343.

among them, which was apt to oblige nearly all of them to disperse from the station in search of the means of subsistence.[1]

In June 1825, Mr Threlfall, one of the missionaries, accompanied by Jacob Links and Joannes Jagger, two of the native converts, left Khamiesberg with the view of proceeding to the Fish River in the Damara country, in order to see whether the people in that quarter, who had previously expressed a wish for teachers, were still desirous of obtaining them. They reached the Warm Bath in safety, but eight or ten days after leaving that place, they were all three attacked at midnight as they lay asleep on the ground around their fire, and were barbarously murdered by their treacherous native guide, assisted by some Bushmen who lived near the fatal spot, and whom he had seduced to assist him in his bloody design. What were the motives which instigated them to this cruel deed does not appear certain ; but it is probable it was in order to possess themselves of the beads and other trifling articles which they carried with them for the purpose of buying food. The principal murderer was afterwards taken and delivered up to the colonial authorities, and after the charge was duly investigated, he was brought to the Silver Fountain in Little Namaqualand, and with the consent of his chief executed.[2]

In July 1834, a station was begun by Mr Edward Cook in Great Namaqualand at a place called the Warm Bath, or, as it was afterwards named, Nisbet Bath. Several families came in a short time to reside at the place, and an invitation was sent, with the sanction of the chief, to the whole tribe to repair thither as soon as possible, that they and their children might enjoy Christian instruction. The governor of the colony took a lively interest in the establishment of this mission, and promised to the chief to make him a handsome present half-yearly, so long as he should conduct himself properly and co-operate cordially with the missionary.[3]

[1] Meth. Mag. 1832, p. 524 ; Miss. Not. vol. viii. p. 570.

[2] Meth. Mag. 1826, p. 631 ; Ibid. 1828, p. 199, 342 ; Memoir of Mrs Ann Hodgson, p. 19.

Upon the death of Mr Threlfall's father, a legacy of £1000, which would have fallen to him had he survived, was, agreeably to his desire, paid to the Methodist Missionary Society, a gratifying proof of his disinterestedness and zeal.—*Miss. Not.* vol. i. (N.S.) p. 315.

[3] Rep. Meth. Miss. Soc. 1835, p. 37.

The people in this quarter were extremely poor. The greater part of them possessed a few cows and goats, and some also had sheep; but as they had neither bread nor vegetables, the little milk and flesh which they obtained from them was not at all adequate to the supply of their wants. As to futurity they scarcely seemed to have a thought. Their young cattle were generally devoured before they attained to maturity, and the man who did not give to his neighbour while he had any thing himself, was looked on as very inhospitable. When their resources failed, as they were apt to do through the dryness of the weather, they were sometimes reduced by hunger to mere skeletons, and lengthened out their miserable existence by any thing which they obtained in the course of their rambles, or by hunting or surprising wild animals as the lion does his prey.

But notwithstanding many unfavourable circumstances in the condition of the people, the stations of Khamiesberg and Nisbet Bath made encouraging progress. The congregations at both places were considerable, and they appeared to manifest much interest in the instructions of the missionaries.[1]

Besides these stations in Namaqualand, the Methodist Missionary Society established many others in South Africa. In Kaffraria, they carried on an extensive mission: the principal stations were named Wesleyville, Mount Coke, Butterworth, Beechamwood, Morley, Clarkebury, Buntingville, Shawbury, and Palmerton. They also established a mission in the Bechuana country: the stations were chiefly among the Barolongs and Basutos. A mission which they attempted in the Damara country was given up after a few years. They had likewise a number of chapels in the colony, and at Port Natal, chiefly for the benefit of the colonists; but the missionaries also directed considerable attention to the instruction of the aborigines, who are found scattered throughout the colony, many of them in the service of the colonists. They are particularly numerous in the direction of Kaffraria, and consist of various races,—Hottentots, Kafirs, Tambookies, Fingoes, Bechuanas, Mozambiques, and others who had taken refuge in the colony, in

[1] Rep. Meth. Miss. Soc. 1852, p. 48; Miss. Not. 1847, p. 192.

consequence of the destructive wars of the tribes in the interior.[1]

The following was the number of church members connected with the stations among the aboriginal tribes, according to the latest accounts :—

Namaqualand, . .	398
Kaffraria, . . .	812
Bechuana country, . .	576
Total,	1786 [2]

SECT. IV.—SOUTH SEA ISLANDS.

ART. 1.—THE FRIENDLY ISLANDS.

IN June 1822, the Rev. Walter Lawry sailed from New South Wales for Tongatabu, one of the Friendly Islands. He was accompanied by two or three mechanics, and he took with him a number of horned cattle and sheep, which were presented by his Excellency the governor, in the hope of their breeding on the island. He also carried with him Indian corn, wheat, pease, beans, cabbages, potatoes, turnips, melons, and various other garden seeds, with a view to their cultivation.[3]

On arriving at Tongatabu, Mr Lawry was received by the chiefs in a very friendly manner: they were greatly delighted with some chisels and axes which he presented to them. Paloo, one of the principal chiefs, under whose protection he placed himself, made at first a very favourable impression on his mind: he represents him as a very fine-looking, remarkably shrewd, discerning, prudent, generous man. But it was not long before he discovered that much of the favourable impression which the chief had made upon him, was to be attributed to the deceitfulness of his character. Some of the mission property he took away by treachery, some by violence: the settlers felt that there was no security even for their life. Every day's

[1] Rep. Meth. Miss. Soc. 1852, p. 49, 57, 59.
[2] Rep. Meth. Miss. 1853, p. 109.
[3] Miss. Not. vol. iv. p. 54, 101.

experience shewed that it was not with them the chiefs were in love, but with their property, a circumstance which shews how unadvisable it is for missionaries to savage tribes to carry much property with them; that instead of contributing to their safety, it only increases their danger. The behaviour of Paloo, indeed, was exceedingly capricious and changeable. When Mr Lawry, after having been upwards of twelve months on the island, was about to return to New South Wales, he manifested, or at least professed, great sorrow at his departure. He was scarcely able to speak for weeping: others of the people also burst into tears. Yet afterwards he ill-treated the two young men who remained behind, and even threatened their lives if they would not go away.[1]

In June 1826, Messrs Hutchison and Thomas, two new missionaries, landed on the island, and after making the chiefs some presents, they explained to them the object of their coming, and the conditions on which they were willing to remain among them, which were readily agreed to. Land to any extent was promised them, the protection of their property, the free and undisturbed exercise of their religion, that all the children of the tribe should be made to come to their school, and that as many of the people as chose should be at liberty to attend their worship. To make such conditions with savages, it is obvious, can serve little purpose. They will not scruple to promise any thing, but neither will they scruple to break every promise they have made.

The new missionaries settled at Hihifo, under a chief called the Ata. It was soon evident that it was merely on account of their property that the chiefs cared any thing about them. The Ata, under whose protection they had placed themselves, broke all his engagements. He threatened to burn their house, and suffered them to be robbed by men and boys of all descriptions. He was quite opposed to Christianity, and prohibited his people from attending divine worship. The few who did attend were ordered to leave the district, and some young women who were learning to read and sew, were taken away by the wife of the chief. It was alleged that the missionaries were bad men, and that they prayed the people to death. As there

[1] Miss. Not. vol. iv. p. 129, 311, 341; vol. viii. p. 462.

was the prospect of a scarcity of food on the island, it was said the Tonga gods were angry with the people for suffering them to come among them; that the Tonga and the English gods had had a quarrel on the subject; and that the Tonga gods being the strongest, were now punishing them for what they had done.[1] By such means as these the missionaries were greatly thwarted in their labours at Hihifo, and their prospects of success, for the present, blasted.

In November 1827, a second station was begun at Nukualofa, under Tubou, who appears to have been the principal chief, and is usually called the king. Here from the very commencement of their labours, the prospects of the missionaries were of the most cheering kind. They had large and attentive congregations: the place of worship was often crowded, and sometimes hundreds sat outside unable to obtain admission. Several schools were established which were numerously attended by men, women, and children. The desire of religious knowledge was very intense, and the progress which many of them made is represented as truly wonderful. It was not long before a number of them were baptized and admitted to the Lord's Supper. Among those who professed to renounce the religion of their fathers were Tubou the king and several others of the chiefs. One ot the principal men, who expressed his determination to cast off the gods of his country, assigned as a reason for this, that when the missionaries first came to the island, he thought that something very bad would quickly befal such as prayed to their God, and that they would all soon die; but having looked a long time, and nothing evil having happened to them, he came to hear for himself, and was now convinced that Jehovah was God, and therefore he resolved to worship him only.[2]

Messages were also received from chiefs of the Vavau and

[1] Meth. Mag. 1828, p. 487, 630; Ibid. 1830, p. 558.

It is remarked by Mr Thomas, after he had been preaching on love to God, that this was quite a new thing to the Tongas. They had been in the habit of dreading their gods, and serving them with a slavish fear; but they never loved them. Such an idea had not so much as crossed their minds. This is probably not confined to Tongatabu; we suspect it is characteristic of heathenism in every part of the world; a circumstance which strikingly illustrates the vast superiority of the religion of the Bible.

[2] Rep. Meth. Miss. Soc. 1828, p. 43; Meth. Mag. 1829, p. 628, 631; Ibid. 1830, p. 563, 629; Ibid. 1831, p. 195.

Habai Islands, requesting the missionaries to come and instruct them in the knowledge of Jehovah. The chief of the former said he was tired of his evil spirits; they told him so many lies, he was sick of them; that he was the only chief on the island, and that when he turned, all his people would turn with him. It was even said that the chief of the Habai Islands had taken an oath that he would give up his lying spirits and turn to Jehovah, and that he had already begun to observe the Sabbath, by ceasing from work and from all his amusements on that day.[1]

In January 1830, Mr Thomas proceeded to Lifuka the chief of the Habai Islands. On his arrival, he found that the king Taufaahau had renounced idolatry and acknowledged Jehovah as the true God, and that the houses which were formerly held sacred were used as common dwellings. The chief had visited Tonga a few months before, and on his return, he was accompanied by a young man and his wife, who were both baptized, with a view to their instructing those who had renounced idolatry in the new religion, and to teaching them to read. Immediately on his arrival, Mr Thomas began to preach to the natives. He also opened schools, both for males and females, which were well attended, chiefly by adults. They were taught principally by the natives themselves: such as had learned a little taught others what they themselves knew. The king and others of the chiefs attended, and stood up in the same ring with their people, to be catechised every morning. There were about eighteen inhabited islands in this group, some of them forty or fifty miles distant from each other, but all under the government of Taufaahau; and they contained, it was supposed, about 4000 inhabitants, nearly one-half of whom had renounced idolatry, but they were, for the present, without the means of instruction.[2]

Mr Thomas, after being some months in the Habai Islands, baptized a number of the natives, among whom was Taufaahau the king. He and his people erected a large building for divine worship, which was usually attended by great numbers of the natives, there being generally from a thousand to fifteen hundred persons present. The king was very zealous in bringing

[1] Meth. Mag. 1829, p. 266; Ibid. 1830, p. 630.
[2] Ibid. 1831, p. 125, 195, 714, 778.

over the people from idolatry, and the influence of the chiefs in the South Sea Islands in matters of this kind commands ready obedience. Young and old, rich and poor, masters and servants, priests and people, might now be seen renouncing the worship of idols, and turning to the true God. Among others was the Tamaha, a female chief of the highest rank, who had been regarded as a deity, and was one of the pillars of the popular superstition.[1]

Idolatry also now received a heavy blow in the island of Vavau. Three years before, Finau the king appeared anxious for a missionary; but afterwards he acted the part of a persecutor, and was mad on his idols. The king of the Habai Islands and some of his people had, however, gone on a visit to Vavau, with twenty-four sail of canoes, and the missionaries wrote a letter to Finau, expressing their love to him and his people, and their earnest desire for their welfare. The king of Habai exhorted him to turn to God, and put away his lying spirits, and he at length yielded, saying, "Well, I will; and I will spend the Sabbath with you in worshipping your God." He then gave orders to his servants to worship Jehovah, and to set on fire the houses of the idols. These orders were promptly obeyed. Some of the houses of the idols were taken by the people for their own use; others to the number of eighteen were burned to the ground, and their gods in them. Some, however, were much alarmed at these proceedings; but a thousand people at least, it was supposed, joined with the king in renouncing idolatry. They shewed great eagerness to hear about the new religion. The Habai people had no rest from them, day nor night; when they had done with one company, another would come, and thus they were kept constantly employed speaking to them.[2]

In March 1831, Messrs Nathaniel Turner, J. Watkin, and W. Woon, three new missionaries, arrived at Nukualofa in Tongatabu, the last of whom was a printer. Hitherto, the missionaries had had great trouble in writing out books for the natives; but now a press was established, at which were printed large

[1] Meth. Mag. 1832, p. 144; Miss. Not. vol. vii. p. 513; Rep. Meth. Miss. Soc. 1833, p. 40, 44; Ibid. 1834, p. 37.
[2] Meth. Mag. 1832, p. 578.

editions of several school-books, select passages of scripture, hymn-books, catechisms, and other useful works. The people were greatly delighted, and not a little surprised, when they first saw the press in operation. Thousands of these little books were in a short time circulated, and were read by them with great interest. The desire for books was very great, and the missionaries, availing themselves of this, did not think it advisable to give them generally gratuitously. They took payment for them, but the people were so poor, that many found it difficult to purchase them.[1]

In prosecuting their labours, the missionaries were greatly assisted by a host of native helpers, not only teachers of schools, but class-leaders, exhorters, and even local preachers. The overthrow of idolatry, and the reception of Christianity in the various islands was, in fact, effected very much through the instrumentality of the natives themselves. In the schools there were some thousands of scholars, of whom a large portion were adults, and about one half females. Several hundreds of the natives, both males and females, were employed as teachers, amongst whom were some of the most influential of the chiefs and their wives. Many of the females, besides learning to read, were taught to sew by the wives of the missionaries; and it was truly surprising to see the rapidity with which they acquired this useful art, and the neatness of their work. There was a great desire among them to dress in gowns and bonnets like Englishwomen.[2]

Though the religious instruction communicated by the natives must of necessity have been very imperfect, and probably often not unmixed with error, yet they appear to have contributed essentially to the overthrow of idolatry, not only in their own and in the neighbouring islands, but even in islands at a great distance. One day the missionaries in Vavau observed three canoes approaching the shore. They were navigated by strangers, and proved to be from the island of Niua-Fo-ou, three hundred miles distant, which no missionary had ever visited. Some of the Vavau converts, however, had visited it, and such had been

[1] Meth. Mag. 1831, p. 857; Ibid. 1832, p. 56, 141, 143, 524, 892; Rep. Meth. Miss. Soc. 1833, p. 45; Ibid. 1835, p. 135.
[2] Miss. Not. vol. vii. p. 226.

the effect of their representations, that intelligence was now brought that the whole of the inhabitants had cast away their idols. One of their visitors they had detained to afford them further instruction.[1]

In July 1834, a powerful religious movement began in Vavau, which quickly extended to the whole of the Habai Islands, and afterwards, though in a less degree, to the Tonga group. Thousands of the natives had before been turned from idolatry to the outward profession of Christianity, and been brought under regular religious instruction, yet the number who gave evidence of being seriously impressed with divine truth was not considerable. There was even much indifference amongst them; but now, in their meetings for divine worship, the greatest excitement prevailed. Hundreds of men, women, and children, including some of the principal chiefs, might be seen in deep distress, weeping aloud and crying to God for mercy. Often as soon as the service commenced, the cries of the people began. Many trembled from head to foot, as if they were about to be judged at the bar of God. For a time, the people laid aside their ordinary employments, and gave themselves up entirely to religious exercises. The missionaries went about among them in their meetings, pointing them to "the Lamb of God which taketh away the sin of the world," and praying with them. Many, it is stated, were soon enabled to lay hold by faith on Jesus Christ as their Saviour, and found "redemption through his blood, even the forgiveness of their sins." After a time, the distress of the people generally subsided, most of them having obtained peace and joy in believing. The work was not confined merely to the principal islands: it spread like fire among stubble through the whole of them. In a short time, every island had caught the flame: every where, it is said, the people were earnestly seeking the Lord, or rejoicing because they had found him.[2]

This religious movement, it is stated, was followed by a remarkable reformation of manners. Among other sins, polygamy was now abandoned; marriage became prevalent; they became more decent and modest in their dress, many of them

[1] Rep. Meth. Miss. Soc. 1834, p. 35, 39; Ibid. 1835, p. 33.
[2] Miss. Not. vol. viii. p. 148.

dressing in the English style. They set a high value on the means of grace. It was not every trifle which kept them from the house of God; and when present, their eyes were riveted on the speaker, and frequently the abundance of their tears bespoke the joy of their hearts. The Sabbath they kept with remarkable strictness: not only was all work laid aside, but the whole day was employed in the public and private exercises of religion. Nor were they less punctual in their devotional exercises on other days. At the first dawn of morning, they presented unto God the sacrifice of prayer and praise, and at night their last employment, before retiring to rest, was to sing the wonders of redeeming love, and to commit themselves to the protection and care of their heavenly Father. In their prayers, there was an affecting emotion and simplicity. Though formerly "hateful and hating one another," they now loved each other "with a pure heart fervently." The missionaries had great pleasure in labouring among a people so affectionate in their dispositions, so attentive to their instructions, and so tractable in their manners.[1]

[1] Rep. Meth. Miss. Soc. 1836, p. 24.

In judging of what are commonly called revivals of religion, we apprehend that great caution is necessary, more than is commonly shewn both by those who report or receive them, and by those who doubt or reject them. We are not prepared to pronounce an opinion in regard to the religious movement in the Friendly Islands, of which the above is an account; but yet we cannot help feeling great jealousy of it. Even supposing it to be, to some extent, a work of divine grace, we fear that the missionaries greatly over-estimated their success, and that they spoke much too confidently both as to the numbers converted, and as to the nature and truth of their religious experience. The work appears to have essentially resembled those movements which have not unfrequently taken place among the Methodists both in England and America, and which they are accustomed to speak of as the work of God, though much of it is probably nothing more than the excitement of the imagination and of the passions acting on numbers by means of sympathy, without being followed by any change of heart and life. To assist the reader in judging of the character of the work, we shall here give a few extracts from the letters of the missionaries :—

"On Tuesday July 27th," says Mr Turner of Vavau, "we believe that not fewer than one thousand souls were converted; not now from dumb idols only, but from sin to righteousness, and from the power of Satan unto God." "For a week or two we were not able to hold the schools, but had prayer-meetings six times a day. We could not speak five minutes before all were in tears, and numbers prostrated before the Lord, absorbed in deep concern about salvation. Frequently their first words were, 'Praise the Lord! I never knew Jesus until now! Now I do know him. He has taken away all my sins! I love Jesu Kalaise!' Some were so filled with joy through believing, that they could not contain themselves, but cried out for 'hearts to praise the Lord.' This has not been like the dew descending upon the tender herb, but as

Not the least remarkable of the converts was Taufaahau, the king both of the Habai and Vavau Islands, and who at his baptism was called George, while his queen was named Charlotte. They both adorned their Christian profession, and were truly zealous, devoted persons. They both met classes and superintended schools. The king was a very excellent local preacher, and never sought to be preferred before others, but went wherever he was sent, fulfilling his appointments with the greatest cheerfulness. Mr Tucker having one day in the course of conversation stated his views to him on the subject of slavery, and mentioned the emancipation of the negroes in the West Indies, he said several of his servants were slaves, having been given to him by his father and other chiefs, but that he would liberate them that very day. In the evening, he accordingly called them all together and set them at liberty. The scene was very affecting. He told them of the many evils which were practised among them during the reign of heathenism, and spoke of the love and mercy of God in sending the gospel to them with all its attendant blessings. He told them how much he loved them, and then said, "You are no longer slaves: you are your own masters, and may go and reside wherever you please."

the spring-tide, or as the overflowing of some mighty river; all the mounds of sin have been swept away; the people have been willing in the day of his power. I may say the Lord has bowed the whole island to his sway. We have to hold two prayer-meetings daily, and many are brought into the enjoyment of pardon and holiness. We have ascertained that the total number in Society is 3066; and the number converted, for the most part within the past six weeks, is 2262."

"In the morning," says Mr Tucker of the Habai Islands, "we repaired to the house of prayer as soon as it was light. The Lord made 'the place of his feet glorious;' the stout-hearted began to tremble; there was a mighty shaking among the dry bones: as soon as the service began, the cries of the people began. O what a solemn but joyful sight to behold! One thousand or more individuals bowed before the Lord, weeping at the feet of Jesus, and praying in an agony of soul! I never saw such distress, never heard such cries for mercy, or such confession of sin before. These things were universal, from the greatest chiefs in the land to the meanest individuals, and of both sexes, old and young. The Lord heard the sighing of the prisoners, he bound up many a broken-hearted sinner in that meeting, and proclaimed liberty to many a captive." "We were engaged nearly the whole day in this blessed work. I attended four services, and witnessed hundreds of precious souls made happy by a sense of the Saviour's love on that day and the preceding evening." "We have not yet received an account from all the islands of the number who have obtained peace with God during this revival, but from the number already brought in by the leaders, we believe that upwards of two thousand were truly converted to God in the course of a fortnight."—*Miss. Notices*, vol. viii. p. 149.

They all burst into tears and wept aloud; the king himself and his queen could not refrain from tears. Two of them begged to be allowed to live and die with him; but he would not consent to their remaining as slaves. "If you wish," said he, "to reside a little longer with us, well; if you desire to go and dwell in any other island, just please yourselves."[1]

The missionaries were indebted to the king for the erection of a very large chapel in Habai. It was 110 feet by 45 inside, and was expected to be capable of holding all the inhabitants of the island. It was probably the largest and most elegant building ever erected in the Friendly Islands, and was a fine monument of the zeal and good taste of the king. It was built in little more than two months, and for several weeks there were about a thousand people engaged in the work. Most of the chiefs and matabules were employed in plaiting kafa or cinet, while the common people did the heavier work. The pillars and other timber used in the framework were brought from other islands. The labour was regularly divided between the inhabitants of the whole group, and each party tried to excel the others in their workmanship. As they had no nails, the timbers were fastened with kafa made of the fibres of the cocoa-nut husk, and dyed black, red, and other colours. These colours they interweave with almost mathematical accuracy, which makes their work appear to great advantage. The king gave several beautifully carved spears which were left to him by his predecessors, and had often been used in war, to be converted into rails for the communion table, and two beautifully carved clubs which were formerly worshipped as gods, and were now fixed at the bottom of the pulpit stairs. At the opening of the chapel, the natives assembled in great numbers from all the islands, on many of which the sick and aged only were left. On this occasion, the king delivered a very appropriate sermon from Solomon's prayer at the dedication of the temple.[2]

In February 1835, Mr Peter Turner, accompanied by some of the natives, sailed from Vavau in a small vessel of seventeen tons for Niua-Tabu-tabu or Keppel's Island, about 170 miles distant. As his proceedings, and others to which they gave rise, furnish an illustration of the hasty and imperfect

[1] Miss. Not. vol. viii. p. 315, 317, 320.

[2] Ibid. vol. viii. p. 318.

manner in which the Methodists, at least in some instances, christianize savage tribes, we shall give a few brief details in regard to them. Previous to this, some native teachers had come to the island and had endeavoured to instruct the inhabitants in such things as they themselves knew. After the arrival of Mr Turner, a work similar to that which had lately occurred in the Habai and Vavau Islands commenced. The people were very attentive, and seemed to drink in the word as the thirsty ground drinketh in the rain. Many were brought under great distress on account of their sins, and, after a short time, professed that they had obtained mercy. Mr Turner remained on the island between three and four months, baptized 514 adults and 200 children, united the former into a Methodist Society, and married 240 persons, while in the schools there were 557 scholars, male and female, old and young. He now left them under the care of the native teachers. Mr Thomas, on a subsequent visit to the islands of Niua-Tabu-tabu and Niua-fo-ou, baptized 778 adults and 403 children, forming probably, with those previously baptized, the greater part of the population.[1]

Among the converts on the island of Niua-Tabu-tabu was Gogo the king, who as one proof of his sincerity put away his wives, with the exception of one to whom he was married by the missionary. He soon began to preach to his people, and expressed much zeal for the spread of the gospel. He even proceeded with a number of his people to Uvea or Wallis' Island, for the purpose of persuading the king, who was related to him, to receive the new religion. The latter, however, was not disposed to do so, and in a few weeks some of the chiefs were offended and commenced hostilities, which ended in the destruction of Gogo and forty-five of his men, besides thirteen of the people of the island. It was apprehended that the party from Niua did not act a very prudent part.[2]

In 1836, auxiliary missionary societies were formed in the islands of Habai and Vavau. At the meetings held for establishing them, there were vast numbers of the natives present; they flocked to them from all quarters. The speeches of the

[1] Miss. Not. vol. viii. p. 314, 327, 426; Rep. Meth. Miss. Soc. 1838, p. 42; Ibid. 1840, p. 45.
[2] Miss. Not. vol. viii. p. 455.

natives on these occasions were exceedingly interesting: the contrasts which they drew between their past and present condition, were at once appropriate and affecting. The subscribers were very numerous, and included persons of all ages, and of all ranks, from the king down to the poorest of the people. Money not being current in the islands, their contributions consisted chiefly of articles of native produce and native manufactures. The most valuable were fine mats, which many of the chiefs presented. A few gave pigs, many native cloth, some native fish-hooks;[1] others oil, yams, arrowroot, tortoise-shell, baskets, ornaments, &c. When the whole were collected together, whatever could be converted into money was sold, while the articles of food and clothing which were not saleable, were applied for the support of the missionaries and their families, thereby lessening the expenses of the mission. Tauhaafau, the king, appears to have been particularly zealous in carrying on these auxiliary societies, and on one occasion he and his queen gave a donation of ten sovereigns, probably all they had in the world.[2]

In March 1839, Taufaahau promulgated, in a large assembly of the chiefs and people, a code of laws which had been drawn up for their government, and appointed judges to hear and decide all cases of complaint which might arise among them. No one, whether chief or private person, was now to take the law into his own hand, but must bring every matter of importance before the judges. The code, as may naturally be supposed, bears the stamp of English origin, or, at least, of the missionaries having had a hand in the formation of it. Though some of the laws relate to religion, a subject on which, we apprehend, civil governors ought never to legislate, and though the punishments are perhaps, in some instances, characterized by over severity, an error which commonly attaches to early efforts at legislation, especially for a savage or barbarous people; yet the simple attempt to establish a code of written laws for any country, and the appointment of judges to execute them, is itself an important step in civilization, and lays a foundation

[1] These are made of bone and tortoise-shell, and answer as the bait as well as the hook, as when drawn through the water they resemble the motion of flying fish.

[2] Miss. Not. vol. ix. p. 12; vol. i. (N. S.) p. 352; Rep. Meth. Miss. Soc. 1837, p. 24.

for the security both of life and property, and for the future improvement and happiness of the people.[1]

In the Habai and Vavau Islands, there now remained little room for the extension of missionary operations. Idolatry had ceased to exist, and almost the whole population had assumed the profession of Christianity, yet much was still required to be done for them. Fully to instruct a people just emerging from heathenism and barbarism in the various doctrines and duties of religion, to give a right direction to their new-born energies, and so to train and form them as that they shall grow up a truly Christian and civilized population, is a task, the importance and difficulty of which it is not easy to estimate. Mr Tucker remarks, "The people in their comparatively infantine state seek counsel of the missionary on all subjects of importance, whether temporal or spiritual. Their wants are numerous; their desire after knowledge is intense; but yet there is still much ignorance among them; much that requires patience and perseverance on the one hand, and decision and strict attention on the other."[2] The imperfection of the work will appear the less surprising, when it is considered that on most of the islands the people were of necessity left chiefly to the care of the native local preachers and teachers, and that they could be visited only occasionally by a missionary.

In Tongatabu, Christianity had made much less progress than in the Habai and Vavau Islands. There heathenism had all along maintained itself in great vigour, particularly in the district of Hihifo, where the missionaries originally settled, but which after two or three years they left in consequence of the opposition they met with. Tonga was, in fact, the centre of the superstitions of the Friendly Islands. Its very name Tongatabu, or Tonga the holy or consecrated, would seem to mark it out as a stronghold of the ancient religion. Though many of the natives, particularly at Nukualofa, embraced Christianity, yet there were thousands throughout the island who clung to idolatry, and from time to time they manifested determined hostility to converts. On one occasion, being assembled at one of their yearly idolatrous feasts, they were roused by hear-

[1] Miss. Not. vol. i. (N. S.) p. 281, 350.
[2] Rep. Meth. Miss. Soc. 1837, p. 23; Miss. Not. vol. i. (N. S.) p. 490.

ing of the insults, as they deemed them, which were offered to their gods by the praying people; and proceeded to burn their chapels in several places, to plunder their houses, and to carry away their little property. No lives, however, were taken. The converts, particularly those in Hihifo, were on other occasions driven from their houses, and obliged to take refuge at Nukualofa, or other parts of the island. Parents, in many instances, rose up against their children, and children against their parents. Such, indeed, was the violence of the heathen party, that it was at one time deemed desirable for the missionaries to remove their families for a time to Vavau; they were in constant dread of war, and appeared to be every hour in jeopardy. War did at length break out; but it was of short duration, being speedily terminated in favour of the Christian party; and among other terms of peace, it was agreed that no one should be molested on account of his religion, a condition, however, which it is obvious would be no longer kept than was judged expedient. Meanwhile the heathen party did not dare to persecute the Christians, and, on the other hand, the Christians did not think it prudent to remove out of their fortresses, lest their enemies, seizing the opportunity, should attack and murder them.[1]

In June 1840, the mission in Tongatabu was broken up under circumstances of a peculiarly painful and disastrous nature. About the beginning of that year, the heathen belonging to the Ata at Hihifo murdered four of the Christians who resided in a fortress about a mile distant while they were at work, and they left another, a little girl, for dead, who afterwards, however, recovered. This atrocious deed they committed while Tubou the king was there trying to persuade the Ata to embrace Christianity, and endeavouring to create a kindlier feeling between the Christian and the heathen parties in that quarter; but on the perpetration of this treacherous act, his brother, apprehensive for his safety, went down with a large party, and brought him away. The Ata and his people now flew to arms, and would not be persuaded by the entreaties of the old king to desist. Tubou sent for Tauhaafou, the king of the Habai

[1] Rep. Meth. Miss. Soc. 1834, p. 36; Ibid. 1837, p. 22; Ibid. 1838, p. 39; Miss. Not. vol. vii. p. 287; vol. viii. p. 18, 152; vol. ix. p. 131.

and Vavau Islands, to come and assist him in making peace between the Christians and heathens of Hihifo; and on his arrival the two kings sent repeated messages to the Ata, entreating him to make up the breach between the two parties, and not to involve the island in war. The Ata evaded giving them a direct answer; but at length he sent messengers to them, wishing apparently to make peace, and accordingly Tauhaafau set off with about five or six hundred men; but it was discovered that a plan was laid for murdering him on his arrival. On making this discovery, he returned with most of his people, determined to subdue the other party by force of arms, if they would not submit to the terms which he offered them. He resolved, however, not to take their fortress by storm, on account of the loss of life which this might occasion, but to reduce it by famine. He accordingly surrounded the place for near a fortnight, guarding every avenue; and every second or third day, he sent messengers to the besieged begging them to surrender and lay down their arms. He at length obtained possession of the fortress and secured its defenders, amounting in all to about 500 persons. He had previously charged his people, if possible, not to shed blood in taking the place, and now he pardoned the whole of them, only removing some of the ringleaders to Habai and Vavau. He also resolved to take up his residence in Tongatabu, and to bring over some hundreds of his people from Habai and Vavau to reside with him. This was in accordance with the wish of Tubou and all the other Christian chiefs.[1]

The heathen party, however, were not to be thus subdued. In various places they attacked the Christians; and in this way, skirmishes were every now and then taking place between them. The United States ship Vincennes having touched at the island, the commodore, at the request of the missionaries, made an attempt to negotiate peace between the Christian and the heathen chiefs; but the latter evaded all negotiation, and did not so much as come to the place appointed for meeting. The whole island was at length involved in the horrors of civil war. Her Majesty's ship Favourite, commanded by Captain Croker, having now touched at the island, the missionaries represented to him the danger they were in, and solicited his pro-

[1] Miss. Not. vol. i. (N. S.) p. 420.

tection. They were anxious for conciliation, and in no way indicated the measures which he pursued. He expressed himself willing to do any thing he could to put an end to the war, and he without delay directed a number of volunteers from his ship to proceed with him on shore, carrying with them three carronades, besides their small arms, ammunition, &c. There were a number of fortresses on the island, some in possession of the Christian and some of the heathen party. That in which the heathen forces were chiefly collected was about four miles distant, and was called Bea. It is described as a well constructed fortification and almost impregnable, the walls formed by the buts of cocoa-nut-trees placed perpendicularly to the height of twenty feet, and being at the same time several feet in thickness. Above this was a kind of net-work of cane or bamboo to increase the difficulty of scaling them. Round the outside of this barricade, there was a deep trench about forty feet wide with water in it; and at certain distances there were loop-holes to afford the besieged facilities for firing at their assailants. The only entrance was barricaded by cocoa-trees placed horizontally, with a carronade within pointing through an aperture made for the purpose. The whole had the appearance of having been constructed and superintended by persons well skilled in the science of fortification, a supposition confirmed by the fact that there were at least two Europeans who took an active part in the present conflict, one of whom was said to have been an armourer. He had been many years on the island, and was known by the significant appellation of Jemmy the devil.[1]

By the orders of Captain Croker the carronades were brought within about a hundred yards of the fortification, quite within the range of the enemy's musketry. A native female bearing a flag of truce was then sent to the fortress, conveying the captain's wish that they would surrender and come to amicable terms with the Christian natives. In a short time she returned bearing the intelligence that they were desirous of peace. A flag of truce was at the same time exhibited from the fortress, and the European Jemmy presented himself on the barricade. The captain called to him, expressing his gratification at their

[1] Miss. Not. vol. i. (N. S.) p. 422, 425.

willingness to come to terms, and informing him that the only condition on which peace could be obtained would be the observation of certain propositions, the principal of which were, that all the fortifications on the island, those belonging to the Christians as well as those of the heathen, should be levelled to the ground, and that both parties should resume their ordinary employments and friendly intercourse. The European then appeared to communicate with the natives; the result of which was that Captain Croker was invited to a conference with the chiefs, and he accordingly proceeded within the fortress, accompanied by his second lieutenant and two or three others, bearing a flag of truce and also the British flag. When they were admitted, the entry was again strongly barricaded, and every thing around them presented the most warlike appearance. There was a vast concourse of natives with fire-arms, clubs, &c. who assumed most menacing attitudes, so much so that the party were at first exceedingly apprehensive for their own safety. They were, however, treated with courtesy, and after a parley of three quarters of an hour, the natives required half an hour to consult with some chiefs who were at some distance, which was granted by the captain, who with his companions were then allowed to retire from the stockade. A little before the half hour was expired, the natives sent to say that they were willing to come to terms, but they could not hold intercourse with their enemies. To this it was replied, that the terms proposed must be observed, and when the time had expired the command was given to make the attack, the captain leading the way to the entrance of the fortification.

The serjeant of marines was now ordered by the captain to scale the barricade and to fire, which was no sooner executed than it was returned by the firing of the cannon at the entrance, and a volley of musketry from various parts of the fortress, by which the captain and several of his men were wounded. He then exerted himself to the utmost to enter the stockade, but being exhausted, he retired to a tree at a short distance, by which he supported himself until he was shot through the heart and dropped lifeless to the ground. All this time the officers, seamen, and marines were within a few yards of the fortress, exposed to a hot fire from the natives, who were themselves perfectly screened from the attack of their opponents. The consequence was, that not only the captain but two officers were killed, and the first lieutenant and nineteen men dangerously wounded. With the utmost difficulty they succeeded in carrying off their dead and wounded, and embarked on board their vessel, taking with them the missionaries Tucker and Rabone and their families, whom they conveyed to Vavau. The rash act of Captain Croker in attempting to take the fort, which was so strongly fortified, is altogether unaccountable. European officers are but too apt to despise the warlike resources of savages, but they sometimes, as in this instance, pay dearly for their temerity. Peace was afterwards restored between the contending parties, and the missionaries again resumed their labours.[1]

Of late years the profession of Christianity has greatly extended in the Friendly Islands. In 1850, the Rev. Walter Lawry, the general superintendent of the missions in Australasia and Polynesia, thus wrote, "All the Friendly Islands are now Christian and in communion with us, except a few heathens at Mua and Bea. Homa also is for the most part heathen still, and a few neighbouring places, but their strength is departed from them: they are not at all respected, and are neither loved nor feared by any."[2]

In 1853, the following was the number of church members connected with the Methodist mission in the Friendly Islands:

Tongatabu, . . .	2204
Habai, . . .	1945
Vavau, . . .	2009
Niua-Tabu-tabu, or Keppel's Island,	393
Niua-fo-ou, . . .	610
Total, .	7161[3]

[1] Miss. Not. vol. i. (N.S.) p. 425; vol. ii. p. 469; Rep. Meth. Miss. Soc. 1843, p. 58.
[2] Miss. Not. 1851, p. 136.
[3] Rep. Meth. Miss. Soc. 1853, p. 110.

ART. 2.—FIJI ISLANDS.[1]

IN October 1835, the Rev. W. Cross and D. Cargill proceeded from Vavau, one of the Friendly Islands, to Lakemba, one of the Fiji Islands. It was but a small island, being only about twenty-two miles in circumference, and did not contain above a thousand inhabitants. With the view of ascertaining the disposition of the chiefs and people, it was agreed that the two missionaries should go ashore in the boat. As they approached the beach, many of the natives were running hither and thither on the sand; and as they drew near to the landing-place, nearly 200 men were standing at the distance of about a hundred feet from it, some armed with muskets, others with bayonets fastened to long sticks, some with clubs and spears, others with bows and arrows, their faces painted, some jet black, others red, some after one fashion, others after another. This was rather a formidable array. However, being told that the chief wished to know who they were, and what they wanted, the missionaries went on to his house, a large building within a fortress, nearly a mile from the shore. Having had their object explained to him, he appeared friendly, gave them a piece of land on which to live, and built a temporary dwelling for each of their families.

The missionaries soon began to preach to the natives, and in a few months they baptized a number of them, some of whom had previously obtained a knowledge of divine truth in the Friendly Islands. The gospel silently made its way among the people; and every week one or more turned their backs on idolatry. A desire to embrace the new religion prevailed among many of the inhabitants of Lakemba; but they were afraid openly to declare themselves, as the chief, notwithstanding his first professions, threatened and persecuted those who embraced it. He was himself only a tributary chief, and appeared unwilling to take any step in favour of Christianity until he knew the mind of the more powerful chiefs of Fiji. "When Tanao," said he, referring to one of their most renowned chiefs, "leads

[1] The number of inhabited islands in the Fiji group is said to be nearly 200. The circumference of the largest island is about 300 miles, whilst the smallest vary from 4 to 30.—*Papers relative to the Wesleyan Missions*, March 1842, p. 2.

the way, I and all my people will embrace the new religion." Indeed, it was remarked by the missionaries, that until some powerful chief should set the example, not many of the Fijians would receive the gospel;[1] a remark which will explain, in many cases, the numerous conversions which have taken place in some of the South Sea Islands.

In the course of a few years, the missionaries, with the aid of native teachers and preachers, some of whom came from the Vavau Islands, introduced the gospel into various other islands of the Fiji group besides Lakemba, as Rewa, Vewa, Bua, Nandy, and some others of less importance. Though, in some instances, they had many difficulties to contend with, yet, generally speaking, they met with a favourable reception from the chiefs and others of the natives; but it must not be supposed that this arose from their having any right understanding of the nature of the gospel, or any love to it. Some were glad to have missionaries residing with them, because they thought it added to their respectability and importance, or that they would obtain axes and other useful articles from them, or reap other advantages by them. On one occasion, a chief made Mr Cargill sit more than two hours with him, while he asked questions about the gospel; and when the missionary inquired if he believed what he told him was true, he replied, "True! every thing is true that comes from the White man's country: muskets, and guns, and powder, are true, and your religion must be true." Such was the way in which he reasoned about the religion of White men. The chief of another island recommended his brother to receive the gospel in order that his life might be prolonged by the power and love of the true God, and by the temporal and spiritual medicine administered by his servants. In fact, the great reason why some were disposed to receive the new religion was that they might enjoy bodily health.[2]

In 1845 and the following year, there was a religious movement in the island of Vewa, which extended also to others of the islands, similar to that in the Friendly Islands which we

[1] Miss. Not. vol. ix. p. 35, 163, 168; Memoirs of Mrs Margaret Cargill, p. 96, 101, 103, 111, 152, 155, 159.

[2] Miss. Not. vol. ix. p. 170; vol. i. (N.S.) p. 151, 154, 353; Rep. Meth. Miss. Soc. 1839, p. 44; Ibid. 1841, p. 57, 61; Mrs Cargill's Memoirs, p. 149.

have already described. "Business, sleep, and food," says Mr Hunt, "were almost entirely laid aside. We were at length obliged almost to force some of the new converts to take something for the sustenance of the body. Some of the cases were the most remarkable I have ever seen, heard, or read of; yet only such as one might expect the conversion of such dreadful murderers and cannibals would be. If such men manifest nothing more than ordinary feelings when they repent, one would suspect that they are not yet fully convinced of sin. Certainly the feelings of the Vewa people were not ordinary. They literally roared for hours, through the disquietude of their souls. This frequently terminated in fainting from exhaustion, which was the only respite some of them had till they found peace. They no sooner recovered their consciousness than they prayed themselves first into an agony, and then again into a state of entire insensibility. The result has been most happy. The preaching of the word has been attended with more power than before the revival. Many who were careless and useless have become sincere and devoted to God. The experience of most has been much improved, and many have become, by adoption and regeneration, the sons of God." "The people, old and young, chiefs and common people," says Mr Watsford, "were heartbroken before the Lord. The cries for mercy drowned every other sound: the struggling and roaring for deliverance by the penitents was of no ordinary character: It was agony indescribable, and bitterness of heart. They felt themselves great sinners, and their repentance was deep and genuine." "The joy of those who were pardoned was as great as their distress had been. One man was so happy that he went away shouting, 'My heart is on fire, and my soul is burning.'" "At some of our meetings, the feeling was overpowering, and the people fell before the Lord, and we were unable to stand because of the glory."[1] We quote these statements of the missionaries, partly as giving some idea of the nature of the movement; partly as furnishing some illustration of the views of the Methodists; and partly as exhibiting some remarkable psychological facts, for whatever estimate any one may form of this as a religious revival, every intelligent person must consider it as a singular

[1] Miss. Not. vol. v. (N.S.) p. 64, 66, 68, 159.

circumstance that savages, some of them probably murderers, and most of them ferocious cannibals, should be affected, subdued, melted in the way and manner here described.

In 1853, the following was the number of church members connected with the Methodist mission in the Fiji Islands :—

Lakemba, . . .	1770
Vewa, . . .	250
Bua, . . .	290
Nandy, . . .	216
Rotumah, . . .	—
	2526[1]

SECT. V.—GENERAL STATEMENTS.

We shall not proceed further with the history of the Methodist missions in detail, as in most of the others which they established there occurs nothing peculiarly interesting or characteristic: we should only have to relate circumstances similar to those we have already stated, or which we shall afterwards have occasion to relate in recording the operations of other denominations of Christians who occupied the same fields of labour. But though, from the accounts we have given, some idea may be formed of the nature of the Methodist missions, little idea can be formed of their extent. For near thirty years, their labours were directed chiefly to the negroes in the West Indies; but after the establishment of the mission in Ceylon, a new and mighty impulse was given to their exertions; and with all that zeal, and energy, and activity, which are so eminently characteristic of them as a body, they not only augmented the number of labourers in the fields which they previously occupied, but sent forth missionaries to most of the other quarters of the globe.

In North America, they sent missionaries to the Indians in Upper Canada, and in the Hudson's Bay Company's territory;

In Western Africa, to St Mary's and Macarthy's Island in

[1] Rep. Meth. Miss. Soc. 1853, p. 102.

the River Gambia, to Sierra Leone, to the Gold Coast, to Badagry, and to the Ashanti country:[1]

In the EAST INDIES, to Madras, to Bangalore, to Negapatnam, to Manaargoody, to Goobee, to Mysore, and to Coonghul:

In AUSTRALASIA, to the aboriginal inhabitants of New South Wales:

In POLYNESIA, to New Zealand.

In 1853, the full and accredited church members in connection with the Methodist missions in different parts of the heathen world, amounted to about 76,532.[2]

In comparing the numbers in the Methodist Societies in successive years, nothing is more striking than the frequent and sudden variations which take place in the amount of their members. In the West India Islands, it was not uncommon for them in the days of slavery to rise or fall, by several hundreds in a year. In 1813, the Society in St Christopher's consisted of 2162 members; in 1814, it had increased to 3024. In 1816, it still amounted to about 3000; but in 1818, it had decreased to 2209. The stability of the Methodist Societies is often even much greater than appears, from merely comparing the amount of their members in successive years, as the numbers who leave them, or who are excluded, are in many instances made up by those who join them, so that though the fluctuation has been considerable, there may be no great variation in the amount of the whole. In 1812, for instance, the members of the Metho-

[1] As in other missions on the Western coast of Africa, there was great mortality among the missionaries at all the stations of the Methodists in that quarter of the world. From 1811, when the mission to Sierra Leone was begun, to 1850, there were sent from England, as nearly as could be ascertained, about 123 missionaries, including their wives; and of these there were no fewer than 54 who died, while many others returned home on account of the failure of their health. Nor was this merely after a lengthened course of labour. In consequence of the unhealthiness of the climate, the committee, after a short trial of *seven* years, restricted the period of service first to *three* years, and then to *two*; and it was only in a few instances that this period was exceeded. Many died within the first year; some in a few months, a few weeks, or even a few days, after their landing. Instances were not wanting of husbands and wives lying ill in different rooms of the same house at the same time, and dying within a short time of each other. The frequent sicknesses and deaths of so many of the missionaries, and the early return of others to England, could not fail to affect materially the progress of the missions. Stations were sometimes left with only one missionary, or without any missionary at all.—*Fox's History of the Wesleyan Missions on the Western Coast of Africa*, p. 224, 276, 330, 411, 417, 436, 617, *et passim*.

[2] Rep. Meth. Miss. Soc. 1852, p. 124; Ibid. 1853, p. 114.

CPSIA information can be obtained
at www.ICGtesting.com
Printed in the USA
LVHW101923170422
716440LV00004BA/256

9 783752 591446